I0676669

DRAGONFIRE

Charles S Jackson

A Charles S. Jackson novel
First e-book edition distributed by Amazon.com - 2018
First paperback edition printed by Amazon.com - 2018
© 2018 Charles S. Jackson

All rights reserved. No part of this publication may be reproduced, stored in a retrieval system, or transmitted, in any form or by any means, electronic, mechanical, photocopying or otherwise, without the prior permission of the copyright owner.

ISBN: 978-0-9872488-9-3

Printed and bound by Amazon KDP,

'*Ægishjálmr*, Helm of Awe' image courtesy of: Bourbon-88/shutterstock.com.

Cover art images courtesy of: Jose AS Reyes/shutterstock.com,
Francey/shutterstock.com,
pixelparticle/shutterstock.com, kwest/shutterstock.com.
Thank you for respecting the hard work of this author.

FIRST OF THE

SHARD WORLD

SERIES

The Keepsakes

All around us, there were places not safe to walk: places where the Old Majik still held power... the places where the Keepsakes lay. Some no more than some small patch by the side of a lonely road, or a place where the careless might trip or stumble over nothing at all: strange, inaccessible pieces of land – sometimes huge, sometimes no larger than a cart or wagon – where nothing lay that could be seen, yet through which no man might pass all the same, and a traveller would strike their knee, chest or face against something invisible that was nevertheless real enough to leave bruise or mark.

Everyone knew what to do. Any man who dared to venture beyond the walls of their village or strayed from the safety of the road in unfamiliar terrain made sure they carried with them a pack of Holding Staves. One placed at each corner, standing waist high with the top painted white to a hand's breadth for better vision at night, with a Rope of Warding strung between. No one would ever speak of it again once that cord was tied, yet there it would remain, a warning for all.

There were cautionary tales – the stuff of frightful bedtime stories – that told of those foolish enough to ignore the ropes. It was said that in the Old Times, soon after The Cleansing, many tested the will of the dragons by climbing atop these invisible places, declaring to the world their courage and power. But just like dragons, so too the Old Majik had teeth, and it was said that one bite from these unseen things *was enough to inflict a fever so brutal and sudden that only the strongest might survive.*

For women there was no such 'concern', of course... our lot was mundane by comparison. Relegated to the role of idle, unknowing bystanders, we would wait patiently – blindly – was the menfolk attended to what must be done. Blindfolds or shuttered carriage windows were there to 'protect' us – to 'save' us from Nethug, and from ourselves – for there were many paths to heresy in those times, and the fear of witchcraft was still very real.

The priests – The Brotherhood of the Shard – told us that this age was founded at the end of a time called The Cleansing... a time when the evil of Nethug, the Bicephalus was rampant and consumed all. The world was a wild and decadent place, and the Shard Gods, having for some time tolerated the wickedness of Nethug and his minions, sent great beasts called the Night Dragons to scour the earth and cleanse it of evil. That is what we were all taught: me... my father... his father before him. These were the histories that were handed down through generations, and we believed; believed because there was *nothing else for so* many *years...*

Doubt began to grow however, throughout Huon and the rest of the known world. The young are ever suspicious of old ways, and I was no different. Science had come to the kingdoms of the Osterlands in my father's time, bringing with it the dangerous seeds of rationale and curiosity within the ranks of royalty and lords alike; and also – more *dangerously – within the minds of those commoners fortunate enough to be blessed with scholarly learning.*

There were mechanical things now, pulled behind horse and ox to help farmers plant and till their lands. In the great mills of Swales and the northern Blacklands, paddles turned by running water in their *turn powered endless rows of 'Jennifers': huge, clattering spinning-wheels that churned out reams of cloth by the cart load. In similar fashion, the great forges of Croweda produced tons of precious iron and steel with the aid of this water-powered revolution, and in the saw mills of Strahn and Zeehn and other working villages across the western reaches of Huon, razor-toothed blades of newly-forged, Crowedan steel sliced the huge trees of the inner highlands into long planks, bound for the shipyards of Burnii and Demon's Port.*

Some began to openly question the old ways and dared to doubt the words of the priests, and although it was true this had happened before, this time *there was less effort from above to silence such whispers of discontent. Like those who'd dared to speak out, some* rulers *whose economies were now irrevocably bound to these nascent technologies had also begun to question... and The Brotherhood looked on, taking careful note of every slight and transgression, for to question The Word was to question the ways of The Shard, and that threatened the very existence of The Brotherhood itself. It is said that even the weakest animal will fight if its life is in peril, and The Brotherhood was anything but weak.*

Introduction
The Collected Writings of Phaesia I
Year 16NE (New Era)

Huon & The Southern Osterlands

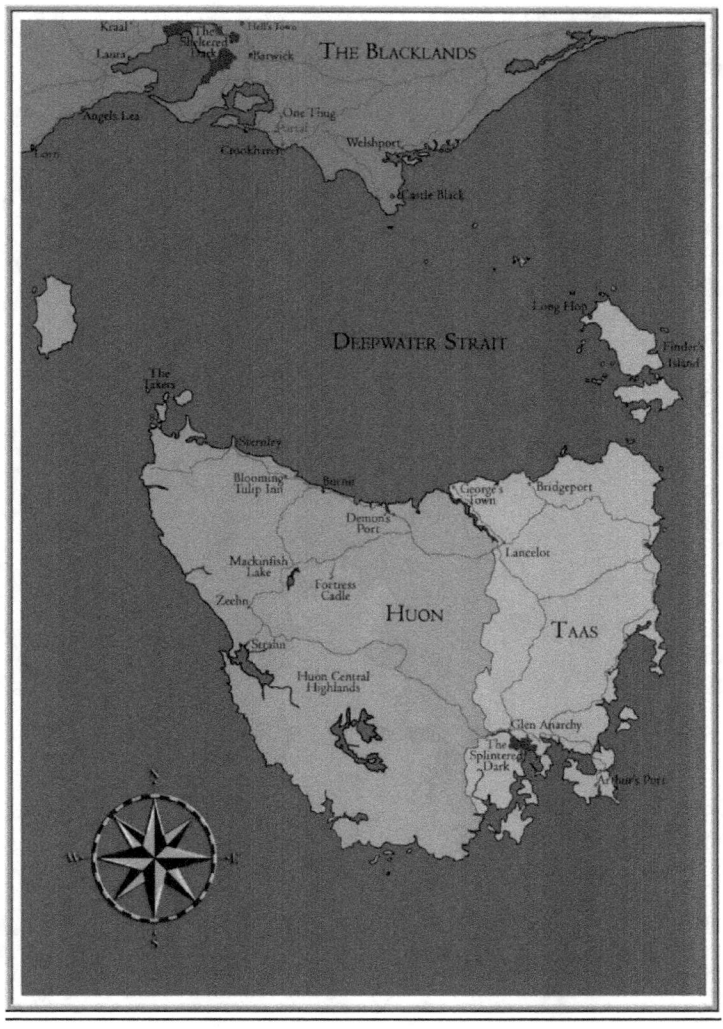

Contents

PROLOGUE

Nev Anderson crashed hard into the tree, collapsing against it and fighting to catch her breath, chest heaving as she gasped at the sudden pain in her shoulder. Years of athletics training and martial arts had left her exceptionally fit for her age, yet even the strongest young body had its limits and she could tell she was reaching the hers after ten minutes of sprinting, falling, stumbling and staggering lost and terrified through dense bushland in almost total darkness.

Her long, auburn hair had fallen loose and now hung wild and tangled about a face that was scratched and grimy from crashing through endless layers of thick underbrush. Her muscles ached, and her elbows and knees were bruised and scraped from numerous trips and falls. A thick layer of low cloud had reduced night-time visibility to almost nil, the situation not helped at all by the heavy, misting rain falling directly into her face through the forest canopy overhead. That she was terrified and also fighting back tears of shock and betrayal wasn't helping her blurred eyesight either.

There was a rather over-dramatic flash of lightning above followed closely by an earth-shaking clap of thunder, and as the sound faded she also heard the frightened neighing of a horse somewhere behind her. It still sounded distant but was nevertheless far closer than the cries of her pursuers had been a few minutes earlier, and Nev realised in horror that they were gaining on her. An initial whimper of fear morphed quickly into a grunt of angry exertion as her survival instincts took over, forcing herself to push away from the tree and run on desperately on into the night.

Her large, black duffel bag dug hard into her back, dragging at her as she ran, yet she refused to leave it behind. Her rational mind screamed at her to ditch it – that she'd run faster and further without such a burden – yet she clung to it tenaciously, some instinct deep within her soul certain its contents would be of far more value than any benefit gained by casting it aside.

She paused again a few hundred metres on, resting against another tree, and took a moment to drag her phone from her jacket pocket. The dim light of the screen was vaguely comforting as it flared into life, but the complete lack of any signal whatsoever still shook the very foundations of her world, just as it had every other time she'd checked in the last few minutes with the same lack of success.

Had there been just one or two men chasing her, she might've considered turning to face them: her youthful appearance hid great strength and quick reflexes, and the wooden practice sword inside her bag could be a dangerous weapon in well-trained hands. Nev considered herself reasonably brave, however she certainly wasn't stupid: there were *a lot more* than just two of them out there, at least one of them was carrying a gun, and it was likely the *rest* were armed with *real* swords made from real steel that was certain to be *real* sharp.

It *should* have been a nice, sunny afternoon according to the radio forecast she'd heard that morning, although the black clouds and the rain had certainly proven *that* wrong. It *should* have been a *fun* afternoon, snacking in front of the TV, watching *Game of Thrones* on cable at Percy's house and fangirling over Jon Snow. Both of them *should* have been at school... but that hadn't happened that afternoon either...

All things considered, Nev Anderson had had better birthdays...

I

A DAY IN THE LIFE

The day had started just fine, her father knocking on her open bedroom door and calling out his usual greeting from the doorway in the minutes before he left for work.

"Time to get up, Lazybones!"

Nev heard that most mornings at six as Drake Anderson bade her a combined good morning/goodbye and headed out the front door for work, although *that* morning he'd at least added a "and Happy birthday, by the way…" in recognition of her having officially turned seventeen overnight.

"Thanks, Dad," she mumbled sleepily, dragging herself into a half-seated position and spilling pillows onto the floor as he entered the room and headed over to her side of the bed.

"Got your present ready for tonight, yeah?" He asked with awkward concern, leaning in and planting a kiss on the top of her head. "Is that okay?"

"It's all good, Dad," she smiled back, trying not to sound too disappointed. It meant having to wait *all day* to see what it was, but she knew he wanted to be there so he could see her reaction when she opened her gift, and she couldn't blame him for that: his work schedule meant they spent little enough time together during the week as it was.

"Gotta go, okay?" He announced apologetically, already halfway to her bedroom door as his face contorted into a badly-hidden frown. "I s'pose you're going to *training* as usual…?"

"You *know* I am, Dad…" she answered with a frown of her own, holding back the comment she wanted to add that would've started them fighting.

"Doesn't he have people of his *own* age to hang around with?"

"We don't '*hang around*', Dad: he's my *sensei*, not my *friend*…!"

"He's an *old man…*" Drake persisted, not happy that she always used the Japanese title for her martial arts instructor, but the disappointment he saw in his daughter's eyes in that moment forced him to rein in his remarks.

Although still technically *not quite* an adult, Nev had been forced to grow up faster than an average teen and her father was well aware of how smart *and* tough his only child was. He knew that in *her* eyes at least, questioning her instructor also questioned her judgement. He *also* knew that at least *some* of his misgivings were based on his *own* racial prejudices, something he sensibly kept to himself, as neither of them needed an argument on his daughter's birthday… particularly one he knew he'd never win. He *also* knew that *Nev* knew how he felt about it, and he wasn't particularly proud of that fact either.

"Just… not *too* long, okay…?" He added finally with a sigh, once again deciding to concede defeat for the time being.

"*Okay*, Dad," she sighed in return, but he was already heading up the hallway for the front door, not wanting to cause any more trouble *or* be late for work.

"Love you…" floated back from the front of the house as he left, as usual carrying the cooler bag she'd prepared for him the night before, packed with a chilled litre-bottle of supermarket-brand water, three small muesli bars and two sandwiches with plain fillings (which was exactly how he liked it). It'd taken two years of constant nagging just to get multi-grain bread onto the menu, and Nev knew there was a harder battle still ahead before something as healthy as salads or vegetables would be permitted to join his preferred staple of sliced deli meat and cheese. She was up for the fight, though… he was starting to put on weight as he got older, and exercise was hard to come by for a man who spent most of his working day at the wheel of a truck.

Her dad hauled coal over at Yallourn, back and forth between the mine and the power station for eight hours a day, five days a week, and that wasn't even counting the frequent 'voluntary' overtime, *or* the three-hour round-trip between work and home. He often griped that most of it seemed to go on the mortgage, but she knew he didn't mind really: they had a home of their own and even if money was tight sometimes, they lived well enough for all that. It mightn't have been this year's model, but he'd given her an *iPhone* for her last birthday, and at Christmas she'd received a mid-range *MacBook* that was a far better unit than her school's standard-issue. Nev never complained: she knew how much overtime he'd worked to pay for it all.

Releasing a frustrated groan that was a reaction both to family issues *and* the fact that she now had to get out of a warm and perfectly good bed, she rolled over twice, buried her head in the covers and toyed with the idea of staying in bed for *at least* another five hours. She got up anyway, threw on her woollen robe and stomped grumpily down to the laundry to stuff a load of washing into the machine and set it running. Realising she'd forgotten to put on her necklace, Nev then returned to her room and took it from the bedside table.

A gift from her paternal grandfather, it was comprised of a chain of finely-made dark links from which hung a single pendant of similar, blackened steel. No more than two centimetres long, the pendant was roughly circular and carried a design of Nordic runes and symbols in a circular pattern, enclosed on both sides by the rearing heads of two dragons, each a representation of the figurehead of a Viking *drekar* longboat. The only small sparks of colour in the entire design were a pinkish colouring for the dragons' tongues and two tiny rubies set into their eyes (which Nev assumed were synthetic).

An old man in his seventies who'd been passionate about his Icelandic heritage, Anders Gunnarson had given it to her for her eleventh birthday, just a few months before he'd passed in his sleep without warning. Her father's names had been anglicised at the time of his birth – at his mother's insistence – but in true Icelandic tradition, he'd always been Dreki Andersson to his father regardless of what his birth certificate said.

Her father had never shown any great love for his Nordic ancestry. Nev had tried to learn at least a *little* out of respect for a grandfather she remembered with great fondness, but it had seemed difficult to separate myth from history as she'd tried to read up on such subjects as Norse gods and the Sagas of Snorri Sturluson, and a lot of it had been *very* heavy reading, even for an exceptionally-bright pre-teen. Interest in her Scandinavian heritage waned as high school arrived on the scene, bringing with it an exponential increase in homework, but Nev at least still honoured the memory of Grandpa Anders in the wearing of his parting gift.

It was the one piece of jewellery she felt any connection to and she *always* wore it *everywhere*, no matter the occasion or situation. Smiling faintly, she stared at it for a moment in her hands then reached back to fasten it behind her head and let the pendant fall down inside the neck of her pyjama top. She felt immediately better with its familiar, reassuring weight resting just below her throat, as if she were finally ready to take on the world and its obstacles for another day.

Heading back to the kitchen for a quick cup of coffee and a light breakfast, she found two opened envelopes on the kitchen table with bills inside for the electricity (quarterly) and a bundled monthly charge for the internet and both their mobile phones combined. Nev wasn't worried about the latter one – she'd already paid that one online the week before – but she did make a mental note to call the power company later and ask for an extension until Dad's payday at the end of the month.

As she looked up, Nev was surprised to find a gift waiting for her on the bench near the sink: a small, flat box that had clearly been awkwardly 'man-wrapped' using far too much sticky tape and a *mortifying* choice of decorative paper that would never be spoken of again (Pink teddy bears and rainbow unicorns, no less!). The box itself seemed intriguingly small: perhaps large enough to hold one of the 'plus-sized' smart phones that had become popular in the last year or two.

"No *way...*" she thought silently, knowing already there really *was* no chance of it being a new phone just a year after she'd received her beloved *iPhone-6*. It *definitely* wouldn't be another phone, so... *what, then...*? She withdrew her phone from her robe pocket almost by reflex, halfway through Instagramming the scene before she remembered how *not* cool the wrapping was and instantly lowered the phone again with a whispered "*...oh,* God, *no...!*"

The note atop the small gift was helpful, at least:

> *I know you're always running out of battery.*
> *Just a little something to keep you connected*
> *'til you get your real present tonight.*
> *Hope you like it.*
> *Happy birthday.*
> *Love you*

"Love you too, Dad," she muttered softly with a faint smile that spoke volumes.

She tore off the paper off in a rush and was pleasantly surprised by what she found beneath. With a smile and a short '*Hmmph...!*' of appreciation, she placed the gift back on the kitchen table, hid the wrapping paper and *then* proceeded to lift her phone to capture the moment.

"*Soooo...* here we have the first present for the day..." she began brightly, engaging video capture on her phone and concentrating on her words as she hurriedly cleared away the unwanted wrapping paper. "A solar-powered phone charger *and* power-bank..." she narrated, switching to dual camera mode to show the gift in the main screen but also keep her face showing in a small box in the bottom corner. "*Not* a new phone... but *very* nice all the same..."

A quick review of the recording, and the footage was immediately uploaded to social media. Her first 'like' a few minutes later was from Percy (*of course...!*); she'd have been *very* put out if it hadn't been.

With the important work now done, she proceeded to make a coffee and butter a few pieces of toast, pausing occasionally to check as a dozen more likes and birthday messages popped up on her phone via Facebook and Instagram, the senders' memories conveniently jogged by her initial post. She read through them quickly, liking a few in return and smiling to herself as she basking in the glow of birthday glory. She then laid the phone on the bench and synced it with the portable Bluetooth speaker already sitting in the centre of the kitchen table. There was always time for a few tunes, played a little louder while she had the house to herself, and some Rita Ora, Selena Gomez or Imagine Dragons would do quite nicely.

She set her phone's music player to shuffle and turned toward the toaster to her left, only to be frozen in place midway through inserting the bread as the *extremely* loud opening lyrics of Led Zeppelin's *Black Dog* blared out from the speaker on the table. Desperately slotting the slices into the toaster as quickly as she was able, she snatched the phone from the bench, killed the music and checked what was actually in her music library at that moment.

"Led Zeppelin... AC/DC... Iron Maiden...?" She muttered in disbelief as she read down the list of latest additions. "Oh... my... God... *Nickelback*...? *Daaaaaad*...!" She moaned in frustration. "*Again*...?"

Her father liked using her laptop to browse sports websites and look for cheap car parts for his never-ending (barely-started) muscle car restoration project, all of which was fine, but he also liked to sometimes change the music selections on his own phone through iTunes. As Nev's device automatically connected to her computer when they were both powered up, he'd also inadvertently loaded what appeared to be an entire gigabyte of crusty old rock songs onto *her* phone while updating his own playlists, something that happened far more often than anyone should have to put up with.

"*Eww... Midnight Oil* now...? Oh, for *goodness sake*...!"

Nothing to be done about it now – there was barely enough time for her to throw together a little something to eat – but that evening after the presents, there would be *serious* words to be had, accompanied *yet another* tedious lecture on '*Using iTunes 101*' for *someone's* dad.

Honda Yoshinori stood on the front porch of his old, weatherboard cottage and stared out at the dawn sky, drawing the air deep into his lungs and releasing it again as his exhaled breath swirling about his head in faint clouds of condensation. He'd experienced some hardship in his seventy-five years – tough times he sometimes doubted many young people today could endure – yet as he stared up into that cloudless blue sky, he knew that far worse was yet to come... and that it was coming soon.

His hand instinctively found itself in the pocket of his dark blue *dogi* training robes, touching the *omamori* amulet he'd travelled four hours by bus to collect. He didn't take out the fabric charm, instead taking some comfort in the feel of it inside the pocket. The amulet was *yaku-yoke* – a ward against evil – and he *always* kept it with him wherever he went. He wasn't sure he believed in the power of such a talisman, but he was also pragmatic enough to recognise it never hurt to hedge ones bets.

Omamori were only intended to last twelve months, and this one was almost due for replacement. Part of him almost felt relief that after waiting for so long, the day he'd been waiting for had finally come: Shinto temples weren't easy to come by outside of Japan, and he'd already made that same bus trip *again* on someone else's behalf in the last month. Making yet another arduous journey back to the city at his age, so soon after the last, was something he was happy to avoid.

With a sigh of thoughtful resignation, he turned and made his way back inside, taking the first door on the left and entering his small, sparsely-decorated bedroom. The curtains were partly-drawn, barely allowing enough light to see what he was doing, but so many years living alone in the same house had left him completely aware of where everything was regardless of what he could or couldn't see.

A long, narrow box of dark, lacquered wood lay atop the mattress on the near side of the bed, its top secured by a pair of shiny, metal latches. The polished lid carried no markings other than the large engraving of a stylized gold dragon that covered almost its entire length. He reached down and felt a sudden shudder ripple through his body as his fingers touched the surface, as if he'd been struck by an unexpected chill. He swayed slightly for a moment, regained control of himself and uttered another prayer as his hand dove into his pocket again for the *omamori*. He drew the amulet out into the open, wrapped about his right hand by its braided cord, and this time there was no ill sensation as he placed his fingers gingerly upon the lacquered wood. He didn't care whether or not it was coincidence that he felt better when holding the charm, just so long as the nausea abated.

Definitely today... he thought to himself *...and I think it* knows, *somehow...* His mouth suddenly felt dry, and he paused again for a moment before lifting the lid and reaching inside. *Still so far away, still* *disconnected from this world, yet it senses* something *all the same. Is it the* knowing *that accelerates everything now...? Is this a cause and effect, or would it happen anyway...?*

An almost overpowering sense of foreboding had swept over him the night before. Similar feelings of nausea and unease had been coming infrequently now for five months or more and had increased significantly in the last few weeks, to the point where he was suffering from sudden attacks of fear and weakness almost daily.

It was the sheer magnitude of the battle he'd foreseen the preceding night – and there was no doubt in his mind that it *was* a battle– that had finally convinced him the time had come. He'd barely slept, spending most of the preceding twelve hours preparing the contents of the box that now lay on his bed... contents he'd kept carefully hidden away for most of his adult life, waiting for just this moment.

Reaching down again, he lifted out the contents of the box and held them reverentially in both hands as if offering to up to the gods, all the while bowing his head low and whispering another prayer to his ancestors. He stood motionless for a few seconds, silently begging the ancients for guidance, before slowly and carefully returning the contents and closing the lid. Flickering images had come in reply to his prayers... nothing coherent, but enough to know that something terrible was indeed going to happen: that it would happen to *her*. He sighed again, saddened by what he'd seen in the vision: it seemed unfair that someone so young and innocent should be dragged into something that would most likely cost them their life.

"Enough pity, you old fool!" He admonished himself grumpily, realising he was wasting precious time. "If you complain long enough, do you think this will wrap *itself*...?"

With a grimace and a renewed sense of purpose, he turned and strode out of the room in search of wrapping paper and adhesive tape.

At the age of twelve, Nev Anderson had found hand-written adverts for martial arts lessons posted on the community notice board of her local supermarket and the idea had stuck. The simple sketch of a stylised, Japanese dragon at the top of the page had captured her imagination in a way that been impossible to shake. Being only twelve, she'd of course been forced to fight hard for her father to even think about letting her try, but she'd persisted and had won out in the end... and had never looked back.

Three times a week, every week since, she'd turned up before school to go through an hour of intense training in *kenjutsu* and other associated martial arts. It had been tough at first, the old man allowing little consideration for her age, but it wasn't in Nev's nature to give up and her determination and natural aptitude had made her an excellent student. The double garage at the rear of Honda's property served as a quite-serviceable training *dojo*, with bamboo panelling on the walls and ceiling, plenty of paper-covered skylights for natural illumination, and a floating floor that was well-sprung to allow for the heavy footwork that went hand-in-hand with *kenjutsu*.

Kenjutsu was an umbrella term covering all forms of Japanese swordsmanship, and unlike the more widely-recognised *kendo*, which made use of protective masks, padding and flexible, bamboo swords (called *shinai*), the old man's open, flowing method combined a range of complimentary and differing styles drawing from a number of schools including *kendo*, *iaido* and even *nitōjutsu* (a style involving the use of two swords simultaneously).

Neither Honda nor his star pupil (his *only* pupil, as far as she could tell) had ever made use of protective padding during the five years Nev had trained with him, and rather than practice with the flexible *shinai*, they instead made use of traditional Japanese *bokken* – wooden swords carved and polished to replicate the feel and balance of real katana. The use of these weapons as training equipment required far more care, as they were heavy, rigid weapons that could cause serious injury or even death, if poorly used in the hands of the inexperienced.

Nev had been badly bruised many times over the years, and even lightly stunned once or twice (although she'd never dared tell her father about that, for fear of being banned from going back). Such heavy blows were rare however and were generally only received in return for an exceptionally poor attack or parry: it was never clear whether her *sensei*'s (instructor's) savage ripostes had been accidental or an unsubtle form of punishment, but she'd always clearly remembered and corrected each mistake as a result.

Both wore traditional *dogi* robes of dark blue: loose-fitting garments tied at the middle that allowed great flexibility and freedom of movement, with Nev's also wearing of bike shorts, T-shirt and a snug-fitting sport crop-top over her underwear, in deference to her own modesty.

Impossible as it seemed, training that particular morning was even more intense than usual. Never one to go easy, Honda drilled her mercilessly, and after forty solid minutes, she was breathless and sweating profusely. He bade her come at him with repeated attacks, launching successive blows from multiple directions, yet try as she might (as always) she'd rarely managed to land a single strike on her instructor in spite of his advancing age and apparent lack of mobility everywhere *except* inside the training *dojo*. In return for her ineffective attacks, she'd received at least half a dozen superficial bruises to take away as souvenirs, as was also usually the case.

Bruises were generally the worst she came away with nowadays: she'd become too quick and adept at dodging or parrying his retaliatory ripostes to receive anything worse than that over the last year or so. Their *bokken* clacked together now and again as blows were parried or deflected, or (more often) slashed through empty air as the dodged and evaded each other's attacks, and as dazed as any connecting strike was likely to leave her, Nev probably would've been even *more* stunned to discover that the *bokken* themselves – one of which she was permitted to take with her for practice at home – were carved from the wood of the Loquat tree, each valued at over a thousand dollars.

"Enough, Tatsuko…" Honda announced finally, lifting a palm as a signal to stop as he stepped away. As usual, he used the Japanese 'pet name' he'd given her by the end of her first week, five years before: one that had stayed with her ever since. "You've done well… *very* well this morning, considering how strongly I have tested you…"

"*Sensei…*!" She acknowledged simply with a deep bow with hands clasped in front of her chest, hiding a proud smile all the while: open praise from Honda was as rare as a diamond, and was to be similarly cherished.

"We shall rest now, but not *too* long…" he added slowly, the hint of a wry smile crossing his lips. "It should not do for your father to receive a call because you were late for school… *already*, he does not like you being here, yes…?"

There was no anger or recrimination in his tone, making Nev feel far more sadness and embarrassment as a result. She was actually a little surprised he'd mentioned it at all; she knew that *he* knew how her dad felt about the training, but it generally wasn't in Honda's nature to openly speak on sensitive or personal matters.

"I – I'm *sorry*, *Sensei*..." she stammered awkwardly, walking over to where her black duffel bag lay against the near wall and slipping the sheathed *bokken* casually inside. "He doesn't mean anything by it... he just..." But her words trailed off as she realised she had no idea what else to say, and she instead followed him meekly out of the *dojo* and along the rear porch to the back door of the house.

"He does not like his daughter... his *teenage* daughter... spending too much time *alone* with an old man, yes...?" Honda asked simply, again with no malice as he stepped straight through into the kitchen, although perhaps this time with notable sadness. "Sit, Tatsuko... sit. We shall take tea and talk, you and I," he added, moving over to where a round, cast-iron kettle of Japanese design sat atop his gas stove. She was so used to hearing that name now that she mostly didn't even register when he said it, and considering how much she hated the long version of her *real* name anyway, it hardly seemed to matter.

The kitchen was as sparsely decorated as the rest of the house, with just the bare essentials of stove top, oven, fridge, sink and benches complemented by a tiny, circular table in the centre partnered by just three chairs of varying parentage. On the other side of the sink, a long, narrow box wrapped in plain, brown paper lay on the kitchen bench, and although it was impossible to actually tell, Nev suspected that considering its shape and length, it might well contain a set of *bokken*. Honda occasionally ordered replacements from overseas, and had there not already been a difficult conversation in progress, she might well have been a good deal more interested in its contents.

"He – he's not a *bad* person, *Sensei*..." she offered apologetically from the doorway, reluctant to enter the house now as feelings of guilt-by-association washed over her.

"What is '*bad*' about being protective of one's only child?" Honda asked pointedly, one eyebrow raised as he turned to glance at her for a moment. "That I am *Nihongo* – *Japanese* – is also a problem, I think, but not for the same reason... *Sit*...!" He urged more insistently, pointing at the nearest of three chairs placed randomly around his small, circular kitchen table.

"His grandfather fought in the war... was taken prisoner..." she tried to explain, suddenly feeling very awkward about how to approach so sensitive a subject as the Second World War with someone of Japanese ancestry. Although Nev's *logical* mind mostly understood that her father, an otherwise decent and reasonable man, was sometimes guilty of racism because of how he'd been raised, it nevertheless always made her feel incredibly uncomfortable and more than a little ashamed.

"...And died at the hands of *my* countrymen, yes...?" Honda asked knowingly, lowering his eyes momentarily as he too felt a fleeting sensation of associated guilt on a far greater scale. "I suspected something like this – I have *seen* such reactions many times in my life, and one should be cautious in assigning blame: these feelings are passed down through generations, and only through the passing of *further* generations will they ease and disappear.

"It may surprise you that I too lost my father to that Pacific War," he added, indeed surprising her with part of his history that hadn't previously been revealed. "He was *kamikaze*... shot down when I was just two years old. Do I blame the American gunners, protecting themselves and their shipmates? Of course not... that war left a stain of dishonour on the history of my people, and shameful acts were committed in the name of the Emperor during those terrible years.

"Hatred is a difficult thing to be free of, *particularly* when it is born out of pain..." Honda observed gently, his back to her now as he checked there was water in the kettle and ignited the burner beneath it. "Your father never knew his grandfather, but it is honourable that he should remember him.   Do *you* not honour your *mother's* memory also?"

"Why so hard at training today, *Sensei*...?" Nev asked, blurting the words out far too quickly. She'd always been extremely sensitive regarding mother and was desperate to change the subject.

"The *truth*...?" He asked, letting the question slide as he waited patiently for the water to boil. "The truth is that you have *already* learned *everything* an old fool such as I can teach. Most of this last *year* has been nothing but practice, and only the loneliness of an old man has prevented me from telling you this a long time ago. I pushed you harder today than I ever have before, and you performed as well as I expected."

"But – but, *Sensei*..." she stammered, fighting to prevent sudden tears from welling at the corners of her eyes at the shocked implication of what Honda had just said. "How – how can there be no more training... *what – what will I do*...?"

"You have learned less than I imagined if you are so quick to believe you need no longer practice to maintain your skills, Tatsuko," he pointed out drily as he used a wadded tea towel to lift the hot kettle from the burner by its handle and carefully place it on a circular heat pad at the centre of the small table. "*Indeed,* more time on practice and *less* with this 'Instagram' and 'Snapchat' would serve you well..."

"Where did you even *learn* those words?" She asked with mild surprise, trying to remove her hand from the phone in her robe pocket as if the thought of Instagramming their tea together hadn't occurred to her for a moment.

"A *wise* man learns much... about his friends *and* his enemies..." Honda pointed out, a momentary sharpness in his tone now as he placed two small, bowl-like cups on the table next to the kettle. "These things you teenagers do now with your phones may be media, but it is *anything* but social: friends are those who are *real... not* those who 'like' your photographs but never show you their *true* selves. But, enough of this..." he continued with a soft growl and a shake of his head, realising he had slipped off-topic. "*Of course*, you may still come and practice whenever you wish: you will *always* be welcome here." He slid down into the chair opposite hers, the steaming kettle between them. "All I am saying to you *today* is that is that I am getting no younger, and that you have come as far as *I* can take you."

"*Is* there no more to learn, *Sensei...*?"

"There is *always* more to learn, child!" He snapped quickly in reply. "What I teach here is not some registered *kendo* class, Tatsuko: here there is no striving for the next *Dan* before a panel of judges. What I teach will never win awards or trophies..." he added shrewdly, fixing her with a strangely intense gaze for a moment, "...but *remember* what you've learned, and when the time comes it *may* save your life. You *still* hold back on your strikes against me, for example, although I doubt you do this *consciously*. You will need to master such things *and more* if you are to grow into the master swordsman you are destined to become..." he advised cryptically, leaving her torn between the meaning behind his words and pride over what had clearly been a great compliment.

"*Sensei...*" she began searchingly, completely confused now.

"Tatsuko-*chan*, there is no need to call me 'teacher' any longer," he observed kindly, bowing his head as a sign of respect. "We may speak as equals now... as *friends*... if that is your wish..." he added

29

quickly, ever aware of the difference in gender *and* the staggering age gap.

Never before had Nev heard Honda attach that diminutive suffix to the name he'd given her. In Japanese culture, the addition of '-*Chan*' to someone's name when addressing them was an indication that the speaker considered the other party a friend or equal, as Honda had just indicated, and Nev instinctively understood the significance of the subtle shift that had just taken place in their five-year relationship as pupil and instructor.

"You do me a great honour, Yoshihiro-*san*," she replied eventually, rising quickly to her feet and also executing a short bow, but ultimately unable to bring herself to use an honorific of similar familiarity. She instead elected for a more formal type of address that suggested equality of a more conservative nature.

"It has been *my* honour to be your teacher," he declared with a smile and a sudden slap of his palm on the table top that made her flinch just a little. "You have been a perfect student, these five years. Not only have you learned and mastered every combination of moves that I have taught you, you have *also* made every effort to follow the *tradition* of my teachings. You have acknowledged me as your master and have always shown the required level of respect. *This*, I did not expect from a 'Westerner'. Along with the training I have given you, you have indulged my lectures, and through them – I hope – you have *also* learned the importance of *Bushido*…"

"Righteousness, *compassion*, respect, duty and loyalty, *integrity*, heroic courage, *honour* and self-control… *these* are the Way of the Samurai…" she declared with a single nod, well aware of each of the eight virtues and emphasising those she knew Honda personally considered most important.

Had he asked her to recite them again in Japanese, Honda knew she could've done that too, with perfect inflection. Either in spite of her family history – or perhaps *because* of it – Nev Anderson was meticulous when it came to learning, something unusual in a modern teenager that was to be applauded and encouraged. He knew that she also excelled at her high school studies for the same reason.

"Because of this…" he continued with a nod of his own, "…*and* because it is your birthday…" he added, rising from his chair and causing her to blush inexplicably as she realised something unexpected was afoot "…I have this small token to give…" And with that, he lifted the wrapped package from the bench behind him and turned back toward her, arms outstretched just as they had been earlier than morning, the solemn offering to her this time instead of his ancestors.

She moved quickly around the table as she recognised the ceremonial manner in which he was presenting it to her. Without a single word, fighting to keep any emotion from her expression, Nev bowed deeply and then reached out and carefully accepted the gift from him with similar solemnity, both of them bowing again to each other in turn at the conclusion of the exchange.

It was wrapped simply in a single layer of brown paper, and she could feel the smooth wood of the box beneath. It was heavier than she expected a wooden sword to be – several kilograms at least – although she reasoned that the added weight of the box itself probably had something to do with that.

"A new *bokken*, *Sensei*... Yoshihiro-*san*...?" She asked, finding that old habits definitely died hard but correcting herself quickly.

"Something... you will find useful," he suggested with a tilt of his head, completely avoiding the question as a faint, almost impish smile flickered across his face in that moment. "All I ask is that you *do not* open until *after* school..."

"Oh, no *way*...! You, *too*...?" She protested, the combination of sudden excitement and dismay over the unexpected gift causing her to lose any show of formality. "I can't open it *now*...? *Sensei*, you *can't* be serious?"

"This is all I ask..." he replied, steadfast. "You go to your friend's house after school, yes...? Take it *with* you and you may open it *then*. You may ignore my request, of course, but I do not believe you would show such disrespect."

"Now you're not playing *fair*...!" She grumped, well aware that he was using emotional blackmail and not happy about it. "Just for *that*..." she added, deciding to return fire in her own way, "...you're going to have to let me take a selfie with you...!"

"I do not believe in such foolishness!" He protested immediately, dismissing the idea with a wave of his hand.

"It's either that, or I open the present *now*, Yoshihiro-*san*..." she pressed on, determined to win *this* battle at least. "Which is it to be?"

"This is unseemly...!" He snapped grumpily, but she knew she'd won in that moment and she was by his side in an instant, the phone already miraculously in her hand and at the ready.

"Smile for the camera…!" She directed brightly, holding the phone at arm's length and leaning in until her face was next to his. It took some effort: although she was little more than average height herself, she was still at least a half-head taller than her diminutive, elderly instructor.

"*Omae ikareteru…*!" He muttered sourly under his breath; but at the same time, just as millions of others were probably doing at that very moment around the world, he swallowed his pride and a affected an obviously-fake smile just long enough to allow the 'crazy person' beside him to take the picture.

"Now, *that* is going on Instagram…!" She declared, triumphant in having finally been allowed her first selfie with him in the five years they'd trained together. "*See…*!" She added, holding the screen up to show him as her phone chirped loudly. "Perce *already* likes it…!"

"I have trained a *demon child…*!" Honda decided, at least partly joking. "Away with you now… you have *school* to attend…!"

She'd returned home just long enough to have a quick shower, get ready for school and hang out the load of laundry that had finished while she was out. With her own lunch also prepared the night before, it was a simple enough task to pack that into her duffel bag with a few school books, her dad's present, the Bluetooth speaker and the still-wrapped gift Honda had given her. She wondered for a moment if perhaps she should leave behind the new *bokken* – it *had* to be a *bokken*, after all – but she wouldn't be back home for hours and she *really* wanted to open at least one major present while it was still daylight.

Taking it with her wasn't the problem it could've been at most schools. Her *kenjutsu* training was well known and the principal himself had given tacit approval for her to keep her practice equipment in her bag or in her locker, including *bokken*, just so long as they *remained* there throughout the day. There'd never been a problem before, and she didn't see any reason for there to be one today, of all days.

"It's not like it's a *real* sword or anything…" she muttered softly to herself, slinging the now-heavy bag over her shoulders and heading out the door again for the second time that morning.

At her school, Year-Twelves were at least permitted smart casual dress, allowing them to stand apart from the serviceably frumpy uniforms they'd been forced to wear the last five years running. That morning, she'd decided to make a special effort to dress up in honour of her own birthday, and had broken out some of her best clothes as a result: a lace-panelled, white peplum top with a beige mini-skirt, worn over brown leggings and matching slouchy calf boots in suede. Over all that she shrugged on her prized dark brown, double-breasted woollen jacket, hip-length and belted at the waist. It wasn't *quite* snug enough to be considered 'figure-hugging', but it was undeniably flattering nevertheless.

It was a favourite outfit that she only wore on special occasions; one of a few special combinations in her wardrobe that had taken a long time and a lot of extra shifts at the local *McDonald's* to pay for. Her dad worked hard to keep them housed and to put food on the table, but a truck driver's wage only went so far and she'd decided early that if she wanted any treats or luxuries that lay beyond the scope of their limited budget, the best way to get anything special was to pay for it herself.

From the moment she'd been old enough to legally work, Nev had done exactly that at the local burger franchise, working as many shifts as she could get to buy herself clothes, shoes and other accessories, and to also take some of the burden off her dad's shoulders by contributing where she could, like paying her own phone plan and contributing to utilities like gas and electricity and the monthly internet bill (which she mostly used in any case).

The school morning had passed exactly as it had on countless other weekdays, with her working hard at her classwork or studying intently until the bell sounded to signal the end of each period, at which point hundreds of students simultaneously stampeded to wherever their next class was, beginning the whole cycle all over again. There'd been the obligatory collection of birthday greetings from a dozen or so of her closer school friends – all of them female – but otherwise there was little to report of any interest. The only minor exception to that routine came during French, one of only two classes this year that she shared with Persephone Koutroulis, her best friend in the entire school (or anywhere else, for that matter).

Persephone had turned eighteen a few months earlier and was already thinking hard about life *beyond* school, with most of her plans revolving around becoming *extremely* rich and powerful without being required to do lots of *anything* resembling actual work. Percy was of above-average height and thin as a reed, and Nev had to admit (if backed into the jealousy corner and poked with a stick) that her best friend was quite attractive in her own, slightly off-centre way. Where Nev had turned to martial arts and athletics as a young teen, Percy had instead taken ballet lessons for years, and somehow always seemed to glide across the floor rather than actually walk.

Nev's hair was a bright auburn colour, tending to a lighter reddish-brown when exposed to direct sunlight, and always seemed to have a mind of its own when it came to styling (leaving Nev with a fight on her hands most mornings), whereas Percy's was long and flowing and hung about her Mediterranean features in lustrous locks that somehow never seemed out of place no matter how much (or little) preparation it received. As attractive as Nev might've been to any unbiased observer, she nevertheless secretly envied Percy for her dark, 'mysterious' looks and her incredible hair.

Sharp, socially savvy and *very* clever, if not *exceptionally* smart in the classic sense, Percy *might* have been the most popular girl in school had it not been for the fact that there was something strange about her; something vague and undefinable that most people found a little 'off'. She was friendly enough when she felt like it, but she generally chose *not* to hang out with the popular crowd (a form of social 'suicide' in itself, as Nev could personally attest) and instead spent a large part of her free time at school either in the library or a spare study room, reading books on folklore and mythology.

Percy was obsessed with the idea of magic and dragons, and liked nothing better than to sit down with a good (or even not-so-good) fantasy novel or non-fiction work on the subject, or curl up in front of the TV watching movies of a similar ilk. It had been at Percy's urging that Nev had first seen the *Lord of the Rings* and *The Hobbit* movies, after which she'd then gone on to reading the novels (which had been hard-going at times but had nevertheless turned out to be surprisingly good). As a self-proclaimed nerd herself, Nev's tastes tended more toward science-fiction but she'd been forced to admit that Tolkien's most famous works had been an amazing experience for any avid reader. That interest had also developed into a shared love of *Game of Thrones*, the release of the latest season on cable having been the cause much excitement for both of them.

Percy's obsession often flowed over into her daily life. She generally refused to dress in the fashions of the day and seemed to mostly get away with it (as much a reason to envy her as anything else

Nev could think of). Dark dresses and carefully-applied make up that might've seemed excessively 'Goth' or (*God forbid*) even *Emo* on someone else, somehow worked for Percy and became something different... a style all her own. Of all the strange little anomalies that somehow made Percy stand out for what a teenager might think were all the wrong reasons however, Nev suspected it was the weird way she *looked* at people that mostly set them on edge.

Persephone's eyes were large and dark, and in low lighting they sometimes appeared completely black – as if she had no irises at all. Whenever she spoke to someone, it seemed her eyes were actually boring straight into their psyche, where she could somehow read every thought and see every dark secret... as if she already knew what that person was thinking. Nev's dad often joked that *boys* were usually only thinking about *one thing* most of the time anyway, so reading *their* minds probably wasn't all that difficult. He said that, having *been* a boy once, he knew what they were generally like, and although *Nev* hadn't had much experience with boys at all, she knew *that* was true enough.

One of the older boys had dared to ask out Percy the preceding year, but his words had simply trailed off half-way through under the assault of that dark, withering stare. A nickname had been coined not long after: NQR... 'Not Quite Right', like that chain of clearance grocery stores that had outlets in the city and up in Morwell. Persephone Koutroulis didn't like being called 'Percy' all that much (although she accepted it from Nev as a symbol of their friendship), but she *really* hated 'NQR'. Something as tame as 'Percy' paled into insignificance by comparison.

One thing Honda had been wrong about however had been his assumption that morning that Nev had been spending most of her afternoons over at Percy's house. Although that might've been true once, her friend had been unusually difficult to catch up with over the last few months, something that'd left Nev feeling strangely ill-at-ease and more than a little left out. Her absences had been due to a sudden and completely out-of-character decision to take up bushwalking and bike riding in the surrounding countryside, and the fact that she generally preferred to go alone made the whole thing stranger still.

"Morning, bitches..." Percy quipped lightly, issuing her customary, cavalier greeting to anyone within earshot and drawing a few sniggers as she plonked herself down into the empty chair Nev had saved for her.

She wore one of her standard ensembles; fashionably-expensive Doc Martens beneath a long, figure-hugging dress of dark blue she'd picked up from a charity shop somewhere. It looked like it had been made in the seventies, based on what Nev could see of the fabric's faded, tie-dye style pattern that was now almost invisible with age, yet somehow – as usual – Percy managed to look a million dollars in it, the effect capped off by a small decorative necklace inlaid with a bright blue, diamond-shaped stone that appeared to be tanzanite or kyanite, if Nev's recollection of their science geology project served her correctly.

"Not feeling the love, *Persephone...*" Kevin Gallagher called softly from the desk behind theirs, childishly emphasising Percy's name just to be annoying. "How come *I* don't get a 'good morning'...? Don'tcha wanna talk to me...?" Seated together as always, Kevin and his partner in crime, Robbie 'Dunkin'' Donat ('Dunkin'... as in the doughnut franchise, obviously...) were two of the usual suspects in those rare times that there was any kind of trouble or disturbance at school. Most of the other students suspected the only reason the pair hadn't been suspended or expelled several times in the last six years was because of their family connections within the local council.

"I *was* talking to you, *biatch*...!" She fired back without a moment's hesitation, turning to fix both of them with a witheringly icy glare that instantly wiped the smug, cheesy grins from both their faces as the pair became the focus of another round of faint laughter.

"That will be *enough* of *that* kind of language, Persephone..." Miss Hoskins warned severely from out front of the class, as she did *every* time Percy entered the room and made a similar, irreverent declaration upon arrival. She then went about the morning's French lesson as if nothing had happened, *also* exactly as she did every other time. "All right, everyone: please open your text books and continue on from where you were up to yesterday. At the end of the class, I'll be asking each of you to give a brief *précis* of what you've read so far..."

"Hope I haven't ruined your *date*, boys..." Percy hissed under her breath, just loud enough for Gallagher and Donat to hear as she delivered her *coup-de-grâce*. "Next time, maybe try somewhere a little more *romantic*...?"

"Nuffin' wrong with bein' gay..." Donat pointed out with surprising open-mindedness, almost sounding genuine in his protest but not at all helping their cause as the laughter at their expense grew substantially.

"Jesus, Dunkin'... *we're* not gay...!" Gallagher hissed back plaintively, rolling his eyes and mightily sorry he'd ever opened his mouth.

"I know *that*..." Donat grumbled softly, the damage already done. "...Just *sayin'*, is all..."

"Class...! *That will do*...!" Miss Hoskins snapped loudly, not at all happy about the noise levels, the giggling *or* the fact that she'd been distracted from her own reading. "I can hand out a snap test instead, if you've all *finished* your work already..."

That threat instantly turned every pair of eyes back to their text books, and a hush settled back over the class room as actual study finally began. Reading like the rest, Percy could feel the heat of Gallagher's humiliated glare burning into her back and she cared not a bit, a self-satisfied smirk the only outward display of the enjoyment she felt over her latest victory against the Neanderthals of the world.

"You *really* know how to make friends, don't you...?" Nev whispered a few moments later, allowing enough passed time to avoid Miss Hoskins' attention. "His dad *is* the mayor, you know... and they *do* know how to use *guns*..." she added as an afterthought, not sure of the relevance but throwing it in anyway.

"Dad kicks their butts at the range every weekend," Percy replied with a snort of derision. Her father had been a regional trap-shooting champion several years running, and was the number one member at the local club. "I don't know why those two morons are even *in* this class, other than boosting numbers and keeping Hoskins in a job! Never mind about *that*, anyway: what *else* did you get for your birthday?" She continued, glancing up just long enough to make sure their teacher had indeed returned to her own book, the class again forgotten for the time being.

"Haven't got my 'big' present yet, *whatever* it is..." Nev grumped softly in return. "Dad wants me to wait until he gets home, *as usual*. *And* he went and put all *his* songs on my phone *again*: my player's *filled* with screaming, old *pensioners*...!"

"*Painful*...!" Percy nodded in sympathy, pulling a face and giving her tone just the right amount of drama to suit the occasion. "Thank you *so much* for *that* mental image..."

"Got a solar charger for my phone though..." Nev added brightly.

"Yes, I already 'liked' *that* this morning... *duhhh*... how boredom...!"

"Well, *I* think it's pretty cool," Nev sniffed in return, "and I got something from Yoshi as well..."

"*Creepy*, if you ask me, but *again*: seen the movie, bought the T-shirt...!"

"Why are you being such a *cow* this morning?" Nev shot back, knowing Percy was just having fun in her own, caustic way but not really in the mood for it on her birthday. "It's not the end of the month *yet*..."

"*Ouch*...!" Percy conceded with raised eyebrows, in deference to their current class adding: "...or maybe I should say *Touché*...! *Sarcastic*, much...? And apparently *I'm* the cow... LOL..." she added, actually pronouncing it as '*loll*' rather than sounding out each letter individually. "*So* over this conversation," she declared suddenly, changing the subject again. "...What are you doing later...? Anything planned...? Meeting up with some *boy* I – and possibly *you* – don't know about...?"

"What, *apart* from *school* on a Monday...?" Nev asked grumpily, ignoring the crack about her well-known, almost complete lack of experience with boys and not quite ready to let her friend off the hook just yet. "Dad's not going to be home until late as usual, so *nothing* I guess, unless I can find a 'friend' to spend time... *for a change*..."

"Oh, *such* melodrama..." Percy sighed, clearly overacting. "I can do better than *that*. You've got a study period after lunch, right? And after *that*, we both have history..."

"With you so far..." Nev replied drily.

"*We-ell*..." Percy continued, dragging the word out for effect. "You *know* we have satellite at home, right? And you *know* it's Monday... right...?" She left the rest hanging for her friend to run with.

"Oh, my *God*, I forgot: *Game of Thrones*...!"

"Latest episode, screening from noon today and set to record..."

"And this helps us *how*...? *School*, remember...?"

"I *thought* that *maybe*... just this once, and considering it *is* your birthday..." Percy went on, lowering her voice to a hushed whisper now as she verged into potentially dangerous territory "...that you *might* consider ditching school after lunch so we can go back to my place and *watch* it. Mum and George are away visiting Nana, and Dad won't be home until well after five anyway, so we'll have the house to ourselves."

"I don't know if that's such a good idea..." Nev recoiled slightly, vaguely phobic about the idea of doing anything even *slightly* against the rules. "We've got projects due soon... and someone will *know*, anyway..." She was thinking of what her father would say if he found out, and nothing she was imagining about that was very pleasant.

"*Seriously*...?" Percy almost laughed out loud. "Nevaeh Anderson..." she went on, purposefully using Nev's full name simply because her friend hated it so much "...you have the *highest* grades of anyone in the entire year, and have done *every* year in recorded history..." She knew there was at least *a little* exaggeration there, but wasn't about to let that get in the way of making a persuasive argument. "Jorgenson sometimes checks his physics questions with *you* before he hands them to the rest of the class, for goodness' sake!"

That was only once, *really*... Nev conceded silently.

"Missing one stupid history class *will not* hurt your marks *at all*..." Percy continued, suddenly feeling that an intervention was in order, "and more than *that*, you *never* do *anything* fun that involves breaking the rules even *just a little*: no cutting class... *no kissing boys*... not even any bloody *swearing*, for Christ's sake, and *any* bastard will tell you *that's* not healthy...!" That she managed to get a suppressed smile out of Nev in reaction to her intentionally excessive profanity was encouraging at least.

As was the way of teenage girls the world over, as attractive as Persephone Koutroulis knew she herself was, in her own way she nevertheless also envied Nev for her athletic fitness, auburn hair, green eyes and her perfectly-shaped nose and smile. Just that little bit older than her friend and *far* more worldly and 'street-smart', Percy was certain that the only reason Nev had never had a boyfriend (apart from never really seeming to have been *interested* in having one for some unfathomable reason), was that she never made any effort to 'put herself out there', as Percy's mum would've put it in her own, classy way.

Admittedly, Percy hadn't shown any interest in boys lately either, past history notwithstanding, but that was of course *completely* different, and what had happened between her and Johno didn't *really* count, anyway. Besides, the fact that she'd decided for the time being to remain happily single was purely an indication that her mind (and heart) were set on far *bigger* goals, something she was quite confident *wasn't* the case with Nev. She didn't *think* Nev was gay, although she'd of course never actually *asked*, and Percy was *pretty* sure her best friend at least *liked* boys, even if she seemed likely to slip into paralysis if she ever actually *talked* to one.

Nev certainly went on enough about how gorgeous Jon Snow was, (adding silently: well, *hello*...who *wouldn't* think that...?) yet she *also* had a tendency most of the time to dress in frumpy, utilitarian clothing that basically *guaranteed* no boy would ever look at her twice. Nev had *at least* shown a bit of fashion sense for her birthday; although it was of a very different style to anything Percy would've chosen for *herself*, it was nevertheless a marked improvement over most other days, when she seemed happy to just turn up in any old thing. Nev was well overdue for a little mischief in her life, and Percy wasn't above using that to suit her own purposes.

"I dunno, Perce... we've got that paper on Ancient Greece due next week..." Nev wavered, her schoolwork foremost in her thoughts as usual, "...and anyway, what would Barnaby say? He'll be in the principal's office *five minutes* after class finishes to drop us right in it."

"*Ahhhhhh*...!" Perce groaned in exasperation, loud enough for Miss Hoskins to lift a warning eye and glare momentarily in her direction. "You know *everything* there is to know about physics and chemistry..." she continued, lowering her speech accordingly. "You speak *French* like a Parisian. *Shakespeare* comes to *you* for spellchecking..." she complained, exaggerating again, but on point at least regarding Nev's tendency to excel in every class "...and you *already* know more about Ancient Greece than bloody Herodoofus did...!"

"*Herodotus*," she corrected automatically, unable to stop herself despite knowing Percy had intentionally mispronounced the name just to annoy.

"What-*ever*...! The point is, missing *one silly history class* will not do you *any* harm whatsoever, and *might* just do you more than a little good!"

As Perce had entered into her little rant, it occurred to Nev that it *did* sometimes feel like she never had the opportunity to actually *live* once in a while. When she wasn't at school, she was usually at training, flipping burgers at work, or at home either studying, doing chores or making sure Dad had his clothes ironed and his lunch packed for the next morning. In that moment, with her best friend raving on about enjoying life, she suddenly *did* wonder what it might actually feel like to break the rules or step outside her well-established routines once in a while.

"*Honestly*, Nev: *Game of Thrones*...!" Percy continued, sensing her friend's defences were weakening and going for the 'kill'. "Jon Snow... Jaime Lannister...!" There was a long pause, Percy's eyes boring into the side of her head as Nev stared hard at the 'virtual whiteboard' projected onto the screen at the front of the class and thought deeply about what to do next. "Dragons, Nev... *Dragons*...!"

"Oh, Perce..." Nev answered finally, turning to face her friend with a melodramatically dreamy half-smile, the decision made. "You had me at 'Jon Snow'..."

II

A MOMENTARY LAPSE

Nev grumbled something unpleasant under her breath for the thousandth time that afternoon as their push-bikes rounded the Reed Crescent corner and trundled on along Chisholm, pushing down hard on her pedals and trying to catch up as Percy began to draw ahead. The thick scrub and long grass of a wetland nature reserve rose up on either side, and as they continued south she could hear the faint sound of surf crashing against the beach somewhere up ahead in the distance.

They'd slipped away from school after lunch, made a quick stop at Percy's house, then headed out of town and turned their bikes south toward the nearby coast. The cloudless sunshine of the morning – something the forecast had promised would last all day – had completely disappeared by that time, gathering dark clouds hanging extremely low, and it was starting to look like an excellent chance of rain in the not-too-distant future.

Rain wouldn't have been a problem had they been seated in front of the 55-inch flat screen in Perce's lounge room, watching cable and snacking guiltily on some of the numerous treats her mum always kept in the pantry. It had turned out however that Percy's mum had come home earlier than expected, and *somehow* (...during a moment of temporary insanity, *clearly*...), Percy had instead convinced Nev to take part in some ill-conceived 'nature ride' that was sounding sillier by the minute, *particularly* now that grey clouds were looming so ominously.

Second thoughts were also starting to raise their ugly heads at the back of her consciousness regarding the consequences of what they'd done that afternoon. Her Dad often said that there was nothing faster than the 'speed of doubt' – Nev was pretty sure he was quoting some comedian from one of his old DVDs – and right at that moment, she was finding out exactly how fast that actually was.

She was now absolutely certain that she'd be in *big* trouble for skipping school. Maybe not tonight... maybe not for a day or two... but *eventually*, her father would find out she'd cut class for the afternoon and when he did, it wouldn't matter in the slightest that she was already 'top of her class', or that one of the periods she'd missed had 'only been a study break anyway'...

"Just one more *fun* fact about living in a small town at the *end of the known world*," she growled as she quickened her pace and tried to catch up. Much like any small, country town, everyone in *hers* always knew *everyone else's* business, and sooner or later that business *always* became public. 'The truth will out', Dad also said, and he'd sure-as-hell found *that* out the hard way. Nev hated her mum for what she'd done to him – to *both of them* – yet although she'd never admit it to anyone, Nev missed her terribly all the same.

"Come on, *loser!*" Percy called laughingly back over one shoulder, sounding like she'd not pedalled a single metre. "You're making it *easy!*

First-is-the-worst...! That strange, irrational catchphrase rose up from some long-forgotten backwater of Nev's brain – something that had been a running joke back when she was younger, play-fighting to be first in through the front door and losing out to Mum or Dad. She'd only been a kid then, back when she'd never have thought twice about saying something so childish... back when it was still the three of them. Nev released a soft growl and forced those memories from her mind, finding extra strength and surging ahead as her bike swayed left and right under all that increased energy.

"'I don't know what happened, officer,'..." she mimicked with breathless sarcasm, jokingly supposing how the imaginary police interview might go after her arrest for murder. "'One minute, she was cycling in front of me... the next, I was standing over her with the blood-spattered road sign in my hands'..."

Nev was almost Percy's height but looked much shorter when standing side-by-side due to her friend's notably slimmer figure. Nev's dad often joked that Percy could be arrested for having 'no visible means of support', after which Nev usually pointed out in return that dad jokes like that were one of the reasons he never got invited to parties. The irony that she'd picked up many of his 'old-fashioned' sayings and mannerisms as she'd grown up with just one parental influence was an irony had eluded her over the years.

Although she too was definitely on the 'lean' side, Nev's fitness regime had given her a figure that was noticeably more solid and athletic than Percy's; one that was clearly more defined when wearing form-fitting clothes (as rare as that generally was). At seventeen, she'd already grown into the beautiful young woman she'd always been destined to become; something her father sometimes lay awake at night worrying about.

His only daughter was smart, funny and full of life... everything her mother had been and more... and that fact was Drake Anderson's greatest joy *and* his darkest fear. She'd been forced to grow up early, forced to take a far greater burden upon her young shoulders than any child should ever have to bear, and even a simple truckie who'd left school early understood well enough that that kind of extra responsibility was bound to take its toll on someone so young.

"It's up here on the right!" Percy called back over her shoulder, releasing a whoop of excitement and waving a hand in the general direction of what appeared to be a narrow track, disappearing into the scrub on the right about two hundred metres further on. The track looked a bit overgrown and marshy where it joined Chisholm Road, didn't look at all safe for bikes, and *definitely* wasn't very appealing as somewhere to 'get back to nature' as Percy had so enthusiastically put it an hour before. The whole thing was starting to seem a bit suspect in Nev's opinion.

"Are you *sure* this is gonna be worth it...?" Nev asked doubtfully as they came to a halt by the side of the road, standing upright astride their mountain bikes in the middle of the track's entrance. The duffel bag that still hung faithfully from her back swung to and fro, dragging at her shoulders faintly as she shifted her footing to keep the bike stable. She'd left her books at Percy's place, but there was no way she was leaving her presents behind and the bag was still quite heavy as a result.

"Of *course* I am," Percy snapped back tartly. "...Been here *heaps* of times."

"The *one* day I decided to wear my *good* boots!" She muttered, feeling *very* dubious about the whole thing and unimpressed by the look of the track as it disappeared into the scrub. "We're not gonna find Jimmy Hoffa in here, are we?"

"*Who*...?" Percy asked blankly, not a shred of recognition in her dark eyes regarding an American union boss who'd disappeared without trace four years before her dad had even been born.

"Donald MacKay…?" Nev tried again, almost hopeful for a reaction as she at least moved to the subject of more *local* missing persons.

"Oh… Em… *Gee*…! I *thought* we were *skipping* ancient history today… can we *go*, please…?" Percy sighed, already bored and not in the mood for Nev's treasure-trove of pointless trivia. Turning the handlebars, she lifted herself off the ground and pedalled off down the track, already heading for the first, bush-lined bend as Nev scrambled to remount her own bike.

"*Where's Wally, perhaps…?*" She offered up with sour sarcasm, knowing that Percy was already out of earshot as she turned around and took a long look back down the slope of the road at the rooftops of her town, shimmering faintly in the waning sunlight beyond the intervening grassland. The wind picked up again in that moment, gusting and blowing her hair all about, and she frowned up at the gathering clouds as she reached back and resecured the elastic hair tie holding it all together in a long pony tail beneath her bike helmet. She could smell the ozone of imminent rain now and silently cursed the washing still hanging on the line at home.

Almost out of instinct, she slipped one hand into the pocket of her jacket and withdrew her phone, checking the time as first point of order, then swiping it open to the weather app on the second screen. Sunny and twenty-two degrees, it clearly displayed in Celsius; the prediction completely at odds with the actual environment.

"Twenty-two in *Fahrenheit*, maybe…" she muttered softly, feeling a little too uncomfortable about it to add much humour to her sarcasm. Nev wasn't sure exactly how to convert between the two temperature scales, but she knew 22°F would be below freezing.

She took a moment to capture a short, panoramic clip for Instagram Stories, considered making a joke along the lines of 'if I'm never seen again…', then thought better of it when she realised that five minutes after posting anything like that, Dad would be on the phone, demanding to know why she wasn't at school. She decided instead to video Percy riding off awkwardly in her long dress, perhaps for use in some good-natured teasing later, but her friend had already disappeared by the time she'd turned the phone in the right direction.

"Oh, *bugger*…!" She blurted to herself, knowing it was something her dad would probably say and not caring in the slightest.

In a rush of renewed effort, she pedalled off in pursuit of Percy, phone once more tucked safely away in her jacket pocket.

Nev had spent a lot of the last six years being on her own for one reason or another, *mostly* while her father worked his long shifts to support what was left of his splintered family. Drake Anderson had nevertheless done everything he could to make sure his daughter wanted for nothing, particularly with regard to reading material to keep her occupied. Although becoming an unexpected single parent had left Drake Anderson little enough spare time to eat and sleep, he made sure that no matter what luxuries they lacked from week to week, there was never a shortage of books for Nev to read.

One entire wall of their lounge room was covered with tall bookcases, each filled to overflowing with every imaginable subject possible, both fiction and non-fiction. She was exceptionally well-read for a teen as a result, although her father's eclectic tastes in reading matter left her with interests in some subjects such as modern history and technology that were probably unusual for someone of her age. It was perhaps the fact that she found it just as difficult to fit in with the 'in-crowd' as Percy did that had resulted in the pair 'finding each other' as friends, in spite of their own obvious differences. There'd been some benefits however to not conforming to social norms, not the least of which being that she'd learned early regarding the benefits of study and had determined to do well at high-school right from the outset.

After another few minutes of bumpy riding around several winding bends, she finally caught up with Persephone once more, the older girl now standing by her mountain bike in the middle of a small clearing that appeared to all intents and purposes to be the end of the track.

"Took you long enough," Percy teased with a smirk, not really meaning anything by it as Nev drew up alongside, poked her tongue out in response and dismounted her own vehicle, laying it carefully on the grass.

"You might've warned me I needed to bring *rations*," she shot back with a sour grimace of her own, casting her gaze about the small, open space and deciding she liked it no better than the overgrown track they'd just cycled down. "You sure it's *safe* here?"

"Oh, my *God*, *get a grip*: we're... like... *a kilometre* from the centre of town!" Percy exclaimed with frustrated disbelief. It was actually more like four or five kilometres, but Nev knew there was no point arguing.

"What are we doing here *anyway*?" She demanded instead, deciding it a better option to cut straight to the chase.

"There's something I wanted to tell you about..." Percy admitted with a weird smile as she rested her bike on its kickstand and fixed Nev with an equally-strange stare. "A secret I've been wanting to tell *someone* for a while now..."

"Ummm... *ohhh-kayyyyy*..." Nev took a single step backward, suddenly feeling *very* uncomfortable and more than a little disturbed by Percy's strange manner as she cast a nervous glance around at bushland that suddenly seemed very isolated and unforgiving. "Aren't you s'posed to come out of the closet *after* you return from Narnia?"

"Oh, *please*..." Percy grumped, pulling a sour face, the mood well and truly broken as she turned and began to rummage inside the large sports bag she'd strapped to the carrier rack behind the seat of her mountain bike. "No offence," she added, pulling a canvas bumpack from the bag and buckling it around her waist, completely ruining the look of her otherwise stylish ensemble in the process "...but if I *were* gay, *you* would *so* not be my type..."

"Geez, love you *too*... you were starting to *scare* me, Perce!" Nev growled in return, allowing herself to relax and release a long-held breath. "I was starting to think you we going to... *Christ on a bike*...!" That last outburst of mild profanity – another of her father's favourite exclamations and *very* out of character for her – came out in a startled cry as Percy drew the barrel and stock of a shotgun from the bag and proceeded to deftly assemble both pieces into one functioning weapon.

"Hmmm...?" Percy asked, barely lifting her gaze and not for a moment acting like anything at all out of the ordinary was going on as she proceeded to take a pair of plastic-cased shells from the bumpack and loaded the weapon as casually as if she were slipping pods into her mother's *Nespresso*. "Oh, this isn't for *you,* silly..." She added, sounding not the slightest bit reassuring as she snapped the action shut and hoisted it over one shoulder. "*This* is for protection."

"'*Protection*...'...?" Nev repeated, incredulous. "Are you *nuts*...? Protection from *what*... rabid *field mice*...? Some rare species of man-eating *possum*...?" Nev's defence mechanisms tended toward nervous sarcasm under stress, and the presence of the rather dangerous-looking shotgun in Percy's unconcerned hands was *definitely* a source of concern.

"*You*… need to lighten up a little," Percy suggested, frowning at Nev disapprovingly over invisible spectacles. "Now, what I'm going to show you…" she went on immediately, getting straight down to business, "is going to be *our* little secret, okay? I chose *you* because you're really smart and you… *know stuff*… and you're the only person I know at school who's likely to *appreciate* what I've found: you're not a total *idiot* like the '*pretty* ones'…"

"Thanks… I *think*…" Nev replied warily, *mostly* confident that'd been some kind of back-handed compliment.

"*Any*-way… *moving* right along, this is a *secret*, like I said… yeah?"

"*What* secret…" she demanded in exasperation. "What needs a *shotgun* for 'protection', *four bloody kilometres* from the centre of town?" (…*other that something illegal*, she was seriously thinking in her own head…) "Do you even know how to *use* that thing?" She added, not knowing which answer would be worse.

"You *know* Dad's a shooting champ…!" Percy sniffed, the subject somehow a matter of family pride now. "*Yes*, he'd have a heart attack if he knew I've taken his five-thousand-dollar shotgun," she conceded, "*but*… he's always made sure I knew how be *safe* with it. Come on…" she urged finally, nodding her head toward an almost undetectable break in the surrounding grass off to her left. "It's over here…"

Being safe *with a gun's definitely* not *the same thing as knowing how to* use *one*! Nev silently pointed out, sensibly keeping that thought to herself as she fell in behind her shotgun-toting friend and followed her toward a narrow walking track leading deeper into the surrounding scrub.

"Oh, for goodness' *sake*, you won't need that *huge* bag: leave it with the bikes."

"As *if*…!" Nev snapped immediately with a shake of her head, the duffel bag swinging from side to side with every step. "I have my Bluetooth and *two* birthday presents in this thing, and I am *not* leaving all that lying around, just so they can be stolen by some passing *bogan* while *we're* trying to find out way out of *Mirkwood*!"

"Fine... *ruin* your back then for all I care..." Percy fired back hotly, at least recognising the Tolkien reference this time, "...and will you *stop* videoing me... *Jesus*...!"

"This is just in case they only find my phone..." Nev joked automatically, unable to help herself.

Percy remained surprisingly and *very* uncharacteristically silent after that remark – suggesting she'd *definitely* taken offence – and instead immediately picked up the pace a little, as if seeking to distance herself from her doubting friend. Nev knew she probably should apologise, but her own pride wasn't quite ready for reconciliation yet and she instead went with the very *teen* response of remaining silent in the hope Percy's mood would shortly blow over, returning everything back to normal. She *did* make the small concession of putting her phone away... for the time being, at least.

The ground was soft and slightly moist under their feet, with long grass and tea-trees growing thick on either side, and it rose above eye level at times, leaving Nev with a distinctly claustrophobic feeling. The hairs on the back of her neck started to rise and she was struck by the strange, unshakeable feeling that someone or – inexplicably – some*thing* was watching them. A soft, chilly breeze swept toward them down that track, and as silly as it made her feel in her logical mind, she was nevertheless suddenly a little happier that Percy had brought the shotgun.

It was darker now, too... far darker than it had any right to be in the middle of the afternoon, and the levels of moisture in the air were almost enough to classify as a fine, misting rain. The sky above was now a solid blanket of grey/black cloud, and as she glanced nervously upward, blinking through the growing drizzle, they seemed so close she could almost reach out and touch them. The patches of sunshine and clear blue that had filled the sky what seemed like only moments before were now completely gone.

"Uhh, Perce..." She muttered softly, suddenly gripped by the feeling that they really should be somewhere else – *anywhere* else. "...Maybe we should..."

"Look... *over there*...!" Percy called back over her shoulder in a sharp whisper, cutting Nev off and pointing directly ahead. "Can you *see* it...?"

Moving forward and peering cautiously over her friend's shoulder, Nev at first saw nothing: just a small widening ahead in the track that was barely large enough to be considered a clearing. Yet as she stared a little longer, she began to wonder her eyes were playing tricks. As grey and dull as everything around them had become in the failing light, the space ahead somehow seemed to be brighter, as if lit by its own faint luminescence. There was a shimmer in the air: something that was impossible to see if you stared at it directly but *almost* came into focus in your peripheral vision if you turned your head.

"*What the...*?" Without even thinking about it, she fumbled for her phone again, starting to record before she was even certain of what it was.

"Come on, chicken!" Percy urged excitedly, taking a few steps forward. "Come and see what all the fuss is about!"

"Perce, I *really* don't think this is a good idea," Nev began, suddenly filled with a fearful certainty that the very *last* place in the entire *world* she wanted to be right now was that small clearing up ahead. Even so, she continued to hold the phone high in one hand, both of them so accustomed to its presence that it was almost invisible.

"Why are you being like this...?" Persephone exclaimed with real disappointment in her tone now as she turned to face her friend, the shotgun held casually across her waist as if it were completely irrelevant. "This'll be *fun...* this'll be *awesome...*! I've been here before and it's *completely* safe! I thought..." she continued, her voice almost cracking at that moment, as if she were about to cry, "...of all people, I *thought* that *you* might *understand...*"

"If it's '*completely safe*'..." Nev began with acid sarcasm, preparing to ask the obvious question about the shotgun, when something interrupted her words and her train of thought.

This one is prescient, *you fool... she cannot be controlled...*

That soft, disembodied voice appeared directly in Nev's mind, the words barely audible.

"*Who's that...*?" She gasped, whirling about in fear with phone raised as if she might use it as a tiny club. "Did you *hear* that...?"

"Well, if you're just going to be like *that...*!" Percy harrumphed as she turned her back on her friend, one free hand placed jauntily on hip in a clear sign of displeasure. She was pouting now and feeling unappreciated, and had decided that maybe certain people *didn't* understand what a *huge* favour she was doing for them.

Are you feeble? She cannot be here! I see... fire... ruin...! *She hears ...she* hears...!

"Someone's *whispering*…" Nev persisted, "…someone… or… some*thing*…" she added finally, not at all sure why she'd made that last statement.

"Look, if you're going to *insult* me, then I'll just go home...!"

Kill them both… the dark one, too: she serves no further purpose…

"Perce, stop it: this *isn't* funny!" Nev growled, angering now and certain her friend was playing some huge prank. "I'm not in the mood for –!"

The rest of her words were cut off mid-sentence as the shriek of a horse's whinny split the air, the heart-stopping sound coming with a sudden burst of blinding white light at the centre of that strange clearing ahead. Even as both girls recoiled instinctively, each raising a protective hand to cover their eyes, they heard the clattering drumbeat of hooves from the same direction.

A huge stallion was suddenly upon them, galloping out of that dazzling light. A dark-clad rider sat astride its back, leaning forward in the saddle with the reins in one hand and a long, curved sabre in the other. With face wrapped in black cloth and only eyes visible, the horseman rose on his stirrups and released a howl of rage, blade held high and ready to strike. The light behind him flared again as he appeared, spreading out like a ripple of searing white from that tiny clearing and sweeping over all of them with equal impact. Both teens were instantly overcome by a strange, queasy feeling that filled them with nausea and caused Nev's vision to blur.

Nev screamed – nothing else seemed appropriate – and as the rider bore down on them, Persephone took a startled step backward, stumbled over something at her feet and fell flat on her backside. The shotgun fired as she hit the ground, its muzzle facing the horseman as he came at them with sword raised. A loud boom filled the air and the rider pitched backward with a cry, toppling from the saddle as his sabre fell away to one side. Shying away from the shot, the now-riderless horse swept past Percy and bore down on Nev instead, her phone still held pointlessly in one hand as she watched the scene unfold with horror and disbelief.

Initially slow to react, the horse's flank clipped her shoulder as Nev finally threw herself to one side at the last moment. The bag flew from her hands and rolled away as she was catapulted into the long grass in a daze, landing on her back and laying there motionless for a few seconds, staring blankly at the darkening sky above. As her ears pounded from the sounds of both the retreating horse and the hammering of her own heart, Nev's mind desperately tried to process what she'd just experienced.

"Nev! Nevaeh! Oh, my *God*...!" Percy's shocked cry began to break through the fogginess of her mind as her friend knelt beside her and helped her into a sitting position. "*No, no, no, no, no*... this won't do *at all*...! I can't mess this up *again*! Are you okay? Are you *alive*...?"

"I *think* so... heard my full name *twice* already today though, so *possibly* in Hell..." Nev mumbled, still not completely in control of her own senses but managing a little sarcasm to at least show she was recovering.

"Yes, you're fine, then... *clearly*..." Percy replied with exasperation, standing up once more and taking a few relieved steps backward.

"The flash... *the sword*...!" Nev exclaimed suddenly, reality elbowing its way back into her consciousness as she clambered to her feet once more and glanced around in fear. "That *creep* on the horse!"

"I... um... I think maybe he's *dead*..." Percy admitted eventually, not sounding at all happy about that as Nev, horror spreading across her face, took a few steps toward where a dark, motionless shape lay crumpled on the grass. "Oh God, Nev... I've *killed* him... They'll be *ever* so angry! What'll I do...? *I've killed him*...!"

"Good job, *too*...!" Nev decided, not upset about that at all as she recalled the whispered words in her head seconds before he'd appeared. "He was gonna kill *us*, Perce... serves him right, I reckon..." Phone amazingly still in hand, she turned and cast her eyes about for her fallen duffel bag, then wandered over on unsteady feet to collect it.

Little of what Nev had said registered with Percy in that moment as nervous tension got the better of her, and she fell to her knees and proceeded to vomit comprehensively onto the grass. Instinct took over however as she dropped the shotgun, and she at least managed to protect her father's prized Beretta by pushing it out of the splash zone.

"Well... *that's* unpleasant..." Nev observed disdainfully, referring both to the body *and* Percy's retching heaves. "I wonder where that horse has got to..."

Part of her realised she really shouldn't be feeling so relaxed about what had just happened, and she wondered if perhaps she might be shock, but thinking about all that was something for the 'too hard' basket at that moment and Nev decided it better to just concentrate on getting her bag back... and the pair of them getting the hell out of there as quickly as possible.

"Kill *me*...?" Perce managed eventually, wiping daintily at her lips with the sleeve of her own dress as she rose shakily to her feet. "Why would he want to kill *me*? Why would he *say* that...?"

"How the hell would *I* know...?" New shrugged, still mulling over how little shock or fear she was feeling and completely misinterpreting what Percy had said as a result. "*True*, but..." she added, those two words a simple statement in itself. "Heard the creepy voice order him to kill us both just before the horse appeared. '*Kill the dark one*', he said... '*she serves no purpose*'..." she mimicked, not making any effort to be complimentary. "*Something* like that, anyway..."

"How *rude*..." Percy decided primly, fighting to regain some of her usual demeanour as her own initial shock began to wear off.

"Mmmm... *I* thought so, too..."

"Keeping secrets... and after all this effort..."

She must not escape.

"Oh, *hello*: it's the 'Creep Whisperer' again...!" Nev added, struggling to hide the sudden fear that rippled through her as she again whirled around, trying to locate the source of that bodiless voice. All too late, part of her sub-conscious decided that maybe the numbness of going into shock wasn't so bad after all.

All may be forgiven... the fair one: kill her and bring the weapon to me.

"Ummm, I *think* we need to leave *now*, Perce," Nev began with a quaver in her voice, her thoughts struggling to catch up with everything that had transpired. "That voice is... wait, *what*...?" She added, suddenly fixing Percy with an accusing glare as a mental penny the size of a small planet finally dropped. "*What* can be forgiven...?"

"Oh, sure... leave me out of the *important* bits of the conversation – like '*kill the dark one*' – but it's all praise and happiness *now*...!" Percy spat bitterly, apparently speaking to the air itself as she turned on the spot, staring up at the drizzling clouds with the flash of anger in her eyes. "What happened to 'she serves no purpose...'...?"

It was only in that moment, as Percy turned toward her, that Nev noticed the pendant she was wearing seemed to be flashing brightly, something that should've been impossible without direct sunlight. The only other explanation she could think of was that it was glowing faintly of its own accord, as unlikely as that seemed, and Nev had seen and read enough sci-fi and fantasy to know that things glowing when they *shouldn't* was *never* a good sign.

What has passed is of no consequence. All that matters is what is now, *and right* now, *I again offer you reward and power in exchange for the weapon and the life of the girl.*

Nev noted for the first time that the bluish glow emanating from that brooch pulsed in sync with every silent world that was 'spoken'.

Definitely not a good sign.

"Persephone Koutroulis, you need to tell me what the *hell's* going on... *right now*..." Nev snarled, hands on hips as anger took over from fear. "You definitely *did not* just talk about making deals with this... *thing*..."

"Just like you promised?" Perce continued, still talking to the heavens and making a great show of ignoring Nev, even though she was quite clearly inching across to where the shotgun still lay a few metres to her left. "No tricks, now...?"

The bargain will be honoured. You will be a queen *of The Shard, with power beyond imagining.*

"Oh, you are *so* unfriended!" Nev blurted angrily over her shoulder, not fooled for a moment and already legging it down the track toward the main road as fast as her feet could carry her. As she ran, she mapped out her escape plan: get back to the bikes, then head for town at full speed and straight to the police station to report her clearly-insane and *totally* ex-friend. She didn't know what that crazy voice in her *own* head had been, but that was something to discuss with a school counsellor at a later date, if necessary. Escape from the immediate danger was a far greater priority... Nev was no doctor, but she was *fairly* certain psychotherapy wasn't all that effective in the treatment of gunshot wounds.

Nev knew she was in better physical condition than Percy, and adrenalin would give her even more speed once she started (*literally*!) pedalling for her life. She was also fairly confident she could make an emergency phone call while riding one-handed, whereas it was unlikely someone could reload or fire a shotgun while keeping up on a pushbike.

The whole thing came completely unstuck, of course, in the moment she burst out into the larger clearing where the bikes had been left and found – *of course* – that they were gone.

"*Ahhhhhh…!*" She howled in desperation, and was then struck by the thought that there might be some accomplice hiding nearby – another sword-swinging weirdo responsible for the disappearance of the bikes.

The renewed fear of that possibility pushed her on, chest heaving as her lungs drew desperately-needed air and she pounded down the main track heading back toward Chisholm Road. Without the benefit of a warm-up, she could tell that her body wasn't happy over the sudden exertion, and her muscles were now screaming at her in protest as she pushed herself harder than she ever had in training.

Lightning cracked for the first time overhead, a ground-shaking clap of rolling thunder following close on its heels, and the mist began to solidify into regular rain, soaking her clothes and chilling her to the bone as she ran doggedly on.

Just a little further… just a little further… She kept telling herself, fighting to keep the terror from her mind now as tears began to stream down her cheeks. *Onto the road and then a downhill run back to town… maybe get a ride…maybe someone heard the shot…*

"Come back, Nev!" Percy's voice cut through the grumble of the wind and rain from somewhere behind. "Don't run off… we're not going to *hurt* you!" It never occurred to her that it probably shouldn't have been possible for a human voice to carry so far through such background noise.

"Lying *bitch…!*" She screamed angrily in reply, knowing it was foolish to react but unable to help herself. The faint howl of indignant rage that floated back to her in response made her feel a little better at least, and she allowed herself a moment of relief as she rounded the last bend and picked up speed in a race to main road.

Lightning again flashed overhead with a suitable level of melodrama, and Nev released one long, lost wail of despair as she finally burst out onto what should've been Chisholm Road and discovered the utterly impossible: that like the bikes and that afternoon's good weather, the road had also completely disappeared. With only hard earth beneath her feet, she stood in the middle of an open expanse of knee-high grass with thick scrub beyond… the road that *should* have been there was most definitely not.

Remembering for the first time in some minutes that she indeed still carried a phone clamped in her right fist, she desperately lifted it and swiped open to make a call for help, only to feel an even greater stab of fear in her heart as she read the pop-up message already waiting for her in the middle of the screen:

No network available.
Please try again when you are connected to a network.

She whirled about in desperation, vainly hoping that she'd simply got her bearings wrong: that some passing car would suddenly appear, its headlights leading the way back toward civilisation and safety. Yet part of her mind already knew that where she was standing *should* have been the centre of Chisolm Road, and that as she turned to the north, the distant lights of the town she'd grown up in *should* have been clearly visible through the gathering dusk.

No network. *No network*! It just wasn't *possible*. Her mind was teetering on the very edge of rationality now. She was with the *premier* carrier in the country – the one that charged half as much again as *everyone else* and always bleated on the TV ads about covering '*ninety-five* per cent of the population'. How could a country town just two hours' drive from the state capital so suddenly and inexplicably fall into that *other* five per cent? *Maybe* one of the cell towers in the area *might* have gone down coincidentally, leaving her without coverage, but if that were the case, *why couldn't she* see *the bloody town...*?

Less than half an hour earlier, she's stood in that the exact same spot and seen familiar rooftops in the distance, not realising at the time how comforting that was. But where she stood *now* had no road, no phone coverage (not even lousy 3G), and the bright lights of home, which should've been clearly visible in the darkness, were nowhere to be seen. There wasn't even the faint glow they always left in the sky above on cloudy nights, confirming her fear that it wasn't just a matter of her not being able to see them... *they simply weren't there at all.*

There was a shout of warning from somewhere behind her, and it hadn't come from Percy. It had clearly been a male voice and it was answered by another shout from somewhere off to the south. Another flash of lighting lit up the sky, again followed quickly by thunder, and the faint whimper of nervous horses came soon after, galvanising her mind and body and forcing her to take some kind of action.

Whatever had happened to the town... wherever she actually was *right now*... the most important fact was that she desperately needed to be *somewhere else*, and needed to be there ASAP. If she was no longer where she should've been for whatever reason, then it followed by the same twisted logic that it didn't really matter which way she ran, so long as it was *away* from danger.

Another flash of lightning, and her decision was made in its fading afterglow. Past the open patch of grass and the line of scrub beyond, she caught sight of thicker bushland that might make it difficult for men on horseback to follow her in the dark. Stuffing her phone back into her pocket, she turned and caught sight of the flicker of burning torches moving back and forth in the distance, above the long grass. Without further hesitation, Nev Anderson sprinted across the open clearing and pushed through the tall grass on the other side, making for those distant trees with as much speed as she could muster.

She'd run blindly on, forcing her way through thick scrub and clumped walls of tall, rough-edged grass that snatched at her clothing, caught her hair and raked her face and her bare hands. Lightning continued to flash overhead, thunder deafening in its wake as she pushed herself desperately onward, sometimes careening from tree to tree with a staggering gait as if she were a human pinball in some hideous arcade game. After ten more minutes of solid running, she halted again to catch her breath, once more checked her phone, and this time something else occurred to her.

"*Restart...!*" She declared to nobody at all, fumbling for the power button on her phone and holding it long enough to prompt the device for the power-down slider. "If I restart, maybe it'll pick up the network again..." she reasoned with herself, not needing to verbalise but feeling more positive hearing it out loud. It was true that reception around the outskirts of town *was* occasionally sketchy, and amid all the drama she'd forgotten that restarting the phone could sometimes rectify any connection issues.

She waited impatiently for the cycle to complete, watching as the device powered down and then jamming her finger on the button once more to fire it up again, the beloved *Apple* logo flashing up onto the screen. Another few seconds' wait, her breath rasping in her lungs, and the home screen flickered into colourful life.

No network available.
Please try again when you are connected to a network.

She fell to her knees then as her remaining strength failed her, and she began to sob quietly beneath the darkened forest canopy. She could hear more hoof beats now, distant but closing fast enough, and it was clear there were at least three or four horses approaching from different directions across a broad arc behind her. She didn't know why that disembodied voice had wanted her dead, or why Percy had betrayed her. She didn't even know where she *was* anymore, and there seemed no point in fighting it… easier just to give up and surrender to whatever terrible fate whoever they were almost certainly had planned.

"*Do you want to live, girl…?*"

The words jolted her back reality, and she snapped her head in the direction of that new voice, eyes wide and fearful as she realised that it had been a *real* one rather than something imagined inside her own head. She immediately spotted a dark figure standing just a few metres away, and as she lifted her phone screen for light, she saw a young man with mud-streaked features above a scruffy moustache and 'almost-beard', both doing their best to cover rough-hewn, youthful features.

"Douse your faerie light, *witch*…!" He growled sharply, lifting an arm across his face in reaction to the pale glow of the phone. "Save your spells for the Black Watch, if you've majik to spare…"

"*Wh – what*…?"

"My question stands…" he hissed with anger born of impatience, taking a few steps forward until his entire body was clear in the faint lighting. "They'll be on us in a handful, and nothing will save us when *that* happens…" he pointed out, almost pleading now as he extended a questing hand. "*Do… you… want… to… live…?*"

Nev had only a fraction of a second to make her decision but there wasn't really one to make, truth be told. Working in league with persons – or *things* – unknown, her former best friend (*bitch!*) had just betrayed her, conspired to kill her into the bargain, and was most definitely *still trying* to accomplish part or all of the above. Even a complete stranger (a *cute* one at that, so far as she could tell in the dim light) was *already* well ahead in the 'trustworthy' stakes, and *anything* seemed like a better idea than hanging about right now, waiting to be captured by Percy and whatever other henchmen she may have conjured out of thin air.

All of that flashed through Nev's mind in the space of a heartbeat and she was back on her feet in another, courage and strength renewed by a suddenly-growing hope that all might not actually be lost.

"Who *are* you...?" She demanded as she took a step forward, raising her voice just enough to be heard over the increasingly heavy rain. As she spoke, she slipped the bag from her shoulder and slid her hand inside, forcing aside Honda's wrapped gift as she reached for the hilt of the *bokken* she'd used at training.

"Name's Godfrey..." the young man answered after a moment's consideration, eyes continually flicking about in search of danger. "I'm a ranger of the Southern Oster, sent to keep you safe..."

"Oh, the *army*..." Nev exclaimed with a little more relief, thinking she'd recognised a military rank and completely missing the distasteful tone he'd used regarding the purpose of his mission.

"The Southern Oster follows *no king,*" Godfrey snapped quickly in return, almost sniffing with disdain at the very thought, "...and I'll be a *dead* ranger and *you* a tortured witch if we're not away from here!"

"Who're you calling a 'witch'...?" She asked indignantly, the irrelevance of the question not occurring to her in that moment as what he'd been saying finally began to sink in.

"Dragonfall take me, this is *no* time for talk! Come... *come now...*! Questions later, when we're *safe...*"

As if on cue, the whinny of a horse again split the air, this time far nearer than the galloping she'd heard earlier, and she needed no further urging.

"And we're still here because *why...*?" Nev asked nervously, giving an excellent impression of someone who thought the idea of a speedy departure had been hers right from the start as she dragged the *bokken* free and brandished it in one hand while slipping the bag back over her shoulders,.

"They warned me you'd be a strange one..." Godfrey observed cryptically, staring at her for a moment with a confused mixture of exasperation and laughter in his expression. "Stranger still for an *enchantress*! Away... let's get out of here...!" He added hurriedly, extending a hand and grasping hers firmly as he dragged her into the reedy grass beyond. "Answers later... *if* we survive...!"

He was off and running then, darting in and out between the bushes and gnarled tea-trees and avoiding each and every one as if they were running in broad daylight. Behind him, he dragged a cold, tired and completely bewildered Nev Anderson, the pair slowly but steadily opening an ever-increasing distance between them and their pursuers.

III

UNANSWERED QUESTIONS

They reached the treeline at the other end of the wood after a few more minutes of breathless running and as lightning cracked overhead, Nev caught a glimpse of open pasture spreading away before them beneath the blackness of a leaden sky. There were two horses waiting nervously, their reins tied together around a thick, low-hanging branch near the very edge of the fields, and they whinnied and stamped their feet in fear as Nev and Godfrey approached.

"We can't go *out there*…!" She howled, her own terror mounting as she turned back to see the faint light of torches still behind them, flickering eerily between the trees. "They'll be able to *see* us as soon as we break cover!"

"Smart thinking, witch," he nodded in agreement, the hint of a smirk suggesting there was more to it than that as he carefully inched his way forward, reaching out for the reins where they wrapped about the branch. "And what'll they be looking for…?"

"What the hell do *you* think?" She barked, her natural talent for sarcasm managing to break through for a moment. "Riders on horseback, escaping across the field!"

"Aye, girl… and that's *exactly* what we'll *give* 'em!" He grinned widely as another flash from above lit the area and she braced herself for the thunderclap that followed close in its heels.

Releasing the reins, he threw them free, raised his arms high and released a bellowed "*Yah*…!" with the intent of frightening the horses.

It was made redundant by a monumental roar of thunder above that completely drowned it out, but the end result was the same. The terrified beasts immediately turned tail and bolted at full speed across the open fields, heading directly away from the trees in a tight group. It was only during the next streak of blue-white brilliance across the dark clouds that Nev realised there were packs of something strapped to each horse's back, and that even at a short distance, in that limited light it looked very much like riders leaning low over their necks at the gallop.

"What are *we* supposed to do now?"

"Run, girl... *run...*!" He hissed in her ear, once again taking her hand and dragging her south along the edge of the treeline, skirting the fields and moving in a completely different direction to that of the fleeing horses.

Perhaps another hundred metres or so along, he ducked behind a thick clump of low bushes and pulled her down with him, cautiously peering out from one side to watch as their pursuers also reached the edge of the trees, torches still in hand, and their own mounts began to mill about in the almost impenetrable darkness.

There was a faint twinkle of blue among the trees then, followed instantly by a coiling snake of light that lashed upward into the sky, struck the clouds overhead and blazed in their midst for a few seconds, the glow expanding outward on all sides for many kilometres and illuminating the ground below.

"*Hag...*" Nev breathed bitterly, thinking she knew exactly who was behind *that* little display.

"Aye, another one indeed..." Godfrey agreed in a whisper. "I've often seen her come and go these last months, but this was only the second time she ever brought anyone back with her. If you've some majik o' your *own* to spare for *that* filth, I'd not complain of y' usin' it right now..."

"I am *not* a *witch*!" She hissed angrily, frustrated and feeling increasingly insulted over the insinuation.

A cry of alert from their pursuers cut off any reply he might've given as one of them caught sight of the horses Godfrey had set free, now a good distance away across the fields but still visible in the fading afterglow of that bolt into the clouds. Without hesitation, every one of them – no less than *five* horsemen that Nev could see – set off a full speed, the rumble of their hooves faintly audible through rain that finally seemed to be easing a little.

"You *knew* they'd follow the horses!" Nev exclaimed with mild surprise.

"Got to thinkin' about it a while back," he replied, more than a little proud that his idea had actually worked. "Been training 'em for a month now for just this occasion. Stole 'em from the local lord's stable fair 'n square and all, and I reckon they'll find their way back well enough: horses have a knack for that kind 'o thing." He gave a low chuckle as another thought occurred to him. "That swine won't be too happy to see 'em though... not with a handful o' the Blackwatch hard on their tails. They're just as like to string him up on the spot if they even *think* he's hidden you somewhere."

"You mean they'll *kill* him...?" Nev asked, horrified at the thought.

""Oh, not *straight away*... not if I know the Blackwatch. They'll want to have some fun first..."

"But... but, that's *horrible!*" She declared, completely aghast. "How could you *do* that?"

"Easy..." Godfrey replied with barely a shrug. "There's more than a few kids disappeared 'round this area the last few years and almost all of' em were servants up at Lord Berwick's manor house. Lot 'o folks here know he's involved in it, but no one can touch him 'cause he's tight with Harald's cousin..." He gave a toothy grin in the weird, turquoise afterglow still haunting the clouds above. "Be doin' everyone a favour if they stretched *his* neck..."

"Harald...? Who's Harald...?"

"'Who's Harald?'... *Black Harald*....?" He repeated, as if hearing the most ridiculous question ever asked. "Do they teach you *nothin'* in 'witch school' or wherever it is you lot go to?"

"For the *last*... *time*..." Neve began through clenched teeth, but she was given no chance to complete the sentence.

"Come on then," he interrupted cheerfully, cutting her off. "No point hanging about. We've not far to go but we'll catch a death if we don't change out o' these wet clothes and get in front of a warm fire. Try and keep up..."

And with that he was off and running again, continuing his path along the edge of the treeline where shadows and the overall darkness of the background bush would best mask his progress from any onlooker. With an indignant grunt of frustration, Nev sprung to her feet and jogged off after him, thinking carefully about all the unpleasant things she was certain to say to him the moment (*The very moment...!*) they were somewhere safe and sheltered from the elements.

The rain had all but ceased by the time they finally left the cover of the trees and turned eastward again, striking out across the open fields well south of where they'd last seen their pursuers. With the storm beginning to ease, it was now possible to hear the crashing of the surf close by, that realisation only creating more confusion in Nev's as it meant that the ocean was still pretty much *exactly* where it *should've* been, leaving her even less able to explain what had happened to the rest of the world she'd known.

A farmhouse appeared out of the darkness as she followed on a few paces behind Godfrey, and beyond that stood a tall barn of thick, rough-cut timbers covered by thick panels of thatched straw to keep out the rain. There was no activity outside that she could see, nor any lights on in the house, but as they drew closer she could at least see a faint glow around the edges of the barn's closed main doors. The flickering of that light and the lazy tail of smoke curling from a plain opening in the centre of the roof suggested a fire might well be burning within.

"Lester…!" Godfrey called softly with a grin, rapping once on the door with his knuckles as he placed his ear upon the wood. "Are y' awake, y' festerin' little maggot?"

"Awake enough to do for the likes o' *you*…" came a soft, surprisingly high-pitched voice from the darkness to their left, and as they whirled to face the sound, a young boy of no more than eleven or twelve stepped out of the darkness, holding a crossbow that was clearly far too large for his physique. "Heard you comin' a mile off…"

"Cheeky sod…!" Godfrey chuckled, patting the lad on the shoulder as they came together. "I told you not to leave that fire unattended: you set this barn alight *again* and McTavish will sell us over to the Blackwatch himself!"

"This the witch then, is it…?" Lester asked bluntly, giving Nev a serious, 'up-and-down' with his eyes and displaying an unpleasantly interested expression she'd *never* have expected from a pre-teen. "A pretty one, too…" he added, not helping matters at all "…after a good *bath*, maybe…"

"I *am* right here, y' know…!" Nev growled darkly, taking a threatening step toward the boy and lifting her *bokken* slightly in one hand without even thinking about it.

"Easy there, deadeye…" Godfrey warned with another chuckle, reaching out and forcing down the crossbow Lester had raised in response to Nev's advance. "Our contract's not for a *dead* harpy, *or* one with too many holes in her."

"Look, if the *whole night's* just going to be spent *insulting* me," Nev exclaimed, giving up on continually denying the whole 'witch' thing as a lost cause, "can we *at least* do it inside where we're safe from pneumonia?"

"Who's this 'New Moanier' then?" Lester squeaked aggressively, the crossbow up and ready again as he whirled about, prepared for attack from any quarter. "They dangerous...?"

"I *think* she means a fever, genius..." Godfrey explained, laughing out loud as he pushed the boy heavily toward the doors in a manner few were likely to get away with. "And witch or no..." he added, tilting his head in her direction and at least finally giving a little ground on the subject, "...she's right: we'll catch our death out here and no mistake." He'd not recognised the word Nev had used, but the way she's said it and the inflection in her tone made it clear she was more likely to be concerned about illness than an attacker with a strange name.

The interior of the barn, musty and smelly and vaguely *filthy* as it was, was nevertheless pure *heaven* compared to the freezing darkness outside. Her body had been too busy expending energy and generating excess heat while they'd been running to really feel the cold, however the human cooling systems that worked so well when overheating had now become a liability and the perspiration that had soaked into her pits and down the centre of her back and chest had quickly begun to chill as they'd stood outside, the cool breezes of the night wafting about them.

Enclosed in a double-stacked ring of blackened stones and broken bricks, the fire inside was simply wonderful. Standing up close enough to feel uncomfortable in its radiated heat, she was at least able to dry her soaked legs and back a little, steam rising faintly from the material. Her clothing, although amazingly intact considering what she'd experienced, was nevertheless soaked through, and her duffel bag wasn't much better despite being nominally water-resistant. She placed it by her feet, set back a little to ensure nothing inside got too hot, and took a moment to look over the two strangers who'd undoubtedly saved her from an unpleasant fate... for the time being, at least.

Godfrey was tall, broad-shouldered, and probably would've been quite handsome had his face ever seen a decent shave... or a recent *wash* for that matter. His tragic attempt at facial hear wasn't a *complete* failure – it was about as uneven and patchy as the attempted beards of *most* men in their late teens or early twenties – and it certainly wouldn't be held against him. His hair – longish and gathered in a thick pony tail at the nape of this neck – was strawberry blond and a little fairer than she'd have liked, but (as she quickly reminded herself) that was hardly her business anyway, having barely met him.

Lester, on the other hand, was short, thin as a rake and almost ferret-like, with an unruly mop of beet-red hair and unfortunate patches of similarly-coloured acne scattered across his face in haphazard patterns. He *looked* completely awkward, but as she watched him more closely she soon noted that he actually moved with a fluid, rather cat-like gait that looked completely out of odds with an appearance that seemed to be all arms and legs.

A sudden shudder of cold rippled through her body then, and as Lester moved about the darker corners of the barn, scrabbling around behind stacked piles of hay and extremely ancient-looking tools and farming equipment, she was happy to turn back to the fire and spend a few silent moments taking in that glorious warmth just as Godfrey was already doing. Eventually, the boy returned with a three-legged milking stool in one hand and a battered wooden crate in the other.

"There's a seat for ya, Haggis…" he offered cheerily, knowing exactly what he was saying and drawing a narrow-eyed glare from Nev in return as he dropped the stool at her feet "…and I reckon a few splinters won't hurt *your* bum, Westacre…" he added, tossing the crate over to Godfrey from the other side of the fire and again receiving a glare for his efforts as the heavy box bumped and clattered on the hard ground.

"You can be a real *arse* sometimes, Lester…" he pointed out, only half-joking as the boy gave a mock salute in reply and plonked his butt down on the floor, his back against one of the pillars reaching up into the centre of the wooden ceiling.

"Only 'sometimes'…?" Lester replied with a smirk. "I must be growin' up." He nodded to himself, as if actually impressed. "Make me dad proud, I will…"

"Finally worked out who he was then, have ya?" Godfrey asked innocently, suppressing a smirk of his own.

"Down to two or three likely fellas now… made me a short list…" He grinned broadly. "Come to think of it, *you* could be me dad 'n all!"

"You *wish*…! You'd be a damned sight more handsome for a start, if I *was*…" Godfrey shot back, chuckling over his own joke.

"I've gone *mad*…" Nev observed softly, staring at the pair in disbelief as she sagged tiredly onto the stool, automatically turning her legs to one side so as to maintain her modesty. "*Completely* insane…!

This is like some great, practical joke... *surely* there are hidden cameras... there *must be*...! *Who* are *you people*...?"

"Us...? Well... I'm Godfrey Westacre, ranger-scout of the Southern Ostermen, and *this* loudmouthed little git over here..."he added, pointing a vague finger "...is Lester Boniface, my apprentice and squire..."

Godfrey's answers were direct and completely honest and explained nothing whatsoever.

"Why..." she paused for a moment, struggling with the enormity of it all as her adrenalin began to subside and her mind began to allow her body to relax. "*Why* have you brought me here?"

"Independent contract... undisclosed client..."

"Well, *that* clears up absolutely *everything*..." she muttered darkly, mostly to herself. "*This* is crazy! I *must* be imagining things. Maybe – *maybe* we *are* at Percy's place and we've actually decided to smoke the 'special herbs' her parents think we don't know about." She nodded faintly, as if seriously considering it as an option. "Yes, that actually sounds *nice* compared to this. A few hours of mellowing out and eating munchies, then off for a nice nap and *all better* in the morning. *That* sounds just *lovely*."

"I think we've got a nutter here, Westy," Lester observed, making an over-exaggerated show of tapping a finger against the side of his head as he dubiously watched Nev muttering to herself.

"She's a strange one all right," Godfrey conceded with a grin, shaking his head also, "but it *has* been a long day, and who knows *what* goes on in the head of a witch..."

It was at that point that a shiver of cold rippled through him, the wet clothes chilling Godfrey's back, buttocks and calves even as the fire warmed his chest and thighs. Now that the thought of cold was at the forefront of his thinking, he noticed for the first time that Nev was also shaking faintly, and it was entirely possible that she hadn't realised it yet either.

"We've some spare duds you can use, if you want to change," he offered with a nod toward a pair of piled rucksacks against a far wall. They'll be a bit baggy, maybe, but I think they'll do well enough until your proper clothes dry over the fire.

"It can't be... it just *can't*... I – *what*...?" Nev stammered, caught mid-ramble and missing what he'd said. "I'm sorry?"

"I *said*: we've got some spare clothes for y' if you want to get changed," Godfrey repeated, again indicating the backpacks across the room. "You can dry *your* gear by the fire while you sleep."

"I – uh – I'm not sure…" she began nervously, not at all comfortable with the idea of taking her clothes off within close proximity of two complete strangers, *particularly* male ones.

"They're fine clothes you've got," he reasoned kindly, tilting his head to one side across the flickering flames and thinking he understood her reluctance well enough. "Not any kind 'o fashion *I've* ever seen, it's true, but it's still clear enough they must've cost you some gold. Be a shame to spoil 'em by leavin' 'em all soaked like that… not to *mention* you maybe catchin' that 'New Moanier' into the bargain. If y'r worried about your honour with *us* around, there's a stack o' storm shutters standing up the back o' the barn there y' can change behind. You've me word we'll not peek…"

"Speak for yerself…!" Lester muttered with a sly grin.

"*Right*, Toadface…! Upstairs and take watch! Off you go!" Godfrey snapped in exasperation as Nev, who'd clearly been intended to hear the remark, reacted exactly as expected and fixed Lester with another glare, gasping softly at the outright rudeness of the horrid little boy.

"It were a joke!" Lester declared, acting as if it were he who were suddenly the victim. "Just a harmless *joke*…!"

"Then you can spend the rest of the night workin' on some new material, *jester*," Godfrey replied drily, shaking his head in disbelief. "You've had *all evening* down here with the fire anyway: get your butt up into the loft *now* and keep an eye out. We're *probably* safe, but I'd rather be *sure* about it."

"Y' could ask nicely, at least," Lester shot back grumpily, trying a guilt-trip now and failing miserably as he rose to his feet and stomped across to where he'd left his beloved crossbow propped against a wall.

"Aye, *please* get upstairs and keep an eye out… before I boot your backside into next week!" Godfrey added with a smirk, the boy blowing a soft raspberry at him in return as he clambered up a short ladder and through a narrow hatchway leading to an upper level above the main, double doors. With the opening's trap door closed, little light from the fire reached the loft, and Lester – wrapping himself in a thick blanket – was able to peer out across the roof of the farmhouse through a small, open window set into the wooden beams. From there he had a perfect view of the fields to the north, and a good angle on anyone who might think to sneak up on the barn's only entrance.

Rising from his crate, Godfrey stepped quickly across to the rucksacks he'd indicated earlier and fished around inside, pulling out a few random pieces of clothing that were all coloured in flat, earthy tans or greens. Turning, he approached Nev slowly and offered them to over as she rose nervously to her feet.

"They're Lester's... but you've come at a good time," he added quickly as she reached out for them. "I make him wash his gear at the turn of each season, and *today's* the first day o' spring."

She stared at him in horror, actually recoiling a little before she noticed the twinkle in his eye and that characteristic smirk again, and this time the sheer cheek of the man finally drew a soft snort of derision from her that she couldn't completely stifle.

"They *are* clean..." he assured, only honesty in his expression this time as he again offered the folded clothes. "I give me word."

"You are... the *strangest* person I have *ever* met!" She said softly, shaking her head as she reached out again to accept them, and then suddenly found herself unable to meet his gaze. She instead turned her head for a moment, actually worried she might be blushing for some reason.

"Well, so far it's been about even for *both* of us, then" Godfrey admitted with a more open smile now, "but we're only young... there's always a chance things'll get *much* stranger."

"Behind the shutters back there...?" She asked, hastily changing the subject and pointing toward the rear of the barn.

"I'll wait here and keep a lookout for y' – 'just in case'..." he nodded, turning his back and making a show of assuming an 'at ease' pose that was stoic enough to seem both comical and just a *little bit* impressive at the same time.

With a thin smile and a faint nod of her own, she tucked the clothes under one arm, picked up her duffel bag in the other and made her way to the far end of the barn, threading a path around wooden barrels, sacks of grain and a clutter of other random, farm-related items, all scattered about in haphazard fashion. She found the shutters easily enough and true to Godfrey's word, they stood upright against one of the central pillars, forming almost a cubicle of sorts up to neck height that was more than sufficient for her purposes.

That it was also further from the fire and bathed in partial shadow was an added bonus as she carefully craned her neck to check once more that Godfrey was still standing where she'd left him, and that Lester was nowhere to be seen. With a deep breath, she placed the duffel on the ground, carefully laid the clean clothes on top of it, and shrugged off her damp jacket.

It was only a few moments before she was out of her damp clothes and slipping on the replacements Godfrey had provided. A little short for her legs, the tan dungaree pants matched her boots well enough and were complimented by a long-sleeved tunic of faded khaki that was a little baggy but was otherwise serviceable. As no stage did she consider removing her underwear: although still vaguely damp, there was *no way* she was going to take *them* off in the present company... not for all the good intentions in the world, *whatever* world that might presently be.

Over the tunic, she pulled on a long, sleeveless leather vest with deep, flap-covered pockets sewn into the front and sides of its lower half, along with a matching belt to draw it all in at her waist and at least accord her *some* kind of figure. With all that done, the last item was a long, flowing cloak of dark green that tied about her neck with a braided cord and also provided a deep hood that was large enough to cover her face in poor weather and hung in loose folds at her shoulder blades when pushed back.

Delving into her bag, she managed to locate a brush and hair tie and tried to work out the multitude of knots she'd accumulated in her flight from the clearing, the dampness of her hair making hard work of it. Reaching a point that wasn't perfect but close enough, she used the hair tie to secure it all in a pony tail of her own, clenching it tight behind her head. It was difficult to gauge properly without a mirror, but she was fairly confident that the ensemble wasn't actually *too* bad considering what she had to actually work with.

"Oh, *God*... I look like *Aragorn*...!" She realised suddenly with a little dismay, not even the thought of an unshaven Viggo Mortensen enough to make her feel better.

She pulled and prodded at the bits and pieces, trying to make impossible adjustments, before finally giving up and deciding there was nothing else to be done. The wet clothing had felt disgusting *and* cold, and if she was being brutally honest, *anything* was better than that at the moment. Sure, the material was rough and a little itchy, but it was otherwise comfortable enough, and she was surprised how much freedom of movement she possessed as she gathered up the wet clothes and carried them back out to the fire.

"I've put up a line for you to hang your gear," Godfrey offered as she appeared form the rear of the barn. He'd taken some cord from his pack and tied it off at eye level between two of the central pillars, only a few metres from the crackling fire. "Should dry faster like that."

"Thanks," she managed with a thin smile, feeling very self-conscious about her new attire as she slung each damp garment over the line and spaced them out neatly. "Aren't you going to change too?"

"Been out in the field long enough to be used to it," he shrugged simply, as if that was all that needed to be said. Having turned around for her benefit, he'd taken the opportunity to warm his back and legs in the heat of the crackling flames. "Fire's nearly dried me off already, anyway," he added. "Come... *sit*..." he continued, gesturing to the stool as he moved to collect his crate and bring it around to her side of the fire while she finished hanging her washing.

"How do I look?" She asked eventually, scared of the answer and not entirely sure why.

"Sure don't look like a... *stranger*... that's for sure," he began, correcting himself pre-emptively and earning a softly-whispered "*Nice save...!*" in response from a faintly-smiling Nev. "Look more like one of us... a scout, maybe..." he continued with another shrug. "You certainly look more *normal* now, although we'll need to do *somethin'* with that hair if you're to go out in public." He caught the flash of dismay in her eyes and, thinking quickly, added: "Definitely look the part though... almost *ranger* material..."

Aragorn: I knew *it...!* Her ever-vigilant self-doubt muttered silently as she returned to her seat. *He* must *know about* Lord of the Rings, *surely...?*

But that thought then led on to other thoughts about home and the world she'd lost, and *that* in turn led to thoughts of her father. Drake would've been home for hours now and he'd have called the police the *moment* he'd found the house empty. She knew he'd be terrified, not knowing where she was, and knowing her dad, she also knew that he'd blame himself whatever happened. She fell into a funk, staring into the flames and fighting desperately *not* to cry as she struggled with renewed feelings of loss and confusion over the unbelievable situation she'd been dragged into.

"I'm *not* a witch…" Nev murmured in a small, weak voice after they'd been alone with the fire for a few moments. With the tension of the chase now gone, a change of fresh clothes and the chance to relax a little, the mental strength she'd been holding onto to keep herself going had now run out, and all that was left was a tired, frightened teenager who badly needed her town, her school and – *most of all* – her dad. More than anything at that moment, Nev Anderson just wanted to go home… the one thing that above all others currently seemed impossible.

"Aye, I'll admit… you're not like any witch *I've* yet seen…" Godfrey conceded, trying to give a comforting smile as he recognised the sudden fragility in her tone.

"How many witches *have* you seen…?" She asked carefully, arms folded protectively across her chest.

"*Including* you and the 'Blue Hag'…?" He asked, receiving a silent nod. "*Two…*" he answered, again no longer able to keep that cheeky grin from his face.

She knew she *should* have been angry that he kept teasing, but somehow she could sense innocence behind the jokes and at the very least, his laid-back manner was helping to put her a little more at ease. This time, she didn't try to cover up the fact that he'd managed to make her smile, weak and fleeting as it had been.

"…Never seen much of *anything* before now…" he went on to explain. "Waitin' for you 's been my first big mission in the Blacklands." He gave a faint shrug, as if conceding another point. "Guess I seen a *bit* of fighting up in Swales when I was a young'un… but *that* was only a border skirmish: clearin' out a few sell-swords and the like… nothin' like a *real* war or anything."

"What *is* this place?" Nev asked finally, again fighting back tears as so many unanswered questions fought for their turn to be asked. "Where's my *home* gone? What about the other towns… the *cities*…? Melbourne… Sydney… *Canberra*…? Surely, they can't *all* be gone?"

"Don't know nothin' like those names," he answered with apologetic honesty, "and I've been *all over* the Osterlands the last few years. We're just north o' Crookhaven at the moment, maybe three miles south o' One Thug. From here, it's a day's *hard* ride to Castle Black and maybe the same to Welshport. More than a *hundred* miles to Eidon, though, but Harald only stays there in summer and no one likes heading that way if they can help it..." He was trying to be helpful, as always, but the place names he'd just reeled off sounded just as unrecognisable to her as the cities she'd mentioned had been to him.

"Hard slog to get there from here, up through the Black Spur from Hell's Town, unless you take the *western* roads," he went on, hardly missing a beat, "but they run too close to one of The Darks for my liking... *no one* likes getting too close to *them*..."

"I don't know *any* of those places..." she admitted sadly, confusion fogging her thoughts. "You carry swords and crossbows and you talk of kings and wars and *witches*..." She shook her head in exasperation, as if trying to clear an overload of bewildering information. "*There's no such thing as witches*," she declared in a desperate, quavering tone. "There *shouldn't* be... but... my own friend... *ex-friend*... *she* used magic...! It *must've* been magic! It's *impossible*... but I *saw* it! One minute, I'm standing in the middle of a *nature reserve*, four 'kays' from *my own house*, and the next..." She paused for a moment, overcome her own frustrated inability to explain what had happened. "The *next*... I'm stuck in the middle of *Sherwood Forest*, running away from sword-swinging *nut-jobs* and getting called a bloody *witch* by a bunch of *Tolkien* fanboys! I just want to go home...!" She wailed finally, her shoulders sagging as she burst into tears, sobbing quietly. "*I want to go home...*"

"You made her cry *already*, Westacre...?" Lester called out nastily from upstairs. "That was quick, even for *you*...!"

"You just keep eyes open and your mouth *shut*, Toadface...!" He barked in return, the sharpness of his tone making it quite clear he wasn't kidding as he glared up at the closed trapdoor. The boy in the loft above for once showed excellent judgement by not saying another word.

"I – I suppose they *burn* witches, do they?" She croaked haltingly between sobs, unable to look directly at Godfrey as she instead stared woodenly into the glare of the fire, hoping in vain that she might see something to ease her growing despair.

"Aye... aye, they *do*..." he began, knowing that wasn't the best possible answer but unable to lie, and instantly wincing at her expected reaction.

"Oh, my *God*...!" She moaned softly, burying her head in her hands again. "Is *that* what you're going to do to *me*...?"

"No, lass…!" He stated firmly, for the first time not even thinking about using the word 'witch'. "No… we're *not* here to harm you… *that* I swear on my life…"

"Then… then *why* were you waiting out there in the bush… for *me*? Why were *they* trying to kill me?" She lowered her head to her hands once more, fighting against the tears that so badly wanted to come. "My *best friend* tried to kill me…!"

"*That* hag at the clearing was your *friend*…?" Godfrey asked quickly, eyebrows raised in disbelief. "I'd be thinkin' you need better friends, if that's the case…"

"Yeah, thanks for the heads up on *that one*, Captain Obvious…" Nev replied sullenly, cheered up just a tad by the discovery that her sarcasm was still in working order.

"Ain't no captain… just a ranger," he replied in an instant, opting for 'Captain Oblivious' instead. "You can say *you're* no witch, but *that* one *definitely* is." He continued, returning to the subject of Persephone Koutroulis. "Seen her here a few times already, like I said earlier, and she just comes and goes as she pleases, vanishing in and out o' there like some bright blue will o' the wisp. The days she's here, there's usually one of The Brotherhood lurkin' about in those robes o' theirs as well, and she's usually got a few of the Blackwatch about, too, but they're easy enough to hide from if you're worth your salt."

"You said before that this was only the *second* time you'd seen her bring someone else through…" Nev asked sharply, the analytical side of her mind taking over as she recalled that piece of information. "What happened *last* time she did that?"

"Well, it was maybe two months ago…" Godfrey began, thinking hard. "*Most* times, she comes in the early evening, usually regular as clockwork. She was *earlier* today, though – lucky for both of us I'd only just got there meself when this all went down."

"Yes, yes… but the *other* person…" She persisted, trying to keep on topic. "Who *were* they?"

"Well, we weren't formally *introduced*…" he grinned in return, displaying his own capacity for sarcasm. "Some older fella… lot older than me or you… He weren't any happier about turnin' up there than *you* were…"

"What happened to him?"

"They took him away," he replied simply. "She did somethin' to him with a Shard Crystal – one just like The Brotherhood always carry

– and he fainted dead away. They carted him off with the witch following on behind."

"They *killed* him?"

"Not *dead*, just knocked out…" Godfrey frowned, as if she'd not been listening to a word he'd said. "He was still movin' and moanin' a little as they put him over the back o' one of the horses."

"And…?"

"And *what*…?" He shrugged. "Dunno what happened after that: never saw him again."

"Why didn't you help *him*?"

"Weren't me job to," Godfrey shrugged again. "Contract was to wait for a *witch*… a *girl*. He wasn't a girl, far as I can tell, and unlike *you*, he was too stupid to try and run. Weedy little bugger he was, too – like Toadface but with grey hair…"

"I *heard* that…!" Lester called out faintly from above, sounding unimpressed.

"Aye, and you were *supposed* to 'n' all," he shot back with a sly grin. "Might o' helped him – *maybe* – if he'd been lucky enough to have run my way, like you did…" he went on, turning back to Nev. "But he just stood there instead, acting all brave and raising his fists to the Blackwatcher that came to tie him up." He snorted with laughter at the memory. "Silly bugger actually tried to protect the hag, pushin' her behind him and acting like he was defendin' her honour or some such silliness."

"He didn't *know*?" Nev whispered, remembering the shock of her own experience with betrayal. "So Percy tricked *him* as well…"

"He hadn't a clue…" Godfrey nodded in confirmation. "'*Percy*', her name is…? Well, she just reached up and touched the back of his head, real gentle, and that was it: down he went."

"*Why*, though…?" She demanded again. "They wanted to capture me, then decided to *kill* me – and *you two* were waiting for me as well." Her eyes narrowed as she realised he'd not answered her original question. "Why *did* you save me from them? Where are *you* going to take me?"

"The 'why' part's easy," he conceded with a tilt of his head. "Got orders from my mob – The Oster – to come and wait here for you to turn up. Collect the 'witch' and make sure she ain't hurt: that was my orders. The *where* part's a bit trickier… *that*, I don't know… *yet*…"

"So we're supposed to just sit around in this barn and chat?" She asked with a half-smile and a raised eyebrow of her own.

"Just for tonight," he grinned back. "We've transport ready, and at dawn tomorrow we'll be making tracks for Welshport – about a day's good ride east of here. We'll be meeting a ship there, but only the captain knows the destination after that. It'll be somewhere safe, though."

"That *still* doesn't tell me *why…*" she pointed out.

"They didn't tell *me* that, either…" Godfrey admitted with another of his characteristic shrugs. "That way, there's no danger of me givin' anything away if I got captured."

"Well, none of that matters," she declared suddenly, sounding determined. "First thing tomorrow, *I* am going back up to that portal or 'wormhole' or whatever the hell it is and I am *going home.*"

"Not a chance," Godfrey said simply, but this time there was the faint hint of steel in his voice. "Too dangerous for a start, and my orders are to get you to Welshport by tomorrow night to meet that ship. They only come once a month, so we've been lucky there, and I'm sure as Dragonfall not waiting around *another* month because we missed *this* one. Going back would do y' no good anyway: they only open it up when that hag comes and goes, and that *ain't* every day."

"I *have to!*" Nev argued desperately, rising to her feet and barely holding onto her tears again as she stomped a few steps away, turning her back to him. "You can't keep me here… you just *can't…!*" She continued, whirling to face him again. "I'm going *home!*"

"That 'port-hole' thingy *won't be open,*" he insisted, calm but firm in tone, "*and* there's the danger of running into the Blackwatch again…"

But he caught the look of desperation in her eyes in that moment and allowed his words to trail off. She was a strange one, that was true enough, but she wasn't unpleasant to talk to in her own, weird way and Godfrey was already fairly sure she *wasn't* a witch. Awful pretty too, truth be told, although that had nothing to do with anything, of course. He could *also* see that she was right at the end of her physical *and* mental reserves at that moment, and pushing her over the edge into hysteria wouldn't make things easier for any of them.

"Tell you what…" he mediated, forcing a more relaxed tone back into his voice. "You're tired… *I'm* tired… why don't we *both* get a few hours' sleep and talk some more about it in the morning. I can scout around first, check if the coast is clear, and maybe *then* we can have a look at that clearing if everything seems all right. How does *that* sound?"

Nev stared him down for a long time, eyes boring into his as she dared him to show any hint of falsehood and was met only with honesty and openness. She *wanted* to go back there right now, but she was smart enough to realise that *that* wasn't going to happen, and although she didn't really trust him yet, perhaps a morning trip *was* a reasonable compromise. Of course, that didn't necessarily mean that she had to go about it the way *he* was suggesting.

"Um… okay, I guess…" she began slowly, making an effort to sound sincere in her desire to meet him halfway. She then stretched rather overdramatically. "I *am* really tired, now that you mention it…"

"There y' go, then!" He agreed happily, pleased he'd gotten his point across. "Like I said, we'll talk it all through tomorrow when we've got full bellies and a clear head. He rose from the crate and moved back to the rucksacks, pulling free a large bedroll from the pile. "Here's a bag for y': you can sleep out back there where those shutters are, if you like."

"Thanks," she replied with a nod as he tossed the bedroll across and she caught it deftly in both hands.

"Take *these* as well," he added, handing across a metal flask and a small canvas bag. "There's water and a few strips of jerky to eat. It's not much, but you won't be able to sleep if you don't eat *somethin'* to keep your guts happy."

"Thanks… *thank you*…" she repeated, giving the words more emphasis this time as she tucked the bedding under her right arm and accepted the food and drink with her left hand, holding it awkwardly. "I – I think I *should* get some sleep, now…" she added, taking a tentative step toward the shutters at the rear of the barn.

"You know, I don't think you ever told me *your* name…" Godfrey pointed out, staring expectantly with hands on hips.

"I – um – my *name*…?" She stammered, suddenly fighting the urge to blush once more. "I'm… uh… my name's Nev… Nev Anderson…"

"Nev, eh…?" He asked rhetorically with one eyebrow raised. "First Percy, and then *Nev*…" He shook his head, the twinkle back in his eyes now. "This world you come from *must* be a strange place…"

"Why do you say that…?"

"Well… so far all the womenfolk seem to have *men's* names…"

"Goodnight, Godfrey…" She said softly, giving a wry smile as she nodded her farewell and turned to move into the rear of the barn.

"G'night, Nev Anderson…" he replied softly, sending an innocent wink with it that went completely unnoticed.

She unfurled a thick, canvas roll that seemed to be packed with down or something similar, with extra stuffing sewn into a separate compartment at one end to form a makeshift pillow, and Nev found it to be surprisingly comfortable once it'd been laid flat and covered by a woollen blanket. She'd taken off her cloak to also use as a blanket, and as she lay down for the night, the shutters shielding her from most of the fire's glow, it made for a reasonable bed, all things considered.

Nev had transferred her phone to one of the pockets of the leather vest as she'd changed clothes, and she took it out now, hoping there might be some last, slim chance of a signal. She was met with the same connection error message, and in frustration she opened its settings and switched the phone over to airplane mode, at least ensuring it wouldn't keep pestering her with notifications reminding her of the lack of a network she so desperately needed.

She thought about maybe making a short video log of what she'd experienced so far, but even as her finger hovered over the button, she found she had neither the heart nor stomach for it. She was tired, confused and almost certainly depressed, and none of those conditions made her feel at all like recording anything at that moment. As she closed the apps and returned to the lock screen once more, Nev noted the time – 11:00pm – and was no longer surprised over the levels of exhaustion she was feeling.

"My god… *eight hours*…?" She murmured, finding it hard to believe that eight hours had passed already since she'd first entered that clearing with Percy. "Almost seems impossible…"

But then, in a strange world where impossible things seemed to be happening all around her, what was the small matter of a few missing hours here or there? Reopening the phone menus once more, she activated her clock app and set an alarm for 4:30 in the morning, then lay the phone down beside her head and finally allowed herself to surrender to the sleep that had been calling out for her for some time now.

As Nev had gone about setting up her bedroll, Godfrey had moved across to one of the pillars near the rucksacks and sat down with his back to it, his sword in easy reach with its scabbard laid atop the rest of the gear to his right.

"You all right up there, Toadface…?" He asked genially, calling out just loud enough for Lester to hear him through the closed hatch above.

"Well enough, Westy… well enough…"

"G'night then, y' ugly little bugger…"

"'Night, Westy…"

Godfrey sat for a while longer, staring deep into the crackling flames of that small fire and thinking even deeper about everything that had happened that day. He didn't come up with many answers, but then his job wasn't to contemplate the meaning of life itself: he was just a ranger with a single mission to complete, and it sometimes paid *not* to think too hard about things. Long after Nev's soft snores could be heard from the back of the barn, he too drifted off into a restless sleep, his dreams filled with strange majik and even stranger women.

Cardinal De Lisle, Chief Primus of The Brotherhood of the Shard waited patiently as a carpenter and three peasant assistants carried out the final assembly of his ceremonial communion chair. He rarely travelled nowadays but when he did, De Lisle always insisted on bringing the chair with him. The quarters he'd been provided at Fortress Cadle weren't as spacious as his private suite back at Kraal, but it would suffice for the next few weeks as preparations were made for the coming celebration.

The cardinal, clearly an old man, had also held a given name once, prior to his acceptance into the life of The Brotherhood, but he'd been a brother so long now that even he could barely say what it had been. De Lisle had been a *cardinal* for so long it was unlikely anyone could even *remember* what life within their order had been like without his guiding presence. For the same reasons, no one really knew his true age either, although the look of his greyed hair and wrinkled features suggested that he's seen at least sixty summers or more… something unusual in itself in a world where most were lucky to make it past forty-five.

Tall and solid of build for a man of his age, he still moved well, although arthritis had begun to set into his joints in the last few years to his dismay, making his movements painful on occasion, particularly during colder weather. De Lisle had faced many challenges *and* challengers during his time as cardinal, and he'd seen all off with similar drive and purpose. Under the guidance of his steady hand, the Brotherhood of the Shard had grown from quite humble beginnings to become a powerhouse of influence and control, spread right across the expanse of the Osterlands and beyond.

He made a particular effort to thank both the artisan and his workers as they completed their job and then personally escorted them to the door, only to find the Cadle prelate waiting for him outside.

"Prelate Roland..." he acknowledged tiredly, standing back to allow the younger man entry. "It's been a long day *and* a long journey before that: I'll ask you to be brief, whatever the issue..."

"Nothing of consequence, Your Grace," the prelate assured, bowing his head slightly in greeting as he stepped through the doorway and past the De Lisle himself as he entered the room. "Nothing more than a few minor matters of state I need your decision on in preparation for Endweek."

Prelate Roland was tall, thin and fair haired, with narrow, angular features and piercing eyes of pale blue. He looked to be in his early-thirties, and like De Lisle, he wore the black ceremonial garb customary of higher ranks within the Brotherhood, rather than the more common brown robes worn by lower level brothers and novitiates. De Lisle had met the prelate just once before, but the man, his zealotry *and* his unbridled ambition were all well-known throughout the Kraal hierarchy and the cardinal's secret and carefully-handwritten personal files on Roland filled a number of thick volumes.

"I believe I was clear in my earlier letters that there was no requirement that any special accommodations be made for this Endweek?" The Cardinal replied coldly, his recollection very clear on that matter.

"Err... Quisitor Silas..." Roland began awkwardly, suddenly left all at sea.

"...Can be *overzealous* at times...?" De Lisle suggested with a raised eyebrow, completing the sentence for him. "One would imagine an occupational hazard on occasion, considering his position, however the Inquisition is *not* tasked with managing *my* daily schedule so far as I'm aware... not *yet* anyway..." He added definitively, '*not while* I *still have any say in it*' remaining unsaid but definitely clear in implication.

"Of – *of course*," Your Grace..." Roland acceded instantly, his face a mask of perfect serenity.

"I *will* be in attendance, *naturally…*" the cardinal continued, giving at least a little ground "…but I do not intend to officiate or be *present* in an *official* capacity. This is *Huon's* time to shine, and the less there's any perceived outside interference the better."

"I understand completely, Your Grace," the prelate nodded sagely, knowing well enough when to cut his losses. "Consider the matter closed."

"Was there anything *else*, then…?" De Lisle ventured with a narrowed stare, *all* matters closed for that evening so far as he was concerned.

"Nothing that can't wait until the morning, Your Grace…"

"Very good, prelate," he nodded with a tired smile, Roland already heading for the door now. "*Tomorrow* I'll be *happy* to be at your disposal for as long as you need me. Right *now* I intend to take my communion with The Shard and retire to bed; as you're no doubt aware, the journey up from Burnii is a long and tiresome one."

Five minutes later, De Lisle had changed into some grey, loose-fitting woollen evening robes and had taken the time to wash his face and brush his teeth before bed, using the gold-handled horse-hair toothbrush he'd been sent as a gift from the then Prelate to the Sun Empire. The only thing that remained to do before he climbed into his badly-needed bed was to make his usual nightly communion before sleep.

Reaching inside the neck of his robes, he took out the Holy Pendant hanging there. Identical to the brooch Percy had worn at the clearing, it was nothing much to look at in itself; little more than a small blue gem set into a metal mounting, suspended from a thin steel chain. Initially dull and seemingly lifeless, the crystal embedded there suddenly glowed with a strange, pulsating light as he slowly lowered himself into the communion chair the workmen had assembled earlier, positioned up against one wall beside his single bed. A similar but larger blue stone was also fixed into the high back of the chair itself, positioned directly above De Lisle's head as he took a seat, and this too began to flicker with life as he took his position and closed his eyes.

The girl has failed… again…

The words boomed like thunder at the centre of his mind, dazing him slightly with their intensity and making him feel happier about the fact that he was sitting down. Although the Shad Gods generally got straight to the point if there was something to be discussed, the news was *disconcerting* to say the least.

"I – I had my *doubts* as to her usefulness from the beginning…" De Lisle reminded quickly, thinking it prudent to at least throw that out there right from the onset. As cardinal, it was *unlikely* the gods would lay fault upon his head without cause, but one could never be too careful.

Your misgivings were noted at the time, it replied instantly – almost *too* quickly – and he was surprised to find a hint of defensiveness in the tone. *This is of no consequence now. The purpose of this discussion is not to apportion blame, but rather to neutralise the damage done…*

"*Damage*…?" He asked quickly, caught off guard. "*What* damage?"

The girl returned through the portal with another… one that I foresee as a source of great *danger to Us…* De Lisle knew instinctively that the Shard God was referring specifically to itself in that sentence, however it mattered little in the long run as the fate of The Brotherhood was in any case tied directly and irrevocably to that of the Shard for better *or* for ill.

"We were *expecting* her to return with *someone*…" he ventured, not yet comprehending. "What is it about this individual that makes him so dangerous? Is he some great *warrior*… some persuasive *heretic* that might challenge our power?"

She *is little more than a child… yet* so much more… It answered cryptically, catching the cardinal completely by surprise. *She has a prescient mind – one that cannot be controlled…*

"Are not *all* witches prescient to some degree… the *real* ones, anyway…?" De Lisle suggested calmly, not seeing any great need for concern. "Surely this - this *girl* is of no greater threat than any *other* witch…?"

The creatures you send to the purifying flame have lived their entire lives *under the guidance and the watchful eye of The Brotherhood…* it shot back instantly, sounding almost exasperated now, as if being forced to explain something simple to a fool. *Were she of* this *world, her years of conditioning since birth might've been enough to nullify her power. She is* not *of* this *world however, and is already at such an age that Endweek conditioning would be of no use. Her mind would not respond to anything short of* burning… it added, referring to one of The Brotherhood's most hideous mental tortures rather than any physical act of immolation ...*and even* that *might not be effective.*

"*Burning* would not be effective?" De Lisle snapped, shuddering at the thought and not sure whether to be sceptical or apprehensive. "When has burning *ever* been ineffective?"

I do not blame you that you cannot understand, it responded thoughtfully, sounding far more magnanimous than the cardinal would've imagined possible. *This creature is something We have never encountered before. Our connection with its mind was momentary during the process of transference through the portal, yet it was enough for Us to see that much at least. There were* others *we encountered in the past – before The Cleansing – who displayed similar powers, but they were all* male *and were therefore easily controlled. This... girl, as you put it... is something very different.*

"What would you have me do?"

Find it and terminate it... it replied coldly. *I do not need to remind you that this is* not *the time for distractions: not when so much is already at stake.*

"Of course... and the *other* girl: this *Persephone...?*"

The Blackwatch have her. Keep her alive for the time being... We feel that she may yet be of use.

"Surely we cannot trust her judgement any longer..." De Lisle began.

Was there anything *in Our last order that was unclear?* A sharp reply came immediate, powerful enough to again leave him feeling slightly woozy.

"No... of course not..." he answered immediately, backpedalling for all he was worth.

You need to understand that We do not see time as you do, it explained further, deciding at least some elaboration was reasonable. *We are ageless. Time does not pass for Us in the same fashion that it does for* your *pointless species. While We cannot* see *the future with certainty, We* can *see the paths of* possible *futures, and at the moment of this girl's arrival, a* number *of possible outcomes were created – utterly improbable as they are – that might foreseeably result in Our defeat. This obviously cannot be permitted, and the creature must be destroyed as a result. You will send word to Harald that it is to be done: she* must not *leave the Blacklands.*

"It will be done…" De Lisle confirmed, asking no further questions.

On another *matter*, it continued without missing a beat, *what progress have you with Phaesus?* No further elaboration was needed on that topic: the cardinal new exactly what it was referring to.

"None, I am afraid. He has refused outright to heed my warnings. Huon is *obsessed* with this new-found 'science', and I do not believe there is *anything* that can be done now to prevent the spread of their machines."

There is one *thing that can be done… that* is *being done…* it pointed out darkly. *If it is permitted* here, other *kingdoms will* also *see this as an opportunity to disregard the will of The Brotherhood.* Already, *there is dissent spreading in Huon: these depictions of the Nethug daubed on city walls and carved into trees of the forests.*

"These machines create spare time for idle hands…" De Lisle mused. "Is it any wonder they turn to the evil one's work…?"

Perhaps you do not take this insurrection seriously? It admonished severely. *You speak as if this were the thoughtless acts of children at mischief, yet so far the Endweek ceremony has uncovered no culprits. These 'pranks' are the seeds of insurrection… of* blasphemy… *and through this the Nethug will seek to gain succour in the dark recesses of a heretic's mind. It is no* coincidence *that the increase of these incidents coincides with the spread of* machines *in this kingdom, and it* will *be purged, one way or another.*

"Then we proceed as planned? The Kings' Council will *not* react well to unprovoked warfare…"

You may make one more attempt to convince him – in deference *to the 'council'…* it growled in return, tone heavy with sneering disdain *…but* do not *cease preparations… We do not believe he can be dissuaded.*

"It will be done…"

One more thing…

"Yes…?" the cardinal asked evenly, taking care to keep any hint of weariness or disinterest out of his tone.

Phaesus' daughter, Charleroi… We suggest you keep her under scrutiny: we have… concerns…

"Surely, she is no heretic nor *witch*…?" De Lisle blurted, eyes open in surprise now as he baulked at the idea. "Roland's an experienced prelate: to *conceal* such thoughts from him would be *impossible!*"

Nothing *is impossible... although it is nevertheless* extremely *improbable.* It conceded reluctantly. *We have no certainty in this, only suspicion... her Endweek patterns have been* 'erratic' *of late. Were there real* evidence *of anything, we would not be having this discussion, however we have none, and as she's a princess, discretion is required. We have also not ruled out the unlikely possibility of read errors on the part of your prelate and for this reason, We have decided that* you *will perform this coming Endweek:* a different *read will allow Us to compare results.*

"It will be done," he acknowledged yet again, quite sourly this time in recognition of the fact that he'd now be forced to do *exactly* what he'd been hoping to avoid.

We have nothing further to discuss. Rest now, and we shall speak again tomorrow.

"As you wish..."

As he pushed himself awkwardly out of the chair, knees threatening him vaguely with the possibility of arthritic pain, De Lisle allowed himself the luxury of an exasperated sigh as the light faded from both the Shard crystal in his pendant and the larger piece set into the chair back behind him. Shuffling over to the door with more confident steps as the stiffness in his joints began to loosen, he pulled it open and turned to the sentry standing at attention outside, exactly where the cardinal had expected him to be.

"Guard; have a message sent through to Prelate Roland immediately..." he began, the man starting with fright over his unexpected appearance. "Tell him that there's been a change of plans, and that I *will* be leading the Endweek ceremony tomorrow."

"At once, Your Grace!" The guard barked far too enthusiastically for that time of evening, immediately executing a regimental-perfect about-face and marching off down the corridor at a cracking pace. De Lisle had already closed the door on his retreating back and turned toward his bed, determined to ensure there'd be no more disturbances that evening.

IV

THE NIGHT DRAGON

Princess Charleroi sat quietly, just one person among a hundred or more as Cardinal De Lisle himself stood before the faithful, preparing to dispense the Shard Blessing that always formed the closing ceremony of the Endweek Service. The Royal Chapel was large and well-appointed, with long, comfortable pews cut from golden pinewood taken from the tall trees that gave the Kingdom of Huon its name. Most of the fittings – the pulpit, choir box and the rest – were all ornately carved from the same stock and all had been stained and immaculately polished as befitting the finest chapel in the kingdom.

Several huge, candle-dotted chandeliers hung from a high-arched ceiling supported by walls of polished basalt that rose dark and lustrous on four sides, all fitted with tall, lead-framed windows of stained glass, while vases of fresh tulips dotted the columns, adding bursts of colour to the polished darkness of the stone. Also known by the commoner's name of 'black granite', the stone was actually an extremely dark grey and was found in abundance right across Huon, particularly in the midst of the country's central ranges where Fortress Cadle lay.

Dominating everything else in the room of course was the great mural, referred to privately by any number of colloquial nicknames throughout the known world that were rarely spoken aloud for fear of denunciation as a heretic. Its correct title was *Cleansing: The Coming of the Night Dragons*, and the original – a dozen metres high and twice as many wide – hung as a great tapestry from the walls of the Great Chamber of The Brotherhood's headquarters at Kraal. The name covered both the castle and the independent city-state that surrounded it, nestled within the south-western provinces of the Blacklands and far away across the Deepwater Strait that separated Huon and Taas from the rest of The Osterlands.

Charleroi had never left the grounds of Fortress Cadle but her mentor, Randwick had told her that just about every chapel or Brotherhood temple displayed a copy of that original tapestry, invariably hung somewhere prominent where it could be seen by all. The one she glanced up at now wasn't as large, hanging behind the pulpit and the ceremonial altar at the centre of the main stage, but it nevertheless measured at least five metres by ten and was quite imposing in its own right.

Every man, woman or child throughout The Oster knew that painting well enough. The ruins of a burning city lay at the feet of Nethug the Bicephalus, screaming his defiance as a multitude of acolytes faithful to Way of The Shard stood witness in the foreground and the destruction of the Night Dragons rained down from the dark and boiling heavens. The followers depicted there were the last survivors, spared by the Shard Gods for their unquestioning piety, and every single one of them held aloft their Shard prayer books as testament to their faith, the glow of the Crystal's holy blue light enveloping both the books and the hands holding them.

The intent of the image was brutally clear: only the righteous would be saved come their time of judgement, and the wicked would fall into the pits of fiery damnation, where they would spend the rest of eternity as playthings for the Dark-Dweller himself.

The Endweek Service was the latest of the hundreds Charleroi had attended in her sixteen summers so far. She was a tall, elegant young woman who'd taken the best of both her parents to combine a flawless, almost tanned complexion with large, dark eyes, long brown hair and a wide, perfect smile. Already almost as tall as her father, the king considered his only child to be the greatest of all his life's achievements.

She turned her head and glanced up as he sat there at her left shoulder, briefly smiling down at her with a faint nod before turning his own eyes forward once more. She did the same: the cardinal was moving toward them now, the king naturally first to receive the blessing and as princess, it followed that Charleroi would be next. Without turning his head, her father reached out his hand and took hers, holding it close at his side between them as he always did during Endweek and squeezing it a few times in silent reassurance as the blessing approached.

Cardinal De Lisle, Chief Primus of The Brotherhood of the Shard halted before them, bowing once as the king automatically slipped from his seat and fell to one knee with his own, crowned head lowered in respect. The cardinal lifted his right hand, his wrist wrapped in the chain of the holy pendant he normally wore about his neck as part of his ceremonial robes. Dangling beneath his open palm, the Shard Crystal flickered softly with a faint, blue glow, its intensity building as he lifted it toward the king's forehead.

"In the name of The Crystal, I absolve your sins, deliver you from Nethug, the Bicephalus, and welcome you back to The Way of the Shard..." he prayed solemnly with eyes closed, the glow pulsing in time with his words as he spoke the Endweek Absolution. "May The Word lead you to paradise everlasting, in this life and the next..."

"In the name of The Crystal..." the king murmured softly in response.

There was a pause of perhaps a second or two, where both cardinal and king swayed together as if two blades of grass caught in the same breeze, before normality returned, the priest took a step back, and the monarch resumed his seat as if nothing had happened.

Taking a step to his right, De Lisle now stood before Charleroi, and she too fell to one knee, accepting his bow with a single nod of recognition.

"In the name of The Crystal, I absolve your sins, deliver you from Nethug, the Bicephalus, and welcome you back to The Way of the Shard. May The Word lead you to paradise everlasting, in this life and the next..."

"In the name of the Crystal..."

Charleroi's head swam for just a moment, a faint dizziness sweeping through her and then immediately dissipating as she slid back up into her seat and her father once more took her hand and squeezed it tightly. For his part, De Lisle gave her no more consideration than he had her father, moving on to the next nobleman in line: with a hundred or more to get through, there was little time for pointless niceties. Behind him and keeping an appropriately-discrete distance, Prelate Roland followed on behind, nodding his own far more familiar greeting to each of them in turn.

Charleroi had never known anyone else to take the Endweek other than Roland, save for just once when the prelate had been ill and it had instead been performed by one The Brotherhood's chief investigators: a Quisitor by the name of Silas who'd been one of De Lisle's most avid acolytes for as long as anyone could remember. She hadn't liked him at all: he'd looked at her strangely as he'd delivered the Absolution, and for a little too long, and it had left her feeling very uncomfortable about the whole experience.

The Absolution took perhaps an hour to complete, meaning it was close to midnight as the king and princess were escorted out at the end of the ceremony, leading the procession of royalty and nobles as they left the chapel and separated, heading for their own quarters for some well-earned sleep. The intention, as always, was to finish as close to midnight as possible, symbolically *and* literally recognising the end of the past week and the arrival of the next.

As they crossed the main courtyard, heading for the palace entrance hall, Charleroi took note of lesser nobles and local barons' families preparing their wagons and carriages for the journey back to their nearby farms and mansions. A palace it might be, but all were welcome at Endweek: no one was refused entry for the service, and that included serfs and workers also, although admittedly there was a larger but less ornately decorated chapel on the opposite side of the courtyard for *their* use.

She frowned as she noticed men and boys helping their mothers, sisters, daughters and aunts to correctly place visards – ceremonial blindfolds – over their eyes and face in preparation for their journeys outside the castle walls. Generally a single, oval-shaped piece of reinforced velvet, the visard was seated around the top of the head by a loose-fitting strap and kept in position by a small bead sewn to the inner face, which could be held between the lips or teeth to prevent the mask from coming away from the wearer's face.

There were a multitude of different, sometimes colourful designs printed to the outer faces of the masks, and some of the beads might be pearl rather than ceramic or metal, however the general effect was the same for all: to prevent the wearer from seeing anything while being worn and, in practical terms, to also limit conversation through the need to keep one's lips closed over the positioning bead. She knew the reasons why, of course: the Keepsake Law... one of the most important of the Shard Laws enforced by the brotherhood. It was in place for one purpose only: to limit the identification of Keepsakes and, by definition, the spread of witches and witchcraft.

She'd seen this process followed after countless Endweeks over the years, and the concept had irritated her for as long as she could remember: the idea of women and girls of *any* age or class being forced to cover their eyes while in open or unknown countryside while they were led blindly by their menfolk either by the hand, on horseback, or inside windowless carriages seemed utterly abhorrent.

Shaking her head, Charleroi turned and headed back toward the palace's main entrance, forced to speed up awkwardly to catch her father, who'd continued on ahead. She was in the lead as they reached the huge main doors, towering two storeys above and thrown wide open for the Endweek service, and she drew near, something new caught her eye. Directly below a burning torch mounted to one of the towering pillars that rose on either side of that great doorway, a mark had been left against the stone for all to see. The princess couldn't recall seeing it when they'd come through earlier, bound for the chapel, and judging by the gasps and frowning comments made by others in the entourage as they also drew near, it was most likely no one else had seen it before either.

Daubed in dark red paint, a hastily-scrawled and very basic drawing had been left of what appeared to be a two-headed serpent, coiled about a sword. There was no need to guess what it represented: everyone recognised a depiction of Nethug, the Bicephalus well enough. Described as the essence of evil throughout the Book of the Shard, Nethug was known as the Corpse-Eater, the Soul-Destroyer… the Dark-Dweller that was the very *reason* the Shard Gods had rained the fire and death of The Cleansing upon the world.

"Have the guards questioned…" she heard her father behind her, speaking softly with one of the Cadle commanders on duty, noting that he was taking great pains not to show any great annoyance or concern. "Find out who did this and report to me immediately."

As she passed close by, she could see that it was indeed quite fresh, with faint trails of wet paint still oozing slowly down the stone below. Charleroi began to slow down again, thinking to stop and take a closer look, but the gentle press of her father's hand at her back instead propelled her onward, the king one step ahead in knowing when to choose discretion over curiosity. Placed at the rear of the main group, De Lisle, Roland and a trio of followers also took note of the fresh graffiti as they passed. Not a word passed between them, yet both the prelate and the cardinal knew there would be dark discussion on the matter soon enough, and as he walked on through those doors and into the palace, De Lisle's expression was one of grim determination.

It was past the hour by the time she made it back to her bedchamber, a fire already crackling in the hearth and spreading its warmth and comforting light throughout the room. Floors of the same polished basalt were covered by a multitude of sheepskin rugs, while at least half a dozen wardrobes were positions about the walls on either side of her huge, four-poster bed. A dresser with a single chair and huge mirror sat close to the fireplace on the other side of the room, while opposite the only entrance, one whole wall was comprised of floor-to-ceiling windows bordered by thick drapes, with a glass-paned doorway leading out onto a wide, walled balcony.

"There's a bed-warmer already inside, Your Highness..." Matron Griselda advised as she carefully made some adjustments to the placement of the gowns hanging in the nearest of the robes. "Your travelling clothes are ready for the morning, and your trunks have been packed..."

"I can't believe I'm *really* going to be gone for two whole Endweeks!" Charleroi burst out excitedly. She'd quite literally spent her whole life growing up within the boundaries of the Fortress Cadle, and the thought of her very first journey outside its walls filled her with an incredible, almost breathless anticipation.

"Aye, Miss... a whole two weeks indeed, and a two-day journey as well, there *and* back..."

Griselda of Westerland, who as a child had survived arduous journeys across the breadth of the Osterlands, had been Charleroi's Matron and primary female mentor the princess' entire life. A simple, no-nonsense woman of forty-four summers, she was short and tending to the plump side, with a broad, open face that could be quite pleasant on those few times she actually allowed her smile to be shown in public.

"And do I *really* have to travel the *whole* way with the shutters closed?" She asked in a softer voice, the faint tone of dismay creeping in now.

"Aye, Your Highness... you know The Law as well as I..." Griselda replied apologetically. "You *know* it's for your own safety as much as anythin' else."

'The Law'... The Keepsake Law: it stood as a linchpin of society, binding the Osterlands together, and its importance was second only to the Book of The Shard itself. Everyone knew The Law, for it was drummed into every child from the moment they were old enough to understand.

"But, *why* must *all* women be covered while travelling? *Why...*?" The princess persisted, standing by the foot of the bed as the older woman finished fussing over the sheets.

"You know *very well* why, My Girl..." the matron snapped in return, shorter than Charleroi by a half-head but intimidating her all the same as she loomed up into the girl's face and waggled an accusing finger under her nose. "You can see the gates from that balcony out there, and I *know* you watch *everyone* who comes and goes. You've seen them all and *you* know that there's not one woman or girl who passes out those gates who don't cover the windows o' their carriages, or blindfold themselves and let their man lead 'em out safe and sound. It's the will 'o The Shard, and no good *ever* came o' gettin' on the wrong side o' The Brotherhood."

"But... but it seems so... *ridiculous...*!" She exclaimed eventually, unable to find any better word to describe how she felt. "What *possible* harm can there be?"

"What harm?" Griselda barked sharply, almost scoffing at the idea. "You *want* to be labelled a *witch*, do you? Trussed up against a pole in the palace courtyard with kindling at your feet?"

"They wouldn't *dare...*!" Charleroi declared regally with all the superiority a spoilt teenager could muster.

"My *word* they would, and don't you *ever* forget that!" The matron shot back immediately. "King or peasant, it makes no difference to The Brotherhood, and there's not a *damned* thing even your *father* could do to stop them! There's *at least* ten Keepsakes we *know of* on the road to Burnii as it is, and there's *always* more turnin' up here and there, '*specially* after a flood or a bad storm. Holding staves only do so much to lock them down, and even then; they don't do *nuthin'* to stop a *witch* seein' 'em..."

It was an old argument Charleroi had had many times with Griselda, her father and any number of nobles and servants alike in her time at Cadle. Normally the whole thing had been rather an academic exercise, considering she'd *never* been allowed to leave the safety of those great stone walls but *now*, with an *actual* journey imminent, the whole thing now seemed very *very* real.

"*Lewis* doesn't believe in witches..." she sniffed grumpily, plonking herself down on the bed as Griselda sat down beside her.

"*Lewis* doesn't *have* to..." the old woman pointed out, her tone softening now. "*Lewis* is a *boy*, who *might* grow into a man – if he's *lucky* - and *he* doesn't have to worry about whether he sees anythin' or not... *no* man does. The fact remains, Princess that The Book of The Shard says quite clearly that witches *do* exist, and such is any woman who can see the Keepsakes. Whether *you* believe in them or no, *bad* things happen when a witch is discovered... both to the witch *and* to her family or friends, if they try to help her."

"It's just not *fair!*" Charleroi muttered, staring at the floor and knowing she was never going to win argument against The Shard... no one ever did.

"No, Young Miss, it *isn't* fair..." her father agreed in a kindly voice, standing in the open doorway to her room with arms folded across his chest.

Hachem Namur, King Phaesus IV, was a tall but otherwise unassuming figure – a man who's almost willowy frame had definitely been passed down to his daughter, although she'd received her mother's finer features rather than his larger, hawkish nose and angular cheeks. He somehow looked ill at ease with the crown and royal robes he wore, and it took real effort sometimes for him to remember to keep his shoulders up and his back straight when walking the palace halls, as befitted the style of a true monarch.

"Your *Majesty!*" The matron exclaimed with a start, immediately lowering herself in a deep curtsey.

"Calm yourself, Griselda," he assured as he stepped into the room, waving a dismissive hand. "Since when have you *ever* needed to bow before *me...?*" The old woman had been almost a surrogate mother for the princess the last sixteen years and Phaesus had never been one for formality at the best of times.

"But, sire, you're *king* now..." She answered as she rose once more, as if that explained everything.

"And I was a *prince*, then..." he countered with a dry grin. "These last six months have been *difficult*," he conceded, not allowing that understatement to dampen his mood, "and I know I've been away from you all far more that I was *before* the coronation, but I promise: I'm still the same prince you've worked for *and* looked after all these seasons past." He crossed the floor to stand with them, Charleroi also on her feet now and standing quietly and respectfully beside Griselda. "You've been almost a *mother* for Charli all this time," he added sadly, "and to *me,* you're family in everything but name alone so *please...* outside of public or *formal* engagements, do not bow to me. You've earned too much of my respect for that."

"You honour me, sire," she whispered, voice thick with emotion and barely managing to catch herself before she curtsied again.

"No more than you deserve..." he nodded faintly, then turned his attention toward the princess with an impish gleam in his eye. "...and what of my smart, witty, beautiful and – most importantly – *argumentative* only child...? Debating again with *Griselda* over the laws of The Shard itself? As formidable as the good woman is, I doubt she'll be able to help: you'd just as well argue with a fisherman over the coming and going of the tides..."

"I was just saying that it was unfair, that's all," she replied sulkily, staring down at the floor just ahead of her father's feet.

"And I *agreed* with you, did I not?" He pointed out, gently, reaching out and lightly lifting her chin with a single finger to look into her eyes. "Did I not say that very thing just seconds ago?"

"I – I suppose..." she shrugged, unwilling to give any ground as teenagers were wont, and not seeing any benefit to be had from her father's admission in any case.

"A moment of privacy, lady, if you will...?" The king asked with a pointed glance at the old woman, nothing but courtesy in his tone.

"Of course, Your Majesty... *of course...*" Griselda blurted, immediately curtseying once more without thinking and heading straight for the open door, closing it behind her as she went.

"Still in your Endweek dress...?" He asked with a smile, noting her attire for the first time. "All the better... come: take a coat and join me out on the balcony."

"I don't need a coat, father," she replied quickly, the need to disagree an almost pathological symptom of teenage years. "I *like* the cold..."

"Yes, you *do* need a coat..." he insisted, and there was no more argument to be had there. "Come out and we'll talk, you and I..."

The balcony was long and narrow, running at least forty or fifty metres across the southern face of the palace's second level, and bordered both the king's and princess' bed chambers, separated by a low wall. With tall ceilings on the lower floor, its stone balustrades stood at least three metres above the ground with burning torches mounted on the outer side of the railing and spaced at regular intervals to provide lighting along its entire length. A squad of the King's Own bodyguard patrolled below at all times, the height and the manpower present acting as great deterrents for any would-be assassin, unlikely as the possibility might be.

From the railing, the king could look out across the palace grounds past the towers of the Fortress and see the four snow-capped summits that formed the Cadle mountain chain, glowing beneath the moon and stars on that clear night. Small Horn, The Osterman, The Smith and Cadle itself, running from east to south-west in a great, ponderous curve of towering, dolerite pillars. They weren't the tallest mountains on the island but they were the most recognised: renown across the kingdom and beyond, they were symbols of the strength and longevity of Huon and the Namur line.

The King's grandfather had long called them his 'Four Dragons', and he'd chosen to build his great fortress in the shadow of their majesty. It had taken two decades for Fortress Cadle to take shape and the king's father – the second in their line – had often recalled with sadness that the building of the fortress had destroyed his father just as surely as the constant fighting with the Blacklands: Phaesus I had died young, broken both in mind and body.

And yet Phaesus II had continued to literally build on the legacy his father had left behind. The palace in which they now stood, although modest by comparison to some the king had seen – particularly those of the Sun Empire in the far north-east of the mainland – was nevertheless a grand and impressive structure, with fine, polished walls and floors of stone throughout. Those walls were adorned with artwork from right across the Osterlands, along with the finest tapestries and beautiful furniture carved lovingly from that same, golden Huon pine.

War alone had taken Hachem Namur's father, killed in a great sea battle off the Blacklands' coast, within sight of Harald's summer fortress. His two sons had mourned the old man's death, yet with it came a crushing victory that had destroyed the Black Fleet and left Castle Black open to attack. The siege that had followed had ended that war – one of many between the two great powers of The Deepwater Strait – and had gone some way toward laying the foundations for the coming, long-lasting peace that Phaesus IV had worked ceaselessly for these last six months.

"They're beautiful, father... as always..." Charleroi observed quietly as she joined him at the railing, and stared out at the moonlit peaks across the silent, silver mirror of Peaceful Lake. She now wore a thick, woollen coat lined in sheepskin and although she'd never have admitted it, she was grateful of its warmth as she stood beside him, their breath swirling in the icy darkness. Neither uttered a word of complaint though; clear nights were as rare as sunny days, and they were to be cherished in spite of the cold.

"Almost as beautiful as my loving daughter..." he replied with a smile, not looking down but nevertheless aware that she would be blushing now. "...Although, *not* as *argumentative*..." he added, releasing a soft sigh that coiled in the air around his head and dissolved in the breeze.

"I know Matron Griselda can't *do* anything about the laws, father," she explained softly. She knew he wasn't angry: that statement had been his characteristic way of giving her an opening – an opportunity to speak. "*I know that...* but sometimes I need *someone* to talk to, and *you're* so *busy* these days, especially now the peace accords have started..."

"Even *I* cannot change a Shard Law," he pointed out honestly, and she was a little surprised to note a faint hint of sadness in his tone.

"*You* don't believe in them either, do you!" She asked, more as a statement than a question as she caught the faint hint of scorn in his voice.

"What I *believe* is irrelevant..." he answered diplomatically, side-stepping that question, "...but I *will* say honestly – as I did inside – that I do not believe them to be *fair*."

"But then, *why*..." she began, faltering in her rising frustration, "...*why* can't you *change* them? You're the *king*! What is there that a *king* can't do?"

"My darling girl..." he began with a rueful expression, the sadness far clearer now, "...there are *many* things a king or queen *can* do, but ignoring the will of their people is not one of them."

"But... but... you can send the kingdom to *war*...!" She frowned, searching for logic in what he was saying. "You could take everyone's lands and possessions for your own... demand tribute... take their grain: as a king, you could do *any* of these things..."

"I would *not* do any of those things, given a *choice*..." he countered firmly, giving a frown of his own in return as he turned to face her for the first time.

"I know that, father, but you *could*..."

"Not without *justification*, Charli..." he explained, his tone even but stronger now. "You've learned much from your tutors and your classes, and there's great intelligence *and* compassion within you – both *vital* to the success of a monarch – but there's still *much* for you to learn about how a kingdom works. You're right," he conceded. "As king, I *could* do any or *all* of those terrible things if I so desired. But a king *cannot* send his people to war – to *die* in war – without reason... *not* if he wishes to *keep* his crown, *or* his head."

"But..."

"*One day... you* will wear this crown... *you* will stand in my place... and when that times comes, *hopefully* many years hence, you will learn that there are *many* things a monarch cannot do, much as he or she wishes otherwise." He turned away again with another sigh, casting an arm out at the mountains and lake beyond the castle walls. "Out *there*, ordinary people live their ordinary lives, *most* of them surviving from day to day with no greater desire than to see food on their table and spend time with their loved ones. *That* is a the essence of a simple life, the life of my subjects – *your subjects* – and the reason they work and toil, pay their taxes and give their share of food and service to the crown is because of what *we* give *them* in return..."

He again faced her, raising an eyebrow in unspoken question and making it clear a response was required. She thought long and hard, recognising that her father expected something considered and well-thought, and it was a moment or two before she finally answered.

"Safety...?" She answered carefully, uncertainty in her voice.

"Safety..." he repeated with a faint nod, filling her with relief. "Safety and security: protection against dangers from without *and* from within the kingdom. They pay their gold and give their services when needed because they know – they *expect* – the crown in turn to keep them safe from bandits and enemy nations. They expect roads and city walls... sanitation and clean water. They expect to see Crown Guards patrolling the streets and the open roads, and warships patrolling the oceans, holding back pirates and invaders alike. *This* is the unspoken contract that *every* king must honour.

"To send your people to battle is to knowingly condemn hundreds – *thousands* – to certain death... *in your name.* This is a terrible responsibility that *must not* be undertaken lightly. If the war is a just one, the people will endure it... If it is *unjust...?* If they do not *believe* in the cause, whatever that may be, then they may persevere... *for a time...* but I tell you this: sure as I'm speaking to you right now, Charli, a ruler who pushes too harshly or unjustly *will* fall in the end. To push the people beyond their limit is to invite revolt and anarchy... there's nothing so certain as this.

"To return to *your* statement that the Keepsake Law is unfair..." he continued, bringing the focus back to the original subject. "This law stands as an integral part of The Book of The Shard. The Book tells us that eradication of evil was the prime purpose of The Cleansing... of the time when the Night Dragons fell from the sky and scoured Nethug from our world with fire. The Book *also* tells us that heeding The Word – to follow the *laws* of The Shard – will provide each and every one of us with salvation in *this* world *and* a doorway to paradise as we pass on to the next."

"Do... do you *really* believe that...?" She asked carefully, knowing that even with her father, the question was potentially dangerous.

"Again, what *I* believe does not matter..." he replied, this time clear in his meaning despite the evasive answer. "It is what the *people* believe that matters. In this, The Brotherhood is all-powerful. The one thing that the people desire in life more than any other is the 'certainty' that all their years of hard work and sacrifice have *purpose.* What point would there be in a peasant's mind to all his toil and labour, giving so much of his earthly life to the land and the state, if there was no hope of a paradise awaiting them in the *next*? The Brotherhood – *The Shard* – gives them that promise, and that is something *no king* can match.

"I know what you will ask next..." he went on, forestalling her words. "You would point out that *surely*, the women of this world cannot *enjoy* being forced to cover their faces – their *eyes* – while outside their own homes and villages? That their menfolk *surely* cannot endure to see their beloved humiliated and controlled in this way? That a princess who will one day become a *queen* – the *ruler of an entire kingdom* – should be able to come and go as she pleased and not be locked up in a windowless carriage in her travels throughout *her own lands*?" His smile then was wan and humourless.

"I would answer only thus: no, they do not enjoy this... *no* decent human being would *without reason* endure such humiliation. However, whether I believe in the law or not, whether I believe in *witches* or not, the fact remains, as Griselda said earlier, that bad things *do* happen to those accused of witchcraft. Aside from *human* actions – the burnings, and the torture of those who give aid – there are *also* the magical powers of the inquisitors: the power of The Crystal in the Holy Pendants they wear. Every Endweek, we *all* receive that blessing willingly, and you and I are no different in spite of our doubts.

"You saw the image of Nethug tonight, yes? Hastily painted against the pillar for all to see? Done on a dare by some foolish youth, no doubt. There's talk going about at the moment how *some* believe that Nethug is 'misunderstood'... that he's a harbinger of *change* rather than destruction..." he sighed with exasperation. "They don't understand how *carefully* the Brotherhood watches. You know the stories of those who fall aside... *we all do*. And you *also* know how those stories end: farms or entire *villages* wiped out, sometimes leaving no more than a smoking hole in the ground... death and destruction for unbelievers and anyone around them, their deaths without explanation by something *other* than human hands. And so we attend every week to accept the blessing."

"It's not The *Brotherhood* you fear..." Charleroi realised finally, no accusation in her words. Everything her father had said suddenly became very clear in her mind in that moment. "It's not them at all, *or* The Shard... it's the *people* that frighten you."

"Indeed..." he nodded, staring out at the mountains. "Challenge The Shard and you threaten the doorway to paradise. Take away *hope*, and you take away *everything* they believe in. To dispute or disrespect the teachings of The Shard – to even *think* of forcing change – would mean death for *any* ruler across The Osterlands... suicide at the hands of his own people. *That* is the power of The Shard. It spans *all* kingdoms, and it needs no army... no war fleet. The 'soldiers' of The Brotherhood are the peasants, the commoners and the nobles alike, and they would answer *any* call, man or woman, in defence of their *hope* for salvation and paradise."

"What point is there in even *being* a king... *or a queen...*?" she mumbled softly in defeat, the reality of what her father had said sinking in.

"There is *much* one can do... so *much* more than just *rule...*" he answered immediately, optimism returning to his tone. "My brother, my father and *his* father before him all ruled this kingdom with fists of iron: the wars and the constant need to defend against our enemies – *mostly* Harald and his predecessors – made this a necessity. *Now* however, as we stand for the first time at a doorway to a lasting peace, *this* will be a new age of prosperity not just for Huon and the Namur, but for *all* the kingdoms of The Osterlands.   Smiths and engineers have already doubled and tripled the efficiency of our farms and factories through the use of science... through the use of tools to better till the earth... mechanical devices that pick cotton... spinning machines that weave linen. *All* these things have improved the lives of our subjects in *real* ways: in *this* life rather than waiting for the next.

"The only problem at the moment is that it is all on such a small scale. Now, as it has always been, the primary industry in Huon is the building of warships. In Croweda, the majority of the foundries there produce steel blanks to be forged into swords, spears and other weapons of war. Rolled plate comes to our own smithies to be fashioned into shields and armour for *our* knights and soldiers, and into arrow- and spearheads to pierce the armour of our enemy. *Most* of our industrial capacity is consumed purely by *military* needs, and because of this there are great delays in the delivery of improvements for our *civilian* population.

"By signing the treaty with Harald, we will *break* this cycle once and for all and *finally* be able to put our efforts as a *kingdom* into making tools and machines that will *benefit* Huon, rather than simply defend it..." He declared finally, pride filling him. "*This* will be my legacy to you, Charli... the legacy of a nation of *wonders* and prosperity that will be the *envy* of the whole *world...*!"

"A legacy I shall never *see* as queen," she pointed out bitterly, stating the obvious. "Not in the fields, or in the factories... not *anywhere* outside of this castle."

There was a long silence then, neither of them able to think of anything suitable to add at that moment, and both instead elected to stare thoughtfully up at the night sky above the dark, distant mountains. A single, brilliant streak of blue-white light appeared at that moment, streaking downward at an incredible rate from almost directly above them and disappearing behind Cadle's summits. It passed without a sound and had vanished completely by the time either had a chance to react.

"*Father…!*" Charleroi gasped, suddenly feeling a sharp, guilty terror.

"A Night Dragon, yes… I saw it …" he answered, more surprise in his expression than fear.

"Is it an *omen…?*" She breathed softly, not sure she wanted an answer.

"You think it appeared because we're talking?" The king asked, trying hard not to humiliate his daughter by showing amusement. "You think your doubts have brought a dragon's wrath?" He continued with a tilt of his head. "Randwick was right, it seems: there *are* no unbelievers in battle, are there…?"

"Is it…? Do you think…?"

"How many Night Dragons have you seen?" He asked with a gentle smile, working hard to dispel the fear in her eyes.

"A few…" she admitted cautiously. "…Always just passing, though… high across the sky. This one *fell…* it seemed so *close…*"

"It *wasn't* close… not really…" he assured, shaking his head. "I've never told you this, but when I was young – younger than you – I was out on this very balcony one night and I saw a Dragonfall that *was* close." Her eyes flew wide in surprise at that revelation. "It came down beyond Small Horn, so close you could hear the shriek as it passed overhead, and I knew it was near because I saw a flash beyond the pass as it struck. The ground shook, I could hear plates and candlesticks rattling on the table inside, and a few seconds later everyone in the castle heard a roar like nothing I've ever heard before or since. I was the only royal there than night – it was wartime, and father and Serge were away leading the troops, of course – and I decided then and there that I very much wanted to *see* this Night Dragon for myself."

"You went out to *look* for it… *alone…?*" She asked with eyes wide, her voice hushed with disbelief.

"Not alone…" he replied with a half-smile. "Randwick was already with us then, although he was far younger… far more reckless than he is now. I convinced him to come with me – to guide and keep me safe – and we took a squad of cavalry, although we left the others at the pass, Randwick and I, and continued on alone. It was after dawn before we reached the top of the pass between Small Horn and The Osterman, and standing there in a drizzling rain we could see all the way down the other side, past the Rodaway Lake. There's a small tarn there halfway down the slope, and it had struck close by. We thought then that the stories *were* true, for it seemed that the 'beast' *had* set the forest alight with fire and brimstone. The rain had since quenched the flames, but some of the nearer trees had burned, sure enough, and right at the centre was a crater three hundred feet across and at least fifty deep. The trees there at the rim hadn't burned at all, mind you: they were all knocked flat and covered with earth thrown out of the hole it had made."

"Was it there? *Was it still there...?*"

"Oh, yes," he grinned, almost chuckling now as he recalled that moment from so many years past. "We found what was left of it right at the centre of that hole, still smoking and hot to the touch. It was a *rock*, Charli... nothing more than twisted lump of molten rock the size of one of the great cornerstones we use for our watchtowers."

"A... a *rock...?*"

"Aye, my girl... a rock, indeed... There were smaller pieces of it lying about here and there, but there was no denying it was the cause of everything. It had never been there *before* that night – I knew that place well enough – and t'was too large for any man to have left there *after...* And so we were left with one other explanation: that this steaming lump of black slag had somehow fallen straight out of the sky. I know not what this thing was," he admitted with a shrug. "I know not what *any* of the Night Dragons are that streak across our skies between dusk and dawn, but from then on, I *did* at least now know something that they were *not*: that they were no living beast, come from the heavens in vengeance and wrath."

"What did you *do?*"

"We did nothing... *said* nothing..." The king gave another shrug. "The men with us were sworn to secrecy, and none had come close enough to see anything of detail anyway. Randwick and I *both* knew that no good could come of telling another soul about what we'd seen, so we shut our mouths and got on with our lives as best we could."

"How could you *not* tell anyone?" She asked, incredulous.

"For the same reason that I would never question the Keepsake Law," he answered without hesitation. "Because to speak of it – to lay claim that the fire in the sky was something *other* than a vengeful dragon, hell-bent on destroying the unfaithful and Cleansing the world of Nethug, the evil one – would be nothing less than a challenge to the power of The Brotherhood and the Word of The Shard. If the Night Dragons that fall from the sky *now* are nothing but lumps of rock, who can say that those that came for *The Cleansing* were anything more?

"Perhaps these rocks come both larger *and* smaller – one of the size I saw did damage enough perhaps to shatter the fortress beyond repair – and perhaps The Cleansing *did* happen just as The Book says, with fire falling from the sky. But… if *every one* of these dragons is just a stone, flying through the void before it either passes our world or *collides* with it, then it follows that *maybe* these encounters are by *chance* rather than design… and random chance has *no place* in religion.

"You'll understand better when you're older," he added with a sad smile. "Give the people more time… more *free time*… and give them an education to go with it… and *eventually* they'll see the world as I do… and as you're *beginning* to: that it's a world where people do not *need* the promise of an afterlife if they have sufficient comfort and happiness in the lives they have *now*. But that will only change over time – over many, *many* years – and I fear that *I* will not live to see that come. You *may*, however, and a king or queen may do much to influence with subtlety, through means far less dangerous than heresy."

There was a soft chiming from within her bedroom as the clock against the wall struck the half-hour, and that fact brought reality back to forefront of the king's mind.

"It is *late* now, and we leave before dawn. You need sleep, so I'll bid you goodnight. Never speak of this to *anyone* – our conversation this night – but I *swear* we'll speak more of it soon enough in private. Promise me however, in the meantime, that you *will not* make *any* attempt to peek out of your carriage or make any effort to see the outside world on the journey?"

"But, *father*…!"

"*Promise me*…!" He insisted sternly, knowing she would never break a promise, once given.

"All right, I *promise*!" She blurted finally, not at all pleased at being forced into giving her word.

"That's my darling girl," he nodded, completely satisfied as he leaned in and kissed her frowning forehead. "Now… off to bed –

there's much to be done this next week and barely enough time for work, let alone *sleep*."

Charleroi found sleep to be an elusive thing as she lay in her huge, comfortable bed, tossing and turning and staring at the ceiling through the fine gauze of the white veil that covered the four-poster frame and hung down on either side. Her mind was filled with confusion and doubt regarding what they'd talked about on that balcony, and it was well into the early morning before she finally sunk into a fitful slumber. Even then, she found little rest, and her dreams were haunted by images of picnics with giants, of tiny horses, and strange, metal carriages being slowly swallowed by a dark and ravenous landscape.

V

THE COLD LIGHT OF DAY

The fire had gone out by the time Nev awoke, the soft rumble of her phone's vibrate alarm eventually forcing its way through to her consciousness after a few final moments of restlessness. She'd fought it initially, her mind fogged by the confusion and displacement of the night before, but it was bitterly cold inside the barn now and the chill was cutting through her cloak and the single blanket that had come with the bedroll.

She rolled over and stared at the darkened ceiling above for a moment or two, the faint light of the pre-dawn visible through gaps in roofing and in the eaves. She didn't spend too much time on the disappointment that came with the realisation that it *hadn't* all been a terrible dream. Nev had carefully honed her capacity for repression and denial a long time ago, and she was able to put it to good use now as she rose quietly, straightened her rumpled clothing and checked that her bag and its contents were all still present and intact.

Godfrey was still asleep, curled up close to the smouldering remnants of the fire, and she took great pains not to wake him as she carefully removed her dry clothes from the line he'd strung up and carried them back to her private area behind the shutters. There, she was able to fold them as neatly as she could and slip them inside her duffel bag, which was now close to capacity and starting to bulge. She kept her woollen jacket, removing her cloak and slipping it on as further protection against the biting cold. The cloak went back on over the top, the brown of her coat blending fairly well with the greens and tans she already wore.

She slipped on her suede boots and stepped carefully around the other side of the fire, making for the door as quietly as she was able. Godfrey shifted slightly in his sleep once and gave a faint snuffle of some kind, freezing her momentarily to the spot and almost causing a minor heart attack, but he otherwise kept sleeping, snoring softly the whole time. There was no sign of Lester, for which she was grateful for a number of reasons. Whether he too was still asleep up in the loft that took up the forward half of the barn's ceiling, or whether he was already up and about somewhere else wasn't really of any interest to her at that moment just so long as he didn't interfere with her plans.

Amazingly, the door made almost no sound as she pushed it open just far enough to slip through sideways, closing it immediately behind her to prevent the icy breeze from filling the barn and possibly waking anyone else. It struck her with such force that she gasped faintly, glad she'd had the sense to put her jacket on and wondering how much worse it might've been without it.

It was the first time she'd had a chance to get a good look at the barn or the farmhouse, the glow on the horizon not much by way of illumination but nevertheless far more than had been present the night before in driving rain beneath a thick layer of black cloud. The house itself wasn't much better than a hut – dry stone walls and a thatched roof – and it looked very much like the old, Scottish blackhouses she'd researched for a school project in an earlier high school year. It did have a chimney at least, but it otherwise seemed almost identical in style to the images she'd seen.

Never mind that, dopey… she admonished silently, wary of wasting any more time. *You've got places to go… people to see…! Tick tock…!*

Slipping the bag over her shoulders as she had so many times when heading out her front door for school, she took off at a jog across the open fields, not *entirely* certain of her bearings but remembering well enough that they'd followed the distant line of trees for some time as they'd come south the night before. It stood to reason that reversing the process would take her in the right direction, and that was good enough for the time being: she'd deal with the details later when it became important.

Nev *did* feel a *little* guilty about just taking off without them – they'd *mostly* been nice to her (well, *one of them* had been, anyway), and Godfrey had almost *certainly* saved her life into the bargain. The chance to get back to her *own* world was too great to ignore however, regardless of how slim that chance might actually be, and whatever guilt she might feel would be easily dealt with once she was safe at home.

She headed west across the open fields as her body settled into a well-known pattern of slow, steady jogging, making directly for the cover of the forest ahead and intending to use it as cover as she turned north. There were a few herds of sheep dotted here and there that scattered as she approached with a chorus of unimpressed bleats of complaint, but the fields ahead seemed otherwise empty.

The distance between the barn and trees was probably no more than five hundred metres, although it had seemed far longer in the rain and darkness, and she was surprised to see how fresh and pleasant her surroundings felt in the growing light before dawn. It took just a few minutes to cross that open space, and only once did she feel a moment of real fear as her eyes caught sight of a dark silhouette looming toward her out of the early-morning gloom.

At first she thought she might be trapped or captured, her heart leaping to her mouth, but as she drew nearer she realised that it was no more than a large, vine-covered mound standing about shoulder height, with low shrubs and thick grass obscuring whatever lay beneath. Someone had placed four wooden stakes around it, all painted white at the tip and joined by a thin, white cord that made it look like some weird, abandoned museum exhibit. With the sudden rush of adrenalin coursing through her system from the fright she'd just received, Nev almost giggled at the strangeness of the sight.

At the same moment, a mob of kangaroos moved eerily across the treeline ahead of her, their presence little more than a procession of graceful, leaping ghosts through the mist that lay across the open fields between. That their appearance *also* sent her heart flying straight into her mouth for a second time went without saying. She'd originally started to wonder, inconceivable as it seemed, if perhaps the flash she's experienced in that clearing as the horseman has appeared had somehow transported them all to somewhere in Britain during the middle ages: the swords, the style of dress and the fact that everyone appeared to be speaking English making any other possibility even more unlikely; the sight of those exclusively *Australian* marsupials however *completely* put paid to that hypothesis.

"What *is* this place...?" Nev mused softly, actually taking time to bring out her phone and record a short video, despite having no social media to upload to. "The buildings *look* primitive... *medieval*... and everyone carries swords and ride horses... but – but there are kangaroos... and *gum trees*..." she added, looking around "...as if I just walked out my own back door! "And they use *Imperial* measurements here!" She remarked suddenly, to camera again as the thought occurred to her. "Miles and yards... and I'm *sure* Godfrey mentioned something about *hours* last night, so they must use the same measurement of *time* as *we* do..." *Aussie trees and animals... and* white *people on horseback... with* swords... *it's just not* possible...! She added silently, deciding the mound deserved no further attention and jogging off toward the treeline as the roos began to scatter into the bush.

She'd already unconsciously began to classify her experience as being between different 'worlds', automatically assigning an 'us and them' mentality when referring to either the world she was in right now or *her* world – the one she'd been dragged out of against her will. Nev knew she wasn't at her best – considering everything that had happened to her during the last twelve hours, she thought it amazing she hadn't lost her mind completely – yet be that as it may, she was nevertheless certain enough of her own self-awareness to be confident she was thinking with sufficient clarity to at least *try* to work out what was happening to her.

The only problem was that nothing likely to actually be *possible* came even *close* to fitting the circumstances of her situation. It was clear the portal hadn't taken her back through time (she'd decided she'd call it a 'portal' from now on until a more suitable explanation presented itself): she'd assumed medieval Britain purely because everyone seemed to be speaking English, but the environment and the presence of Australian flora and fauna had killed off that idea pretty quickly.

Nev was an avid reader with a particular love of science-fiction, and that interest had started with piles of second-hand books her father had picked up here and there (a combination of old classics and 'not-so-classics') from discount book bins, many of which had probably been out of print for years, while E-books had later provided access to an even greater variety of subjects and genres.

As she reached the treeline and paused again for a moment, she wondered if perhaps this was instead some kind of parallel universe, like those she'd read about in Pratchett and Baxter's *Long Earth* series, or H. Beam Piper's *Paratime* novels. That would go a long way to explaining a well-established, pre-industrial *Caucasian* presence on the South-East Australian mainland that – if Godfrey was to be believed – was far more extensive than the few British colonial settlements that had started with the landing of the First Fleet in 1788.

Her train of thought was broken in that moment as the faint sound of horses filtered through to her from the north. With a soft gasp, she instinctively ducked down behind a low line of bushes, sliding her bag from her shoulders to reduce her overall height, and peered out across the open fields, shifting layers of mist shimmering faintly in the morning half-light. Like the kangaroos she'd seen earlier, the horsemen seemed little more than ghostly wraiths through that mist, appearing for just a few seconds as they passed in an easterly direction. They disappeared again as quickly, although the sound of their travel continued to fade for some time after any visible trace had gone.

They'd been riding in completely the opposite direction by Nev's reckoning, and that was all well and good in itself, but it nevertheless reminded her that there were potentially far more unpleasant characters than Lester roaming about in the general area – there certainly had been the night before – and that she needed to take a lot more care to remain hidden than she probably had been. Fumbling inside her duffel bag, she drew out the *bokken* and slipped it through the belt of her jacket, snugging that tighter about her waist to keep the scabbard in place. Much as her stomach lurched queasily at the thought of actually using the thing as a weapon, she knew how much damage one could do if used properly... something she *also* knew how do to.

She'd held off at least ten minutes before leaving the cover of those bushes, waiting patiently to be certain no further movement could be seen or heard. With just birdsong and the rustle of the wind through the trees as accompaniment, she shrugged the bag over her shoulders again and moved off at a far more cautious pace. The *bokken* felt comforting resting against her left side and she kept the hilt clear of her cloak, ready to draw it with her right hand in an instant, should any threat present itself.

At least half an hour had passed at a slower, power-walk pace by the time Nev reached what she believed to be the area where Godfrey had set the horses free the night before. There was no way for her to be certain, but her instincts told her it was close enough for her to turn west and head into the forest proper, intending to repeat the path of last night's escape in reverse and – *hopefully* – find the original clearing again.

She was down to a slow walking pace now, heart pounding in her chest as she picked her way between the trees and cringed at every sound as her boots crunched softly through the underbrush. It was a small mercy at least that the morning seemed to be bright and clear, with patches of clear sky visible through the forest canopy overhead. True sunrise was probably still an hour away and there were clouds gathering about the distant horizon, but she was nevertheless now able to see reasonably well in the half-light, although Nev was a little disappointed to find that wasn't really helping in her attempt to retrace her steps.

She found very quickly that (*surprise, surprise!*) one tree looked pretty much the same as another, and that while she knew she was heading in *basically* the right direction, the complete darkness of the preceding night had not provided her with any significant landmarks to use as a guide. Her ever-present speed of doubt began to set in then and as she headed deeper into the forest, she grew increasingly worried that she'd never be able to find the clearing again.

Amazingly, the compass app on her phone still seemed to function (she had no *idea* why *that* was still working, considering she was still getting no network connection whatsoever), however while that could certainly confirm she was moving in a westerly direction, that was about *all* it could do and Nev knew she'd need to be far more accurate with her navigation than that if she was going to ever find the site of that portal again. She still wasn't at all happy about the lack of network, but it was more of an extreme inconvenience now than the earth-shattering shock it had been the night before.

"At least I know I'm not in Hell..." Nev muttered softly, thinking of the joke her dad always made about having to sell your soul to sign a contract with their phone provider. "I'd *definitely* have coverage there..."

She'd hoped a little sarcasm might boost her spirits, but it ultimately only served to increase her overall nervousness as fears over what Godfrey had said resurfaced; that the portal might not even be there. She forged on, refusing to surrender to her own negativity and making an effort to push those thoughts from her mind and stay positive.

She'd travelled perhaps three hundred metres by her own rough reckoning – a little more than that in *yards*, maybe (she was already trying to remember how her dad had taught her to covert between the two) – when she came out of the forest and into a more open section of tall grass and thorny scrub, with trees spread about with less regularity.

The ground also felt softer – even a little spongy – and she could once again hear the faint crash of the surf somewhere off to her left.

Even in the alien darkness of that strange place, something about that sound and the smell of salt water in the air felt vaguely familiar and some deep, rarely-used instinct within Nev's sub-conscious somehow knew in that moment that she was too far south. Checking her phone compass and turning toward the north-west, she continued on, feeling far more exposed now and moving almost at a crouch as she threaded her way between shrubs and bushes. With the growing light of the impending sunrise, she was at least able to see where she was going, and this time managed to avoid any major scratches or scrapes for the most part as she headed toward a western skyline that was still far darker.

Ten minutes more of painstaking, wayward movement and she burst out into a more recognisable spot: the same open strip of shorter grass that she'd come across the previous night while looking for Chisholm Road. Her instincts again served her well; she was definitely further south than she'd been ten or twelve hours earlier, but at least she'd now found a landmark she recognised. Following that grassy strip north now, she set off again with renewed enthusiasm, a flutter of nervousness in her heart as she began to dream beyond all hope that there might actually be a way back home to her own world.

Nev almost missed the track as she strode on, all thought of concealment forgotten in her growing excitement, and she was forced to stop, take stock and backtrack a few dozen metres to find it again. It seemed so much more overgrown than she remembered from the bike ride, although she wasn't sure why that thought was even relevant considering she was probably in another universe entirely.

"Here we go…" she confided to her phone, recording another snippet of something she promised herself would one day become *the* most awesome 'travel' vlog *anyone* had ever posted. "It's been fun here in 'Weird Medieval World'… in a terrifying, *not-fun*, 'trying-to-kill-you' kinda way, but it's *definitely* time to go home! Time to find this portal thingy and get the heck outta here…!"

She changed camera modes, took one slow panoramic image of her surroundings, then put her phone away and jogged off down the track, more than ready for a nice warm shower and time in front of the heater with some conciliatory ice cream.

Time seemed to pass surprisingly quickly after the morning's journey from the barn, although the pre-dawn sky became a little murky as she moved back into the wetlands beyond the long grass, passing through patches of heavy, low-lying mist and fog that collected in hollows and bends in the track. The hair at the back of her neck again began to prickle and rise, and having experienced the sensation already once before, Nev now got the distinct feeling that there was definitely something wrong with the area – that there was somehow something bad… something *evil* about it, if that were even possible.

"Not much chance of any Native American burial ground, at least…" she muttered facetiously, with a mental nod to Stephen King's *Pet Sematary*. "…*Although*… God knows what *else* might be buried around here…"

That thought didn't help her mental state at all, although it *did* push her to increase speed as she found the larger clearing where their bikes had disappeared and immediately veered off down that last track toward the site of the portal. She was almost at a run as she entered that final, smaller clearing, hoping for some hint of an unusual light… a strange voice… of *any* indication that the connection back to her world still existed.

The body of the horseman still lay to one side, the dark, bloody wound in his chest as gruesome as a pair of lifeless eyes that continued to stare blindly into the sky in a fixed and quite terminal expression of sudden shock, and from what she recalled of the preceding night's events, it didn't seem difficult to work out where the actual area of the portal had been: the point from which the horse had first appeared.

Dropping her bag in the middle of the clearing, Nev moved quickly from place to place, pushing through grass and between bushes and trees as she searched desperately for something she might not even recognise. The heavy breathing of exertion became soft whimpers of despair, her movements more frantic as her fear of failure grew greater with each passing second.

It took just a few short minutes to realise that there was definitely no portal, exactly as Godfrey had predicted, although actual *acceptance* didn't come immediately. Much as her rational mind had thought itself prepared for the possibility, the *reality* of it still dealt her a crushing emotional blow and with a soft, low moan of despair, she sank to her knees beside her duffel bag and began to sob softly, head in her hands.

Slim as her chances had actually been, she'd hung the entirety of her hopes on them simply because there'd been no other option. With all hope now in tatters, she awkwardly, jerkily took out her phone once more and began to search through her saved images, tears pouring down her cheeks as she found a random selfie of her and her dad taken a few months before. She even remembered the evening – a Saturday night dinner for Drake's fiftieth – and there they were, Nev dressed almost identically in the clothes she'd worn yesterday, and her father looking happy but a little awkward in a jacket and tie.

Searching further through her gallery, she found a video this time: one her father had made for her on their old computer almost exactly two years earlier as part of his gift for *her* fifteenth birthday. It was short video just four minutes long, and she'd pretended it had been an embarrassment when he'd posted it on his rarely-used Facebook page for everyone to see. Taking her headphones from her jacket pocket, she plugged them in and played it now though, the tears already building in intensity as she set it playing.

A new-born baby crying on a delivery table, swaddled in blankets, and the opening bars of Rob Thomas' *Little Wonders* chimed melodically in Nev's ears as she heard her father's own voice in the background, filled with emotion. He'd worked for weeks on it, all by himself, and produced a short movie of clips from the first year of Nev's life, all of it set to that Disney soundtrack song, and as much as she'd made a great show of how humiliating the whole thing was in front of her friends, deep down she'd loved it more than *anything* he'd ever bought her, before or since. Her dad knew it too – she'd made sure of that – and watching that video now, the emotion of the song sweeping over her, she felt completely overwhelmed.

Danger and the simple process of remaining active had allowed her to keep anxiety and depression at bay for most of the last twelve hours, but that all came crashing down now as she knelt there in that silent clearing, hearing her father's voice through the headphones and not knowing where he was or if he still even existed. She felt broken and completely alone, and she threw her head back in that moment, allowing a mournful wail of despair to rise unchecked into the coming dawn, the terrible sound carrying with it all the loss and betrayal she'd carried with her since first fleeing that clearing the night before.

"And here was I, thinking maybe there was a dyin' *wolf* out 'ere or somethin'…" a completely unexpected voice called out laughingly from behind her. "Whaddya reckon, Dimble…?" He continued unfazed as Nev outright cried out in fright and leaped to her feet, whirling on the spot and backing quickly away with her bag in one hand and the phone in the other. "This one might be a *pure breed* from what I can see…"

There were two of them… two dirty, scruffy and intimidatingly *tall* men dressed in what appeared to be some kind of pre-industrial soldier's uniforms: plain, tan-coloured pants and tunics of thick cotton, covered by heavy, oversized vests of boiled leather. Even in the dim light, she thought she could see the faint shimmer of chain mail beneath the vests, and both wore large, flat-brimmed helmets of polished iron that looked almost like misshapen prototypes of the 'tin-hats' she often saw being worn by soldiers commemorating the First World War.

It was the swords in their hands however that attracted most of her attention. Short and broad-bladed, they looked similar to a Roman gladius and although they'd never have been of much use against something like the far-longer sabre the dead horseman had been wielding the preceding night, Nev had no illusions as to how lethal they might be as a melee weapon if used in combination with the round, iron shields the pair also carried against their opposite forearms.

"Reckon y' might be right there, Kane…" the other observed with a nasty grin. "Hard to tell in *this* light, but might be a pretty present indeed, once the *packing's* all taken care of…"

"Now… now, I don't want any trouble…" she began falteringly, not at all liking the dangerous way they were looking at her as she stuffed her phone back into her jacket.

"Oh, no trouble at all, missy…" the first one – Kane – assured, taking a step forward as Nev matched it in slow withdrawal. "Thought we was bein' *picked* on by the squad sergeant, makin' us get up so early just to bring Cragelen's body back…"

"Not like he was *goin'* anywhere," Dimble pointed out with a morbid chuckle.

"…But *now* it looks like maybe we're the *lucky* ones…" Kane continued, taking another step. "No need for any silliness, lass…" he added, noting with some amusement that her right hand had reached down across her body to close around the hilt of a sword at her belt, partially hidden beneath her cloak.

"He *said* it weren't no trouble..." Dimble pointed out, a cold edge to his voice.

Watch both of them... watch their movements... watch their eyes..." she thought quickly, struggling to recall her training in a sudden moment of stress. *Their eyes will give them away... warn you when they're going to move...*

"How 'bout you put that bag and the sword down and we have a nice little chat... just the four of us, like...?" Kane suggested genially, his eyes leaving hers only once as they flicked momentarily to a point just beyond her shoulder, and it was then that her mind registered what he'd just said and did the required math.

She was spinning again, dropping her duffel bag and turning away from the third soldier even as she heard his footsteps behind her. The *bokken* was instantly pulled free from its scabbard and rising in a tight arc, drawing speed and power from her turning body as she went with it and completely wrong-footing her would-be attacker as he suddenly and unexpectedly found empty air where she'd been standing just a split second before.

Instinct and muscle memory guided her movements, accelerating her reflexes with the help of many years' practice, and the wooden 'blade' of the *bokken* cracked against the side of the man's neck just above his chain-mail collar. That same training however had also instinctively taught her to pull her strike at the last moment, something she'd always done for fear of seriously injuring Honda during their regular sparring (although the number of times she'd *actually* connected with him could be counted on one hand).

As a result, although the contact was *extremely* painful, it wasn't the debilitating blow it should've been. Staggering awkwardly away from the strike, the newcomer released an exceptionally foul curse in response, clutching at his bruised neck and falling to his knees as his helmet toppled from his head and rolled away into the grass.

"Ooh, you're a *quick* one, aren't ya...!" Kane growled, a little surprised but still ready to enjoy himself with a little harmful fun at her expense. "Get up, Perry, you whining git!" He barked, cutting the third man no slack at all. "It's *wood* for Crystals' sake! Hate to see ya in *real* battle, if that's how easy a *girl* can take you down! Come on now, missy... let's have a little *fun*..." he added, turning back toward Nev and advancing faster this time as Dimble split off to one side, opening the gap between them and forcing her to keep track of separate threats.

"I don't want to hurt you…" she tried to warn, but her chest was still heaving from her earlier sobbing, and her voice sounded too frail and croaky to sound at all convincing.

"Oooh, don't *tease* me, now…" he growled as Dimble sniggered over the comment and moved wider still, intending to flank her from one side as Perry, now back on his feet, made a move toward her other flank.

Be ready… she warned herself. *Keep the* saya *hidden from view…*

They were lessons Honda had taught her time and again: keep the scabbard against your body and hide it as much as possible – never let an enemy see how long your blade was or how far you could reach with it. Never draw your sword until you were ready to strike… until there was no turning back and you were ready to *end* the fight.

Kane lurched forward, slashing the sword from left to right without any real conviction but forcing her backward with a gasp all the same.

Not yet… not yet… Now…!

He lunged a second time, slashing vertically this time, but Nev had seen his muscles tense and predicted the move. She was ready as the sword arced down, stepping lightly to one side and deflecting the blade with a deft flick of her wrist. As he stumbled forward on the follow-through, wrong footed and over-extended, she whipped the *bokken* sharply downward to rap him hard on his exposed knuckles.

He cried out in pain, the sword falling from his grip as if he'd been stung, and stood motionless and staring for a moment, too surprised to react. Her tactical mind immediately recognised a perfect moment to step in and 'finish' him with a quick thrust straight to the throat: even the blunt-tipped *bokken* could've caused enough damage to put him out of action for some time. Yet she again hesitated and backed away, instead sliding the *bokken* back into its scabbard at her belt in a text-book *noto* manoeuvre, using the webbing of her left hand as a guide around the scabbard and drawing the flat of the wooden blade across her hand until the point automatically found the sheath and she was able to slide it smoothly back inside.

"You little *bitch…!*" Kane howled, not so much hurt as humiliated in front of his mates, which was probably far more dangerous. Snatching up his sword, he charged again, the rage in his eyes a clear indication of his desire to cleave Nev's head from her shoulders. He slashed downward again, surprisingly fast for his size, but he was no expert swordsman, and he was also far too committed to his own strike as Nev again deftly sidestepped him to his left side, this time forcing herself *not* to hold back as she again drew the *bokken* at the last moment.

"*Hyah...!*" Nev barked loudly, releasing a *kiai* shout to focus and increase her power as she drew the wooden blade and snapped it sharply downward against his outstretched forearm. Her placement was as precise as the amount of force she applied as she struck quickly then instantly leaped back and away into a classic samurai 'ready' stance, her weapon raised high above her head and pointing toward her enemy with its blade inverted. The blow caught the middle of his forearm, cleanly snapping Kane's ulna with a sickening crunch that turned his cry of rage into a howl of agony, and he collapsed onto the damp ground, unable to do anything other than clutch at his broken arm and wail in frustration and pain.

She instantly turned to engage Dimble as he too leaped forward, hoping for a chance to strike while she was dealing with his colleague, and Nev *very* quickly showed him the error of his ways. He was a *little* smarter than Kane at least, and he made no attempt to overreach or unbalance himself, but he was also markedly slower and Nev was easily able to dodge his first, short jab at her mid-section. As his sword sliced through empty air where her left side should've been, she stepped *into* his blow and clamped his outstretched arm beneath her left armpit, trapping it and him against her.

Dimble stank – *badly* – and her revulsion over his sudden proximity was almost as complete as the look of shock and surprise that flashed across his face as he realised what had just happened. Nev didn't give him any time to react as she released a sharp, loud "*Yah...!*" and brought her right fist around in a tight arc, smashing the pommel of the *bokken* hard into the side of the man's head and sending him staggering away with stars flaring across his vision.

Perry had learned from his earlier mistake, and he had no intention of underestimating Nev again as he came at her from her right while she sent Dimble reeling. This time, he kept his shield arm high and held his sword low and tight against his body, keeping it out of harm's way until he found an opening to strike. She dived away from him, looking for space to manoeuvre and ignoring the mucky ground as she rolled once and rose instantly to her feet again on the other side of the clearing, the *bokken* once more sheathed and ready with her hand resting on the hilt.

"*Kill* the bitch…!" Kane howled in agonised fury, still lying where he'd fallen and clutching at his right arm. "Run her through…!"

"Aye, I'll do that soon enough…" Perry grinned darkly, his eyes never leaving hers as he moved from side to side, forcing her backward with every step. "Not *right* away, though… this one's going to *suffer* first!"

"You got her, Perry… you got her!" Dimble joined in, shaking his head to clear his vision as he staggered back into the fray without hesitation. "I'll take her on the left: you take the right…!"

"*Get away from me…!*" She snarled, nothing but anger in her hissing tone now as adrenalin once more coursed through her veins. "*Get back…!*"

Her foot caught as she took another step backward without turning her head, realising she'd unwittingly allowed herself to be pushed back against the corpse of the man they'd called Cragelen. She attempted to side step, misjudged her movement and for just a split-second was forced to glance down and back to confirm her surroundings. Even as she turned, Perry was already lunging, waiting for that very moment, and this time she was forced to bring the *bokken* up in desperation to block his blade in mid-swing, the tough Loquat wood taking the full force of that powerful blow.

A *bokken* wasn't designed for *actual* combat and strong as it was, it couldn't hope to stand against two pounds of solid, sharpened steel as the sword bit deep, the force of the blow snapping it in half. It'd been enough to at least deflect it away to Nev's left, but the flat of Perry's turned blade still slapped her brutally against her shoulder, drawing a cry of pain and surprise.

He followed up immediately with a savage thrust of his shield, its reinforced centre crashing into Nev's chest and toppling her backward over Cragelen's body. She fell hard onto her back, winded and gripped by a sudden terror as she realised how vulnerable she was without a weapon of her own. She still held what was left of the *bokken* in her right hand, but little remained other than the hilt and perhaps a foot of wooden blade, tapering to a jagged, uneven point where Perry's sword had snapped it off.

"That's it, Perry!" Kane crowed with triumph. "Show her who's boss *now*…!"

"Please…" she wheezed, somehow knowing full well that any chance of negotiation was long gone, had it ever existed at all. "*Don't…!*"

"Make her wish she'd ne'er been born!" Dimble hissed darkly, sounding far too eager.

"When I'm done with her, she'll curse her own *mother…*" Perry whispered in a soft, angry voice, displaying an evil smile to match.

There was a sudden sound: a soft, whooshing noise followed by a far louder, wet *thud* to Nev's right, and as both of them turned their eyes in that direction they were presented with the sight of a *very* surprised Dimble standing a few metres away with a rather large, black crossbow bolt jutting from his chest at the centre of a spreading dark stain. He fell without another sound, already a lifeless lump by the time he hit the ground. There was only one person Nev had *ever* seen with a crossbow, and as unpleasant as the little creature had been, she couldn't have been happier that he'd appeared in the nick of time.

"I already *do…!*" She snarled, anger returning and overcoming her fear as she realised the 'cavalry' had arrived. As a momentarily distracted Perry turned back toward the sound of her voice, she drew back her right foot and kicked hard between his legs. There was no chain mail or protective armour at that angle, and her heel dug deep into his flesh, sending excruciating pain and nausea rippling through his body. He collapsed with a gurgling scream, clutching at his stricken groin as she pushed herself onto her feet and backed quickly away.

"No… no…! I yield… *I yield…!*" Kane screamed in terror, raising his one good arm high as a sign of surrender as Godfrey charged out of the scrub toward him, brandishing a long-bladed sabre so lightly curved that it almost seemed straight. His pleas fell on deaf ears however as the young man ran him through without a second thought. His death was longer than Dimble's, and was neither quick nor quiet.

She felt her stomach lurch at the sight of blood and death, yet she was unable to turn away as Lester also appeared out of the surrounding bush, his crossbow reloaded and at the ready. She could tell he was headed Perry's way, and terror spread across the Blackwatcher's features as he too worked out what was about to happen. He struggled to his feet, fear and desperation driving him, but was able to take just one step before his legs gave out and he fell again, wracked with pain and an urge to throw up.

"Please…!" He moaned weakly, reaching out to a horrified Nev as he dragged himself across the muddy ground toward her on his elbows. "*I don't wanna die…!*"

But there were no words in that moment that could possible make any difference, and as abhorrent as the idea of taking life was, there was also no denying what Perry and his colleagues had intended to do to *her* had they been given the chance. Much to her own silent shame, Nev found that she didn't *want* to speak out in his defence, and she could only turn slowly and face the other way as Lester raised the crossbow to his shoulder with an evil grin.

There was another thick, wet *thud* and a soft groan of surrender, and in the awful silence that followed, Nev bent double with hands on her knees for support and threw up on the grass in dramatic fashion. That she'd hardly anything in her stomach to shift was of little consequence, and the painful dry retching that followed continued for some time before finally fading minutes later into a faint, recurring shudder. She miraculously managed to keep her hair out of the firing line, but her face was pallid and coated in a thin sheen of perspiration as she stood upright once more and turned toward the other two, both already motionless and waiting expectantly for her to finish with arms folded.

"Are you *mad…*?" Godfrey barked angrily, advancing on her with his bloody sword in hand and similar stains sprayed across his face and chest. "Do you have even a *clue* how *stupid* this was?"

"Not real smart for a *witch…*" Lester muttered – not softly enough – as he casually placed a foot against Dimble's chest and forcibly wrenched the crossbow bolt from the dead man's chest.

"For the love of The Shard, Boniface, *shut up* would you?" He snarled in frustration, turning back toward Nev as the younger boy simply shrugged matter-of-factly and uses his shirt tail to clean blood off the bolt he'd just retrieved.

"I want to go home…" she croaked hoarsely, the after-taste vile in her mouth as she wiped at it with a corner of her cloak.

"You want to be *dead* if you're crazy enough to come back *here* all by yourself… *in the dark…*!" He raged, almost unable to conceive how anyone could've been so foolish. "There's no *reasoning* with scum like that. They would've taken you, then *killed* you!"

"Taken me…?" She stammered, still weak and trying to focus on what he was saying. "Taken me *where…*"

"*Right here*, y' fool! *Then killed you!*" He repeated, glaring at her as what he actually meant finally sunk in and she cringed in horror and disgust.

"Oh… *oh*…!"

"They were Harald's watchmen… *king's guards*: in the Blacklands, they've licence to do anything they want… to *kill* anyone they want… to *take* anything *or anyone* they want…! They don't like you; you die… *resist* one of them and you die… *slowly and painfully*…!"

"I just wanted to go *home*…" she moaned, tears flowing again as shock once more began to take over from adrenalin.

"*There is no home*…" He hissed viciously, his patience wearing thin, and the savagery of his words made her flinch. "Whatever… *wherever* it was you and that blue *harlot* came from, it's *gone*… and *you* need to get that into your pretty little head *fast* before you get yourself *and* me and Lester killed. I have a *mission* to complete, and I will *fail* that mission if I don't deliver you to our client… *alive and in one piece*…!"

As she self-consciously tried to wipe tears from her eyes, Nev suddenly realised that he too was shaking faintly, as if he were barely in control of his own rage or…

…*Or something else*…? A strange idea flared in the back of her mind. She could understand him wanting to keep her alive to fulfil whatever task he'd been assigned, but why get some worked up over that if it were just a job? What *else* was going on inside his head? Anger and frustration was starting to build again inside her now though, and she pushed the thought out of her mind, not in the mood to think about anything other than her own situation.

"I – I'm *sorry*, alright…?" She snapped, desperately trying to control her sobbing as she stepped around him and stalked across to where she'd dropped her bag. "I thought maybe it would still be open… I *thought* I could still find a way to get back…" She snatched up the bag and shrugged it over her shoulders once more, feeling just a little better now that the reassuring weight of her belongings once more hung against her back. "*You're* not the one who just got dragged out of her own world, *betrayed* by her best friend – *who then tried to kill her* – and then got attacked by a bunch of goons while trying to get home again… *who then tried to kill her* again!" She was shouting now, hands clenched into fists at her sides as she glared at the pair of them and angrily stomped her foot for emphasis. "This has been *the* worst birthday I have *ever* had, and having *you* criticising everything I do *isn't* helping!"

"The 'worst birthday you ever had'...?" Godfrey asked coldly, lowering his voice and trying hard not to lose his temper again. "Nev Anderson, this was very nearly the *last* birthday you ever had, and if you don't start paying attention and *listening* to my instructions, it *will* be!" He took a few steps toward her again, taking a cloth from a trouser pocket and wiping the blood from his sabre before sliding it back into the sheath at his belt. "I am here to keep you *safe*, *not* to pander to your every command. Maybe you're a witch, and *maybe* you're *not...*" he continued, cutting off any protest she was about to make "...but *acting* like a *princess* doesn't *actually* make you one, and *I* do not take orders from *you*.

"When we got here, *they* were about to *kill* you." He added bluntly, deciding the obvious needed to be stated. "Had *we* not come to your rescue, you'd be *dead* by now, or dying, so... before you start *complaining* about me '*criticising* you', *maybe* you should think about *thanking* me first – me and Lester, here – for *saving your stinking life... twice...*!" That last sentence was laced with venom, and whatever else might've been going through his mind a moment or two earlier, there was only anger in his eyes now. The impact of it was enough to break through her own stubbornness for a moment and force Nev to think about what he'd actually said.

"Now... we have *maybe* an hour before the nearest post sends out another patrol to find out what happened to *this one...*" he continued, maintaining his intensity "...and if we're *lucky*, they'll be on foot the same as *this* lot. If *not*, then we might have the *Blackwatch* to deal with, and *that* would be *very* bad. *I* intend to be well away from this area when they *do* arrive, and complain all you like, one way or another you *will* be coming with us, even if I have to tie you up and throw you over the back of my horse! Lester and I are going to spend the next five minutes hiding these bodies as best we can... after *that*, we're leaving!"

With those last angry words, he stalked off toward Kane's fallen form, taking the corpse by the feet and grunting with exertion as he dragged it slowly toward the long grass on the opposite side of the clearing.

Still experiencing a range of conflicting emotions including fury, fear, pride and confusion, Nev was momentarily left without any idea what to do. Still angry over the way he's spoken to her and with her system still flooded by the adrenalin that had returned because of it, the very *last* thing she wanted to do was what Godfrey was telling her, or to spend any more time around him whatsoever. Not even her own *father* has ever spoken to her with such rudeness or disrespect, and her natural instinct was to rail against it: to do precisely the opposite out of spite and stubbornness.

Yet as she stood there completely alone, shuddering from the after-effects of tears and shock, her rational mind was also well aware of the fact that the closest person she could call a friend right now – the *only* person – was Godfrey Westacre. Save for Lester, who was horrid anyway, everyone else she'd met so far had tried to kidnap or kill her... or *worse*. Being left to fend for herself wasn't really an option at that point – that was pretty clear – and she wasn't left with too many viable alternatives.

As the other two went about the unpleasant task of moving the bodies out of plain sight, Nev made a great show of thinking hard about a making a decision that really shouldn't have needed any thought whatsoever. She made it more difficult than it should've been, however considering it was the only thing she seemed to have control over at that moment, she wanted to at least fool herself into believing exactly that, if just for a little while.

VI

THE DRAGON'S DAUGHTER

The sun was well above the eastern horizon by the time they made it back to the barn, and the cloudless blue sky of morning had been replaced by dull, leaden sky filled with a blanket of grey cloud. It wasn't raining – yet – but those clouds were definitely threatening with a palpable sense of moisture in the air. There were signs of activity about the area too now, and Nev was surprised to see that the farmhouse was one of a number clustered about within a few square kilometres. She could see two or three off in the distance, smoke rising from chimneys and cooking stoves as farmers and their families went about the beginning of their daily chores.

She saw the owner of their farm just once as he set off across the fields with a small sheep dog that was definitely part kelpie, crossing paths with them as they arrived and passing Godfrey a single nod of greeting before continuing on his way.

"Does he know what you're doing here?" Nev asked quietly, riding behind Godfrey on a large, black stallion while Lester followed on astride a smaller mare of brown.

"He never asks…" Godfrey answered with a shrug as he slid off the horse and then reached up to take her by the waist as she swung her leg over, lifting her down to the ground without too much effort. "He knows we're against the Blackwatch, and that's enough for him…"

"Doesn't he worry they might find out?"

"Soldiers came calling here one evening…" Godfrey explained coldly as he moved over to Lester's horse and dragged Nev's duffel bag down from its position behind the boy. "Garry was away in Norfoster that night on business… was just his wife and daughter home…" He grimaced as he walked back over and handed her the bag. "You can work out the rest, no doubt. That was years ago… before I was born, I think," he shrugged again, stopping for a moment to stare after the distant shape of the shepherd as he continued on in a slow, ambling gait.

"I don't think he *cares* what we do, long as we're doin' something the Blackwatch don't like. Don't think he'd care if he were caught either…" he added with another shrug. "Stickin' it up Harald's men's all he's got left now, anyway… that, a dog and a few sheep…"

"I'll need a hand to hitch up the wagon," Lester pointed out as he led the mare past them, taking her around to the far side of the barn.

"Comin', Toadface…"

"Can… can *I* help…? With anything…?" Nev asked after a moment's pause, Godfrey already halfway to the corner of the barn. He stopped for a moment and turned in her direction, a thoughtful expression on his face that almost included a smile.

"Aye… I guess you *could*…" he decided after a moment's thought of his own. "Hitching a wagon's not for the untrained, but there's our packs and stuff inside, waitin' to be loaded." He offered a genuine smile then, smart enough to recognise an olive branch when he heard one. "It'd be a *big* help if you could give us a hand loading the rest of our gear while we work."

"I – I can do that," she replied, not really managing a smile in return but at least making an effort. He gave a simple nod and disappeared around the corner, and she soon heard sounds of activity from that direction that presumably signalled the hitching of a horse to wagon.

Turning toward the barn, she walked stiffly over to the door and opened it wide, cringing at the shooting pains in her aching muscles with every step. Nev had never ridden a horse before, and she'd been forced to hang on for dear life, hands wrapped tightly about Godfrey's waist as they'd travelled most of the way back at a steady canter. The experience had left her jarred and sore and she was fairly certain her butt was going to ache for a week. Although she was fit and active, horse riding used her muscles in a manner completely different to anything she was accustomed to and she was now feeling it quite painfully through her backside and inner thighs.

Didn't really seem like anything worth complaining about though… certainly not after what Godfrey had told her about the old shepherd, Garry. What were a few aches and pains to a man who'd had his whole family taken from him in the most brutal and horrific fashion? A bit of soreness was definitely a first-world-problem by comparison, and despite Godfrey having made it clear earlier that she *wasn't* one, maybe the term 'suck it up, princess' might apply under the circumstances.

With her own bag on her back, she bent carefully and collected one of their backpacks; a crude design of stitched canvas with toggles to hold the top flap. The actual pack itself wasn't large but its outside was sewn with a number of pouches and loops that held two leather-wrapped glass canteens, two smallish daggers and several other small implements she couldn't identify. Strapped beneath, it also carried the bedroll she'd slept on the previous night, leading her to presume that it was Godfrey's gear she'd picked up.

With a few grunts and wheezes to go with her aching muscles, she lugged it outside and around to the same side of the barn the others had disappeared to. There Nev found them to indeed be in the process of hitching up a wagon to the brown mare. The wagon itself was a small, wooden-sided design no more than two or three metres long, with iron ribs rising in loops above the cargo bed supporting a tough, canvas cover as shelter against the weather.

Leaving the pair to their work, she headed straight for the rear of the vehicle and stood on tip-toes to peer inside over the high backboard. One or two large crates inside lay up toward the front, and there was an open, empty space at the rear that seemed perfect for the luggage. Reaching up with both hands, she awkwardly lowered the pack inside, placing it carefully and resting it against the rear of the wagon. She then shrugged off her own bag and also lowered that in beside the rucksack. With a single stretch, Nev then turned and went straight back to collect the other backpack and a few other loose bits and pieces stacked with it.

They'd finished by the time she'd come back with the second load, and Lester was already seated up in the driver's position, feet propped against the buckboard as Godfrey mounted his own horse around and cantered around to join them.

"All set...?" He asked as Lester loaded his crossbow and placed it down on the floor beneath his feet, out of sight but well within reach if needed.

"Right enough, Westy," he replied with a grin. Garry's left us supplies and a barrel o' water, so we'll not starve at least. "Which way you lookin' to take...?"

"My first thought was to take the northern road, through Tarwin and on through Stony Waters to Norfoster, but we've lost a lot of daylight already…" He shrugged. "I don't want to push the mare too hard with the wagon and we've no time to spare, so it'll have to be due east to Verlock and Ponder Creek, then on to Norfoster through Fishwaters instead. Straight run through to Welshport after that either way."

"First leg…?"

"Midwin at least, but I'd *prefer* Fishwaters before we rest: shorter run home after that and the further we can get before break, maybe the longer break we can take. In you get, lass… there's no room back here on a long ride, and you'll be more comfortable in the wagon anyway."

"There's the bedrolls to sit on if you've a need," Lester offered helpfully, grinning with less unpleasantness than usual, "or you can sit up here with *me* if you prefer… promise I won't bite…" he added, spoiling the friendly mood just a little.

"There *was* that old woman in Mowl…" Godfrey pointed out, but she was starting to pick the glint in his eye now when he was teasing "…although, she *did* mostly deserve it…" he finished, giving a wink to make certain she caught the joke.

"Last time I do *that*, n' all… I think she gave me gum rot!"

"In the back, I think…" Nev decided, suppressing a smile and moving to the rear of the wagon as the others chuckled loudly.

"Prob'ly best…" Lester agreed as she tested the strength of the backboard, then hoisted herself up and over in a reasonably fluid movement that surprised both of the others. "You'd have to have yer mask on anyways if you was sittin' up 'ere with me, and I'd reckon that wouldn't be much fun. Sing out if you need to stop for a leak or anythin'… no need to be shy…"

"Charming…" Nev muttered drily, deciding that a bedroll was an excellent idea and unrolling the same one she'd slept on, spreading it across the width of the rear cargo area and plonking herself down on top of it with her back against one side.

"Alright, Toadface… let's be off…" And with that, Godfrey kicked his heels into the side of his mount and took off at a trot as Lester flipped the reins into the mare's backside, giving it a signal to also move off at a slower pace.

Their journey proved completely uneventful for the first few hours, with little sound other than birdsong, the wind and the steady rumble of the wheels along rutted dirt tracks as they headed east. The sky had cleared by that time, and Lester wore a wide-brimmed felt hat to keep the sun out of his eyes as he sat at the buckboard, placidly guiding the mare on and passing the occasional comment as to how lucky they were to have a sunny day... the first one in some time, judging by frequency of his observations. Godfrey would appear briefly every now and then, reining in his mount beside the wagon and exchanging the occasional detail with Lester regarding the road ahead and the lay of the land in general. Most of the time, however, he was away scouting their path and nowhere to be seen.

The dirt tracks they'd been travelling along had been quite rough and bumpy to begin with but had smoothed out after a few hours. Trees lined the southern side of the road, and apart from the very rare appearance of the occasional farmhouse there'd been little sign of life other than sheep and dairy cattle roaming about the open fields on either side. Although her view of the outside world was severely limited from inside the covered wagon, Nev would nevertheless have thought they'd at least have seen a *few* other travellers or farmers during the course of two or three hours' travel.

Nev had quickly found the rear of the wagon to be quite boring. She was running low on phone battery, which meant no listening to music, and browsing wasn't going to happen anyway because of that whole 'no network' thing, so with nothing else to do she decided to move further forward, finding a seat on a small crate positioned just behind the driver. With the sun streaming brightly down on that warm, spring day, she was now at least able to set up the power-bank her father had given her for her birthday, placing it on the front seat beside Lester and connecting it to her phone to recharge while it at the same time soaked up solar energy to recharge its own internal battery.

"Is that thing safe?" Lester asked warily, trying not to look nervous as he stared down at the electronic devices beside him but clearly having a difficult time of it.

"Perfectly safe... so long as you don't touch them..." she replied, grinning slyly when he wasn't looking.

"And if you *do* touch 'em?"

"Hmmph..." she shrugged simply. "How badly do you need *two* hands?"

"*What...*?" Lester blurted quickly, reacting before he could catch himself *and* before he caught the wry smile on her face. "Oooh, you cheeky *cow*…!" He grinned in return, not at all offended. "You 'ad me there…!"

"I'm a *cow* now, am I?" Nev asked with a chuckle and a shrug. "Well I guess that's a step up from being called a *witch*. They won't hurt anyone…" she reassured with a nod toward the power-bank and phone. "They run on something called electricity and my phone – the one with the pictures on the front – is running out. The *other* one can use the power of the sun to get its energy back…"

"Oh, aye…?" Lester asked with a smirk and a raised eyebrow. "And which bit 'o *that* don't sound like witchcraft?"

"Would you rather I turned you into a toad?"

"Happy to go without, thanks all the same… Godfrey would probably reckon someone's already done it anyway…" he pointed out with a chuckle of his own.

"When we were leaving the farm…" She began, recalling something she'd heard earlier "…you said something about me needing to wear a mask if I were riding up front with you?"

"Only 'cause of the Keepsake Law, 'course… nuthin' personal…"

"The 'Keepsake Law'…?"

"You've *not* heard o' the Keepsake Law?" Lester asked blankly, the concept beyond him.

"*Should* I have?"

"Well… *everyone* has…!" He shot back immediately, seeming almost shocked. "It's one o' the biggest laws in the Book o' The Shard: no woman or girl of any age shall travel the open road or walk beyond the walls of her village without the wearin' of a closed hood or visard, lest they be travelling by walled wagon wi' out windows."

The concept was so archaic and ludicrous to Nev that it took a few seconds before the fact that he wasn't kidding sunk home.

"You *can't* be serious…!"

"Do I *look* like I'm foolin'…?"

"What on earth *for*…?"

"Well… the *Keepsakes*, o' course…" he stated simply, as if she were mad to have even asked. "You sees one of 'em, you're a witch *for sure*… dead certain."

"Keepsakes…? What are *they*…?"

"*Well*…" he blustered for a moment, taking on the high-pitched air of a young man knowing all there was to know about a particular subject without *actually* having ever needed to explain it. "They're... they're... *Keepsakes*...!" It was a question no one in The Osterlands would ask, and as such there'd never been a need for an answer. "No one *really* knows *what* they look like – no *man* does, anyway – and they turn up anywhere... on the side of the road... in the middle of a field... sometimes they wash up on a beach somewhere..." He shuddered visibly. "They're *bad* omens, them, and its only *witches* can see 'em... that's mostly how y' *tell* someone's a witch in the first place."

"So..." Nev began slowly, trying to get her head around the whole thing as she went over what he'd just said in her mind. "...Only *witches* can see these... *Keepsakes*...?"

"Yup..."

"Then why is it only *women* need to be blindfolded...?"

"'Cause *they's* the only ones that can *see* 'em...!" Lester shot back, staring directly ahead, and she could near the hint of frustration in his tone now.

"*Why*...?"

"*Because... they're... witches*...!" He spelled out slowly, making it as simple as he could manage. "Only *women* can see Keepsakes... *anyone* who sees keepsakes is a witch... so: only *women* can be witches... stands to reason!"

"And these laws are written in this book... the *Shard* book...?"

"Aye – that's it..."

"And this Church of the Shard or whatever it is..."

"Brotherhood..." he added helpfully.

"So this *brotherhood* runs the whole deal...?" Nev asked shrewdly, thinking she could see a pattern emerging. "...And this *Brotherhood* of The Shard – *spoiler alert* – is made up completely of *men*, I'm guessing?"

"It were the 'brotherhood' bit that gave it away, right...?"

"So: why can't *men* see them?"

"...'Cause *they're* not witches..."

"Silly me..." Nev nodded sagely, happy Lester was sometimes a little slow in picking up subtle sarcasm "...sorry I asked..."

Godfrey arrived a few minutes later, having ridden hard from somewhere up ahead, reining in sharply beside Lester as the boy brought the wagon momentarily to a halt..

"We've got Blackwatch on the road… half a mile, just north of Ponder Creek!"

"How many…?" Lester asked quickly, all business.

"Small troop – no more than three or four, but enough to cause trouble and they're headed our way."

"Run or hide?"

"No running with the cart," Godfrey shook his head. There's a copse of trees up ahead where the creek crosses the road – we can turn off there and take shelter… wait for 'em to pass by. There's that farm track a bit further on that runs south of the main road: we can use it to cut below Ponder and get back onto the main road on the other side."

"That's not an easy road…" Lester pointed out. "We'll lose an hour going that way – maybe more…"

"Not my first choice, but if there's Blackwatch on the prowl there's bound to be others, and that damned Harmon is well-known to be sweet with 'em – there might even be a few patrols watering at his keep, north of Ponder. Losing time's better than not arriving at all – we'll just have to make it up later if need be. Follow me…" he added, calling over his shoulder as he turned his horse away. "We'll be turning right up ahead…"

Lester urged the mare on, picking up the pace and bringing the wagon up to a jarring speed as Godfrey forged on ahead. Nev was forced to quickly collect her phone and the power-bank as they started rattling their way across the wooden seat toward the open side opposite the driver. The phone was only at fifty per cent but it was better than nothing, she decided as she stuffed both devices back into her jacket pockets.

"Are these bad guys up ahead?" She asked nervously, her voice trembling in time with the jarring of the road.

"Bad as they come…" Lester answered grimly, concentrating on the road ahead as the mare continued to gather speed. "Blackwatch: same bastards as what were chasing you last night."

"The same ones…?" She gasped, suddenly much more afraid. "Will Percy – uh – the *witch* be with them…?"

"The *other* one…?" He shot back with a faint grin, not able to help himself. "Not the same *mob* as yesterday – *probably* – but riders from the same army. Harald's Blackwatch is everywhere. They're cavalry, policemen and bully-boys all rolled into one, and they roam all over the Blacklands, keepin' the 'peace'… even where there weren't any trouble to begin with. Only a small troop of 'em, Godfrey reckons, but that's still enough to give us trouble we don't need. We're gonna try hiding out up ahead where the bush is thick and see if we can wait 'til they pass by. Here he is…" he continued, nodding toward the road up ahead a hundred metres or so, where Godfrey and mount waited patiently near a particularly thick line of trees that appeared to veer off across the fields in a crooked line.

He began to ease the mare back down to a less hectic pace and had the wagon at a slow trundle by the time they reached Godfrey's position. With no more than a nod between them, Godfrey turned the stallion and walked him in between the tall trees, and Nev could now see a small creek ahead, crossing the road at a narrow ford. Heavy growth followed either side of the water as it ran off to the south-east, and once anyone was within that thick bush they'd likely be very difficult to see from the road or the surrounding countryside, even from a relatively short distance.

Short and slight-of-build as he was, there was no denying that Lester was an excellent wagon driver. With careful precision, he worked the reins and flicked them encouragingly to turn the mare off the road in the same direction, allowing the horse to find its own way between the trees in pursuit of Godfrey. With just one very minor scrape against the rear corner of the wagon, the whole set up was secure within the dark cover of the scrub within seconds.

"This should do us here," Godfrey decided with a soft voice, dismounting and tying his reins to the rear of the wagon. Lester also dropped to the ground, and each dragged a large feed bag from the rear cargo bed which they then hung over their respective horse's noses. With the prospect of a meal presented to them, both animals promptly forgot all about whatever else was going on, rendering them about as silent as they were likely to get.

"Hope they've no dogs with 'em," the boy observed quietly as he climbed up onto the front bench and he drew out his crossbow, laying it across his lap.

"We're done for if *that* happens," Godfrey admitted without emotion, clambering over the backboard and taking a knee in the rear of the wagon, "although I've not seen any hounds out this far from the larger towns for many a season now… they don't venture far from easy food, and times are tough out here in the countryside; farmers have prob'ly been *eatin'* 'em, if y' ask me… If they *do* have one, take it down first… those evil sods will have your throat out soon as look at you." As he spoke, his eyes never left the direction of the road they'd just left, barely visible in the distance through the intervening undergrowth.

"So, we just wait?" Nev hissed softly, her voice shaking with nerves now rather than the rattle of the road.

""Nothin' else for it," Godfrey shrugged. "At least it was rainin' last night, so there's no dust on the road to give us away. The fresh wagon ruts might be a problem if they've a smart bugger with 'em, but they're fragile little swine at heart: there's not a single Blackwatch rider *I've* seen who'll get his boots dirty unless he has to. Unless we give ourselves away or they're on the hunt for us in particular, we should be right enough. *Hark, now*…!" He added in a hushed warning. "They're *coming*…! Not a *sound*…!"

The faint rumble of approaching hooves rose in Nev's ears a moment later, and she held her breath, actually clamping a hand over her mouth in a movement that was equal parts fear and precaution. The sound seemed endless, growing louder and louder until finally the troop were there beyond the trees, cantering past in tight formation, heading west.

It was difficult to see much, craning her head around Godfrey and the bush beyond, but she did catch fleeting glimpses of black-clad riders who were indeed very much like the man Percy had accidentally killed the preceding night – the man Kane and the others had come to collect. Each man held the reins in one hand and a long, curved sabre in other, the shining blade held vertically with its tip pointing skyward as if they were all in the middle of some formal, military parade. They were gone again in a moment, the sound of their movement receding now as they carried on along their merry way, seemingly completely oblivious to the fugitives they'd just passed by.

"No hounds, at least," Lester observed softly, allowing himself to relax a little.

"We'll wait twenty minutes before we move out," Godfrey nodded, releasing his own sigh of relief. "Follow the creek on the eastern side and come out onto the fields a bit further on. It'll be slow going for a few hundred yards, but the track's beyond that that'll take us south of Ponder. I want to make Fishwaters by mid-afternoon so we can get a good few hours' rest before heading out for Welshpool after dusk."

"Rough going to start with," Lester agreed, "but this old girl will manage…" With a sly grin, he then added: "…the *horse'll* be alright, too…"

Godfrey had the good manners to turn his face away before an uncontrollable smirk spread across his face, and it was a good few seconds before Nev caught up with what the boy had actually said.

"*Hey*…!" She grumped softly, frowning and reaching out without even thinking to punch Lester gently on the shoulder in protest.

"Oh, no…! Touched by a *witch*…!" He mourned mockingly, all three of them a little euphoric now after their experience as the tension began to dissipate, leaving adrenalin behind. "I'll wake up a *toad*…!"

"Now… with *most* folks, that's *not* an improvement!" Godfrey joked in return, trying not to laugh too loudly as Nev fought to prevent a smile from crossing her own lips.

"…Toad's too good for the likes of *you*…!" She pretend-pouted, making a show of crossing her arms in a huff but not really managing to show any conviction. "Maybe a *slug* instead… or a wriggly little *worm*…"

"There's no fish alive that'd lower its colours enough to take *him* on a hook…" Godfrey declared with a chuckle, and they were all smiling now, happy to enjoy a moment or two of relief after a near-miss with danger.

"You are *so* mean to each other," Nev observed with a shake of her head and a wry grin. "It's 'reassuring' that boys are pretty much the same here as they are where *I* come from."

"What… big, strapping, *handsome* lads there too, are they?" Godfrey asked jokingly, striking a ludicrous pose that was somehow intended to show off his muscles but to Nev looked more like he was painfully constipated. "Bet *your* man's a fine-looking fella…" he added, carefully choosing his words. "…A *lord* o' some kind no doubt, with plenty of acres and a brace o' servants to look after 'im…?"

"Oh… I – uh… I don't…" Nev faltered then, completely flummoxed over what to say next and mortified to realise that her cheeks were suddenly burning red. So unexpected was the outwardly innocent statement that she completely missed the veiled interest behind it. "There's… I *mean*…"

"What, you don't have a fella…?" Lester asked in a surprised voice. "Surely a lass such as yourself has 'em *hammerin'* on yer family's door, seekin' yer hand in marriage…?" He threw a cheeky wink in Godfrey's direction while Nev wasn't looking: much as the statement *had* been *mostly* innocent, Lester knew his friend and mentor well enough to know that there was nevertheless at least a *little* interest behind it.

"Um… no… not *exactly*…" *…or* not at all*, being honest…* her mind added silently, for no one's benefit.

"Mad bloody world *you* come from, then…" Lester shrugged as if it were the simplest of logic, and Nev was doubly dismayed to realise she'd begun to blush even harder as it became clear he'd just given a surprisingly subtle compliment. Godfrey said no more for his part, and was happy to close his eyes and lean back against the sideboard of the wagon with a faint, thoughtful smile on his face.

They'd set off again after perhaps half an hour, the first few hundred metres as rough and jarring as predicted as Lester carefully guided the mare across the open fields beyond the treeline at the creek (which turned out to be more like a string of elongated lagoons than a free-flowing waterway). They found a scrubby dirt track soon enough however, and the ride – although definitely not perfect – at least settled down a bit after that.

Nev again put out her power-bank and phone to charge, then tried to settle in as comfortably as she was able. Lester was happy to watch the road ahead, and he launched into song for his own entertainment, although his words were loud enough for Nev to hear. He was half-singing, half-reciting words that fitted somewhere between poetry and true song, and laying down on the bedroll behind the driver's seat, she let her mind drift as she listened, surprised at the depth of feeling the boy gave those strange yet somehow familiar words.

> *No chance for me to act a wise man*
> *Nor live a thief among the poor*
> *No more the burden of a blind man*
> *No more this heartless life of yore*
> *Remind me now what came before*
>
> *Remind me now what came before*
> *Before those heartless days of yore*
>
> *Ask not falsely for forgiveness*

Or give those lies I've heard before
Ask me not for trust mistaken
Or hearts too broken to ignore
For lying near the broken barrel
Supping wine spilt on the floor
Here lies the husk of how you left me
The day you turned me from your door

Remind me now what came before
Before those heartless days of yore

You always knew how much I loved you
I still do now, just like before
Had I been there the day they took you
We might yet have those days of yore

Remind me now what came before
Before those heartless days of yore

"That was *lovely...*" she said after he'd finished, and this time it was Lester's turn to redden slightly, having been so lost in the recital that he'd completely forgotten she was even there. "What's it called...?"

"Uh... dunno, really... it's an old song me ma used t' sing when I was a little kid... *all* the oldies in my village know it. I think *their* parents sung it to them to in their day. Us kids just call it the 'Remember Song'... dunno if there was ever a *real* name for it."

"Well... it was very nice... although I think it must be a sad song..." Nev observed, thinking more about the few lyrics she could recall.

"Sad enough..." he shrugged. "Old Garry likes hearin' that one. You'd think he'd *hate* it, with what happened to his family... but he reckons it makes him feel *better* to hear it. I dunno..." he repeated, shaking his head vaguely. "Life's tough all 'round... maybe singin' about it makes the hard parts a little easier..."

"Maybe it makes people feel better to know there are *others* that have had sad experiences too... to know that someone else understands what *they* feel..." She suggested, thinking of something her father had once told her about why he liked listening to Pink Floyd's *The Wall* so much.

"Never thought o' that…" Lester conceded, smiling as if they'd just shared a bonding moment – which they pretty much had "…but I guess that sounds fair enough."

"Know any others?" She asked, happy to spend the passing hours listening to anything other than whispering winds and birdsong.

"*Heaps…*" he declared, eager to show off now he had an appreciative audience.

"Can you sing some more?" She asked eagerly, happy for something to relieve the boredom as she took up the *iPhone* and activated the camera.

Clearing his throat, he began another song in a similar vein and Nev lay back on the bedroll, holding up the phone and taking it all in. The boy's voice was quite soothing when he sang, and it wasn't long before she'd fallen asleep in spite of the bumpiness of the road, the phone lying by her side as she dreamed of home and strangely-familiar songs.

The rest of the journey to Fishwaters was almost as long and far less eventful. It was well into the afternoon – after three according to Nev's phone – as they arrived at another small farm, this one on the outskirts of a smallish village. They'd quickly unhitched the mare and set both horses roaming free in a small field while all three of them, with help from a farmer and his teenage son, pushed the wagon inside a far larger barn than the one they'd stayed in the night before.

The house itself was almost identical in construction to one they'd seen yesterday and from a distance of a kilometre or so, it seemed that the entire village was comprised of similar dwellings with just one larger structure rising above rooftops at what appeared to be the centre of town. There was no symbol or icon she could see from that distance, but the tall, angular steeple was enough to make it obvious she was looking at a church or similar place of worship.

"Best stay in here to be safe…" Godfrey suggested, standing beside her at the barn's open doorway as she looked out across the village. "We're closer to the main road here than in Crookhaven and it'd be bad news for any passing travellers to catch sight of an unknown woman out and about without a blindfold."

"This *Keepsake* thing again," she huffed in exasperation, turning and stomping back inside as he nodded sympathetically.

"It's a rum gig," he shrugged, "but that's of no matter if someone makes a report. That wouldn't go badly just for *us* either: there's Andrews and his family to consider."

"The farmer...?" She asked, less grumpy now as he closed the large doors, leaving them open just enough to allow a breath of fresh air.

"Aye, the very same... He'll be back with some food shortly, but other than that we'll likely not see anyone else at all while we're here. They don't know what we're doin' *or* where we're going, and they don't *want* to know. They're riskin' their necks just helpin' us as it is..."

Something to eat *would* be nice..." Nev admitted, suddenly realising her stomach was rumbling, and she couldn't remember when she'd had anything to eat at all other than those few strips of dry jerky Godfrey had given her the night before.

"Shouldn't be long," he assured, moving across to the wall near the door and sitting down on the hard-packed, earthen floor. "Get some more rest: there won't be much chance of any more during the night."

"Long way to go, still...?" She asked, taking a small barrel from a pile of junk near the wagon and dragging it over as a seat.

"Long enough," he shrugged again, resting his head back against the barn wall with eyes closed. "A little more than twenty miles but we'll not travel as fast at night, and it'll take longer still when the clouds come back, *which they will*: first clear skies in many a week and it can't last much longer.

"Welshport's a big town too, so we'll need to be more careful when we arrive: lots o' people coming and going means we probably won't look out of place but it *also* means there'll be lots of town watchmen about, checking papers and making a general nuisance of 'emselves. A lot of goods come and go there, and where there's business there's also graft and corruption: we'll fare no better taken for smugglers than we will if we're taken as spies."

"Where to, after that...?" She asked after a long moment of thought, not sure she actually wanted to know.

"Dunno yet... Like I said; captain o' the ship we're meeting tomorrow morning will though, and he'll be in charge from thereon."

There were a number of concerns boiling over in Nev's mind at that moment, foremost of which was a fear that had suddenly blossomed darkly at the thought of what might happen once they met that ship.

"And – and, what will *you* do... um... once you've handed me over...?"

There were a number of reasons she wanted to know the answer to *that* question, not the least of which being that he and Lester were the only two people she actually knew in that world, and she knew them well enough to also know that she could trust them with her life *and* her 'honour' (or whatever Godfrey had called it the night before). For her to be expected to just walk away from that trust and place her fate in the hands of a complete stranger was not a pleasant idea. There *was* more to it than that of course, but none of that was as important right at that moment in comparison to her safety in the immediate future.

"I'll go where I'm told," he answered softly after another long pause, but she did note that he wasn't able to look at her in that moment – that he continued to stare almost woodenly at the roof above. "I don't *want* to just leave you with some stranger though," he continued, echoing her own concerns, "so I'm *hoping* I'll continue on as your escort for the time being..."

"That..." she began, then paused as she became a little lost for words. "...I'd like that..." she said eventually... *honestly*... and this time, Godfrey did look at her, their eyes meeting in a gaze that showed hidden relief on both sides and a bit more than just that.

"What... ah... what've you got in that *bag,* anyway..." he asked eventually, feeling almost as uncomfortable as Nev and desperately seeking some way to change the subject. "You haven't let it get more than two feet away from y' the whole time you've been here. I already *know* its heavy... you carrying *gold* in there or something?"

"*Hardly...*" she admitted, also happy to change topic. "Just my change of clothes, some bits and pieces and... *and a* present *from my trainer...*" she finished, having thought of the wrapped box for the first time in quite a while.

"A 'present'... a *gift,* y' mean...?" He asked with a frown as she suddenly snatched up the bag with interest and zipped it open. "What were y' training for?"

"*Kenjutsu...*" she answered without thinking as she drew out the wrapped box, then went on to explain: "It's a martial art where I come from... it's a form of self-defence using swords..."

"So *that's* how you were able to hold off those three fellas? We managed to catch part of the show and I *was* wonderin' where you learned to fight like that." He frowned as he thought a bit deeper. "Not much for defence if they only give you a *wooden* one though…"

"*That* wasn't a sword…" she answered slowly, suddenly fascinated as she carefully tore the plain, brown wrapping away to reveal the long, lacquered box Honda had prepared, covered in its dragon motifs. "That was just a *bokken*: a *training* tool for practice…"

The latches had been unclasped at some stage during the trials and tribulations of the last 24 hours, but the box had remained closed, secured by loops of plain, white ribbon tied tightly at each end. As Godfrey rose to his feet and came over to watch with interest, she slowly slipped the ribbons from each end, forced to take some time about it due to +how tightly they were secured.

For some inexplicable reason, she found that her breathing was now shallow and rapid, and although she had no clue as to what was actually inside – her initial guess of a new *bokken* still stood – she realised she was suddenly feeling quite nervous. Having seen the ornate design and obvious quality of the box's construction however, it now seemed far too luxuriously constructed to house even the most expensive wooden practice sword. With a shaky hand, she laid the box across her knees and lifted the lid.

It was a sword… a *real* one, of course. She later suspected that her sub-conscious has always known somehow, but the idea had been so inconceivable that she'd not been able to even consider it. As Godfrey looked on eagerly from above her right shoulder, she removed the weapon, sheathed in an equally black, lacquered wooden scabbard (*saya*, in Japanese) that was engraved with two golden dragons identical to the one that adorned the lid of the box.

It was almost a metre long overall, a third of which was the wooden *tsuka* (the hilt), traditionally covered in ray skin and wrapped tightly in criss-crossing bands of black silk that matched the darkness of the *saya*, and hanging from the pommel was a small *omamori*, similar in design to the *yaku-yoke* that Honda always carried with him. The meeting of hilt and blade was encircled by a circular handguard – the *tsuba* – formed out of solid, blackened steel inlaid with more golden dragons, this time a pair set into the outer circumference, chasing each other's tails. She carefully, almost reverentially took the *tsuka* in her right hand and lifted it, preparing to remove the *saya* with her left.

Nev had seen numerous images of the katana – the premier weapon of choice for the samurai – on the web and in reference books. She'd even seen real ones once or twice – *authentic* swords – at museums and such like. None of that could've prepared her as she carefully drew the blade clear of the scabbard, the sound little more than a metallic whisper as it came free and shone dully in the half-light of that musty barn.

"Now… *that* is beautiful…!" Godfrey breathed softly, almost as in awe of the thing as she was.

"'Beautiful' doesn't even come *close*…!" She replied in a similarly-hushed tone, placing the duffel bag back down on the ground and then laying the box and the *saya* carefully across the top of it.

Rising suddenly enough to force Godfrey to jump backward slightly, she took a few steps out into the centre of the barn, moving away from both the walls and the wagon, and held the katana out in front of her in both hands, testing the weight and feel of it. Wary of her movements despite having made the same ones countless times in training, she went through a few simple practice strikes and blocks, the blade slicing through the air with soft swishes as she slashed at the empty air.

"That's a *beauty*, alright!" Lester observed from a seated position up inside the rear of the wagon. He'd been catching up on rest there but had been roused by her movements.

"It's… it's *heavier* than the *bokken*…" she observed softly, mostly to herself. "Maybe *twice* as heavy, but it's so wonderfully balanced you hardly notice…!" She completed a few more strokes, the greater mass and superb balance of the weapon quickly making her feel very confident.

A sword that was too heavy toward the point might carry great striking power but would also suffer from inertia and prove more difficult to wield quickly, whereas one with greater mass at the hilt might be faster in one's hands but would trade power in return. The principle was the same for *bokken*, although at least in training that wasn't potentially a life-or-death matter

"*This* one…" she muttered, thrusting and slashing at invisible opponents, "*this* one is *perfect*…!"

"There's a note in here…" Godfrey called out, fishing through several various bits and pieces at the bottom of the box and pulling out a small, rolled-up piece of paper, tied with a similar white ribbon.

"*What… where…?*" She demanded, everything else forgotten in that moment as she almost leaped across the space between them and snatched it from his hands.

"You – you wanna give *me* that thing while you read?" He suggested, ducking out of range of the swinging blade and watching her almost slice her own throat as she simultaneously tried to keep hold of the katana and open the tiny scroll.

"I'll… I'll put it away…" she decided warily, not particularly imagining he might damage anything but nevertheless suddenly very protective of it as she took up the *saya* once more and carefully slid the katana's blade home.

Placing the sheathed sword back inside the box, she was then able to unfurl the note and pay it proper attention. The words were handwritten – she wasn't sure Honda had ever *used* a computer – and they filled the page in neat, spidery script that said much about the care and patience of the writer.

> *My dear Tatsuko…*
>
> *I know not when you will read this, but I feel it will not be soon enough. There is much I cannot explain to you… so much that <u>cannot</u> be explained in mere words. I have lived a long life and I have trained many during this time, but none have come close to displaying the skills you have shown. I have always believed that fate brought me to your town… to find and to train you, so far from my own homeland. I hope that in time you will forgive me that I did not warn you of what was to come… I pray that in time you will understand why I could not.*
>
> *There are some who walk this earth… a very few… who sometimes sense the future before it happens. I have met some of these people over the years, and I myself am one of them. Why have I never told you this? Because your training was far too important to jeopardise by being thought of as a crazy old man. What I have seen of your future is limited – little more*

than glimpses of fire and death — but I have also seen hope… hope that there is a chance to regain what by now you will have lost. I cannot lie: the road I have seen for you is a hard one indeed… but never doubt there is hope.

This weapon has remained in my family for generations. With no heir, there exists none more fitting it should pass to than you… you, who have studied well the history of the samurai and culture of Bushido. This weapon is Sōshū Sadamune, and you will know what that means. It carried a name once in the service of my ancestors. Name it again now for yourself, and it will serve you well. It is all I have to give, and I give it freely. Like the training, use it well and it will save your life.

I do not know if we shall ever meet again, yet I remain hopeful.

Live well, daughter of dragons… find strength in the way of the samurai.

Godfrey, standing beside her and unashamedly reading over her shoulder, glanced up and was surprised to see that there were tears in her eyes as Nev finished the note and crumpled it into a ball in her right fist.

"He knew…" she almost choked, tears streaming down her cheeks now as the words' full impact sunk home. "He knew something was going to happen… *and he did nothing…*!"

"You sure that was for you?" Godfrey asked carefully, trying to be helpful. "That wasn't *your* name at the top of the note: it was written for someone called 'Tatsuko'…" To his credit, he made a reasonable job of the pronunciation into the bargain.

"That *is* me," she snapped angrily, casting the crumpled note aside and dabbing self-consciously at her damp eyes (although the question had at least broken the mood and diverted her attention for a moment). It was a nickname he called me… *Tatsuko*… in his language, it means 'Dragon Child'…"

"'Daughter of Dragons'..." he mused softly, regarding her with a curious eye, "...that's *you*, is it? Why *dragons*...?"

Godfrey was genuinely interested – dragons were a huge part of Osterlands culture and mythology after all – and he'd also come to realise that Nev tended to forget about her problems when she was concentrating on other issues, as if her mind was better able to remain calm and focussed when there were puzzles or problems to be overcome.

"It's my *name*..." she repeated with vague exasperation, understanding that there was no way he could know what she was talking about but not in the mood for stories. "None of this will make much sense to either of you," she added, sitting herself on the barrel once more and burying her head in her hands, "but my family on my *father's* side has Icelandic heritage. Iceland is a small, volcanic island covered in fjords and glaciers, and in Iceland, family names aren't like *ours*... instead, they simply take your father's *first* name with 'son' or 'daughter' added to the end.

"My father *should* have been called Dreki Andersson – it was what Grandpa Anders always wanted – but my grandmother insisted the family take more *Australian* names to match their new home, and Dad became *Drake Anderson* instead. I don't remember much more about it: dad never talked about it, and they divorced when I was very young."

"And you...?" He ventured, sensing there was more to the story.

"And *me*...?" She asked with sadness. "Dreki is Icelandic for 'dragon', and by that same tradition, I wouldn't be called Nev *Anderson*: my family name should be '*Drekansdottir*'..."

"Daughter of Dragons..."

"*Literally*..." she agreed darkly, glancing up at him for the first time. "My trainer – the one who wrote the note – started calling me Tatsuko soon after he'd worked out what my ancestral name would've been. I thought it was just a harmless nickname all these years... it seems now that maybe I was wrong about that: that he really *meant* something by it."

"Seems like he was *right*..." Godfrey shrugged, taking a step back almost inadvertently as she lifted the sword from the box once more and turned it over in her hands, examining the gold filigree of the engraved dragons in more details.

"If he really believed something was going to happen, why didn't he *warn* me?" She asked with bitterness through clenched teeth, Honda's perceived betrayal as awful in her mind as Percy's. "If he *really* believed, why did he *do nothing* to help me?"

"Dunno about doin' *nuthin'*..." Godfrey observed in a gentle voice as she glanced up sharply, mid-way through drawing the blade once more from its *saya*. "...Gave y' that *sword* there, didn't he...? *I've* seen what you can do with a piece of *wood*...!"

VII

DIFFICULT JOURNEYS

They rested for three hours, Godfrey and Lester managing to spend at least half that time sleeping as Nev sat alone and despondent against a far wall of the barn, completely confused regarding the sword she hadn't been able to put down. She'd spent the entire time alternating between staring at the katana and at the crumpled note Honda had left, and at the end of it all she was no closer to finding any rational explanation than when she'd first opened the package.

The only thing she *was* certain of was that her earlier statement was entirely correct: the sword was about as close to perfection as any edged weapon could be. One *extremely* light touch of a finger had told her the blade was razor sharp, and staring along its length she could clearly see that there was not a single blemish or imperfection. That it was a *Sadamune* (surely, Honda wouldn't have lied about something like that?) made the fact that she was holding it even more unbelievable.

A different wagon entirely had arrived at the farm around dusk, this one a large, six-wheeled affair pulled by a four-horse team. Instead of a canvas cover, this one's cargo bed was a fully-enclosed wooden box with small, louvered windows set into the sides and a low hatchway up front allowing access to an open-sided driving position that was provided with an overhanging roof as basic protection against the elements. Everything was painted in dull green, over which was stencilled a single name in white: *ARLEIGH.*

"Better transport to take us the rest of the way," Godfrey explained with slightly bleary eyes, having been woken prematurely by the rumble of its arrival. "*Safer* transport: Arleigh here's known to the local watch at Welshport and they're used to him comin' and goin' at all hours with goods and supplies, both for the merchant fleet there *and* for Harald's war galleys over at Long Pier."

"Can he be trusted…?" Nev asked suspiciously as she stood near the open barn door and Godfrey freshened up just outside, making use of a large bucket of cold water standing on a thick, off-cut log perhaps a metre high.

"Could you have asked that *any* louder?" He snapped, more surprised at the question than offended as he splashed water over his face and rubbed it into his eyes and beard. "I don't think they heard y' down at the town square."

"I – I'm sorry…" she blurted, realising after the fact how rude that question must've sounded.

"These are people either I or other Ostermen have worked with before, and we *know* who we can trust: mistakes tend to cost *lives* in this business."

"Of course… I didn't mean…"

"I know…" he nodded with a dismissive wave, softening his tone as he took a grubby towel hanging on a nail in the barn wall and dried his face and hands. "You're nervous, and all this is *very* new – I understand that." He stopped for a moment, turning to face her with hands on hips. "Do you trust *me*…?"

That question left her momentarily lost for words, and (*damn it!*) she felt her cheeks flush again.

"I – I… *yes*… yes, I trust you…"

"Then you don't need to worry about *them*, do y'?" He grinned simply, as if that was all settled. "I'll not see anything bad happen to y' while I'm still drawin' a breath, and with that there 'pig-sticker' of yours, it'd be a brave bugger indeed that tried anything funny anyway."

"You lot ready to go, there?" Arleigh called from the other side of the horses, in the middle of checking their running gear. "We've some way to go yet, and the Welshport Watch have been showin' a tendency to lock the gates at midnight of late. I'd prefer not to be caught out for the rest o' the night, and I'd warrant neither would the rest 'o ye!"

Hammond Arleigh was a bear of a man in his late thirties. Huge and round and looking like there was some serious muscle underneath his rotund form, his tiny, bloodshot eyes, thick moustache and mutton-chop sideburns decorating a face that was otherwise dominated by his huge and decidedly bulbous red nose.

"*Some* of us are ready…" Lester chimed in unhelpfully, already seated on the bench next to the driver with his ubiquitous crossbow across his lap.

"We're comin', brother…" Godfrey called cheerfully in return. "…just collecting our gear…"

"Yer *no* brother o' *mine*, Godfrey Westacre," Arleigh pointed out genially as he hoisted himself up into the driver's position, "…and a good thing that is, too! *My* brother's a *pig* of a man I'd nary take a leak on if he were burnin'…!"

"*Charming…*" Nev muttered to herself, frowning at the unpleasant imagery that comment conjured up as Godfrey dived inside the barn and came out with two armloads of packs and belongings, including Nev's duffel bag and the lacquered box the katana had come in.

"You're a gentle soul indeed, Hammond," he shot back with a chuckle as she hurriedly took her gear from him and hoisted the bag over one shoulder. "You're happy to suffer the Toad up front?"

"I like a song now and then," Arleigh shrugged with a dry smile of his own, "and I can box his ears well enough if he gets out o' hand."

"We'll ride in the back then," Godfrey nodded in agreement, striding across the space between the barn and the wagon at a speed that forced Nev to run to catch up. "You takin' the Raised Road?"

"None quicker I know of, and plenty of traffic these days between Welshport and the western Blacklands, meanin' less random patrols… most o' the buggers can't be arsed checkin' papers when it means stopping a hundred wagons a day."

"Sounds like a plan to me," Godfrey called out from the rear of the wagon as he opened the large, double doors and clambered up inside, making use of a set of built-in steps that hung down from beneath the cargo bed. "Up y' come!" He called pleasantly, extending a hand for Nev and hoisting her up into the rear before closing the doors behind her.

The cargo area was remarkably spacious, even with quite a number of crates of various sizes stacked and tied down within, and a long, low box had been laid along each side at the rear for use as benches, each topped by surprisingly-comfortable cushions stuffed with straw. After stowing their gear securely between two crates toward the middle of the wagon, Nev and Godfrey took seats on opposite sides and he banged lightly on the wooden wall with his fist.

"Good to go back here, Hammond!" He called out, and the horses fussed and grumbled and moved off a few seconds later at a reasonable pace, setting out along the dirt track leading away from the farm and back down toward the main road.

"It's a fine weapon, that's for sure..." Godfrey observed from across the rear of the cargo bed as Nev once again fidgeted with the sheathed katana, still unable to put it down for more than a few minutes at a time.

"'Fine' isn't the word..." she muttered, correcting him for a second time regarding the sword and this time at least managing a half-smile. "The blade is *pristine*...!" She continued, drawing the weapon fully this time and giving it another once-over before *very carefully* reversing the hilt and offering it across to Godfrey. "Almost *seven hundred years old* and there's not a single mark on it!"

"It's definitely clean," he conceded, dubious and frowning over her statement. "How can you be sure it's so old?"

In that note, Honda – my trainer – said that it had been made by Sōshū Sadamune. He was a master swordsmith who was born... seven hundred and *nineteen* years ago..." she explained, doing the math quickly in her head, adding quickly "...in *my* world, anyway. He only lived for about fifty years, so if it *is* one of his swords, then it *must* be that old."

"He must have been a great swordsmith to still be remembered so long after his death," Godfrey observed, vaguely impressed.

"One of the best," she nodded enthusiastically. "I studied a *lot* about these – they're called *katana* – and Sadamune was right up there with the greatest of them all. Only one man – a guy called Masamune – was thought to be any better, and *he* was Sadamune's *father*... either by blood or through adoption, although no one's sure which, nowadays..."

"It *looks* a lot like some of the blades you find up north, although I've *never* seen anything this good in the Sun Empire. There are *kings* who'd pay a lifetime's wages for something as well-made as this."

"I just wish he'd *told* me!" She sighed sadly, mind veering back onto the less pleasant topic of Honda's note. "Maybe I could've done something to *not* end up here... like just *stay at school* instead of taking off with Percy."

"So this other girl – the 'Blue Witch' – was your *friend*, yes?" He asked with interest, handing the katana back and watching her sheath it carefully as she nodded in dark agreement. "And she's from *your* world, rather than ours... d'you have *any* idea why she would've done this to you? Why she's doing *any* of this?"

"Not a clue," Nev shook her head sadly, feeling that terrible sense of betrayal once more. "She said she wanted to go for a 'nature ride', led me to that clearing, then all hell broke loose without warning: weird voices in my head, and her talking back to them..."

"Voices in your head...?" Godfrey frowned, checking which pocket he kept his tiny prayer book in and fighting an urge to touch his forehead in the sign of The Shard as superstition momentarily got the better of him.

"I don't remember *much*..." she continued, laying the sheathed sword gently beside her on the cushioned bench. "I could hear a voice inside my mind, but there was no one else there I could see at the time. It said something about how I wasn't any use, although I don't know *what for*. It said I was... um... *'precedent'*, I think – *prescient?* – and that I couldn't be 'controlled'..." she shrugged. "Then it ordered that swordsman to *kill* both of us..."

"It ordered a Blackwatcher to kill the *witch*?"

"Aye... uh... *yes*..." she agreed, faltering momentarily as she frowned over her unconscious use of his terminology. "Then Perce fell over, the shotgun went off – by accident, I'm pretty sure – and the rider was killed. It was only *after* that I realised she'd been working *with* whatever it was to bring me there in the first place. That was when I took off..."

"And you ran into *me*..." he finished with a grin.

"And I ran into you..." she nodded.

They shared a silent but important moment then, intently matching each other's gaze with a greater openness that hadn't been there before... with a deeper level of trust that hadn't existed before.

"Thank you..." she murmured eventually, glancing down at her feet then.

"For...?"

"For everything..." she admitted, knowing it was something she should've said a long time ago. "For saving my life... for coming back to rescue me *again* when I was too stupid to listen to reason... for looking after me..." she lifted her eyes once more, and he was surprised to see that they were moist with painful honesty. "For *everything*..."

"You'll get home again..." he stated with more certainty than Nev would've thought possible. "I don't know *how*, yet... or *when*... but I can feel it in me bones: you *will* get back to your world somehow."

"I wish I could believe that…" she sighed, shaking faintly as she struggled to hold her emotions in check.

"That'll come in time…" Godfrey assured, and there was only sincerity in his tone and expression now. "You're a lot stronger than you think… you just need to *know* it. *I* can see it, and I reckon that Honda could see it too, or he wouldn't have given you the sword. My ma used to say that everything happens for a reason – the damned *Brotherhood* says the same thing all the time, for *different* reasons – and maybe… *maybe* it's just that before you get home, there's a few things need to happen *first*… things that need a fine blade, a sharp eye and a good heart."

"I wish everything was that simple," she sighed in frustration, leaning back until she was wedged into the rear corner of the cargo bed between the wall and the back door. "I trained for five years with *wooden* swords, practising against a *seventy-year-old*. I don't know anything about *fighting*. I don't even kill *spiders* when they come in the house. This isn't some fantasy movie with plucky hobbits or sparkly vampires… I might get killed… *you* might get killed, trying to protect me…"

"People die every day," Godfrey shrugged, not at all caring that he had no idea what a movie or a hobbit was. "Not meanin' to take that road meself for a few summers yet, but you don't always get to pick your time… particularly in the Blacklands. Soldier, farmer or king… *any* day could be your last: no point walkin' around the whole time, actin' like y'r already dead. All the more reason to make the most of what you've got *right now*, *I* say…"

"That's… that's a pretty cool perspective," New replied eventually, staring at the roof of the wagon after reconsidering the sarcastic remark that had flared in her mind about him trying to sell life insurance.

"And *you* were going to say something *else* at first," he pointed out, not missing a thing. "What's a shotgun?" He added, throwing her off track with a change of subject before she had a chance to feel embarrassed. "You said this thing 'went off' and that the rider was killed… is it some kind of crossbow?"

"Oh… *er*… not *really*… It's… well, it's a gun… that fires shot…" she tried to explain, cringingly awarding herself a 'Mastery of the Bloody Obvious' award within her own mind as Godfrey raised an eyebrow and she realised the statement was no help whatsoever. "It's like a hand-held cannon... not good at long distance like a rifle would be, but lethal at close range."

"What's a 'cannon'?" He asked blankly, giving her no help at all.

"Oh, jeez... *cannon* don't exist here either? *That's* not good: a shotgun loose in a world without firearms... not good *at all*." She paused for a moment, then soldiered on. "It's basically a long, steel tube that fires big lead balls *really* fast out one end – faster than the eye can see. It's *far more* deadly than a crossbow at close range – maybe fifty to a hundred meters... uh... *yards*..." she corrected, switching to a rough approximation of imperial measurement. It'd *probably* punch through anything short of metal armour, and I'm not sure if even *that* would be strong enough to stop it at close range. Sorry... I don't know a lot about guns..."

"More than *we* do, though," he conceded with a serious expression. The description Nev had given was vague at best but it nevertheless painted a grim picture of a weapon far more dangerous than any crossbow. "I'll need to get word to my local command about it: they might be able to..." his words trailed off as he realised Nev's eyes had closed, and that her head was beginning to nod slowly forward.

"Wha – *what*...?" She mumbled, shaking her head in a vain attempt to clear her thoughts.

"Come on..." he grinned, taking the sword from the seat beside her and laying it down on top of her bag. "You need some rest: you got hardly any sleep at all last night, and you've had none since..."

"I – I'm *fine*..." she insisted, her words slow and slurring.

"Of course you are..." he agreed with a silent chuckle, placing a guiding hand on her shoulder and sliding her along the seat just far enough to leave space for her to lay down "... now *rest*...! That's an order!"

Her response trailed off into nothing as she lay her head down on the straw-filled cushions and drew her legs up almost into a foetal position. She was asleep and snoring lightly by the time he'd sat down again on the other side, watching her with a thoughtful expression.

They were already through the town gates at Welshpool as Nev awoke with a start, six hours later. A second cushion had been placed beneath her head as a pillow at some stage during the journey, and a blanket laid across her against the cold, and the fact that she'd remained asleep for almost the entire trip spoke more of her levels of exhaustion than it did of the smoothness of the ride.

A few seconds of waking panic dissipated quickly as she realised Godfrey was standing at the front of the cargo area, looking out through the central hatch there and engaged in quiet conversation with Lester and Arleigh. Rising into a seated position, she gave herself a moment or two for her thoughts to clear before also standing and staring out through one of the small, louvered windows on her side. The smell of the town had already filled the inside of the van, hinting at volatile combinations of refuse, stagnant water and human waste… none of it good.

The view that presented itself wasn't much better as she wrinkled her nose in disgust. As with the other houses she's seen so far, most of the dwellings that filled the town were one- or two-roomed blackhouse-style structures with open windows and thatched rooves. Narrow, muddy alleys ran between clusters of them, with little or no yard other than spaces set aside for livestock such as pigs, chickens and even the occasional cow. There were dogs everywhere of all shapes, sizes and cross-breeds, and all of them running loose in the streets with barks, yips and howls as they chased each other about and otherwise begged or stole scraps of food from the local populace. Nev noted with interest that several of the animals looked to be purebred dingo or something very close.

Smoke filled the air. It dominated and pervaded everything, even eclipsing the markedly less pleasant odours of refuse and waste that that were notable but at least dulled by its overpowering presence. There were few lights on inside the houses – most hard-working commoners had been asleep for hours by now – but dark, wispy plumes of smoke and the occasional spark nevertheless rose from almost every roof as hearth fires continued to warm those cold, Spartan houses of stone, wood and mud brick. It was dark now and clouds had indeed gathered once more above as predicted, but there were lit torches burning along the main roads, set into posts perhaps a metre-and-a-half tall on either side of the street that gave light enough to get some idea of what was going on around them as they passed.

Very few civilians seemed to be out and about that late but the local military were prevalent, wandering about in twos and threes and armed with swords and crossbows. As Arleigh's van continued on through those narrow, winding streets, Nev noted several times that soldiers had stopped civilians in the street, and the body language and general stance clearly suggested they were 'checking papers' or otherwise making official enquiries as to their reasons for being out and about at such a late hour.

On one occasion, she witnessed three uniformed troopers kicking a fallen civilian – a teen of possibly fourteen or less – who could only lay there and cover his head against the worst of their blows. No one came to his aid and not one of his attackers seemed the slightest bit self-conscious about assaulting an unarmed boy in the middle of the street. She turned away momentarily as one of them aimed his crossbow, preparing to deliver a killing shot, and steeled herself against the faint scream that came next, the cry cut terribly short soon after.

"Just another regular night in Welshpool," Godfrey observed darkly as he joined her in the rear of the wagon, staring out through the next louvered slot next to hers.

"What did he do?" She asked in an angry whisper, as enraged as she was sickened by the experience.

"No idea…" he shrugged with a grimace, his tone of resignation conveying his own disgust well. "Probably not much; maybe they caught him thieving, or maybe he was just some poor sod they didn't like… doesn't *take* much to find yerself dead in a Blacklands town if you get on the wrong side of the city watch. Luckily, Arleigh here's well-known to 'em and he slips a few coins to the local commanders here now and again to keep in sweet: they'll not bother us, long as we keep out of their way."

"This place is *brutal*…!" She muttered with a shake of her head.

"Aye, it can be," he conceded. "It's a hard life for a peasant here, that's for sure. *Some* kingdoms are kinder on their subjects – down in Huon, where me and Lester come from, Phaesus is well known to be a fair and decent ruler so far as *kings* go – but all the same, there's nowhere *I've* seen where common folk have it much better."

"I used to think *we* had it tough…" Nev admitted, considering her father's unrelenting work and the fact that she rarely even *saw* him outside of weekends. "…I'm starting to change my mind about that, now…"

She still wasn't completely sure of the truth behind the world in which she was currently trapped, but it was already clear that it wasn't far removed from the historical middle-ages of her own. The squalor in which common folk of previous centuries had lived in *her* world had seemed distant and unreal when printed in the pages of a history book, and Nev was discovering that seeing it first hand was a sobering experience indeed.

"We're *here*…!" Arleigh called sharply from the front of the wagon at that moment, and both of them were jolted into forced sitting positions together as the wheels below passed unexpectedly over something large and uneven in the middle of the road.

"Heads down and not a *word*…" Godfrey warned immediately, throwing the blanket she'd worn over her sword and bag and taking a seat across the other side as the wagon began to slow to a halt. "They'll *have* to check his goods, but they'll not put much effort into looking so long as they don't see anything *interesting*. They'll expect to see our faces, but *don't* look 'em in the eyes – just look straight at me: staring at 'em would look like defiance and we don't need that kind of grief right now."

"What – what if they *ask* me something?" She hissed, suddenly terrified over this new and unexpected information.

"They *won't*," he answered with certainty. "They'll think you're back here 'cause of the Keepsake Law, and *no one* cares about what a *girl* has to say anyway… just *keep quiet* for a few seconds and we'll be *fine*…" he added, cutting off a reaction to his last remark that he knew was coming.

"It would've been *nice* to know about this *earlier*…!" She seethed quietly, the rational part of her mind knowing he was only commenting on how women were treated in *general* rather than making any personal statement, but finding herself no happier about it.

"What… and give you time to *worry* about it? *Nahhh*…!" He shot back with a grin, somehow – as usual – managing to defuse her temper with a single, cheeky remark.

The rear doors flew back a few seconds later to reveal the unpleasant faces of three guards, none of them likely to be appearing on *The Bachelor* in Nev's considered opinion. One held a burning torch raised in his hand while the other two carried loaded crossbows, neither weapon directly pointed at them but both nevertheless aimed close enough to make a none-too-subtle statement.

"What's all this then, Hammond?" The crossbow wielder called out with lazy suspicion, laying eyes on Godfrey and Nev. "You operating a cab service as well, now?"

"They're me niece and nephew, Derek, come across from Fishwaters..." Arleigh called back, not even bothering to turn around. "Got 'em some work on a ship headin' out tomorrow."

"Lucky sods," the man presumably named Derek harrumphed with a shrug. "Better a life at sea than bein' knee-deep in cow pats, I'll warrant. You, boy: what's yer name?"

"G-Godwin, sir..." Godfrey answered immediately, affecting a nervous tone and, to Nev's surprise, lightening his voice slightly so as to sound younger. "Godwin Arleigh... and this here's me sister, Jenna..." he added, nodding toward Nev as she spent the entire time staring woodenly at a point over his left shoulder.

"Fine lookin' girl there, Godwin..." Derek observed with a little more interest than any of them would've liked. "Looks to be *at least* eighteen summers – why's she not married off already, 'stead o' takin' away a *man's* job...?"

"Poor thing's ma was afflicted by the fever while she was carryin' her," Godfrey answered without a moment's hesitation. "Left her a bit soft in the head when she were born y'see, sir... she can follow simple orders and cook well enough to be o' *some* use, but there's no man willin' to take the risk of fathering *idiots*." That remark dulled the guards' interest somewhat... children born with intellectual disabilities generally didn't survive long in that world, and those few that did were also of little use later in life for looking after invalided parents as they grew too old to work. "She's *mute* as well, sir, which don't help..." he added quickly, well aware of how much effort Nev must've been expending at that moment to *not* react or pass enraged comment over what he'd just said. "One of the ships here needs a cook, though, and she can do that well enough, sir, like I said."

"Alright then, kid – wasn't askin' for her bloody *life story*," Derek growled, already losing interest as he waved a dismissive hand. "Just keep yer noses clean while you're here and we'll get along fine. Off you go, Hammond!" He called out, louder now. "See you at Endweek with the next payment, yeah?"

"You know it, Derek..." Arleigh agreed with a forced smile, waiting just long enough for the guards to close and secure the rear doors before gently urging his horses on through the gates leading into the Welshpool docks.

"You are *so* in trouble right now!" Nev hissed, glaring at a grinning Godfrey as Lester – being unhelpful as always – burst into fits of muffled laughter the moment they were clear of the gates.

"You'd rather they ask you directly or – even *worse* – take you over to the *barracks* for 'questioning'…?" He asked pointedly, making a huge effort of his own not to laugh.

"That's not the point at all and you know it!" She shot back, also smiling now in spite of herself. "'Soft in the head'… *seriously*…!"

As they all shared in a moment's relief, the serious part of her inner consciousness tried to tell her that the situation wasn't amusing at all: that having had a close call with soldiers who'd have executed them on the spot as spies, had they known who she and Godfrey really were, most *definitely* wasn't a laughing matter. Yet the sudden adrenalin that the unexpected encounter had sent coursing through her system combined with the relief of making it through unscathed had brought on a kind of euphoria that she'd never known before.

With no prior experience of combat or similarly life-threatening situations, Nev was also being given her first glimpse of intense bond that could be formed between individuals in the face of extreme adversity. She already trusted Godfrey with her life, and despite knowing that at least part of that trust came from superficial things like the fact that that she found him very attractive physically, there *were* also some far deeper reasons behind it.

There was definite proof in that particular pudding, in that he'd already saved her life twice and had made efforts to defend what he called her 'honour' in protecting her modesty. Both his actions so far *and* his inactions – the terrible things he *might* have done to her had he *not* been the man of honour and decency she firmly believed him to be (things that she'd almost certainly not have been able to prevent) – had clearly established Godfrey as a man of integrity. He also had the uncanny ability to defuse almost any situation by making her laugh… by making her feel good… to feel better about herself… although that same part of her mind was *also* trying to tell her that *that* had nothing to do with anything *either*.

The wagon moved beyond the gates to the port, the horses threading their way between torch-lit barns and larger warehouses that, apart from one church, were the only structures Nev had so far seen that were of anything more than rudimentary, single-storey construction.

Although still relatively empty, the port itself was definitely more active than the rest of the town, covering an area of several thousand square metres with four long, wooden piers stretching out into a large, sandy estuary that was sheltered by a large island to the south, and opened out into the wild expanses of Deepwater Strait to the east and west.

Other carts and wagons moved this way and that, with dockworkers loading and unloading by completely inadequate torchlight. All four piers were crowded on both sides with a huge variety of vessels large and small that included, Nev realised with surprise, both sailing ships and oared galleys. Many appeared to be civilian ships, but there were definitely a few warships among them and *all* of those were larger triremes and quadriremes, their tiered banks of oars set in a raised position as they lay at anchor.

"There's somethin' big afoot," Godfrey noted with suspicion, staring out at the moored vessels through the windows on his side. "Harald usually keeps his navy over at The Long Pier – they wouldn't be anchored *here* unless they've run out of room…"

"There's a bit been going on while you've been coolin' yer heels over Crookhaven way," Arleigh advised, calling back from the driver's position. "Harald's reached agreement on a treaty with Huon…"

"A *'treaty'*…?" Godfrey snorted, making no effort to hide his disbelief. "Is Phaesus so simple he believes *that* would ever happen? Harald would sell his own grandmother into slavery… *and* kill his ma to get to her…"

"Aye, that's *my* thoughts on the matter too," Arleigh agreed with a shrug as he hauled back on the reins and once again brought the horses to a halt, this time at the jetty, close to the easternmost pier. "No one *asked* me what I thought, though, and there's to be a signing all the same… the whole bloody fleet's setting sail for Huon to attend some big ceremony in a few days' time, where they're gonna sign this thing and be done with it all. Everyone's crowin' about how it'll be the 'end of war', or some such rubbish…"

A 'war to end all wars'… We all know how that *turned out…* Nev thought with silent interest, recalling her knowledge of First World War history.

"Well… all power to 'em, but I'll believe it when I see it," Godfrey replied to Arleigh, pulling a face and sounding uncharacteristically negative. "It'll be a cold day in The Underworld when Harald bends his knee to *anyone*, right or wrong. We here, are we?"

"Second ship on the right… the *Sea Skimmer*…"

"Cameron Garbutt…?"

"Right enough," Arleigh confirmed with a nod as he dropped the reins and poked his head through the hatchway for the first time.

"Been a few years since I saw him last," Godfrey admitted, recalling fond memories with a faint smile. "He still drink like a fish?"

"Like the man had gills of his own…"

"Don't worry," Godfrey assured Nev, expecting the fleeting, unseen expression of concern that flickered across her face in the darkness. "Cameron Garbutt's a better skipper drunk than *most* are when they're sober. Now I know they *all* say that…" he added quickly, leading Nev to wonder who 'they' were more than anything else "…but in *this* case, I promise you it's true. I worked with him off the northeast coast a while back, and he's *solid*. *Sea Skimmer's* a good ship – she'll see us right."

"And he can tell us where we're *going*?"

"Probably," he grinned, shouldering his rucksack and pushing the rear doors open as Nev scrambled for her own bag. "Keep that sword hidden if you please, and pull the hood down over your eyes 'til you get on board: the guards'll ask questions about a *woman* being out this late carrying a sword, and they're well known to pay bonuses to informants…"

"What a *wonderful* world this is…" Nev growled, zipping the katana inside her bag and slipping it over her shoulders. With a little manoeuvring, she was able to hang the cloak over the whole thing as camouflage: it was still obvious she was carrying a backpack, but at least the appearance of her very *modern* duffel bag wouldn't raise any unwanted questions.

"You've got no idea," Godfrey muttered drily, jumping down onto the hard concrete of the docks and waiting with Lester's pack in his free hand as Nev joined him.

"Let's not hang about eh, Westy…" Lester suggested in a far more serious tone than usual as he collected his own pack and shouldered both it and the crossbow. "Too many strange eyes about for my liking…"

"I hear ya, brother…" he agreed with a dour nod. "Hammond! Many thanks, my friend: we owe you…!"

"I'll send the bill to Harris, shall I?" Arleigh called back with a chuckle. "Take care o' yerself, boy – you and your own there."

"Is it a Westacre I see before me?" Another voice called out from behind them as Arleigh flicked his reins and the horses moved off again, dragging the van behind them. They turned as one to see a smallish man standing a few metres away who looked to be in his mid-thirties. Reed-thin and weathered of face, he was smoking a huge, hand-rolled cigarette and wore ragged blue clothes that might've passed for a naval officer's uniform in years past.

"Captain Garbutt," Godfrey acknowledged immediately, stepping forward and shaking the man's hand, both clasping the other's wrist firmly as part of the greeting. "A long time between voyages... good to see you're still hale and hearty."

"Hale and hearty... *ale* and hearty..." Garbutt chuckled in a voice at least two octaves deeper than should've been possible from such a small-framed man. "All one and the same to me, boy, and you know it! Good to see you're well also. Is that *Lester* now?" He added, staring around Godfrey as he took in the other two. "He was shorter than *me* last I saw him! What's it been, lad: three years?"

"Close enough, Skipper," Lester nodded, beaming as he too stepped up and shook the man's hand in similar fashion. "Growin' big and strong these days," he declared with pride, flexing a scrawny arm as if to show off non-existent muscles. "Those greens Westy keeps makin' me eat are doin' some good."

I can see that," Garbutt laughed out loud, slapping a friendly hand on the boy's shoulder before gently moving him aside and taking a few slow, purposeful steps toward Nev, who was now standing alone and watching the exchange with suspicion. "And who do we have *here*...? Is *this* the person we've been waiting for all this time, Godfrey... *finally here*...?"

"That's what they keep telling me..." Nev answered softly, standing up straight and making a show of not appearing scared.

"Aye, Westacre: there's *definitely* somethin' *interestin'* there, and no mistake," the captain observed shrewdly, his eyes narrowed as he regarded her with an intense stare. "...Not sure what her purpose is... and not my *business* to know... but there's definitely *somethin'*...! Enough about that though..." he continued, nodding vaguely in her direction as a subtle show of greeting and respect before turning back to the other two. "There's naught gain and *much* danger in hanging about on these docks without purpose. Get yourselves to the ship and we can talk more in private."

"We're of a similar mind on that score, Cam," Godfrey agreed, moving to stand beside Nev once more, hovering close off her right in an overtly protective manner. "We've been lucky so far but there's no need to tempt fate too much in one day."

"Let's be away, then," Garbutt suggested, turning and extending an arm in guidance as he addressed Nev personally. "Miss, be so kind as to fall in between us and we'll escort you to my ship, such as she is. I'd feel better that you were safe and sound there rather than out here in the open where idle hands *and* eyes look too readily for mischief."

Glancing across to Godfrey and receiving an imperceptible nod of approval, she did exactly as he requested, moving off in the direction he'd indicated as the three men formed an informal guard around her. As a group they moved at a steady, purposeful pace toward the nearest of the piers, where a number of single and dual-masted sailing ships lay moored, activity all around.

The *Sea Skimmer* wasn't a large ship… at least, not by comparison to the ocean liners and super-tankers Nev knew of from her world, although the vessel appeared to be at least the equal of the smaller warships moored nearby. Perhaps twenty-five metres long and eight metres at the beam, she was a round-bottomed craft of simple, clinker design known as a cog, fitted with a single, square-rigged mast and carrying around fifty crew.

It was built to open-hull plan, with cargo stored on the central main deck, and was fitted with neither forecastle nor quarterdeck, although there was a small covered area at the very stern. It was there that Garbutt guided them, sheltering beneath the wooden bridge deck and seated at a large, round table that appeared to have been built directly around the steering gear than ran directly between the rudder below and the wheel mounted on the open rear deck above their heads.

Glass-enclosed candles hung from the ceiling for illumination, and a small, cast-iron stove popped and crackled at the rear of the covered deck, its chimney bending backward and venting through the wall close to the sternpost. It generated minimal warmth at best in such an open environment but it was welcoming all the same as the faint sounds and smells of burning wood filled the air around them.

"It's not much…" Garbutt admitted apologetically, casting a hand around to encompass a half-dozen wooden cots topped with ragged bedrolls, "but what we have is yours as long as you need it. We've plenty of fresh water and smoked meats, and we'll be away on the morning tide at dawn. Four days' sailing – *maybe* five if the wind isn't in our favour – and we'll be at our destination…"

"Any chance of tellin' us where that *is* exactly, Cam…?" Godfrey asked immediately, pre-empting Nev's own question regarding the same.

"West… bound for Despair…" he replied without hesitation. "The Coven's been waitin' for you for some time, miss…" he explained, directing his next words at Nev personally. "They've not told me *why*, but wherever it is you're from, they knew you were coming right enough."

"*Despair*…?" Godfrey repeated with surprise. "What on earth would The Coven want with her? I didn't even know they still *existed*: didn't Harald and the Crowedans burn them out of Kings' Coat a few years back?"

"That they did," the captain agreed with a wry expression, "but you know how it is: you can find 'despair' *anywhere* if you go looking for it. Seems they didn't get *everyone*, and the survivors have set up shop again sure enough. Get some rest now… we'll need y'all up bright and early to help get her out to sea before sunrise."

"'*Despair*'…?" Nev asked nervously, the moment Garbutt had left them alone. "This is a place I want to go to because *why*…?"

"It's just a name…" Godfrey assured quickly. "I knew of it when I was a boy, but I honestly thought it had been destroyed years ago, if it ever even existed at all…" He took a quick breath and released it as a short sigh. "Despair isn't just one place, really… it's wherever The Coven is, and a *coven* is where…"

"Where *witches* meet, *yes*… *I know*… how could I *not*…?" Nev growled in exasperation, having believed they'd gotten *beyond* the whole 'witch thing' by now.

"That's where the name *comes from*," he countered evenly, "but it's *not* what they *do* in this case… at least, not what I've *heard*…."

"Which is…?" She asked, not ready to stop being annoyed at this point.

"Well, Despair *used* to be something mothers frightened their kids with to make 'em behave: somewhere they'd end up, captives of 'the witches'…"

"How *lovely*…" she muttered sourly.

"When I got older however, I found out that there *might* actually be a real place behind the stories. The stories go that in the 'Old Days' – *hundreds* of summers ago – there were a *lot* more witches around than there are now… that just about one in every third or fourth woman or girl could see the Keepsakes and The Brotherhood and the local armies were being run ragged just tracking them all down."

"How terribly *inconvenient*…"

"Well, the story goes that it was often *impossible*. Families and whole *villages* at times refused to give up their womenfolk to the Quisitors, hiding them away instead, keepin' 'em safe and claiming they'd run off or outright disappeared in puffs of majik. The Brotherhood probably *knew* they were talking rubbish most of the time, but they could hardly argue with claims of majik when that was what they were accusing the witches of in the first place…"

"*Were* these women all 'witches', then?" Nev asked with scepticism.

"Haven't a clue," he answered honestly, "but stands to reason *some* of 'em weren't. Even *nowadays*, it's not unknown for the Quisitors to conveniently discover that people who've been giving them trouble for some *other* reason turned out either to be a witch or *married* to one: it's amazing how quickly disagreements can disappear when there's accusations of witchcraft getting thrown about. Anyway, it goes that there ended up bein' a problem with what to do with all these women in hiding…" he continued, getting back to the topic at hand "…and someone came up with the idea of sendin' 'em somewhere *safe*; as far away from the prying eyes of The Brotherhood as could be managed. That was when Despair came into being: a place – a *secret* place – where women accused of witchcraft could go to live out their days in safety. They may not be with their families, but at *least* they were still alive and able to make lives for themselves somewhere else."

"And this Brotherhood found out where they were: this 'King's Coat'…?" Nev asked thoughtfully, recalling history lessons on the Underground Railroad of the 18th and 19th Centuries, sneaking African-Americans out of the US Slave States and away to the relative safety of 'free states' and to British North America (Canada).

"So the story goes," he nodded. "Back a few years ago, the Crowedans and Blackwatch were a lot friendlier with each other than they are now, and legend has it they joined forces to land at both ends of the island and drive everyone to the centre, killin' anyone who got in their way. Surrounded and slaughtered the rest at the end of it all and left 'em to rot. No one goes there now: the Crowedan navy don't let boats anywhere near it, or so it's said.

"It *is* just a story," he added with a shrug, "but old tales like that often have a grain or two of truth in 'em. The Coven was the name for the small group 'o women who were running the whole thing: the ones who organised everything and kept contacts throughout the Osterlands. Many of 'em weren't accused of bein' witches themselves, but that was useful 'cause that meant they were still able to move around in relative safety without fear of the Quisitors."

"Quisitors... as in, 'The Inquisition'...?" She asked slowly, momentarily forgetting that no one else present would have any knowledge of the history of the Catholic Church.

"Witch hunters..." Godfrey almost spat. "The Brotherhood's bully-boys, with *all* the authority that comes with The Shard at their back, and no one *dares* get in their way for fear of denouncement. There was a time not so long ago when no one would *think* about criticising The Shard or The Brotherhood: anyone who questioned 'em often ended up 'disappearing' or being found to be heretics, like I said. I've heard tell things have been less strict of late – that people have started using these new *machines* in spite of The Brotherhood denouncing them as evil, and there's been talk of some silly fools paintin' images of Nethug himself on city walls here and there – but it don't pay to take the Quisitors for granted, all the same."

"So they maintain control through *fear*, mostly?" Nev observed, deciding questions about the 'machines' and this mysterious 'Nethug' were best left for another time.

"*Everyone* fears the Quisitors," Lester observed darkly from the other side of the table. "They're no better 'n *animals*, the *bastards*...!" He'd been happy to simply sit and listen until then, but the tone of his voice now suggested a personal connection, and not a good one.

"Lester's sister was accused a witch..." Godfrey explained, drawing a surprised reaction from Nev as the boy turned away from them, hiding his face in the relative darkness. "T'were a long time ago, when he was only little, but he remembers well enough..."

"She *weren't* no witch…" he mumbled haltingly, and it was clear he was fighting back tears as he spoke. "Only thing she did wrong was refuse a *lord's* proposal… a lord who was in good with the Brotherhood. Those dogs took her… *took her away…*"

"How *awful…*!" Nev said softly, realising the statement was completely inadequate but not knowing what else to say. "How awful for you *and* your mum…!"

"Me ma kicked me out after that…" he sobbed softly, all the bravado and pretence of a twelve-year-old melting away in that moment of vulnerability. "Said it were *my* fault they'd taken her… that she should 'a just *married* that prancing git, and that it were *my* fault somehow that she'd said no…"

That unexpected revelation struck Nev like a physical blow, her stomach tightening and churning as the boy's heartfelt admission landed far too close to home. Even from the few basic details he'd given, it was already clear that Lester's mother had probably been suffering from grief – possibly some kind of mental health issue like PTSD, from what little she knew of that condition – and otherwise decent people often did wild or irrational things when placed under moments of great stress… or loss.

His words had also dredged up a mountain of her own unpleasant memories however, and sitting there in that *other* world so *completely* different to her own, having just faced life-threatening danger several times in the space of twenty-four hours, Nevaeh Anderson found that for the first time in six years she was able to look at what had happened in her own life with a totally different perspective. Every part of her being from the old world she'd grown up was howling for her to remain silent – to do *anything* other than share her own pain with strangers – but she instinctively knew that what she'd already been through *with* them during that last twenty-four hours had nevertheless formed a bond that deserved better.

"You know, Lester…" Nev began haltingly, surprising Godfrey with the emotion in her voice as a single tear formed and trickled down her cheek "…when I was ten, *my* mother did something *terrible…*"

There was a moment or two of loaded silence before Lester turned on his seat toward her, snuffling and using his sleeve to wipe self-consciously at his nose and eyes.

"What… what did *she* do…?"

"Well..." Nev continued, voice almost breaking in that moment, "...my father caught her cheating with another man... somebody she knew from work..."

"Did – did he beat her, your father?" The boy asked carefully, imagining reactions he'd seen so many times in his own world over such transgressions. "Did he throw her out...?"

"*No...*" she breathed softly, shaking now as she fought against the emotion that was building up inside. "He didn't do *anything*. He loved her very much, so he tried to *forgive* her... we *both* did..."

"What...?" Lester began to ask, but Godfrey could see there was far more to come yet in the tale she was telling, and he quickly leaned across and rested a gentle hand on the boy's arm, silencing him.

"They tried *so* hard to work things out, but... but my mother couldn't stand the guilt... couldn't forgive *herself* for what she'd done..." Tears were streaming freely down her cheeks now as she went on. "It was six months later she killed herself... Dad came home and found her lying on their bed, as it it'd been no fuss at all. He said – he said it was like she was just sleeping... just taking a nap in the afternoon..."

The terrible, shattering pain that Nev had hidden and bottled up inside for so long came flooding out now, eager to be set free after so many years locked away. She couldn't look at either of them as she spoke, instead staring fixedly at a point on the back wall of the deck near the crackling stove.

"There wasn't *really* any right or wrong about what she'd done... the cheating, I mean. I didn't know at the time, but I think they hadn't been happy for a while and that if it was *anyone's* fault she looked for love somewhere else, it lay with *both* of them rather than just with her alone. I think that was why Dad forgave her... that he understood... but Mum... Mum had always been fragile... she'd *never* been a strong woman, emotionally, and I – I think in the end, him *forgiving* her actually made things worse... made it *impossible* for her to forgive herself." For the first time, Nev was voicing fears and suspicions she'd carried silently for far too long – dark theories developed over teenage years that had never really seen closure over her mother's death. "I think that maybe... *maybe*... if he'd shouted at her... thrown her out – even just for a little while to punish her for what she'd done – she might've been able to deal with the guilt over what'd happened and move on... to feel like she'd paid some kind of penance for what *she* saw as her own sins. Instead, the demons inside tore her apart...

"You see, Lester... good people – caring, *wonderful* people – sometimes do awful, *terrible* things after they've suffered some shock or loss that's too great for their mind to bear. They don't *mean* to hurt or betray the ones they love... they just can't help it. Nicole was my mother's name, and she hurt my father and I *terribly* when she took her own life... but there isn't a *day* goes by I don't miss her *so much*, and I know my Dad does too. I don't think *your* mum meant what she said about *you* either: she was just so hurt and lost after your sister died that she couldn't cope without finding someone – *anyone* – to blame. I think she'd be sorry for what she's done..." she added, suddenly realising something else that seemed relevant both for Lester *and* for herself "...and I don't think there's *any* shame or anything to feel guilty about in admitting you still miss her... that you still love her *no matter* what..."

Part of her had known all of it – understood all of what she'd just said – for a very long time, but that moment as the three of them sat around a table beneath the bridge of the *Sea Skimmer* was the first time she'd ever had the courage to face that fact and put what she'd felt about her mother's suicide into words... to *express* it to others. As raw as Nev now felt, her own pain and vulnerability exposed, part of her rational mind also somehow understood that it was probably something she should've done a long time ago.

For Lester's part, there seemed no words at all he could think of: in that moment, the larrikin, outwardly tough exterior of a lost boy forced prematurely into the streets to fend for himself had all been stripped away, leaving just the fragility of a twelve-year-old who still desperately needed his mother's love and comfort... a boy who'd never been given the opportunity to properly grieve for his own sister in the aftermath of her death.

There was no bravado in his expression now, and his eventual reaction was the most honest Godfrey had ever seen: Lester almost leaped from the bench he was sitting on and threw his arms around Nev, hugging her tightly and burying his face into her shoulder as he tried to stifle the sobs that were now wracking his small frame. She returned the embrace without hesitation, as if some latent maternal instinct already knew exactly what to do. They remained that way for some time, the boy sobbing quietly and Nev staring blankly into the middle distance, thinking deeply and with a very new perspective on the demons of her own past.

Godfrey was the first to move, knowing better than to ruin an important moment with words as he rose to his feet and moved around the table, intending to settle down for some well-earned rest. As he passed where Nev sat, he stopped for a moment to lay a reassuring hand on Lester's shoulder, at the same time fixing her with an honest and clearly thankful stare as he silently nodded his appreciation of what had just happened. She could only stare back with tear-filled eyes and return a faint nod of her own, along with a 'what-else-could-I-do?' shrug, at which point he nodded faintly again and turned toward the nearest of the nearby cots.

"Come on, Lester..." she suggested eventually, patting him gently on the back as he reluctantly opened his embrace and drew back a little. "...We need to get some sleep: there's a long voyage ahead for all of us tomorrow..."

"D'you *really* think me ma still misses me?" He asked in a soft, broken voice, again wiping at tears with his sleeve.

"Of course I do," she answered without hesitation as she rose from her own seat and laid a reassuring hand on his shoulder. "Of course I do. Let's get some rest, now... okay...?"

The other two were snoring softly in their cots within ten minutes, and a shaken Nev was left to stare at the deck above her, wondering what on earth had come into her to have shared anything so personal. At a whim, she drew out her phone – for the first time not even bothering to check for a network that still wasn't there – and recorded a short 'segment' for her imaginary vlog.

"At the moment I'm lying on a rough bed on the deck of some sailing ship, waiting to be taken off to a God-knows-where place rather disturbingly named 'Despair'..." she began, thinking over her current situation carefully. "I'm still no closer to finding my way home... if there *is* a way home... but I think at least I've made some friends here I can trust: friends who've already saved my life twice and – I *hope* – won't have to again.

"*Sensei* Honda has given me an incredibly beautiful katana..." she continued with a frown. "He seemed to have somehow known what was going to happen to me, or at least had *some* idea. I *should* be angry with him... should *hate* him for not warning me..." She paused, thinking about that for a long time. "I'm *not* though, although I'm not sure why. This morning, all I could think about was getting back to that *portal* thing – whatever it was – and getting home. That didn't work out, and I *nearly* got myself killed into the bargain. I *still* want to get home more than anything, but I think I need to listen to Godfrey for the time being: he seems to know what he's doing, and he's kept me safe so far.

"Who's Godfrey...?" She smiled coyly at the camera, her face vague and almost ethereal in the dim light of the screen. "More on *him* later, at a more appropriate time when I work out how I actually *feel* about him, but newsflash: *he's gorgeous...*!" She whispered, simultaneously excited and scandalised by the fact that she was admitting it even to an inanimate recording device. "If you get to see this, Dad, don't worry: I *think* I know what I'm doing, and I won't do anything silly." Her expression darkened then, showing much more sadness.

"I miss you, Dad... more than you can imagine. All I can think about is seeing you... of hugging you and being home safe again. Last night I was scared that'd never happen, but now..." she paused again, searching for some reason for her sudden certainty "...*now*, at least I have some *hope* that it's still possible. Godfrey says he thinks I'm strong enough – that he has faith in me – and *I* have faith in *him*... so maybe I *can* find a way."

With her recording done, she tucked her phone away, made sure her bag was secure beside her, and lay back once more, a thousand wild thoughts circling in her mind over what she'd experienced and what else might still lay ahead. She too was asleep minutes later, lost in strange, hopeful dreams.

It felt as if it were just moments later that she was shaken roughly awake once more, although it had in fact been three or four hours and there was now a glow behind the clouds on the eastern horizon. Birds were already singing all around as Godfrey shook her again, this time calling her name softly as her mind fought to clear the sleep from her thoughts.

"Nev... Nev, wake up *now*...!" He hissed urgently, and she could also hear Garbutt calling desperate orders from some distance away over the shouts and calls of the crew hurriedly going about their business.

"What – *what is it...*?" She blurted, forced into a suddenly nervous state by the unexpected nature of her waking. 'What's wrong?"

"It's the Blackwatch!" Godfrey whispered, crouched by her right side as she sat upright with a start. "They're taking over the ship!"

And as she looked out in fear across the open deck forward, she could already see Garbutt standing on the pier, arguing with a helmeted officer as a line of black-clad soldiers waited by the gangplank for the order to go aboard.

VIII

SECRETS

Standing thirty metres tall, Fortress Burnii's central keep was a simple, hexagonal affair with crenelated turrets at each corner for use by archers. A single keep wall surrounded the entire structure; roughly circular and around a hundred metres in diameter, it stood ten high and was also adorned with crenelated battlements and firing slots both for crossbowmen, their shorter-ranging iron bolts lethal against even the thickest armour.

At six equally-spaced points around that outer wall, squat, stubby towers rose a few metres above the battlements, each of them aligned with one of the hexagonal keep's corners and mounting a single large trebuchet seated on a rotating platform. At least four could be brought to bear on any target within range, allowing their well-trained crews to strike at landward targets up to three hundred metres away and even further out to sea to the north, firing as they were from atop a steep cliff that towered over two hundred metres above the road and the narrow beach below.

There were also defences for Burnii itself of course, with similar stone walls and towers surrounding most of the city and the docks, but the fortress to the east on Round Hill was the linchpin that held the rest together, having so far proven impregnable in three major sieges since its completion some fifty summers before.

Even from the lower ramparts that looked out over the framework of the chain-car platform, Princess Charleroi could pick out the faint smell of the city and the Burnii Docks below, teeming with life in much the same way – as she'd heard her old mentor, Randwick mutter unkindly once or twice – that a festering carcass writhed with maggots and other parasites as they feasted on its inevitable decay. Below them lay the largest city in Huon: a tainted jewel that was the kingdom's economic centre and one of the major ports connecting it to the rest of the world via trade ships and fishing fleets that sallied forth into Deepwater Strait and beyond every day to make their livelihoods. Her father often said that Fortress Cadle, the ancestral home of the Namur lineage, was Huon's 'heart', and by the same analogy, Burnii was the kingdom's 'lungs', breathing life into the nation through trade and through the tonnes of fish its ships brought in every evening to feed nobles and peasants alike throughout the land.

"Matron won't be pleased to see you out and about, young one..." Randwick observed, stepping up at her left shoulder as she stared down at the coastline below. "You *know* the law, and it applies to princesses the same as it does for fishwives! The King gave express orders you were *not* to be out in public on the journey from Cadle, and he'd have a heart attack seein' you standing like this at the railing. Heads'll roll if he finds out, more 'n like, and I've *no doubt* Madam Griselda will find way to blame *me* for it..." he added with an almost impish grin, a happy participant in the competitive rivalry that existed between the Princess' two primary carers.

Slightly stooped with age, the man must've once towered over most others, and his barrel-chest and broad shoulders still showed some of the immense strength and fitness he'd carried with him in his younger years. He made use of a thick, wooden staff now for support, its tip gnarled and battered like the head of a war club, and no one really knew exactly how old he was. Angelo, the First Lord's firstborn and one of Charli's few friends in court back at Cadle, thought Randwick might even be as old as sixty summers. She didn't really believe it, though – *no one* lived *that* long, after all – but he was certainly older than the King or anyone else the young princess had ever met, save perhaps for Cardinal De Lisle... or possibly Chief Quisitor Silas.

"I'm not *in* public," Charleroi pointed out proudly, making every advantage of the fact that the battlements from which the mechanical elevator rose and descended were still *technically* part of the castle's outer walls. I know father doesn't *really* believe any of that *anyway...* he's just being over-protective."

"Fortress grounds or not, you're *still* out in the open and away from *home*, Princess," Randwick countered evenly, trying to hide a wry smile, "and what *I* or His Majesty think of Keepsake Laws aside, I doubt a *Quisitor* would care for the finer points of your argument. I'll concede in *this* case but you should learn *not* to take these laws for granted. Why *has* 'The Grizzler' left you roaming about on yer own?" He added, changing the subject.

"*Matron* was too *scared* to ride the chain-car, so she left with the royal carriage *hours ago* to make the journey down by road," Charleroi added, making great show of an outward lack of fear over her first ride in this new, mechanical creation.

"And it frightens you *not*, I take it?" He asked in return with a faint smile still gracing his features, not believing such an insincere display of bravado. "But look, you: it draws near! Behold, whelp: here comes a wonder of this mechanical age!"

The old man leaned almost precariously over the railing as they looked down at the approaching chain-car, and The Princess – 'Charli' to her father and a precious few she considered close enough to be friends – flinched slightly in reaction to both his actions and the clatter of its rise toward them. The Princess generally hated being called such names and there were few who might get away with such a slight without reprimand or worse from The King. Randwick was one of those few, however.

"I've never ridden the chain-cart before, Randwick..." She remarked softly, trying to sound as brave as a sixteen-year-old was able but not really managing.

"You've never been *anywhere* beyond Cadle before..." Randwick observed kindly with a tilt of his head, "but aye, there's been a few 'firsts' on this trip, sure enough."

"It's *very high*... is it safe...?"

"Never heard tell of anyone ever dyin' from it..." he shrugged simply, as if that single sentence settled things in his mind. "I've ridden it a few times meself this last two weeks, and I came out no worse than I went in." He neglected to add that it nevertheless also frightened the living Crystal out of him every time he had.

On a viewing platform set at a slightly higher level, no more than a dozen metres away, three whiskered old men stood with grave expressions, all dressed in identical hooded robes of thick brown wool. In unison, all three chanted softly and without falter, the words too soft to be intelligible although the unmistakable meter of prayer in the faint thrumming of their voices carried well enough across the intervening distance.

Charleroi knew well enough what they were doing – protesting the use of an 'infernal device' (the chain-car) – and they didn't need to be loud or to make a scene for their presence to be felt: *everyone* already knew where the Brotherhood of The Shard stood on the 'evils' of mechanical invention. In their hands they carried their personal prayer books, each one wrapped in the chain of a Holy Pendant identical to the one De Lisle had used at Endweek.

"Merry and Annabel think it's a 'tool of Nethug'..." She whispered nervously as she sent the murmuring monks a sidelong glance, recalling the overheard conversation between the two maids

"'*The Corpse-Eater*...?" He asked in a tone that tried unsuccessfully to sail a steady course directly between scorn and amusement as she nodded quickly. "Well, people think and say all sorts o' things, not all of 'em true or even sensible... Look now for yourself and tell me what *you* think..." he added, more thoughtful this time as he nodded toward the rattling cage of wood and iron that was now little more than a few metres away, below the edge of the rampart to their right.

"Well... the carts are fashioned by smithies and carpenters..." she reasoned cautiously, understanding – as was usually the case – that there was something deeper hidden within the old man's question. "So *they're* just iron cages on wooden frames... just like *any* old wagon."

"And what carries them up and down the mountainside? Do they fly on the wings of *dragons*...?" He asked impishly, the gentle sarcasm evident in his tone.

"A pair of *bullocks* turn a wheel, and that winds a chain..." she frowned in mild exasperation, suspicious that he might be teasing her "...with that big rock 'thingy' tied to the other end..." she added, pointing down to the left at the parallel track that carried the cart's large, stone counterweight on a similar set of cast-iron bogies."

"And what is it that the '*rock thingy*' does...?"

"It..." she began, staring down over the iron railing now and thinking very hard until the light of realisation blossomed in her eyes. "It *balances* everything!" She declared triumphantly, looking eagerly up and Randwick and receiving a nod of approval that filled her with hard-won pride. "It makes it easier to move the cart up and down!"

"And, does *that* seem like 'Majik' to you?"

"*That's* not Majik... that's just... just..." she paused, trying to remember a new word she'd heard her father use two nights ago on the balcony... "Science...!"

"Science, indeed..." he nodded, hiding most of the pride he felt over Princess Charleroi's display of logical reasoning. "Concepts called 'engineering' and 'mechanics', and other ideas: yes, that *is* science..."

"So…" she began again, hesitant now as she ventured back to a subject that she instinctively understood was far more contentions (and possibly dangerous into the bargain). "If it's all just *building* things… *science* and… '*mechanics*'… and stuff, why do The Brothers say it's something else… that it's *bad*…?"

"The Brotherhood wants everyone to believe that *true* power rests solely with the Gods of the Dragon Shard…" Randwick growled softly, giving the deity its full name, and Charleroi was surprised to note that even *he* carefully lowered his voice as he threw his own furtive glance in the priests' direction. "*Through them*, of course," he added caustically, unable to keep the sneer from either his face or tone, "and they're not short of tryin' *anything* to keep us all believin' that."

"But… but, the chain-car, the spinning wheels, the ploughs and all the other machines *help* people… help them to work *better*…" she pointed out, again recalling the conversation her father. "If these mechanical things *aren't* Bad Majik, why would they *say* that…?"

"I'll let you think on that a while and tell me yerself," the old man suggested instead, nodding toward the safety gate to the chain-car as its roof appeared over the parapet for the first time and it shuddered to a loud, clattering halt. "You can give me the answer another time: it's time to put your visard on and take the ride down…"

Of course, she peeked. The chain-ride was the highlight of the entire journey for Charleroi, mostly because it was the only time during the last two days she'd been allowed into the open to actually look around her kingdom, even if that *was* only for a moment. The journey from Cadle had been comfortable but boring, travelling as she was within a specially-fitted royal carriage flanked by a company of elite cavalry for protection. The honour guard was mostly for show as Huon was currently at peace, after all, but it paid to be careful nevertheless and King Phaesus wasn't about to risk the life of his only child in any way.

Being accustomed to having the run of the castle at home and being naturally curious in any case, Charli hated being locked away inside that wagon and Griselda's protestations notwithstanding, the only thing that had *truly* stopped her from throwing open the carriage's bolted shutters was the fact that her father had expressly forbid it in no uncertain terms. Huon was changing, as were the rest of the Osterland Kingdoms to varying extents, but the one constant that applied to kings and emperors alike was that *no one* dared test The Brotherhood on The Keepsake Law.

They'd arrived at the fortress the night before, approaching via the inland route from Cadle, and it was dusk by the time the entourage completed its journey up the long, winding trail that approached the summit of Round Hill from the south. With a few hours' rest and a good nights' sleep, the intention had been to end their journey the next morning at the Burnii Longhouse: a huge structure that it was said predated even Cadle, and had once been the seat of Huon's government prior to the completion of that great fortress above Peaceful Lake.

Travelling with her matron and mentor – both charged with providing their own style of protection against any threat the Princess might face – Charleroi has been completely honest in her statement regarding Griselda's fear of taking the chain car. Faced with the two-hour downward journey back along the southern trail, she'd argued, pleaded and cajoled in her attempts to have Charleroi accompany her in the carriage but it had been all in vain. Out in the world for the first time, the first in line for the Throne of Huon had remained resolute in her desire to experience this new mechanical wonder that had been in operation now for just a few short weeks.

The chain-car itself was a rather basic contraption, little more – as Charleroi had so perfectly described – than an iron cage on a wooden frame. Barely large enough for more than five or six people at a time, the ride was loud and bumpy and sometimes terrifying in bad weather, with most of the passenger area open to the elements save for a half-hearted attempt at providing at least some kind of thin, wooden roof that might be hard-pressed to keep out even the lightest rain. There were hand-rails built into the inner sides of the cage, and the entire thing was canted forward just enough to remain basically vertical as the bogies attached to its base trundled slowly down a pair of thick, steel rails set into a wooden framework that was fixed into the sides of the very cliff itself.

On the opposite side of the castle, the single, southern access track wound its way down Round Hill to the farmland below, curving around and finally ending up at sea level not far from the main coastal road running between Burnii and Demon's Port, forty kilometres east. It was an arduous and time-consuming journey of at least three kilometres down that undulating hillside and the construction of the chain car had been a direct attempt to speed up the journey down to the city for anyone important enough to deserve such consideration.

The final run from Cadle to Burnii was similarly spent locked away in the comfortable but oh-so-claustrophobic confines of her royal carriage, with a grumpy Matron Griselda her only companion the entire time – as usual – although that last leg of the journey was at least a far shorter one of just a half-hour or so.

Charleroi had been allowed the freedom to roam the halls of the Burnii Longhouse upon arrival. Her father, who'd arrived midway through the preceding afternoon with his own cavalry escort, had ensured all the ground floor windows had been boarded up in an attempt to walk a middle road between upholding the law and allowing his only child to wander about without restriction. The nature of the coming meetings meant there were plenty of guards posted at every exit anyway, inside and out, leaving no likelihood of any accidents or misunderstandings with regard to her whereabouts.

The Longhouse was a truly gigantic building that covered hundreds of square metres, built on the western bank of the Mu River as it opened out into a shallow bay. It towered over the docks and warehouses that lay to its west: three storeys of sprawling magnificence constructed around the single, central meeting hall that gave the entire structure its name. Charleroi's private chambers were on the third floor overlooking the bay, and the one concession to her confinement that her father had permitted was the wide, covered balcony that allowed her to at least look out across great expanses of Deepwater – the wild, stormy strait that separated Huon from the rest of the Osterlands.

It was well into afternoon as the princess walked that balcony, sea birds filling the skies and wheeling this way and that as she stood at the wooden railing and stared out longingly at the choppy surf below. A full moon was already visible, a blotted disc of pale white at the centre of a narrow strip of clear blue that lay between the northern horizon and the customary blanket of grey/white clouds that covered the rest of the sky above.

To her left, the town spread out beyond the docks, a hive of activity that was faintly audible in the calls of market hawkers and the clatter of wagons as the chaotic symphony reached her softly at the balcony railing. Down in the bay itself, the ships of Huon's war fleets could be seen at anchor, their oars raised at rest and their crews nowhere to be seen save for one or two men on watch.

"We're fortunate there's a breeze coming off Deepwater this afternoon," Matron Griselda observed with a pinched expression, going about the business of fluffing the princess' pillows and sliding a long-handled bed warmer beneath the sheets for later, the flat, lidded pan leaving a faint trail of grey smoke in its wake from the hot coals she'd just shovelled inside.

"*Much* nicer than this morning, Matron, yes," Charleroi agreed with a frown of her own, happy there was no longer any hint of the vague but nevertheless potent stench of the town that she'd experienced earlier. Human waste, random garbage and the rotting remains of fish left over from the preceding day's catches had all added their own individual and varied bouquets to the general malaise of smells that had wafted across the balcony and into her chambers, and the wind change after midday had been welcome indeed, bringing with it the cool freshness of the open sea.

For all that, there was still part of Charleroi that longed to be able to venture out on her own: to experience what it was truly like to walk among her people and *see* the sights for herself… *experience* those smells in person, good *and* bad. Considering the town itself was reported to be completely free from Keepsakes, she'd argued during the morning that perhaps she might at least be allowed out to ride through the streets, taking in the sights for herself. Matron had refused, *of course*, and had threatened to tell the king when Charli had persisted, leaving the princess in a huff that had lasted at least an hour.

Griselda had never married, instead pledging her servitude to her royal charge, but she had sisters and she knew *exactly* what men were like. Brutes, most of them, and now that the princess had well and truly come of age it was *her* duty more than any other's to protect the innocent young woman from the unsavoury advances of footpads, servants and conniving young noblemen alike. There might not be *Keepsakes* within the city, but there were plenty of *other* dangers a beautiful young woman would do well to avoid.

"I still don't understand the harm of walking *inside* the walls…" Charleroi observed evenly, no longer angry but persisting nevertheless as she drew a deep breath of air in through her nose and savoured the refreshing tang of saltwater that came with it.

"You'll understand better when you're older, Your Highness," the old woman answered almost by rote, not even thinking about it. "The commonfolk are often exactly that – *common* – and there's plenty of sights inside these walls a young woman'd be better off *not* seein'."

"I'd have an *escort* with me, Griselda... how dangerous *could* it be?"

"It's not often I'd admit to bein' in agreement with the Matron, but I do in *this* case..." Randwick observed drily from her chamber door, bothering to knock only after they'd both turned in surprise toward the sound of his voice.

"Yes, *brutes*..." Griselda growled softly in affirmation, fixing him with a severe gaze. "It's *customary* for a man to knock *before* entering a young woman's chambers, Master Randwick," she added, instinctively placing herself between the newcomer and any potential view of the princess, regardless of the fact that the girl was fully clothed and that the man in question was undoubtedly the most trustworthy in the entire kingdom, with the exception of His Royal Majesty himself.

"It's *also* customary to keep a young woman's chamber door *closed* if one requires privacy, Mistress Griselda," he countered with a wry half-smile, executing a bow in her honour that was *just* formal enough to avoid any accusation of humour at her expense. "I come at the king's bidding in any case," he added with a flourishing sweep of his hand to round out the bow. "He's requested your presence, Princess, as an observer to his afternoon audiences..." he paused for a moment as a soft set of melodic chimes rang out in the hallway behind to signal the turn of the hour, and he leaned back to throw a glance at a free-standing tower clock pushed against a nearby wall, its long, polished pendulum swinging slowly back and forth. "...Although I'll warrant we've a little time to kill yet..."

"You'll no doubt make yourself at home, then..." Griselda grumped for the sake of it, not having any particular gripe against Randwick *per se* but having decided a long time ago that as mentor of the princess' *womanly* development, a Matron should by definition stand opposed in principle to the man tasked with instruction in the more *manly* arts that were an unfortunate necessity of being next in line to the throne, regardless of gender.

"You're welcome to stand by, Mother..." he offered with another grin, using a term that was *technically* respectful but was nevertheless somewhat insulting coming from a man who was clearly her senior in years. "We've no conversation between us you cannot hear…"

"And spend a handful listening to the pair of you argue at length over the right tension for a bow or the most advantageous number of tiers for a war galley?" Griselda asked disdainfully, having sampled their conversations before. "I'll respectfully decline, good sir," she conceded with a hand raised in tacit surrender. "I've staff to attend to in any case, so I'll bid you both farewell for the afternoon. In bed before the ninth hour if you please, Master Randwick…" she warned as an afterthought.

"I'll assume it's the *princess* you're meaning, Mistress…?" He asked with one eyebrow arched, as much innocence in his tone as he could manage without laughing as she pushed past him in a huff, Charleroi seemingly none the wiser regarding the potential hidden meaning he'd included in that reply.

"*Brutes…!*" Griselda declared once more in exasperation as the door closed behind her, and Randwick turned back toward the princess with a self-satisfied grin over an annoyance well done.

"Why d'you think I'd not be safe in the city, Randwick?" Charleroi asked pointedly, not about to let him get away without explaining his earlier comments. "What could *possibly* hurt me while surrounded by a troop of cavalrymen?"

Apart from the cavalrymen themselves… he asked silently, knowing as much about a man's darker side as Griselda and probably more. "You've *forgotten* that your uncle was assassinated just six months ago? Another time for *that* discussion, perhaps…" he declared, not waiting for a reply as he crossed the room in a few strides and stepped out onto the open balcony, also electing to stand at the railing a few feet to her left. "An impressive view, I admit…" he added, then changed the subject entirely. "Have you thought about our earlier discussion… about the machines…?"

"I have…"

"And you have an answer for me?"

"I – I *think* so…" She replied, less confident now, standing before a man whose opinion she respected more than any other save for her own father's. "I *think* The Brotherhood's dislike of these new machines *isn't* because they make life easier for the peasants, but because…" she paused for a moment, thinking hard on how to word the next part "…because The Book of the Shard says that *all* power to give and take life – to reward or to punish – remains with The Shard Gods... that The Dragon Shard is the only true way, and that all others are false." That part, she was basically reciting by rote from the religious classes that were compulsory for all children not yet come of age.

"And why is that important...?"

"Because..." she continued, thinking on the fly "...*because... every* Endweek, peasants, commoners, nobles and royal families alike *must* go to the temples for The Service: where they present their tithe for the week and receive The Blessing in return... and the prelate presides over baptisms for any newborns."

"It's the *one* constant in *all* our lives..." Randwick observed with a wry smile. "I've travelled far in my younger days, and I can tell you that the Endweek Service is the *one thing* that's kept sacred throughout *all* the known kingdoms. Few dare to defy The Brotherhood on this... we all 'know' what happens otherwise..." he added pointedly, raising one eyebrow.

Everyone knew the stories, handed down through the generations. Somewhere – usually far away in another part of the Osterlands – some small hamlet or village had begun to fall by the wayside: to turn away from their spirituality and the True Path. Endweek attendances began to drop... tithes became smaller and smaller... and eventually – the story always told – no one came to the services at all.

The Shard Gods tolerated this for a time, hoping that the people might see the error of their ways and come back to the fold, and all was well for those who did. For the others, however there was invariably disaster. The actual 'punishments' varied dramatically – bushfire, disease, or (in some extreme cases) a Night Dragon falling from the sky to destroy an entire farm in thunder and flame – but the result was always the same: death and destruction for the infidel. Neither subtle nor apologetic in its delivery, the message was simple: defy The Shard or turn away from the True Path and sooner or later there'd be consequences of a most extreme and terminal nature.

"Do *you* believe the stories?" Charleroi asked in return, trying to sound mature and logical but nevertheless not quite able to shake the fear of retribution that was drummed weekly into every man, woman and child by the Endweek Service.

"There've not been many such stories lately I've heard of," Randwick conceded with a frown, his expression darkening

187

momentarily, "but I *did* see the aftermath of one such incident many years ago." He shook his head faintly, almost shuddering even now as he recalled the experience. "I'll not frighten you with details of what I saw, but I *will* say that the poor devils who'd lived at that farm all suffered *terrible* deaths." He raised another eyebrow then. "What *caused* those deaths is another thing entirely. If it were an animal, then it was one of the like *I've* never seen before, and whether it had *anything* to do with The Shard or those farmers not turning up at Endweek? Well... who can say...? Either way, it serves the purpose of The Brotherhood to speak of it as vengeance, and it's safer for everyone else to accept that explanation and maintain their piety: in a sense, *everyone* 'wins'..."

"But if these things *aren't* sent from The Shard, what *are* they?" She asked pointedly, thinking back over the story her father had recounted of his search for a Night Dragon and remembering that Randwick had been with Phaesus at the time. A far darker thought the followed, unnerving her a little. "If it *isn't* the work of the gods, then who or what *did* do it...?"

"Your father's personally ordered a *number* of investigations to determine exactly that," Randwick ventured cautiously, having often *privately* wondered exactly the same thing, "and he's had word that similar such 'independent' queries have also been made in other kingdoms. My *own* experience with such an incident was while leading one of those investigations and as has always been the case, no clear evidence of *human* involvement was ever *proven*..." He paused, then added with even greater caution: "...And I should think twice – nay, *three times* – before speaking of these matters with *anyone* else: there are *many* ways to 'anger' The Shard Gods, and missing Endweek is but *one* of them. The greatest enemy of piety is doubt, and as easy as it is to forget in these modern times, a cardinal may raise an Inquisition *anytime* he so desires.... The Brotherhood will *never* tolerate *doubt*."

"Then for *them*, every new machine – every invention like the spinning wheel or the chain-car – must seem *filled* with doubt," she mused softly, her conviction firming as she thought deeply on what they'd discussed. "If *machines* make life easier for the commoners – and in turn for the nobles too – then perhaps they fear the people will see no *need* to pray to The Shard for benevolence. How many times have pious farmers been faced with drought and pestilence, only to be told that it was the 'Will of the Gods'; that it was 'Part of the Plan'?"

"They *tolerate* these new inventions at the moment," Randwick admitted, "but only *grudgingly*. I *think* only because they know how much dissent they'll create amongst farmers and factory hands alike who would lose so much now if machines were taken away. It's *difficult* to take something back once given, and there's *always* bad feeling afterward. I know De Lisle *has* spoken to your father at least twice about *limiting* the use of machines throughout the kingdom, but the king didn't seem to think he was all that serious. The Brotherhood's biding its time at the moment, perhaps *hoping* everything will settle down, but they'll not stand for a *moment* if they think their authority is being questioned."

"But machines *do* threaten them! A *machine* can perform the same duty in the same way *every single time*... day in, day out..." Charleroi continued along her original train of thought, opening her mind to new ideas now as they came thick and fast. "*Machines* don't need *prayers* to provide service, and that service isn't dependent on the benevolence of a god. A 'believer' in machines... in *science*... has no need for *other* gods, and if the *people* no longer need gods, then *neither* do those who rule them."

"There is *so much* of your mother *and* father in you..." Randwick said softly, turning to stare down at her as pride filled him as never before.

"I never knew her..." Charleroi whispered, the sadness in her voice born of emptiness rather than a sense of loss.

"I had that honour..." Randwick declared softly, lowering his head out of respect for The Queen's memory, "and so wise and beautiful a woman I've never seen, before *or* since... save for *one*..."

The Princess opened her mouth as if to speak, realised what her mentor had meant by that last statement, then decided instead to remain silent, turning modestly away to hide the reddening of her cheeks.

"I think we should go, Your Highness," he added quickly, glancing back inside at the clock inside once more. "Your father will be expecting to see you..."

"Am I presentable, good sir?" She asked nervously, suddenly very concerned she mightn't be dressed well enough for an official audience.

"I'm no judge, Milady, as you're *always* perfection to me," he replied gallantly, giving another flourishing bow, "but I'll warrant

Matron would never have left you for me to take to court if she'd not thought you dressed properly."

He took a step back and regarded her with a critical eye for the first time. Clothed in a long, flowing dress of pale blue silk adorned with intricate lace patterning, and with her dark hair tied and gathered in tresses at her back, she looked every bit a noblewoman of royal lineage.

"The courtiers may be struck dumb upon first laying eyes on you, Princess," he suggested impishly, "so I'd wear your tiara to remind them of their place... but *otherwise*, a *picture* of grace and beauty."

"Your gallantry is a credit to you, sir," she acknowledged playfully, almost drunk on the endorphins of flattery as she executed a curtsey in response. "Will you do me the honour of escorting me to the Longhouse?"

"The honour is all mine, Your Highness..."

The actual proceedings were terribly boring, with Charleroi spending most of her time watching quietly from an upper viewing chamber, seated alone in the front row of a small cluster of padded seats set at a second-storey level that overlooked the main hall below. There were a number of such chambers along each wall, their express purpose to provide comfortable seating for guests and nobles to look on from a discrete distance as affairs of state were discussed below. She'd barely had time to say hello to her father before they'd begun – no more than a single kiss on the cheek, a hug and a kind word before he bade her retire to the chamber in which she now sat to simply 'observe'.

She watched her father now as he sat at the head of a cluster of curved tables, assembled in the centre of the room to form a great ring with dozens of seats positioned about its outer circumference. Directly opposite the throne, a narrow opening between the tables allowed passage, and custom held that whether there were two present or two hundred, anyone addressing the royal party would stand, bow to the king, then enter that ring of tables and stand at its centre to make their case.

Most of the ceiling, which stood three floors above the hall itself, was comprised of stained glass fixed into iron frames. The design produced a stunning effect of decorative illumination that sent beams of multi-coloured light across all four walls surrounding that circular table, and set into each wall, large fireplace also spat and crackled as piles of thick logs burned atop glowing embers. Paired guards with swords at their belts stood at each entrance – of which there was one in each of the four walls – and in several of the empty audience chambers on Charleroi's level, she noted with interest that one or two of the king's elite archers were also lounging quietly in the semi-darkness, able to watch over the whole show without appearing too obtrusive.

Phaesus had ruled Huon for just six months, having been forced prematurely into the role after the murder of his older brother, Rizal at the hand of an unknown assassin. There'd been only one ruler likely to have ordered such a killing and in earlier times, war between Huon and the Blacklands would've been a certainty after such an act. Phaesus IV however was a ruler with very different ideas to those of his brother and father before him, and in spite of great personal grief he'd pushed ahead with a softer approach with the hope of a better future.

Alliances forged with the Crowedans and the Westerland, followed by similar agreements with Swales and the Sun Empire soon after, had gone a long way toward laying the groundwork for this final treaty with Huon's only remaining enemy. The Osterlands as a whole was tired of the almost constant conflict that had engulfed it for more than two generations, and although Huon still suffered the occasional raid from Westerland pirates on occasion, tensions had generally eased across the entire continent.

It was this very real opportunity for lasting peace that made this final accord so important. The only remaining enemy – ever Huon's greatest and most dangerous – was Harald the Black, his kingdom twice the size and able to muster a similarly greater number of men. Three times in a generation, The Blackwatch had landed on Huon soil, only to be beaten back and defeated by the effectiveness of the Huon war fleet in destroying supply and halting invasions on the beaches themselves.

It stood to reason however that this good fortune couldn't last forever and Phaesus was now working hard to secure a final, binding treaty with the men of the Blacklands that had eluded his predecessors throughout their reigns; the very same one they'd all come to Burnii now to settle so that once and for all, there could finally be peace throughout the whole of the Osterlands.

The real ceremonies were yet to come. King Harald and his entourage were due to arrive within days, at which time there'd be much rejoicing and celebration at the completion of this last step toward lasting peace. Yet as always, a king's work was never done and there were a multitude of far less interesting yet no less important matters of state that required consideration, whether the king held court at Cadle or anywhere else.

Discussions went on for hours. Charleroi couldn't tell exactly how long, for the only clock in the room was positioned well below and outside her line of sight where the king could see it, however servants had brought a tray of bread and meat at one point, suggesting it had been close enough to dinner time. What she *did* know was that it was incredibly boring, sitting up and not *really* listening as a procession of nobles and wealthy guildsmen bleated on about minor issues affecting their own, tiny little worlds.

Each had sat patiently, waiting for a turn to present his case, and Phaesus listened intently to each and every one, nodding here and there, passing soft comment or asking the occasional short but pointed question before handing down his royal verdict, everything recorded by the royal scribe that always sat at the king's left hand, scribbling away in his own coded, scratch-like scrawling as he recorded every word and detail of what had transpired.

Randwick sat at the king's right, one of just a handful of the king's trusted advisors present that evening. Her father had also grown up under Randwick's mentorship and it was no surprise that the king at times still sought the counsel and support of one of his most trusted men. The princess understood how important it was for him to be down there at that moment, but it also meant that she was left all alone, and she definitely wasn't enjoying it as the third guildsman in a row droned on about how vagrant boggans had been breaking into his factories, stealing his wares and vandalising his new machinery.

As that too came to an end, Phaesus paused the proceedings for just long enough to have a quiet word with Randwick, the two whispering together for just a few seconds before the older man nodded once, rose from his seat and bowed deeply as he took his leave. He moved directly for the nearest door and slipped through quickly as a guard held it open for him. Down below, Phaesus continued on with the next order of business without a second thought.

Randwick stepped through the small door at the rear of her audience chamber a moment later, and she rose to meet him, happy to finally have company.

"Your father sends his apologies regarding the standard of discussion this evening and tasks me to send you away to bed," he advised immediately, disappointment showing on her face as she realised that he meant for her to go alone.

"You're not to escort me?"

"I'm sorry, Your Highness... the king needs me back downstairs: there are important matters yet to be discussed before this night's done."

"So I'm to find my way back *all alone*..." she grumped, making a statement rather than asking a question.

"Aye, if y' so choose..." he replied with a smirk, not falling for her feigned indignance for a moment, "*or* I can call one o' the courtiers to show you the way. Might take a while to find one at this time o' night, but you've nowhere *else* to go, after all..."

"You're *mean*...!" She observed, fighting a smile of her own and not at all looking forward to the idea of listening to any more talk of trade deals and petty vandalism. "Don't bother... I can find my own way back."

"Straight down these steps..." he advised helpfully, turning back toward the stairs he'd just climbed beyond the open doorway, "...then take a right, head straight down the end of the corridor, *another* right, then up two flights of stairs and your chambers are right there on the left. Can you remember all that?"

"Of *course*...!" She frowned, already struggling to commit his rapid-fire directions to memory but not about to admit defeat. "You just go off and do *whatever it is* that you must..."

"Believe me, Princess..." he confided honestly with a grimace, once more refusing to take the bait of her attempt at sympathy. "If I were given a choice, I'd take being your escort over sitting in on this drivel *any time*, but the king commands and I must obey..." he added ruefully. "And so must *you*! Away with you, now, or I'll have the scruffiest guard I can find take you instead."

"*Eww*...!" She bleated softly, mostly sure he was joking but not willing to risk it as she slipped past him and made her way down the stairs at a good pace.

"To the *right*...!" He called helpfully, only to be met with a faint squeal of exasperation as the princess reached the bottom, veered right as instructed and disappeared from view.

Of *course*, she'd gotten lost. It had taken all of perhaps ten minutes to realise that fact as Charleroi rounded a hallway corner and came face to face with the same painting of a rider on horseback she'd now seen three times. Steeling herself against a powerful desire to loudly and rudely verbalise her frustration and embarrassment, she turned and stalked slowly back the way she'd come, attempting to backtrack to a point where she once more recognised her surroundings in the maze of rooms and corridors that filled the spaces around that great, central hall.

There was no way she could safely seek help from anyone else. Word was certain to get back to Randwick, and she'd never hear the end of it: it just wouldn't do! There was nothing for it but to soldier on, suffer in silence, and find her way back to her chambers alone, even if it took all night. She was still on the second floor and as she passed a wide set of stairs leading both up and down, she paused for a moment to gather her wits, collect her bearings and try to decide which way she needed to go next. Downstairs again, she decided, to find her starting point and begin again from scratch.

It was at that point, halfway down and leaning on the thick, wooden bannister, that she heard voices below accompanied by the clatter of many footsteps as whoever it was made their way along the long corridor at the bottom of the stairs. She considered for a moment whether she should bite the bullet and ask for directions, but her pride was too great and it also dawned on her in that moment that there seemed to be *a lot* of people down there... certainly more in one place than one might expect, so late into the evening.

Curiosity got the better of her then, and rather than show herself or withdraw, Charleroi instead decided to creep carefully down to the landing between floors, crouch down behind the corner of the balustrade and peer around it, silently observing the scene that was unfolding below.

De Lisle was of exceptionally poor mood as he stalked along the corridors about the Great Meeting Hall, followed as usual by a half-dozen lesser brothers; his own personal collection of customary retainers, social-climbers and hangers-on of a generic type that invariably gravitated toward men of power. It was within *his* power to dismiss all of them... even have them tortured and executed, should he have so desired... yet as much as the idea appealed on occasion, he generally refrained from ordering such brutal activity. Those aspiring to greater things were often better kept close where they could be observed, rather than allowed to hide dark places where plots and conspiracies grew faster than mushrooms ever could.

It was true – at the moment, at least – that none would dare challenge him while he held direct counsel with The Shard, however all things were subject to change and even a cardinal could still grow old, become infirm... or choke on a thimbleful of poison, slipped into his cocoa on a cold, winter's eve. De Lisle's position came with its own set of challenges (and an official food taster), but he mostly enjoyed his duties and he *definitely* enjoyed the comforts, perks and luxuries that came with them (his taster, perhaps less so...).

It was however the cardinal's firm belief that The Brotherhood currently faced the greatest threat to its existence he'd ever encountered. While that frightened him more than a little, in a way he was also glad that this perceived crisis had come while he was still in charge. The world they currently knew might've been doomed, had its fate rested with some inexperienced successor, whereas De Lisle, concerned as he was, was nevertheless supremely confident in his own ability to successfully guide The Brotherhood through the current crisis.

"Silas...!" He barked sharply, halting without warning and causing some of his posse to collide awkwardly with each other rather than sign their own death sentence by bumping into him instead.

"Your Grace...?"

Quisitor Silas wasn't one of the cardinal's usual entourage, but he was rarely out of earshot when travelling in Huon and *always* managed to appear when De Lisle called, seemingly almost of thin air on occasion... which even the cardinal sometimes found a little disturbing.

Short and frail enough to be described as wizened, Silas was one of The Brotherhood oldest members, yet rather than seek power for himself, he'd instead carved out a niche for himself both as Chief Quisitor and as one of De Lisle's most indispensable movers and shakers. Pinched features, watery eyes and a laughable pair of *pince-nez* spectacles were excellent camouflage for a sharp, calculating and *exceptionally* cruel mind, and it was the very fact that Silas had never shown any ambition for further advancement that made him so perfect as an assistant and confidant.

"Send word to Furphy and Connor immediately that the audience with the king went about as well as was to be expected – which is to say '*badly*' – and confirm they're to proceed as planned."

"Of course, Your Grace…" Brother Silas nodded immediately, making a clear mental note for later.

"Any word on the witch…?"

"Nothing yet I'm afraid, Your Grace…" he replied immediately, with less enthusiasm. The news over the last forty-eight hours hadn't been good, and he knew how much had been riding on the success of *that* particular operation. "I have Brother Trabant holding direct communion through The Shard as we speak, awaiting any further developments. As soon as our brothers in the Blacklands know more, we too shall be informed."

"See to it…" De Lisle suggested coldly, neither man at all concerned that extended direct communication with The Shard might eventually destroy Brother Trabant's less experienced mind. "We need to deal with this before she falls into the wrong hands: we *cannot* allow *that* to happen."

"Our men are clear in their orders, Your Grace… they will not fail you."

"And *Gregor*…?"

"Already done, Your Grace… word of his incompetence will not spread. What of the *other* one?" Silas added eagerly, a dark smile flickering momentarily across his lips. "She's still being held at the Welshport temple. Is she also to be disposed of?"

"She's to be kept alive for the time being," De Lisle countered with a shake of his head, frowning as he noted the dark disappointment that showed in Silas' face at that moment. "Those are orders *direct* from The Shard, so you can *forget* any designs you may have in *that* regard… for the time being, at least…" he added eventually, thinking that perhaps it never hurt to keep one's hopes alive. "Although it may be of some use to question her regarding the other one," the cardinal decided suddenly, changing his mind. "You can take care of *that* personally. Have her thrown on the fastest ship you can find and meet them at Long Hop… from *there*, whatever means you use to extract information is at *your* discretion, so long as she's not *badly* damaged…"

"Your Grace…" Silas acknowledged finally, mostly hiding his excitement as he bowed in farewell. He moved to depart, paused for a moment as if distracted by something, then cast his pale gaze directly up into the darkness of the nearby stairwell, trying to decide whether he'd actually heard something or not.

"All's well, Brother Silas...?" De Lisle inquired softly, noting the man's momentary hesitation and recognising it as being out of character.

"Nothing... nothing, Your Grace..." Silas replied instantly, shaking his head as he turned to stare at his superior once more. "Probably just rats... by your leave..." This time be departed without hesitation, disappearing down the hallway almost as quickly as he'd originally appeared.

"You'd all do well to learn from that one..." De Lisle observed with a wry smile, enjoying the fact that each one of his gathered lackeys flinched noticeably as his gaze fell upon each of them in turn.

"Cardinal...!"

His name had been called from the far end of the hall, cutting off anything else he might've said, and he forced a smile onto his face as he turned to face the newcomer, insincerity oozing from every pore.

"Deputy-Viceroy Garrick, a *pleasure* as always..." he declared loudly, extending his right hand in greeting as Edward Garrick accepted it with equal formality and made a show of kissing the man's ceremonial ring.

"You honour us with your presence as always, Your Grace..." Garrick conceded with a tilt of his head, before extending an arm down the hallway in the direction he'd come. "I trust your audience with the king went well?"

"As well as was expected..." De Lisle answered coldly, seeing no need to elaborate as he had just moments before.

"A shame that no accord could be reached," Garrick offered with a shrug, already aware of what had transpired. "Huon has *always* been a tireless supporter of The Brotherhood's fight against evil and their selfless provision of counsel and redemption for all."

"Mmmh," the cardinal mused dubiously, not buying any of it for a moment. "Can I be of *assistance* in any way, viceroy?" He asked finally, deciding there was no reason *not* to be blunt and get straight to the point.

"I come as the proxy of His Excellency, Prince Baal, and request a private audience." Carrick answered immediately. "The prince is at sea aboard *Rapier* and will not likely return before Endweek, however he's tasked me to speak on his behalf regarding a favour… one believer to another…"

"And this is something that cannot wait until his return…?" De Lisle asked tiredly, not at all impressed by a summons from someone as lowly as a mere prince. "You're aware, of course, that there's still much preparation to be done in the lead up to the signing of this most important treaty? As you can imagine, there's *also* much for a *cardinal* to do at such a time…"

"I understand completely, Your Grace," Garrick placated profusely, showing nothing of the offence he'd taken at the obvious slight, but deciding to make a point of his own. "I assure you I shall need no more than a handful of your time: the prince bade me promise to speak to you this night…" he paused for effect "…he *is*, after all, on business that benefits *both* our houses…"

The implication was right there for all to hear and several of the cardinal's followers stifled gasps over the impudence of the man to have so issued so blatant a threat. De Lisle glared at Carrick for a long time, trying to deciding whether there could be *anything* worthwhile that Baal, a pathetic effort of a king's cousin at best, might *possibly* have to offer. The decision was made for him in the end however: after several seconds of awkward silence, there was a single, faint flash from the stone set into the cardinal's pendant and a single word boomed loudly within his mind, crisp and clear as winter sunlight on a cloudless morning.

Accept…!

Accustomed as he was to such random events, De Lisle managed to show nothing of the disorientation that always accompanied so powerful a message, and it seemed completely natural as he reached out one arm and rested casually against the wood panelling of the corridor wall, a long sigh of resignation escaping his lips.

"*Very well*, Carrick…" he acceded eventually, dragging the whole thing out long enough to make it seem as if it had been his own idea all along. "I shall be along presently…"

"Your Grace…" Carrick acknowledged, bowing deeply and then striding off down the hallway the way he'd come.

"To the temple," De Lisle groaned weakly, sagging visibly against the wall now that they were alone and there was no longer any need for pretence. "I need to commune! Help me!" With a follower each taking one of his arms across their shoulders, the entourage carefully turned their leader around on the spot and carefully led him away in the direction of the Longhouse's small but ornate Shard Temple.

Backed up against a wall at the very top of the third floor stairwell, Princess Charleroi jammed a fist against her mouth and struggled to stifle a terrified gasp of her own. He'd *seen* her! Somehow, he'd *known* she was there, eavesdropping. That evil creature, Silas had somehow sensed her presence and had stared up at her through the darkness, his eyes boring into her soul. How she'd managed not to scream in fright right there and then was a miracle in itself, Thank the Crystal. As she thought back over the strangeness of what she'd just overheard, it never once occurred to her that as princess and daughter of the king, she had every right to be walking those halls *regardless* of the time of day.

What were they talking about? She mused silently, giving herself time to calm down as her chest rose and fell with her laboured breathing. *Who's this 'witch' Cardinal De Lisle was talking about? Why was finding a witch loose in the Blacklands so important to the man in charge of the whole Brotherhood? And what does* that *have to do with his meeting with Father…?* The *rest* of what De Lisle and Silas had discussed had slipped completely past without consideration, and wouldn't come back to her until much later.

She jumped in fright, crying out sharply as a door right next to her was suddenly thrown back, only to reveal the concerned and questioning face of Matron Griselda.

"What *are* you doing out here in the corridor alone, Your Highness?" She asked with a frown, hands on hips as she stepped out through the entrance to Charleroi's chambers and stood in the hallway with hands firmly on hips. "I told Master Randwick that you were to be in bed *no later* than nine!"

"He – he was detained by the king, Matron…" She stammered, adrenalin causing her body to shake faintly now as her mind attempted to simultaneously process sensations of sudden shock and immediate relief. "It's not his fault: I got lost on my way back. He wanted to get a courtier to escort me, but I said I could find my own way…" Griselda was the one person she could trust with such information, for there was no way she would *ever* tell Randwick.

"Well, that's as may be…" the old woman conceded grudgingly, "but it's *still* well past your bed time! In with you now and get changed! There's a *long* day ahead tomorrow for *all* of us and you're going to *need* a good night's sleep.

As she lay in her huge feather bed some time later, Charleroi stared up at the dark ceiling and let her thoughts run wild, playing the scene over and over in her mind as she recalled the conversation between Silas and the cardinal. Nothing made sense.

Could there truly *be a witch on the loose in the Blacklands?* She wondered to herself. *Does anyone* really *believe in witches anymore…?*

Nobles and peasants alike were always scaremongering and spreading rumours about demons and witches and other disciples of Nethug – particularly whenever something bad happened that they either couldn't explain or didn't want to accept responsibility for – but she couldn't even recall the last time there'd *actually* been an inquisition. Certainly not in Huon in the last ten years or more that she could remember, although it allegedly still happened in the Blacklands every second week.

I should ask Randwick about it… she decided, eyes drooping as exhaustion fought to overcome her senses. *So much to do tomorrow… ask Randwick…*

The oblivion of a deep sleep took her seconds later.

IX

LONG HOP

An officer and nine troopers boarded the ship in those cold hours before dawn, officially commandeering *Sea Skimmer* in the name of Harald the Black, ruler of all the Blacklands and its territories. The official reason given was the great need of shipping in support of the upcoming treaty celebrations, and the ship was therefore now temporarily part of a conscript merchant navy and would sail for Huon as soon as sufficient cargo had been loaded. Garbutt had protested, raged and pleaded in turn to be exempted from service – that he would lose precious contracts in Swales if he were not there in three days' time to load up – but it was all to no avail: the troop commander remained completely unmoved by threat and cajolery alike.

Nor were any crew permitted to leave the vessel once the Blackwatch had come aboard. The troopers cared little for whatever items of cargo the ship was already carrying nor did they seem particularly interested in the crew itself – neither matter was part of their standing orders – however they *did* ensure that anyone already present aboard *Sea Skimmer* remained there. Although they seemed happy to leave Nev, Godfrey and Lester to their own devices, still seated quietly as they were beneath that rear bridge deck, there was no way the trio would be able to get off the ship without raising far too many awkward questions.

And there they'd been forced to remain, tense and terrified of discovery at any moment as a steady stream of huge wooden crates arrived by horse-drawn cart over the next four hours, each loaded in turn onto *Sea Skimmer's* open cargo deck and carefully tied down. A hundred and fifty large boxes, each around two-metres long (Nev actually counted them, as there was literally nothing else to do) along with thirty more crates that were more square in shape – perhaps 150cm along each side – and appeared to be far lighter judging by the way dock workers were able to manhandle them far more easily into place. She videoed a few moments of footage on her phone but quickly hid it away again, too scared to continue for fear of being discovered with some 'magical' device that might warrant *another* accusation of witchcraft.

Godfrey had hoped they might perhaps make good their withdrawal once the loading had been completed, but the opportunity never presented itself. Rather than leave after the last crate was secured to the deck, the Blackwatch troopers and their commander had settled themselves in forward in preparation for the voyage. Armed with crossbows and the same short swords Nev had encountered the day before, nine huge and rather serious-looking armed men were more than enough of a potential threat to keep the ship's fifty-man crew on best behaviour. It was clear the Blackwatch officer intended to escort his important cargo all the way to its destination without ever allowing it out of his sight.

Although it was well into the morning by the time *Sea Skimmer* was finally able to weigh anchor, the voyage itself proved relatively uneventful. An hour or so to clear the eastern channel around 'The Snake' – the large island that formed a natural shelter against the elements to the south of Welshport – and then south into the open reaches of Deepwater Strait with the good fortune of a strong wind at their backs. They made excellent time, passing west of their first navigational waypoint, the small and unremarkable Hog Island, after four hours' sailing. It was then just two more to reach The Deals, a larger cluster of islands that stood two thirds of the way to Long Hop, an island port that Garbutt had been informed was their final destination for the time being – something he'd only been told *after* they'd put to sea.

The morning was bland and overcast, with a cool, gusting wind coming out of the north and seabirds shadowing the ship for most of her journey. Peering out over the side at the passing waves, Nev had even seen dolphins escorting them for an hour or two, the happy creatures leaping in and out of the water with not a care in the world for the trials or misfortunes any human might be experiencing. She'd only ever seen dolphins once before during a family trip to Sea World when she was eight, and the joyful surprise of the encounter had been great enough to momentarily distract Nev from her nervous tension. Had it not been for the oppressive presence of those black-clad soldiers, the entire voyage might otherwise have been reasonably pleasant.

It was evening as they'd arrived at Long Hop, only to be held out to sea for many more hours as several ships ahead of theirs in the queue took their turn at being unloaded at the docks. Little sleep was had by any that night and the sun was once more rising over the eastern horizon as *Sea Skimmer* had finally pulled into the pier, the approach made without sails as the crew deployed long oars on either side of the ship and rowed her in across that last few hundred metres. The town – if it even deserved to be called such in Nev's opinion – was little more than the port itself collected with a few dozen buildings of solid construction, all of that surrounded by what appeared to be hundreds of large, military-style tents with their own campfires and groups of off-duty soldiers standing about.

The piers were filled with shipping in various states of loading and unloading, while dozens more vessels, large and small, lay at anchor in the wide, shallow bay that swept around to the south-east from the port. Long Hop lay on the northern coast of Finder's Island, the largest of a cluster off the north-western coast of Taas, the vassal kingdom that lay along Huon's land-bound eastern border. The last time Godfrey had visited it'd been little more than a supply station used as a rest point for galleys whose oarsmen were exhausted from the 'long hop' across the Deepwater from Welshport. He'd never seen the place as active or filled with such a heavy military presence. Neither had Garbutt, it seemed.

"This isn't good *at all*, Westacre..." he'd observed darkly as they'd stood together at the railing, watching the dockworkers tie the ship up at the pier. "All those warships out in the bay... all these *soldiers*, and *all of them* Blackwatch: this is no *celebration* they're planning here..."

"Sure don't look like it," Godfrey had agreed with similar misgivings. "This place is run out of *Taas*, though: *surely* this couldn't all be happening without Baal knowing about it?"

"It's no pretty sight for Huon, that's for sure," the captain had conceded, concerned but not overly so considering the situation hardly affected him personally.

It quickly became apparent however that their plans had also been thrown completely awry by whatever was going on. Their cargo was unloaded within a few hours of arrival but the troopers who'd come with it remained much to everyone's dismay, and it was only then the commanding officer, a weasel-like creature going by the name of Hanssen, had advised that *Sea Skimmer* was to be held in reserve, waiting at Long Hop to support operations over the next few days.

The ship would be anchored offshore for the time being and the crew was given the choice to either come ashore now or remain on board. Either way, the vessel wasn't going anywhere anytime soon. A pair of war galleys remained on constant patrol, cruising back and forth across the upper reaches of the bay, and it was made very clear to Garbutt and the rest of them that *any* attempt to put to sea would be met with the *sternest* measures. Hanssen had also taken great delight in recounting tales of two vessels they'd already been forced to ram and sink over the last few days as their captains had tried to sneak away during the night.

Some of the crew chose to go ashore and anyone doing so was issued with a stamped piece of paper that listed them as sailors and gave authorisation for them to be out and about, allowing them free rein within the town itself *within reason*, although it was made very clear they should stay away from both the port and the military marshalling areas further inland if they knew what was good for them. The trio went with them, holding to some vain hope that other transport might be found or chartered that could take them somewhere else... *anywhere* else. It was all to no avail however; the tiny layover port for tired oarsmen had been transformed into a huge military staging base and as Garbutt had pointed out on arrival, it was clear that there was more going on here than any *peaceful* celebration.

The permanent structures built near the port were mostly single-story, with the largest being an administration building and a rather bawdy tavern, *both* of which they avoided completely as they were naturally filled with Blackwatch soldiers. The streets themselves were filled with workers and other non-military personnel, most either milling about or moving this way and that as they went about their business. No one paid them any mind in any case and Nev generally managed to pass unnoticed by keeping her hood over her hair and eyes, and drawing her cloak about her body to hide her figure, looking for all the world like any other boy seeking work in the service of Harald and the Blackwatch.

Rather than risk any larger establishments, Godfrey instead sniffed out a small food stall that was little more than a shop-front attached to the side of someone's house (meaning it likely belonged to one of the original residents), and stumped up enough silver to secure a triplet of home-made bread rolls stuffed with braised lamb and thick, salty gravy. It was heavier food than Nev would've eaten back home but she'd never gone so long without a proper meal back home either, and she couldn't imagine *anything* tasting better as she wolfed it down in just a few huge bites.

The stall stood back from the street in a narrow alley that lay a good few hundred metres from any main thoroughfare and it was relatively private as a result, with just a few tables and chairs set about a small, walled courtyard for the few customers that occasioned to wander past either by accident or design. It gave them the chance to sit back for a few hours in relative safety and consider their extremely limited options, the provision of a single gold coin buying them another round of lamb rolls (*two* for Nev, at her request) with plenty of profit left for the cook.

"So... what do we do *now*...?" Nev mumbled unintelligibly, using two fingers to daintily keep the hood pulled down over her eyes while at the same time making a valiant effort to stuff half a roll into her mouth in one go.

"Try to find a way off this stinking island, *obviously*..." Godfrey growled, pouring some water from a large jug into a ceramic cup. "Although *how*'s another question altogether. Garbutt's already checked with three different harbour masters and *no one's* being allowed to leave. There's *thousands* of soldiers here – none of the locals are even *sure* how many – and apparently they've been here for *weeks* yet *nobody's* heard a word about it *anywhere else*. The Southern Oster doesn't take sides – *usually* – but they need to know if Harald's planning a surprise attack on Huon... no telling *who* might get caught up in *that*. Comes back to the question of how to get away from here, though..."

"Head south to Redhead or Stressleck...?" Lester suggested, sitting back in his chair with a noticeably full stomach, having already polished off both his rolls. "Maybe we can bargain or steal a boat down there and make for Taas: only thirty miles' sailing..."

"Maybe..." Godfrey mused, not entirely convinced. "*Another* thirty miles overland first to get there, though... no easy walk, and then no guarantee there'll even *be* a boat waitin' for us." He shrugged in vague resignation. "Not sure I can think of anything better though, tell you the truth: I don't think any of the ships *here* will be leaving any time soon and even when they *do* weigh anchor, where they're *goin'* may not be safe…"

"Not likely to be much chance of getting away from here, *anyway*…" Lester pointed out, clearly thinking hard on the matter as Godfrey took a drink from his mug and Nev searched for a relatively clean piece of her cloak – one that wouldn't be readily visible afterward – to wipe some left over gravy from her face. "Maybe we should head back to the docks and find somewhere to hole up: keep an eye on who or what turns up. If nothing presents itself, maybe we can head south for Stressleck after dark…"

"Sounds as good as anything *I* can come up with," Godfrey conceded. "What do *you* think…?" He added, including Nev in the conversation for the first time and catching her completely by surprise.

"Um… sounds okay, I guess…" she stammered, thinking quickly. "I don't fancy a thirty mile walk *either*: I'm happy to look for *other* options…"

"Guess we're in agreement, then…" Godfrey nodded, the decision made in his mind. "Been a while since I was here last but I remember there bein' a small storehouse at the western end of town that boat crews used to go to for a few hours' rest: there was a ladder up to the roof and they had a few benches set up so you could sit and have a smoke… watch the world go by, if that took yer fancy. I think I saw the same building there when we docked… if that roof's still vacant, might be a good spot to rest up and keep watch over proceedings."

"How close are we likely to get with *these* things?" Nev asked, drawing the flimsy shore pass from a jacket pocket and holding the crumpled paper up for all to see. "They made it clear no one was s'posed to go near the port unless they were coming back to their own ship."

"There's a few tracks running below the ridgelines to the west of the town we can use that should keep us out of mischief for most of the way…" Godfrey suggested, working more on memory than any solid intel, then conceded: "but we'll need to be careful, *yes*. It's well away from the tavern at least, so there's not much likelihood of running into any wandering Blackwatch… just the *regular* patrols we'll need to look out for…"

"And that's good because *why*?" Nev asked with eyebrow raised, raising a mug of her own.

"Not something to be taken lightly..." he admitted with a wry grin "...but better *that* than a score of drunken, lecherous morons – also known as *soldiers* – who're actually out *looking* for a fight rather than just following orders. Now... if we're all done stuffing our faces...?"

"I was *hungry*, okay?" She shot back, instantly self-conscious.

"I don't believe I named any names..." Godfrey shot back, that cheeky glint in his eye again as Lester snorted with laughter and almost sprayed a mouthful of water over the table. "Shall we be off, then?"

The storehouse was as Godfrey had remembered, although the area – a few hundred metres back from the nearest pier – seemed to have fallen into disrepair since he'd last visited. There were blackened scorch marks at one corner of the building from a previous fire and the ladder at the rear that led up to the roof was rusted and loose enough to make the climb a nervous one. The roof itself was little better, with piles of collected leaves and debris in the corners and a large hole toward the centre, exposed beams showing beneath the rotted planking where it had collapsed into the darkened space below.

There were no other tall structures nearby, lowering the risk of being spotted from below, but Godfrey was taking no chances, making sure they all kept to a low crouch as they carefully negotiated their way across the creaking roof toward the front of the building. A low wall roughly a metre high ran around the entire perimeter of the structure, providing more than enough cover for all three of them to sit in reasonable comfort with their backs up against the brickwork.

As the others settled in he produced a pair of brass binoculars from his rucksack. They were quite small, folded flat into a pancake-like casing, and when deployed were little more than a two matching pairs of lenses held in an open frame with a focussing mechanism mounted between. They provided low magnification only, although in return they were also compact and easily concealable.

"Ships are still coming in," he observed softly, taking in the scenes below on the docks. "Warships now, too... now, *that's* strange..." he frowned, silent for a moment as he watched something unusual unfold below. "Here, Toady..." he continued, offering Lester the glasses. "What d'you make of this, down by the near end of the pier there..."

"Whaddya got...?" Lester muttered, taking the offered binoculars and raising them to stare down at the port below.

A sleek galleass lay moored at the near end of the closest pier, its ram bow adorned with a carved eagle figurehead and ornamental shields mounted along its sides in a decorative display. Troops of soldiers were clustered about the wharf, working hard as they broke open a pile of crates identical to those that had accompanied the trio on their voyage aboard *Sea Skimmer*.

The smaller, cube-like crates had been broken open to reveal pairs of large, wooden-spoked wagon wheels, which the men below – engineers, Godfrey was assuming – moved with large pivots and lifting ropes to attach to long, wooden frames mounting even longer cylindrical tubes that appeared to be forged from some kind of metal. Lester had never seen the like before – he assumed Godfrey hadn't either from his earlier comments – yet based on the manner in which those men assembled and manoeuvred the strange units, the boy instinctively felt that he was looking at something dangerous.

"Gonna sound silly, but it... It kinda *looks* like a weapon..." he muttered, not sure what to make of his own statement.

"Thinkin' the same meself..." Godfrey admitted, feeling just as foolish. "Dunno if this makes sense, but they look too damned *simple* to be anything else..."

"What are we talking about...?" Nev asked, as interested as anyone could be when there was literally nothing else to do save join in the conversation.

"Take a look..." the boy suggested, handing the glasses over.

It took Nev a moment before she was able to master the strange layout of the glasses, accustom herself to their operation, and then turn her vision toward the ship below. As her eyes took in what was happening, she instantly released a short, soft gasp of surprise.

"Oh, my *God*... those are *cannon*...!" She exclaimed, amazed that she actually recognised something in that world that made sense. "Cannon, Godfrey! The guns I was telling you about earlier..."

"You mean like that 'shotgun'...?" He asked sharply, recalling the discussion. "So they *are* some kind of weapon! Are they dangerous?"

"I can't believe I'm having this conversation," she muttered as an aside, finding it difficult to accept there was even a need to explain what cannon were. "It's a gun... a *huge* gun that fires either cannonballs or exploding shells over *really* long distances..."

"*How* long...?"

"What do you have at the moment for ranged weapons... *catapults* or something like that?"

"Aye, catapults," Godfrey nodded, not happy about where the conversation was going. "Catapults and trebuchets..."

"Not sure what range trebuchets have but I'm gonna assume they're about the same as catapults," Nev shrugged, knowing a little about military technology from a historical standpoint but never having had a great interest in it. "Not sure how big those guns are down *there*," she added, "but they'll probably fire a solid iron ball a lot further and *a lot* faster than any catapult! *Those* things can blast through castle walls! They were the reason that they stopped *building* castles in *my* world!"

So... those *things*..." Godfrey repeated slowly, trying to keep the disbelief out of his tone "... can fire an iron ball hard enough to punch holes in solid stone?"

"Yup... out to – oh, I dunno – maybe a mile... maybe more. Weapons were never my strong point..."

"Hard to believe something could do that... *but*... seein' as you're the only one who has a *clue* what these things are, and all o' them *down there* seem to think they're important, I guess there must be *somethin'* in what y'r sayin'..."

"Westy, there's – like – *ten* o' those 'cannon' down there already..." Lester observed, able to count the assembled weapons easily as Nev handed the binoculars back.

"If they're the same crates we brought on the ship with us," Godfrey pointed out bluntly, "there could be *hundreds* of 'em!"

"That's *Rapier* down there!" Lester called out suddenly in surprise, still looking through the glasses. "I swear: I can see the name on her prow!

"Gimme...!" Godfrey demanded instantly, taking them from him and checking for himself. "I do believe you're right, Master Boniface..." he declared eventually, having studied the vessel hard for a good few moments. "Prince Baal's own transport... s'posed to be the fastest ship in the whole Huon war fleet..."

"Aren't Huon supposed to be the Blackwatch's *enemies*...?" Nev asked thoughtfully.

"You *have* been listening," Godfrey observed with a dry smile, turning to face her and placing the binoculars down on the top of the wall, "...and that *definitely* raises questions about what *Rapier* is doing *here,* taking on a load of these so-called '*cannon*'..."

"All of this info has to rub off eventually," she shrugged with a grin of her own, sliding into a seated position once more with her back to the wall. Taking out her phone on a whim, she decided to take a few panoramic shots, then zoomed in on the cannon being loaded and recorded perhaps thirty seconds of grainy, magnified footage as engineers fussed over their assembly. They watched for a few moments more until the activity down below became repetitive enough to lose their interest and all three instead turned and settled into as comfortable a seating position as they could manage below that low wall.

"Not much we can do about it right now, I guess..." Godfrey conceded, stifling a yawn that was partly exhaustion and partly full stomach and craning his neck to stare up at the sky. "Be a good idea to get some sleep while we can. Looks to be around mid-afternoon, so a few hours yet before dusk – best we've had *some* rest if we're forced to set off on that bloody march south tonight. Someone probably oughta keep a lookout though..." he added, glancing at each in turn as if seeking agreement... or volunteers.

"I'll take watch," Lester shrugged, earning himself a nod of thanks and approval. "Only a few hours 'til sunset anyway... no problem..."

"Good lad..." Godfrey declared with a grin, slapping him on the shoulder. "Wake me if you see anything interesting, right?"

"'Course I will..."

Godfrey laid his pack down on the roof a metre or two away, using the strapped bedroll as a makeshift pillow. It wasn't anywhere near as comfortable that way, but Nev could see the logic in keeping everything secure and ready for a quick getaway if necessary. She did the same, finding her own space and laying down with her folded clothes stuffed inside one end of her duffel bag as cushioning. Fortunately it was a cloudy day that was warm enough to be pleasant without a blazing sun shining down in their faces. Godfrey – like any soldier worth his salt – was already snoozing by the time she'd laid her head down, and Nev smiled faintly to herself at the sight: with so much going on, she was amazed *anyone* could sleep at all.

That idea, along with her own consciousness, lasted all of five minutes.

Left to his own devices, Lester looked about for a moment and fixed his eyes on a small pile of old crates and building materials piled up in the roof's opposite corner. Tiptoeing over as carefully as he was able, he picked out a suitable box and carried it back to his original position. Using it as a makeshift seat, he was able to look out over the lip of the roof wall and take in everything that was happening down below. Every now and then he would take up the binoculars and sweep his eyes across the port, making sure there was nothing of any particular interest going on that Godfrey should know about.

It was almost sunset by the time Nev woke, rising slowly and stretching the sleep out of her mind and body before kneeling down beside Lester and gazing out across the port with him, the pair sharing a silent nod of acknowledgement.

"Nothing happening...?" She asked conversationally, not sure she'd know what she was looking at if something *was* going on.

"Boring as..." he shrugged in return. "Ships come... ships go... back to the start again..."

"Should we wake him?"

"Nahh, give him a bit longer..." the boy replied with a grin. "Too early to head off yet... he might as well get as much rest as he can."

"Fair enough..."

They settled into a comfortable silence, Lester maintaining his watch on the docks as Nev turned and gazed up at the nearby hills that seemed to tower dramatically over the western edge of the port. She could see smoke from what looked like a signal fire or beacon burning at the northern end overlooking the bay, and the flicker of torchlights here and there as people – presumably soldiers – moved about on the summit.

Still scanning the ships below with the field glasses at that moment and completely unnoticed by Nev, Lester suddenly stiffened with shock and surprise, his entire body turning ice cold. He'd turned his attention back to *Rapier*, this time panning forward of the bow, where he'd noticed a small group of men clustered near the near end of the pier. At least three of the men were dressed in the black robes of Brotherhood officials, and as one of them turned toward him, Lester realised with a combination of rage and fear that the man's face was terribly familiar.

"I – uh – I need to take a leak..." he announced bluntly, no emotion in his words as he placed the binoculars, on the wall, rose from his kneeling position and immediately made for the ladder at the rear of the, slinging his crossbow over one shoulder as he skirted around the hole in the centre of the roof.

"Well... thanks for sharing, I guess..." Nev blinked, surprised that *she* was actually surprised he'd come out with such a statement. In another moment he was gone, disappearing down the ladder at an urgent pace.

"Where's the Toad got to...?" Godfrey asked a few moments later, only mildly startling Nev as he too rose from his sleeping position and joined her at the wall.

"...Said he needed to relieve himself..." she explained with a grimace, not at all comfortable with discussing other people's bathroom habits.

"Hope he doesn't hang about too long down there..." Godfrey muttered softly, taking up the abandoned binoculars and beginning his own surveillance, looking for anything that might serve as a possible way off the island. "Too many patrols out and about..."

He was still staring down intently at the port below when he noticed unexpected movement off to the left of the docks where tall stacks of crates and sacks of goods were piled up in the gathering darkness, waiting for a suitable ship to become available. His eyes picked out a small, furtive figure moving quickly among those crates, darting from shadow to shadow with the unmistakeable shape of an oversized crossbow across his back.

"*What the...*!" He muttered with a deep frown, his tone alerting Nev, who also turned to stare down in the same direction. "What the *hell* does he think he's doing...?"

"I did *wonder* what was taking him so long..." she admitted with a grimace, having initially imagined the boy might've decided he needed more than a simple pee break "...but I didn't want to ask..."

The hair rose on the back of Godfrey's neck then as he scanned back toward *Rapier*, wondering what could possibly have dragged Lester away so foolishly without a single word.

"Dragonfall *take me*...!" He breathed, horror in his voice as his gaze fell on the same small group of men down on the pier, and he too recognised one of them.

"What... what is it...?" Nev asked nervously, not at all liking the fear in his voice.

"For the love of The Crystal, it's Silas... *Silas*...!"

"Who's 'Silas', for goodness' sake?"

"He's the priest..." Godfrey explained, his voice hollow with shock. "The *Quisitor* who executed Lester's *sister*...!"

"Oh... *no*...!" She moaned softly, her heart sinking with the news. "He's going to do something *really* stupid, isn't he...!"

"Not if I can stop him first..." he declared, leaping to his feet with his rucksack already in hand and bolting for the ladder, not caring a whit for who might've heard or seen him.

"Oh... *crap*...!" Nev blurted, thinking of any number of words far worse that were immediately blocked by her overactive conscience. With a sigh and a groan of frustration, she gathered up her own bag and took off in pursuit.

Down below, Silas and a small escort of Brotherhood novitiates had arrived from Burnii with the sole intention of making De Lisle's ordered rendezvous with the fastest vessel they'd been able to secure: *Rapier*. Their own ship had docked an hour earlier, the oarsmen pushed beyond all limits in a desire to get them to Long Hop in a record time of just ten hours. Six men had died from exhaustion during the voyage and another four weren't expected to last the night, none of which mattered in the slightest to the men of The Brotherhood as they stood about on the wooden boards of the jetty, waiting for the arrival of *Rapier's* owner.

Silas was first to notice Baal as the prince finally made an appearance, striding casually across the main deck and down the gangway as if out for an evening stroll. Fit, tall and strong of limb, he looked to be in his mid-thirties and wore a closely-trimmed beard and moustache that matched the colour of his thick, dark hair. The king's first cousin on his mother's side, Amun Baal was the current Viceroy of the Taas Hegemony, a small vassal nation that had splintered from Huon during an earlier war some years ago and had at the time foolishly aligned itself with Harald.

The Black King had been quite happy to sit back and watch while both sides engaged in a particularly bloody civil war from which Huon had emerged the eventual victor, and Taas had immediately been returned to the kingdom as Huon's vassal, ruled by a crown-appointed viceroy. Baal had seemed the obvious choice, and had reigned over that small nation ever since.

"Brother Silas!" He called from some distance away, all smiles and welcoming arms. "I take it the cardinal received my message?"

"He did…" Silas replied with distaste as they drew near, bowing slightly in recognition of the man's royal standing "…although he wasn't shown any information he didn't already know." He added, bursting the prince's bubble. "Your highness, do you think The Brotherhood wouldn't *notice* that you've been spending so much time at Castle Black these last few months, presumably *without* your cousin's knowledge? You forget, perhaps, that we have prelates *everywhere* across The Osterlands, including the Blacklands – *particularly* the Blacklands considering that Kraal exists within its borders. Be *thankful* we priests know how to keep secrets, or your head might well be hanging from a pike above the Burnii Longhouse."

"I'll warrant there'll be *other* heads up there soon enough," Baal countered with as little temper as he could manage, "but that's not what we're here for tonight, is it? Your Brotherhood found the presence of my ship *convenient enough* when it turned out we could bring that cursed *witch* to you faster than anything afloat on the other side of The Blackwater…"

"'*My*' Brotherhood…?" Silas repeated as a question, almost sounding scandalised as he raised a querulous eyebrow. "Surely you mean *our* Brotherhood, good sir: it would hardly do for the king's *cousin* to be accused of *heresy*…"

"Yes, *that* might happen when I'm of no further *use* to you and your lecherous lot," Baal sniffed, utterly unimpressed, "but *not* anytime soon, I'll wager. We're loading these 'guns' and are taking on the last of our supplies now… all we've been waiting on otherwise was your good self. The captain plans to be away again on the high tide… shall I give the hag to you *now*, or shall I take her as far as Bridgeport?"

"Leave her be for the moment," Silas replied a little too quickly, not entirely hiding his interest and surprising Baal a little. "The cardinal wants her questioned, but better she isn't seen on a *Brotherhood*-chartered vessel. *I* shall come with *you* instead, aboard *Rapier*… there'll be time enough for interrogation on the voyage back…"

"As you wish, Brother…" Baal acceded with a faint bow. "My ship's at your disposal. Shall I have quarters made up just for yourself, or for – ?"

He was cut off mid-sentence as he noticed the Shard Crystal at Silas' throat begin to glow brightly, and a moment later the priest suddenly and quite unexpectedly threw up an arm and physically elbowed Baal to one side, following him as he pushed the prince to the ground and all the while displaying an expression of surprise over actions even he seemed not to have expected.

Even as they fell, there came the faint, ripping sound of a passing crossbow bolt followed immediately by the unmistakably wet *thud* of it striking flesh. One of the novitiates standing behind both of them screamed shrilly, clutching at the bolt that now protruded from his lower abdomen as he collapsed backward to the cold ground, blood already pouring out between his clenched fingers. An alarm was raised instantly, Blackwatch troopers running in from every direction with swords and crossbows ready while a quartet of the prince's own bodyguards also sprinted down the gangway from *Rapier* to form a protective cordon around their charge.

"Three-Squad: search that cargo!" A nearby sergeant barked sharply, four men instantly peeling off toward the darkened stacks of crates and sacks near the abandoned storehouse. It hadn't taken long for an experienced eye to work out the rough direction of the shooter, and a crossbow couldn't range long enough for the would-be assassin to be far away.

"It may be that I owe you my life, Brother Silas..." Baal conceded in a shaky voice as he dusted himself off, a dozen Blackwatch now clustered about the group as a human shield.

"Not *you*..." Silas replied, sounding as if he were in a daze as he stared blankly down at the screaming man. "The shot was aimed at *me*, but we couldn't risk *your* safety either..." The pendant at his neck was still glowing, although not so brightly as before as he turned and knelt beside the novitiate, the prince already forgotten. Working quickly, he took the pendant in his fingers and lifted the chain carefully over his head.

"Brother Silas... *please*... the pain..." the young man moaned through clenched teeth, most of his shirt soaked in blood now below the waist. The iron tail of the bolt was visible between his fingers and it was clearly a large projectile capable of inflicting great damage. There were desperate calls for a medic already spreading about the area, but those soldiers nearby with combat experience knew well enough how bad a wound like that could be.

"Peace, Brother Chan... *peace*..." Silas soothed softly, reaching out with the glowing pendant wrapped about his open palm and resting it upon the man's heaving chest. There was power enough in the crystal to save him, and Silas knew what to do well enough, but that kind of effort would've left the old man drained with exhaustion and he had neither the time nor the inclination to waste that amount of time and energy.

"Fear not, for you shall soon be One with The Shard and *soar* with the Night Dragons... *peace*, now..." he continued, trying to sound sincere. The glow beneath his open palm grew brightly for a moment and at the same time, Brother Chan's moans and struggles began to settle and his eyes closed. "Peace..." he repeated, moving his hand now to hover over the man's forehead. There was a faint flutter from Chan's eyes then, only white showing beneath the lids, and his chest and legs gave a few final spasms before he slipped away into a final, painless oblivion.

"Remind me never to come to you with a *headache*, brother..." Baal observed with cold humour, resisting an urge to make the sign of The Crystal following that eerie display of power.

"A brother's life was just forfeit at the hands of an assassin..." Silas hissed sharply, sounding more himself now as the pendant's glow faded to nothing and he returned it to its place about his neck. "Prince or not, I'll warn you *once* to show some respect for a death in The Shard's service! *Who is in command here?*" He snarled then, as loudly as his old lungs would allow as he cast his eyes about the area beyond their cordon of guards. He'd already ceased to have any interest in Baal, and the prince could only stand there and glare at him in complete impotence.

"Duty Officer Hanssen at your service, brother," Hanssen advised nervously, appearing almost out of thin air and right at that moment rueing the fact that he'd pulled 'short straw' on the afternoon roster.

"I want whoever it was captured and brought to me aboard *Rapier*..." he snapped angrily, seething now over both the loss of a fellow brother and the attempt on his life. "The ship will be leaving on the hour: have him in custody by then, or *your* life will be forfeit in his place!"

"At *once*, Brother Silas..."

"...And do not damage him *too* much..." the old man added with an evil smile, stopping Hanssen as he turned to leave. "I want him *conscious* enough to *suffer* through what I'm doing to him!"

"By your leave…" Hanssen bowed faintly, making as speedy an exit as he could manage.

"*Are you* trying *to get us all killed*…?" Godfrey hissed as loudly as he dared as they met in a narrow alley, halfway between the storehouse and the cargo holding area Lester had fired from. The boy was running at full speed and was almost past as Godfrey snatched at his collar with one hand and hauled him back.

"Let go o' me!" Lester snarled angrily, slapping his hands away and backing against the opposite wall. "That bastard murdered Emily: he *deserves* to die!"

"Oh, aye… and that's worth all of *our* lives in exchange is it?"

"My bloody *oath* it is!" the boy screamed in return, crying now as all of his repressed rage and sorrow burst to the surface.

"Well, thank The Crystal you *ran* instead of hanging about, you bloody fool…!" Godfrey barked in frustration.

"Could we *possibly* discuss this *somewhere else*…?" Nev asked pointedly, no happier than Godfrey over what Lester had done but perhaps feeling his pain a little more keenly. "Somewhere *safer*…?" Already, the shouts of men in pursuit were growing nearer and she wasn't at all pleased about the concept of being involved in what amounted to her *third* brush with death in the space of just forty-eight hours.

"Here… *over here*…!" The accusing cry came from the far end of the alley, where a trio of soldiers with swords and burning torches had paused to take a breath and noticed the altercation.

"Time to leave…!" Godfrey decided, not sure where they *could* run to but deciding in a split second that *anywhere* was a better option than staying put. "Ridgeline to the west," he added, drawing his sword and breaking into a run with Nev at his side. "If we get separated, we can meet up there…"

Lester paused just long enough to raise and fire another bolt downrange at the soldiers now running toward them, then turned and ran also, struggling to catch up on the other two's head start. There was a cry of pain behind him, providing him at least a little solace. The shot had been made too quickly to be accurate but it had struck one of their pursuers in the leg all the same and sent him tumbling to the ground in agony, followed by the other two who immediately tripped over his falling body and left them all writhing in a pile in the middle of the alleyway.

With the other end of the alley drawing near, Godfrey was starting to think they had at least a *chance* of making good their escape. There were just a few more buildings to pass by on that western side of the port and beyond them was nothing but empty scrub that offered far better cover. His hopes lasted just long enough for the three of them to burst clear of the far end of the alleyway, only for Godfrey to be taken low in a flying tackle as an unseen Blackwatcher crashed into him at full tilt.

They were suddenly surrounded by bellowing soldiers, and Nev screamed as an already winded Godfrey was knocked out cold, his head intentionally smashed against the hard ground by his far-heavier assailant. Lester was a howling dervish, struggling and fighting for all he was worth, but his lack of strength and body size left it all to no avail. It took but a few seconds for two equally-large troopers to manhandle him forcibly to the ground and produce some rope with which to bind him.

Even in the middle of her frightened cry, Nev was already trying to reach into her bag for the katana. She was never given the chance. A barrel-chested thug in chainmail and boiled leather crashed into her from behind, slamming her brutally against a wall at the mouth of the alley they'd just exited. Dazed and disoriented by the impact, she was completely unprepared for the blow that came next, delivered with savage precision to the back of her head and sending her instantly into unconsciousness as she crumpled to the hard earth.

X

THE KEEPSAKE

Charleroi was up again and breakfasted not long after sunrise, and by mid-morn she was already clothed in one of her finest dresses: a long, flowing gown of silk inlaid with gold highlights and tiny, precious jewels in layers about its neck and long, puffed sleeves. An accomplished hairdresser had been brought in from town to wash and style her long, dark locks into a tight, decorative bun affixed low to the back of her head, leaving just the hint of a pony tail hanging down beneath her tiara. It was a special time – a momentous time – and *everyone* was expected to look their best for the celebrations to come.

Charleroi watched thoughtfully from her balcony as peasants and commoners scurried this way and that below, oblivious to the greater world of which they were such a tiny part. She suspected few of them could've understood what this new treaty really meant for them and for everyone else – some probably didn't even know the *king* was in town – and it was more than likely that fewer still cared about either. Down on the docks, workmen carried sacks of cargo in every direction, loading and unloading a wide variety of commercial cogs and galleasses from near and far while across in Burnii itself, townsfolk too went about their daily business, never once looking up from the narrow scope of their own tiny lives. From *her* position on that balcony however, the princess imagined she could look down upon it all with a far keener eye and *definitely* take in the bigger picture.

More ships had arrived during the morning: freighters, nobles' pleasure craft and warships alike filling the bay in preparation for the coming ceremonies. She recognised some of the insignia and flags that flew from their masts, while others were a complete mystery; most likely vessels belonging to guests from the other side of the Deepwater. The journey across that wide, forbidding strait was a long and arduous one: that much, she knew.

Sailing ships could risk a direct run south from the mainland of the winds were in their favour and the Deepwater not too rough, but for oared vessels the journey was by necessity a coastal run from Welshport or The Long Pier, then down along the south-east coast of the Blacklands, past King's Beach on the Great Promontory, where Black Castle, Harald's summer fortress stood atop the central mountain there and looked down on everything for miles around.

From there, galleys would strike out across the strait itself: a day of solid rowing at best before landfall at Long Hop for rest and re-supply, then on to the Taas, the small vassal nation on Huon's eastern border. From George's Town or Bridgeport, it was then just another short coastal cruise west to Demon's Port or, more likely on to the great port of Burnii itself.

It was the main leg of the trip that usually caused problems for oared vessels: even with the aid of favourable winds filling their small, triangular sails, anything more than a half-day's journey was likely to leave rowers drained and exhausted. The stretch between Welshport and Long Hop had been known to claim lives if oarsmen were pushed too hard, and the only viable alternative was to carry replacement crews; something that seriously cut into the space left over for water, supplies or, in the case of a war galley, for marines or land armies.

It was that problem that had always plagued Harald's forces when attempting to mount invasions across the Deepwater, and it'd played its part in a number of successive defeats during the last three decades. Although the triremes used by the Huon navies were often smaller, they were also faster as a result and none of them were forced to travel far to engage in battle, leaving their crews fresher and more prepared. Extensive and regular crew training in ramming manoeuvres and in the operation of their deck-mounted ballistae also helped.

One vessel in particular caught Charleroi's eye, if only because it seemed to have separated completely from the rest and run itself aground on an empty section of Burnii beach, perhaps a kilometre or two around the bay to the east. It was difficult to make out any detail at that distance – part of the vessel was hidden from view by intervening trees – but what she *could* see clearly belonged to a ship of some sort. Now that she thought about it, she wasn't sure when it had actually arrived. She'd not been out onto the balcony since the afternoon of the day before: in theory at least, it might've been there all night and she'd not have known... although surely someone else must have noticed...?

She had no idea why the sight of it had so suddenly and completely captured her interest, but something about it looked strangely out of place even from such a distance, and once again her curiosity began to get the better of her.

"Annabel..." she called softly, turning toward one of her younger handmaidens currently tidying inside the room.

"Yes, Your Highness...?" She asked meekly, stepping out onto the balcony and presenting a curtsey.

"You're a friend of Guard Captain Hakim, are you not...?" She asked innocently, carefully choosing to ignore the faint reddening of her handmaiden's cheeks over that question.

"We... we have spoken on occasion, Your Highness..."

"I'm wondering about that ship over there on the beach..." Charleroi went on regardless, lifting a finger to point in the indicated direction. "I'm *mostly* wondering why it's beached itself over *there* rather than finding a mooring like all the others... do you think the captain might know anything about it?"

"I – I don't know, Your Highness..." Annabel replied with a blank expression. At eighteen summers, she was roughly the same height as the princess, a little more solid of build and not the slightest bit more mature in any real sense, particularly considering she'd been given only the most rudimentary education necessary for the performance of her daily duties, as was often the case for commoners in the employ of the state. "I could ask him later if you like, Miss..." she added, trying to be helpful and staring out past Charleroi's extended finger as a frown formed on her face. "*Which* ship was that, Your Highness...?"

"That one *over there*...!" The princess insisted, electing to point again with a more pronounced jabbing motion, as if that were certain to do the trick. "Just through the trees there, on the beach below the castle..."

"I'm not sure I see which one you mean, beggin' your pardon, Miss..." Annabel eventually admitted, not for a moment wanting to disagree with her royal charge but unable to lie about it all the same. "What does it look like?"

"It *looks* like a *boat*...!" Charleroi shot back, starting to become vaguely annoyed now. "A big *brown* boat...! Can't really see *that* much from here, but the stern it sticking out past the trees, half out of the water and lying right near where the beach ends and the rocks come out into that little promontory there... oh, you *must* see it, surely!" She insisted with exasperation, but as she turned to glare at the serving girl, ready to accuse her of playing tricks, the look of fear she received in return made it quite clear that Annabel was telling the complete truth.

"I – I'm *sorry*, Your Highness..." she stammered, well aware now of how annoyed the princess was now and trying to hold back tears.

Charleroi wasn't usually the vindictive type, but she *was* prone to rather savage mood swings at times, and most of her personal staff – save for Griselda of course, who simply didn't put up with any of it – quickly learned to keep out of her way during certain times of the month. The secret marked calendar the whole staff shared had indicated there was no danger of that for at least another week or more however, and Annabel was going to have a *very* stern talk to Merry if that girl had somehow marked the dates wrong. Matron Griselda knew about the calendar of course – very little slipped past her without notice – and she tolerated it for the sake of the other staff, although she nevertheless found the whole idea quite unseemly. No one dared let on that they kept *another* calendar for *her* too.

"How can you *not* see it?" Charleroi demanded plaintively, unable to reconcile the girl's apparent innocence with the findings of her own two eyes. "It's *right there...*"

Pointing wildly *again* of course worked about as well as it had the last two times.

"Is everything alright, Your Highness...?" Griselda inquired with a frown of her own as she stepped out onto the balcony to join them, having overheard Charleroi's raised voice from out in the hall.

"I don't *understand*, matron," she moaned plaintively, an almost childish whine creeping faintly into her tone. "There's a ship out there on the beach – *a big, brown ship* out past the trees there, near Round Hill – but *Annabel* says she can't see it!"

"Girl, if you've been teasing the princess, I *swear...*" Griselda warned darkly, glaring at Annabel as she pushed past her and took a position at the railing right beside Charleroi. "Now let me have a look my dear, and we'll sort this all out. *Now... where* is this ship of yours..." she asked optimistically, squinting her old eyes and staring off in completely the wrong direction to the point that the princess was forced to point again, this time adding an exasperated growl into the mix.

"Over *there...*" she explained again in frustration, overemphasising her words as if speaking to simpletons. "Over there behind the trees... the big, brown boat over there *behind the trees...!*"

"Well, I'm sorry to say, Milady, that *I* can't see anything *either...* are you sure that you –?"

But Griselda cut herself short in that moment as something else occurred to her: a dark and terrible idea that she'd never have imagined possible but now felt the need to rule out all the same.

"Annabel..." she began again slowly, trying to maintain a level tone and thereby show none of the vague concern that was beginning to build in the back of her mind. "Be so kind as to go and fetch a spyglass from one of the sentries on the roof, if you would..."

"Mistress...?" The girl asked in return, completely bewildered by the request.

"*Now*, if you please: there's a set of stairs directly around the corner to the left that lead up to the nearest watchtower. Be *quick* about it, would you... and tell them that if they give you any trouble, they'll answer to *me!*"

It took Annabel just five minutes to climb the stairs up to the small, rounded hatchway that led out onto the roof, approach the nearest archers on duty and return to the chambers where the others still waited. There'd been no trouble at all in securing a spyglass from one of them: Griselda was well known throughout the court and *no one* – save perhaps Randwick – was foolish enough to get on her wrong side.

"*Right,* then..." the old woman declared, trying to sound confident once more as she opened up the collapsible telescope to its full length of half a metre and raised it to her right eye, the other one shut tight as she cast her magnified gaze down toward the section of beach Charleroi was talking about.

She saw nothing at first. Away to the east, the bright sands of the beach stretched calmly away in a wide, shallow curve before ending in the small, rocky promontory the princess had mentioned earlier. She could see no large ship of any kind, anywhere along that pristine strip of sand. There weren't even any smaller vessels – dinghies, rowboats and the like – that one might expect to be out and about on such a lovely, lightly-overcast morning, although the complete lack of *anything* on the water in that area *did* begin to strike her as unusual.

It was then that Griselda noticed a strange indentation in the sand, positioned roughly in the same area Charleroi had insisted the 'boat' had run aground. It was difficult to pick out at first at such a distance and on such a sharp angle, but as she watched for a little longer, the uneven shape of it began to appear out of the background. It looked to be wide and quite shallow, like something flat and heavy had pushed down the sand there, and there were the hint of drag marks a little further up.

She also noticed that waves that were otherwise coming in gently everywhere else just never seemed to reach land in that particular section, instead prematurely spraying upward into the air for no apparent reason at all perhaps ten metres or so out from shore. The water there shimmered, giving off strange reflections, and as she moved the spyglass back to the beach she noticed for the first time that three men had appeared from behind the trees and were walking slowly out toward that strange mark on the sand.

They all appeared to be carrying something, but it was only as one of them raised one of the long, narrow poles he held in his hands and positioned it point-down into the sand that fear truly found Matron Griselda of Westerland, stabbing at her heart as a dark, creeping horror oozed slowly into her mind.

"Oh... oh, *no*..." she breathed softly, barely managing to speak at all as she lowered the telescope for just a moment and glanced at Charleroi with a mixture of fear and sorrow. "It can't be... it just *can't*...!"

"What is it, matron?" The princess asked urgently, also suddenly terrified by the old woman's unexpected reaction. "You see it, don't you? *What's wrong*...?"

"It's not possible...!" Griselda continued to mutter, lifting the glass to her eye once more and taking another desperate look, hoping beyond hope that she'd somehow imagined the whole thing. "It just *can't* be!"

"Matron, you're scaring me!"

There was no mistaking what she was seeing or, more importantly, what she *wasn't*. Out into the water as far as knee height, the trio were hammering long, iron stakes into the sand at intervals of roughly two metres. She didn't need to guess about the distance... she already knew all too well what they were doing. As two placed the posts and hammered them deep into the ground, the third proceeded to tie off a thin, white rope to the first and follow them as they went, extending the thick coils he was carrying and tying it off at the top of each post in turn as his colleagues moved on. She couldn't see the colour of the posts from that distance, but Griselda already knew that each one would be painted white at the very tip to the thickness of a hand's breadth.

"Annabel..." She croaked softly, her throat suddenly dry and rasping. "Go and fetch Master Randwick if you would... *go now*, please, and tell him he must come *urgently!*"

"Matron...?"

"*Now*, girl... and don't take 'no' for an answer! Tell him it's *me* who's askin' him, and tell him I ain't *asking!*"

"Griselda, you need to tell me what's going on *right now!*" Princess Charleroi Namur of Huon demanded with as much regal anger and severity as she could muster, her attempt at the use of authority the only thing she could think of to combat the unknowing dread building within her, threatening to reduce her to tears at any moment. "You *must* tell me *exactly* what's happening! *What did you see...?*"

"It'll be alright, my girl..." Griselda offered, the hollowness of her voice not really doing anything to convince the princess of anything of the sort. "Let's go inside my little love, and we'll have a sit down..."

Griselda, *please...*" She pleaded, unable to maintain her façade of anger as tears began to trickle down her cheeks. Without having any clue as to what was actually going on, something in her matron's tone and expression had convinced Charleroi that whatever was wrong must somehow be her fault. "What *is* it...? *What have I done...?*"

"Come, dear..." the old woman urged gently instead, shaking her head sadly and reaching out an arm to guide her toward the door back into her room. "We just need to wait for Randwick, *then* we'll have a chat..." But it was what the matron said next that truly frightened Charleroi more than anything she'd heard or seen so far: eight words formed into a sentence she'd never before heard from the old woman's lips, nor ever believed she could possibly utter. "Master Randwick..." Griselda repeated, nodding slowly to herself as if lost in a trance. "Yes... *he'll* know what to do..."

It quickly became apparent ten minutes later however that Master Randwick had absolutely *no* idea what to do as Griselda explained everything and he too went through the process of scanning the beach with the spyglass, grimacing and frowning and trying to hide the awful, sinking feeling in his gut as his eyes took in dozen or so

Holding Staves that had been positioned around the huge *thing* on the beach that they simply couldn't see... the thing that could only be a Keepsake.

"What does it look like, girl?" He asked quietly, still staring through the lens of the telescope as Charleroi stood meekly beside him, her cheeks stained by the tracks of tears that still trickled occasionally from the corner of her eyes.

"I – I couldn't see *much*..." she began haltingly, trying to remember the details she'd picked up before all the drama had begun. "It was big and mostly brown, with a little green on top..."

"And it was a *boat*...?" He confirmed, releasing a soft grunt of displeasure as his magnified view picked out the point where the staves and the white Rope of Warding they supported became fuzzy and indistinct, partially obscured by the otherwise invisible object they'd been placed around. That he could still somehow see the *beach* beyond it was an anomaly that was common to all Keepsake sites, and it was one Randwick had given up trying to figure out years ago... although it still irked him that it couldn't be explained.

"I – I *think* so..."

"Here, girl...!' He snapped with frustration, thrusting the spyglass into her hands. "Take a *proper* look and tell me what you see!" He was angry at the situation rather than at her, but was unable to keep his temper completely in check, so shocked had he been when the old woman had first revealed the truth.

I – I see a boat..." she began nervously, lifting the telescope to her eye with shaking hands and seeing the thing right up close for the first time. "A *ship*, really..." She corrected, considering the vessel's size. "It's run aground and looks like its lying on its side a bit, with at least a quarter of it is still in water. The bottom – the *hull*, is it? – is all brown... *like it's rusty*!" She exclaimed with realisation, smiling for a moment then sinking back down into the funk of fear once more as she remembered what was happening. "There's... it looks like there are things *growing* on the deck... it looks all green and *leafy*..."

"How big is it?" He asked carefully, watching her now for her reactions rather than staring out across the water. "As big as a war galley...? Bigger...? Smaller...? *How big*...?"

"Um..." she began thoughtfully, lowering the scope for a moment and turning her head to glance over at the warships moored down at the docks. *"Bigger*..." she determined eventually, after repeating the exercise a few more times. "Not by *much*, but *definitely* bigger. Randwick, *what is it...*?" Charleroi demanded again, anger once more rising with her fear and frustration. "No one will tell me *anything*. I'm the *princess*!" She added, moving to stand directly in front of him and stomping her foot. "I *order* you to tell me!"

"Did you learn *nothing* as a child... from all those Endweek classes at the chapel?" He asked tiredly, the sad light of resignation in his eyes as he took a step back and turned away.

"Don't you *dare* turn your back on me, sir...!" She snarled, finally determined to get some kind of clear answer and drawing on every ounce of her sixteen summers of privileged upbringing and royal lineage. "Answer the question!"

"It's a *Keepsake*, you young *fool...*!" He fired back sharply in return, whirling to face her once more and making her flinch in the process. "You *saw* the staves, yes? The *rope...*?"

"But... *but...*" It didn't register: even after everything she'd seen, and all they'd said – albeit indirectly – she simply found it impossible to accept the ramifications of what he was saying.

"*You're a witch...*!" Randwick hissed angrily, forcing his voice lower out of fear of spies or eavesdroppers as he took her firmly by the arm and dragged her back into the relative safety of her chambers, the telescope slipping from her grasp and clattering to the floor with the clink of broken glass. "You can *see* a Keepsake... which part of that do you not understand?"

"But, I *can't* be! I don't know any Majik... I'm not evil..." She wailed, tears again streaming down her face as the reality of it finally sunk in. "I'm the *princess...*!" She moaned, almost collapsing into a seated position on her bed as Randwick stood over her and the two other women present cowered back against one wall. "I'm not *evil...*!"

"I *know* you're not, lass..." He agreed with a sad, knowing smile, kneeling down before her and laying a comforting hand on hers. "You're the furthest thing from evil I've seen in this world in a long time, but that's not gonna make a lick 'o difference to the Inquisition."

"*Inquisition...*? By The Crystal, *no!*" She almost shrieked, forcing him to gesture quickly for her to lower her voice. "They can't do *that*... I'm the princess...!"

"You keep saying that like it means somethin'," he observed sadly, "and aye, it *does*: it's *because* you're a princess – *because* you're the king's own flesh and blood – that they'll *have* to do it... they'll have no choice. *Every* witch must be dealt with evenly: De Lisle could *never* allow any suggestion that there'd been special treatment for the daughter of a king…"

"Oh, Randwick: *the cardinal*…!" She exclaimed, remembering for the first time the conversation she'd heard the night before on that stairwell, and she proceeded to recount all that she could remember, fearing suddenly that perhaps the witch De Lisle had been referring to had somehow been her.

"It's a strange tale, alright," he agreed, not doubting her for a moment, "but I canna see how he could'a been talkin' about you when you're right here at Burnii rather than running wild somewhere in the Blacklands." Both were a little calmer now that the conversation had shifted to other matters. "Damned weird coincidence though, I'll grant ye. You'd not credit the mention of a witch in the Osterlands, only to discover *this* the next morning. Steady yerself and keep your courage, lass…" he assured quickly, seeing the tears well in her eyes once more. "I'll not see you locked in a dungeon or standin' atop any bonfire while *I* still draw breath. There's hope yet – we just need to find a solution. Either way," he decided suddenly, seeing no other option, "we need to tell the king before anything else happens."

Her father…! Her stomach lurched then, and she feared she might be sick. How could she possibly tell *him*; the man who'd been her hero and whole world for her entire life?

"There's no other way, lass…" Randwick confirmed, reading her expression perfectly. "I've an idea of what *might* be done, but there's nothin' can happen without the king's order. Well take a private audience and talk it through. Trust in your father, and trust in *me*: we'll see this fixed, all right…?"

"All – All right…" she surrendered meekly.

"Good mother," Randwick called out, rising to his feet once more and turning to address Griselda. "Can I trust you to say nothing if this?"

"I'd speak never a word!" She answered steadfastly, her pride at stake. I've raised this one from birth, and I'll not see a hair on her head harmed."

"Aye, I guessed as much," he nodded with an appreciative smile, both of them in complete accord over something for possibly the first time ever. "I thank y' for that: I'll handle everything from here. What about *you*, girl…?" He then asked with a far more serious expression, fixing Annabel with a sharp glare as he took a step in her direction and caused her to flinch. "You have anythin' you wanna tell me at this point?"

"I swear, I'd never tell a *soul*... swear on my *life*, Master Randwick!"

"Aye, you're swearin' on yer life alright!" He warned softly, taking another step forward purely to intimidate. "The torturers o' the Inquisition will be *nothin'* compared to what I'll do to y' if any loose talk gets about!" Griselda was someone he knew, respected and trusted regardless of the verbal sparring they sometimes engaged in, but the handmaiden – one of a number who worked on and off looking after the princess – was another thing entirely. Randwick knew how easy it was for even the most virtuous servant to be tempted by the lure of reward or favour, particularly if those seeking information were able to argue that information provided was for the 'good of the people'.

"There's no need for making threats like that, sir," Griselda declared firmly, pushing her way between the two as Annabel sagged back against the wall in relief. "*I* take care of my staff, and they do *exactly* as I say. There'll be no more mention of this, and that's that."

"You're word's good enough for me, Missus," Randwick nodded eventually. Turning, he glanced across at the standing clock and noted the hour for the first time. "Dragonfall take me, it's *already* almost noon! Come, girl!" He continued, turning back to Charleroi and extending both hands to help her to her feet. "Let's have the ladies here get you all cleaned up and looking pretty: we've perhaps a half-hour before the king finishes his next appointment, and I'd rather we were waiting for him when he does..."

It was almost an hour before Phaesus, having concluded his latest round of meetings with inconsequential local land owners, noblemen and unashamed social climbers, was finally provided the opportunity to take a short recess and partake of a late luncheon. A small antechamber had been set aside as a private dining room, leading directly off from the main hall behind the throne, and it was there that the king sat down alone to enjoy a large platter of roasted meats, bread and local cheeses, all complimented by a fine selection of red wine. He was seated at the table, facing the only entrance as Randwick knocked softly and slipped inside the room, a very pale and subdued Charleroi following close at his heels.

"I *had* thought I'd directed the guards to allow entry to *no one…*" Phaesus observed drily, knowing full well that no sentry with any sense and a desire to keep his vulnerable parts intact and unbruised would *ever* refuse Randwick passage. "No matter… there's plenty for all. Come… *come…*!" He added, beaming now as he spied his daughter for the first time, but that smile died on his lips as he caught the sorrowful expression on her face and the tracks of tears on her cheeks that she's not been able to stop. There was clearly something wrong – something he didn't know about – and that it might involve his only child caused his stomach to lurch slightly as his appetite left him.

"I've some news, Sire…" Randwick began carefully, nowhere near prepared for what was to come next as he and Charleroi took adjacent seats on the opposite side of the table. "News regarding the Keepsake found out on Round Hill beach this morning…"

"Oh, yes…? The 'sea monster' that was washed up overnight…?" Phaesus asked cautiously, using the standard nickname for any such Keepsakes brought in on the tides. They were rare nowadays – far rarer than they had been in his father's time, were the histories to be believed – but they did still turn up from time to time, sometimes creating havoc and sinking ships as the waves carried their invisible bulks inshore and smashed them against rocks, beaches or city wharves alike.

"Aye, Your Majesty: the very same…"

"It appears this may be ill news, judging from your expressions here," the king observed seriously, pushing the plate of leftovers off to one side and leaning forward, elbows on the table and propping up his goateed chin as his eyes bored deeply into Randwick's soul. "Come on, man: out with it. There's no service to either of us in beating about the bush."

"Sire, I've no words…" he began, faltering a little, before biting the bullet and going on. "Mistress Griselda called me to the princess' chambers this morning, and…" he paused again, swallowing deeply as the hairs on the back of Phaesus' neck rose in fear. "Your Majesty, your daughter has *seen* the Keepsake…"

Even as he uttered that last sentence, Charleroi began to sob softly and buried her face in her hands beside him. He'd steeled himself for some kind of outburst from the king – some raging denial or sorrowful wail of anguish – but instead received just the barest flinch of reaction in return, as if Phaesus had suddenly slipped completely into shock. It was a reaction – or lack, thereof – that Randwick had *never* expected.

"Sire… the princess… your *daughter*…" he began, lowering his voice to a whisper and leaning in as if proximity might somehow aid the man's hearing. "She can *see* Keepsakes!"

As silence once more reigned, the king's sad eyes stared into his for a moment and then moved on to his daughter, the pair meeting each other's gaze through a curtain of Charleroi's hair that had already managed to break loose from the pack and dangle down in the front.

"*Sire…?*"

"I hear you, Randwick… I hear you…" Phaesus assured finally, reaching out both arms across the table and taking his daughter's hands in his. "Charli, my beautiful one…" he began slowly, "I am *so* sorry…"

An apology was the last thing either had expected, and Charleroi was shocked as she realised a tear had also formed in the corner of her father's eye and trickled its way down along the forward edge of his left sideburn. Sitting there and allowing the scene to play over and over in his mind, it was a few more seconds before the rest of the picture came into focus for Randwick.

"You *know*…?" He asked simply, losing all sense of royal protocol momentarily from the shock of that realisation. "*You know*…!"

"I've known for a very long time, Randwick, yes…"

"But, father… *why*…?" Charleroi demanded, sorrow and anger filling her equally now as she too realised the truth. "Why is this happening to me? *Why didn't you* tell *me*…?"

"What was there to tell, my dear?" He asked with simple resignation, releasing her hands and raising one of his own in supplication as emphasis to his point. "I discovered what you could do when you were still *very* small… no more than three summers," he began slowly, seeing no point in withholding the story now. "I doubt you'd remember any of it. You'd been given your first pony… a little Shetland with a tiny saddle and reins tailored to size, and you could already ride him like a champion. You were a natural on horseback and I'd promised to take you for a ride that morning…" he paused then for a moment, wiping at his suddenly-dry lips and deciding to take a small sip of wine from the goblet at his right hand before continuing. "I *shouldn't have* – not beyond the walls – but you were so young and I'd *promised*, after all: what could be the harm? We'd travelled perhaps two hours or more and stopped to take a meal by a creek that emptied into the far side of Peaceful Lake…" He almost smiled then, thinking of it. "I remember it well… I was *so* proud of you that day, riding like a true horseman already…" He smile disappeared again as he continued the tale. "It was midway through our meal that you looked up and pointed at a clearing at the end of a narrow track, leading off into the scrub. 'Wagon!' you said… 'Funny wagon…!' I'll *never* forget those words…" he breathed softly, another tear making its way down to his chin.

"I didn't think anything of it at first, but you kept saying it over and over again… and *eventually*, I got up, drew my sword and moved closer to where you were pointing, using my blade like a blind man's cane." His voice broke then, he lowered his head to his hands, and it was a moment or two before he was able to continue on. "Sure enough, right where you'd been pointing the whole time, the blade catches hard against something I cannot see: a phantom of clanging metal in the forest."

"And you did nothing about it," Randwick nodded knowingly, sympathy and understanding in his voice now as Charleroi simply stared on in shock and disbelief. This was no king seated before him in that moment… only a desperate father instinctively trying to protect his child.

"What *could* I do?" Phaesus asked, his voice shaking. "So soon after what happened with Illyra, I couldn't bear to lose my *child* as well. Just the thought of it was too much to bear. There was no one else present, so I decided there was no need for *anyone* to know. We packed up our picnic, rode back to Cadle, and all was well again…"

"And you've been hiding *me* from the whole world ever since, father!" The princess hissed bitterly, so many things now making sense where none had before. "All the chaperones and the shuttered windows… all those times I couldn't come with you because it 'wasn't safe' or the roads were 'too rough' for a carriage. I see one of these stupid things when I was a baby, and since then you've done *everything* you could to stop me from *ever* seeing *anything* again! And *to what end*, father?" She demanded in the end, somehow feeling that part of an entire lifetime had been cheated from her without recompense. "What have all these years of 'protection' gotten me?"

"You were only supposed to be here for *two weeks*…!" He tried to explain, desperate to water down the terrible guilt he already felt.

"There hasn't been a sea monster wash up on one of our beaches in a *ten-year*. How could anyone have *possibly* guessed?"

"Sire, *something* must be done," Randwick ventured, cutting off pointless recrimination and returning the conversation to the present. "I've a proposal... something that *might* work for all of us... but we'll need resources that only *you* can give."

"Tell me, sir..." Phaesus urged, trusting the man completely. "Whatever you need, you shall have it..."

"A fast cog for a start, with a loyal crew and provisions enough to make landfall anywhere in the Osterlands that we so desire." He answered immediately. "She can't be here for the Endweek service – that's assured – but neither can she leave too early either: a missing princess would raise too many questions. I know just the ship and crew for the task, but I'll need your order to allocate supplies."

"Leave...?" Charleroi asked sharply, shock once more filling her words as the concept of going somewhere came up for the first time. "Why should I *leave*...? I'll go back to Cadle..."

"There's *nowhere* safe in Huon right now, lass..." Randwick replied sadly, turning to face her with a serious expression. "Much as I know *most* of it's smoke and mirrors, there's no denying there's *some* kind of power behind those crystals they carry with 'em and we can't risk you taking part in another o' the weekly blessings; not now you *know* what's wrong. One *hint* of what's happened and you'll be locked up where even a *king* can't save you."

"But... but, it's *my home*...!" She pleaded desperately, unable to even conceive of being away from Cadle and her father.

"Not anymore, lass..." Randwick said sadly, shaking his head.

"There's nothing to be done, my darling," Phaesus confirmed, fighting to hide the heartbreak filling his own soul. "Randwick's right... it'll not be safe here. I would defend you with my life, but if the truth is revealed and I defy The Brotherhood, there'd be no *hope* of a treaty: the Kings' Council would disavow me and every kingdom in the Osterlands would stand with Harald as he wiped us out. *Thousands* would die...the kingdom would be destroyed..." another tear coursed down his cheek then. "And you would *still* be dead at the end of it all."

"Father, you can't... *you can't*...!" She wailed, becoming more frantic as she realised he might actually stand by his decision. "I'm the princess... *your daughter*... you *can't do this*...!"

"I cannot bear this, Randwick… go now, please… I *beg* you…" Phaesus moaned softly, turning his head away now so as not to show the weakness of a king in tears.

"Come on, lass…" he sighed sadly, nodding to the king as he rose from his chair and turned to the sobbing princess. "There's no gain to be had talkin' more on this while everyone's upset."

"Father, *noooo*…!" She moaned, overcome with feelings of abandonment as Randwick placed his hands gently in her shoulders and guided her to her feet, at which point she immediately collapsed against his chest sobbing uncontrollably.

"Who else knows, Randwick…?" Phaesus asked softly, never turning his head back to face them for a moment.

"Just Griselda and one of her handmaidens, Annabel, Sire…"

"You trust them…?"

"I trust the old woman," he answered with cold honesty, laying a steading arm around the stricken princess as comfort. "As for the girl, I know not, but it was *promised* she'd be kept in line…"

"Thank you, Randwick…"

"Your Majesty…" he nodded simply, then returned to the task of guiding Charleroi toward the door.

"*Daddy… please…!*"

The king collapsed to the table the moment the door had closed behind them, sobbing silently with his head in his hands.

She woke late into the night, startled at first in the semi-darkness of the crackling fireplace set into the opposite wall, only to find her father seated beside her on the bed, tears in his eyes.

My beautiful girl…" he whispered softly, reaching out to brush the hair from her face and instead accepting her embrace as she threw her arms about him and buried her face in his chest. "My poor, beautiful girl…"

"What shall I do, father… what shall I *do*…?"

"You'll *survive* for the moment, my darling, while I find some way to fix this. I must away with the official party to Demon's Port tomorrow morning and shan't be back until nextday, for the official ceremony. You *must* be seen at the celebration, but you shall be away from here directly after… you *cannot* be part of the Endweek service."

"No one knows, father… how *could* they…?"

"You've never seen them use the crystals to uncover a witch," Phaesus observed, pausing for a moment before recounting a memory that had just come to him. "*I* saw it once... back when I was about your age. It was an Endweek service, and the prelate was moving about the congregation as usual, Shard necklace in one hand as he delivered the Holy Blessing. There was a young girl there –no more than eight or nine, she was the daughter of a nobleman – and when his hand touched her skin, the crystal in that necklace flashed brightly and there came a sharp, keening like the unholy buzz of some great insect."

He paused again then as unpleasant memories came to him.

"They took her away there and then," he continued, shaking his head faintly at the recollection. "The father – old Prendergast, I think it was – screamed and raged against them but it was to no avail. He pleaded and wailed as his daughter screamed for her daddy and his wife collapsed in a faint over the shock of it all; yet they would hear none of it. What else could he do... to save his own flesh and blood? Enraged and devoid of all reason, he drew the dagger at his belt and tried to kill the prelate, as if that might somehow put everything to right..."

"What happened?" She asked slowly, not sure she wanted to her the answer as she pulled back, staring up into his sad eyes.

"He was shot down by the Captain of the King's Guard: his own *brother*..." Phaesus answered after a moment, and she felt him shudder at the memory. "*His own kin* took a crossbow and fired a bolt into his back, in front of his screaming daughter and a hundred fellow nobles, and not *one* of 'em raising a hand against it... *myself* among them!" There was guilt in his tone, now. "The mother killed herself in grief that night and they burned the girl next morning, with no family to say goodbye. Her name escapes me, now, I'm ashamed to say, but I would think of what happened to her often in the early years, as you were growing up... after I found out what you could do..."

"How *horrible*...!" She murmured, then a thought occurred to her. "But... father if I *have* been a witch all this time, how is it that the brothers have never found *me* out? I've sat through *hundreds* of Endweeks..."

"*That*, I do not yet know for certain," he shrugged, "but I *suspect* they can only see what the *person* knows. *You* were too young to understand at the time, and *I* never told you... in your own mind, you were as innocent and pure as you truly are, and there was no darkness in your thoughts for the crystal to find. Most men *aren't* like Randwick," he continued darkly with a grim expression. "Most of us are foolish, *stupid* creatures, and ignorance is easily led. If my own guard thought for a *moment* I'd betrayed the Laws of the Shard, *every one of them* would strike me down in The Brotherhood's name without a thought.

"I know The Brotherhood fears this age of machines – fears that their congregations will turn away from the 'old' gods – but those fears are groundless, really." He continued tiredly. "There are no unbelievers when the battle rages, believe me… and in *this* life, people *need* something to believe… something that promises *some* kind of 'paradise' they can look forward to when their days are short and their time approaches. *Machines* can give them none of that."

"Do *you* believe them, Daddy? *Am* I a witch…?" She asked in a soft, broken voice that tore at his heart. "*Am I evil…?*"

"I don't know *what* to believe anymore, darling girl," he admitted, almost managing a wry smile then, "but I *do* know this, Charleroi: that *you* are the kindest, smartest, most *wonderful* girl in this whole, wide world and the *one thing* you are *not* is evil. I may not yet be able to prove it, but I am as certain now as I was that afternoon we went riding, all those years ago: witches may exist or they may not but *whatever* The Brotherhood say, seeing Keepsakes is *no* proof of being one for *you* are no witch, and if *you* can see these things, there must be – *must be* – some *other* explanation. You must go away for now to be safe, but I'll do *everything* I can to find out what that explanation is… *this* I promise on my very soul, as a king, and as a *father*…"

XI

CATALYST

There was pain and dizziness as Nev struggled back toward the unpleasant reality of consciousness. Not quite ready to open her eyes, she could already feel a dull ache at the back of her skull where she'd clearly been hit by something hard, and a growing migraine threatened to split it in two whenever she moved her head. It was also quite clear that she was tied to a chair, her hands secured behind her back in a position that was quite uncomfortable, if not actually painful. It took just a few seconds for fear to take over from confusion and although she knew it would make no difference whatsoever, her first instinct was to keep her eyes shut tight as if not being able to *see* what was happening might somehow make it all go away. In the end, it was the sound of other voices that gave her the strength to overcome her mounting terror and open her eyes.

She'd originally thought it was the blow to her head that was making the room move around her but it turned out that they were actually on a ship, and at least *some* of that movement was the vessel cutting through a mild ocean swell. The room was darker than she'd expected with just a few glass-enclosed lanterns hanging about the walls for light, and the air stank vaguely of kerosene, sweat and the faint but unmistakably coppery smell of blood. It had originally been used for dining, and a long, narrow table still consumed most of the room's centre although it was unlikely to have meals served on it anytime soon. Most of its length was at present taken up by the prone bodies of Lester and Godfrey, both strapped down tightly with their heads almost touching near the middle.

An old man wearing black robes stood over them on the far side of the table and just behind him, a bearded man in fine, colourful clothes watched on with dark interest. Taller and far younger, he rested against the opposite wall, a long-bladed dagger in his hand and a sword at his belt. To Nev's right, a small porthole opened out into the blackness of the night beyond while on her right, the only door out of that room was currently closed and flanked by a pair of guards, also armed with swords and wearing plain uniforms of green leather beneath fine links of blackened chainmail.

Lester had been gagged tightly and was currently struggling hard against his bonds to no avail. He was being completely ignored by all concerned as he glared in the old man's direction, all the while spewing forth an almost unending stream of profanity that although unintelligible because of the gag, was nevertheless clearly quite vile and filthy judging by the tone and meter of his muffled words. Godfrey had not been gagged however, and he was currently speaking freely as he desperately attempted to salvage what he could from the situation.

"Have y' not heard what I've been saying...?" Godfrey growled at that moment, facing away from Nev as he addressed the priest. "We came here lookin' for work, that's all... tryin' to make a few coins to feed the family, for Crystal's sake...!"

"By operating as *assassins*, it appears..." Silas hissed darkly, eyes narrowed with hatred, "...how *else* would this explain the crossbow in the boy's possession? There are far *safer* ways to earn 'a few coins'..."

"*It weren't him...*" Godfrey insisted, trying to include as much sincerity in his exasperated reply. "A man would have t' be *insane* to take a shot at The Brotherhood!" He added plaintively. "Dunno *who* it was that killed that poor feller of yours *but it weren't any of us...*"

"Just 'poor, law-abiding citizens'..." Silas observed, his words dripping with sarcasm. "Can't *imagine* why you'd need to run from the Blackwatch... *surely* all just some *huge* misunderstanding..."

"Yeah... yeah...! Misunderstanding... *that's it*...!" Godfrey offered enthusiastically, clutching at any straw the priest was ready to offer. "It was dark: we couldn't rightly *see* it was the Blackwatch when they yelled out – thought it was robbers, we did!"

"*Mmmh...*" the old man mused, displaying a distinctly evil smile "...and this has *nothing* to do with the fugitive *witch* you've been harbouring?" He added sharply, pointing an accusing finger at Nev and glaring in her direction for the first time as Godfrey's slim hopes of talking his way out of the situation evaporated completely. "We *know* who you are, Westacre! A *mercenary*...! A minor lackey of the damned Southern Oster, working under James Harris! The Blackwatch have been looking for you for a *long time*!"

"Perhaps we should hand him over..." Prince Baal observed from behind Silas, well aware of the kind of tortures Harald's men might think up for a wanted man and smirking at the thought. "No doubt they'd pay a handsome reward for such a prize..."

"We may do just that..." Silas agreed with a thoughtful nod, moving slowly around the bottom end of the table, circling Godfrey's feet. "We've our *own* information to extract *first*, however..."

"I – I dunno what yer talkin' about..." Godfrey stammered in vain, making one last, desperate attempt at holding to his original story. "Dunno *who* this 'Westicker' is, but he ain't *me*..."

"You see how *clever* they are, Your Highness...?" Silas observed with grudging admiration. "...How *smoothly* the lies slip from his tongue? How the tiny *details* make the difference; like the mispronunciation of his own name as if he's *never* heard it before in his life. You'd make a fine politician, boy..." he added, his face hardening into a cold, pitiless expression "...but some advice from one who knows: *never play out of your league...!*"

Silas was beside him again in an instant, this time with his back to Nev as his right hand flashed out, the crystal necklace wrapped about his palm. The moment it neared Godfrey's face, it flashed into life and his body went rigid as if suddenly wracked with a seizure. Grunts of discomfort and fear escaped his clenched teeth as he struggled to turn his head just a few centimetres toward Silas, defiance alive and strong in his eyes.

"You think you can fool *me*, sell-sword?" The old man hissed venomously. "*I*, who have served The Shard for *half a century*...? You'll *beg* me to hand you over to Harald by the time I'm done..." he continued, withdrawing his hand in that moment and releasing Godfrey's body from its stricken state.

"I... don't... *know*... anythin'..." he wheezed in between deep breaths as the crippling pain he'd just experienced began to fade.

"What were you doing with the witch?" Silas asked coldly, not buying any of it. "*Where* were you taking her?"

"I told you, I don't.... *uhhhhh...!*" The crystal flashed again and Godfrey gasped, arching his back in agony for a second time as his body was gripped by an unseen force that sent slivers of pain lancing through his skull and threatened to crush his chest.

"You have *no idea* what I could do to you with this. It's been a *long* time since you were last at Endweek, boy... *I can tell*..." Silas noted, almost smiling then as he acknowledged a silent thought within his own mind. "I shall have to be *careful*: you're tolerance will be low and I can't afford to lose you *before* I've got what I need."

"There are always more *traditional* methods..." Baal pointed out, casually picking something from his fingernails with the point of his dagger. "I've one or two men aboard who are skilled with such things..."

"Indeed, I may ask for your assistance if need be, Your Highness," Silas conceded with mocking grace, "however I've some ideas of my *own* I can try *first*..."

"Leave them alone, you... you *bastard*...!" Nev snarled angrily, no longer able to hold her tongue as she finally found something (or some*one*) worth swearing properly over; the volume of her words made her aching head spin a little, but she fought to conceal her dizziness as the old man turned slowly in her direction, his face a mask of hatred.

"I'll deal with you in due course, *witch*...!" He snapped in return. "*Your* demise with be *breathtaking* in its brutality but you'll need to show some patience: there are *others* to be dealt with first."

"They don't know anything!" She shouted in return, struggling to keep the fear or emotion out of her voice. "And I'm *not* a bloody *witch*, you crazy old *fool*...!"

"You *dare* to speak to a *Quisitor* with such disrespect?" Silas hissed with indignant fury, taking a single step forward and lifting his fist as if might strike her, the crystal still wrapped about his knuckles.

Hold...! *Desist*...!

Those dark, earth-shattering words roared in Silas' mind in that moment, staying his hand as he used every ounce of his remaining strength to *not* stagger backward and reveal any weakness.

There is danger here... you cannot – must not – *use Our power against this one...*

He'd experienced direct communication with The Shard once or twice on his life, but never with such intensity as in that moment, and the force of it came as a huge shock to his system. Silas knew that De Lisle dealt with such incidents on a daily basis, and he admired the man as much for his ability to retain his sanity in the face of that as much as anything else.

"I – I will *enjoy* watching you *burn*..." he growled, recovering quickly and turning back toward to the table. "It *speaks*, Westacre...

sounds almost *human*...! Was it a *spell* you were under, or is this simply another Osterman contract?"

Nev was the only person in the room other than Silas who'd heard that warning boom inside their mind, and the hint of fearfulness it contained surprised her as much as his unexpected withdrawal. She'd recoiled in shock initially, preparing for the blow that had never come, but she'd then seen the fear that had also flashed in his eyes briefly upon hearing that silent command. The revelation that either the old man or the faceless voice that controlled him might actually be *scared* of her was a confusing one indeed.

"I *told* you..." Godfrey began again, completely oblivious to what had just occurred. "I don't..."

"...Don't know *anything*... *yes*, I know, I know..." Silas sighed, finishing the sentence for him with a dismissive wave. He was tiring of the cat-and-mouse, and the sudden contact with The Shard had also left him feeling slightly drained. "Perhaps you could explain *these* to me, instead?"

He moved back to the foot of the long table again, turning toward a narrow bench running the length of the cabin below the porthole, and Nev for the first time noticed that their belongings had been dumped in a pile on the deck there, her duffel bag amongst it all. He withdrew the katana and held it up, drawing the blade halfway to show the rest of the room.

"*This* is no *mercenary's* weapon..." he observed sharply as Baal nodded in silent agreement. "What nobleman did you steal it from? Did you stab them in the back like the coward that you are?"

"Didn't kill no one for it... it ain't mine," Godfrey shrugged simply, telling the absolute truth for the first time.

"You expect me to believe this belongs to the *boy*?" Silas scoffed, not for a moment considering Nev as an alternative.

"You're gonna kill us *anyway*," he replied, finally giving up on any hope of pretence and deciding for Nev's sake it was better not to argue regarding the sword's ownership. "I don't give two stuffs *what* you think!"

"Oh, there are *so many* different ways to die... some *far slower* than others..." Silas pointed out softly, placing the sword carefully on the bench and returning his attention to the duffel bag. "You *will* tell me what I want to know or I will show you *exactly* how long it can take for a man's life to fade...

"What are *these*..." the old man continued, his hands diving inside once more and drawing out Nev's phone and her portable Bluetooth speaker. "Devices of *witchcraft*, no less..." he decided scornfully, holding them aloft for all to see. "Who *knows* what evil might come of such things?"

What I would give *for* Highway to Hell *to start blasting out at full volume right now...* Nev thought angrily, sending a death stare in his direction.

"Perhaps I could use them to steal your *soul*...?" She asked instead, forcing a sweetly insincere tone into her voice. Something in the way he'd reacted earlier gave her the distinct feeling the old man was scared of her, and as unlikely as that seemed, it occurred to Nev that that might just give her something to work with.

"The Shard protects me, *harpy*..." Silas replied, almost throwing the devices onto the bench in his hurry to be rid of them as the rest of those present, Baal included, shifted uneasily at the thought. "Your threats are meaningless to me..."

"So 'meaningless' you couldn't get rid of them fast enough?" She muttered under her breath, her volume calculated to be *just* loud enough to be heard by everyone else in the room. The remark drew a snort of derision from Godfrey, and even Lester stopped struggling just long enough to give a muffled laugh of his own.

"How I would *love* to *burn* you..." Silas snarled, his wrinkled face reddening with humiliation, and the way he raised his hand in her direction, palm open and crystal on display, suggested he wasn't talking about physical flames. "Alas, my orders are clear in that regard..." he shrugged, sweeping past her close enough to make Nev flinch all the same, much to her own dismay.

"I doubt any *direct* threats of torture or harm against *either* of you would be particularly effective," he continued, his tone calmer now although everyone could nevertheless hear a hint of foreboding behind his words. "How much you care for *each other* however, is yet to be proven..."

He'd also walked straight past Godfrey and instead came to a halt beside Lester, you boy's struggles intensifying dramatically with the old man's presence.

"I *remember* you..." Silas declared, tilting his head in Lester's direction. "The Boniface family... *Such* a shame that sister of yours turned out to be a 'witch'..." Lester screamed then in rage rather than fear, and it seemed he might dislocate his own limbs in his desperate attempts to free himself and attack the old man. "Calm now... *calm* now, child..." Silas suggested firmly, extending his hand and holding the glowing crystal over the boy's head, and this time Lester was afflicted with the same seizures that had gripped Godfrey earlier.

"Leave him alone, you *dog*...!"

"*Where* were you taking the witch...?"

"Go to hell!" Godfrey spat darkly, Lester all the while fighting against the pain and shaking his head violently, urging him to reveal nothing.

"*Who* ordered the contract to escort her?" With a single flex of Silas' fingers, the crystal brightened and the pain intensified, arcing through every nerve of Lester's body as he screamed in agony.

"He's just a *boy*, damn you...!"

"And he can go in peace... all you need do is tell me what I want to know..." Silas clenched his fist slowly, and behind the gag tied tightly about his face, Lester screamed it agony, his body arching off the table as he jerked his head from side to side, his mind trying to cope with something far beyond its capacity.

"His mind will die first..." the old man said casually, as if discussing the weather. "His body will follow soon enough... he may *already* be beyond hope..."

Through her own tears, Nev could see Godfrey was breaking. As strong as his sense of honour and duty was, he simply couldn't ignore the fact that a boy who'd become almost a brother to him was suffering at the hands of this torturer. She knew he'd break eventually and she also knew he'd never forgive himself.

"*Despair*...!" She wailed, not needing much pretence to affect an expression of misery and defeat. "They said they were taking me somewhere called 'Despair'..." She elaborated as Silas turned slowly in her direction again and the boy's pain suddenly ceased, his body sagging back to the table as he slipped into blissful unconsciousness.

"Tell 'em *nothing*...!" Godfrey howled, anything else he might've said cut short as the old man lifted a single finger without even turning back and again sent his body rigid.

"*Despair* was destroyed *years* ago. It's nothing but a fairy tale that crones use to control their grandchildren..." Silas sneered, taking a single step in her direction.

"Believe what you like, but that's where they were taking me. Despair: a place where accused witches go to hide from The Inquisition, yeah? Despair; the same group that The Blackwatch and the Crowedans *thought* they'd wiped out on Kings' Coat, *'years ago'*...?"

"My word; you've learned much in the last few days..." Silas conceded, almost impressed. "...Do go on... *please*..." He urged cautiously, suspicious that Nev was offering up the information far too easily.

"Nothin' else to tell..." she shrugged, working hard to bring her emotions under control once more now that she had his full attention. "They don't know where this place is and neither do I. They told me they don't know – that they weren't told *specifically* because of the risk of capture..."

"You lie...!" He declared, inadvertently taking another step toward her then almost leaping backward again as he realised what he'd done.

"You think so?" She asked shrewdly, her confidence beginning to grow with the knowledge that he really was scared of her for some reason. "Aren't you guys the 'All Powerful Brotherhood'? Surely you can use that crystal-thingy of yours to check if I'm telling the truth?"

She knew it was a dangerous game she was now playing, but some long-buried instinct within her sub-conscious was now coming to the fore, guiding her actions. She'd spent the last three days in almost constant danger and she was suddenly shocked by the realisation that it was all starting to become a bit of a bore. With so many potential enemies already inside that room and all three of them tied up like Christmas turkeys, the situation was already hopeless from any logical perspective, so what could possibly be lost by acting in an *illogical* manner?

"Th – The very *thought* of using The Shard Crystal in such a fashion is an insult," he stammered quickly, and this time everyone heard the sudden indecision in his voice – something *completely* unexpected from a man of Silas' formidable reputation.

Nev found that she was beyond caring anyway. As she looked across at Lester's unconscious body, blood trickling in thin streaks from one nostril, she was filled with a rage that overwhelmed everything of the fear and confusion she'd experienced almost constantly since being dragged into that world.

"Well... *that's* convenient, isn't it!" She shot back with equal speed, including as much scorn and attitude as she could manage. "I don't think that's it at all... *I* think you're *scared* of me...!"

The shocked hush that enveloped the room in the seconds that followed that outlandish statement was palpable. Godfrey stared on in disbelief, while one of the guards' jaws literally dropped in surprise.

"You have *no idea* of the pain you will suffer before you die..." Silas hissed with barely-suppressed fury, well aware of how greatly he had been humiliated in that moment. "You will *beg* to be burned at the stake..."

"Maybe..." she conceded, managing to keep her tone light and control her own rage. "Bet you'll get someone *else* to do it, though..." she added, knowing with all the innate viciousness of a teenage girl *exactly* how to plunge a verbal 'knife' into someone's heart. "...*You* wouldn't have the *guts*...!"

"You little *whore*...!"

Silas almost screamed those words, so incensed with rage now that he was actually shaking as he took another involuntary step forward, his right hand struggling to force its way toward her with the crystal suspended from its palm. The old man had no experience in the use of *physical* violence – he'd never *needed* it – and his first instinct was always to fall back to the power of The Shard, either in defence or attack. To be deprived of that power now for the first time in his living memory left him feeling completely defenceless in the face of her verbal assault.

"Think you're so *tough* while we're tied up and helpless, don't you...?" She taunted scornfully, nodding her head faintly at the quaver in his right arm. "I see you thinkin' about it. *Big*, tough guy you are when no one can fight back...!"

"For the Crystal's Sake, Brother Silas, we need not endure any more of this drivel!" Baal called from the other side of the table, taking a step away from the wall now and resting his hand on the sword at his belt. "Give the word and I'll cut out that tongue of hers... give us *all* some peace..."

"*Do not* presume *to interfere*...!" The old man barked savagely, momentarily casting a fiery glare in the prince's direction and *very* unhappy about any suggestion he was unable to fight his own battles. "You think I am *incapable* of dealing with this creature?"

"I *know* you're not capable…" Nev muttered, just loud enough for everyone to hear. "Is that what it is…?" She added, suddenly seeing the trigger her sub-conscious had been searching for all along. "Is *that* why you like torturing women and little boys…?"

"I will *destroy* you…!" He snarled as loudly as his old lungs could manage, but there was the quaver of uncertainty in the words now too, as if his sub-conscious was silently pleading to be left alone.

"Go on, then…" she goaded, almost drunk on the power as Nev realised it was *she* who was completely in control of the current exchange. "Cut me free and try to take a swing at me…" she paused then, glancing momentarily toward the bench to her right before returning her gaze to Silas, a thin, smug smile spreading across her face. "*Pick up that sword* and we'll *see* who's tougher… you, or a *girl*…"

"She's *goading* you, brother," Baal warned, taking a few steps toward them and half-drawing his sword, but Silas heard none of that as Nev continued to speak, his entire, enraged focus solely on her words alone.

"…But you're *not* going to do it, are you?" She sneered, forcing derision into her tone and expression as she added in a hiss: "*You don't have the balls…!*"

Something inside Brother Silas broke in that moment. In all his years of solid service to The Shard… with all the terrible, unforgiveable things he knew he'd done in Its name… *no one* had ever been allowed to speak to him in such a manner. *No one* had *ever* disrespected him or derided his authority so blatantly and without fear of retribution. That this attack should come from a woman – from one who was barely *even* a woman – magnified the insult far beyond the capacity of his self-control.

Silas' rage pushed him beyond any rational thought. Had he been a soldier or an assassin, his first instinct might've been to reach for the decorative dagger at his belt and had he done so, Nev's life would almost certainly have been over *very* quickly. He was no warrior however, and Silas instead made use of the most powerful weapon he had at his disposal – a weapon that had served him flawlessly over many decades in the service of The Shard.

Do not attack… Step away: I command it…! Those thundering words boomed in Nev's mind, filled equally by anger and fear, and the power of it was enough to leave her dizzy.

Silas was beyond any ability for coherent thought however, and the strength of his rage was such that he was able to shrug off the restrictive, mind-numbing force that came with its command. Releasing a guttural roar of primal rage that seemed to explode outward from his small, wizened frame, the priest stepped forward, lifted his right hand and pushed his open palm down hard on Nev's forehead, the glowing crystal pendant pressed beneath his fingers.

No...! The booming voice howled in desperation, far too late to be of any use. *This cannot-*!

Nev had recoiled back into her chair as those words rang in her mind, convinced the next seconds were the last of her life in spite of all her anger and bravado she'd been displaying (although some small, raging part of her inner mind nevertheless howled in jubilation over the absolute mental victory she'd just won). She felt his hand touch her head... felt the rough shape and faint warmth of the crystal as it pressed against her skin... registered a muted flash of brilliant blue through her closed eyelids, and then...

...nothing, to begin with: silence... darkness... and an overpowering sensation of somehow being nowhere *and* everywhere at the same time. Seemingly unbidden, a vision rose in her mind; a memory of her childhood, long-forgotten and shrouded in the camouflage of hiding from family pain and anguish. A memory of when she was just six years old and her world was a *very* different place.

Nev thought Grandpa Anders talked funny, but that was okay 'cause he was an old man, and anyway, Mummy said he came from a country all the way around the other side of the whole world. Daddy said it was a place called Iceland, which sounded *really cold, but he'd also told her that there was lots of volcanoes and bubbly, hot pools there (which didn't really make much sense, if the whole place was made out of* ice...*). Grandpa Anders was taller – much taller than Daddy – and he always talked about how his thick hair and beard had been bright red when he was younger, not grey like it was now – and he always talked about funny people called 'Vikings' who rowed everywhere in long boats with dragons at the front. At six years old, Nev was already incredibly bright and well-spoken, and her paternal* grandparents spoilt Drake and Nicole's only child shamelessly whenever they visited.

Sometimes, when they were in alone in the spare room and they thought no one could hear, Grandpa Anders and Grandma Jeannette argued and shouted at each other (...you really could hear them through the rest of the house anyway...). Nev didn't like it when they shouted. They were so nice, and she couldn't work out why nice people would even want to yell and scream at each other.

The strange thing was, even though you could hear everything, Mummy and Daddy always acted like they couldn't. At first, Nev had wondered for a while if she was the only one who could hear: like maybe it was her own, special 'superpower'. As she'd grown a little older however, she learned how to pick up the subtle changes in her parents' body language during those private arguments and she eventually realised they were only pretending not to hear. Mummy and Daddy shouted sometimes, too, but that wasn't very often at all. Nev really didn't like it when that happened, and when it did, she pretended too.

She loved all her grandparents dearly, but everyone knew that when the Gunnarsons visited, Nev was 'Grandpa's Girl'. Drake's father could think of nothing better than to spend time playing games with his only granddaughter, listening to her childlike ramblings with sincere interest and delighting in her squeals of enjoyment as he carried her about on his huge, bearlike shoulders while her parents called warnings about banging her head on the lounge room light fittings.

It was one of the games they'd played one day that had been only time Nev had ever heard Daddy arguing with Grandpa. They'd been playing in her room with a deck of playing cards; a well-worn, chequered blue Queens Slipper '500' pack with all the extra elevens, twelves and thirteens, and the colourful jokers that Nev loved the best. Nev didn't really know any proper card games – her parents had forbidden her learning poker or pontoon, she was too young to grasp five hundred or euchre, and she simply didn't have the patience for patience – so Grandpa Anders had instead hit upon the simple idea that each of them take half the pack and hold single cards up in turn, facing away from the other player, who would then attempt to guess which card it was.

Nev tried her best. Grandpa would hold up a card and she'd think really hard, trying to imagine a picture of its face in her mind.

Sometimes she'd guess correctly (most of the time, she didn't), but Grandpa was always encouraging and supportive, urging her to try again and again. Grandpa was really good at that game. Most of the time he'd correctly guess which card she was holding, and even sometimes when he made a 'mistake', Nev got the feeling he was giving a wrong answer on purpose.

Nev loved it. She laughed and giggled and clapped her hands, pleading with Grandpa to tell her how he did it, but all he would say was that it was 'magic', and that magicians didn't tell their secrets. Nev replied (not very certain about the whole thing) that she didn't think magic was really real, and Grandpa told her in return that magic was just stuff that people couldn't explain yet: that there were lots of things today that people in 'The Old Days' would've called magic or witchcraft.

That was when Daddy came into the room and saw what they were playing. He got angry with Grandpa, shouting louder than Nev had ever heard before and telling him that it 'wasn't fair'; that Grandpa had 'no right'... Grandpa yelled back that Daddy was turning his back on something called his 'ancestors', and that someone had to do what was 'best' for the family. Nev didn't understand any of it. It had just been a card game after all and it seemed really unfair for anyone to be arguing over some silly game.

Grandma Jeannette had joined in then, standing in the doorway and telling Grandpa off too, and Nev had pleaded and pleaded for them all to stop and be nice... but no one would listen to her at all and Mummy had to come and take her to another room. Nev cried and cried, saying she was sorry over and over because playing cards had been her idea, and now Daddy and Grandpa were shouting because of it. Mummy tried to tell her that it wasn't her fault but she knew that wasn't true.

It wasn't long after that Grandpa Anders and Grandma Jeannette started visiting on their own instead of together, and Grandma didn't come as often as she had before, which was very sad. Grandpa still visited regularly, but he also seemed a little sadder and less talkative than he had when they'd turned up together. He and Daddy never shouted at each other again like they had that day, but even Nev could tell things weren't the same... that something had changed.

Nev had no idea why that memory had suddenly flared into such vivid life within her mind, and as she fought to clear her thoughts, sadness flowing through her thoughts, a single, booming word thundered in her consciousness, louder and stronger than anything that had come before:

Interesting...

"What... who are you...?" She demanded angrily, flailing wildly and unable to see a single thing in the blackness surrounding her, but there was no answer... only a continuing, oppressive silence as she staggered forward into nothingness. With tears streaming down her face, she raised her fist and shouted: *"Answer me...!"*

A thin arc of blue-white electricity sparked from her hand and crackled away into the darkness around her, shorting on random, invisible points of light with diminishing intensity as it spread out in all directions, and for a fraction of a second it was possible to see the faint, flickering movement of ill-defined, shadowy shapes as they shied away from the flash. There seemed to be a faint glow at the edges of her fingers now and as she opened her palm, she inexplicably found Silas' pendant lying there, glowing brightly with the chain coiled around it in a tangle. Tiny crackles of static electricity arced from the gem to the tips of her fingers, making them tingle, and coiled about her wrist as she stared down at it in wonder.

"What *are* you...?" She asked softly, almost mesmerised for a few seconds by the miniature light show as she ran her other hand over the top of the pendant and the intensity of the discharge increased, creating a translucent ball of energy that sparkled and flickered much like the tragic old plasma ball her father kept in his room as a night light – the same one he'd picked up as a kid in the 1980s when the thing was still thought of as a cool novelty item. The momentarily pleasant memory of her father was then followed by memories of all the other, far less pleasant experiences she'd survived since arriving in that strange, new world and the fleeting smile that appeared briefly on her lips disappeared as quickly as it had come.

"What are you...?" She screamed, the words a demand as much as they were a question.

The crystal flashed brilliant white, leaving a flare at the centre of her vision as a faint shockwave of blue light surged away from her in all directions, a ripple of time and space following in its wake. The blackness itself parted fleetingly and for just a moment she was able to see something else before her... something that seemed small only because of the vast distance that lay between them.

Translucent to the point of being almost invisible, it glowed faintly with the same azure hue as the crystal in her palm; an ill-defined, amorphous shape that seemed to change and shift without warning. As the darkness coiled about her once more, her last impression was of it lashing out toward her across that vast expanse of nothing and she was suddenly engulfed by a wave of pure, unadulterated hatred.

There was a sharp, sudden shock to her consciousness, like the shunting of her train of thought, and Godfrey, the torture table and the rest of it all snapped savagely back into focus with brutal reality. Silas still stood before her, right up in her face, however the rage he'd previously displayed seemed to have been supplanted by an expression of abject fear. There was complete silence otherwise and Nev realised within that first fraction of a second that the eyes of every conscious person present were currently focussed directly on her. It was at that point she realised that the fingers of her left hand were tingling.

Her arms *had* been tied behind her, and they'd seemed quite secure when she'd tested the rope earlier. The bonds that had held her now lay in pieces on the floor however and she was surprised to discover that rather than locked down and unable to move, her left hand was instead clamped firmly about Silas' wrist, the dangling pendant caught beneath her palm. He was struggling desperately to pull back from her vice-like grip, all to no avail, and all the while, tiny crackles of energy arced across both of their hands, leaving the hair on her arm standing straight and tall with static discharge.

For her part, Nev knew she *should* have been terrified right now and part of her sub-conscious was *very* surprised that she actually – *surprisingly* – felt nothing of the sort. Experiencing a level of clarity she'd never known, she instead felt sharper and more aware than ever before and as she glanced down, she could already quite clearly envisage the *exact* amount of strength necessary to crush the old man's wrist – a level of strength that she was *certain* she could apply if she so desired. Turning his arm away and pushing him backward with a single, sharp flex and twist of her muscles, she rose quickly from the chair (no one had bothered to tie her legs) and forced Silas backward to her left, her right hand clamped firmly around one arm of the chair for extra leverage.

"Release me, *hag*...!" He croaked in fright, knowing the true meaning of fear for possibly the first time in his entire life. "Release me, I *command* you...!"

"My *pleasure*...!" She hissed in reply, an evil smile flashing across her face as she fixed him with a steeled gaze and squeezed down hard on his frail wrist.

It didn't take much to force Silas' hand open –pain and the fear of a broken wrist were incentive enough – and she deftly caught the pendant as he released it completely, its glow increasing to almost blinding intensity as her fingers closed fully around it. A turquoise glow flared between her fingers and writhing bolts of tiny lightning crackled and flashed in all directions as the old man staggered backward, crashing into the corner of the table and collapsing to the deck beyond with a cry as agony lanced through his lower back.

"Baal...! *Your sword*...!" He shrieked, terror filling him now as he realised what had happened – that Nev had taken the crystal from him as easily as one might steal a toy from a newborn child.

"*At once*, Brother...! *Guards*...!" The prince acknowledged immediately, casting away the dagger in his hands and reaching for the rapier at his belt. The shocked tension of those first moments broke then as they all came to their senses, the two guards also reaching for their weapons as they charged forward.

"*Guards*...!" Nev snapped at Godfrey, the young man staring up at her with no small amount of shock and fear in his own eyes as his mind tried to process what he was seeing. With a single nod of warning, she cast her eyes across the ropes tying his wrists and instinctively swept her left hand down across the point where they disappeared beneath the table's near edge. There was a flash and tiny crackle of lightning and the ropes tore apart in a burst of flame that stank of smoke and of something intense and almost *chemical* in nature.

Godfrey needed no further urging: he launched himself from the table the moment his body was free, sliding nimbly off to Nev's left and planting a heavy boot into the groin of the nearest guard in the same, fluid movement. The man fell backward, waves of pain and nausea sweeping over him as Godfrey snatched the short sword from his loosened grip and dived forward under the swing of the second guard, driving the blade deep into his chest.

As he dealt with the guards, Nev turned her attention toward Baal as he rounded the other end of the table with murder in his eyes.

Without even really thinking about it, she dodged around Silas' fallen body, spinning through 360 degrees and bringing with her the chair that was still clamped in her right fist. The prince had *expected* the girl to flee... that she came *at* him instead was a mild surprise to be certain, but what he *truly* hadn't expected was the manner in which she attacked.

A trained swordsman (if somewhat lacking in actual *combat* experience), he was prepared for *some* kind of assault – a punch or kick or perhaps even a hidden dagger at worst – but something he definitely *didn't* expect was to find a heavy, wooden chair coming at him in a wide, around-the-shoulder swing from Nev's right. Already in the process of raising his own weapon to strike, he was suddenly forced to completely abandon that idea and instead throw his arms up to his right to defend against the incoming furniture.

"*Hyah*...!" Using her body weight and centrifugal force to increase the power of her swing, Nev screamed a short, sharp *kiai* shout and smashed the chair hard into her attacker.

Baal's reflexes probably saved his life. Had he not thrown his arms up at the last moment, the thick wood of the chair would almost certainly have caved in his skull. As it was, there was enough force to snap his forearm and still strike the side of his head hard enough to knock him senseless. He collapsed against the table where Godfrey had lain moments before, landing in a pile on the floor with the weak and wailing Silas.

"Packs... *weapons*...!" Godfrey barked urgently from the other side of the room, having finished off the first guard with a series of cracks to the back of the head, using the pommel of the man's own sword as a club. "We've a *minute* or two at best before all hell breaks loose out there, and we need to find a way *off* this ship before that happens...!"

With a nod and not a single word, Nev stepped lightly over Baal and the croaking Silas, both of them completely forgotten for the moment, and moved straight across the table where their belongings lay strewn. Working at a feverish, adrenalin-fuelled pace, she hurriedly stuffed everything back into their respective packs, strapped the katana to her belt and slipped her duffel bag over her shoulders. She had no idea what she *should* do with the necklace itself, but she was *certain* that giving it up would be a bad idea at that point. Instead, she took a moment to wrap the chain snugly around her right wrist and tie it off, tucking the crystal pendant into her sleeve.

As she turned, Godfrey's sword and rucksack in hand, she found him bent over Lester on the table, carefully cutting the boy's bonds with his sword.

"Come on, mate… wakey-wakey… time to get going…" he whispered in sad desperation, shaking Lester's shoulders and trying in vain to rouse him from his unconsciousness.

"*Oh, no…*" she breathed softly, her heart wrenching with sudden emotion as Godfrey fought his own tears and used a sleeve to wipe away the blood that had trickled from the boy's nose.

"Come on, Toadface…" he pleaded softly, continuing to shake the boy and not ready to accept what seemed to be the inevitable.

"Is he…?" She asked in a lost, lonely voice, dreading the answer.

"Still breathin'… no thanks to *this* bastard…!" Godfrey spat bitterly, sudden anger in his eyes and tone as he glared at Silas, who'd taken the opportunity to drag himself away from the table and was now cowering in a far corner of the room, near the table their belongings had rested on. Lifting himself away from the table for a moment, Godfrey raised his sword and received a whimper of fear in return.

"If he's still breathing, then there's still *hope*…" Nev insisted, feeling some of the same killing rage she saw in Godfrey's eyes but fighting against it for the sake of reason and their own, continuing safety. "What do we do about *these* two…?" She added, knowing *something* needed to be done but not sure she liked the idea of killing defenceless human beings… even ones who probably deserved it.

"Much as I'd *love* to lop the heads off these two, it'd be more than my life's worth …" Godfrey growled, glaring at Baal's crumpled form. "This one's a king's cousin, and the Southern Oster don't need *that* kind of grief…"

"But he's *betraying his own country*…" Nev pointed out, illustrating the man's shortcomings rather than any real desire for execution.

"Aye, and there's only *our* word for that right now, yeah…? I'll not start a blood feud against Huon if I can avoid it." Godfrey countered with a raised eyebrow, knowing well enough the harm that would come of *another* royal assassination. "And as for *this one*," he snarled darkly, levelling the blade of his sword at the old man cowering in the corner. "Southern Oster's little more than a minor irritation for The

Brotherhood right now… *kill* one o' their head honchos though, and they'll come after *all of us* with the force of a *crusade*…! He'll get his for what he's done to Lester here…" he added, glancing down with sorrow at the boy's unconscious form "…but that'll have to wait…"

"You'll die a *thousand* deaths… *both of you*…!" Silas hissed, emboldened by Godfrey's words.

"Only takes *one* death…" Nev observed coldly, almost working on reflex as she extended her right hand toward Silas, his body instantly wracked with rigid convulsions. "…even a *monster* like *you*…! Heart attacks happen all the time, I'm sure… there'll not be a *mark* on you…"

All she needed to do was *imagine* his heart in her hand… his heart being crushed as she slowly squeezed her open fingers tight around it. A faint glow shone from inside her sleeve, and a few tiny crackles of static discharge arced across the back of her hand.

"I'll tie 'em up…!" Godfrey suggested hurriedly, breaking her concentration as he gathered scraps of rope from the floor and moved toward Silas. The old man sagged to the deck once more, again staring at Nev in abject terror and disbelief over what she'd just done to him. It'd also concerned Godfrey, although he was more disturbed about what she was suddenly able to do with the power of that crystal rather than any danger of Silas or Baal being harmed. With the moment gone, Nev almost staggered backward a step or two, a horrified expression appearing on her face as she realised what she had been about to do… and how *easily* it'd been able to do it, both in technical *and* moral terms.

"We… we need to get out of here… *now*…" she stammered softly, skin crawling and feeling deeply ashamed as she wrenched the warm crystal from her wrist and stuffed it into a pocket, well away from her bare arm.

"Now *that* I can't argue with…" Godfrey agreed, making a show of roughly pushing the old man's face against the wall as he tied his hands. "I'll just gag this bastard and we can be off. Do you think you can carry Lester? I'd rather I had my sword arm free, in case we run into any opposition."

"Just lead the way…" Nev assured, instantly stepping over to the table, slipping her arms beneath the boy's legs and shoulders and hoisting him from the table. With the bulk of the bag on her back already, an extra thirty kilos or so of unconscious human being required a fair amount of exertion but she managed it well enough as Godfrey ditched the guard's sword in favour of his own, buckled it to his waist and then took up Lester's crossbow, taking the time to load it with one of the boy's heavy iron bolts.

"This is the prince's *personal* transport..." Godfrey observed, pausing for a moment at the closed door at the opposite end of the room. "Stands to reason there *must* be lifeboats or *something* like that aboard, somewhere. We just need to find a way up on deck without being seen and make our escape..."

"Sounds *easy* when you put it like that..." she remarked in return, trying to make her sarcasm sound light but unable to keep the quaver out of her voice.

"It's still night out there..." he grinned, glancing over at the darkness beyond the porthole in the far wall. "They'll have the oarsmen going ten to the dozen, but likely as not there'll only be a skeleton crew up on deck... *if we're lucky...*" he admitted eventually.

"Now, I *really* feel confident..."

"You'll be fine," he assured with another of those grins that somehow made her feel that everything was right with the world. "You got the boy, so I'll keep myself between you and any threat if things do go south. Just follow my lead and keep to the shadows where you can."

"Okay..." she muttered, staring into his eyes for support but mostly speaking out loud for her own benefit. "Okay... I can do this..." *God, I hope I can do this...*! "I can do this...!"

With the crossbow raised and ready in his right hand, Godfrey carefully unlatched the door leading out of the room and drew it slowly open. The fact that it *was* the prince's personal vessel at least meant that everything was well-maintained, and he released a sigh of relief as no sound came from the hinges as the door drew inward.

"Ready...?"

"No..." she answered honestly, shifting Lester awkwardly in her arms "...but let's get it over with..."

"Then let's go..." he grinned, and stepped out into the corridor beyond.

The hallway was short, narrow and surprisingly empty. Four metres to their left stood a pair of closed doors while a similar distance to their right, the corridor ended in another, rather solid-looking wooden door reinforced with thick bands and bolts or iron. An ornate emblem depicting a blue bird of prey on a golden background adorned its centre, and it was obvious even to Nev that they were looking at some kind of official emblem.

"Royal Crest of Huon," Godfrey explained in a whisper, momentarily at a loss as to which way to go. That'd *have* to be Baal's private quarters. Doubt there's any escape in *that* direction, so I guess that means the only way out is through *there*..." he added, nodding toward doors at the other end of the hall.

"You're not *sure*?" She asked nervously, clearly struggling with Lester in her arms; he'd started moaning softly now – *hopefully* a good sign.

"Well, *I* was out cold when they brought me here... don't know about you..." he shot back with a faint smile. "Come on... let's..."

He was cut off as those same doors flew suddenly open, revealing a set of steps that presumably led upward in the direction of the main deck. The matter of the two guards now standing in the doorway was not an insignificant one however, although the collective shock regarding the presence of *both* parties left each staring at the other in surprise for an excruciatingly long moment.

"Guards...! *Intruder*...!"

The cry of alarm galvanised everyone into action and Godfrey was first to react, lifting the crossbow and firing a bolt straight into the chest of that man who'd called the warning. Instantly casting the weapon aside, he raised his sword, preparing to charge forward, however the second guard had other ideas. As his colleague died without a sound and collapsed to the deck beside him, he raised his own crossbow and fired at Godfrey in return.

The next moment passed too quickly for Nev to think about crying out, either in fear or warning. Far smaller than Lester's huge weapon, the guard's compact, stockless model nevertheless packed enough force to twist Godfrey sideways and slam him into the wall as it struck him in the right shoulder. He tumbled to the deck, grunting in pain as his blade flew out of his hand and landed almost at the guard's feet. As it happened, her first instinct wasn't to cry out at all. Instead, with a single, apologetic thought of '*sorry, Lester*', she allowed his body to slump to the deck and leaped into attack past Godfrey's fallen form, the katana already out of its scabbard and slashing downward.

The second guard *should* have done exactly as Godfrey had done – cast away the now-useless crossbow and reach for the cutlass at his belt – however the sudden, unexpected chaos of combat being what it was, the man was a long way from thinking clearly. There was a weapon in his hand – one that required reloading – and his first flawed instinct was to reload the crossbow he already held. He'd barely grasped the bow string and drawn it backward as Nev darted forward, and his left hand was reaching down toward the small quiver at his belt as the blade flashed down.

With Godfrey down and wounded, Nev's reaction hadn't been thoughtful or considered. Pure and simple, it had been born of the instinct and reflex of many years of training and practice and there was no conscious hesitation now as the two-handed stroke sliced through the man's wrist, severing it cleanly with a far greater spray of blood than she could ever have imagined in her worst nightmares. His hand clattered to the floor, fingers still grasped pointlessly around the grip of the crossbow, and there was a moment's silence as everything paused around one stunned guard staring with growing shock and realisation at the bloody fountain where his right hand had once been.

The pain hit then and he fell backward with a hideous, piteous scream, clutching vainly at his severed stump with his left hand as blood poured between his fingers in torrents. Nev was stunned – *horrified* – by what she'd just done and she found herself frozen to the spot and filled with nausea as Godfrey stumbled past her, grunting with the pain of his own wound and nevertheless managing to let fly with a savage kick to the screaming man's head that knocked him senseless.

"Damn the luck…!" He snarled, seething with frustration over the futility of the situation as he confirmed that both men were out of action and then pushed the doors closed once more, securing them as best he could with a flimsy wooden bar. Already, there were calls of alarm filtering down from above and the sound of boots ringing on the deck overhead was drawing noticeably nearer. "Never a *single* thing goes our way…!"

"I – uh – maybe we can…?" Nev stammered, confusion and rising terror clouding her mind. Instinct had been fine in the heat of the moment when she'd perceived Godfrey to be in immediate danger, but that moment had passed and she was now left with a terrible, awful guilt over the violent act she'd just carried out against another human being. "Oh, God… oh God, oh God, Oh God, *oh God*…!"

"*This isn't the time…!*" He barked in her face, recognising the signs of someone slipping into shock and snapping her out of it. "Pick up Lester and we'll go *that way...*" he continue, nodding toward the door that presumably led to Baal's quarters.

"But... but, we'll be *trapped...*"

"...And we aren't *already...?*" he asked pointedly, casting an arm toward the sound of approaching enemies from the other direction. "There'll be *dozens* of 'em against us, and we'll not last a *minute* here *or* up there in the open. Barricade ourselves *in there* and *maybe* we can buy some time..."

"Time for what...?" She moaned, barely controlling her hysteria.

"*Move...! Now...!*" He shouted, placing a hand on her shoulder and pushing her heavily backward. The action obtained its desired result, and as her left hand caught his wrist and twisted it upward, away from her body, she fixed him with an almost murderous stare.

"*Nobody* puts their hands on me!" She snarled back, actually causing pain with the force in her grip.

"*Good...!*" He nodded with a thin smile, immediately withdrawing his hand now her focus was back where it needed to be. "Now... I can't manage this on my own," he added, clutching at the bolt still protruding from his shoulder as a dark stain continued to spread on his tunic around it. "Pick him up and let's get moving..."

Hurriedly wiping her blade clean and sheathing the katana, Nev crouched down and hoisted Lester over her shoulder in an improvised fireman's lift as they heard the first crash of shoulders slamming hard against the opposite side of the opposite doors, bulging them inward slightly.

"Come on..." he urged tensely, hissing in reaction to the agony in his shoulder as he pushed the door to Baal's private quarters inward, then turned and collected his own pack in his good hand. "That won't hold them for long."

It took some manoeuvring for Nev to slip through that narrow hatch, awkwardly bringing Lester with her and a pair or rucksacks (Lester's and hers), and she almost staggered through and into the huge cabin beyond. Godfrey slammed the door shut after her and barred that one also, however this time he noted that both the door itself and the bar securing it were both *very* thick and solid, and it would take a great deal more effort to break through than the ones closed at the other end.

The cabin was surprisingly large, presumably stretching the width of the ship with tall windows that spread across the entire length of the back wall. There was only darkness beyond those glass panes, but it at least clearly showed that the cabin was at the very stern of the vessel. A single lantern flickered, hanging above a large, ornately-carved desk in the centre of a room that was otherwise shrouded in darkness. The hint of other furnishings showed faintly within the gloom – a table and chairs, wardrobes and the ghost of a large bed – and everything that *was* visible was clearly quite luxurious and expensively made.

"That should hold 'em for a *little* while," Godfrey conceded with a wry smile, backing away from the door as Nev lowered Lester into the upholstered armchair that stood on the other side of the desk. "Looks like the prince doesn't trust his men all that well…"

"And what're we supposed to do *now*…?" She asked bluntly, still sickened by what she'd just seen *and* done out in that corridor and starting to shake faintly now with the shock of it all.

Any reply he might've given at that point was stopped cold by the unexpected chuckle that suddenly arose from a far corner of the darkened room, somewhere beyond the shape of the bed to Nev's right.

"Nevaeh and a *hot boi*, trying to flee… K-I-S-S-I-N-G…" Godfrey instantly tried to reach for his sword, then groaned with the pain of sudden movement and staggered back against the barred door, but there was no mistaking the soft, scornful sound of Persephone's voice as it sent a chill through Nev's bones.

XII

CATHARSIS

"Perce...? *Persephone*...?" Nev growled, slowly turning in the direction of that voice and consciously resisting an urge to reach for her own blade in that moment.

"Well, who *else* would it be...?" Percy asked with rhetoric sarcasm, stepping out of the shadows in that corner of the room just enough to become a shadowy wraith against that stygian background. "Think you might want to look after *him*..." she added, and Nev *really* didn't like the unpleasant sound of approval in her tone. "Wouldn't want to let *that* one slip away..."

"Shut *up*...!" Nev growled petulantly, deciding it might indeed be a good idea to forget Percy for a moment and tend to Godfrey's wounds. "Oh, God; it's *everywhere*..." She breathed in horror, realising for the first time exactly how much blood had soaked the entire front of his tunic. "What do I do...?"

"Need to take that bloody *arrow* out first, I'd think... no pun intended..." Percy shrugged, being purposefully annoying.

"I *said* 'shut up'...!" She snapped in return, her hands hovering over the embedded crossbow bolt in Godfrey's shoulder as she worked up the courage to even *think* about doing exactly that. "I'll need some bandages..." she added, glancing desperately around for something of use. "Something like those 'shell dressings' they always go on about in Dad's war movies..."

"There's an artery in there..." Godfrey croaked, knowing all too well how bad the placement was. "I've lost too much already... The bolt's the only thing stopping me from bleeding out: pull *that* out and I'll be dead in minutes..."

"*No*..." Nev moaned softly, as the magnitude of what he'd just said sunk in. "You'll bleed to death *anyway* if we don't take that out and put pressure on the wound."

"Aye, lass..." He nodded weakly, empty acceptance in his eyes as he met her gaze then. "I know that..."

Nev fell backward into a sitting position as her strength abandoned her, part of her soul dying in that awful moment. It wasn't possible... *it couldn't be...!*

"It's all right..." he whispered, face so pale now he was almost blue. "*None* of us get to choose... but I met *you*, at least..." he added, struggling for the strength to lift a hand and place it gently on hers, resting on her knee. "I'll be at peace..."

"But *I* won't...!" She breathed softly, tears filling her eyes now as the inevitable came rushing toward her.

"'Nevaeh'..." Godfrey mumbled, fighting to keep his eyes open now as he forced a faint smile. "*That's* your name...?" His smile widened as she could only nod jerkily in agreement, feeling useless as the tears streamed down her face.

"*Yes...*" she croaked, her voice thick with emotion as she clasped his hand in hers, not knowing what else she could do.

"It's *Heaven* spelt backwards..." Percy interjected, sounding a little bored already "...it was her *mum's* idea..."

"I like that..." he decided, closing his eyes now and ready to accept his fate as his head fell gently back against the door. "*Much* better than *Neville*..."

He couldn't help himself. Even as his life slipped away, Godfrey couldn't resist one last joke and the smirk that flickered fleetingly across his features drew a momentary cough of choked laughter from Nev despite her grief, leaving her completely and utterly conflicted as sobs began to wrack her body.

"Oh, for *goodness sake...!*" Percy exclaimed, sickened to the point of nausea by what she considered to be a pathetic display of drama. "Will you do us *all* a favour and just *save* him already?"

"I can't *do* anything...!" Nev moaned despairingly.

"You've got one of the crystals, haven't you?" Percy asked pointedly, knowing the answer to that question already. "*Don't* even *bother* denying it – I can almost *smell* it on you!"

"Why...?" Nev asked nervously, suspicion instantly filling her mind. "What do *you* want it for?"

"Oh, give it a rest..." Percy shot back, rolling her eyes. "I'm hardly going to start chasing you around the room, screaming '*My Precious...!*'... Have you *used* it yet?"

"It helped me break the ropes... helped us break free, " Nev explained cautiously, barely able to make sense of what had happened herself, let alone to explain it to anyone else. "It *showed* me what to do... it *showed* me how to squeeze an old man's *heart* with my own mind... how to *kill* him..."

"Bet you didn't *do it* though, *did* you? Percy offered dryly (guessing who Nev was talking about and adding *'more's the pity'* under her breath) then raising an eyebrow as Godfrey groaned faintly and slid a little lower. "It can show you how to *heal* too... although I'd not leave it much longer, if *I* were you..."

"What...? *What do I do...*?" Nev asked, suddenly filled with desperate urgency as hope rekindled faintly in her heart.

"Just hold the thing over his *shoulder* and *think hard* about the wound getting better," Percy directed condescendingly with an exaggerated sigh. "Don't mess about though – you'll need to pull that bolt out first, and I doubt he'll last long when *that* happens. I'd offer to help, but... *eww*...!" She added, shrugging and making a face.

"Okay... *okay*..." Nev muttered, steeling herself as her right hand slipped inside her pocket and withdrew the pendant. "I can do this... *I can do this*..."

"I'd bloody do it *quickly*..." Percy suggested, not particularly caring about Godfrey in the slightest but *very* interested to see what Nev could actually do. "Be careful not to let it take control, though..." she added, not at all helpfully "...I've seen what one o' them can do... they can *burn* a mind to ash..."

Nev ignored her as she transferred the crystal to her left hand then reached out gingerly with her right to grasp the rear section of the crossbow bolt, protruding from his shoulder. Only semi-conscious, Godfrey moaned softly and shuddered from the pain as she took hold of the iron shaft and tensed her muscles in preparation.

Okay... on three... she told herself silently. *One... two... "...three...!"*

With eyes closed and teeth clenched, she tightened her grip and wrenched on the crossbow bolt as hard as she could. It resisted at first, threatening to pull Godfrey's shoulder with it as he groaned even louder, then came free with a wet, sucking sound that was followed by a sickening spurt of arterial blood that left a half-metre spray across the door by his arm.

"Oh, *eww*...!" She grimaced, desperately fighting the urge to vomit as she shakily stretched out her left hand and lowered it over the wound, which was now bleeding profusely.

Closing her eyes, she tried to open her mind instead, concentrating hard on the crystal dangling beneath her down-turned palm and searching for the same sensation she'd felt earlier when she'd threatened to use it against Silas. In her concentration, Nev never noticed that Percy had also closed her eyes at that point, a frown of concentration creasing her forehead as she too reached out with her mind. She could feel the power of the pendant simmering nearby and although she couldn't control it from that distance, Percy could at least nudge Nev gently in the right direction.

Nev felt nothing for a few seconds, desperation rising as each passed with agonising slowness, before a single pinprick of bright blue light flared in her thoughts and a connection with the crystal came rushing toward her. Her eyes flew open wide and she stared down at her hand and the wound beneath it as discharges of static lightning crackled and coursed up and down the length of her arm from elbow to fingertips.

Her focus shifted to Godfrey now – on the damage wrought on his punctured shoulder – and suddenly she could *see* everything beneath his tunic *and* skin: see torn flesh and muscle around the puncture; the fracture in the shoulder blade where the bolt's tip had come to rest and, more importantly, the ragged tear in his axillary artery and the stream of rich, oxygenated blood that was still pumping out at a rate of over a hundred bursts per minute.

Nev was neither a doctor nor a surgeon, but she could 'see' clearly enough that what was there looked about as *wrong* as anything could possibly be. She had no reason to trust Percy (she was far too inexperienced to realise that the girl was at least partially aiding her mental picture of what needed to be done) but there really was no alternative at that moment, and all Nev could do was close her eyes once more and concentrate clearly and completely on one *single* thought: *fix whatever's wrong…*

The chill that rippled through Nev was tangible, drawing from her a soft, shuddering gasp as the crystal's intensity flared to uncomfortable levels, the light bright enough to show faintly through her closed eyelids. Almost immediately, she could see everything happening inside her mind as the tear in Godfrey's artery folded and sealed itself together again in a second, ending the outpouring of the boy's life blood. Behind the wound, the crack in his scapula fused and sealed, leaving a faint scar but now as strong as it ever was, while directly beneath the hole punched through his tunic, the ragged edges of his flesh began to knit carefully back together until – after just thirty seconds or so – there was nothing more than a livid, coin-sized scar surrounded by a large, livid bruise.

The crystal's glow began to fade then, its job clearly done for the time being, and it was only as Nev allowed herself to finally relax and sit back on her own haunches once more that she realised she still held the bloody crossbow bolt in her other hand. She cast it aside with a groan of disgust, returning her gaze to Godfrey to find him staring weakly up at her, his expression an exhausted mixture of surprise and happiness.

"Hello, you…" she breathed softly, not able to think of anything more eloquent that could possibly have conveyed the same amount of raw emotion.

"Hello, yourself…" he replied with equal intensity, considering the idea of trying to sit up for a moment but quickly deciding against it. "That was *you*, wasn't it…" he added, glancing down at the fading light of the pendant in her left hand.

"I…" she began, then faltered as she fought to hold back tears again, this time out of joy. "I don't know *what* that was…"

"My God, you really *can* use it, *can't you*…!" Percy exclaimed in disbelief. *"What happened…?* It took months for me to manage anything even *close* to that… what did they *do* to you…?"

"They were torturing them…Godfrey and Lester…" Nev mumbled, unable to take her eyes of Godfrey as they stared deeply into each other's eyes, transfixed and barely hearing Percy's words. "The old priest – Silas – tried to hurt *me* with it…" She managed a faint shrug. "That didn't work out too well for him... The voice – the one in my head – it warned him not to, but he tried it anyway… I – I'm not really *sure* what happened after that…"

"He *touched* you with it… tried to *burn* you…?" Percy almost gasped as Nev nodded dumbly. She'd seen the damage an experienced brother like Silas could do with one of those pendants, and there was real excitement in her voice now. *"What did you see…?"*

"There – there was *nothing*… *lots* of nothing, to start with… and then I had a vision of something from when I was a kid… some random memory of Dad and Grandpa fighting… After that, it simply said '*interesting*' and I was back in the real world again, but somehow *I* was holding the crystal instead… like I'd somehow gotten myself free and taken it from him without even knowing it." She shrugged again. "I used it to break free and we got out of there… I *still* don't know exactly *how* I did it…"

"Well, it *worked*, so *I* don't really care…" Godfrey decided, forcing himself to sit up now as he stretched out an arm and braced against the doorway. It was at that moment that an almighty crash beyond the other side of the wall gave a fairly clear indication that the doors at the other end of the hallway had just been smashed in.

"*That* door should hold them a bit longer…" Percy observed airily from her position in the shadows, "…but I'd not leave it too long in making my escape…"

"And *how* exactly do you suggest we *do* that?" Nev growled darkly, anger returning to her now as the immediate danger of Godfrey's demise had now passed, and she was able to concentrate more on her own betrayals of the last few days.

"There's a trapdoor behind the chair there," she answered without hesitation, giving an unseen nod toward the desk at which Lester still lay slumped. "Far as I can tell, it leads down to a small boat hidden below in the… the *stern*, is it…? When I checked earlier, it looked like there was fresh water and food too: I don't think that prince trusts his own men much…" she suggested, echoing Godfrey's words from moments before.

"Making deals with Harald the Black, I'm not *surprised*…" He muttered, grunting with exertion as he struggled unsteadily to his feet upon hearing that news, Nev rising with him. "Why tell *us* about it?" He demanded more sharply, taking a step toward her now with one hand still resting against the wall as he voiced a question that had also occurred to Nev.

"Do you *want* to still be here when they break through that door?" She asked bluntly, at the same moment that the first crash of something heavy battered against the other side of the thick door to their makeshift refuge. "*That* door's a *bit* tougher than the other one, but I'd not want to push my luck."

"I want to know why you'd *help* us," Godfrey countered, taking another step and resting his hand on his sword now, trying to look as threatening as he was able in his extremely weakened state and not managing it very well at all. "It's no secret you've betrayed close friends *already*, and *I've* seen you using witchcraft of your *own* in that clearing, these last few months. What do *you* get out of helping us get away, eh...?"

"Been *stalking* me, have you? I'd not let *this one* near Instagram, old mate..." Percy quipped at an increasingly-infuriated Nev, almost giggling at her own joke as Godfrey tried to draw his sword a few centimetres from its scabbard. "Oh, take your hand off that thing before you fall over...!" She shot back in a far darker tone and as she turned her head in the darkness, just for a fraction of a second, Nev thought she'd caught the faint flash of red from Percy's retinas, reflecting the glow of the lantern on the desk behind them. It couldn't possibly have been intentional, yet it gave the girl the aura of something demonic all the same.

"I don't get *anything* from helping you two escape," Percy answered eventually, being completely honest. "Not *immediately*, anyway, but I *definitely* get nothing out of seeing Nevaeh caught by that *filth* outside."

"That doesn't answer *anything*...!" Nev snapped in frustration as a second crash thudded against the door and they heard the frame creak slightly. "Why help us? Are you their *prisoner* or their *guest*...?"

"Do I *look* like a *guest* to you...?" Percy snarled angrily as she took several long strides forward, stepping fully into the light for the first time and drawing close enough to reveal to reveal a trio of livid wounds torn across her left cheek at a rakish angle. The sight of her damaged face silenced Nev for a moment, her next words catching in her throat as she instead released a shocked gasp.

"Not pretty, is it...?" Percy asked bitterly, a mirthless sneer forming. "*Is it...?*" She barked again, loud enough this time to make Nev flinch. "No more 'pretty face' for poor old Percy... *poor* Perce, who only wanted to share a little excitement and *adventure* with a friend... her *best friend* who *abandoned* her and left her to suffer at the hands of these *morons*...!"

"*I* abandoned *you*...?" Nev almost roared incredulously as her building rage finally overflowed. "*You brought me here*...! *You* betrayed *me*, lured me to that *bloody* clearing *and* nearly got me *killed* in the process!"

"Oh, *puh-lease*...! That sleaze told Cragelen to kill *me* too!" Percy shot back immediately, her words laced with bitterness. "I'd have *never* let them *do* anything..."

"You chased me... *you all chased me...*!" Nev spat in accusation, taking an angry step forward as Godfrey held fast, taking in the exchange with great interest. "You *tricked me* into ditching school just so you could lure me to that clearing, *kidnap* me and bring me *here*... here to this *hellhole* of a world! We were *friends*, Perce... you were my *best friend*... how could you? *How could you...?*"

"Of *course* I tricked you: you've never have come if I'd told you the *truth*. I did it *because* we were friends..." Percy croaked, emotion filling her words. "Do you have *any* idea of the *power* they have? Of what they *promised* me... *promised us...?*" There was real loss and disappointment in her tone now. "We could've been *queens*... could've ruled this world like no others! I could've smoothed things over with the *Shard*! All you had to do was just *go along with it*, and we'd *both* have been powerful beyond our wildest dreams!"

"I don't *want* to be powerful... I don't *want* to be a queen!" Nev shouted, Godfrey's earlier insult about acting like a princess flaring in her mind for a moment. "I just want to go *home...*!"

"Well, *that's* not going to happen..." Percy muttered dryly, showing surprisingly little sympathy in Nev's considered opinion as she nodded scornfully at the crystal in her hand. "You'd *never* have the power to do it yourself with *that* pathetic little thing: *they* alone control access between worlds and they'll *never* let you back through... you're *far* too dangerous for *that...*"

"But why, Perce...*why*...?" Nev pleaded now, not understanding a word of what she was saying as her mind continually came back to the same unanswered question. "Why me... *why me...?*"

"*Because I was nothing* without *you...*!" Percy bellowed in return, her shouted words punctuated by another crash against the door that this time produced an audible cracking sound. "Oh, boo hoo...! '*Why me... why me...?*' They came looking for someone useful... someone *smart...*" she continued, the *very* uncharacteristic sound of sorrow and insecurity seeping into her voice now as she explained further. "*Instead*, they got *me*, and my *only* purpose was to act as bait to lure in *someone else* that they really *could* use..."

"But... but... *why...?*" Nev moaned, unable to move past the overwhelming feelings of betrayal.

"*Because you're smart...*" she repeated "...the smartest person I know. They needed science and technology and help with how to *make* things, and *you* know *all* of that crap..."

"I'm just a *kid... we're* just kids..."

"And I don't *know* any bloody *scientists...*!" Percy almost shrieked. "I know *schoolkids* and *farmers* and *country people*, and most of *them* are barely literate! And then there's *you...*" she added, her sneer laced with a deep, irrational envy "...*you*, who could *sleep* through *every* class for the *entire year* and *still* come home with high distinctions.

"My *God*, Nev, do you think you were the *first* person I tried to get? Why do you think you hadn't *seen* me at all these last few months? I *tried* looking for older people to bring back... tried *so hard* to find someone – *anyone* – with intelligence in that Godforsaken town of ours. We have a TAFE, Nevaeh... a *TAFE*, for God's sake... not even a *proper* university! Do you have *any* idea what it's like trolling *that* campus in search of someone with even *half* a brain? 'Technical And Further Education' my *bum*: that was the *last* thing on the tiny minds of most of the men *there*, I can tell you..." she added with a shudder, remembering having to fend off their pawing hands on far too many occasions. "Although considering the general lack of intelligence, I'm amazed *some* of them even knew what *sex* was...!

"In the end, I chose *you* because you were the *only* one I knew with even the *slightest* chance of being acceptable..." she continued, making a conscious effort to slow her words and lower her intensity as the door groaned under yet another assault. "Because if there was *anyone* I knew who could *possibly* impress these *things*, it was Nevaeh *bloody* Anderson..."

"And *now* you want to help us escape out of the 'goodness of your innocent, misunderstood little heart'... is that it...?" Nev sneered, not buying any of it.

"Hardly..." Percy grinned, the deep scratches on her cheek a macabre sight as they twisted and deformed at the edge of a mirthless smile. "You ruined *everything* for me, but *they* did this to my face..." she explained, touching a finger tenderly against her wounds, "...and I'll be *damned* if I'll let *them* get you before *I* have my chance. Watching you die quickly would be no fun *at all*..." she continued, her toothy grin becoming decidedly evil and more than a little insane. "I want you to *suffer* first... at *my* hand... and in exchange for *that*, helping you escape *these* losers is a deal I'm *happy* to make."

"We *could* kill you right now," Godfrey pointed out darkly as he staggered awkwardly around behind Lester, pulled back a large rug with his boot and found the trapdoor Percy had described. "Believe me: I'd lose not a *wink* o' sleep over the doin' o' *that* deed…"

"I love you too, gorgeous…" Percy replied with sweet sarcasm, noting that that small effort had already exhausted him as he almost collapsed against the desk. "Oh, if you could find the *strength*, I doubt you'd hesitate for a *second*," she added, then nodded toward Nev who, in spite of her own rage and indignance, knew that every word Percy spoke next was completely and utterly true "…but *she* would. Nevaeh's no killer, and 'though you *might be*, you'll do *anything* not to hurt her feelings… I can see *that* already…" she observed with an unpleasant smirk that might've had both of them blushing, had the circumstances been different.

Another crash of a battering ram beyond the doorway, and this time the frame around the top corner cracked and pushed inward a centimetre or two, sending splinters flying into the room under the impact. Godfrey could see that door had perhaps one – maybe *two* hits left in it at the most, and that time had most definitely run out for pleasant conversation.

"We need to go… *now*…"

"How do we know she's not lying?" Nev wavered, not ready to believe Percy just yet.

"If she's lying, then we're in no *more* trouble than we are if we *stay*, are we…?" He pointed out tersely, crying out in pain as he used his good arm to haul the trapdoor open and let it fall backward with a loud bang against the floor. "Besides… I think *this time* she *is* telling the truth… it *sounds* crazy enough to be real…"

"Crazy like you wouldn't *believe*, babe…" Percy almost cackled then, backing away again until she was once more in the shadows.

"You get down there first, then I'll lower Toadface to you…" He suggested, distracted momentarily as Lester moaned and shifted in the chair. As little as the reaction was, it was nevertheless at least *some* sign that the boy might be improving. "…if there *is* a boat down there and we can get on it…" Godfrey went on, voice almost catching with emotion as relief surged through him "…they'll have *no* chance of finding us in the darkness. It's all we've got."

"I really *should* kill you…" Nev growled, knowing very well it wasn't going to happen as her own hand instinctively touched the hilt of the katana at her waist.

"Oh, you really *should*..." Percy agreed without hesitation. "Is that a *real* katana, by the way? Did the old man give you that?" She actually sounded impressed. "That crusty old fool is *way* cooler than I gave him credit for: samurai swords are *so* hot right now...!"

"Nev, *now*...!" Godfrey warned, the door pushing away from the frame even further now with the next impact.

"I *hate* you...!" Nev hissed finally, turning on her heels and sweeping up her duffel bag as she moved quickly to join Godfrey. Stretching her foot tentatively down into the open hatchway, she found the first rung of the narrow ladder below and began her descent with as much speed as she could muster.

"You don't know what *hate* is..." Percy muttered softly, glaring at Nev as she disappeared below the level of the deck.

The ladder led down to a long, narrow platform enclosed on three sides and open at the far end, where Nev could faintly pick out the glint of the ship's wake in the moonlight as it cut through the dark water. That being said, there was nowhere near enough light to see what she was doing and she immediately took out her phone and activated its torch app. With a wide beam of white light glaring from its rear-mounted flash, she was finally able to make out the rest of her surroundings.

What she stood on was indeed a narrow platform perhaps a metre wide and twice that in length, beyond which was an empty space filled by the small, wooden boat Percy had mentioned, set on a pair of iron rails. It was mounted facing the same direction as *Rapier* and Nev quickly noted a large lever close to its starboard side, amidships, which appeared to be connected to the rails beneath. It took no great leap of logic to make the connection that a pull on that lever would drop the boat's stern into the water rushing past below and allow it to slip out and away behind as the galleass continued on its merry way.

Nev had to admit that the whole thing seemed quite ingenious. With a good wind, there'd be no chance of finding them on a dark night, and with a little good luck thrown in they might be well away before anyone even realised where they'd gone.

"Is it *clear*...?" Godfrey called down in a hushed whisper, barely audible over the rustle of the water rushing away below the boat.

"It looks okay... *narrow*, but okay..."

"He's coming down…" he warned loudly, and Nev quickly shrugged off her duffel bag and tossed it into the bow of the boat in preparation for Lester's descent.

She was surprised to find the boy climbing down of his own accord, albeit slowly and with a number of pauses as he rested for a few seconds at a time, breathing heavily as he waited for his head to clear. Nev waited patiently for him to reach the bottom, standing with feet braced apart as he descended and ready to catch him should he fall. Lester indeed missed his footing on the last step, but managed to catch himself as she leaped forward and carefully lowered his feet to the platform.

"Good to have you back…" she grinned, and he gave a silent nod and a smile in return. He looked pale and worn out and weak as a kitten, but he was awake and clearly lucid, and that was enough to be thankful for, for the time being. "Hop in – we're getting out of here!"

He nodded again, and as he slowly tumbled himself over the side and into the boat, Nev glanced up toward Godfrey again just soon enough to see Godfrey's rucksack plummeting down toward her. She caught it awkwardly in one hand, staggering a little close to the edge of the platform for her liking as she continued to wave the phone light around with the other, then tossed it into the bow next to her own.

"Nice catch…" he offered with a weak smile, sliding one-handed down the ladder so quickly it could almost be classified as a fall and grunting at the pain that came with his landing as the heavy trapdoor slammed shut above them.

"Do *you* trust her?" Nev asked warily, standing firm with hands on hips as Godfrey heaved himself into the boat behind Lester.

"Not in the slightest," he answered honestly, "but I *believe* her… in *this* case, at least. Anyway," he added, his words interrupted by the muffled sound of a crash and the tromping of many boots above, "we've not much choice, as she pointed out. Any reckoning can be had later on if you've both a mind to, but *right now* we need to get as far away from here as we can…"

"I *know* I'm going to regret this…" She growled, finally pushing aside her reservations and climbing into the boat ahead of the other two. There was a folded mast lying right down the centreline of the boat, a canvas sail wrapped and tied around it, and she found herself seated on the opposite side.

"Regrets can be fixed..." Godfrey pointed out with a thin smile, lifting his eyes skyward as they all heard the creak and thud of the trapdoor once more being pulled back "...*decapitations*, not so much! Wanna hang on to something?" He suggested, working out the purpose of the lever on the starboard side as quickly as Nev had and grasping it with his good hand.

"I *already* regret this..." she corrected, mostly muttering to herself as she dragged her duffel bag in between her legs to keep it secure and latched both hands tightly around the folded mast.

With a nervous chuckle that was no reassurance whatsoever, Godfrey tensed his body against the agony he knew he was about to experience and hauled back on the lever for all he was worth. He cried out through clenched teeth as stabbing pain instantly flared through his wounded shoulder, yet the mechanism gave way with surprising ease for all that and the small boat instantly tipped downward at the rear, its stern hitting the water with a jolting splash.

A marine dressed in leather armour and brandishing a short sword dropped through the trapdoor and landed heavily on the platform at that moment, followed quickly by a second, however the boat was already under control of the passing sea now, dragged by its stern as it jerked backward at speed and lurched out into *Rapier's* wake as the warship carried on regardless.

Another alarm was raised immediately, but it took time for news to travel from one end of a ship to the other and it was three full minutes before the crew had managed to lower the sails and stow the oars: *Rapier* continued on for more than a kilometre before she was able to completely slow down and come about. Cloud had completely obscured the moon by that time, leaving it no more than an indistinct, muted glow in the sky, and there was no hope whatsoever of spotting something as small as the sailboat against the backdrop of a dark sea.

"Are you *insane*...?" Silas almost shrieked, advancing on Percy with a noticeable limp as guards stood on either side, restraining her tightly enough to make it uncomfortable. "Do you know what you've *done*, helping them escape...?"

"Well, I've pissed *you* off for a start, so that's *some* consolation..." She replied proudly, lifting her head in defiance and standing taller by a good half-head.

"I'll have you *executed* for this," Baal snarled angrily, the agony he felt clear in his tone as he perched precariously on one corner of his huge desk and allowed the ship's medic to splint and bind his broken arm. "Not *quickly*, though..." he added with a dark smile. "... I've no doubt our oarsmen would find great delight in filling your final hours with any *number* of tortures..."

"You'll do none of that, and you *both* know it," she fired back without hesitation, more than ready to meet his gaze with one as cold as iron. "This crusty old *turd* has orders to bring me back to the cardinal in one piece, and he'll follow *those* orders if it *kills* him! Disobey De Lisle, and it's *your* life won't be worth a pinch of *crap!*"

"She speaks the truth..." Silas spat disgustedly, seeing no point in continuing with the charade. "She *must* not be harmed... not before the cardinal has done with her at least. After *that*..." he added, almost promisingly "...she's yours to do with as you wish..."

"I look *forward* to that..."

"So do I, *bitch...!*" Percy shot back, never one to give an inch in an argument, regardless of the consequences.

"*Enough...!*" Silas barked angrily as Baal leaped to his feet, fumbling for his sword with his left hand and grunting at the pain that instantly lanced through his right arm as the medic dived to once side. "Enough of this stupidity: it solves *nothing!* You...!" He continued, glaring at Percy now, taking a quick step forward and making her flinch in spite of herself. "They were *trapped* here! You've *no* love for the girl after what she's done... why did you do this...?"

"*Now* we're asking the right questions," she observed with an evil smile, pulling her arms free of the guards as Silas gave them a silent, grudging not of consent regarding her release. "Why did I help them escape?" She shrugged. "*Partly* just for shits and giggles, but *mostly* because if *anyone*'s going to make that bitch *suffer* for what she's done, it's going to be *me* and *no one else!*"

"Revenge... I *see*..." Silas mused softly, his faint smile quickly became something far more dark and malevolent. "And *for* that revenge, you would *willingly* jeopardise *everything* The Brotherhood has been working toward for *years*. For *this*, you would risk *everything* we are...?"

"*Your* Brotherhood... *not mine*..." she fired back with defiance, not about to let him stare her down. "I was promised power and title and riches beyond my wildest dreams, and I *delivered*...! The *Blackwatch* let her escape, and gave *me* up as the scapegoat when it all went down the toilet. Then *you* used that crystal to ruin my face and mess with my head… *God knows* what damage you've done in *there*."

"Your thoughts were filled with chaos and a *thousand* senseless images…" Silas shuddered, recalling in mild horror the wild and inexplicable things he'd seen in the thoughts of a 21st Century teenager.

"Yeah…? Well don't think for a *moment* I don't know how much fun *you* get out of hurting people… *especially* young women," she growled, sneering at him with disgust clear in her face and tone. "It's a *two-way* street when you use one of those things on someone, and I *saw* the sick things that live in *your* mind too, so don't get all sanctimonious on *me,* you dirty old *bastard*…!"

'None of this is of *any* consequence," he dismissed nervously, unsettled by the thought that someone might actually have looked into the dark corners of his thoughts and seen the ugly truths living there. "The only fact that remains is that *you* allowed – nay – *helped* them get away, and you've placed the entire Brotherhood in danger as a result. Cardinal De Lisle will need to know about this and I can promise you he *will not* look on your actions kindly."

"Shame you're gonna have to wait 'til you get to port to let him know, Nev having taken off with your *crystal* 'n' all, isn't it?" She shot back with mocking sweetness. "I bet the cardinal will be *rapt* when he hears about *that*… and she'll be *long gone* by then."

"The other witch will be caught, and she will die…" Silas stated with simple conviction.

"Oh, she'll die alright…" Percy agreed coldly, her eyes filled with hatred and vengeance "…but by *my* hand, *not* yours…"

"The sail…!" Godfrey called urgently, not wasting a moment as he struggled to get his good arm under the lowered mast. "We need to get the sail up, *now*…!"

Nev didn't need any further urging. As quickly as she was able without tipping them over, she shifted position and added her strength to his as they both strained to raise the folded mast and slot it into its mounting socket at the centre of the boat. It slipped into place easily and Godfrey locked it securely with a large, steel pin.

"You know how to sail…?" She asked breathlessly, sounding impressed as he rose awkwardly to his feet and began to unfurl the canvas.

"They teach us a little bit of everything in the Oster..." he shrugged, allowing the sail to billow out and fill as the cool, night breeze surged around them out of the east. "Gotta get out of this area as fast as we can," he continued, turning to cast a wary eye up at a large moon half covered in cloud. They'll *never* find us if we can get far enough away in this darkness... no, sit down, y' silly bugger...! You'll have us *all* in the drink with your carry on!" That last remark was directed at a weak and very woozy Lester, who'd automatically tried to stand up and help and had sent the boat rocking wildly in the process.

The sail caught almost immediately, bulging as the wind propelled them forward. Godfrey seated himself at the rear and turned the tiller to starboard, bringing the sailboat around and turning her west beneath the cloudy sky.

"How can you *possibly* know where you're going?"

"I don't," he shrugged again. "Not really... but if *Rapier* was headed to Bridgeport or George's Town, which they *had to be*, then they were headed pretty much due south. That puts us pretty much in the *middle* of Deepwater Strait, so there'll be no major islands or anything else likely to get in our way. Won't be sunrise for a few hours yet I reckon, but we should be able to see the Huon coast when it comes and we can find somewhere safe to land then. Before *that* happens, I want to make sure we've put enough distance between us that when we *do* make landfall, it *is* somewhere safe. Come in too soon and we'll still be in Baal's territory... but if we can make it to Huon, I've got Oster contacts there who can help."

"And *then* what...?"

"Then...?" He asked rhetorically, the faintness of the moonlight giving his face an eerie glow as he grimaced. "Not sure. The Southern Oster don't usually concern 'emselves with the politics of nations, but this alliance 'tween Baal and Harald won't be good for *anyone*. Need to check with the local command when we arrive, but I reckon we *might* need to have a talk to the king..."

"And what...? We just call his secretary and book an appointment?" Nev suggested with sarcasm.

"Not *quite* what simple, no..." he conceded, not sure what a secretary was but getting the point well enough. "We'll have to cross that bridge when we come to it."

"Never seen the king..." Lester muttered to no one in particular, only half-conscious as he lay back amidships, staring glassily at the stars and clouds above. "Never seen *any* royalty before tonight, and that ugly git, *Baal* don't really count..." He sighed softly, his thoughts floating off to a far more pleasant place. "They reckon the *princess* is *real* pretty, though..."

"You just rest yourself, Toadface!" Godfrey grinned, chuckling softly and thinking his friend *must* be feeling better. "Pretty or not, she's too good for the likes o' *you*..."

"No harm in dreamin', is there...?" The boy pointed out, eyes closed and drifting off to sleep even as he spoke.

"Aye, lad..." Godfrey conceded, gazing thoughtfully at Nev as, none-the-wiser, she stared out at the dark waters ahead of the sailboat's bow. "No harm indeed..."

XIII

MACHINATIONS

Although far smaller and less busy than Burnii docks, the main pier at Sternley stank just as badly. That's what Randwick's nostrils were telling him at least as he waited at the far end and watched the *Ocean Breeze* approach slowly under oars. The left-overs of the day's catch lay strewn about the pier and surrounding rocks, unseasonably-warm weather and another surprisingly clear day ensuring the discarded fish guts had rotted nicely beneath the glare of the afternoon sun.

Sternley was westernmost of the major fishing villages along Huon's northern coastline. Most of the town was built around the north-western end of the bay and was overshadowed by the towering Nutt Hill, a volcanic plug that rose more than 140 metres above the beach and the clustered houses below. The pier was all but completely in darkness now, the great hill rising imposingly above as the sun continued its journey toward the western horizon.

'Ocean Breeze'… now that *name's an irony, and no mistake…*! He thought ruefully as a miasma of odours surrounded him and carried out what felt like a combined assault against his five senses. His sense of smell had already surrendered under the onslaught, his eyes were burning of it, he could *taste* the foetid reek to the point of almost throwing up… surely it was only a matter of time before numbness set in and his hearing went out in sympathy.

He'd found somewhere shady during the afternoon, standing in the lee of a large, hand-operated crane surrounded by a pile of the large wooden crates he'd brought with him, and had waited patiently for the cog to make its way into port, drop anchor and tie off at the dock. The ship too was in darkness by the time its captain was able to step off the gangway and onto the wooden planks of the pier.

"Well met, Farouk," Randwick declared with a smile, shaking the man's hand firmly as they met. "Two years now I think, if memory serves…"

"And a pleasure it still is, good sir," Ismail Farouk acknowledged with a grin and a flourishing bow. Short, stocky and olive-skinned, the thirty-year-old wore a loose-fitting tunic and pantaloons that gave at least the appearance of a military cut. "My apologies on the delay of our arrival – we were beset by a storm on our way into Strahn that put us two days behind schedule: I only received your rider's message yesterday morning – we're not too late, I trust...?"

"*Any* delay is unfortunate," Randwick admitted without any apportion of blame, "but not critically so. Arrival in the 'nick-of-time' would be a better term than to say you were actually *late*. I've work needs doing that requires *exactly* your level of expertise and discretion..."

"My ship is yours, as always..." Farouk conceded with a faint bow. "What would you ask of us?"

"Only to wait... for the moment... I have cargo here that needs loading, but none of it as important as what's to come. Let your men get some rest and find what entertainment they can over the next twenty-four hours, for *tomorrow night* you'll have a delivery of the most *precious* cargo imaginable... something requiring *special* delivery of a similar nature to that which you've assisted in the past..."

"It'll be an honour, Master Randwick. Have them bring aboard what you have while we take a drink together, you and I, and we remember old times and lost comrades..."

"Now *that* would be *my* honour..." Randwick countered with a grin, deciding a drink or two might not be a bad idea at all.

As the two spent time in Farouk's cabin, reminiscing old friends and past battles, dockworkers and ship's crew alike went about the task of loading a half-dozen crates of varying sizes into the cog's hold, carting each box up the long, wide gangplank on loading trolleys with two or three men on each, pushing and pulling all the way. There was a great, communal cacophony of songs, grunts, catcalls and swearing as the crews unceremoniously dumped each crate into the main hold, leaving it for their replacement shift to lock the cargo down in a few hours' time.

One of those crates, rather precariously perched atop another, tipped over as the loading crew passed by on their way out, toppling it to the deck with a crash and a splintering of wood. The last man in line, dockworker Darius Moore, by chance also filled in part-time as an administrative cleric with the Sternley harbourmaster's office. He'd been tasked with the completions of the cargo manifests due out that day, and remembered no such shipment listed for departure with *Ocean Breeze*. As he paused for a moment, feeling guilty by association as he inspected the damaged corner, he was very surprised to find what appeared to be dresses of extremely fine material stored inside.

Moore knew who Randwick was well enough by reputation – there were few men throughout Huon who didn't – and the fact that an undeclared cargo was being loaded aboard at the behest of the princess' personal mentor was an intriguing one indeed. There were others within the administrative corps who paid good money for 'intriguing' information, and Darius was always interested in any opportunity to better his own finances. The moment he was back up on deck, he made his excuses and made a quick exit: the local message-rider's office would be closing soon and there was not a moment to lose if he was to get a letter away to Burnii that evening.

Bridgeport was little more than a small village attached to a large port and naval base on the north-eastern coast of Taas. With a population of less than two thousand civilians – most of whom worked at the base itself – it existed only because of its strategic value as the first port of call available for rest and resupply on the long journey south from Long Hop. Ramshackle huts and simple stone houses lay clustered around the obligatory small church of The Shard, all of that tucked up against one of the long, wooden walls that surrounded the military base. Smoke from cooking fires and from a number of blacksmith's forges filled the air, its acrid, choking blackness a small mercy for many in that it went some way toward nullifying the stench of the nearby sailors' camp.

Pulled by a team of six horses, De Lisle's personal carriage was far better appointed than most and it generally carried him about the landscape in quite reasonable comfort. One thing it's fine fittings and upholstered leather seats could *not* do however was filter out the smell that he would've sworn had infiltrated his nostrils while still at *least* a mile from the town. He generally eschewed personal travel wherever possible, and it was environments such as the one he now found himself in that had pretty much put him off the concept. Attending to important matters *personally* was sometimes unavoidable however, and *this* was definitely one of those times.

The carriage had taken him straight through the village that afternoon and on into the base, where it had trundled its way along wide, hard-packed dirt roads between barracks, foundries and other associated ship-building industries to the docks themselves. It was the nearest of those piers that interested him – the one at which *Rapier* was currently tied up, her banks of long oars at rest and lifted high into the sky. The driver brought them to a halt as close to the dock as was humanly possible, in deference to limiting the cardinal's need to walk across open, dirty ground, and De Lisle appreciated the effort.

An escort of Huon cavalry had accompanied him on the day-long journey from Burnii, their polished armour glistening in the failing sunlight as the long, grey-green plumage in their helmets swayed this way and that. He dismissed them with a single wave to their captain, making it *very* clear it was unnecessary for them to accompany him aboard *Rapier*: having an audience for the discussion he was about to have would've been 'awkward' at best.

A pair of ship's marines led him below decks and through the length of the ship to Baal's private rooms at the very stern, and as he approached the hallway outside, De Lisle was visibly shocked by the damage caused as *Rapier's* own crew had broken down both the outer door and the heavier one leading directly to the prince's quarters. The troopers left him at the entrance and he stepped inside gingerly, lifting the hem of his priestly robes as he was forced to step over some left over debris.

"I was not aware that war had already broken out..." he growled at the three people already inside that room, no humour at all in the words as he regarded each in turn with a savage glare. "It seems I was mistaken in my belief that two *grown men* in command of *trained soldiers* would be able to deal with *one girl*..."

"Had I *known* the creature we captured actually *was* a witch, I might've taken greater precaution...!" Baal shot back with venom, lying atop the covers of his huge, queen-sized bed with his fractured arm in a bandage and sling. "A 'waif of not even eighteen summers', I was told by this *lackey* of yours," he added, glaring in return at Silas, the old man seated very uncomfortably behind the prince's desk, "and this *fool* practically *hands* her his Shard Crystal..."

"You did *what*...?" De Lisle roared, the force of his words shaking Silas to his core. "You let that *heathen* take your pendant?"

At any other time, the insults and disrespect Baal had just levelled at one of his brothers might've earned the prince a one-way trip to the inquisition, however the cardinal was so stunned by the man's revelations that such thoughts never crossed his mind. Instead, he rounded on Silas and reached the desk in two great strides, towering over him across its expanse with such rage in his eyes that the old man recoiled in terror, cowering almost into a ball on the chair despite the constant pain in his back.

"I *suspected* something was amiss when there was no reply to my attempts at communion, but I could *never* have imagined you could be so *incompetent*...!" De Lisle howled, displaying an intensity he'd never before shown. "Are you senile... *insane*...? I *know* The Shard's orders... I *know* you were *specifically* instructed *not* to use the pendant on this girl!"

"I – I was *tricked*...!" Silas stammered desperately in return, his voice little more than a whine as covered his head and face with his arms as if afraid he might be physically assaulted – something that had definitely crossed the cardinal's mind. "She *is* a witch... with powers beyond *any* we've seen! She *twisted* my mind and *forced* me to strike her – to give her a chance to take it from me!"

"She *goaded* you with your own pride!" Baal interjected then with scorn, completely ruining the tale Silas had spent the last twenty-four hours honing and perfecting as best he could. "I've seen the wenches at the George's Town *Tavern* do no different with drunk troopers on Endweek leave. There was no *witchcraft* in *that*... only a clever *girl* with smarts enough to use a fool's *pride* against him..."

"A girl *also* capable enough to best you in *combat*, damn your eyes..." Silas snarled in return, finding a little backbone now that his honour and intelligence had been questioned. "She used the power of the Crystal to break their bonds, found strength to use a heavy, pine chair as a missile and threw it with enough force to break your sword arm: have you seen a tavern wench do *that* on one of your Endweek prowls?"

"I've arm enough left *for you*, old man, if you've a thought to try me," Baal growled darkly, swinging his feet over the edge of the bed and leaning forward as threateningly as one was able with a bandage and sling. "I doubt I'd need *both* to deal with the likes of you!"

"*Enough*...!" De Lisle screamed, so incensed with rage now that he was forced to steady himself against the desk. "Do *any* of you have any idea how *crucial* the next three days will be? The planning for this goes back *years*! The Shard *itself* has foreseen this... has worked toward this for a *decade*... and you sit here, squabbling like spoilt *children*...? This will succeed... *must succeed*... there *is* no acceptable alternative! All of us, *myself included*, live or die in the success or failure of this: *no one* walks away from the outcome!"

The cardinal was shaking, his eyes scorching the others with their glare as he cast it upon both men with equal disdain. A stab of pain flared within him as his chest heaved with adrenalin, but De Lisle ignored it, unwilling to show any sign of weakness in his moment of righteous fury. Silence reigned for seconds that seemed like hours, only to be broken – finally – by a soft, slow clap of hands from the far corner beyond Baal's bed.

"Now *that* was impressive!" Percy declared with a thin smile that barely held itself back from the brink of condescension. "Kinda reminds me of that Hitler guy on the documentaries my dad likes to watch... 'course, you're not speaking *German* – which is *such* a hot language when talking *angry*, by the way..." she conceded, rising from the chair she'd taken in the shadow of that corner and stepping out into the light. "*That* still sounded pretty good, though..."

The statement was so light, so out of context and had come so randomly out of left field that De Lisle almost blinked, left speechless for a moment as his mind attempted to process what the girl had just said and came up wanting. That she'd *dared* to interrupt him was inconceivable... that she'd dared to speak to him in such a tone even moreso... yet for all that, it had broken the intensity of the mood and he was shrewd enough to suspect that had been her intention all along.

"Could someone so young be so tired of life that you would insult *me* in such a fashion...?" He asked simply, raising an eyebrow and almost sounding amused by the concept as Baal and Silas stared on in horrified silence. "Who is this 'Hitler' you liken me to?" He continued, with *real* interest and intent behind the casual tone of his questions. "A buffoon, perhaps... some court jester, kept for a king's amusement?"

"Well, silly me, you *wouldn't* know who he was, would you?" She shrugged, chiding herself for forgetting her audience. "He was no fool..." she explained, assuming an expectant stance in the centre of the room with hands firmly on hips as she unflinchingly met his cold gaze with one of her own than was equally intense. "He was *crazy*, yes... but smart enough take over a country, personally order the extermination of six million people and start a war with the rest of my world that killed fifty million more..."

"A *formidable* enemy..." De Lisle conceded with a faint nod, willing to allow her some latitude now that he could sense there was a point to what she was about to say.

"And *Nev* thought I wasn't listening in history class..." Percy muttered proudly to herself. "Now, *you boys* have *also* managed to get yourselves a formidable enemy..." she continued, bringing herself back on track.

"The torture has twisted this one's mind," Baal scoffed in disbelief, regarding Percy with a scornful eye. "I'll call a guard and have it taken away."

"You've *already* underestimated *one* teenage girl and had your arse kicked for it," she fired back sharply, piercing his heart with her dagger-like stare as she took a threatening step in his direction, fists clenched at her sides. "You wanna have it handed to you a *second* time...?" In spite of himself, Baal actually flinched in reaction to her unexpected advance, something that wasn't missed by anyone else in the room.

"The girl's *clearly* insane," Silas broke in with a sneer of his own, saving the prince from his own humiliation as he drew the cardinal's attention. "She's of no further use for *anything*, save perhaps as a plaything for the soldiery..."

"Surprised *you* can remember *how*, you old perv..." Percy snarled, her cheek still stinging from the rawness of the wounds Silas had inflicted there. "I *told* you: I got a free look inside *your* head when you used that crystal on *me* the other day, and there was some *sick shit* down there, mate... it reads like a *demon's* diary! I know *exactly* how *he* likes to hurt people..." she added, turning toward De Lisle. "I could tell you *all about* the dirty little secrets he keeps hidden in that black, shrivelled little heart of his, Roger..."

"You can't *seriously* consider anything this harpy has to say," Silas screeched desperately, not at all happy about the idea of his deepest thoughts being revealed to the eagerly-waiting world. "She *helped* them escape – she *admits* it!"

"Too *right*, I admit it!" Percy replied defiantly, not backing down for a moment. "Unlike *you* lot, *I'm* not afraid to take responsibility for my actions..."

She has something... knows *something...* the deep, resonating words echoed through De Lisle's mind in that moment, shaking his soul to the core although he outwardly showed no reaction.

"Get out..." he ordered instantly, directing his words at Baal and Silas.

"I'll remind you these are *my* chambers, sir..." Baal began sharply, not at all pleased with being ordered about on his own ship. "I'll leave by *my* choice and no other's."

"I *do* give you a 'choice', you simpering fool..." De Lisle snarled, thrusting out his hand toward the prince as the ring on his pointing finger glowed and crackled with tiny arcs of purple lightning. For a second – just a *fraction* of a second – Prince Baal felt a sudden, tight constriction around his heart and the expression of shock, pain and terror that flashed across his face was telling. "You can leave here upright or *feet first – that* is your 'choice'; now get out, *both of you...*!"

Baal wasted no time getting out of the room as the sensation receded, ignoring the pain in his arm as he pushed between both of them as quickly as possible and not pausing for a moment to look back or catch anyone's eye. For Percy, the sight of the prince being 'force-choked' to all intents and purposes was absolutely delicious.

"You know, I found his lack of faith *particularly* disturbing..." she observed tartly, unable to help herself despite being well-aware that no one still present would have *any* chance of recognising a *Star Wars* quote.

Surprisingly made of sterner stuff, Silas rose from his seat but paused for a moment before De Lisle, pointedly throwing a caustic glare in Percy's direction before addressing his superior.

"Your Grace, this 'girl' is as wretched and duplicitous a creature as any I've ever seen... I have... made *mistakes*..." he admitted eventually, forcing the words out through clenched teeth, "but I have nevertheless served you well these many years and you've *always* trusted my judgement. I *implore* you... do *not* trust this creature: she hides agendas of her own devising that none of us can see..."

"You will need this, Chief Quisitor..." the cardinal advised evenly, drawing a small, wooden box from a large pocket inside his robes. "Use it to heal that fool's bones as you go out: he's no use to us without both hands..." Silas took it from him and opened it carefully, finding within a Holy Pendant identical to the one he'd lost to Nev almost two days earlier.

"Your Grace, I thank you for your – !" The rest of the sentence was cut off as De Lisle slapped him hard across the cheek, sending the old man staggering backward as he fumbled to hang onto the box and its contents.

"Your *incompetence* is beyond measure!" He hissed softly, rubbing his striking hand with the other to ease the pain he'd felt in dealing the blow. "It's only your *'years of service'* that's kept me from crushing your heart where you stand. I do not give you this as some pathetic symbol of forgiveness; simply that you're no use to me at all *without* it: keep *this one* from falling into the wrong hands, and *perhaps* I shall forget the damage you've done here. Now, *get out...*!"

There was shame and embarrassment in the old man's eyes, but De Lisle could also see a surprising amount of defiance as Silas clutched at his cheek with one hand and glared daggers in the cardinal's direction. Just as had been intended, it was a lesson the man wouldn't forget anytime soon, and the fact that the incident had occurred in the presence of a woman only served to make the whole thing that much more humiliating. Without another word, Silas stalked out of the room, his stiff, stilted footsteps sharp and clear as he continued on down the hallway and up the stairs at the far end.

"Much as a glimpse into Brother Silas' psyche *does* sound vaguely interesting," the cardinal admitted, forcing a wry smile, "I'm *far* more intrigued by the idea that you *admit* helping the witch and her accomplices escape, yet made no effort to go with them when the opportunity presented itself. Don't think for a *moment* that my *current* focus on the mistakes of those other two fools in *any* way diminishes *your* failures," he added, his expression and tone making it quite clear he was deadly serious. "In accordance with the will of The Shard, The Brotherhood persisted with its support of your operations in the other world *long* after it became apparent to *me* that there was no *real* likelihood of success: only *twice* have you actually returned with possible subjects and *both* occasions have now proved to be unmitigated disasters.

"I'm *not interested* in whining or excuses..." he continued, cutting off the protest she was clearly about to make. "The fact remains that you were on borrowed time *before* you were brought aboard *Rapier*, Mistress Persephone, and that situation hasn't been improved in *any way* by your actions since. Amusing jibes and verbal sparring are fine diversions for a village tavern, but they won't save you from the sword *here... unless...*" he added quickly after a momentary pause "...you have *something* to offer that is still of use...?"

Percy might've been more than a little crazy even by her own standards but she certainly wasn't stupid, and it was patently clear at that moment that any sarcasm or disrespect in the words she next spoke would almost certainly result in her very quickly finding herself on the wrong end of a *very* terminal cure for dandruff. Much as it rankled that she 'bend the knee' to *any* man, she could see that discretion was the better option here.

"Cardinal..." she began, giving a textbook curtsey and affecting a picture-perfect expression of sincere obedience "...I helped the three of them escape for one reason and one reason *only*: revenge. She was my friend... I trusted her with the secret of this world, and she spat it back in my face... and I will see her *suffer* by *my* hand and mine alone...!"

"Now, *revenge* is an emotion I can understand..." De Lisle conceded after a moment's thought, making his way slowly around the desk and sliding into the chair Silas had vacated. "It can be a *powerful* motivator, but *only* when used with judgement and *control*. Releasing the girl and her companions... *that* displayed neither. Did it not occur to you that perhaps, had they been recaptured, you might *still* have been allowed your vengeance?"

"Honestly...?" Percy asked in return, receiving a nod as she considered the question seriously. "No..." She shrugged. "Two men, both of them *fools* who've just been humiliated... no, I was *pretty* certain I *wasn't* going to get a look-in there..." It was De Lisle's turn to consider for a moment then, and he eventually returned a similar shrug along with a grimace of grudging concession.

"Possibly..." he admitted in the end. "*Possibly*... You're a shrewd creature – that much is true. Are *all* the women of your world so aware at such a young age?"

"A lot of us," she replied after another pause. "Not *enough* of us, but it's getting better. Women have more rights in my world – more *freedom* – but it's no *paradise*. *Some* men are still savages. There are too many of 'em who think they can still treat women as possessions... who think they can *hurt* women whenever they please. There's still a lot to learn..."

"A 'lot to learn'...?" The Cardinal repeated with a wry smile, thinking momentarily on Phaesus' misguided attempts so far to educate his own populace. "Do you think that better learning for women – better *education* – would make a difference?"

"Who said anything about *women*...?" She countered quickly, a faint bitterness in her voice now. "It's *men* who need to learn... who need *education*... in my world *and* here..."

"An *interesting* idea... and who would be the one to *teach* them...?" He asked with a raised eyebrow, very interested in what response might follow.

"Are you trying to trap me?" Percy shot back, raising an eyebrow of her own. "Do you want me to say *I* would do it, giving you some reason to fear me... to *condemn* me later, should the need arise?"

"I am Chief Primus of The Brotherhood of The Shard and subordinate *only* to The Shard Gods themselves," De Lisle declared slowly, a faint tinge of iron in his words now. "I need give a single word to have you disposed of... I need *no* evidence. Your ideas *intrigue* me however, and I would know more of them... know more of your world so that I might better deal with this *other* 'witch' you've released upon us."

"Well, she's *far* more dangerous than I would be..." Percy admitted, hiding her disgust just as De Lisle hid the sudden stab of fear that lanced through his heart over that revelation.

"How so...?"

"She's smart... *way* smarter than I am..." she shrugged again, seeing no point in denying it. "She's smart and *fit*, and she *really* knows how to use a sword... spent the last five years learning from some crazy old 'Samurai' guy. I'll bet you the only reason she's not *killed* anyone yet is the fact that she's so bloody *nice*. Now she has one of your crystals too. She doesn't know what she can do with it yet – not everything, anyway – but that'll come soon enough..."

"Use it to control others, perhaps," De Lisle mused, considering worst-case scenarios and not at all pleased with the idea this new girl could be *smarter* than Percy. "Control a rebel force and make them rise against us."

"*That* shows you're thinking like a dictator to begin with," She pointed out drily, moving to take a seat on the bed. "She won't *need* the crystal to bring people together... to convince them to rise up against you lot..."

"And *why* might that be...?" He asked sourly, not at all pleased with her remarks either.

"Well... because she's *nice*, like I said..." Percy replied, sounding as if it were the most obvious answer in the world. "She *cares* about people... she's *open* and *friendly* and *likes* to help others..." she continued, spitting out each 'compliment' as if it were poison on her tongue. "The crystal might let her *show* others the truth of what your 'Brotherhood' is like, but if something like that *does* happen, it's *she* who'll *inspire* them to rise up... all by herself..."

"We shall need to stop this *quickly*..."

"Yes, Captain Obvious... you *will*..."

"You're insolence *will* bring you undone eventually," De Lisle observed sourly, too preoccupied to find serious insult in her sarcasm.

"But *not* before I catch Nevaeh for you..." Percy suggested, sounding almost smug.

"*So* sure of yourself for one so young..." The cardinal shook his head in exasperated amusement. "I have *hundreds* of brothers to command, *all* with a direct connection to The Shard and the power it holds... with a *snap* of my fingers, I could also order the mobilisation of *thousands* of soldiers from *every* kingdom across the Osterlands... what makes you *so* certain that it will be *you* who gives me what I want?"

"Because... *Your Grace*... unlike Nevaeh Anderson, *I* am *not* nice..." she began slowly, picking her moment to show respect as she rose from the bedside and stepped slowly, purposefully toward him, "and there is *nothing*... in this world or *any other*... so cold, vindictive or *dangerous* as a teenage girl..."

He paused for a moment then, their eyes locked as each dared the other to look away first, and in the corner of his mind, that terrible, all-powerful voice echoed faintly:

We will consider this...

"I will think on it..." he advised eventually, fighting off a shuddering wave of dizziness that rippled through him in the wake of those words. "It is sufficient for the moment for me to say that your execution has been *postponed* and nothing more. Much will happen in the next few days and I will not risk what is already in play by concentrating on *diversions*. Once this Huon matter is done, we will consider this *other* matter of the witch... *if* it too has not already been resolved. It may be that she's already captured and disposed of by then."

Good luck with that… Percy thought silently, but she knew when to keep her opinions to herself, and simply added: "Of course, Your Grace…"

Annabel Martin's parents had worked in the kitchens at Cadle for many years, and she'd grown up surrounded by royalty and nobles alike as a result. She'd taken a job as one of the princess' handmaidens at just thirteen and had been a valued and trusted member of the royal household ever since. Five years later, she'd developed into a reliable, friendly and down-to-earth young woman who, although never provided with any formal education, was nevertheless bright enough in her own way, had been provided with knowledge of at least basic reading and writing by her parents, and generally displayed a relatively level-headed approach to the performance of her daily duties.

Annabel loved working for the King's family; she was provided all the comforts a commoner of her standing could ever hope for, and her days – filled with hard work as they were – were also generally filled with the pleasant companionship of her peers and the princess herself. That had all changed however with the revelation that Princess Charleroi had seen a Keepsake. She'd been sworn to secrecy and she'd never have broken a promise given to Matron Griselda, but that hidden, terrible truth weighed heavily on her soul.

Annabel loved her princess dearly, and truth-be-told, she also held Matron in the highest regard, yet she was a Gods-fearing person too and she'd been raised to respect and believe in the principles and the teachings of The Shard. It seemed impossible to believe that Charleroi could be evil – that she could be a *witch* – yet the evidence had been clear all who'd been present that morning: the girl had seen The Keepsake and stood accused by her own admission. To say that Annabel now felt conflicted would've been a significant understatement.

Deputy-viceroy of Taas and *very* distant cousin to the king, Edward Garrick also felt conflicted, although admittedly for less altruistic reasons than those affecting Annabel. Tall and athletic and in the prime of his life at thirty-three summers, he's served under Prince Baal in one form or another for most of his adult life and during that time, the pair had developed an almost symbiotic relationship. That being said, Garrick was nevertheless as shrewd, conniving and ambitions as Baal had ever been, and having come across information that might now be valuable and – more to the point – *useful*, he was now of two minds as to how he should proceed.

Garrick, a man whose career connections provided many and varied sources of intelligence from right across the length and breadth of Huon and beyond, knew that *something* was going on with the princess. He didn't know exactly what that was as yet, but the fact remained that something unusual was afoot and he was now torn between the potential to turn *any* unexpected revelation to his own, immediate benefit and the recognition that *any* such information would also likely be useful to Baal in their support of greater, overarching plans of The Brotherhood as a whole. Rumours that Prelate Roland was *already* keeping a watchful eye on the girl for unknown reasons only added to the confusion of the whole thing.

Garrick wasn't even sure what he was looking for *yet*, but he was a clever man with a predator's instinct for cunning and he could almost *smell* opportunity in the wind. His sources hadn't been able to work out *exactly* what was about to happen, but they'd certainly been able to tell him *who* was involved ('someone' who'd be dealt with properly in good time), and that knowledge alone was enough to make it worth investigating further.

Garrick's opulent quarters at the Longhouse were on the second level, not far from the stairwell up which Charleroi had escaped after having overheard the conversation between Silas and the cardinal. His two large rooms were spacious and well-appointed, with luxurious, hand-carved furnishings and drapes of the finest silk that overhung windows opening up onto a balcony similar to the princess'.

The sitting room contained a large desk, a number of upholstered armchairs, a large fireplace in one corner, a dining table in the middle with seating for eight and two doors – one as entry and the other, opposite, leading to an equally-large bedroom. A piled plate of fresh fruit stood atop a low buffet near the main door and beside that, a narrow rack held a small selection of swords of varying sizes, supplied for his practice and amusement.

It was through that door that Annabel was ushered, escorted by a pair of large and rather intimidating troopers from Garrick's own, personal bodyguard. She'd been told nothing of why she'd been brought before him and fear of the unknown *and* the known-but-secret was painfully clear in her expression and nervous demeanour.

"Mistress Martin..." Garrick declared with all the welcome he could muster, "so kind of you to come and see me at such short notice... I know you've your duties to attend to..."

"Weren't nothin', sir..." Annabel replied instantly, bobbing her head slightly as a sign of respect keeping her eyes fixed firmly at Garrick's feet as he walked casually toward her around the dining table, "...nothin' of any importance, sir..."

"'No importance'...?" He repeated with kindly, mocking scorn as he silently waved away the guards behind her. "Don't sell yourself short, mistress: without the hard work of our servants, there's not a keep in the kingdom that would last more than a day before falling into chaos!" He reached out and gently placed a finger beneath her chin, lifting her head until their eyes met. "There are *some* who might underestimate the worth of their staff..." he added, nothing but sincerity in his expression now, "but *I* am not one of them. There's a great failing in *anyone* who confuses 'subordinate' with 'inferior'..." ...*or with* dangerous... he added silently in his mind. For her part, Annabel could only nod silently in that moment, although she wasn't sure about one or two of the bigger words.

"Now, as you probably know, mistress, *I* am deputy-viceroy to Taas..." he continued brightly, as she again nodded mutely, "...*and* a member of the Namur family. It has come to my attention that something – and I stress the word *something* – may be lurking in the shadows regarding a possible threat to the princess..."

"I – I don't know nothin' about anythin' like that, sir..." Annabel answered far too quickly, and all the denial in the world couldn't hide the start she gave at the mention of the princess, or the quaver in her voice.

"No... of course you don't..." Garrick nodded slowly, giving what he hoped was a reassuring smile as he lowered his head in acknowledgement of her words and stepped away, moving around behind her as she stood rooted to the spot, staring straight ahead and frozen with fear. "You're a handmaiden... why should *you* know anything about the dangerous politics of a monarchy? *I*, on the other hand, know *exactly* how easily an enemy can rise from within to *strike* at the heart of a kingdom..." he added, barking out the word 'strike' loud enough to make her flinch and whimper faintly "...just as was the case when king's brother was assassinated six months ago.

"The *king* is *not* his brother..." he continued, trying to keep the sneer out of his voice as he spoke. "Our sovereign is a mild and *temperate* man, who – in a *sane* world – should have no enemies at all..." He grinned then, dark and evil and unseen behind the girl's back as he stared unfocussed at the door and wall before him. "*This* however is *not* a sane world. I've been advised that *someone* has requisitioned a ship from the Western Merchant Reserve in the king's name, along with sufficient supplies for a small army. That same ship left Strahn a few days ago and docked at Sternley yesterday afternoon. Now I'm a close friend of the royal quartermaster and even *he* does not know who has set aside these assets... something I find *very* strange considering he is, after all, the man charged with the administration of those same assets *in the king's name...*"

"I – again, sir... I..."

"Yes, yes, yes..." he dismissed quickly with a wave of his hand, cutting her off and not really hiding the exasperation in his tone. "You 'don't know anything'... you've already said. With the *wealth* of resources available to *me* however, I *have* been able to determine who's behind it all, but more on *that* a little later... Instead, can you guess what *else* is rumoured to have been stowed aboard this ship after it arrived in port yesterday? No...? *Apparently*, a large trunk filled with clothes for the princess was *also* brought aboard... aboard a ship I am told on good authority is set to depart *tomorrow* evening to 'destinations unknown'..." He paused for just a moment, entirely for effect and to increase tension.

"Now *that* interests me *very much*," he went on, reaching out almost absent-mindedly and running his gloved hand across the jewelled hilts of the swords that stood at the rack by the main door. "We have Endweek tomorrow night and Princess Charleroi is expected to be attending a *plethora* of official engagements over the course of the next week as part of the treaty celebrations: the one place she *definitely* shouldn't be is *anywhere else*, rendezvousing with a ship full of supplies and her best dresses. Perhaps she's *not* intending to depart with this vessel, however a *devious* mind might think all this were some kind of contingency plan – a standby for the princess that offers some safe avenue of escape in case of danger...

"It may *all* be a complete coincidence, of course," he conceded with a shrug, not believing that for a moment, "but as a *loyal* member of the Namur, I take *any* threat to the king or his family *very* seriously.

And so we come to the point of my asking you here today…" he declared brightly, turning to face her back as he rested his against the sword rack. "You may not know much about politics or power, girl, but you *do* spend a *lot* of time with the princess and if there were something happening in which she was involved, I'd imagine it would be impossible for you *not* to know about it… *hmmm*…?"

"I – I don't know what to say sir…" Annabel stammered softly, the terror in her voice a siren song to Garrick's predatory instincts as she turned to face him. "I'd *never* want anything to happen to the princess. If I knew anything, I'd be *sure* to tell you right away."

"Oh yes…" he nodded in solemn agreement, his fingers closing about the hilt of a sword behind his back. "I *know* you will…"

XIV

CHANCE ENCOUNTERS

Darkness... and someone with catlike movements passed silently in the shadows, keeping low to avoid detection. Little more than a wraith in the moonlight, a hooded figure all in black crept slowly beneath the window sill, pressed flat against the outside wall of the inn. It was a warm enough night and a window left open in search of some elusive breeze provided a perfect point of entry. Reaching up carefully, he pushed the wooden frame high and peered in, squinting against the deeper darkness of the room beyond.

With extreme caution, he hoisted himself up onto the sill and brought around the small crossbow he'd hung down the centre of his back. There were rooms filled with sleeping guests... and his mission was to kill all within, with one of them the primary target and the rest an unfortunate case of collateral damage. When the deed was done, a fire would destroy the inn and *the evidence, and all would appear to be some terrible, tragic accident...*

The crossbow rose, catching the light of the moon through the open window as he paused to steady his aim and pulled the trigger...

Nev awoke with a soft gasp, her chest heaving with the fright of the nightmare, and she found she'd broken into a cold sweat that had left her clothes faintly damp. It took a moment or two for the shock to dissipate as her sleep-addled brain struggled its way back to the reality of waking... of remembering where she was as the sound of the water and the rocking of the sailboat brought it all back to her in a rush. Nev rarely experienced bad dreams – surprisingly enough, she sometimes thought, when she thought about it at all – and that one had been far more vivid – far more *real* – than any she could remember.

The sun hung low on the western horizon below a layer of thin, wispy cloud and she was surprised to find that the boat was headed straight for a small, curved beach, skating across the tops of the moderate waves with the help of a gusty northerly wind. She glanced nervously about as her clarity returned, then sighed with both relief and a little melancholy as she received reassuring nods from Godfrey at the rudder, and Lester too, the boy reclining in the middle of the boat not far from where she'd been laying.

Nev suspected there was no more than an hour or so to sunset and as she looked up to her left, her breath caught again at the sight of cliffs off the port bow, towering above her to a height of almost two hundred metres. The heights on that side sloped sharply down toward the narrow sliver of sand they were heading for, approaching at a steady pace that seemed a little too fast to her untrained eye.

"Ready with the sails, Toadface," Godfrey called softly, his voice barely audible above the roar of the surf surrounding them.

"Ready, Westy…" the boy assured with nervous excitement, already upright with his hands gripped tightly around the rigging.

"Righto…" he warned, waiting for the right moment. "Haul 'em in… *now*…!"

With a few deft movements, Lester quickly loosened the billowing mainsail and hauled it in, spilling the air within and bringing it down in a cascade of folding canvas. The boat began to lose momentum almost immediately, slowing noticeably as Godfrey turned the rudder slightly and brought it in close to the beach.

"Hold on there, Nev… there'll be a bit of a bump when we hit…"

She barely had time to brace herself before the bow bit into the wet sand at an oblique angle and sent her lurching forward. Even so, Godfrey's warning had probably saved her from losing a few teeth as she managed to stop short of smashing her face into the gunwale.

"Anchor away…" Lester called out eagerly, already knowing what needed to be done as he leaped over the side with the thing snugged under one arm.

Fast as a rabbit, he sprinted at least a dozen metres up the beach with the ten kilogram anchor trailing a rope behind that remained tied to the bow near where Nev lay. Finding a suitably-large rock sticking out of the sand, he raised the implement over his head with both hands like a huge, barbed hammer and drove it hard into the ground, making certain one of the hooks connected with the stone so there was no chance of it coming loose.

"Alright then," Godfrey declared, already slipping his own pack over his shoulders as he jumped over the side and into knee-deep water.

"We've at least ten or twelve miles to cover and *no time* spare to do it in… we need to find ourselves some horses…"

"Where are we going to find horses *here*…?" Nev asked, sounding very unimpressed as she shouldered her own rucksack and clutched the katana tightly in one hand. She stood unsteadily up at the bow, eying the very shallow water beyond with some serious doubt and heavily overthinking the best way to avoid getting her boots wet.

"We've a friend who runs a tavern near here: serves as a rest-stop for travellers heading east or west on the Huon High Road…" Godfrey explained with a wry smile, moving around to the bow and extending a supporting hand as she awkwardly launched herself from the boat and, much to her own amazement, indeed landed on the wet sand beyond the line of the actual water. She was then forced to bolt up the beach with an inadvertent squeal as the surf immediately and rather uncharitably decided to come rushing in at her with surprising speed.

They'd sailed for the rest of that first night and most of the following day, heading steadily west under the mild but constant winds surging down across the Deepwater from the mainland. As Percy had suggested, there was indeed plenty of water and a box full of sealed jars containing a plain variety of preserved meats and fruits that was more than enough to survive on.

Godfrey had stayed well out to sea for the first twelve hours or so, a succession of light easterlies pushing the little boat along at a good four or five knots for most of the journey as he made sure they stayed clear of any possible search area. They encountered few other ships during that part of the voyage: the deeper areas of the central Deepwater were rarely travelled by anyone other than the fishing trawlers and they generally worked west of Huon in the wide expanses of the Great Bite, south of the central Osterlands.

Only as the sun was well past noon had he turned the boat to port, making for a distant shoreline that was little more than an indistinct smudge across the southern horizon. Navigation had been aided immeasurably by a sextant and set of nautical maps included with the supplies, and Nev had been amazed to find that Godfrey was a reasonably accomplished navigator. It was another three or four hours before they'd made landfall, during which time she'd fallen into a fitful and uncomfortable sleep in the bow, where she'd remained for almost the entire trip.

All three were able to stretch their legs and backs now as they walked upon the wonderful solidity of dry land for the first time in almost twenty-four hours. A difficult hike up the steep slope leading away from the beach brought them out onto a large, open plateau that lay cool and silent before them in the fading twilight and stretched away for what seemed to be miles in every direction.

Godfrey set out south across the open fields, already knowing his way with the surety of an experienced tracker as Lester and Nev trailed on behind. The night air was crisp but the steady pace soon warmed them all as they passed through almost endless rows of flowers, set into lines far too accurate to be anything but man-made.

"Tulips...!" Nev exclaimed, her curiosity getting the better of her as she picked one from its stem in passing and examined it closely. "Rows and rows of tulips...!"

"They keep 'em for the palace..." Lester advised with a shrug. "Had tulips growin' here fer as long as anyone can remember: me ma reckoned they like to decorate the halls with 'em at Cadle..."

"You come from around here?"

"Well... not 'round *here*..." he shrugged again, slowing just enough to allow her to draw level as they walked on. "Me family lived near Burnii – worked the land there for a local lord..." His voice faded into silence then as less pleasant family memories returned, and Nev knew better than to press the issue.

They marched on for at least another hour, the night definitely upon them now as they passed over a shallow rise in the landscape and caught sight of the main road in the distance: a faint, dirty-brown ribbon stretching east-to-west across an otherwise virgin landscape of fields and trees with dark, towering ranges in the distance. Godfrey's sense of direction had been true enough, and almost directly ahead lay the faint flicker of lights twinkling in the windows of a small, wayside tavern.

"That's the place," he affirmed, openly proud (and a little surprised) over the accuracy of his navigational skills.

"Not bad work, mister..." Nev conceded, giving due credit and swelling his pride exponentially.

"Bloody *miracle*, considering how long it's been since he came here last..." Lester observed as they all stood together in a group, the casual remark a grudgingly backhanded compliment that nevertheless brought Godfrey back down to earth just a tad.

"Come on, big mouth," he grinned, slapping the boy on the shoulder. "Time for a few hours' rest and a decent meal while they work out where they want us to go next..."

"So this friend of yours is a fellow Osterman?" Nev asked as they set out once more, this time at a cracking pace as excitement over the thought of food and rest gave them all some additional reserves of stamina.

"No... not *quite*..." Godfrey admitted "...but he's *sympathetic*, *and* he gets paid a regular retainer to keep supplies aside for us if we're ever in need. He's got no love for the Brotherhood, that's for sure."

The Blooming Tulip was a small, single-storey structure with a tall, thatched roof and just four guest rooms tacked onto the rear of the main bar area. The largest room in the place, it was still barely big enough to fit tables for perhaps a dozen guests, all jammed in tight between the bar at one end and a crackling fireplace at the other. A small, covered corral out back served as a stable and as they entered the premises that evening, six horses were present along with two empty carriages parked directly outside. It stood perhaps two dozen metres apart from the tavern itself, with hard-packed earth in between that had been scuffed and rutted by hoofmarks and the tracks of wagon wheels through many years of seasonal rains.

The interior was about what Nev might've expected of a medieval tavern (from the extremely limited knowledge she had of such things) and the only thing that struck her as odd about the entire scene wasn't anything to do with the room at all... it was the fact that the innkeeper – a man of short stature and looking to be in his late thirties – was clearly of Asian ancestry – the first such person she'd seen since she'd arrived in that world.

"Well met, good sir," he called out jovially to Godfrey as he stepped through the door at the far end of the room, the others close behind. "Are y' in need of lodgings this night or just a little rest and replenishment before you get on your way?"

"I've a mind for both, Mister Nguyen," he replied with a matching smile as they approached the bar itself, making certain they paid no attention to the single other guest, currently seated in the shadows over in one corner, away from the fire. "Lookin' for a little o' the *southern* hospitality this place is famous for..."

"Why..." Nguyen stammered, recognising Westacre for the first time as the emphasis of that coded phrase sunk in "...why, it's surely not Master Godfrey...? It's been – what – over a *year* now?"

"Close enough to make no odds, Pham," he grinned, extending a hand that was accepted instantly and shaken with gusto across the benchtop. "You remember The Toad, no doubt?"

"Aye... how could I forget?" Nguyen faltered again, at least managing to keep the discomfort out of his tone as he recalled the terrible blows the Boniface family had suffered so many years before (well-known around the local area as proof of the brutality of The Brotherhood). "Good to see you too, Lester, me boy..." he added, maintaining his smile without missing a beat. "And *this* young *lad*...?" He added, turning his attention toward Nev for the first time and – having noted that she was clearly female – making a loud declaration of her supposed 'manliness' to avoid any awkward involvement regarding a lack of blindfold with the other guest present.

"...is a *friend*, whose identity is of *no* consequence..." Godfrey countered quickly, lowering his voice then to ensure his words graced no unintended ears. "It's news we have – *urgent* news I need to get to my lord, back home – and yes, we'll *also* need some beds for the night and three horses at dawn..."

"Well, I can manage the *horses* well enough," Nguyen explained, reluctant to disappoint, "but the *beds* may be a problem. We've two families already turned in for the night and they've *women* with them so they've taken the rooms without windows. That leaves me just two rooms more and one of those – the only one with three beds – has also been taken. I'm left with just a single bed between you – there'll need to be some sleepin' on the floor, I'm afraid. I can bring in some fresh, dry straw and some extra blankets if it'll help..."

"You've a need for the larger room, friends...?"

Those unexpected words came from the stranger in the corner and as they all turned in his direction, he rose from his table and walked slowly toward them, a gnarled staff in one hand that clunked on the floor boards in time with every second step. Tall and broad-shouldered and possibly the oldest man Godfrey had ever met, he was an intimidating figure in non-descript civilian clothes that clearly and not very effectively hid thick chainmail beneath.

"I thank y', sir, but there's no need to bother yerself..." Godfrey began, sensing instinctively there was more to the fellow than met the eye and deciding he wanted no part of whatever that was.

"If t' were a bother I'd have nay come over, lad..." Randwick countered evenly, the hint of a smile quirking the edges of his lips beneath the tavern's dim lighting. "I'll admit, I *do* like me space when I'm alone, but I'd not take my luxuries in exchange for another's hardship. Besides..." he added quickly before anyone else could butt in "...it'll be a *tight* squeeze for *three* o' ye in the other room and it wouldn't do for *lads* such as yerselves to be crushed in there together so snug..."

There was something in the way he'd uttered that last sentence – the stress on one particular word – that sent a shudder through Godfrey's body. It was plain that the old man had seen beyond Nev's cloaks and disguise and had come to a similar conclusion as Nguyen: that there was a female in their midst who'd clearly arrived without blindfold or mask and was pretending to be male to avoid discovery. As disconcerting as that realisation was for Westacre, the most telling part was that this stranger had chosen not to denounce them, making him either a friend or someone *very* dangerous.

"Truly, sir, it's a fine gesture, but..."

"I *insist*, young'un..." Randwick declared loudly, not sounding at all displeased yet nevertheless able to slip some hard steel into his tone that would allow no negotiation. "I'll hear nothing more on the subject!"

"I – I *thank* you, sir... we're in your debt..." Godfrey conceded eventually with a faint bow, accepting with as much grace as he could manage and suppressing his concerns.

"A small thing, to be certain..." he replied with a wave of one hand. "Buy me a drink, and we'll call it square."

"Easily done, sir," Godfrey acknowledged, managing a smile this time as he turned back toward Nguyen. "Innkeeper: a glass of your best for this good gentleman!"

"*Four* glassed of Green Fairy, or nary a *one*..." Randwick countered immediately. "A toast to The King – I'll accept no less – then I'll move my pack to the other room and leave you all in peace."

But of course, 'one' drink became another and another as a far-too-friendly old traveller plied them with drinks and also plied them with subtle, indirect questions. Nev had tried desperately to sit on her first and not drink too much, knowing how little exposure she'd had to alcohol in general, and Lester's mugs were heavily watered down at Godfrey's order, in deference to the boy's young age and in spite of his unending complaints. What should have taken just a few moments ultimately took over an hour, and all three were absolutely exhausted by the time Nguyen was able to finally convince the old man that the bar was well and truly closed.

Randwick knew the movements of a female well enough when he saw one, even one disguised with hood and heavy clothing, and He'd also noticed the shifting shape of a sword at her waist, hidden beneath the folds of her cloak. That in itself had been enough to pique his curiosity, boosted substantially by the realisation soon after that she'd been travelling under the pretence of being a man; without blindfold or anything else to cover her eyes as they'd entered the tavern.

Giving up the larger room was no great sacrifice – he'd have done that anyway as the decent thing to do – but the insistence of a drink beforehand would give him a few extra minutes' of time in their presence, perhaps presenting a chance to gather more intelligence. The King's Mentor hadn't lived this long by taking chances or ignoring his instincts, and right now his instincts were telling him that there was something *very* unusual about this trio of strangers.

They'd been forced through toast after toast and downed each drink as quickly as had been humanly possible without arousing suspicion then – *finally* – waited for what felt like the passing of an age as the old man gathered his belongings and shifted across to the next room down the hall, at the rear of the building. There were indeed three mattresses as promised, and rough as they were they were the most wondrously inviting and comfortable beds any of them had seen in a long time.

"That old man's trouble... I can feel it in me bones..." Godfrey whispered softly as they lay there in the darkness on either sides of the room while between them, Lester was already snoring softly. "He *knew* you were a girl... he *should* have denounced us! Why didn't he?"

"We were three to one, for a start," Nev suggested, too tired to really think about things deeply but trying to help all the same. "*Four*, really, if you count Nguyen..."

"Somehow, I get the feeling four-to-one wouldn't be odds that'd *worry* that old bear all that much," Godfrey mused, recalling how broad and intimidating the fellow had seemed as he'd stood before them. He wasn't scared of us," he continued, shaking his head, "and he wasn't challenging us either, but he insisted on that drink for a reason. He had a careful way of asking things – all innocent like – but he was fishing for information all the same... working us with more and more of that cursed Green Fairy...!" Godfrey wasn't a complete stranger to alcohol – it was almost impossible *not* to be a drinker in military service – but he was smart enough to moderate his intake and remain in control of his own faculties.

"Green Fairy..." Nev mumbled softly, having lost the thread of the conversation midway through as her mind wandered off on a tangent regarding the drinks they'd been served. "*Green... Fairy...*" she repeated carefully, giggling to herself softly for reasons not readily apparent even to herself. "Tinkerbell ..." she rambled, veering off topic completely. "I'm drinking *Tinkerbell*, ha-ha..."

"For Crystal's Sake, you're *drunk*...?" Godfrey exclaimed in a hushed voice, trying very hard *not* to sound amused and not really managing it. "*One drink*...? Dragonfall take me... *just one*...?"

"Drunk...?" Nev managed, her attempt at indignance falling flat as she slurred her words. "That, sir, is an *insult*...! Can't be... *can't*..." She shook her head vaguely, her face a mask of confused sincerity. "What's that saying...? I'm not... I'm... *How does it go*...? I'm *not*... as drunk... as you *think*... constable! Wait, no... no, *that's* not right..."

Nev had never been drunk, having voluntarily lived a life of an extremely sheltered nature. She'd barely even tasted alcohol more than once or twice in her life and that had only been beer, which had tasted awful and had put her right off the whole idea of drinking in general. She'd never in her life encountered a drink as strong as absinthe, an extremely-potent, aniseed-flavoured spirit. Even with water added, her mind and body were completely unprepared for its effects as the alcohol began to work its way through her unsuspecting and generally defenceless bloodstream.

"Well..." Godfrey sighed, conceding defeat regarding any chance of sensible conversation "...I s'pose that's that for the night..."

"Peter Pan... Captain Hook... Mister Smee..." Nev muttered softly to herself, lost in her own world as she rolled over on her mattress and stared up at the ceiling with wildly-unfocussed eyes. "Knock-knock... Who's there...? It's *Smeeeeeeeee....*!" She added, giggling softly again.

Staring at his own part of the ceiling, Godfrey was torn between whether to go with annoyance over there being no chance of any sleep tonight or outright amusement regarding what was clearly Nev's first experience of being drunk. He was dog-tired and should have been grumpy about the situation but in her defence, the sight and sounds of the drunken teenager in the bed opposite were *incredibly* amusing.

"If I knew how to work that infernal 'phone' of yours," he whispered softly to himself, glancing across at her with a caring smile, "there'd be some fine 'moving pictures' of you looking *very* three-sheets-to-the-wind…"

He was let off the hook a few moments later as Nev's muddled brain negotiated with her body over whether to go with falling asleep or passing out: the result was a combination of the two as she slipped restlessly into snoring oblivion.

The assassin again… reaching up to the window sill with his crossbow at his back… lithe movements and the swish of the bolt as it thuds home…

Nev woke in the early hours of the morning, moonlight streaming through the large, open window set into the upper half of the room's outside wall. She'd rolled over during the night, the sheathed katana uncomfortable beneath her left side, and was now facing the wall, where the glow of the moon had bathed the plaster above her in stark illumination bright enough to cause her to squint for a moment or two as her vision cleared.

She thought about the strangeness of the recurring dream, more perplexed the second time around than shocked by it, although she still had no idea where such ideas might have come from in the depths of her subconscious. The vivid nature of it receded from her thoughts however as she became increasingly aware of the pounding headache that was now quickly building behind her forehead. Having experienced drunkenness for the first time, Nev was now also experiencing her first hangover.

Water… She told herself seriously, wincing as even her thoughts seemed to be conspiring to worsen her aching head. *That's what dad used to say: a good drink of water should fix any hangover…*

There was a jug and a few cups on a side table at the foot of her bed and it would be a simple task to get up and pour herself a drink or two… as soon as she'd prepared herself for the assault that was likely to bring down on her suffering frontal lobe. Just a few more seconds to gather her strength, she reasoned, and she'd be right as rain.

It was at that point she noticed the unexpected shape appear above the shadow line left against the wall by the lower window sill behind her. Pausing for just a second, it then rose quickly to reveal itself as the silhouetted shape of a human being climbing onto the window sill in almost complete silence. Terror gripped her along with the realisation that it was her nightmare made *very* real, and it took every ounce of Nev's self-control as she forced herself to not cry out or make any obvious movement.

Moving just her eyes, she watched with rigid fear as the shadowy shape perched itself on the sill exactly as she'd foreseen and raised the crossbow, taking a moment to check its readiness before lowering it toward its intended target. Trying to compare the positioning of the shadow itself, along with the fact that what she was seeing was actually happening behind her, Nev was unable to work out at that point whether the bolt was being aimed at her or Godfrey, although *neither* target presented in her mind as a preferred option.

Turn to the left, aiming the crossbow…

A vision of his attack flared in her mind, galvanising her into action. Her right hand, folded across her chest and invisible to the would-be attacker, was very near the hilt of her sword but there was no way she'd be fast enough to roll, draw the weapon and attack in the time it would take for the assassin to loose his bolt. All this occurred to her in a fraction of a second as her brain kicked into automatic pilot in its search for options. There was only one way to speed up her reaction time, and that was to cut out as many movements as possible: the only obvious alternative wouldn't be particularly effective as an attack but it at least stood *some* chance of success.

Distract… throw off his aim… divert, then *attack…*

The images flashed in her mind again, but her system was too charged with adrenalin to even think about what was happening. Even as his finger began to squeeze lightly on the trigger, Nev began to roll onto her back, the fingers of her right hand sliding around the *tsuka* and bringing the katana with her as she came around. With her index finger pressed down on the scabbard, holding it in place, she was able to use her own movement to whip the sword downward toward the masked man at the window in a tight arc.

Lifting her fingertip at the right moment, she released the scabbard and allowed it to slip straight off the blade with substantial centrifugal force. Even as he turned his head and the crossbow toward her in reaction to the unexpected motion, it was already too late to react. The lacquered *saya* launched itself from the rest of the weapon, spearing across the short distance between them and then cracking against the centre of his forehead with full force.

The killer's head jerked backward under the impact, the crossbow discharging by reflex and sending its bolt deep into the wall to Nev's left as she rose from the bed and lunched toward him with a bellowed "*Hyah…!*", her unsheathed blade stretched out before her.

The point of the katana caught him in the shoulder, slicing through his clothing and punching deep into the flesh beneath. He toppled backward with a scream, cracking his head on the upper sill as he fell heavily onto his back on the hard earth outside

"Assassin… *assassin…!*" Nev howled at the top of her lungs, Godfrey and Lester already leaping to their feet, roused groggy and disoriented by the killer's cry of pain. They were in the process of reaching for their own weapons as the door to their room burst in with a crash, revealing two more black-clad assassins with weapons drawn.

Parry, lunge and strike…!

Too hyped to even think, Nev followed her instinct blindly and thrust forward, slapping the first attacker's sword-thrust to one side with the flat of her blade, then punching upward into his throat with the heel of her hand as his own momentum brought him into range. He fell backward into the corridor with a strangled cry and Nev prepared for the next attack, only to be confronted with the second killer standing against the far wall with a *very* large crossbow already aimed right at her chest.

Pause… then strike…

She was going to die: there was no denying it. The third killer in black was too far away to strike and he had the drop on her anyway, the crossbow already loaded and ready. There was no way around it. Whatever her instincts and those strange, flashing images in were telling her, there was no ignoring the fact that it was all over.

That realisation crackled like lightning through her mind in that first fraction of a second as the assassin's eyes flicked momentarily toward his fallen comrade, then instantly back to her in the doorway. His eyes were the only part of his face visible behind the hood and wrapping that he wore, and they narrowed with hatred as he lifted his weapon slightly and squeezed at the trigger.

That moment of pause between them had probably been enough. A long, wooden staff crashed into the side of his head at that moment, having been flung with some considerable accuracy from the doorway of the next room down from theirs. The crossbow bolt went wide, sizzling past her left ear, then miraculously also missed Lester and Godfrey completely as it disappeared into the darkness beyond the open window.

Nev didn't hesitate any longer as he crashed to the floor in a heap. She instantly leaped forward and fractured his right forearm with a solid kick that sent the crossbow spiralling out of his grasp. He released a cry of agony, curling into a ball of semi-conscious pain and clutching at his broken arm, and Nev – recognising that he was no longer any immediate threat – would've been happy to have left things as they were for the time being.

Neither Randwick nor Godfrey were of similar mind, however. As Godfrey pushed past her, thrusting his sword deep into the man's chest before he could even raise a hand in protest, the old man had also covered the distance between his room and the second assassin – the one Nev had struck in the throat – and despatched him in a similar manner with a thin-bladed dagger.

Nev's initial over the fact that they'd just killed two defenceless human beings in cold blood was one of cold disgust. Sickened by the sight of such brutality, it didn't matter to her that the assailants had been trying to kill *them* just moments before – to her mind, the fact remained that they'd since been disarmed and were now completely harmless, and as such there'd been no need for more killing.

"Fire... *fire*...!" A cry of alarm rose up from beyond the doorway to their left, leading out into the main tavern area, and as they turned in that direction they could clearly see wisps of grey/black smoke wafting into the hallway from around the edges of the closed door. There was a flickering glow beneath its bottom edge that suggested it a fine idea that doorway was left shut for the time being.

"There's families here..." Randwick remarked to Godfrey, all that was needed as he received a nod of understanding in return and both men turned toward the remaining guest rooms further down the hall. Already, there were screams of fear coming from at least one of the other rooms, along with the unmistakable wail of a crying baby.

"Lester: you and Nev secure our gear and get yourselves out the window to safety. Watch yourselves out there – there might be a third one of those buggers still about. The gentleman and I will see to the others…"

The tavern was burning heavily at the other end of the building as Nev and Lester tossed out their packs and then followed them through the open window. After quickly scouting the area to make sure the remaining, wounded assassin wasn't still lurking in the area, she headed back to help the others as Lester stood guard over their belongings.

The other two rooms had been taken by an older couple, both looking to be in their fifties at least, and a young family of three that included the crying baby, definitely no older than six or eight months. Godfrey and Randwick were respectively helping both groups to climb out through their own open windows, with smoke already streaming out beneath the upper sills as it spread right through the building.

That there'd been no back door to be found seemed dangerously amiss as she jogged up and assisted Godfrey in lowering first the old woman, then her husband to the ground, both coughing heavily because of the smoke. The tavern had been built on stumps to keep the floor raised and away from any moisture, and the window sills stood at least two metres from the ground outside – a difficult drop for the young or infirm. With Nev now present, she was at least able to guide the terrified woman safely to the ground and gently lead her off to a safe distance as her husband followed through the opening behind her.

At the next window along, Randwick had first helped the father out into the cool, night air, where he was then able to safely reach up and take his screaming child into his outstretched arms. The mother came next, by which time Nev had been able to return and help her to the ground as her partner looked on anxiously, trying in vain to settle his terrified baby son.

Smoke was now filling every room and it poured out around both Godfrey and Randwick as they came out last, coughing and wheezing with scorched lungs, blackened faces and watering eyes. As a group, the eight of them then staggered together to a safer position a good thirty or forty metres away near the main road as Godfrey searched desperately about for a few moments as he realised Lester had gone missing.

"Where in the name of The Crystal were *you*?" He demanded angrily as the boy appeared a few moments later, looking shaken with his face as dirty and coated in soot as any of them.

"The whole place is goin' up…" Lester explained, almost sounding tearful, although it was difficult to tell if it were from emotion or smoke stinging his eyes. "Went to let the horses out… be a damn shame to see 'em hurt for nothin'…" he paused for a moment, considering what else to say. "Found Nguyen out near the corral…" he added, shaking his head meaningfully. "Mongrels cut his throat…"

"*Why*…" Godfrey spat angrily, asking no one in particular. "Why kill him… why target *us*…? How could The Brotherhood even know we were even *here*…?" He could see no sense to it. There was no way their exact whereabouts could conceivably have been known, even if news *had* come through regarding what had happened aboard *Rapier* the night before.

"Not you, lad…" Randwick growled sadly, shaking his head and carefully drawing him to one side, away from the other guests, as Nev and Lester followed close behind. "T' weren't *you* three they were after."

"And how d'you figure *that*?"

"Because you took *my* room, boy… simple as that…" Randwick answered with anger of his own now, not pleased that an innocent man had been murdered because of his presence there. "Those three went for *my* room first and found you three instead. We were lucky you were quick with your sword there, lass…" he added, giving a nod in Nev's direction "…and I'd warrant *all of us* owe you our lives this night. I'll ask you more on where you learned to fight like *that* another time, but right *now* we need to get as far away from here as we're able."

"You presume a lot, old man," Godfrey snapped, far too tense to be open to taking orders from a stranger. "Why should we trust a *stranger* so… 'specially if he's one hunted by assassins, as you seem so ready to declare. Why should we *trust* you?"

"For a few reasons, *boy*…" Randwick growled in return, lifting himself up to his full, intimidating stature in the stark moonlight. "*One*: because without thinking, you let slip a moment ago that The *Brotherhood* was after you, and you'll need all the help you can get if they *are*… *Two*: you've been travelling on the road with this lass here, her eyes uncovered – which might explain at least *partly* why those bloody 'Brown Robes' are after ye – and she's *something* special, judging by the way I saw her fight; so there's a story there I'm going to be wantin' to hear soon enough… and *three*: …three?" He repeated, lowering his tone just enough for fear of being overheard. "Because, *three*: I knew you lot were something unusual the moment you walked in that tavern, and I know *you* knew I knew it…" he pointed out, locking eyes with Godfrey and daring him to say otherwise. "I didn't denounce you for heretics then, and I'm not going to do it now… I've *bigger* fish to fry today."

"I… I think we *can* trust him…" Nev whispered slowly, her strange new instincts telling her there was good in the old man, and that he might somehow be of use to them. "I think we should tell him what we're doing…"

"Are you *insane*…?" Godfrey hissed in return. "Have you breathed too much smoke? We've just met this fellow, and I do *not* think it a good idea that we share our secrets with a complete stranger – no insult intended, sir…" he added quickly in deference to the tall and clearly powerful man standing beside him.

"Oh, none taken…" he replied evenly, his eyes narrowing slightly all the same. "Perhaps it might help if we were properly introduced? My name is Foucault Randwick, sword-master and Mentor to the Crown of Huon, and unless you've lived your entire life 'neath a *rock*, somewhere out in the Great Momofan, you'll *know* that name well enough." His tone hardened now as shock and recognition flared in the eyes of two out of the three present. "You'll *also* know that as Mentor, my word is honour-bound…

"Now, whether by design or just damned good fortune, your arrival here this night *probably* saved my life. *Why* those assassins were after me I know not for certain *yet* – although I could hazard a guess or two – but the fact remains it were *my* room they came for. So like it or not, I'm somewhat in your debt and I swear to you, *anything* you tell me now will *never* pass to another soul…"

"Master Randwick…" Godfrey acknowledged eventually, falling to one knee in a flourishing bow the moment his motor impulses had caught up with the realisation within his own mind. "I offer my apologies: I could never have guessed…"

"How would you…?" He conceded genially, almost smiling at the sudden turn around as Lester too fell to one knee, almost in reverence, and Nev stared on from a short distance, completely dumbfounded over the fawning display the two boys had suddenly put on. "And *you*, lass…?" He added, turning a raised eyebrow toward her.

"I guess I must've been living under one of those *rocks*…" she shrugged as casually as she could manage as she fought *not* to wither under that expectant stare "…for I've never *heard* of you. A pleasure, I'm sure, but I *don't* think I'll be getting down on one knee just yet…"

"Yet it was *you* who first vouched for me…" he pointed out, nodding faintly in recognition of her trust as the other two hurriedly regained their feet, looking a little embarrassed in the process. "You need not bow down to me, lass… t' were *you* who raised the first alarm if I'm not mistaken and despatched two of those blackguards without help from me or *anyone* else. That sword 'o yours is a fine one and no mistake – one I've not seen the like of in many a summer – and you're welcome to stand at my side anytime.

"But first to the dirty business at hand," he added quickly, bringing everyone back to the present. "If there were three of these footpads about, there's sure to be more soon enough and I'll not feel at rest until I've got the walls of Burnii around me once more. Let's see to the rest of these poor travellers and then be off as quickly as we're able… time to talk later, when we're somewhere *safe*."

The family and the old couple were gathered together and hurried as much as was possible as the three men worked at hitching the right horses up to the right carriages and seeing them on their way. Godfrey and Lester also had taken the time to quickly bury Nguyen's body and perform a basic ceremony of sorts; it seemed the least they could do under the circumstances.

The others' departure left three horses still, which they found saddles for in a small shed at one corner, and there then remained only the matter of who was going to share with whom. With Nev not knowing the first thing about riding a horse, there was little choice to be made: with Lester being too light of frame to make it feasible for her to ride behind him and Randwick still being an old man they still didn't really know (*Ew*…!), it therefore again left Godfrey as the only logical option.

"I know of a place near hear – perhaps ten minutes' ride – where we might hold up safe and wait for morning," Randwick suggested, glancing around warily from the saddle as the remains of the tavern continued to burn, albeit at a far lesser intensity than it had had half an hour before. "It's a bit out of our way but I'd prefer *not* to be on the road at night any longer than necessary: if my enemies have any friends lurking about, I'd much rather face 'em in daylight rather than in darkness."

"I've no objections," Godfrey conceded, giving it some thought as he threw glances at the other two, "and I doubt anyone else has either. Lead on, sir: we'll follow…"

Randwick turned his horse north and they set off at a steady canter across open fields that lay well away from the main road, looking to avoid any watchful eyes in the darkness. They travelled on for perhaps two kilometres or so, everyone following his shadowy silhouette in the moonlight, until they happened upon a narrow dirt track and then followed that instead, continuing in the same general direction. The air was cool and refreshing and it at least went some way toward easing the thumping headache that had plagued Nev the entire time since leaving the burning inn.

Never again! She told herself, unknowingly echoing the words of countless millions of teenagers the universe over on the morning after their first serious encounter with alcohol. *Never again will I subject myself to* that!

They could hear the sounds of surf again as they rode on along with the faint smell of the sea, and it occurred to Nev, based on what little she'd seen of the landscape on their walk earlier, that they probably weren't that far away from where they'd left the sailboat. That suspicion was borne out as the track took them to the very northern edge of a huge, rounded cape with cliffs towering hundreds of metres above the sea below, and she realised in a flash of clarity that it must be the very same cliffs she'd seen as they'd sailed into the beach.

They followed Randwick to a point right at the very cliff edge itself, where a lone, towering ruin stood overlooking the sea. In the shimmer of moonlight against water and the waves crashing against the rocks at the base of the cliffs, there was no denying it was a stunning view that must've been absolutely amazing during daylight. The ruins themselves were little more than a tall, partially-collapsed tower of stone standing perhaps twenty metres high – possibly used as a lookout for enemy ships or something similar, Nev mused as they tied the horses to a tree some distance away and walked the rest of the way.

She found that the base was actually surrounded by a narrow trench perhaps two metres deep, with just one doorway set into the stone at ground level. The entrance would have been inaccessible save for the fact that the trench had been filled in just enough below the doorway to allow precarious entry in single file. The interior was cramped and musty, but it was secure and it was warm enough in their cloaks to avoid the need for a fire that might otherwise draw attention to their presence.

"I'll take first watch if y' like…" Lester volunteered, receiving an appreciative grunt from Godfrey as the boy disappeared outside with his trusty crossbow.

"Hardy lad…" Randwick observed softly, taking a seat on a fallen lump of stone, directly across from the entrance.

"Aye, a roughie, but a good 'un," Godfrey acknowledged in return, his grin a flash of pale white in the otherwise almost complete darkness. "Been lookin' after him these last few summers and he's come a long way. Knows how to handle himself."

"I'm sure he can," Randwick agreed, a wry smile flickering across his lips. "Most Southern Oster boys are pretty well-trained by their second year as squire; I've no doubt the boy's as capable as any…"

"That obvious…?" Godfrey asked immediately, crestfallen that the old man had pegged him so easily.

"Took a little thinking on account of you havin' a woman with y' as well, but with yer dress and the age difference of you and the boy, it seemed logical were a ranger and apprentice. We're well aware of the Southern Oster's training practices at Cadle: it pays to stay informed o' these things."

"And does that change your attitude?" The question wasn't aggressive but it was definitely direct. Godfrey wanted to make sure all cards were on the table.

"Me word's me word and I gave it freely," Randwick shrugged, admiring the boy's forthrightness and taking no offence. "If you've a mind to ride with me, I'll see all of you safe wherever you need to go. There's a guard garrison the other side of Windward – maybe five miles from here – and I know the commander there. He'll see us right with an escort at least as far as Burnii. If you've a mind to travel on from there, provisions and fresh horses can be arranged also."

"We'd be in your debt," Godfrey suggested, tilting his head slightly in thanks.

"We'd be *even…*" Randwick corrected, alluding back to the attack at the tavern.

"And why is it that someone might send *assassins* in the middle of the night against one of the most renowned advisors to the House of Namur?" Godfrey asked pointedly, using the little-used, official title of the royal family of Huon. "I *know* the 'misfortune' that befell the king's brother last fall-season, but to put it bluntly, sir: what might warrant an attack on the king's advisor rather than the king himself?"

"A fine question deserving of a similar answer," Randwick nodded as Nev stared on with interest, seated between the two with her back against the curved stone wall. "I'd be inclined to answer in good time, but I'd *first* ask why you want to know." He again raised an eyebrow. "I've a suspicion there's more than polite interest behind it…?"

"You trust him…?" Godfrey asked, turning his attention to Nev now in the darkness. For reasons he wasn't completely able to explain, he was becoming more and more ready to consider her opinion on matters. With what he'd seen her capable of when using that pendant, and with her actions in saving them from attack earlier (not the first time she'd saved them all, either), he was slowly coming to realise that there was a great deal more to her than he'd originally suspected, even taking into account what he'd already learned those last few days.

"*Me…?*" She blurted, caught unawares as she felt the withering power of *both* men staring at her expectantly. "I – *uh…*" She paused for a moment then, settling her mind and reaching out blindly for the same instincts she'd felt earlier during battle. She still had no idea what they were but they'd not steered her wrong so far and she therefore saw no reason not to heed them. At she stared back at Randwick in the darkness and continued to reach out with her mind, she received nothing in return save for a warm and comfortable sensation of well-being that was more than good enough for her.

"Yes… yes, I trust him…" She confirmed again, echoing her words back at the tavern. "Tell him… tell him *everything…*"

And *everything* was exactly what Godfrey went on to disclose, spending at least a good hour as he ran through all they'd experienced since he'd first taken Nev's hand in the middle of that forest near Crookhaven and led her to Garry's farmhouse. Randwick listened with great interest as they told of the journey to Long Hop, the loading of the cannon aboard *Rapier*, and their subsequent capture and interrogation at the hands of Silas and Baal.

"It seems our encounter is *doubly* fortunate this night," the old man declared eventually, after considering the story for a long time in complete silence. "You say that having seen all this, your first thought was in fact to make your way to Burnii and find some way to warn the king?"

"You've reason to be sceptical," Godfrey agreed, hearing the man's tone. "The Oster's never been an ally to *any* king, it's true, but if what Nev says is true about these cannon Harald has, then it's not only Huon will fall. Having the *whole* of the Osterlands crushed beneath the boot heels of the Blackwatch will do *no one* any favours, *including* my boys. The Oster knows Phaesus to be a moderate – probably the most even-tempered monarch anyone's yet seen – and as we'd no alternative but to make landfall in Huon *anyway*, warning him seemed the sensible thing to do."

"I know an honest answer when I hear one," Randwick nodded, having again taken some time to consider those words in silence. "I've no love for mercenaries either but the Southern Oster *generally* operate with honour and decency, and they've often been of help against Harald in the past – truth be told – in times when there were deeds needed doing by less 'official' means.

"You're *sure* about Baal...?" He continued, changing back to the topic at hand. "I've heard all you've said well enough, but to accuse the cousin of the king himself is no small matter – I'll need *evidence* for such a denunciation."

"We've none other than our word," Godfrey admitted, not happy about it. "We barely escaped the ship with our lives – there was no time to think of bringing proof..."

"There's proof..." Nev interrupted, surprising both men. "*A little*, at least..." She added as an afterthought as she reached into her cloak and drew out her phone. "Try not to be *too* shocked..." she explained, noting Randwick's surprise as she swiped the screen open and it flared into light. "I know *everyone* seems to think I'm a witch, but this is nothing more than a simple device where I come from... it's *not* witchcraft..."

"This... *this* is a *machine*...?" He asked warily, reluctant to touch the *iPhone* as she opened the gallery and brought up the latest video taken.

"Here…" she offered, rising and moving to stand next to him so she could hold the phone out for both of them to see. Adjusting the volume to a lower setting so as not to startle him too much, she hit play and allowed the video to run.

Randwick gasped openly as the screen flashed into life, playing back the images Nev had recorded from the roof of the warehouse at Long Hop. A panorama of the surrounding landscape showed massed campfires to the east, suggesting the presence of hundreds of troops if not more, and the camera then zoomed in on the work taking place down on the docks. Although the footage wasn't great quality at full magnification, it was nevertheless clear enough to show the cannon being assembled, along with the name *Rapier* emblazoned across the bow of the ship behind.

"These are the cannon you saw…?" Randwick asked immediately, knowing the look of a weapon when he saw one. "These things can shatter a castle's walls from a *mile* away?"

"Maybe *more* than a mile," she answered with a shrug. "I don't know enough about guns to be sure but I *do* know they can outrange any catapult or trebuchet. They can *also* fire something called grapeshot: hundreds of little balls the size of your thumb or less that can spray advancing troops at closer range and kill dozens at a time – like a great volley of crossbows firing all at once."

"This is *real*…" The old man croaked, clearly shaken by what he'd seen and heard. "I can *see* Baal's ship, *Rapier*… I can *see* the weapons of which you speak, as if it were with my own eyes!"

"They *also* have a smaller weapon called a shotgun… one easily carried by a single man. It's like nothing you'll have ever seen before – like a piece of iron pipe stuck onto the stock of a crossbow or something like that – and it's not as powerful as a cannon, but it's *lethal* at close range: I think it could probably punch straight through the armour of *anyone* trying to get within sword-fighting range."

"We *mostly* think she's not a witch…" Godfrey grinned, earning a scowl and a poke of the tongue from Nev in response.

"As for *our* story…" she continued, closing the video and putting her phone away "…you can check for yourself next time you see this Baal: I'm pretty certain I broke his arm when I hit him with the chair. *Also*… there's *this*…" she added, diving one hand inside her cloak once more. This time, she drew out Silas' pendant, letting it drop in front of Randwick's eyes, suspended from her fingers by the chain.

"Dragonfall take me!" He breathed, finding it difficult to cope with the overload of shock and surprise he was experiencing in such a short period of time. "No brother would *willingly* allow another to take their crystal..."

"He *didn't* give it willingly," Nev pointed out, more than a little proud of herself in that moment. "He was quite *annoyed* about the whole thing, to be honest."

"This is damning proof..." Randwick conceded, almost breathless with excitement over the magnitude of what they'd told him. "*Yes,* it's mostly circumstantial, but it *fits* the story better than any other I could think of... and I'd be *very* interested to see what explanation Baal might give as to why his personal warship was taking on *Blackwatch* weapons at Long Hop, *or* why Taas was allowing Harald to station an *invasion force* on the island, for there can be no denying that's what it must be..."

"Then you see why we must warn the king?"

"Indeed... warn him, we definitely *must*..." the old man agreed, but a dark expression flashed across his face all the same. "The only thing that remains to be seen is, even *with* this warning, whether the armies of Huon will be able to do a damned thing about it! *You*...!" He exclaimed, turning to Nev as another thought suddenly springing to mind. "*You're* the witch they were talking about!"

"...*Aaaand* we're back to being a witch again..." Nev sighed in exasperation.

"The princess... she overheard the cardinal speaking to that monster, Silas, not three days past, regarding the search for a so-called 'witch' running loose in the Blacklands. That *must* have been *you* they were speaking of..."

"I guess that stands to reason," Godfrey nodded as Nev retook her original seat and fumed quietly in the corner over being called a witch again.

"Even *then* they were frightened of you... of what danger you might represent..." Randwick observed, thinking deeper on the subject. "I've no love for The Brotherhood, *believe me*," he added with a sneer. "We *follow* the Book of The Shard here in Huon for we know well enough what consequences come of falling by the wayside, but there's *plenty*, I'd warrant, who'd shed no tears to learn of those bastards' demise. I shall *definitely* take this to His Majesty... and *you* three are coming with me...!"

XV

HARBINGERS

It was no surprise that the ground inside the tower was hard and uneven, and Nev awoke early the next morning with a stiffness through her entire body. She found herself alone as she lifted her head from her duffel-bag pillow and looked around in the gloom, although soft sounds of conversation were audible from somewhere outside. Her phone lay beside her bag, having spent the night connected to the power-bank and recharging, and as she collected both devices she checked the time and found it to be just after seven, meaning she'd had all of about five hours' sleep. With the power bank stowed in her bag and the phone secure in her pocket, she rose to her feet, stretched long and hard to relieve the tension in her back and joints and then walked slowly and stiff-legged out into the early-morning sunshine.

She found Godfrey sitting beside a small campfire, a dozen metres or so away in the middle of an open, gravelled area directly to the south while Lester had set up some makeshift targets nearby to practice with his crossbow. Some distance behind them lay a large, crescent-shaped lake and beyond that could be seen the undeniable, multi-coloured beauty of the same wide, rolling fields of tulips they'd walked through the preceding night. Blue sky showed infrequently through gaps in the clouds above and the soft crackle of the fire was a friendly, welcoming sound as faint wisps of smoke curled into the still air. Even *more* welcoming was the unmistakeable smell of bacon frying.

"Where's Randwick?" She asked directly as she drew near the fire, accepting the offer from Godfrey of bacon clamped between two thick slices of bread with a nod of thanks.

"Rode out just before dawn," he replied through bites of his own breakfast. "Said he wanted to go scouting, and that he was going to make contact with the local garrison and bring back some escorts." He shrugged. "Been gone for a couple of hours now... shouldn't be much longer..."

"You still trust him?" She asked, chowing down on her own rough-and-ready sandwich and almost gasping at how good it tasted.

"Yeah... I think I do..." Godfrey replied thoughtfully. "The fella comes with a bit of a reputation – all good – and he's been with the King's family for as long as anyone can remember... that much I *do* know. It's more of a question whether *he* trusts *us*." He shrugged again. "Just dumb luck we swapped rooms with him last night, but it's come out in our favour and no mistake!"

"This place is *amazing*...!" She exclaimed, giving herself some time to appreciate the view as she walked off in Lester's direction with food in hand. "The colours are incredible!"

"Pretty, ain't they...!" The boy called out in a friendly 'I told you so' tone.

"Wait, let me take a picture!" She decided, stuffing the rest of the bread into her mouth and fishing in her pocket for the phone. "Stand over by that target thing: I can get the flowers in the background!"

"What... like *this*...?" Lester declared, moving to stand beside the small, concrete mound he'd placed his targets on and intentionally striking a ludicrously exaggerated pose with the crossbow. "Something 'big and strong' to show the girls...?"

"Well... let's not get ahead of ourselves..." She muttered drily in return, walking up close to take the shot as Godfrey chuckled through a mouthful of bread. "But it'll make a lovely picture, I'm sure! Wait... that's it... *got it*...!" The deed was done with a synthesised '*click*' from the *iPhone*, and Lester jogged over, desperate to see his own image on the tiny, colourful screen.

"Aww, that's a *beauty*...!" He exclaimed with excitement, glancing over at Godfrey with a glint of real emotion in his eyes. "Makes me look like a handsome young warrior, off to do battle..."

"That thing *is* witchcraft...!" Godfrey muttered under his breath, deciding it kinder to keep that to himself as he grinned and nodded in mock agreement.

"You be nice!" She admonished with a frown, knowing exactly what he was up to as she gave the image another look. "What's that you're putting them on...?" She added, for some reason feeling the need to zoom in and take another photo of the targets themselves. She suddenly found something very familiar about the shape of the overgrown, concrete mound that stood little more than thirty or forty centimetres above ground height and seemed to be surrounded by what was once a low, wrought iron fence before rust had set in and nature had reclaimed most of it beneath a mass of grass and weeds.

"Dunno *who* it was…" the boy shrugged. "I don't read real good, but it's got a name and a thingummy' written on it… you know; the stuff they write on peoples' headstones…?"

"You mean that's someone's *grave*…?" She asked, quickly taking a few steps back and mortified by the thought of using someone's final resting place for target practice.

"Well, *he* ain't gonna mind, is he…?" Lester asked matter-of-factly in return, hearing the disapproval in her tone and correctly deducing the reason.

"Well, I don't know if that's the *point*…" she continued, not really seeing that as justification, but any further discussion on the matter was ended there and then as the sound of approaching horses rose from the south-east.

They all turned to look in that direction and immediately caught sight of Randwick returning on horseback, this time at the head of a six-man escort of king's cavalry, each carrying a three-metre wooden lance with a blue and white pennant fixed just below each pointed steel tip. As the troop drew to within a hundred metres, five of the riders spread out to take up guard positions across a wide arc while Randwick and another man – presumably the troop commander – rode on toward them at a steady canter, a spare, riderless horse trailing behind them.

"Well met, all…" the old man called out as the horses drew near, bringing his mount to a halt and sliding out of the saddle just a few paces from Godfrey and the campfire. "We're in luck… I caught these boys as they were preparing to ride out on patrol. Everyone…" he added, as Lester and Nev completely forgot about the gravesite and wandered over toward Godfrey "…may I present William of Zeehn, captain of the King's Guard and as fine and loyal a man as you're likely to lay eyes on…"

But Nev already *had* laid eyes on William of Zeehn, the young man looking every bit the image of a textbook cavalryman. Looking to be in his mid-twenties and standing just a few centimetres short of two metres in height, he was clean-shaven and carried a short, neatly-tied pony tail of golden hair that hung beneath a plumed white stockman's hat that had the right side of its brim pinned up in a style very much like the slouch hats she always saw soldiers on the TV wearing during ANZAC day ceremonies. The colour of his uniform matched that of the hat – pristine white with blue piping – although it seemed likely there was some chainmail or other armour hidden beneath.

"At your service, gentlemen... *and* lady..." he added gallantly, removing his hat the moment he spotted Nev and sweeping it downward in a flourishing bow as she giggled in response (mostly in disbelief that it had actually happened) and both Godfrey *and* Lester gallantly fought the urge to vomit.

"I hear the Sun Empire use peacocks as watchdogs..." The older of the two muttered sourly under his breath, drawing a snort of laughter from Lester over something that was most definitely *not* a non-sequitur.

"...About what might be expected of a *mercenary*..." William observed coldly, managing to keep a sneer from his expression as he regarded Godfrey with a withering stare.

"But *less so* of the grace and humility expected of a *Guardsman*..." Randwick shot back immediately, cutting off Godfrey's response as he raised an eyebrow sharply in his subordinate's direction. "These three are *my* guests, captain, and as such I'd expect you to accord *all* of them the same level of respect *regardless* of their background..."

The old man was surprised by the man's impolite reaction, although based on what little he knew of the officer's reputation, he suspected the presence of an attractive young woman had something to do with it.

"Of *course*, sir," William responded with a faint bow of acknowledgement, not missing a beat as he flicked an *almost* imperceptible wink in Nev's direction and completely confirmed the old man's suspicions at the same time. "My apologies, gentlemen... I *am* at your service... Master Randwick tells me you've come to him with information *vital* to the safety of the king *and* kingdom, and the King's Guard needs no greater assurance than that. My sword and lance stand ready at your defence."

"Can't argue with that, I guess..." Lester shrugged, almost sounding disappointed that a possible conflict had been nipped in the bud so prematurely. "Your mob gonna get us to see the king, all safe and sound like...?"

"William's troop will serve as escort as far as the Burnii gates..." Randwick cut in again, impatient to be away and not in the mood for delays due to small talk. "From there, *I* will get you all to the king. However, *none* of this will happen while we're standing about, remarking on the weather..." he pointed out tersely. "William tells me that Harald's arrival has been brought forward to this afternoon – we *must* see the king before then. If you're all packed and ready to go, I'd prefer we were on the road again without further ado: we've some miles to cover this morning and little enough time spare to do so..."

They were mounted and riding within five minutes, a pair of guardsmen galloping off to scout the way ahead as the other four gathered about their charges, alert for any danger that might lurk in the shadows of roadside hedges or in gullies beside the road. Randwick rode at the head of the group, with Godfrey and Lester on either side behind as Nev trundled along between them, her reins tied to Randwick's saddle. Being only her third ride on a horse in her life (and all three of *those* in the last few days), she'd absolutely no idea how to sit properly, and as a result she was left with a rather sore backside after the first few miles.

The problem of a woman travelling out in the open had come up immediately, with Nev no happier about the idea of being blindfolded during their trip than she had been when first hearing about it from Lester days before. There was no wagon to hide within this time however and she was forced to concede the danger of bringing too much attention upon themselves if something wasn't done – more attention, at least, than they were *already* likely to attract in company with an escort of the King's Guard.

Gallant as William clearly thought he was, it also quickly became apparent that he wasn't about to sit quietly regarding the breaking of any Shard laws, and Randwick had taken Nev aside in the end and explained to her privately how important it was they went along with at least the pretence of following the rules in this particular instance.

A compromise was reached at his suggestion, and he subsequently produced a long, silk scarf of jet black from one of his saddlebags. The material was so fine that when pressed up against Nev's eyes it was still possible for her to see almost as well as without it, although the images were all slightly pale and fuzzy. From an outsider's point of view however – William's for example – it looked for all the world like she'd been securely blindfolded as Godfrey had carefully tied the scarf behind her head, quickly jumping in as he realised William was about to offer his services. The speed at which he'd reacted drew a raised eyebrow from the young officer, a cheeky grin from Lester and a silent note of interest from Randwick, who immediately filed the information away for future reference. As she trundled along behind him now, the leading of her reins – albeit in reality for a completely different reason – served to give even more credence to the façade of her being unable to see where she was going.

The troop had moved off at a steady canter, passing through a number of small seaside villages and hamlets. Most of them were home to no more than a few dozen people and all were involved in some kind of farming judging by the attire of the locals and the tools being carried as they went about their daily tasks. Most paid little heed to the military escort passing on the highway, and those few who did saw little of interest other than a cavalry troop and four civilians, the only female travelling with eyes covered exactly as they should've been.

The road followed the coast for most of the journey, with the lands to the south predominantly dotted with small herds of sheep and cattle, interspersed with the occasional field of crops here or there. It was difficult for Nev to see distance clearly through the silk covering her eyes but most of the food being grown appeared to be 'ground-based' types like potatoes or onions... or other crops more suited to the colder, overcast climate that seemed to hang like a pall over the countryside through which they passed.

"Is it always like this...?" She asked Godfrey loudly as they stopped to water their horses, roughly two-thirds of the way into the journey by Randwick's reckoning. They stood on the eastern outskirts of a small village that William had called Summerset, and the name had indirectly got Nev thinking about the seasons in general. A check of one of her *iPhone* apps showed the ambient temperature to be a paltry twelve degrees centigrade, and she was definitely feeling every one of them beneath her jacket and cloak.

"'Like this'...? How do you mean?" He asked in return, standing by his mount as the beast drank deeply of the clear, running water at the river bank.

"So grey and cloudy all the time..." she explained, raising a hand toward the skies at the same time. "I've barely seen a clear night or half of a sunny day since I got here. What season *is* it?"

"Season...? I was joking about Lester's duds back at the barn at Crookhaven," he grinned, one hand on hips as he left the horse and moved in closer, "but I wasn't when I said it was the first day of spring."

"But... but, it's so *cold*..." she went on. "Spring in *Australia* should be warm and *mostly* sunny: I don't think it's gotten over fifteen degrees the whole time, and it's been *really* cold at night."

"They don't grow much down here that doesn't like cold weather," Lester offered helpfully as he wandered over to stand beside Godfrey. "Mostly spuds, lettuces or sprouts or suchlike..."

"Don't know much about farmin'," Godfrey shrugged, "but I know they grow a *little* wheat and stuff up north on the mainland. The weather here's *always* like this..." he shrugged again. "Even in summer, you're lucky to get more than two or three clear days in a row. Dunno what 'degrees' are, but it's *always* cold down here and not *much* better across the Blackwater..."

"*Used* to be a *lot* worse..." Randwick observed from a distance, having risen from a crouch after washing his face in the cool water. "These boys aren't old enough to remember, but when *I* was a lad – *fifty* summers gone now – there were *weeks* without sunshine and the nights seemed to fall halfway through the afternoon and linger on until well into mid-morning. When I was the boy's age, we'd not be able to read without a light if we were standing where we are now at this time o' the day."

"So, this is an *improvement*...?" She asked incredulously, arms spread wide now as she turned to take in her surroundings. "This is *better* than it was fifty years ago? What *happened* here?"

"The Book of The Shard tells us the world's still recovering from The Cleansing..." Randwick shrugged this time, and she could tell from his tone that even he wasn't entirely convinced.

"And 'The Cleansing' is?"

"A time of fire and death," William of Zeehn answered darkly, seated on a large rock a few metres back from the river bank. He was fiercely loyal to his commander but was nevertheless far more of a believer than any of the others present. "The world was evil and depraved and the Shard Gods saw the wickedness of man and decided to cleanse the earth. They sent the Night Dragons, falling from the sky in their thousands to purify the world with fire. Only the worthy were left alive."

"Purify the world with fire, eh?" She repeated carefully, noting the zeal with which he'd recounted those words and making a huge effort not to sound sceptical or mocking in any way. "In *our* world, it was a *flood*... but I get the idea. And how long ago did this 'Cleansing' happen?"

"No one knows for certain," William shook his head, the belief of it clear in his eyes and tone, "but the brotherhood believes it was thousands of summers gone, when the world was new. Sometimes the Night Dragons still fall somewhere, but now mostly alone – never in mass, as they once did..."

"Fall out of the sky, do they...?" Nev asked carefully, and the young officer nodded in response as Randwick – the only one present who picked up the faint change of inflection in her voice – pricked up his ears and waited intently for what she was about to say next. "And... does anyone ever *see* the Night Dragons when they fall?"

"No one would *dare*..." William answered quickly, surprised the question even needed to be asked. "It's rare for one to fall on or near a village – *very* rare – but it *has* happened in the past. The Brotherhood has told us many times of the destruction they cause... how no man who laid eyes on one has *ever* lived to tell the tale."

Or *any woman, I don't doubt*... She thought silently, smart enough to keep that thought to herself.

"So... if no one's ever *seen* one..." she ventured instead, realising too late that she was still venturing out onto thin ice "...how does the Brotherhood *know* that it's a dragon that's fallen...?"

"But... of *course* it's a Night Dragon..." William blinked, sounding quite perplexed as a vaguely suspicious expression flickered across his features for a moment. "What else *could* it be...?"

"I – uh – of course, sorry..." She backpedalled quickly, recognising his reaction for what it was and deciding tact was a better option at that moment.

"We need to keep moving..." Randwick announced almost too quickly, suspecting he already knew what Nev thought about Night Dragons and at the same time recognising that it was time to move away from a potentially dangerous subject. "We've only an hour or two left to travel but it's at least noon now and there's no time to waste!"

Burnii was pretty much exactly as Nev had imagined it might be, in the worst possible way. Approaching from the west along the coastal high road, she'd been able to see a dark haze on the eastern horizon long before they reached the higher density of farms and outlying stone huts that belonged to the 'lesser' residents, forced to make their homes outside the city walls due to expansion and the resulting lack of space within. For purposes of industry, warmth and any other possible use Nev could've imagined, chimney stacks throughout the 'suburbs' (as she quickly came to call them, for want of a better term) pumped a constant stream of soot and smoke into the air and she was starting to think that perhaps the fires were in operation as much for a general provision of comfort and security as they were for any practical reason.

Those sights were nothing compared to the city itself however as their horses crested the summit of that last, low hill coming in from the western high road and it was finally laid out before them in full view. The road passed close to the beach at that point and a great watchtower rose there where the surf met the sand, twenty metres tall at least with a trebuchet perched at its top. From there, city walls half that height ran away to the south, curving back around to protect the citizens within as similar towers dotted its length at regular intervals.

The western gates stood before them, just five hundred metres away as they came down the other side of the hill, and beyond that – above the ramparts of the walls themselves – Nev could just pick out a mass of roof tops, chimneys and other structures that stretched away beyond for several kilometres at least. Smoke and soot again hung heavy in the air, thicker and more acrid than it had as they'd passed through the suburbs, moments before.

A queue had gathered at the gates; at least a hundred people along with their possessions and a many and varied cluster of accompanying horses, oxen, carts and wagons. A dozen uniformed guards were running about as they approached, trying desperately to organise the gathering throng into some semblance of order as an increasingly exasperated junior officer shouted orders from the ramparts of the wall above, for the most part completely ignored by all.

"Endweek at the city gates…" Randwick observed with a wry smile, finding the scene all too familiar. "Oh aye, lass… that'd be the Burnii bouquet right there…" he added with an even broader grin as he looked back and caught sight of Nev wrinkling her nose over the insipid and cloying stench that had finally managed to force its way through the generally smoky tang in that seemed to constantly pervade the background of every breath. "It's only the wind's been in our favour so far: normally you can smell it as far back as Summerset."

"Oh, that's just *charming…*" she almost coughed as all three boys – all of them by and large completely desensitized to the smells of the only environment they'd ever known – grinned and chuckled over her displeasure.

"The king's workin' toward cleanin' up the streets… *literally…*" Randwick offered with unusual optimism, "but it's a slow process, changin' people's way of life…"

"Some things never change…" she muttered softly, thinking of her own world.

"Ahoy, guardsman!" William called loudly, riding ahead with his troop falling in behind as they drew up at the rear of the gathering crowd. "Official escort for Foucault Randwick, Mentor to the Namur… make way, if you please!"

It took one look at the King's Guard and the well-known face of the old man behind them to galvanise the officer on duty into frenetic action. Taking just a moment's pause to gather his wits, he again began screaming orders, however the rest of his men seemed to be taking far more notice now as they banded together to forcibly push the crowd away from the gates, making way for the cavalrymen and their charges.

"The Opening Ceremony, lieutenant!" Randwick called up to him from below as he drew near, forced to bellow at the top of his lungs to be heard over the general din of catcalls and complaint. "How go the celebrations? Have they begun yet?"

"Not yet, My Lord, but *soon…*!" He shouted in reply, taking a few seconds to turn and throw a glance off to the north-west, taking in sights that were invisible to anyone on the ground. "Even now I can see Harald's flagship standing out to sea, but you've time enough yet, I'd warrant…"

"Here's hoping, for all out sakes…" The old man muttered darkly, before forcing a smile back onto his face. "Send riders to Cadle and Demon's Port and all in between!" He continued, shouting again. "Call the garrisons to alert – any who aren't here already. Have them ready to march on Burnii as soon as they're mustered!"

"But… the ceremonies, My Lord…? Surely there are men enough here as honour guard already…?"

"Do as I say, lieutenant... do it *quickly!*" Randwick shot back, his tone making it clear he was not to be argued with. "And mark my words, now: they're to make ready for *battle,* not celebration!"

"But – but, *sir*...!" The young man called down, voice quavering as he found himself torn between direct orders and what seemed simple, common sense. "The *king*... the peace treaties...?"

"If I'm wrong, man, then blame shall lay on me and me alone for this, but I *beg* you do this now – *immediately* – for if I'm *right*, then we may *already* be too late."

Everyone in military service knew Mentor Randwick, a man who'd served the Namur family through three generations of kings and who carried a name as respected and revered as any in the entire kingdom. No matter how wild or unlikely his words might seem, he was not a man to be ignored lightly and it grated against the officer's instincts to disobey an order from such as he. Much as he hoped Randwick *was* wrong, something about the intensity of the man's gaze told him otherwise.

"My Lord, I shall send warning at once to any garrison we can reach and have them mobilised by sunset. We shall prepare for the worst and *pray* that you are wrong."

"And I'll pray the same, lieutenant... thank you, and fare you well!"

"And you, sir!" The officer called back with a salute, but Randwick was already galloping away through the open gates with Nev in tow, the guardsmen forming an escort ahead to clear the way as Lester and Godfrey held on tight to their reins and struggled to keep up. Behind them, atop the wall, the lieutenant began screaming his orders again and this time *everyone* was listening.

Standing apart from the multitude of working docks and wharves that comprised the Burnii port, one particular jetty was always set aside for the mooring of one special craft. King Phaesus' personal flagship, *Wyvern* normally found its home there when not in use, while *Rapier* might often be found at anchor behind it at times when the prince was in town. Although *both* men were indeed currently present on the docks, neither vessel was anywhere in sight that day: both had been moved out into the bay to make room for a very special guest, the gesture itself a sign of honour and respect.

The rest of the docks had also been emptied for the celebrations with much grudging and disgruntled acceptance from the owners of their usual occupants, their vessels also forced either to moor out to sea or relocate to Summerset or Demon's Port for the duration of the Endweek ceremonies. A multitude of warships and royal craft from a number of Osterland kingdoms instead lay at anchor; transports for the dignitaries and invited guests come to take in the spectacle of it all. Yet that last, royal dock remained empty and waiting for the most important guest of all.

Pennants of bright blue hung from every post and window, all displaying the clean, white image of a falcon's head that was the Namur family crest, and down at royal dock a grandstand had been constructed on the long, wide boardwalk that linked the wharves together, along with a dais from which both kings would soon be making their historic speeches. The seats rose in tiers six-high, stretching out to either side with room enough for hundreds while directly behind that dais stood two identical thrones; one for the king and one for his only child.

The stands were covered by a brightly-coloured canvas awning but Charli wasn't sure what it was actually supposed to accomplish. There was rarely any sun anyway and it was far too flimsy to keep out any rain (which had fortunately held off *so far* despite the ominous look of the clouds above). It certainly did *nothing* to protect her from the chill of the cool breeze as she sat there with her father, already regretting a choice of dress that was stunningly elegant and cut from *far* too thin a material to be sensible for the weather at hand. At least someone had seen fit to fix torches to each corner of the small box set aside for the two of them, the heat of the flames flickering behind her left shoulder providing irregular warmth as it crackled and spluttered that was far better than nothing at all nevertheless.

Her father was nervous. She could tell by the sharp edge in his tone as he spoke to everyone and by the way he unconsciously fretted with his ceremonial uniform and fidgeted in his chair, waiting for what seemed an age as a nearby band prepared to play and everyone else in the stands waited eagerly for Harald's flagship to make its way into the bay and drop anchor at the royal dock.

The king *should* have been nervous about the coming ceremonies and the fact that he was about to meet for the first time in friendship with the greatest enemy that Huon had ever known, and he was to some extent, but the princess knew that her father was also heavily preoccupied by the same, completely unrelated problem that was of great concern to her: the 'Keepsake situation'. Just before midnight that evening, Charleroi would be expected to take a knee before the local prelate as she had every other Endweek for as long as she could remember, the problem being that *this* time she was carrying a dangerous secret; one that couldn't be hidden from the all-powerful 'eyes' of The Shard.

Randwick was supposed to be organising something... some desperate bid for freedom of his own devising, the details of which – for her safety and his – even the king did not know. He'd been gone for two days now and had been expected back early that morning but was now many hours overdue. As confident as she was in her Mentor's ability to look after himself whatever the situation, Charli couldn't help fearing for his safety... couldn't help worrying that his non-attendance there that afternoon was no coincidence.

Her attention was drawn for a moment as a hush and a murmur of fearful awe rippled through the grandstands. Craning her neck to see past the dais, she eventually caught sight of what had caused the reaction: Harald's great quinquereme, *Devastator* had appeared beyond the breakwater protecting the eastern approaches to the harbour, cruising slowly toward the docks with its long, multi-layered banks of oars dipping in and out of the calm waters with military precision.

Although she hated to admit it, it was indeed a grand and terrifying vessel with a huge, silver-plated ram projecting from its bow and a brass-nozzled projector mounted on either side, each able to spray jets of flammable black liquid known as seafire, a weapon used by both sides that was devastating to enemy ships at close range. Randwick had told her once that the ship housed almost five hundred men, most of the oarsmen, and she could hear the drum beat as it drew near... thrumming over and over in time with the constant dip of the oars.

The huge warship was almost fifty metres long with a single mast amidships, its sail currently stowed for in-shore manoeuvring, and displaced close to 200 tons in mass. It was an impressive vessel to say the least, yet as the princess looked on she began to feel as if there were something unusual about the warship – something very different to any other she'd seen. Charleroi was no expert on naval matters but a healthy curiosity for knowledge in general backed up by many daily hours of regal boredom meant that she read widely and asked many questions about a wide range of different topics.

It had arrived with a veritable fleet of smaller Blackships – fifty triremes and quadriremes at least – that followed on behind, taking up a huge area of ocean as their crews pushed them on in tight formation. There was no chance of accommodating all of them within the harbour itself and as the flagship rounded the breakwater, the rest of them turned away, forming into long lines and standing off to sea to await further orders.

As she looked across at the smaller vessels already moored at the other wharves, she eventually came to the realisation that *Devastator* was missing the archery towers that were almost invariably fitted fore and aft to every other oared warship she could see. The towers were vital during close-in fighting as they gave archers and crossbowmen a tactical advantage when firing down at the decks of an attacking enemy. Yet on *Devastator* there were none, nor could she see any of the catapults or ballistae that were also found on most other vessels. Instead, all she was able to see behind the bow were one or two flat, slightly-raised platforms upon which sat what looked to be pieces of machinery of some sort: although it was impossible to make out any detail at such a distance, they clearly *weren't* catapults or any kind of weapon Charli had ever seen.

Devastator was drawing closer now, coasting slowly into the harbour itself, and there was another soft shudder of awe through the crowd as her mainsail unfurled, rolling downward almost to her deck to display a huge image of Harald's family crest: a stylised picture of a roaring lion with the world clasped in its paws, all in bright red against a black background.

The sound of tromping feet rose above the general background noise and Charleroi turned her hear to watch as two platoons of Taas' elite guard marched up along the boardwalk in single file, all of them in immaculately-polished armour with swords at their belts and crossbows slung across their backs. At their head was Prince Baal himself, Viceroy Garrick following close behind and both of them resplendent in their own ceremonial livery of blue and gold, wearing their swords in similar fashion to those of the men they led.

Garrick also carried a slung crossbow, however Baal instead carried something else Charli had never seen before: it seemed to have a wooden shoulder stock similar to that of a crossbow but it was far longer and seemed to end in two long, thin tubes of dark metal that (much like the machinery aboard *Devastator*'s deck) looked nothing like any weapon she'd ever encountered. Some ceremonial staff or sceptre of esoteric and no doubt *boring* origin, she concluded in an instant and paid it no further heed, instead turning her attention back to the approaching warship.

As the troops broke into platoons and moved to stand in formation on either side of the dais, Baal took up a standing position opposite Charli, behind the king's right shoulder. With a single glance and formal nod of recognition between them, he removed the strange 'sceptre' from his back and held it diagonally across his chest as he stood at stiff attention with eyes forward.

The Brotherhood was also there now as she looked around again. De Lisle had moved to stand by her side, glancing down once with a condescending smile as he stood waiting in stunning robes of bright red silk she'd never before seen any brother wear. The Crystal hung at his neck, glowing faintly beneath the overcast sky as a half-dozen more brothers filed in to stand in line to his left, all clothed in similarly gaudy ceremonial garb (Prelate Roland among them). To Baal's right stood another seven in similar dress, one of them Silas. Their presence undoubtedly obscured the view of those seated in the first few rows behind but not a single soul voiced any objection: no one was that stupid.

Baal's right arm still hurt. Silas had worked his magic, disturbing as all that had been, and his arm was now definitely good as new... possible *better*, if that were possible. But it still *hurt* all the same... and *itched* like nothing he'd ever experienced. He supposed that made sense if one thought about it deeply enough: whatever power those infernal crystals drew from The Shard and whatever miracles they worked beneath his torn and swollen skin, there was no way a man could shrug off that kind of injury overnight. Bones still needed to knit and muscles to recover, and there was always some price to pay in return.

None of that made it any more tolerable however as he stood stiffly at the king's side, doing his best impression of someone *not* holding a loaded shotgun right next to a reigning monarch. That no one else present other than Silas and De Lisle knew that it was actually a weapon was irrelevant: *he* knew it was a weapon, and had the quartet of Phaesus' personal bodyguards standing just two metres away on either side known what it was (*and* what he was intending to do with it), he'd already have been lying on the boardwalk in more pieces that was generally considered healthy.

Devastator was nearer now, and it wasn't even close to being a warm enough day to excuse the fine layer of perspiration that his nerves had produced, tiny droplets twinkling across his forehead below the base of his crown and running uncomfortably down the back of his neck below his high collar. The stage was set... his own men were in place... and all that remained was for Harald to give the signal to let slip the dogs of war.

There was some faint sound of a commotion off to the west, a disturbance of some kind out beyond the nearer warehouses that might presumably be some dispute amongst the peasants and commonfolk as they vied for a position with any kind of view, held back by painted ropes and most of Burnii's local garrison. None of that mattered now: most of them would be dead before sunset, like as not.

The latest estimates placed the city's regular population at close to ten thousand and most of them had filled the nearby streets and gathered at the edges of the more distant wharves in some vain hope of seeing some of the momentous spectacle. They'd get more than they bargained for soon enough, and Baal almost smiled as he considered the irony that it would indeed be a day that any survivors would remember for the rest of their dramatically-shortened lives.

Most of the honoured guests would not likely survive the hour either. That was an unfortunate but necessary sacrifice in the grand scheme of things, and whatever apologies might need to be made could be delivered once the dust had settled and the Kingdom of Huon had been scoured from the pages of history. Few of the other nations with representatives present would kick up much of a fuss in any case: the terrifying reality of these new weapons the Blackwatch was about to unleash would ensure most of them came running back to the negotiating table, and woe betide any kingdom that dragged its heels.

And then the moment was suddenly upon them. While still at least a thousand metres out from the wharves, Harald's great warship began to come about, turning unexpectedly to starboard rather than continue on toward the royal dock as planned. With just seconds left before hell itself was unleashed, Baal moved the fingers of his right hand slightly and clicked off the safety catch on the Beretta shotgun exactly as Persephone had instructed the day before. Not a single guard or honoured guest – the king and princess included – took any notice whatsoever as he casually lowered the weapons' muzzles to point directly at the back of Phaesus' crowned head.

It was a mere two kilometres between the western gates to the Burnii docks, but covering that distance meant forcing their way through narrow and winding city streets that were packed with thousands of revellers and other commonfolk either trying to get closer to the ceremonies or simply trying to go about their business as Endweek day carried on regardless.

They'd passed through the gates and galloped along the high road as it curved back to the south-east, toward the harbour, where Randwick and the others had caught sight of *Devastator* between the rows of shops and houses that lined the heights there. She was close now – close enough for him to pick out the unmistakeable shape of cannon mounted on her open deck. He wasn't sure exactly what the weapons could do but if even *half* of what the girl had told him were true, their power would be more devastating that *anything* the Osterlands had ever seen.

Urged on at his command, the King's Guard surged ahead, breaking into pairs and using the bulk of their own horses to force the crowds aside. Each pair would pause at an intersection, clear the way on either side, then wait for the next two pairs to power through with Randwick and the others close behind. The moment they were clear, the first pair would then charge ahead once more as their colleagues clear two more intersections further on.

For Nev, who'd now been allowed at last to remove her fake blindfold once they'd passed within the city walls, it looked very much like the kind of operation motorcycle cops carried out back home at times when an escort was required to clear the way through busy traffic for some visiting dignitary. Although the mode of transport was far more archaic, their movements were carried out with the same tight, military precision, making their progress immeasurably faster than it would've been otherwise.

Shotgun... Baal... A crowned head... The shotgun...!

A brief succession of momentary images flashed through her mind, almost too fast for her to register, but the intent was clear all the same: Prince Baal was about to use Percy's shotgun to kill someone else wearing a crown, and considering where they were and what was about to happen, it didn't take a genius to work out who the likely target was.

"The king…!" She shouted ahead to Randwick, the old man turning his head just enough to improve his hearing as they galloped on. "Baal has the shotgun! He's going to kill the king!"

"William…!" He barked loudly, reining in for a moment as they drew level with the young man's horse at one crossing. "The king… get to the king! Baal's going to kill him with a weapon you won't recognise…" There was doubt in the officer's eyes for just a moment, but the intensity of the old man's gaze and his respect for his old commander were enough to burn through any misgivings. "Protect the king and princess at all costs and don't let *Baal* near *either* of them… go… go now…!"

"Riders… the King's in danger! Rally to the king…! *Hurrah*…!"

"*Hurrah*…!" The rousing call came back to him in return and leaving the rest of them behind, William of Zeehn surged forward, pushing his mount to full gallop with sword raised at the charge as the rest of his troop fell in behind.

Nev and the others followed on as best they were able, but as the crowd had immediately parted to allow passage for a troop of screaming cavalrymen at the charge, it just as quickly came together again behind and the chaos left in the guardsmen's wake was such that it was actually far more difficult for the rest of them to push on.

As they rounded another short bend, the buildings suddenly disappeared on their left and they were left with a clear view of the docks and the harbour beyond, able to look out quite easily from the saddle over the heads of the milling crowds around them. Nev spotted *Devastator* in an instant – there was no mistaking the size and power of such a warship – and something familiar flickered in her mind as she took in the fearful emblem of the roaring lion emblazoned two-storeys high across her great sail.

There was no time for any such distraction at that moment however and she pushed the thoughts away for consideration some other time. *Devastator* was coming about, turning her huge bow toward them as the vessel heeled around to starboard, with dozens of long, spindly oars rising and dipping in unison to the thrumming beat of a distant drum. With her vision clear now, she could also see tiny figures in red and black milling about on the deck, fussing about a single line of eight cannon like ants about their latest catch.

"Oh God, the cannon… *the cannon*…!" She shrieked, pointing wildly and almost falling out of the saddle, the reality of what was happening reaching her a split-second later as *Devastator* prepared to unleash her first broadside. "Mister Randwick, *they're going to fire the cannon*!"

Devastator had made the turn – the first part of the signal Baal had been waiting for – and just seconds later her sail began to fold away as dozens of deck hands hauled it upward, releasing the captured breeze and immediately lowering the vessel's forward motion. That was the second signal – the alert that the ship was preparing to fire – and it was also the moment that Baal was expected to curl his index finger around the shotgun's trigger and ascend to the throne through two simple and rather brutal acts.

Just point, aim and fire and the weapon will do the rest … the witch had told him. *Turn toward the princess and do the same, and all his dreams would become reality.*

There'd been no time to practice, but he was standing just a few feet away and surely couldn't miss…

"*The king*…! *Protect the king*…!" That call rang out from somewhere off to his left and a chill speared his heart as he turned and saw that a troop of white-clad cavalry – *King's Guard*, no less – had broken through the front of the crowd at the far end of the boardwalk and were now thundering toward them at full gallop, lances lowered at the charge.

There was no time to lose… no time for any more distractions. The horsemen were still too far away to be of any danger and he could see that a platoon of his own guard were already turning to face them, taking a knee and preparing to meet the charge with crossbows drawn. Turning back to the king, who was also rising from his seat now as the alarm was raised, Baal lifted the shotgun loosely to his right shoulder and took aim once more at the back of the man's head.

Charleroi had also heard that warning call, along with most of the nearby crowd and every other guest in the stands. Unlike most of them however, who instinctively turned toward the sound of commotion, she immediately turned toward her father, suddenly fearful for his safety, and was presented with the unmistakeable sight of Baal aiming something at his back.

That it was some kind of weapon was now quite clear – she could see the prince's finger curling about a trigger that looked much like one found on any crossbow – and it took no genius to recognise that it was pointed directly at the back of her father's head. What happened next was born of pure instinct. With no weapon of her own, she turned her head in desperate search of anything she might use and her eyes settled on the only thing that was in reach.

A flaming torch struck Baal savagely in the side of the head a fraction of a second before he pulled the trigger, throwing off his aim as the shotgun discharged with a deafening blast and tore a plate-sized hole in the wooden decking at Phaesus' feet. Percy had decided it would be hilarious *not* to warn Baal about recoil, and the shotgun had slammed into his shoulder like the kick of a mule, twisting him backward even as the impact of Charli's thrown torch sent him staggering away to one side.

Initially shocked by the roar of the Beretta, the king's bodyguards leaped forward in the seconds that followed with their swords drawn. Three were instantly cut down by a volley of crossbow bolts fired by the prince's men, while the fourth and nearest to Baal was run through by Garrick's blade. Everything descended into a melee at that moment as two squads of Huon soldiers standing further back joined the fray, crossing swords with the Taas troopers as they attempted to push their way through to the king.

"Traitor…!" Phaesus barked, rage growing in his eyes as he realised what the prince had just attempted. "*Assassin…!*"

Fists clenched, he took a single step forward and drew the sabre at his own belt, raising it to strike at Baal. Garrick darted in, placing himself between the two men and slashed wildly at the king, who deftly parried the strike with his own blade and kicked the viceroy under the knee in return, drawing from him a cry of pain as he collapsed onto the boardwalk. Charleroi screamed at her father, shouting at him to back away – to get to safety – but Phaesus knew it was far too late for that as the prince's guards gathered around them

William and his lancers struck the Taas ranks at that moment, leaving men speared and screaming on the ground as their horses smashed them out of the way and powered on through. With lances wrenched from their grasp, they drew their sabres instead and began hacking their way forward, desperate to reach the king – now just metres away – before it was too late.

Everything seemed to slow down for Princess Charleroi in that moment. Sounds faded away, peripheral vision blurred, and all she could see was the image of her father striding forward, blade raised as he advanced on Baal with murderous intent. He'd made it all of a metre and a half as the prince aimed the shotgun from the hip, fired again in a roar and cloud of smoke, and Phaesus IV collapsed to the boardwalk in a crumpled heap.

Baal stood for a moment, transfixed as his mind tried to take in what had just happened – what he'd actually just done. As emotions that were equal parts fear and elation began to ripple through him, he looked up and locked eyes for a moment with the princess, her cries drowned out now by the screams of the panicking crowd around her. Without even thinking, he raised the weapon to his shoulder once more, aimed straight at her face and barely registered any reaction at all when no more shots were forthcoming.

The moment was gone then, the pair of them suddenly separated by a wall of blue and gold as Baal's personal guard closed ranks around him and prepared to face the troop of cavalry currently hacking their way toward the dais. The prince seemed almost in a daze, as if unable to believe what had just happened, however Garrick, sporting a distinct limp from the blow to his knee, was under no such impediment. Whichever way the battle turned from hereon in, there was much danger and no benefit to be had in either of them hanging about. With all the strength he could muster, the viceroy slipped his hand into the back of Baal's collar and forcibly dragged the prince away, seeking to put much-needed distance between them and the King's Guard.

There was a terrible wound in the king's side as Charleroi fell to her knees beside him seconds later, rolling him over as he groaned in agony. Whatever the weapon had fired had been powerful enough to punch straight through the silver chainmail of his ceremonial armour, the garb primarily intended as decoration after all rather than as any *real* manner of protection.

"Father…! *Father*…!" She wailed, tearing a huge segment from the hem of her dress and pushing it firmly down over the wound as a makeshift dressing, although the fine white silk, which turned crimson within seconds, was far too thin to be of any real use.

"Help me! *Save the king...*!" She screamed as loudly as she could, casting her eyes wildly about for aid as her words were lost in the clamour of hysterical crowds streaming away in all directions, seeking safety from the developing skirmish on the boardwalk.

Phaesus was struggling to talk as he lay there in her arms, staring skyward with his arms waving feebly. A pink froth had gathered at one corner of his lips, joining the faint trickle of blood that had already wound its way down his cheek on the same side. Charli had no idea how bad his wounds actually were – although they looked terrible indeed – but it was fairly clear all the same that without immediate medical attention he wasn't likely to last long at all... assuming it wasn't already too late.

It was at that moment that *Devastator* released her first broadside.

XVI

HAVOC

The panic that had begun to spread throughout the crowd degenerated into complete chaos as the roar of *Devastator's* guns reached out for them across the water. Thick grey smoke billowed from the muzzles of all eight guns as they fired in sequence from bow to stern, the power of their roar so great that even from a distance of five hundred metres or more, it struck Nev and the others with physical force like a slap to the chest.

The shriek of artillery came next as eight huge projectiles arced across the intervening distance in a fraction of a second and smashed apart the walls of harbour warehouses and office buildings like matchwood, followed moments later by powerful explosions as the shells detonated. Splinters and debris ripped through the air in all directions, killing and maiming dozens of screaming bystanders and adding to the hysteria that was already spreading throughout the city.

More cannon opened up from the next line of Blackships, adding the weight of their fire to the carnage as *Devastator's* gun crews went about the process of reloading. Their targets were the crewless warships moored at piers and wharves throughout the rest of the harbour area, peppering them with successive broadsides of explosives and incendiaries that tore the vessels apart and left their wreckage burning heavily within minutes. There was more firing further out to sea as several more squadrons of Blackships engaged patrolling Huon warships beyond the bay, quickly destroying them also as the attackers powered on toward the west, seeking out more targets.

Nev would've been the first to admit she was terrified by the whole thing, and there was every likelihood she'd have taken the first opportunity to flee in the most opposite direction she could find had her horse's reins not been securely tied to Randwick's saddle. The old man had been forced to spend a moment or two bringing his mount under control as the first cannon had fired, the animal rearing in fright at the sound, but he'd settled her quickly enough and then galloped on once more, heading straight for the distant dais in the wake of William's guardsmen.

Devastator fired her second broadside and eight more shells screeched deafeningly overhead, smashing into the shattered remnants of the dockside buildings behind as William and his troop hacked their way through toward the king's position with sabres swinging on either side, leaving blue-clad Taasi troopers screaming beneath their horses' hooves.

Three of his men had fallen to crossbows during the charge; the rest – him included – had struck the clustered infantry with a roar, smashing them aside with the impact of almost a tonne of armoured horse and rider. With Huon guards joining the fight on either flank, they were able to force a passage through to the dais in just a few agonisingly slow moments, and the young man's heart leaped into his mouth as he caught sight of Phaesus lying there on the boardwalk in a crumpled heap, his head cradled in the princess' arms as she wailed and screamed for help.

"Guardsmen, *the king…*!" William bellowed at full voice, sliding from his saddle and finding a knee at the princess' side in an instant. "Defensive positions… clear a path…!" He called out again, quickly taking in the environment around them before turning his gaze to the king's condition.

What he saw clearly wasn't good at all. The folded material Charleroi had pressed against the wound in his side was already sodden, and blood had seeped out and stained his clothes from chest to groin on one side. He reached out to lift the dressing for a moment, wanting to see for himself the severity of the wound, only to have his hand slapped away by a young princess who was wide-eyed and bordering in the verge of hysteria.

"Your Highness, we're here to protect you…" he assured quickly, catching her wrist firmly in one hand as she instinctively swung at him again. "We're here for the king but I need to see… to see how bad it is… *please…*"

"Charli… it's *alright…*!" Phaesus croaked softly, managing to raise a hand and lay it gently on her shoulder in reassurance. "Everything will be alright…" There was strength enough in his words to bring her back to her senses for a moment, and with a sobbing sigh she relaxed her arm and withdrew, allowing William access.

He carefully reached down and lifted the bloodied rag just enough to see the wound beneath and gasped at the sight. There was no arrow nor crossbow bolt to be seen, yet a large hole had been punched straight through the chainmail and into the man's side... quite *deeply* so far as he could tell. It looked almost as if he'd been speared, although there were no lancers present other than his own, and he was at a loss to find any other explanation. Either way, there was no avoiding the fact that it was almost certainly a mortal wound, and the flicker of shock and fear that flashed across his face was enough to reduce Charleroi to tears once more as the king met the young man's horrified gaze and simply nodded in solemn recognition.

"What*ever* the outcome, you must take us from here, captain..." Phaesus advised weakly, eyes flicking to his sobbing daughter for a moment. "*Whatever* happens, *she* must be safely away from here. Randwick... *Randwick* will know what to do."

"Indeed, Your Majesty, we came with Master Randwick this very hour but – but we came too late..." William exclaimed, fighting to hold back tears of his own as his king continued to die before his very eyes.

"Not too late... not *yet*..." Phaesus assured, shaking his head. "Get my daughter to safety and you'll have my blessing."

"We'll have you *both* to safety yet, Your Highness," Randwick declared gruffly as he reined in how own beast and dropped to the boardwalk beside William, sabre in hand as more guards joined the fray with every passing second, rapidly overpowering the dwindling ranks of Baal's troops. "We need to make for the safety of the fortress... can he ride...?" He asked quickly, turning to William.

"Not a chance..." The officer answered honestly, also rising to his feet, "...and I'd not rate his chances of making that journey even as a passenger. If he *is* to die though," he added with a humourless smile, "it might as well be in the saddle as lying her on the boardwalk."

"More chance on the move than standing to face *those* hell-spawned things," Randwick agreed darkly as a third broadside struck warehouses and factories further to the west. Fire billowed skyward in huge clouds as a distillery was set alight by exploding shells, sending burning spirits flying in all directions and adding dozens more to the already-mounting casualties. "He can take my horse," the old man added with a shrug. "We'll not make much better than walking pace anyway until we clear the chaos in these streets..."

"There's mine as well… for the princess…" Nev added loudly, having already dismounted and deciding that walking would be a better option moving forward. Her backside and thighs sore in ways she'd not imagined possible and she was happy to stay well away from horses for the time being.

"We can't! We can't move him!" Charleroi wailed, sharp enough to know the damage that was likely to do as William took the scarf from his neck, fashioned it into a rudimentary bandage and slipped it around the man's waist to secure the dressing already there. "He'll die!"

"We'll *all* be dead if we stay here, Your Highness," Randwick pointed out urgently, extending his hand and helping her to her feet as William and another guardsman took up positions on either side of the king, preparing to lift. There were more explosions along the docks, closer now and illustrating his point perfectly as debris clattered around them and they all flinched.

"Ready, your highness…!" William warned, receiving a pained nod in response as the pair steeled themselves and hoisted the king between them with a grunt of exertion and a muffled cry of agony from the king. "Up… up with him!"

"Here, bring him across," Randwick directed, taking his horse by the reins and mane and guiding it slowly around until they were able to lift the king across the saddle from behind. "Can you ride, Highness…?"

"Well enough, sir… well enough… Let's be away now: first to the Longhouse to gather as many as men as we can, then on to the fortress to plan our counter-attack." Phaesus croaked with determination, forcing himself to sit upright as best he could as his old mentor passed the reins to William.

"Aye, and a savage one indeed," the old man growled darkly as he gave the junior officer a quick nod. "See him safe… guard him with your life…"

"Always…" was all the reply that needed to be given. "Guardsmen – *with me…*!"

"The princess with me…!" Randwick barked then, climbing into the saddle of Nev's horse and bringing it around as William remounted his own mount and led the king quickly away. "Come on, young lass: up you get…"

"The doctors…! The doctors at the Longhouse will know what to do!" She sobbed, barely coherent as he reached down and lifted her into the saddle ahead of him.

"Aye, lass…" he agreed, already knowing how bad the wound was and hating himself for the lie he'd just given. "Aye, they will. Let's be to safety now." He turned toward Nev, still standing to one side with bag on her back and sword at her hip. "And you, girl? You'll be safer with us: we owe you that much at least…"

"She can ride with me, My Lord," Godfrey called out from some distance away as he and Lester rode up at a canter, both of them sweaty and stained with soot and smoke. They'd become separated during the race to the king after fire from *Devastator's* guns had shattered the boardwalk and forced them to backtrack through the city streets.

"How far to this Longhouse?" Nev asked, reaching up and accepting Godfrey's hand as he leaned down on the saddle and hauled her up behind him.

"A half-mile or more," Randwick answered, steadying his mount as another broadside howled overhead and exploded somewhere deep within the town itself, "and a dangerous ride at that! Away now! Keep up where you can! *Yah*…!" And with a shout and kick of his heels, he urged his horse forward, following after William, the guardsmen and the king as they pushed forward behind a wall of white-coated Huon soldiers.

A kilometre east of their position beyond the city walls, six large assault ships had coasted up to the beach, the easternmost of them taking great care not to come too close to the white-painted staves pinned into the sand there to denote the Keepsake that had been the cause of all the princess' problems earlier in the week. Each ran aground in turn with oars raised, then dropped loading ramps on either side of the bow to allow mounted cavalry to come streaming out in waves.

The Burnii guards, although initially posted further back from the dockside ceremony itself, were strong in number all the same, and once the initial shock of the attack had passed they'd been quickly able to overpower their Taasi counterparts, forcing them away from the harbour and back against the city wall there. Many had managed to escape through one of two of the gates on that side while just as many had fallen against those towers of black-grey stone, left with no avenue of retreat and given no quarter by Huon troopers incensed by news that the king had been betrayed.

Those who'd managed to slip free were now running headlong to the east along the beach, Baal and Garrick among them, and they were met halfway by the advance guards of the newly-landed cavalry. The prince was immediately given a horse and sent back to a makeshift command post close to one of the grounded boats where – somewhat miraculously, in Baal's opinion – Silas, Roland and De Lisle were already standing around a large map table, engaged in serious conversation with Harald the Black himself. Behind them both, remaining aloof at a discreet distance, Persephone also stood watching the proceedings, outwardly calm but with eyes alight as she watched the cavalry form and move out toward the impending battle.

Harald was a huge bear of a man standing as tall as Randwick and markedly broader across the chest and shoulders. He was also of similar age to the mentor and his face and arms carried a number of battle scars earned during some of the many battles he'd led personally over his thirty-year reign. It had been *expected* that Harald would arrive aboard *Devastator* as part of the now-aborted peace talks... it was of no surprise whatsoever to Baal of anyone else who knew the man that he'd instead arrived with his own assault forces, ready to place himself at the forefront of battle.

"The Burnii garrison holds the upper hand!" The prince barked breathlessly as he slid from his horse and jogged across to join the gathering, his arrival barely raising a glance or even an eyebrow from anyone else. "My bluecoats are being forced out of the town and back toward us, here..."

"No great surprise," Harald grunted, not bothering to look up from the map of Huon he'd spread out across the table top. "Their numbers are greater: it's to be expected." This time he *did* look up, fixing Baal with a cold, soulless gaze. "Those *fops* you call a bodyguard have served their purpose well enough in keeping them within the city walls. We've landed heavy-horse without opposition, with shock troops coming in with the next wave: there'll be nought that can stop them now with support from *Devastator's* guns."

"They've *more* men at the Longhouse and atop the hill..." Garrick chimed in, catching up with Baal and also breathing heavily with exertion and excitement. "It can be only a quarter-hour or less before they march out to meet us..."

"The Longhouse is of no concern..." Harald shrugged with little interest, casting a cursory glance over his shoulder at the looming shadow of it through the smoke and haze of battle that was already floating past their position. "The fortress may prove a harder nut to crack but they'll not sally forth from there in force. The walls are their strength, and they'll not sacrifice that advantage; better for them to wait out a siege while armies are raised throughout the rest of the country to march against us."

"They'd risk *everything* on such a plan?" Garrick was dumfounded at the thought, while Baal simply nodded, deep in thought.

"Aye... and in *any* other battle, they'd be *right* to do so, for we'd never have been able to hold a beachhead against such numbers. *This* time however it shall be their end... *Cardinal*...!" Harald turned to De Lisle and barked is words with such force that any lesser man might've flinched. "A message to your man aboard *Thunderbolt*... tell the captain he may fire at will on the Longhouse: with Phaesus and the whelp gone, I've a mind to see it burning..."

"My Lord..." Baal began haltingly, the chill of fear rippling through him at that moment. "Did my messenger not precede me...? The king is not dead or... at least... he still lived when last I saw him..."

For the first time since he'd arrived, the prince had Harald's *full* attention, and he found it to be an *exceptionally* uncomfortable experience.

"Are you telling me you *failed*...?" The huge man demanded, his words becoming a roar of rage at the end of the sentence. "...That even with this magical killing machine of yours," he continued, slapping Baal's shoulder heavily near where he's slung the shotgun, "you *still* could not accomplish the *one thing* with which you were tasked?"

"There... there was confusion – *interference*..." Baal griped evasively, searching for excuses. "He was mortally wounded when I left him: he'll not last the night, I swear it on my life..."

"Your life *indeed*," Harald snarled darkly, ice in his tone. "And the *daughter*...? What of her...?"

"She... she was not harmed, so far as I know, sire..." Baal admitted eventually, terrified of the man's expected reaction but unable to avoid the truth of it.

"You *fool*...!" De Lisle snapped, pre-empting anything Harald was likely to have said next. "Do you *realise* the position this leaves *you* in? Not only have you tried to kill a king and *failed* but you've left alive his only *rightful* heir. Regardless of the circumstances, *you* should've been next in line for the throne... with *her* alive, all you are *now* is a usurper... a *traitor*. She was *already* a beautiful young princess and now *you* have made her an orphan... the orphan of a *martyr*...! Stories like this are the stuff of *legend*, you stumbling clod! *Empires* are lost because of them!"

"She's a *girl*, preacher, not a Shard God," Harald pointed out, almost amused by the rabid fervour of the cardinal's rage. "She'll die as quick as any other with a blade at her throat. Let's not mourn our battles before they're lost just yet. Get this idiot out of my sight..." he added gruffly, turning to the nearest guard and clearly referring to Baal. "Better yet... put him in with Third Cavalry and send him up to the fortress with the scouts..." he added, grinning evilly as a flash of fear again flickered in the prince's eyes. "Maybe you can see for yourself if Phaesus still lives, and if you come back from *that* alive, then *perhaps* I'll forget about your incompetence. You'll leave that infernal 'hand-cannon' behind as well: I'll not have you make things *worse* by losing *that* the moment you're out of my sight! Take him away, boy..." he ordered the guard, "...and give these orders to the commander of Three-Cav: they're to ford the Mu the moment the Longhouse is done, then circle east up Round Hill from Wyvern Hole via the Stewpot Road. Tell him not to spare the horses: that's where he'll be heading if the king *does* still live, and our task will be a good deal easier if they're caught *before* they reach the safety of the fortress."

"*She's* with them..." Percy observed softly, speaking for the first time as she stepped cautiously forward and whispered in the cardinal's ear at a quiet moment as the others returned to their maps and Baal was taken away.

"The *witch*...?" De Lisle asked in surprise, fixing her with a suspicious glare. "You have no power now: how could you *possibly* know that?"

"I don't know how," she answered with more honesty than usual, managing to affect a shrug as if it were no big deal but throwing Silas an evil glare all the same. "Maybe it's because 'Satan's house-elf' over there burned us *both* with the same crystal – or *tried* to, in her case... don't know how; I just *know*... She's there and she's going to help them... she *has* been helping them..."

"Being touched by Dragonfire alone isn't enough for such a connection," De Lisle shook his head slowly, regarding her with a cautious eye of his own, "although it may be *part* of it..."

She speaks the truth... The words boomed in the cardinal's head, jumbling his thoughts for a second or two as he struggled to show no outward effect.

"See...? Told you..." Percy pointed out, as if nothing out of the ordinary had just happened.

"*You* heard that...?" De Lisle croaked, his voice almost breaking with shock as he took her by the arm and drew her a few metres away from the group. "They have spoken to you *directly*...?"

"I've heard *him* before," she shrugged again, then conceded: "...first time without a crystal, though. I figured he was just working through yours..."

"It's *rare* for the Shard Gods to speak through another's link... although not *unheard of*..." he admitted reluctantly. *Extremely* rare, he didn't add, but the fact remained that for whatever reason, the Gods had decided to trust this girl enough to speak directly with her, and if that was the case it was most likely in *De Lisle's* best interest to do the same. "It seems they have some use for you yet, as I suspected might be the case. What would *you* do next?"

"I'd send a crystal up to the fortress with Prince Idiot for a start," she answered immediately, having been thinking about exactly that subject for some time as the others had talked, trying to decide how best to turn it to her own purposes. "She may not know how to use that thing properly – *yet* – but it could still be dangerous in the wrong hands." She paused for a moment for effect, then added: "She might *also* use it to heal the king..." *That* terrible thought hadn't even occurred to De Lisle, and it frightened him more than a little now as he considered the possibility. "...You *could* send *me* up there with them, but *that* would mean giving me another pendant and I doubt I've been forgiven enough yet for *that* to happen..."

"And the alternative might be...?" He asked almost tiredly, well aware there was already another idea waiting behind her calculating gaze.

"Send the old fart instead..." She suggested evenly, certain the cardinal would know exactly who she was referring to. "She wouldn't even *have* a crystal if it weren't for *him*: the *least* he can do is make amends..."

"With a brother nearby, we *might* be able to block the witch…" De Lisle mused thoughtfully, liking the idea more the longer he considered it. "We should be able to raise a wall against her, but we'll need a point of focus close to her position and there's not many experienced enough to handle that kind of power. I doubt Brother Silas will be *pleased* with such a decision…"

"And which part of that is *my* problem…?" She responded coldly, arching one eyebrow. "Is there anyone *else* could do it…?"

"Yes, but not as well…"

"Then hey, it's a dirty job, but *someone* has to do it…" Percy shrugged again, not caring for Silas' well-being in the slightest.

"Indeed…" De Lisle conceded, unable to fault her logic. "Brother Silas!" He called out, turning toward the old man and gaining his attention immediately. "A word, if you don't mind…"

They'd been forced to move inland, use of the coast road made far too dangerous by the arrival of Harald's assault ships, and it had taken far too long for William, Randwick and the others to draw within sight of the Longhouse as a result. Circling around from the south, they'd reached the meander of the Mu River and turned to follow it north again, back toward the towering structure from behind where they were safe from the prying eyes of their enemies on the beach.

"A quarter-mile now… no more…!" William called back with excitement, still leading the king's horse at a canter as Phaesus, against all odds or reason managed to somehow remain upright and conscious, although the agony of the ride was written clearly across his ashen features. "I can see archers firing from the ramparts!"

The Longhouse had never been intended to withstand heavy assault but it had been provided with reasonable defences all the same. Trained archers with longbows manned the rooftops, firing down at anything coming within 200 metres with deadly accuracy, while ballistae mounted at each of the building's northern corners were currently engaged with the nearest of the landed assault ships. The only vessel in range, it'd quickly been set alight by their huge, flaming arrows and was now burning merrily even as crewmen and soldiers alike struggled desperately to disembark.

"They're still holding …" Randwick muttered breathlessly, riding close at the king's side with Charleroi seated before him. "Perhaps *some* hope remains…"

In the moment that followed, a great explosion rose from the river bank fifty metres east of The Longhouse and the ground shook as the roar of it reached them seconds later. Earth and smoke blossomed into the air, startling their horses and forcing all of them to rein in hard and bring the party to a complete halt. Most of them could only look on in blind terror, completely unaware of what was coming. With the limited knowledge of modern warfare she'd learned from her school work, the History Channel and her father's old, non-fiction books on World War Two, only Nev had any understanding of what was about to come.

"Away… we need to get away…!" She called desperately, dragging at Godfrey's tunic as she tried to get his attention. "We need to get out of here… *now*…!"

"But they've *missed* their mark…" William called back, seriously underestimating her in a manner Godfrey had quickly learned never to do. "They've shot their bolt and come up short…"

To his credit, Godfrey was already turning his horse away in the seconds that followed as the building's central section disintegrated in a shattering barrage of fire and debris.

A thousand metres offshore and well out of range of any land-based weapons, the purpose-built bombardment vessel *Thunderbolt* had fired a single ranging shot from one of two large, cast-iron mortars mounted at her bow. Upon noting the fall of that first round – long and to the left – some minor adjustments of traverse and elevation had been made during reloading before both had fired again in quick succession, completely obscuring the vessel for several moments in great clouds of muzzle smoke.

Intended specifically for the bombardment of fortifications, the weapons were of heavier calibre than the cannon being used aboard *Devastator* and the other Blackships, trading range for greater explosive power and higher angles of attack. Identical in design to the smaller explosive-filled projectiles used on those other vessels, the spherical shells fired by *Thunderbolt's* huge pair of 32-pounder guns were detonated by a timed gunpowder fuse ignited by the flash of the propelling charge.

The shells had punched their way straight through the wooden walls of the Longhouse and buried themselves deep into the structure before their fuses had burned down, and the resulting explosions had shattered and collapsed a huge section at the centre, sending debris and wreckage spiralling into the air and setting off a number of smaller, secondary fires as stored oils and other flammables within also caught alight.

"There's a crossing half a mile upstream!" Randwick roared, bringing his own horse about and urging it past Godfrey and the others at a gallop. "Nothing for it now but to cross there and make for the fortress…!"

Charleroi was sobbing in the saddle before him, overwhelmed completely by the thought that anyone still inside – Griselda among them – was almost certainly dead. Everything was clear in Randwick's mind however: terrible as the situation was… no matter how horrific the losses, their primary goal at that moment was to get the king and the princess to safety. There'd be time enough for mourning later if any of them survived the day.

Two more shells exploded inside the ruined structure a few moments later, collapsing the entire north-western corner and sending a dozen archers and the ballista mounted there tumbling to destruction amongst the wreckage. Fire continued to spread, already flaring up in sheets through the building's shattered centre as a tower of thick, black smoke rose high into the air.

They rode on at a gallop, following the river bends south to a low bridge of stone and rough-hewn wood planks, clattering across without slowing and then turning east once more with the towers of Fortress Burnii already visible in the distance through the treetops. Their progress slowed then as they left the track and rode on into the surrounding forest, Randwick and William at the lead and finding their way through instinct and memory alone. A few hundred metres and they were clear of the trees once more, galloping again through rolling hills of open farmland as they began the slow climb toward the summit of Round Hill, still at least two kilometres away by Nev's fearful reckoning.

They reached a wider, more travelled track a few moments later, coming to a halt at a nearby crossroads and resting the horses as William pulled in close to the king and checked his condition, making sure he hid his reaction from the princess behind. Sloping upward toward the south-east, a stacked pile of fallen trees lay in the fields behind them, leftovers of local loggers who'd dropped their tools and evacuated the area earlier that afternoon.

"Not long now, Your Majesty," he assured, trying to sound as confident as possible.

"Indeed, young sir," Phaesus agreed weakly, his words rasping in his throat as he lay forward against the horse's neck for support and clapped his own reassuring hand on the captain's shoulder. "Not long indeed, I fear... but time enough yet to see the rest of you safe..."

"Don't lose hope yet, sire," William shook his head, trying to remain positive and using every ounce of his manly strength to prevent a tear forming at the corner of his eye. "There's medics at the fortress – the best in Huon."

"Best in the whole of the Osterlands, no doubt," the king smiled ruefully, whispering softly: "but they still may not be enough, I warrant. See us safe and sound behind those walls, captain, and we'll take anything that follows as it comes..."

Fire... death... destruction...! A momentary vision of catastrophe flashed through Nev's mind as she too rested against the neck of her horse, causing her to gasp and sit rigidly upright, glancing about herself in sudden fright with wide, unfocussed eyes.

"We need to leave... *now*...!" She barked instantly, her conscious mind snapping brutally back to reality as she turned toward the others.

"Another moment or two and we'll be on our way up the hill to safety," William assured, imagining he'd managed to hide his patronising tone.

"Not the fortress," she shot back with a shudder. "Nothing *that* way but disaster...we need to flee – get out of here... *now*...!"

"Fortress Burnii is *right there*...!" William of Zeehn declared boldly, pointing up at the distant castle with disbelief in his eyes. "Surely you'd not have us turn away now when we're so close to safety?"

"*No one's* safe *there*," she insisted, her words more urgent now as Randwick brought his horse in close, concern spreading across his features.

"Ready to go when you are," Godfrey offered without a second thought, giving a single nod of recognition. He knew well enough by now to listen carefully when Nev sounded that certain.

"I think perhaps we need to think about this..." Randwick began, not entirely convinced but clearly moved by her conviction all the same.

"Surely, sir, you'll not *retreat* on the advice of a *girl...?*" William persisted, almost sounding petulant now as he turned to Randwick for support.

"The same 'girl' who saved *my* life and brought news of this damned invasion to us in the *first place...?*" The old man asked pointedly, not bothering to hide his annoyance. "*I* for one am willing to keep an open mind after what I've seen this last twenty-four hours, and it's *my* advice that *you* should too."

"But, My Lord: *the fortress is right there...*" William blurted, convinced there must be *some* option other than following a woman's orders.

There was a banshee-shriek in the sky in that moment as a shell fired from *Thunderbolt* arced overhead, off to the east, exploding on the far slope of Round Hill beyond the fortress itself in a spray of earth and smoke.

"You were saying...?" Randwick asked rather unnecessarily, catching the young officer's eye again in that moment and raising a single eyebrow that spoke volumes. "I've no objection to heeding good advice *regardless* of who it comes from. I can make it a direct order... *from me...*" he added, his voice hardening "...if it makes is easier to swallow your pride..."

Anger and embarrassment flared in William's eyes for a moment, but fear took over quickly enough as a second shell struck the walls of Fortress Burnii low at the base of one of the trebuchet turrets a few seconds later, exploding in a flash of flame and a huge upheaval of earth and shattered stone that sent that whole section of battlement tumbling downward in its wake. A third landed directly after, striking the roofs of the inner keep and shattering the ramparts there as debris rained down over a wide area, some of it landing disturbingly close.

"Prepare to move out...!" Randwick barked loudly, seeing no point in further discussion as he turned his horse about to face the rest of them. "We'll head inland and stop for assistance the moment we're clear of danger..."

"*Alarm... alarm...!*" A cry of warning came from one of William's guardsmen then, positioned a few dozen metres north to keep watch at a bend in the road. "Blackwatch approaching at the gallop...!" He shouted urgently, circling his horse as it was filled with excitement over the possibility of battle. "Making straight for us... *yah...!*" And with a single battle cry, he lowered his lance and charged forward into the fray, disappearing from view almost immediately even as William called desperately from him to hold back.

"Not alone, you *fool*…!" He barked angrily, the order far too late as the rumble of approaching hoof beats began to reach their ears. Remy, Diego: with *me*…! Master Randwick, we'll hold them as best we can. Get the rest safety, sir!"

"What, and miss all the fun…?" Lester cawed with wild enthusiasm, sliding from his horse and making for the nearest pile of sawn tree trunks, stacked a hundred metres or so away up a gentle incline leading away to the south-east. "Let's see how many of these buggers we can send back in a box!"

"Guess I'll need to keep an eye on him," Godfrey sighed, resigned to what was about to happen as he climbed down from his own horse, leaving Nev not at all happy in the saddle. "Stay with the king and the princess! Get clear and keep riding!"

"Are you *nuts*?" She shrieked, dropping to the ground seconds later and drawing the katana. "I'm not leaving you lot here to take them on alone…"

"Too late anyway," Randwick called darkly, reining in his own horse and charging up the hill toward the same slope Lester was making for. "They have us surrounded!"

Turning as one, they all stared up toward the top of the summit to the south-east beyond the fallen trees. A six-man troop of black-clad cavalry had already formed across the ridge there, no more than two hundred metres distant and barring their way. With more approaching from the north, it was clear now that there was nothing for it but to fight.

"Fall back, man!" Randwick calling out to William as he and his remaining two troopers prepared to charge in unison. "There's too many of 'em to throw your life away. Stand *with* us instead and defend the Royal Family!"

Although reluctant to pull back, William could see the logic of it well enough and conceded the point. He turned with his men and followed the rest of them up the hill to the abandoned logging camp as six more Blackwatch appeared around the bend of the road, lances held high as they rode at the canter. That there was no sign of William's third cavalryman was as sure a sign of his fate as any evidence of a body.

Randwick rode on behind them all, his gaze alternating between the newly-arrived enemy cavalry and William's retreating form, riding on ahead.

Need to watch that one… He thought darkly to himself, thinking on the younger man's earlier words. *If he can't take orders from a woman, who's to say he'll take them from a* queen…?

The second Blackwatch troop spread out in an east-west line across the Stewpot Road, and as Randwick and the others looked desperately back over their shoulders they could all see the bright blue tunic of Prince Baal as he and two other riders turned the corner and came into view behind them. He'd brought his horse to a halt at the left of the formation and even at that distance, the prince's body language seemed to suggest he'd much rather be *anywhere* else at that moment.

Nev paused then in mid-flight for a moment, her focus shifting slightly as her eyes were unconsciously drawn to the other two other horsemen beside Baal, all three waiting patiently in shadow near the hillside at the bend in Stewpot Road. Although she couldn't make out any features, the faint twinkle of blue that flashed at the centre of one of those silhouettes told her it was a member of the Brotherhood she was looking at, and the sudden flicker of images that appeared fleetingly in her thoughts at that moment left her in no doubt whatsoever that she was staring straight at Chief Quisitor Silas. A warning call came from Godfrey then, breaking the momentary spell that had fallen upon her, and she once more broke into a run, working hard to catch the others up.

As they reached cover, they found some small good fortune in that some of the felled trunks had been stacked in large, squared-off piles, effectively forming solid walls on all four sides that stood at least a metre or more high – more than enough to provide at least *some* cover. There were smaller logs and branches piled within, and all of them save for Charleroi and the king immediately set about piling those between the stacked trunks, creating smaller but no-less effective barriers intended to make any assault on horseback close to impossible.

"Cop *that*, y' *mongrels*…!" Lester howled wildly, loosing his first bolt in the direction of the horsemen on the hill. "I got a bag *full* o' these here for ya!" The shot had fallen well short – the weapon's effective range little better than 150 metres at best – but the shot served a warning all the same that coming closer would present significant risk.

"Damn you, Roberts!" William muttered darkly, sliding from his horse and sending it running with a slap on its rump. "You'd have been more use to us alive and no mistake. Standard formation: two troops of forward scouts..." he observed as Randwick appeared beside him, sword in hand.

"Aye... and plenty more of 'em will arrive soon enough: if we're *lucky*, we might get ten minutes alone with this lot. How's your aim?" He asked drily, nodding at the crossbow in the younger man's hands.

"Fine on the barracks range," William admitted with a rueful smile of his own, basically admitting he'd never fired the weapon at another man before. "I'll shoot true enough. We only carry twenty bolts apiece though – I pray that's enough."

"As do I," Randwick nodded. "We've reasonable cover here and they'll *have* to come in after us to finish us off... we've a *chance* at least. It's the reinforcements that worry me – I'd prefer an attack *now* rather than holding until the rest of them arrive."

"Where do you want us?" Godfrey called from a position further down toward the far corner of that stack of logs.

"I'll have you cover that opening if you would, Master Westacre," the old man answered instantly, "and your boy there can shoot at anything coming down from the hill. "How many bolts do you hold, lad?" He asked loudly.

"Maybe *fifty-odd*..." Lester shot back gleefully, slotting one into his crossbow as he spoke. "Dunno for sure, but *at least* that many..."

"Not well, that boy..." Randwick grinned, shaking his head and not at all unhappy about it under the circumstances "...and all the better for it! Aim true, lad: don't waste 'em."

"And me?" Nev asked, standing on William's opposite side with a determined expression and one hand on the hilt of her sheathed katana.

"I'll have you mind the other end of the logs if you will, mistress..." Randwick answered quickly with a nod of thanks, cutting the young officer off before he could say something stupid like suggesting she stay out of trouble. "Keep your head low: it's of no use to y' with an arrow through it."

With that sobering remark, Nev steeled her nerves as best she could and took up a crouched position a metre back from the branch-filled opening at the western end of the logs, taking care to do exactly as the old man had said and keep her head down below the level of the barricade.

"They're gonna charge…!" Lester called loudly, voice wavering with a mix of excitement and fear as the troop of Blackwatch that had arrived by the Stewpot Road tightened their formation, lowered their lances and kicked their mounts forward into a slow trot. At the same time, the original troop at the top of the hill also spread out, cantering across the upward slope before coming to a halt just out of shooting range. Pausing just long enough to allow their colleagues to begin their charge from the north, they too then wheeled around and spurred their own mounts to the gallop, powering down the hill from the east at similar speed.

A roar rose up from both directions, barely audible over the thunder of the horses' hooves but frightening all the same. Four crossbows fired together, toppling two riders from the saddle as the rest came on. The defenders frantically went through the reloading cycle, lowering their crossbows to the ground to steady them as they worked the push-pull action of the cocking levers to draw their bow strings back for another bolt. They all knew the enemy was close – far too close – and in the end, only William and Lester were fast enough to reload and raise their weapons in time, each felling another rider from the northern troop before the last two were upon them, leaping their horses straight over the barricade and into the enclosure itself. One of their lowered lances found a target as they came through, skewering the guardsman named Remy through the chest and pinning him against the ground, screaming.

Nearest of all of them, neither Godfrey nor Randwick wasted any time. Both men instantly leaped forward and slashed at the horses with their blades, forcing the animals to rear back and toss their riders heavily to the ground. William and Diego made short work of them as they landed, darting in and despatching them without hesitation or mercy.

"The flank… *the flank*…!" Godfrey shouted, crossing to the eastern barricade in an instant as the remaining six horsemen also reached their defences. Three more vaulted their mounts over the logs and dived into the fray while the others pulled up short, slid from their saddles and drew their swords as they charged forward on foot.

A slashing blade caught Diego in the back of the head, killing him instantly and sending his lifeless body sprawling to the ground even as the attacking rider was himself knocked out of the saddle at point-blank range by Lester's third shot. Another rider caught William in the shoulder with a long, iron-headed mace, fracturing his collar bone, knocking him senseless and sending him crashing backward against the piled logs. Randwick slashed his assailant across the back with his sword a second later and sent him tumbling backward with a scream of agony, only to be pounced upon by Lester, brandishing a long dagger in each hand.

Downward strike: deflect, side-step and riposte...

The third rider crashed straight through the middle of them, knocking Godfrey flying with his horse as he leaned forward to slash wildly at Nev, his first available target. A momentary image of the impending attack had already appeared in her mind however and she was waiting for him with her defence prepared.

The katana flashed from its scabbard, arcing upward as she stepped to her left and deflected the blow with a turn of her wrist, keeping her grip loose enough to ensure the sabre slid along her own and away to the right rather than risk taking the full force of the strike and snapping her own weapon in half. Twisting her hands in the middle of her follow-through, she pivoted and slashed diagonally downward as he passed, opening up the entire length of the man's outer thigh with her razor-sharp blade.

Caught by surprise and overcome with the agony of the wound, the rider completely misjudged the timing of the jump he'd intended to make that otherwise would've carried him straight over the other side of the enclosure to safety. His horse stumbled heavily at the end of its leap, casting him from the saddle and slamming his body into the base of a tree where he fell crumpled and motionless, either dead or unconscious and of no further concern either way.

Slash... backhand... thrust and strike...

"*No...!*" She barked sharply, whirling in place and realising she was already too late as images of what was to come flashed through her mind.

Nev tensed, refusing to accept the inevitable, and prepared to dive into the fray once more only to be forced to suddenly dive away to her right, twisting her body awkwardly and rolling to avoid the slash of an unexpected sword blade that cut viciously through the air where her head had been just a split-second before. Less surprised by the attack itself than she was by the fact that it had come without warning, she was on her feet again in an instant and turned to meet her new and unexpected attacker, only to find herself face to face with Edward Garrick.

With both guardsmen dead and William out cold, only Lester, Randwick and a very dazed Godfrey stood ready to meet the three remaining Blackwatch troopers as they leaped over the log barricade and came slashing at them with sabres, round shields in their other hands. Armed only with daggers, Lester was outmatched from the start and it was only his lightning reflexes that saved him as a Blackwatcher came howling at him with sword raised. He ducked away from the blow, rolling to one side and crunching heavily into the barricade in the process, jarring his shoulder and forcing a grunt of pain from between his clenched teeth.

He was still on the ground and at a great disadvantage as his opponent turned and swung at him again, slashing the sword downward in a deadly arc. The blow was stopped cold with a loud and jarring clang as Godfrey, still woozy on his feet, stumbled in from one side and blocked with his own blade, snapping it in the process. Momentum alone was enough to carry him on as he dropped his shoulder and collided hard with Lester's attacker, sending both of them crashing to the ground in a tangled heap of arms and legs.

There was a moment's desperate struggle before the black rider gave a wheezing moan and fell limp, the jagged stub of Godfrey's broken blade jammed between his ribs. A large man of close to a hundred kilos even without his armour, the dead horseman still had some fight in him however in that he was still rather inconveniently lying on top of Godfrey, leaving him pinned beneath and struggling to free himself in his already weakened state as the battle continued around him.

Randwick met the second of the three with his own sword raised, parrying the initial strike against him and following up quickly by swinging round with the staff he carried in his other hand and dealing the fellow a solid crack to the side of his helmet. The padded iron took most of the blow but it was nevertheless still strong enough to send stars flickering across the man's vision and leave him staggering backward for a fraction of a second.

Randwick counter-attacked immediately, thrusting forward with his own sword only to be unceremoniously upended as Godfrey and his opponent rolled past in the midst of their own struggle, collecting the old man's ankles in the process. He landed hard on his backside, unhurt but caught off balance as his own opponent recovered quickly and attacked again, stabbing downward with as much force as he could muster.

The sabre point found Randwick's right shoulder, forcing him back hard against the ground with a hiss of painful breath. The light mail beneath his leather tunic held, preventing an actual puncture wound, but the point dug deep all the same, damaging the muscles beneath and sending fiery agony throughout his upper body. Even so, he was able to strike with his own sword in return, taking the man in the throat and rolling him away to one side with a stunned expression on his face as his life's blood poured out onto the ground around him.

The safety of the king and princess remained paramount in Randwick's mind at that point, and regardless of the pain burning through his right side, his first thought was to leap to their aid. It was therefore a complete and terrible surprise in the seconds that followed as the old man attempted to lift his body from the ground and suddenly realised he was unable to move. He found that he was also unable to speak, able to utter little more than a few unintelligible croaks no matter how hard he tried.

He fought desperately with his own body, trying to find some way to free himself from whatever dark magic had afflicted him, but struggle as hard as he might his nervous system simply refused to comply, and turning his gaze to one side (his head appeared to be the only part of him that he *could* control), he realised that Godfrey, lying no more than two metres away, appeared to have the same problem. They passed a meaningful look, which Randwick followed with a faint shake of the head that received a nod of agreement from you younger man.

Neither of them were subsequently able to intervene as the third Blackwatcher lurched forward to attack the king, and the princess howled in fury as she leaped toward him, ready to defend her father. As she appeared to be a young girl with no obvious weapon in hand, the attacker initially dismissed her as any kind of credible threat as he slashed downward with his sabre, roaring with rage and meaning to cleave Phaesus' head from his shoulders as he lay propped with his back against the logs to one side of the enclosure, clearly in no condition to fight back.

Charleroi had no time to think about what she was doing. Her questing hands found the nearest available weapon almost by instinct, fingers curling about the handle of the same mace that had struck William moments earlier, now lying discarded after falling from its dead owner's grasp during the melee. With a roar of anger and exertion, she swung it now in a wide arc and brought it crashing against the side of the trooper's head. The man's helmet crumpled under the heavy impact, crushing his skull beneath and killing him instantly.

"Charli...!" Phaesus croaked, eyes wide and struggling to regain his own feet in spite of his injuries. *"Behind you...!"*

She whirled, mace at the ready, and gasped in shock as Amun Baal strode purposefully toward her with a grim expression and sword in hand.

XVII

NEMESIS

"You're the witch: the one who's been causing all the trouble…" Garrick observed coolly, keeping a discreet distance and holding his blade before him at chest height as he eyed Nev up and down. "You're practically *famous*, girl…!" Markedly different from the broad-bladed sabres the Blackwatchers had carried, Garrick's rapier was long and relatively thin. Its primary use was as a thrusting weapon, although many were often also honed with razor-sharp cutting edges, and Nev was more than happy not to find out whether his was any exception.

"Well that makes *one* of us, then," Nev fired back with a sneer, "cause you're *nobody* to *me* …" She could see in her peripheral vision that there was trouble where the king lay but she daren't turn to look for fear of losing concentration. Unlike the troopers that had come before him, *this* man had the poise and manner of a trained swordsman and instinct told her she couldn't afford to show him any weakness.

"Do the insults work… generally…?" He countered evenly, actually almost sounding interested as the hint of a smile quirked at the edge of his lips. "Do they make the other morons angry… make them careless…?"

"Haven't really *had* time to *talk* before," she shrugged, almost grinning herself as her hand rested on the hilt of the katana at her belt, her eyes never leaving his. "Usually I've only needed to *kill* the *other* morons…" She'd intentionally emphasised her words to cast another slight in his direction, thinking he was probably sharp enough to pick up her changed inflection.

"Oh, you're *good*…" he chuckled softly. "I *do* so appreciate a rapier wit… moreso a *real rapier*, though…!" He added, words straining with sudden exertion as he lunged forward, taking two short leaps forward in quick succession and thrusting at her face with the tip of his blade.

Nev drew back immediately, side-stepping his first thrust and flicking upward with her own weapon just enough to deflect the second. She held the katana ready in both hands as they drew apart once more, keeping it drawn in to one side of her body just enough to shield it from clear view.

"There's no *need* for this, *really…*" she ventured, her breathing elevated by the sudden burst of activity. "We *could* go our separate ways: I don't *particularly* want to kill you…"

"Ahh, well *that* is where our opinions differ *dramatically…*" Garrick pointed out with a sneer of his own. "What was that phrase you used…?" He continued thoughtfully, tensing his body for another assault. "…'That makes *one of us…*'…?"

Another lunge and thrust forward, and Nev parried again before spinning away to the right, trading ground for safe distance. She'd seen his muscles preparing for the attack and managed to evade again (barely) but all the same, she recognised she was dealing with an extremely experienced swordsman. Perhaps not as accomplished as Honda when the old man was in his prime, Garrick was nevertheless a very dangerous opponent, that fact far more frightening when Nev considered that unlike Honda, *this* opponent *really* was trying to kill her.

"I could cut you in *half…*" she threatened, trying to sound intimidating and not really managing it that well.

"If you could do *that*, girl, I'd be dead *already…*" he pointed out quickly, probing her defences again and this time catching the sleeve of her jacket as she twisted out of reach once more.

He was getting closer with each attack and Nev knew it was only a matter of time before one of his thrusts found its mark. Fleeting opportunities for her to strike back were appearing and disappearing again just as quickly as they moved cautiously around each other, but she was finding it impossible to commit to any attack of her own. This was no training *dojo* – making a mistake *here* would likely see her either dead or seriously maimed – and the extra layer of fear and uncertainty that came with that realisation was putting her off her game just enough to prevent her from taking the risk.

Nev also realised in that moment that the surrounding battle had suddenly turned extremely quiet with very little motion at all showing in her peripheral vision. She still didn't dare glance away for fear of leaving herself open to attack, but she began to get the distinct impression that something had gone *very* wrong.

"Cousin, don't to this...!" Charleroi begged, the thought that Baal had betrayed his own family too terrible to accept in spite of what she'd seen at the docks. "Father's *dying*... please... *help me*..."

"I'm afraid the king's death is *inevitable*, dear..." the prince replied calmly, almost smiling now (and not in a pleasant way). "...Inevitable *and* necessary... as is *yours*..."

"How could you *do* this...?" She demanded, anger showing through her tears now as reality came rushing back hard and she swung the mace awkwardly in front of her. "Betray your own *family*...your own *people*...?"

"I'm going to *save* our people..." Baal snarled in return, a sneer flickering across his face. "Phaesus has hurt Huon more in six months than some kings manage in a *lifetime*! You think all these new inventions have gone unnoticed? You think the Brotherhood and the rest of The Osterlands would turn a blind eye to the *heresy* being committed here in the king's name? The cardinal feared for our people – that they would suffer the eternal damnation of The Bicephalus for the sins of *your* father. He came to me for help..." he added, rising to full height for a moment and almost sounding righteous "...and I was *happy* to give it!"

"You never *were* satisfied as viceroy, Amun... I knew *that* well enough..." Phaesus wheezed sadly, shaking his head. "I know father promised you The Blacklands in the last war, and that you felt cheated when Harald unexpectedly sued for peace. De Lisle may have dressed all this up in enough rationalisation to ease what shreds of conscience you have left, but this was *never* about 'saving' our people..." he croaked. "If you're going to kill us both, let's speak plainly on it at least."

"I was *stripped* of glory... of my *destiny*...!" Baal shrieked, all of his long-held anger, entitlement and feelings of betrayal bursting forth now that they came to the truth of the matter. "Harkon was heir-apparent, curse him, and the only reason *you* weren't given Taas was because you didn't *want* it... didn't want *any* throne. The Blacklands was to be *mine* to rule as I saw fit... but then the *peace* came, and all that was left when the dust settled were the cast-off *scraps* from the negotiating table…"

"You were a *brother* to me, Amun… an *equal…*"

"*I was never an equal…* not to Belil *or* Harkon!" Baal screamed, fury in his words now as spittle sprayed from his lips. "*Never* good enough for the Namur…! Damn you, Garrick, *finish* that little bitch and be done with it…" he bellowed, momentarily turning his attention toward duel playing out between Nev and his deputy-viceroy off to his right "…there's *work* to be done here!"

"You'll never be good enough for De Lisle either, cousin…" Phaesus pointed out coldly, recognising now that there was no hope of bargaining and feeling too weak to bother. "They'll use you *just* long enough to get what they want, and soon enough it'll be *you* lying here and someone *you* trust will stand over you with murder in their heart."

"Time to die, cousin…" Baal hissed bitterly, cursing inwardly as he fought to hold back the tears that came with a decade spent dealing with feelings of rage and betrayal.

"You'll have to come through *me* first," Charleroi snarled, planting her feet carefully and standing ready with the mace. "I'll *die* before I let you touch him…"

"That, my dear, is the general idea…" Baal observed with an evil smile as he raised his blade and took a step forward.

Charleroi's training had never included the use of such a weapon, but she raised it now as best she could despite her limited strength, swinging it around to intercept Baal's attack. The mace's superior weight worked in her favour now as she rose to meet him with a wild shriek of her own, absorbing most of the blow and turning the attack away to his right.

She parried his second attack a moment later, swinging the mace awkwardly and blocking Baal's blade with a loud, ringing clang of clashing metal. She wasn't prepared to face a seasoned fighter however, and Baal pressed forward even as she blocked his first strike, swinging his free left hand back around in a return arc and smashing the back of his clenched fist into the side of her head before she could react. She fell backward with a scream that was equal parts shock and fear, collapsing dazed against the logs beside her father and overcome with the pain now burning across her head and shoulders.

Gravely wounded as he was, Phaesus wasn't about to allow such an attack against his only child. With as croaking snarl of fury, he struggled to rise to face the prince, drawing back his fist to strike. Too slow, he was pinned to the barricade a moment later as Baal ran him through the shoulder on his left side, the point of the sabre digging into the wood beneath as the king grunted with pain and rage. Wrenching the blade free, the prince drew it back once more, meaning to plunge it straight into the Phaesus' heart as Charleroi screamed in terror.

"Can... you move... boy? Randwick croaked hoarsely, managing to find some voice now as they both continued to struggle against the invisible bonds retraining their bodies.

"Not... yet..." Godfrey wheezed in return, his head twitching as he tried to shake it to reinforce his negative response. "Can... feel my... fingers loosening... though..."

"Aye... lad... me too..." The old man agreed, giving up on any attempt at a nod. "Can... you see... what's happening...?"

"William... still down..." Godfrey hissed, the expression on his face suggesting that he wasn't at all happy with what he could see. "Can't... see... Lester... don't know. Baal... attacking princess..." he continued. From the angle at which he was laying, he was the only one able to observe the fighting that was about to unfold behind Randwick's back. "Another... sword... facing Nev... rapier... *good*..."

"That... will be... Garrick..." Randwick replied slowly, no happier than Godfrey was about being a captive audience under those circumstances "...dog... never strays... far from its master..."

"Need... to help..." Godfrey strained desperately, not knowing who Garrick was but able to see clearly enough that the man knew how to handle a blade.

"Too good... for... *any* of us..." Randwick said with a hollow tone, well aware now that there was no chance of getting free soon enough to be of any use. "It's a... *miracle*... we need now..."

"Come on, little one... still waiting for you to cut me in half..." Garrick goaded, moving slowly to Nev's right with the intention of placing himself between his opponent and Baal's attack on the king. "A young woman skilled in swordplay: something so unusual *does* get noticed."

"You're *really* starting to piss... me... *off*...!" Nev hissed through clenched teeth, unable to contain her frustration despite knowing that letting Garrick see he was getting to her would only urge him on. He tried another careful prod at her defences, but Nev simply sidestepped his thrust rather than showing her katana, which she suspected was what he wanted all along: to force her to engage him.

"Really... all these acrobatics...? I've heard from a number of sources now about your supposed prowess with a blade... I should *very* much like to actually *see* some of that..."

Nev would've very much liked to have shown him some of that skill herself right at that moment, but the truth was she was more than a little scared now and wasn't ashamed to admit it. Her defences were strong, but most of her training had been against fighting styles that were *very* different to that best suited to the type of blade Garrick now held.

A katana was primarily a cutting or slashing weapon in stark contrast to Garrick's rapier, and the man's *very* different fighting style was making it difficult for her, leaving Nev feeling nowhere near confident enough to mount an attack of her own in response.

"*Damn you, Garrick, finish that little bitch and be done with it: there's* work *to be done here!*"

Baal's angry call reached their ears in that moment, drawing a dark smile from Garrick and a gasp of held breath from Nev as she was brutally reminded that the king and princess were still in grave danger. The images of what was about to happen flooded back into her mind once more, just as they had moments earlier, and the realisation that there was nothing she could do only served to fuel the rage that had been building inside her for some time.

In the desperation of that moment, with her anger rising in sync with the urgency of it all, Nev's reflexes – probably for the first time since arriving in that world – screamed for her to attack... for her to raise the katana and unleash her fury on the enemy standing before her.

It is the unemotional, reserved, calm, detached warrior who wins, not the hothead seeking vengeance and not the ambitious seeker of fortune. The voice that came unbidden into her head was Honda's, although Nev knew at the time that he'd been quoting Sun Tzu's *Art of War*.

The quote had come at the end of a particularly intense training session, during which her *sensei* had left here with at least half a dozen bruises on different parts of her body. She'd lost her temper after the first few strikes, slashing and striking at him with wild abandon and earning herself some additional, equally-painful blows for her trouble without ever coming close to landing a hit in return.

She knew why he'd inflicted those additional bruises – to ensure she'd always remember the lesson he'd just taught in self-control – and it was clear in her memory now as she emptied her mind of her growing anger and frustration, replacing it with the cold calculation that came with years of training. Rapier... sabre... katana, it made no difference: neither fear nor anger could help her now but Nev knew that if she kept her head, she had the skills to deal with whatever they could throw at her.

"Not *my* head that needs keeping..." she muttered softly out loud, the words coming with a faint, wry smile that left Garrick feeling vaguely unsettled in spite of his own self-confidence. There was no way to know what was going on inside the girl's mind but the complete change in body language he'd just witnessed as she'd spoken those words somehow made her seem a foot taller.

"Getting tired, little one...?" He ventured, hiding the fact that he'd needed to fake a sneer for the first time as he thrust forward again and bounced backward again on the balls of his feet, catching her cloak at the shoulder, although this time she barely moved enough to avoid the strike. "Time's a wasting and there's more to be done yet. I think it's time we finished this..."

"Lucky I'm wearing my good boots then..." Nev observed drily, raising an eyebrow and tensing her body in anticipation of the full assault she was now certain would come next.

"And *why* is that...?" He asked in exasperation, not interested in the slightest but unable to help himself all the same.

"Because I'm gonna *kick* your *arse*...!"

The words came not as an angry shout nor as a wild taunt, but rather as a simple, muttered aside that would've been far more frightening to Garrick had he been given a moment to think about it. He was afforded no such luxury however as the blade of her 700-year-old katana flashed upward and slashed down again like silver lightning, carving through empty air with a soft hiss where the deputy-viceroy's chest would've been had he not thrown himself backward out of harm's way.

"The child has *fire*..." he exclaimed shakily, trying to maintain his bravado but struggling as Nev drew back for a moment then lunged forward again, this time with a feinting thrust that morphed into a spin and slashing cut from the left as she whirled through 360-degrees and again forced him to leap backwards out of the way. Inside her pocket, the crystal was glowing with a far brighter intensity than usual, and Nev had no way of knowing it was already tapping into her nervous system, silently aiding her as it heightened her senses and sharpened her reflexes.

She came on with another thrust at his mid-section that he barely turned aside with his own blade, gasping at the jarring impact as pain flared in his hand and up his forearm. Nev's own momentum carried her forward and lowering her shoulder in anticipation, she crashed heavily into his chest and sent him sprawling to the ground, winded and wheezing for breath as he scrambled to take his feet fast enough to avoid her next strike.

It was Garrick now who felt real fear for the first time, realising far too late that the thin blade of his rapier, while perfect for thrusts against armoured opponents, was dangerously inadequate in defence against the thick, heavy steel of a katana. The weapon had never been designed to take that kind of impact and a few more forced deflections like the one he'd just experienced would be more than enough to snap his blade like a twig.

The feared next attack never came however as Charleroi's panicked scream pierced the air to Nev's right. With Garrick down and no longer an immediate threat, Nev bolted straight past, charging toward Baal as the prince drew back his sword to deliver his *coup-de-grâce* against the king. She was upon him before he could react, blindsiding Baal with a *mawashi-geri* spin kick that took him in the back near his kidneys and sent the prince staggering backward, sword flailing. He found his balance quickly and turned to face her, fury growing exponentially with his damaged pride as he realised that a girl – *this girl* – had once again gotten the better of him in combat.

"*You again…*! " He roared, drawing an intentionally-smug nod and grin from Nev in return. His rage was intense and she knew she could use it against him. "You *dare* to challenge me again…? I am of *royal* blood! *Kneel* before me…!"

Dodge, turn and strike…

"Mate, I haven't '*challenged*' you: I've *beaten* you… *twice…*!" Nev shot back with a sneer, drawing on her connection to an inherently *Australian* ability to show others the *complete* lack of respect they deserved. "I've wiped things off my *boot* that were more 'royal' than *you*!"

She held the katana out before her in both hands, stepping cautiously around to her right – toward Charleroi and the king – as she waited for the attack she knew was coming. At the same time, she also made a point of keeping Garrick within her peripheral vision as he regained his own feet a few metres away and took stock of the changed situation, already certain that he was by far the more dangerous opponent.

"Die, *bitch*...!" The prince snarled, charged forward with his sabre drawn high and slashing downward with all his might. Nev side-stepped quickly, seeing the movement in his tensing muscles and already knowing how it would come. She spun around him as he followed through and her katana slashed upward at the end of her turn, its razor-sharp blade sliced easily through the leather armour Baal had shrugged on over his robes.

He whirled on her awkwardly, howling in pain over the deep wounds her blade had left on his back and left arm, and charged in again, staggering now as his sabre sliced from side to side in an attempt to force her retreat. Taking a step or two backward as she gauged the timing of his blows, Nev blocked his blade on the fourth strike, deflecting it away and to the left as she spun inside the reach of his arm before he had time to react.

Just as she'd done with Garrick moments earlier, she smashed her shoulder hard into his chest, winding the prince and sending him reeling backward again as he fought desperately to keep his feet, instinctively knowing that losing his balance in that moment would also lose him his life.

Nev gave him no chance to recover, striding forward with him fire in her eyes as the katana arced in like lightning at Baal's neck. He threw himself backward and to one side, stunned by the speed of the strike, and screamed shrilly as the tip of the deadly blade that had been aimed at his throat instead ripped across the surface his left cheek in a spray of blood.

He was down now, sprawled across the hard earth, and this time Nev didn't hesitate for a moment as she leaped forward, ready to deliver a killing stroke.

Blindside… pain… *danger…!* The next few terrible, heart-breaking moments flashed through her mind far too late to be of any use as a warning.

"*Noooooo…!*" She shrieked out loud again, twisting herself in mid-leap as Garrick – momentarily forgotten – came flying at her from her right and cannoned in to her using a heavy, wooden shield he'd found lying discarded amid the dead Blackwatchers. Backed by over a hundred kilos of fit, muscled bodyweight, the impact lifted her from the ground and slammed her against the nearest of the high log walls, smacking her head against the wood, knocking the wind clean out of her and leaving her dazed and wheezing for air as she slid to the ground.

Squashed between her body and the logs, her left arm had taken the brunt of the impact and that wrist now burned with a spearing pain that suggested a sprain at the very least… possibly worse. Stars flickered in her vision as she struggled unsuccessfully to find her feet, yet after all that the katana remained clenched firmly in her right hand.

"*Still*, she won't let go of that infernal blade…!" Garrick snarled, actually quite impressed she'd managed to keep hold of her weapon considering how hard he'd hit her. "*No more games…!*" With a howl he lunged forward, smart enough to go for the kill before Nev had any chance to regain her strength or her wits. She was barely able to raise her good arm in defence as the blade came smashing down toward her head.

Lester pretty much felt sore all over. He suspected that at the very least he'd wrenched his shoulder, and judging by the amount of pain coursing through his whole right side he was rather concerned that something in there might actually be fractured. Every attempt at moving his right arm produced searing agony and he found himself unable to stand upright as a result; forced instead to move with a hunched-over crouch, favouring his injured shoulder.

He'd landed hard against that log barricade as Godfrey had come to his aid, and had scrambled awkwardly out of the way during the melee that had followed, forgotten by all during the heat of the battle. He'd since seen what had happened to both Randwick and Godfrey – that they'd been mysteriously afflicted by some kind of unseen paralysis – and hadn't needed any great leap of logic to work out that majik was involved… by definition also meaning a *brother* was somewhere close.

Creeping down to the western edge of the defences, he'd taken a moment to peer carefully over the top of the stacked logs there and immediately caught sight of Silas, still astride his horse no more than ten metres away. The old man's eyes were screwed tight, his hands outstretched in apparent supplication, and wrapped carefully around one of them was a brightly-glowing Shard pendant.

Lester didn't know why that vile rodent hadn't been able to keep *him* imprisoned in the same way he'd taken hold of Randwick and Godfrey. Maybe the fact that Lester had already experienced the priest's wrath left him immune... maybe he'd been forgotten about... *maybe* the old lecher simply wasn't strong enough to control more than two people at any one time... Lester couldn't really care less at that moment. The only thing he *did* care about was that the great nemesis of his short life so far was now standing just a few yards away with eyes closed and no obvious way to defend himself.

His beloved crossbow was gone, lost somewhere in the chaos of battle, and he dearly missed it now with Silas so close within range. The boy cast his eyes downward, searching the surrounding earth, and quickly came up with a discarded dagger its deceased owner no longer had any use for. It wouldn't be easy making a killing thrust with his weaker left hand, but he was confident there was enough rage within his tiny frame to compensate for his current condition. Taking a moment to glance around and make certain there was no other threat, he began to climb carefully up over the logs toward his prey. It was at that moment he'd heard the princess cry out, and instinct alone forced him to turn back toward the sound.

He saw Baal strike Charleroi and send her sprawling, then watched in growing horror and rage as the prince stabbed the king through the shoulder as casually as one might pin paper to a board. He watched as Nev downed Garrick and rushed in to her aid, almost allowing himself a smile at how terrifyingly dangerous she was with a blade when she wasn't worried about actually *hurting* someone. It was only as Garrick sprang to his feet once more and began to move toward her, clearly now outside the range of her vision, that Lester realised his friends were in terrible danger.

It *could* be said that a thousand wild, adrenalin-fuelled thoughts flashed through the boy's mind in that split-second, swirling and fighting with each other for attention, but the reality was that there were only *two* conflicting alternatives presenting themselves to his conscious mind and demanding a decision on what to do next: on the one hand the opportunity – *finally* – to avenge his family with Silas' death *or…* do something to help Nev and the princess *here and now*.

The mace once again blocked a killing stroke, this time intercepting Garrick's blade and snapping it neatly in two as Charleroi stood fast, pushing her body between him and Nev and buying her time to recover. More prepared this time, she immediately followed the block with a wide, ponderous swing that sent the weapon's spiked head swishing past Garrick's nose as he threw himself backward out of its path.

"Traitors… *traitors…*!" She shrieked, eyes wide with rage and adrenalin. "I'll kill *all of you…*!" The princess' cheek was bruised and swollen from Baal's earlier blow, and a trickle of blood had left a thin trail beneath a cut at the corner of her mouth. Half of her hair had come free from its intricate bindings and now hung loose about her face, adding to her wild demeanour.

"My Lord, if you would…?" Garrick asked with mild amusement, stepping lightly back out of Charleroi's path and bending momentarily to scoop up a discarded sabre as she advanced on him, swinging a weapon that was clearly too heavy for her. "I've a far more dangerous specimen to skewer here than *this* little butterfly…"

There were *very* few situations in which Baal might consider taking orders from a subordinate however direction from Garrick during battle was definitely one of them. The man's reputation as a swordsman was legendary amongst the Huon military and in any case, having been almost killed by that damned witch *twice* now, the prince was perfectly happy to step back and let his deputy-viceroy take care of business.

"A pleasure, good sir," Baal quipped with a forced grin, leaping forward with a sudden thrust as Charleroi turned and tried to bring the mace around, barely meeting his blade in time to deflect it to the left side of her midsection. He followed up immediately, crashing his shoulder into her chest as effectively as Nev had done to him earlier and sending the princess sprawling backward to the ground as the mace flew from her hand from a second time.

"Stay your hand, girl…! Time enough to savour your death once the *others* are done…" Garrick warned, stepping in once and holding the sabre point before Nev's eyes as Baal lurched past behind him, ignoring the wounds on his cheek and back as best he could and intent on finishing off the princess.

"Lester, *no...*!" Nev screamed, still groggy but catching movement out of the corner of her eye and somehow knowing the damage was already done.

"*Really*, girl...?" Garrick asked with a shake of his head. "Do you *really* think I'd fall for *that* old trick?"

The boy was on Baal's back in an instant, launching himself at full speed from several metres away and plunging the dagger deep into the man's shoulder as he landed. The prince screamed, the sword falling from his grasp as he twisted and turned, desperately trying to shake Lester loose. The dagger rose and stabbed downward a second time, again plunging deep and only prevented from delivering a mortal blow by the added difficulty of aiming as Baal threw himself from side to side and writhed in agony.

"Oh, for Crystal's Sake, stand *still*, man...!" Garrick sighed, pausing only long enough to choose his moment as he stepped forward and drove the point of his sabre straight into Lester's left side beneath his armpit.

There was no cry... no word of protest; as Garrick withdrew the blade and backed off, Lester simply fell away and crumpled to the ground in a heap, his eyes closing one last time as a final breath wheezed from between his lips.

"*Bastard...*!" Nev bellowed, drawing on whatever remaining reserves of strength and adrenalin she possessed to force herself to her feet once more.

Garrick was fast enough to be able to block Nev's first strike but he *wasn't* quick enough to counter that *and* deal with Charleroi also as the princess attacked with the mace for a third time, swinging at him from a kneeling position. Even as he deflected the katana and turned it away to his left, the spiked head smashed into the back of Garrick's calf, shattering it and bringing him crashing to one knee with a shriek of pain.

"*Yyyyyyy-ah...*!" Nev barked loudly, drawing on a *kiai* shout to boost both her strength and courage as she swung in with her follow-up attack, planting her feet firmly and easily adjusting her point of aim to compensate for Garrick's sudden change in height as she swung the katana with all the force she could muster. There was the soft hiss off the slashing blade punctuated by a louder, far more terrible sound as it momentarily came in contact with something far more solid than empty air.

Nev turned and stalked away without waiting to see the results of her strike, frightened she might lose control of her stomach at the sight and almost gagging all the same as the soft *thud* of Garrick's head hitting the ground reached her ears. Concentrating *very* hard on not throwing up, she instead cast her eyes about for Baal, only to find that the prince had made good his escape during the confusion and was lurching awkwardly toward Silas and the waiting horses. Moments later they were both riding at full speed for the treeline near the bend on Stewpot Road.

Nev knelt by Lester's lifeless body, sobbing softly as she reached out and laid her fingers gently against his dirt-stained cheek. Tears streamed down her own cheeks as a dazed Godfrey and wounded Randwick drew near, their mental bonds having dissipated with Silas' hurried departure. William still lay groaning off to one side, still not completely conscious but at least able to open his eyes and struggle into a seated position, clutching at the side of his head where a large lump had most definitely formed.

"Godfrey, I... I'm so *sorry*..." she moaned, staring up at him and unable to find anything even close to the right words.

"I saw it all..." he croaked, voice breaking with emotion and guilt as he knelt down at her side and laid a reassuring hand on her shoulder. "Couldn't move... but I *saw everything*..."

"I... I should've... I didn't..."

"It's *we* who should be askin' *your* forgiveness, lass..." Randwick observed solemnly, his expression dark with anger as he looked on from a distance. "...left to fight alone for *all of us* against the finest swordsman in the kingdom, while the two of us lay there like a pair of trussed-up boars awaiting slaughter..."

"But... but I *saw*... I wasn't *fast enough*..."

"Nevaeh, *listen to me*..." Godfrey insisted, struggling to control his own sorrow as he reached up with one hand to gently turn her face toward his. "I *saw* you... I *saw*... and there's not a man alive could've fought any better or any harder. There's no blame in this other than with Garrick and Baal and that *bastard,* De Lisle... *this was not your fault*..." He drew her toward him then, embracing her in his arms and holding her tight as both of them spent a moment softly sobbing in shared grief.

The moment was short-lived however as the king groaned softly behind them, bringing everyone sharply back to the reality of the moment.

"Father... oh Gods, *daddy*...!" Charleroi wailed, borderline hysterical now as she scrambled across the bloodied grass and knelt at his side, desperately pressing down on the terrible new wound in his shoulder as if that might somehow make a difference. The damage from the sabre was terrible and the fact that it had completely penetrated his entire body meant that it was bleeding profusely from both front and back, making her efforts to stem the flow all but useless.

Randwick moved to kneel beside her while behind both of them, Nev and Godfrey stood hand in hand at a discreet distance, the shared experiences of battle and loss having forged a far deeper connection than had previously existed. A very groggy William staggered up to join then at that moment, dismay on his face as he took in the king's current condition.

"No tears, now, darling girl..." Phaesus murmured softly, staring up into his daughter's eyes as she cradled him in her arms and leaned back against the log stack at the rear of the enclosure. "Terrible enough there'll be thousands dead at the end of this... what's the life of *one man* against all that?"

'You're *not* going to die!" She bleated mournfully, trying to wipe at her eyes with her free hand. "There are doctors..."

"...All too far away, love..." he continued, shaking his head sadly. "I was never the warrior your uncle was, but I've seen enough of battle to know a mortal wound... You'll be queen sooner than *any* of us expected..."

"Nev, for Crystal's sake; the pendant...!" Godfrey hissed suddenly, able to take a moment to think clearly for the first time since the battle had started.

"What...?" She asked blankly, too tired and distracted by what was happening to pay enough attention.

"The *king*...!" He repeated urgently, nodding down at Phaesus. "*Heal him*... like back on the boat...!"

"Oh god, I'm such an *idiot*...!" She exclaimed with sudden, urgent embarrassment as she stuffed her hand into her jacket pocket and fumbled for the pendant inside. Drawing it free, she wrapped the chain about her left hand with the crystal firm against her open palm and knelt down at the king's side, opposite the princess.

"That – that's a *Shard Crystal*...!" Charleroi exclaimed, her words as shocked as William's expression as they watched her bring the blue gem into the open for the first time. "Women aren't *allowed* to have them…!" She blurted, speaking before she'd had a chance to think about it.

"Aye, and neither are they s'posed to see *Keepsakes* either, lass…" Randwick growled tersely, just loud enough for the princess to hear. "Let the girl do what she must, Your Highness…" he added, addressing the king now as Phaesus stared weakly up at him with a quizzical expression and Charleroi wisely decided to forego further comment. "She knows what she's doing, I think…"

"A *woman* using a Holy Pendant…" William muttered softly, lifting his hand to his forehead in a Sign of The Shard in nervous superstition. "Not right… this *isn't* right…!"

"You think it's '*right*' to stand by and let your king *die*, you young fool…?" Randwick snapped angrily, in no mood for discussion. "I'll thank you to keep your bloody opinions to yourself if you've nothing *useful* to say. Let the girl get on with what needs to be done!"

"I just hope I'm not too late…" Nev muttered softly, nodding her respect to the king as he met her apologetic stare with a faint smile. "Your – uh – Majesty… I *think* I can help you… but I've only done this *once* before… it *might* hurt a bit…"

"Or possibly *a lot*…" Godfrey murmured unhelpfully, unable to help himself.

"You've fought well and with honour, mistress…" Phaesus observed breathlessly, his words slow and frail. "…As well as *any* man here today. Do as you will: you've *already* guarded me with your life and I see no reason for distrust *now*..."

"Sir… I'll do my best…" She nodded humbly, not at all sure how to properly address a king.

Extending her left hand and holding the pendant over the wound in Phaesus' shoulder, she closed her eyes and reached out carefully with her mind, searching for the half-remembered feelings she'd encountered as she'd healed Godfrey two nights before. It took longer this time without Percy right there to nudge her in the right direction, but eventually she again felt that same sensation sweeping in and enveloping her in its power as she found her connection.

She opened her eyes once more and stared down at the wound, sparks of blue Dragonfire crackling up and down the length of her forearm as both William and Charleroi gasped in fear and *everyone* present took an involuntary step backward.

Show me... she thought silently, and her vision was instantly taken down through successive layers of flesh, bone and muscle as the power of the crystal flared and pulsed beneath her outstretched palm. She saw the damage... saw the ragged hole punched through the man's body where the sabre had run him through... watched as what precious little life's blood he still possessed continued to pump out through the exit wound in his back.

Heal...! She demanded, forming the idea as simply as possible in her mind and once again trusting the power of the crystal and the king's torn body to work together to return everything to its original state. Just as had happened with Godfrey, arteries and veins linked up and reconnected as organs healed and flesh and muscle knitted and fused themselves back together, the strange warmth of it drawing a soft grunt from Phaesus as he bore the discomfort.

"It's working...!" The princess burst out incredulously, almost unable to control herself as she watched the skin over the wound seal itself and gloss over into a reddish-pink scar. "Father, it's *working...!*"

"That's fine, dear... that's just... fine..." Phaesus mumbled, trying to smile and almost fainting from blood loss as everyone's moment of hope once more sunk back into fear for his life.

"He'd fading...!" Randwick urged desperately, all of them deeply concerned now by the greyish-blue pallor of the king's face.

"Princess... some room, please..." Nev barked quickly, giving no thought to protocol or niceties as she shifted her position and used her empty right hand to take Charleroi's shoulder and guide her out of the way. "There's still more to do..."

"Come, lass... give her some space, now..." Randwick suggested, holding out his hand and drawing the reluctant princess back to stand with the rest of them.

"Alright, Your Majesty..." Nev continued to mutter as she settled in at his left and cringing, gingerly removed the sodden rags pressed against gunshot wound he'd received at the docks. "You're not going *anywhere* just yet... just a *little* bit more to do..."

She raised her hand again, lowering the pendant to within a few centimetres of the ragged, angry hole the Beretta had blown through his chainmail and tried not to look too carefully at the damage that'd been wrought beneath. Blood started pumping out through the wound again the moment she'd removed the covering, and Nev stifled a gag as she closed her eyes and reached out again, far more confident this time now that she had a better idea what to 'look' for. All she found this time however was a solid, impenetrable wall of nothingness with no hint of light or sensation in any direction.

"Wait... no... *not right...*" she mumbled, the confidence dissipating quickly as her speed of doubt instantly stepped forward and took control. "Where... *where is it...?*" She hissed softly, stretching out with her mind again, only to find the same deep, overwhelming emptiness. An occasional spark flickered across her fingers as she searched, the intensity so negligible as to be almost non-existent, as was the faint glow emanating from the pendant itself.

"This isn't *right...!*" She growled, shaking her head with eyes still closed as fear spread anew amongst the others. "It worked before... it *did...!* *Heal...!*" She insisted, sending her thoughts outward with much more force this time, boosted by the mental weight of frustrated anger.

We do not permit it...

The dark, hollow words echoed frighteningly inside her mind, causing her to sway slightly with dizziness as she struggled to cope.

You...! *You* again...! She shot back with quick fury, recognising the same voice from both her arrival in that world and her vision aboard *Rapier*. *Get out of here!* *You can't stop this!*

Of course *we can stop it...* *we already* have... it countered evenly, too disinterested to bother gloating.

"No...! *Hyah...!*" Nev screamed, instinctively using her *kiai* shout to bring her extra power as she hurled the full force of her thoughts against that mental wall, imagining herself smashing at it again and again with her feet, her fists and her sword, pounding away in search of some weak point where she might somehow break through.

You're not strong enough to challenge us... the voice boomed again, although there was a faint brittleness to it now, as if weakened and speaking under tension. *You will not* live *long enough for* that *to happen.*

"*Hyah...!*" She shrieked again, battering the wall a second time and sending ripples of blue energy coursing outward in all directions.

To the rest of the group, the scene being played out was an unsettling one to say the least. Eyes closed tight and both hands outstretched with fingers splayed, Nev had begun to rock faintly backward and forward, Dragonfire crackling and sparking up and down her right arm with far more intensity than it ever had as she'd healed the previous wound. With each loud and very verbal *kiai* (everyone flinching in fright each time the shout came) her left hand would push sharply forward and release a short, lightning-like bolt of blue energy that sizzled away from her palm at incredible speed and scorched the wood of the nearby barricade wall. All of them had quite sensibly positioned themselves *behind* her after the first of those blasts.

It serves no purpose... we will not allow it...

But – but I have to save *him...!* Nev pleaded now, realising she simply didn't have the mental strength to break through whatever the barrier was. *He needs to live...!*

No... it replied simply, without the slightest shred of emotion. *He needs to die...*

"No... no... no...*noooooo...!*" Nev wailed, straining with as much mental force as she could muster despite already knowing beyond doubt that she wasn't strong enough.

Dragonfire flared and grew, blossoming into a crackling, churning ball around her left hand that expanded out to at least a metre in each direction as the pendant itself lit up with a blinding intensity, turning from bright blue to an almost pure white as power that should've been channelled into healing the king was left with nowhere to go.

Below her hand, the mental block was now clearly visible as an invisible wall standing between her hands and Phaesus' body, preventing any of that sparkling energy from penetrating far enough to have any effect. She felt him pass then... sensed it at the very moment the king's heart finally gave up its valiant struggle and surrendered to the inevitable. With one last soft and almost mournful sigh, Phaesus' head fell to one side and his mind and body were released into final oblivion.

XVIII

Dragonfire

De Lisle and no less than five brothers of varying experience had all collapsed to the ground, their legs no longer able to bear their weight as mental and physical exhaustion overcame them. Two of the younger novitiates were already unconscious while a third lay writhing on the sand, dragged feebly at his own hair and clothes and moaning incoherently with eyes wide and empty. It was obvious the man's mind was gone, and judging by the intensity of what they'd just experienced, the cardinal would be very surprised if the other two recovered either.

The three who remained were extremely lucky to have survived mostly intact. De Lisle had actually felt his own sanity slipping away in those last few moments as they'd channelled the Shard Gods' power into blocking the girl's attempts to heal the king, and it was an experience he wasn't likely to forget any time soon for the worst reasons. Had Phaesus held on for just a few seconds longer, *all* of them might've been left dying or mindless.

"He's gone..." The cardinal wheezed softly, managing to prop himself up on one elbow as Harald and a small group of advisors all stood about, looking on with varying degrees of professional disinterest. "By The Crystal, it nearly did for *us* too, but he's gone... I felt him slip away..."

"I thought you said this witch was a 'nobody'... that she was 'harmless'...?" Harald observed darkly, mostly hiding his apprehension over the fact that it had taken six members of the Brotherhood working in concert just to *prevent* this girl from using a crystal of her own.

"And so I believed..." De Lisle admitted sourly, casing a suspicious, sidelong glance toward Persephone, standing off to his left. "It appears though that this is *not* the case."

"And what of the old one – the brother you sent with Baal...?"

"His fate is his own," De Lisle shrugged matter-of-factly, not particularly happy about the situation but recognising there was nothing he could do about it. "It'd *kill* us to try reconnecting with him right now... we'll need *at least* a half-hour's rest before I can risk trying anything else." In fact, he felt like several *hours'* sleep would be far more likely, but there was a war on after all and sacrifices had to be made all round.

"Can you give me a location at least?" Harald rumbled darkly, not at all impressed with that answer.

"*That* I *can* do..." De Lisle nodded weakly, nodding toward Percy for assistance and almost as surprised as she was as she instantly leaped forward without even thinking about it and took him by the arm, helping him to his feet. "They've taken refuge at a logging camp inland, not far from here..." he continued, limping slowly across to the huge map table with Percy at his elbow for support. "You'll find them... *here*..." he said eventually, jabbing a finger down on the map at the appropriate place. "You have something in mind, Your Majesty...? *Thank you, girl, I can manage from here...*" he added in a whisper, passing Percy a genuine nod of thanks and bidding her step back, which she did quickly.

"I have in mind to blast her and everyone *else* there straight back to Nethug himself..." Harald snarled, turning to throw a pointed glance at the gunboat still cruising close in to shore, not five hundred metres away. "The rest of Third Cavalry should be in position any moment now, in any case... does the Crystal give you the power of an *exact* position?"

"Right *here*, as I said..." De Lisle replied tartly, not pleased with being asked to repeat himself. South-eastern corner of this crossroads with Stewpot and the trail leading up to the castle; my sight of them was clear – are your *maps* as accurate?"

"Accurate enough," Harald growled, bridling at being spoken to in such a manner but wearing it for the time being, knowing no good would come of antagonising The Brotherhood. "Dirty: mark the range for *Thunderbolt*... I want shells falling on their heads in *five minutes!*"

"Your Highness...!" the king's second-in-command answered immediately, leaping forward to the table with a ruler and pencil already in hand.

General Bertram 'Dirty' Deeds was a tall, solid man in his early forties whose wartime experience was well displayed by his scarred features and the three-pronged hook that had served as replacement for his left hand over the last ten years. His abilities as a fine tactical commander under Harald were matched only by an equal reputation for brutality: Deeds regularly spent the first hours after a battle roaming the field and personally despatching any enemy wounded with sword, axe or anything else that came to hand.

"I make it two thousand, three hundred yards south-south-west – grid reference A-H-fifty-five…"

"Good enough…" Harald grunted with a single nod. "Cardinal… if you're strong enough now to pass on a simple message…?"

"I *think* I can manage…" De Lisle replied drily. "What about the rest of your cavalry?"

"What about them…?" Harald asked bluntly in return, caring not in the slightest; he had thousands of horsemen, after all…

Standing back from the main group and mostly forgotten by everyone else, Percy reached out with her thoughts as carefully as she was able, attempting to connect with the crystal hidden inside the robe pocket of the nearest of the surviving brothers, now standing directly in front of her. The mental equivalent of picking someone's pocket, she'd taken to developing an ability to remotely link with the Shard over the last few months, initially just as something to pass the time during periods of boredom.

She called it her 'psychic Bluetooth' (pun most definitely intended), and it was coming in very handy now as she crept about on the fringes of the brother's Shard Link, not a hint of expression on her face the whole time. There'd have been no hope had the thing been hung about his neck – the glow of it would've alerted everyone present to the illicit activity in progress – but the attempt was at least *possible* while the crystal lay hidden away inside his robe.

Eventually, she found the conduit she was searching for – the one Percy was *mostly* certain belonged to Nev – and gently opened her mind, letting it flow through her just as she had back on *Rapier* a few days before. There was no longer the confusion and uncertainty in Nev's thoughts that'd been present on that previous occasion. This time there was just one emotion – rage – and it was coming through *loud and clear*. It was exactly what Percy had been hoping for and she was forced to catch herself before a self-satisfied smirk could make its way to the outside world. Silently forming the concept of what she wanted to accomplish in her mind, she reached out again and cautiously and carefully pushed Nev's mind toward a stronger connection.

Charleroi fell to her knees, wailing with grief as the rest of the lowered their eyes in sorrow and respect and Nev, who'd seen the same clichéd act in *so many* movies, wept bitterly as she reached out with her right hand and gently closed Phaesus' eyes for the last time.

"I – I'm sorry..." She mumbled, barely heard and knowing full well that nothing she could say could mean anything in that moment. "They – they blocked me... the 'Shard Gods' or... or... *whatever* they are... they blocked me from helping him... I could have... *could have*..." A sob wracked her body then as she was left speechless, fighting to retain control of her emotions, determined not to show any weakness.

The blast of a war horn met their ears, rising from somewhere to the north and sounding far too close for comfort. The lead elements of a far larger cavalry unit appearing seconds later from behind the nearest hill, approaching around that same bend on Stewpot Road. The horsemen rode jauntily toward them, all dressed in the cold, dark uniforms of the Blackwatch with lances held high and sabres at their belts as they cantered forward in two-abreast formation, bugles signalling their approach for all to hear.

Nev looked up with tear-stained cheeks as those horns sounded a second time, turning her gaze first to the king and then to Lester's ruined body, and she suddenly found herself filled with a rage she'd never before experienced... a wild and righteous fury that drew not only from the wholesale murder of so many innocents that day but also on the long-suppressed anger of every slight and misfortune the world had handed her over her seventeen years... from her betrayal at Persephone's hands right back to the death of her mother so many years before.

Be careful not to let it take control: I've seen what it can do... Percy's warning echoed in her mind then, just as sharp and clear as it'd been in that dark room aboard *Rapier*. *It can* burn *a mind to ash...*

But her fury was so great now that Nev could think of nothing other than revenge... revenge over every wrong she'd ever suffered through, brought down against *anyone* who dared to stand in her path.

Feel for the connection... reach out... let it in... New thoughts called to her, strange and alien as if they came to her from somewhere else… some strange, unknown place she couldn't identify. That fact might've worried her if she'd been thinking clearly at that moment, however every rational thought had already been swept aside by the rage overflowing from within.

Nev's hair tie had come away, lost somewhere in the melee, and her long, brown hair now hung loose and unkempt both at her back and in her eyes. There was no point looking for the tie (with so many bloodied bodies lying around, Nev wasn't sure she'd want it back anyway), and instead her hands searched almost instinctively for a spare, tucked away inside her jacket pocket. Deciding she needed more than simple elastic however, she then also reached for the scabbard of her katana.

She knew it'd be there (there was no way an authentic *Sadamune* would've come without one), and she found it exactly as expected in a small pocket carved into the outside of the *saya,* just below the weapon's handguard. No more than fifteen centimetres long, the *kogai* was a thin wooden spike traditionally used for arranging a samurai's hair. Drawing it from its socket, Nev laid the sword across her knees and reached back with both hands.

She approached the process almost as if part of a ceremony, using the moment of relative silence to focus her thoughts as she gathered her hair into a single thick band, then twisted it into a tightly-curled bun far different to her normal repertoire of preferred ponytails. Slipping the spike straight through the centre of the bun's mass, she then used the remaining elastic to tie the whole thing off, leaving it positioned high at the back of her head with not a single strand hanging free to interfere with her vision.

With this done, she took the katana between both hands (one near the tip and one at the hilt) and lifted it horizontally, bowing her head for a moment with eyes closed and offering up a silent prayer the same way she'd watched Honda do at the beginning of every training session. Nev had no religion… she believed in no God that she might've sought out in time of need or trouble… and instead she gave thanks and respect to both the master swordsmith who'd created that superb blade she now held in both hands and to the *sensei* who'd taught her the skills that would now aid her in her time of greatest need.

Bugles sounded again – a distinctly different tune now – and the riders responded as one, dismounting and taking a collective step forward as one in every four stood back to collect the reins of their horses. Lances were staked into the ground, useless as a weapon for foot-soldiers in close quarters, and a half of the eighty that remained each took a knee instead, readying their longbows as the rest drew their swords and began to march forward at a steady pace.

The sparkling blue ball of Dragonfire that had enveloped Nev's left hand as she'd struggled to heal the king had mostly dissipated in the moments of sorrow that had followed. It flared back into blinding existence now as she again reached out for her connection to the pendant and for the first time, Nev allowed it full access to her mind and strength. There was a low, almost infrasonic thrum like the sound something of immense weight being dropped to the ground from a great height, and as she rose slowly to her feet once more, sparks arced from her glowing left hand and crackled their way along the length of anything within range.

Arrows... front and flanks: reach, turn and twist...
Repeat...
Incoming blade: block. Parry and thrust...
Target to the left... turn, feint and strike...

A flood of almost subliminal images rushed toward her, filling her mind with a virtual slideshow of the coming battle, and she absorbed it all with a gasp of expelled breath that curled away from her lips in a faint cloud of condensation that was completely incongruous to the warmth of the afternoon. A chill rippled through her body at the same time, the shock of it producing a momentary look of surprise that morphed quickly into a predatory smile as she saw *exactly* how it was all going to go.

"They're *coming...!*" William called as warning, taking up his own crossbow from the ground where it had fallen earlier and awkwardly drawing back the string with his good hand to reload.

"Let them come...!" Nev snarled, vaulting cleanly over the barricade as the rest of them turned toward her in horrified surprise, and with that ancient blade in one hand and her other a crackling ball of blue fire, she marched straight for the Blackwatch cavalry with nothing but hatred in her eyes. "*You want 'em so badly...?*" She screamed, breaking into a run. "*Come and get 'em, you* bastards...!"

"Nev, *no...!*" Godfrey shouted, not close enough to stop her as she'd gone over the barricade. "For Crystal's sake, *wait...!*"

"Dragonfall take us, boy... is it an invitation you need...?" Randwick snarled, drawing his own sword and clambering over the logs after her with surprising speed considering his wounds. "If this day is our last, then let it *at least* be an *honourable* one…!"

"Ah well…" Godfrey signed in resignation, throwing one last glance over to where Lester still lay and taking a discarded sword from the ground near his feet, "guess I'll be seein' y' soon, little brother…" With a whoop of excitement intended to boost his own courage, he threw himself up and over the fortifications and charged after Randwick,

"Princess… *My queen*…?" William asked searchingly, correcting himself at the last moment and torn between his desire to join the fray and his duty in ensuring her safety.

"Worry not for *me*, good sir," she assured, forcing a thin smile below tear-stained cheeks as she took up a discarded longbow and a quiver full of arrows. "Do what you must… you're of more use out there than *anyone* could be alone here at my side…"

"Your Highness," he nodded, giving thanks as he tossed the crossbow aside and instead drew the sabre at his belt. "*For Huon and the queen*…!" William howled loudly, and he too leaped over in pursuit of the others, blade held high as he charged forward.

A ripple of shock and surprise flowed through the lines of dismounted cavalry as Nev appeared over that barricade of fallen logs and stalked toward them with a sword in one hand and Dragonfire sparkling from the fingertips of the other. They didn't hesitate, lifting their weapons at high angle to compensate for the extreme range as they loosed their first volley. A mass of arrows hurtled away with a rattle and thrum of bowstrings discharging released tension, whistling softly skyward and then nosing down toward her in a shallow ballistic arc as forty black-clad swordsmen broke into a run toward the barricades with blades held high.

Arrows…reach, turn and twist… Nev recounted in her mind, already prepared as the roar of their charge reached her ears. She paid it no heed, her face a tight-lipped mask of concentration, and without missing a single step she reached up with her left hand and swept it from left to right as if intending to swat the incoming projectiles out of the air and toss them aside…

…which was exactly what happened…

A thin finger of blue-white lightning arced across the space between her hand and the incoming arrows, sweeping across their path in time with the movement of her arm and smashing them apart. Sprayed to the four winds, the incoming arrows were sent flying in all directions and plunged back to earth spread over a wide area as Nev ran on. A similar fate met the second volley moments later, although rather than be cast aside by a whiplash of blue-white light, these were instead dragged directly downward to fall upon the heads of the charging Blackwatchers that were almost upon her.

At least half of them fell beneath the unexpected assault, dead or down and screaming as they were struck by misdirected friendly fire. Several terrified archers tossed aside their weapons at that point and turned tail in fright, unable to process what they'd just seen but nevertheless certain a powerful witch was indeed coming straight for them.

Nev met the assault head on, charging forward at speed with Randwick, Godfrey and William a few metres behind her. The enemy's charge had slowed dramatically as she'd drawn closer, many of the remaining Blackwatch troopers having by now also realised they were up against something very unusual in the shape of a young woman with one hand gripping a sword and the other engulfed in a ball of blue Dragonfire.

She met the enemy centre at full speed as the line began to fold in around her, releasing an elongated *kiai* that was more like a scream of rage as the katana came slashing downward, opening the chest of the nearest trooper in the line. The Dragonfire dissipated as she took the weapon in both hands, fading and spreading out into her wrists and forearms as she felt it flow back into her, once more sharpening her concentration and focus into pinpoint clarity.

Incoming blade: block, parry and thrust…

Even as he fell away, mortally wounded, Nev was already twisting to her right to block and deflect her next attacker, sending him to the ground with a kick to the groin and following up with a lightning-fast thrust at his throat to keep him there.

Target left… turn, feint and strike…

Spinning back around to her left and still advancing with every step, Nev thrust forward to draw the man's sword out in defence, then whirled through 360-degrees to deliver a completely unexpected strike from the opposite direction, burying her katana deep into his left side before using one foot to kick it free again and move on to her next victim.

Two of them… too late…! Left and right…!

Two troopers leaped at her simultaneously from different directions and Nev committed herself to defence against the nearer on the right, raising her blade to meet his downward stroke even though she knew she couldn't hope to avoid the second strike from her left. A flick of her wrist turned his sabre aside, the point tearing at the shoulder of her cloak as she lifted her left hand from the hilt of the katana and jabbed forward with her right, punching the swordsman hard in the face and sending him reeling backward.

Nev next turned to her left, using that moment of respite to deal with the attacker coming from that direction and registering surprise as she found him already down and writhing in agony with an arrow buried deep in his chest. Another arrow sizzled past to her right at that moment and felled another Blackwatcher, and as Nev quickly threw a quizzical glance over one shoulder, she instantly spotted Charleroi standing high atop the log barricade with longbow in hand and a full quiver over one shoulder.

"Tired already, lass…?" Randwick called with a dry half-smile from a few metres to her right, laying into a pair of enemy troopers simultaneously with sword in one hand and staff in the other and grunting with every swing as pain lanced through his injured shoulder.

A guttural growl was all the reply he got as Nev passed a faint, unseen nod of thanks in the princess' direction, then turned back to the battle and instantly slashed upward, blocking the swing of her next attacker and following up with a savage kick that shattered his kneecap and sent him falling backward in a crumpled, wailing heap.

Dodge, block, turn, side-cut…! In the blink of an eye, Nev had blocked the next assault and opened his stomach with a powerful slash. *Feint, deflect left, sidestep right… strike…!* A second later and she'd faked out the next attacker with a move to the left, wrong-footing him, then back to the right before slashing downward at his exposed throat.

Confidence growing with every successful attack, Nev's blows and movements became faster and faster as her conscious mind began to fall back and allow instinct and muscle memory to take over completely. Of the forty men who'd commenced the charge against them, no more than a quarter remained standing, the rest either dead or dying. The sounds of the battle itself were horrendous, but the battle-crazed howls of charging men had been mostly supplanted now by the terrible screams of the mortally-wounded, and fear and indecision was now filling the hearts of those few Blackwatchers who'd so far escaped unscathed.

With Randwick, Godfrey and William to either side now, protecting her flanks, Nev had become an unthinking whirlwind of destruction, her blade flashing this way and that at almost superhuman speed as she carved her way through three more and the handful who remained finally turned tail and fled, their courage broken. Realising that the battle was lost, the rest of the archers ran too, many casting aside their weapons as they scrambled for their horses and rode for the safety of the bend in Stewpot road. Six more would fall with one of Charleroi's arrows in their backs before they disappeared from view.

"*Huon...! Huon...!*" William screamed after them with wild elation in his eyes and a bloody sword held high over his head.

"Now *there's* a thing I've never seen in all my days," Randwick mused softly from a discreet distance, taking a moment to catch his breath in the aftermath of battle and regarded Nev with a thoughtful gaze.

"Dragonfall take me, she was incredible...!" Godfrey breathed, standing close by with nothing but awe in both his voice and gaze. "*Incredible...!*"

"Aye, that she was lad," the old man nodded, his tone betraying an underlying concern as he considered the mass of torn and broken bodies lying before them, "but at what *cost...?*"

For her part, Nev heard none of it. Standing at the centre of a ring of ruined bodies with her clothes and face drenched in others' blood, she could barely move as the rage continued to burn within her. Eyes wide and chest heaving with surplus adrenalin, she was almost rigid with tension as Dragonfire continued to flow unchecked through her mind and body.

This 'victory' means nothing...! The words came to her once more, as deafening in her mind as usual, righteous and enraged but for the first time there was also the hint of fear behind it.

The first of many... Nev replied with confidence now as she reached down without thinking and pinched a section of her cloak between two fingers, using it to clean her katana as she drew the bloody blade carefully between them.

It means nothing...! It roared, so powerful now that for a moment she feared she might lose her mind.

I'm going to kill *you...!*
I am ageless; a devourer *of worlds*!

...And I'm going to make you choke *on this* one...! She replied darkly, still seething with the rage of battle as she sheathed the weapon, yet also vaguely heartened in that moment in now in the realisation that whatever it was, it was *frightened* of her. Everything *dies...* she added with a shrug *...and* you *will too.*

Do you think that swords *are the best that I can do...*? It asked smugly, and those last words flared in Nev's subconscious as the connection was lost, replaced by a flash image at the forefront of her mind of what was coming. She realised then that it had been stalling... playing for time until the final pieces of its endgame were in place.

The first shell exploded without warning, falling short by a few hundred metres and bursting amid the trees near the bend in Stewpot Road, the blast shattering trunks and sending splintered branches spiralling away in all directions.

"More incoming..." Nev stated blankly, eyes barely focused as she glanced around at the rest of them. "Gather the horses," she growled softly, turning back toward the north. "I'll hold them as long as I can..."

Godfrey didn't argue this time. The look she'd given them all had been enough to show she was deadly serious, and he was still too much in awe of what he'd just seen to even think about disobeying. Even William gave no resistance this time, already feeling weak and struggling as he was with the pain radiating from his damaged collar bone. The pair turned together and jogged back toward the log barricades, veering off in separate directions as they made for the nearest of a number of riderless horses standing about, grazing mindlessly now the battle was done.

Randwick coughed softly, thinking for just a moment that *he* might reason with her – try to bring her with him in retreat – but the single glare he received over her shoulder in return silenced him completely as Dragonfire again flared into life around the palm of her left hand. Instead, he did exactly as she'd ordered – for an order was exactly what it'd been – and he too loped off up the rise behind the others, struggling with a pronounced limp and using his staff for support.

A second shell also fell short, but closer now as earth and grass sprayed skyward, falling around her as she was buffeted by the heat and force of the blast. Following right behind it, the third shell was on target and Nev could see it in her mind, striking the ground not two metres in front of her in a gout of flame and smoke and a huge upheaval of earth. There was no way she'd let that happen.

She could still feel power coursing through the crystal in her left hand, the rawness of it filling her with a restless energy that seemed almost to be *searching* for an outlet as if operating with its own free will. She flicked her eyes upward, reaching out through the raucous background clutter of countless minds and singling out the incoming shell, the hurtling iron ball a brilliant spark of light in a faint and endless field of stars. With a grunt of frustrated rage, she reached upward once more with her left hand and flicked it angrily to one side, the crackle of Dragonfire flaring brightly for a moment at her fingertips and arcing away into the sky as she brought her arm sharply back to her side once more.

Still a thousand metres away and hurtling through a smoke-laden sky, the thirty-two pound shell was suddenly snatched out of its downward ballistic arc and slapped sideways, veering away to the west so sharply it was almost as if it had ricocheted from some invisible, impenetrable wall. Leaving a shriek of displaced air in its wake, it slammed into the ground to one side of the Stewpot Road, still at least five hundred metres short of its original intended target. There was a roar and a huge upheaval of earth as shrapnel filled the air around it, killing at least half a dozen Blackwatch archers as they continued their headlong retreat away from the heat of battle and that deadly witch's blade.

"Crystal save me, she *is* a witch!" William breathed softly, having stopped for a moment at the barricades to stare in wild disbelief.

"Witch or no, she's *savin' our lives* and I'd pay more attention to making an escape if I were you, lad!" Randwick barked angrily, his own exasperation boiling over in that moment. "I'll leave The King in your charge, boy: make sure he's with us when we leave!"

"Come on, old mate..." Godfrey murmured softly, slipping his arms under Lester's limp body and lifting it gently over the rear of his horse before proceeding to take a length of thin cord from his saddlebag and tie the boy down. "Sorry for the ropes, mate: I know it ain't dignified but it's all I can manage right now..." He was clearly struggling to control his emotions, and it was only the constant, one-way conversation that kept him from losing it altogether. "No place to be left here, is it? Gonna take you home, brother... home for a proper rest somewhere *nice*..."

"I've a mount here, Randwick," Charleroi called sharply, bow and quiver now stowed across her back as she brought a Blackwatch horse up to the rear wall of the barricades. "I'll ride with father if you can help me with him..."

"Aye, Your Majesty..." the old man nodded in an instant, giving the young officer beside him a none-too-subtle shove toward where the king still lay, his face almost peaceful now that his pain was no more. "Young William here will see to it..."

"At *once*, Your Highness!" William blurted nervously, rousing with a start but recovering quickly – to his credit – and leaping forward to lend a hand. "Allow me to lift His Majesty for you..."

Randwick watched her carefully then, taking in every twitch and nervous tic of emotion as Charleroi coldly waited for her father's body to be lifted over the back of that horse in a similar manner to that which Godfrey had just managed with Lester a moment earlier. He'd known her most of her life and he knew exactly how much it must've been tearing her apart inside to see Phaesus like that, yet she showed none of it to the rest of the world.

Aye, she's a strong one there and no mistake! He observed with grim pride, his own face a mask of stone as he turned to gather his own horse. *A fine queen she'll be too... if we can get her out of here alive, this day...*

Another shell, and Nev was ready for it; waiting with arms akimbo and the pulsating blue ball of Dragonfire once more crackling about her left hand. The trajectory flashed into her mind once more in advance, and this time she was able to push her mind even further, tracking the ballistic arc all the way back to its point of origin.

Just like the Predator *did,* she thought darkly with an almost wry smile, thinking momentarily of the alien in that cheesy old Arnold Schwarzenegger movie her dad used to love watching as she punched out with her left hand once more and sent another bolt of energy sizzling upward into the sky to meet the incoming shot. Again, the cannonball deflected away, this time blasting out a crater in the middle of a small clump of trees on the rise running up on the eastern side of Stewpot Road, close enough for Nev to once more feel the warmth of the blast as it washed faintly past her a few seconds later.

This time she didn't retract her hand, instead holding it outstretched above her head as she closed her eyes and focussed on concentrating another charge of energy. The glow about her hand pulsed, flashed and grew quickly in size as she continued to hold back, gathering it within her mind and body until she feared it might consume her entirely. Tracking back down that same trajectory she'd already mapped out from the previous shell, she released it all in a single huge burst.

A brilliant bolt of blue-white lightning blasted skyward from her outstretched fingers, searing the very atmosphere around it as it arced upward above the battle-scarred landscape, following back down the track of the last shell fired. It reached its zenith a fraction of a second later and turned downward once more as it homed in unerringly on its intended target. Nev saw none of what followed: the moment the blast had left her fingertips, her eyes rolled back into her head and she collapsed onto the bloody grass, the oblivion of unconsciousness rushing up to meet her.

Thunderbolt was preparing to fire again as a flash of blinding light struck the stubby barrel of one of the 32-pounders, turning it white hot in the last seconds before it disintegrated in a violent explosion that set off a nearby stack of shells and gunpowder propellant, the resulting chain-reaction tearing the ship apart forward of its central mast. Wreckage and debris spiralled high into the air, splattering the surrounding area with deadly lumps of jagged wood and glowing-hot iron as everyone on the nearby beach – De Lisle and Percy included – dived desperately for cover.

"Reports... *reports*, damn you all!" Harald bellowed in rabid fury, the only man still standing as he stomped angrily about the upturned map table and the others cowered around him. "Is this the first time any of you have seen combat, you cowering filth! I want that pathetic little hell-spawn brought back here *now*... dead *or* alive! Send everything we have spare: let's see this '*witch*' of yours fight off an entire bloody *battalion*!"

"Incompetent *fool*..." De Lisle hissed angrily under his breath as he regained his own feet just a few metres from where Percy still lay. "...letting that damned pendant fall into the wrong hands..."

It didn't take a genius to work out whom he was referring to, and had Percy been feeling a little less exhausted she'd probably have managed a *particularly* cruel, self-satisfied smile at Silas' expense. As it was however, she was still reeling from the after-effects of having been in at least partial control of the connection that had supplied Nev with such a huge burst of psychic energy.

That last counter-attack on *Thunderbolt* had hurt – *physically* – and Percy had been forced to break her link completely, leaving Nev to deal with whatever was left. She was now weak at the knees, her hands shaking slightly as the realisation of how close she'd come to losing her own mind finally struck home. She was also dealing with a splintering migraine in the aftermath of breaking connection and finding it difficult to focus properly on anything more distant than a few metres.

Sorry, sweetie... she thought darkly, a shudder rippling through her entire body as she struggled to her own feet and began an awkward but nevertheless methodical stagger toward De Lisle. *That's me done for a bit: you're on your own, for now...*

"I have her!" Randwick assured, sliding Nev's limp, unconscious body face-down over his saddle and climbing up behind. "Let's be gone now: the Blackwatch'll come back soon enough and we'll need to be far from here when they do." He had no illusions about how well they'd fare when their enemy returned in force.

"Where to, good sir...?" Charleroi asked, reining her horse in beside his and trying as hard as she could to ignore the fact that her father's broken body was tied down behind her.

"South for now," he replied quickly with a shrug. "It matters little *where* for the time being, so long as we put some distance between us and the 'Watch. I've a mind to try for Cadle to begin with – to take stock and perhaps rally our troops – but I've *also* no doubt that *Harald* will march on the fortress as soon as he's able. With these Nethug-spawned *cannon* at the head of his army, I fear even *Cadle's* walls will fall..."

"And what of *Baal*...?" She asked pointedly, her eyes dark with anger and betrayal.

"Aye, what of him *indeed*, Milady," Randwick conceded solemnly, no happier about the situation. "There'll be precious few survivors left to spread the truth of his treachery and we've no way of truly knowing who will stand with us or against... at Cadle *or* anywhere else for that matter."

"Spies and traitors at every turn," William growled with venom, drawing level with the old man on the other side.

"Aye, no doubt: and with Garrick gone, who knows how many will rise in their desire to take his place at Baal's right hand." He turned back to Charleroi. "Your Majesty, I'll see to Huon's defence but I've a mind to see you somewhere safe first: without you as queen, *everything* falls apart..."

"And what disservice to a kingdom to be *abandoned* by their queen at their time of greatest need?" Charleroi snapped, arching one eyebrow.

"*Less* of a disservice than to suffer a *regicide*, I suspect, Your Majesty..." Randwick shot back drily, not about to back down. "We'll head south..." he repeated firmly, cutting off any reply she was about to give. "At least as far as Cadle if the roads are clear, Shard willing, and from *there* we can think hard on where to go *next*. By your leave, Ma'am...?"

Charleroi eventually gave a reluctant nod and with that, Randwick gave a loud "*Yah*...!" and urged his horse forward, the others falling in behind single file as he galloped away along the Stewpot Road, heading south toward the safety of the distant mountains. On the hill behind them, the fortress burned fiercely.

"Another failure, brother..." De Lisle growled softly, skewering Silas with his gaze as the old man stood beneath the re-assembled command post tent and stared at his awkwardly-shifting feet. "You were our conduit – the linchpin of our power..."

"And I held *firm*, Your Grace!" He shot back immediately in a plaintive tone, almost daring to sound indignant but ultimately knowing better than to show insubordination in front of others – particularly such others as Harald and his entourage. "Phaesus is dead because of us!"

"And the princess – *the queen* – still lives!" The cardinal shot back fiercely as Percy smirked from a safe distance of a few metres away, behind the main group. "Deputy Viceroy *Garrick* is dead however," he continued in a dark tone. "Three of your *brothers* have also been left mindless – they'll be lucky to last the night – and you've brought that idiot, Baal back wounded as well... although it appears he *will* last the night, more's the pity!"

"The witch was too *powerful*... *no one* could have imagined it... that this could happen...!"

"Indeed, Brother Silas, none of this *should* have happened...!" De Lisle snarled in return, the old man realising far too late the trap he'd laid for himself. "And none of it *would* have happened had *you* not allowed one of our sacred Holy Pendants to fall into the wrong hands in the *first place*...! *Years* of planning to bring us to this day and *your* thoughtless actions have thrown the fate of the Osterlands and even the Brotherhood *itself* into jeopardy!"

Nethug take him... the words dropped into the cardinal's mind like great blocks of lead falling to earth from stratospheric heights. *He has no further use to us... his mind is too old and inflexible...*

"Give me your Shard!" De Lisle demanded sharply, taking a step forward with hand extended.

"Y-your Grace..." Silas croaked nervously, an incredibly well-tuned sense of self-preservation telling him exactly how dangerous the current situation had become. "Your Grace, I..."

"*Give it to me*...!" The order came almost as a scream in its intensity and the old man flinched visibly, taking an unconscious step backward in response. A small but growing group of onlookers had begun to collect near Percy as the heated exchange had attracted their attention, Harald, Deeds and a number of other senior Blackwatch officers among them.

The girl... give it to the girl...

Devout as he undoubtedly was, even the cardinal baulked at *that* idea and he momentarily froze on the spot, uncertainty in his mind as Silas eventually – *reluctantly* – reached into the pocket of his robes as drew out the Holy Pendant, his face a mask of bitter defeat.

Do you *dare question my commands now, cardinal...? Which part was not clear to you? Give... it... to... the...* girl...!

"Your grace, I *beg* you..." Silas quavered, clearly shaking now as the magnitude of what was happening began to sink in; that after so many decades enjoying the power and luxury the Brotherhood had provided, he truly stood at the precipice of losing the only thing that had made all that possible. "I can *mend* this... I can take the Shard back and make this *right* again..."

"The matter is out of my hands," De Lisle answered coldly, his hand snaking out with remarkable speed to snatch the pendant from the old man's wretched fingers. "The *Shard Gods* have decided, and you *know* what that means... I could not change this even if I wanted to..." the clear implication of course being that he did not.

"My *lord*...!" There were tears in the old man's eyes now, his hands reaching out in supplication as if they might somehow take the precious crystal back. "My lord; a *lifetime* I have served you, your most *faithful* of brothers... you cannot *do this*..."

"You would have me *transgress* against the word of a Shard God?" The cardinal asked sharply, eyes narrowing as he turned back toward him for just a moment. "A *millennia* of loyal service wouldn't justify an act of *heresy*, Brother Silas... you *of all people* should know *that*...!"

"But... but what's to become of me...?"

"Brother..." De Lisle began tiredly, turning his back on the old man as if he were already forgotten and muttering an unfamiliar but *exceptionally* fitting phrase he'd heard earlier "...which part of that is *my* problem...? The Shard Gods have spoken..." he continued, this time speaking to Percy as he strode forward and pressed the pendant into her unsuspecting hand without warning. "This is yours... *for now*..." he added, leaning in close as Silas released a soft wail of despair. "Serve me well – serve the *Shard* well – and you will be rewarded. *Failure* will bring you more pain that you could imagine. Are we clear...?"

"*Completely…*" She answered in an instant, the coldness of her tone in stark contrast to the fire of excitement that now shone in her eyes. "What about *him…*?" She asked, already knowing the answer as she threw a faint nod in the old man's direction.

"He's *yours…* do with him as you will…" The cardinal answered bluntly, Silas definitely forgotten now as he walked away without another thought.

"Sweetie…" Percy began, turning toward a cowering Silas and flashing a predatory smile "…this is going to hurt you *way* more than it's gonna hurt me…" The old man screamed as she advanced toward him, the blue-white glow of Dragonfire flaring around her clenched right fist.

"A word, Your Majesty…" De Lisle growled, dragging Harald's attention from the spectacle momentarily. "I think we need to discuss how best to proceed regarding the princess and this 'witch' of hers…"

"Aye, cardinal…" the king snapped curtly in return, barely able to take his eyes away for more than a second or two. "I'd welcome *any* suggestion at this point…"

Even Harald flinched in that moment as Silas released another shriek of fear and pain that was abruptly and quite brutally cut short.

XIX

LAST LIGHT

Bad news had travelled as quickly in that world as is does in any other, and the keep at Cadle was already in chaos by the time they'd rode through the main gates in the evening of the day after the battle at Stewpot Road. Many nobles, merchants and others of the middle class wealthy enough to own their own transport had already evacuated, prepared to take their chances along the winding, mountain passes of the Bolivar Road as it took them west to the Burnii Crossroads.

Most of that first night and much of the next morning was lost to sleep as they all took the opportunity to get their first decent rest in quite a while. Drained beyond mere physical exhaustion, Nev had slept well into the second afternoon and the sun was already well on its way toward the western horizon as she'd finally opened her eyes, staring dazedly at the tarred thatch of the roof above. A moment's blank fuzziness in those few seconds after waking was quickly replaced by shock and adrenalin as memories of the day before came flooding back.

"*The princess*...!" She exclaimed, sitting bolt upright in bed, her chest heaving with fearful gasps.

"She's all right..." Godfrey assured with a faint smile, mostly managing to hide the relief that washed over him as she'd first opened her eyes. "We're *all* fine... thanks to *you*..."

"Oh... my... *God*...!" She breathed emphatically as she remembered the part she herself had played in the battle. "Did I *actually* do all that...? *How* did I actually do all that...?"

"I gave up wondering *that* a while ago..." he shrugged, smiling faintly, "...and *yes*, you *did* do all that. Never seen anything like it my entire life; never seen a *brother* manage anything even close..."

"The *crystal*...!" She blurted, lifting her left hand almost in reflex as if the pendant might still be wrapped about her wrist.

"On the table beside the bed..." he reassured, nodding to her left. Turning her head in that direction, she found both the Shard crystal and her dragon pendant coiled beside each other on a ceramic plate that lay atop the small side table by the bed. "No one's been game to touch it since we came in... to touch *either* of them..."

She took in the rest of the room as she self-consciously slipped both pendants over her head and made sure they were positioned property about her neck. The space was small and functional with a single window looking out across a large courtyard, the angle of the view clearly suggesting they were at least one or two storeys above ground level. Two narrow beds were the main feature, the other being unoccupied, along with a fireplace, a set of narrow shelves and a single dresser on the far side of the room accompanied by a free-standing mirror.

"How long have I..." she began, then stopped as her eyes came to rest on the shelves and she realised that they currently held all her clothing, neatly cleaned and folded, her sports bag placed on the floor below with the hilt of her katana poking out of the zipped-up opening. "My clothes..." She blurted, looking down for the first time and realising she was dressed in a plain cotton shift with a wide collar and loose sleeves to her elbows. *"My clothes...!"* She repeated, more urgently this time as she realised she was literally wearing nothing else beneath and fixed Godfrey with a glare that was equal parts fear and suspicion.

"You were unconscious when we arrived..." he replied quickly, raising his hands in supplication as his cheeks reddened faintly with embarrassment. "The princess... uh... the *queen* ordered a pair of handmaidens attend to you while your clothes were taken and cleaned."

"So... so – uh – how long *have* I been asleep...?" She finally asked, allowing most of the intensity to fade from her accusatory glare as she self-consciously drew the covers up about her chest.

"Maybe seventy-two hours, give or take..." he shrugged. "You collapsed straight after the thing you did with the cannonballs, and we've not been able to wake you since. The medic here was starting to worry you'd *never* wake up: that maybe the crystal had burned your mind."

"I feel... *fuzzy*..." she stated slowly after much deliberation. "Like everything around me is a *little* out of focus and I have to strain my eyes in a weird way to see properly. "I remember the arrows... remember the cannonballs... the *blood*..." she added, grimacing as her stomach churned faintly over those gruesome memories.

"Here... a drink..." he suggested, rising quickly from his chair by her bedside and stepping across to a low table in the centre of the room, where a ceramic pitcher lay with three large, wooden mugs.

"There are some here who escaped Burnii..." he ventured, not sure if he wanted to know the truth but unable to hold back as he poured her some water and brought it back to the bed. "Some say they saw a bolt of lightning come out of the sky and destroy one of Harald's ships... one that was firing its cannon at something inland..."

"That... that was *Thunderbolt*..." she confirmed with a vague nod as she sipped at the mug, her gaze unfocussed now as she recalled more of what had happened. "I *remember* the ship... remember *seeing* its name on the bow... *remember* imagining the metal heating up... the gunpowder exploding..."

"Dragonfall take me..." Godfrey breathed softly, again fighting an unconscious urge to lift his fingers to his forehead in the Sign of the Shard. "*How...?*" He managed eventually. "How are you able to *do* all this? Even *Randwick* claims he's never seen the like of it, and the queen says she thought he'd seen *everything*! How is it possible that you – who've never even *heard* of a Shard crystal until a few nights ago, let alone ever held one – can do things even *The Brotherhood* can't explain...?"

"I... I *don't know*..." she answered finally, having thought hard about the question for some time. "After Percy showed me how to do it that first time, aboard *Rapier*, it just seems to... I dunno... *happen*...? I think about what I want to do and the crystal just... 'makes it happen'. After the king died... after *Lester*... I was angry... *enraged*. Before then, I'd been afraid to let the power in... afraid what might happen it I let it take control." She took another sip, her hands shaking faintly. "I guess we found out..."

"I've never seen *anyone* swing blade than fast..."

"I could feel it flowing through me; following my commands, but at the same time guiding and *enhancing* my movements..." she gave a grunt of frustration, struggling to find a way to explain what she'd felt. "*God,* this would be *so* much easier to explain to a *Star Wars* geek..." she added softly, almost managing a wry smile as she fell back onto the pillows and stared up at the ceiling once more.

"Don't care how it happens..." Godfrey shrugged, coming to a very pragmatic decision regarding things he knew he was unlikely to understand any time soon. "Don't care *why* it happens... all I know is, whatever you did saved *all* our lives, and not for the first time. Call it Dragonfire... call it 'majik'... *whatever* it is, what worries me most is what *price* you had to pay to tap into this power. There's *always* a price – that much is clear – and *this* time it knocked you out for more than three days!"

"There wasn't any choice..." Nev replied quickly, lifting herself up onto her elbows once more as a wave of inexplicable guilt swept over her. "There were just too many of them for us to fight on our own!"

"I *know* that…!" He answered sharply, body language making it clear it wasn't her he was angry with. "I know that, but that doesn't make things any *easier*! I think that's the worst part about it: that without you – without this *power* you're somehow able to draw on – we'd have been completely *helpless*. What happens *next time*… or the time *after that*…? Are you out for *four days* afterward… *five*… a *week*…? Maybe…" he faltered, his voice almost cracking with a depth of emotion Nev had never expected "…*maybe*, next time you don't wake up at all… *ever*…"

"I… I – !"

Completely flustered and no longer knowing what to think, any answer Nev might've given was cut short as there was a sharp knock at the door on the opposite side of the room followed immediately by the appearance of Randwick's face as he opened it and poked his head in.

"Ah, lass… you're *awake*! You've no idea how happy I am to see that! We've a great deal to discuss, all of us... the queen *particularly* wants to speak to you… but we'll come to that when you've had a chance to get yourself dressed and get a bite to eat. Right *now*, I'm here for the lad…" He turned his attention toward Godfrey now. "Best get yerself out and about too, fella: Madam Boniface has arrived and I thought it best she speak to *you* before anyone else…"

"Gods on high… *already*…?" The boy blurted, leaping to his feet as a sudden wave of nervous fear washed through him.

"Aye, lad… already; and I've made sure no one's spoken to her yet. It's a raw deal for ye, but I know the Osterman's code well enough to know you'd want to be the one to tell her, whether you *want* to do it or not."

"I – uh…" Godfrey stammered, hugely conflicted now between honour and the magnitude of what was required of him. "I'll be out directly. Much as I'm not looking forward to it, it *should* be me all the same…"

"Good lad…" Randwick nodded approvingly. "She's waiting in the servants' chapel, 'round back near the ice well…" He grimaced. "Not a long walk from there, at least. I'll be in the main hall afterward, if you've need of counsel."

"You have my thanks, sir…"

"And *you, mine*…" The old man nodded in return, then turning to Nev and adding: "Milady…" by way of farewell before closing the door and striding off along the hallway beyond, boots ringing faintly on the stone.

"Who is it? Who do you need to see?" Nev asked, easily picking up the discomfort he was now displaying.

"It's Astrid: Lester's ma..." he explained, still staring at the closed doorway with fists balled tightly at his sides. "They must've found her among the peasants fleeing and brought her here. *Someone* has to tell her what's happened, and I was his mentor..."

"I'll come with you..." she declared without hesitation, moving to throw the covers off then remembering at the last moment her current dress – or lack thereof "...just *as soon* as I can get dressed."

"The duty falls to *me*..." he stated sadly, turning to stare at her with obvious pain in his eyes and tone.

"And *I'm* going to be right there with you when you do..." Nev countered firmly, not about to accept any argument. "Now *get out* while I put some clothes on!"

The servants' chapel, while decorated far more plainly and inexpensively than its nobleman's counterpart, was nevertheless far larger in actual area, the size necessary to accommodate the legion of maids, carpenters, groundsmen, guards and other hard-working 'ordinary' folk kept on staff to ensure the smooth running of the fortress' daily operations. Seats for at least five hundred filled almost endless rows on either side of the central aisle and even then there were usually two services performed on any given Sunday evening. As was the case with the smaller and more luxurious Royal Chapel, the one constant was another depiction of *Cleansing: The Coming of the Night Dragons*, this time a grand tapestry hung on the back wall, reaching all the way to the floor.

A simple structure of concrete, brick and iron, it was almost entirely empty now as Godfrey entered, Nev following close behind and now dressed in her original suede skirt and jacket, matching blouse and, for added warmth against the cool evening, the green cloak she'd been given on the first night of her arrival. As they stood at the main entrance and looked straight down the main aisle toward the small wooden pulpit at the far end, there was just one other person waiting inside.

Astrid Boniface looked to be in her early sixties, although Nev wondered how much younger the woman might actually be considering she'd undoubtedly experienced a far harder life than anything Nev had experienced back in her world. Short and stocky, her broad, weathered features were capped by a thick shock of once-red hair that had mostly faded to silver-grey, all tied down beneath a large scarf of plain white. Standing not far from the central dais, she turned toward them as they approached and both could see the streaks of tears on her face.

"He's gone, ain't he, Master Westacre…" she moaned softly, the words more a statement than a question as they drew near. "Cheeky little sod never would stray more 'n six feet from y' unless he was sick or dead, and it ain't the infirmary they've brought me to…"

"I'm sorry, missus…" Godfrey croaked thickly, bowing his head as he reached out and took her wrinkled hands in his. "T'were the heat of battle… I weren't fast enough t' save him. Silly bugger never would do what he was told…"

"Don't blame yerself, young'un…" She shook her head jerkily, shaking from emotion as she reached out and laid an unsteady hand on his shoulder. "He'd a' never been with ye in the first place if I hadn't turned him away… me own stupid fault and no one else's."

"Had he not been with us yesterday, good lady, *I* would not be here *now*…"

All turned at that completely unexpected voice to find Charleroi standing at the chapel entry, Randwick and William close behind her as escort.

"Your *Majesty*…!" Astrid exclaimed, almost overwhelmed with shock as she instantly sunk to her knees and lowered her eyes to the ground out of respect for the new queen.

"Your son saved my life, Mother Boniface…" She continued, walking slowly down the main aisle toward them in a flowing gown of dark blue cloth and simple design. "…saved *all* of us in our moment of greatest need…"

"…L-Lester…?"

"Your son is a hero of Huon, and he shall be remembered for it…" she continued, as both Nev and Godfrey pulled back to let her through. "Rise now, madam…" she added, reaching out to take Astrid's hands reluctantly in hers and guide the old women to her feet. "We're friends here, all: no need to kneel when you've already given so much."

"I abandoned him, Your Majesty…" the old woman croaked softly, tears streaming down her face now as Charleroi – standing at least a half-head taller – drew her in to a comforting embrace without hesitation. "I turned him out in my madness and grief, when he was all I had left in the world…"

"He loved you very much," Nev ventured then, her heart breaking as she saw the pain there in the eyes that stared back at her over the queen's shoulder. "Spoke about you just a few days ago, and *anyone* could see how much he still missed you…" she continued, thinking back over the discussion aboard *Sea Skimmer* that seemed an eon past now.

"We *all* carry with us the mistakes we make in this life, madam..." The queen murmured, tears in her eyes now too. "Things not done... words left unsaid until far too late. They'll haunt you by and by, at quiet times when you least expect it, but think not on them *now*: everything that happened before played its part in bringing your son to me these three days hence, and when I needed him – when *Huon* needed him – he didn't falter. I owe him my life, and I *promise* you the kingdom shall know of it. Long after this Blackwatch *scourge* is gone from our land, songs will be sung of how Squire Boniface saved the life of a queen."

"You – you're too kind, Your Majesty..."

"The honour is mine..." Charleroi countered quickly, hiding her nervousness over what next needed to be asked. "Now... if it's your wish – and *only* if it's your wish – it would *also* be my honour to escort you to the ice house so that you might pay him your last respects..."

"He – he's *here*...?"

"How could we have left him behind?" The queen croaked, voice thick with emotion as she thought of her own father's body, lying beside Lester's in that dark, cold resting place. "We've tended to him best we can, but it's *your* choice and yours alone whether you wish to see him before we send him to Dragonfall."

"I – I think it best that I do, *ma'am*..." Astrid decided reluctantly, clearly torn between the two options as she drew back slightly. "Much as it sickens me to think of him lying there, I owe him that at least... you'll come with me, won't you, Master Westacre?" She added, turning toward Godfrey with pleading eyes. "You always looked out for him... the *brother* he never had. I know he'd want you to be there..."

"'Course I will, missus..." he replied quickly, managing a weak smile. "...'Course I will..."

They moved off together as a group of three, the queen on one side and Godfrey taking the old woman's arm on the other as they moved toward the rear entrance, hidden behind the wall hanging behind the dais. William was there in an instant, pulling back the tapestry and opening the door to allow them passage before slipping out behind them, one hand on the sword at his belt and prepared for any danger.

Randwick, still limping slightly and otherwise labouring with recovery from the injuries he's taken during the battle three days earlier, had ambled down at a far slower pace and came to a halt beside Nev as she looked on with deep concern, not at all sure whether she should've stayed or gone with them. She stared at the huge tapestry for a moment, not really paying much attention to a faint rumbling within her subconscious that there was something disturbingly familiar about the whole thing.

"Good man you've got there, lass..." He observed quietly, also staring up at the wall it fell back into place, covering the door behind.

"Mmmh... wait, *what*...?" She almost yelped, not quite registering what he'd said at first, then managing an epic double-take. "I – *what*... no... I don't... don't know what you're talking about..." She blustered eventually, wondering exactly how badly she was blushing, as her traitorous cheeks suddenly felt *very* hot indeed.

"Aye... 'course you don't..." he smirked faintly, making a good job of keeping any sarcasm or condescension out of his tone. "...And that colour in y'r face is 'cause of the *sweltering* heat in here, I'm sure. He's the only one who's nae slept a wink since we got here..." the old man continued, softening his tone slightly. "The rest of us dreamed like babes, but not Westacre. I asked the palace staff when I awoke, and they told me true: never left your bedside once the whole time. Just sat there, lost as a lamb and *desperate* for a sign you was going to wake up again..."

"I..." she began, then her voice trailed off completely as Nev realised she had *absolutely* no idea what to say to any of that. It was all she could do to stare woodenly at the far wall, well aware that to look directly at the old man in that moment would be to give far too much away.

"Don't fret about it too much, lass..." he went on, accepting her silence with good grace. "I'll not give *your* secret away either. Written across your face for *anyone* to see, if you've a keen enough eye..." he confided, causing her heart to momentarily leap into her mouth with fear. "Takes a 'witch' to spy a Keepsake right enough, and I reckon it takes a man of a certain age – a certain *experience* – to recognise *real* love when he sees it."

"I – uh... I couldn't... this isn't..."

"...A good time...?" He finished for her, neither of them taking their gaze from a fixed point on the wall behind the dais as they spoke. "There's *never* a good time for these things," he shrugged, "but they often seem to work 'emselves out anyway. You're a smart lass... smarter than any woman *I've* ever met save for the queen, maybe... and you've got a few years' *life experience* on her too, which is nothin' t' be sneezed at. No doubt you're sharper than any *man* of your age *and* a good many *twice* as old." He gave a soft snort then. "*Not* that that's too difficult, most of the time. What I'm tryin' to say is..." he continued, almost sounding exasperated with his own meandering for a moment "...that the lad there would travel to the end of the known *world* if you bade him, and lay down his life for you when he got there. Now, that's not *necessarily* a bad thing..." he added, catching the soft gasp of drawn breath as she'd heard those words "...but it means that *you* need to be careful."

"I... I'm not sure what that means..." she admitted finally, forcing herself to turn her gaze to meet his for the first time as her voice and body shook with far too many conflicting emotions. "I'm nothing... *nobody*... just some *kid* who got caught up in someone else's insane dream."

"Well, you're no woman *yet*... not by the standards of *this* world at least," he conceded, managing to say so in a kind enough tone that she took no real offence. "But you're no *bairn* either, and *any* man with eyes and a heartbeat can see *that* well enough. One thing you're *also* not..." he continued, moving on quickly before what he just said could sink in completely "...is a *nobody*... and whatever it was you did out there on that battlefield... whatever power you were able to draw on through that crystal... *that* was a *long way* from *nothing* too. Mark my words, girl; you're bound for greatness before this is done. You've a way about you that commands loyalty in others... that brings inspiration... and even these last few days I've seen enough of it to see how *easy* it sits upon your shoulders, whether *you* know it or not. Seen it before: the kind others *believe* in... someone they'll follow to the house of Nethug himself and back..."

"I didn't ask for this..." Nev breathed softly, almost pleading with him as if Randwick might have some say in it all. "I didn't want *any of this...*"

"Course y' didn't... none of us do... but it's gonna happen regardless." He shrugged again. "Mebbe y' can't see it yet but you're a leader, not a follower, and it's that learning curve movin' from one t' the other that's usually the problem... does the most damage. Take it from someone who *has* lead men into battle: far too often, there's a time when a leader needs to make a choice between doin' their duty and protecting those they care about. If you're lucky – *really* lucky – you'll never have to face that choice, but *that* lad there: mark my words, he's gonna be either your greatest strength or y'r greatest downfall."

"Jesus, *no pressure...*!" Nev snapped eventually, feeling arising annoyance over the old man's words, not in the least part because of the accuracy of some of the statements regarding her own hidden feelings. "We've known each other – *what?* – a *week...*? I'm *seventeen*, for God's sake! Maybe that's old enough to be married off in *your* world, but in *mine* it's *barely* old enough to not be a *kid* anymore. I still go to *school*... used to hang out with my now *ex-best friend* (*the bitch!*)

watching HBO... *did kid's stuff*...! He's – *Godfrey's* a nice guy...*really* nice..." *gorgeous, actually*... she added silently, unable to stop herself for almost ranging off-topic for a moment, "but – but I can't think about *any* of this! I want to go home... *need* to go home! *Nothing else* matters!"

"Aye, you *say* that," he countered, recognising a fragile moment when he saw one and choosing his words carefully, "but you're *here* all the same. When you lot ran into me back at the inn, you were ready to follow the lad all the way back to Burnii to warn the king, and when the Blackwatch was streaming toward us at Stewpot Road, you charged at 'em without even a thought for your own safety. Like I said already; y' may not *know* it yet but there's a greatness in you that's *ragin'* t' be let out: y' can barely keep it inside y' even *now*. Your *head* tells you that *home's* the thing y' want, but *any* fool can see plain enough that y'r *heart's* cryin' out for *somethin' else*... something that's naught to do with the world you came from."

"I – I don't know what to say about *any* of that..." she mumbled, eyes lowered once more as she struggled to find some explanation for it all.

"I know y' don't, lass..." he grinned kindly, reaching out and placing a reassuring hand gently on her shoulder. "This is all new to ye and you're still findin' y'r feet sure enough, but you're only seventeen summers old and you've *already* won your first battle, saved the life of a queen and – *maybe* – saved an entire *kingdom* into the bargain! Dragonfall take me, what've we to look forward to *next week*...? Your fate's your own..." he added quickly, cutting off any likely reply "...just keep in mind there are *others* around ye, and *some o' them* are already hangin' off your every word. Men of honour – *decency* – are few and far between in this world: just don't take it for granted when you *find* one..."

Any response Nev could've given at that moment was cut short by the others' return as the door at the rear of the dais creaked open once more and William again threw back the drapes, holding them wide as Charleroi, Astrid and Godfrey came through behind him.

"This conversation is *so* not over..." She warned, glaring up at Randwick feeling *very* uncomfortable now that the primary subject of their discussion was present once more.

"Aye, lass... y' know how to find me well enough if you've a need..." the old man nodded with a half-smile and a faint wink that somehow eased a great deal of her embarrassment in spite of Nev's determination to feel vulnerable. "Just *think* on it rather that worry... but more of that *later*..."

"All's well, then...?" Godfrey asked openly as he left the old woman with the queen and approached the pair. Although he wasn't conscious of it, the body language they were displaying left his subconscious feeling that something was markedly different to when he'd left.

"Aye, lad, well enough..." Randwick replied evenly, not a hint of intrigue or secrecy in his tone or expression.

"More to the point, how are you...?" Nev asked quickly, honestly concerned and also not ashamed to use that feeling to head off any otherwise awkward questions by changing the subject.

"I – yeah, well enough..." he answered finally with a sign, a mixture of conflicting emotions flashing across his face. "She's taking it hard, but she's a tough old thing... she'll manage, I guess."

"And how are *you*...?" Nev persisted, completely genuine now with on ulterior motive as his emotional guard softened. "That can't have been *easy.*"

"It weren't..." he admitted, eyes flicking downward as he was momentarily unable to meet her gaze.

"Never is, lad..." Randwick agreed, having had to deliver such bad news too many times himself. "Takes a *special* kind o' courage, *trust me...*" They locked eyes then, and it was all the young man could do to prevent himself from breaking down completely as he gave a single, shaky nod of thanks.

"Come have some dinner with me...?" Nev asked softly, seeing the need for a change of subject. "I've not eaten *anything* in *days* and I'd *prefer* not to do it alone."

"Aye, there's a find idea indeed," the old man declared. "We've the funeral ceremony at sunset, but you've at least an hour or two before then. You *both* need a meal and *you* need some rest as well, lad! We're off at first light with a long ride ahead of us, and we'll *all* need our wits about us on the road now. Get out 'o here, *both o' ye*: I don't want t' see *either* of y' before dawn."

They'd set a funeral pyre for Phaesus later that night. There was no priest to speak at the ceremony – word had already spread that Cardinal De Lisle was in league both with Harald and with Baal, the usurper – and any members of The Brotherhood still at Cadle at the time of the invasion had been dealt with quickly and, in some case, quite terminally. Instead, it was Charleroi herself who'd officiated, giving a short, broken speech interspersed with numerous pauses as she fought to compose herself then forged on. Many of those who'd gathered about on that first night to pay their respects had shed a tear with her as their new queen bade her father farewell.

She'd stood on a small, wooden platform at the centre of the main courtyard as the fires had burned twenty metres behind, insisting Astrid Boniface stand at her side as the new, young queen extolled not only the virtues of her lost father but also the bravery of a young boy who'd given his all to protect her in her time of need. True to her word, Charleroi had declared Lester a Hero of Huon, had led three cheers to his memory, and had held his mother close as the roar of the crowd in return had reduced the old woman to tears.

Neither Nev nor Godfrey saw a moment of it. After sharing a hearty meal of thick lamb stew, both had retired to her room to talk, each taking one of the beds in turn and staring across at each other by the light of the crackling fire on the other side of the room.

"Your pendant – the one with the dragons..." Godfrey began slowly, broaching a subject that had been on his mind since he'd first laid eyes on it the day before. "Where did you come by it?"

"*This* one...?" Nev asked, lifting the heavy pendant from inside the neck of her blouse by the chain. "I've had it for *years*: it was a gift from my grandfather when I was little..."

"Does it *mean* something, or is it just for show?"

"It's based on Old Norse mythology. The central symbol with the radiating tridents represents the 'Helm of Awe': *Ægishjálmr*..." she explained softly, pronouncing it as '*eye-gis-hyowl-mer*' as she turned the thing over in her fingers. It's named for a magical helmet intended to paralyse or strike fear into the hearts and minds of your enemies."

"Fitting enough," he conceded with a nod, taking the information in his stride "...and the dragons?"

"They're the figureheads of longboats – ships traditionally rowed by Vikings in ancient times... my ancestors... why do you ask...?" She added, sensing there was reason behind his question.

"Brotherhood's been worried the last year or so about people getting about in the middle of the night painting stuff on doors and city walls... pictures of two-headed dragons..."

"Seriously... graffiti...? Have they nothing *else* to worry about?"

"Is that what they call it in your world?" Godfrey asked in return, getting the gist of what she was saying. "Everyone *thought* it were just wags mucking about at first..." he continued with a shrug "...but the – *graffiti?* – started to turn up more frequently... *especially* in places where there were more machines coming into use. My local command was definitely aware the Brotherhood were *very* concerned about the spread of machinery, and I *think* the two issues are linked in their minds."

"But, what's wrong with *dragons*...?" Nev pressed on with a frown, not seeing the point. "Aren't they an integral part of your whole mythology...*er*... *religion*...?" She added, correcting herself quickly.

"*Normal* dragons is one thing... *two*-headed dragons are a different thing altogether..." Godfrey explained with a wry grin. "You have churches where you come from, yeah? Like the Brotherhood...?"

"Not like the Brotherhood..." Nev answered hurriedly, *mostly* comfortable with that response "...but *yes*, we do have religion there... a number of them."

"They have an *evil* one? Someone or something at the centre of it that's the exact *opposite* of your gods... rotten to the core...?"

"Well... where *I'm* from, there's a creature they call 'Satan' or 'Lucifer'... a fallen angel in the mythology of that particular religion..." she replied, not bothering to mention she wasn't sure in *her* opinion that 'rotten to the core' ruled *anyone* out of being part of church hierarchy back home.

"Uh-huh..." Godfrey nodded, as if an expected piece of information had just dropped into place. "Well, *here* we have Nethug the Bicephalus..." he went on, giving another shrug.

"Let me guess: two heads...?"

"Got it in one..." he grinned. "The Book o' The Shard says that *Nethug* was the cause of the evil the Night Dragons were sent to wipe clean. There are prophesies in there that tell of a time when he'll rise again and try to destroy the Shard Gods, drawing all the evils of the world to his side."

"You sure that hasn't happened already...?" Nev asked with a wry smile, drawing a chuckle from him in return that left her feeling all warm in side. "The painting in the chapel...!" She exclaimed softly then, pleased she'd made the link all on her own. "*That's* Nethug? Nasty-looking thing," she added as Godfrey nodded in reply.

"Charming fella all 'round... they call him 'Soul-Destroyer' or 'Corpse-Eater': the story goes that he lives in the underworld, gnawing at the bones of the evil ones he's led astray..."

"Wait, say that again..." Nev urged suddenly, something he'd said resonating in the back of her mind.

"Say *what* again... that he lives in the underworld, gnawing at the bones of the evil ones he's led astray...?"

"Yeah... yeah, *that*...!" She nodded seriously, brows furrowing as she thought hard now, searching for the final link she knew was hiding in her thoughts somewhere. "*Why* does that sound *so* familiar...?"

"Well, maybe you heard someone..."

"*Niðhöggr*...!" She blurted suddenly, roughly pronouncing it as '*nithoggre*' in as close an approximation to the original Icelandic as she could manage. "This world *must* have a connection with *my* world somehow! It's not '*Nethug*'... it's *Niðhöggr*! They call him the Malice Striker: in Norse mythology, he's portrayed as a dragon-serpent who gnaws at the roots of *Yggdrasil*, the World Tree. The stories tell that he *also* chews on the corpses of murderers, adulterers and oath-breakers... all terrible crimes in Norse society of the time..."

"The *corpse-eater*..." Godfrey nodded thoughtfully, seeing where she was going with it. "Nethug and ... '*Nithogger*'...?" He ventured, not quite managing the pronunciation but coming close enough to see the similarities clear enough.

"Of course in the legends, *Niðhöggr* doesn't actually have *two heads*..." she conceded, willing to accept a little poetic licence, "but what else could it be...?"

"The Book predicts an 'evil one' 'll rise from the underworld one day, trying to destroy the Shard Gods and the world with them..." he mused, expanding on the original idea as a cheeky grin formed at the edge of his lips "...and now *you're* here, come from another world with a power The Brotherhood's never before seen and an *amulet* round y'r neck showing a two-headed dragon. It *does* seem an unlikely coincidence..."

"Are you implying I eat *souls*, sir...?" Nev asked with mock indignation, head falling back onto her pillow as she stared up at the ceiling and tried not to laugh.

"*Never*, Milady..." Godfrey shot back in an instant, also laying back on his own bed with hands behind his head for support. "Although..." he ventured tentatively, trying to maintain his cheekiness but suddenly feeling much more nervous "...I warrant the soul comes *willingly* once you've taken the *heart* captive..."

"I – !" Nev began, starting to speak before the impact of what he'd just said actually hit home, and she was left *completely* speechless, certain her cheeks were positively *glowing* in the dark room.

"I'm... *glad*... you're awake... that you're all right..." Godfrey murmured eventually, turning his head toward her as she met his gaze.

"I'm... glad you're *here*... *with me*..." Nev replied falteringly, unable to think of anything more to say at that moment that could've better conveyed how she felt.

They lay silent for a long time, staring into each other's eyes as the fire across the room crackled softly in the hearth and cast a faint orange glow throughout the room. Nev imagined that if only it were possible to forget for a few moments the terrible events of the last few days, the two of them lying there alone, talking so softly and deeply might've seemed *incredibly* romantic. Both of them were of course snoring heartily five minutes later.

She awoke shivering in the early hours of the next morning to find the fire had died in the hearth, although enough of a glow remained for her to restart it with some kindling and another large log taken from a pile stacked to one side. Taking a moment to drag a thick quilt over Godfrey as he slept on the other bed, she quickly rummaged through her bag, still shivering, found her phone and then returned to her own bed and snuggled back under her own covers, waiting for the warmth of the fire to return.

She thought for a moment that perhaps it might be worth getting undressed, but a check of the time on the *iPhone's* lock screen put paid to that idea. Already five in the morning and dawn couldn't be more than an hour away, something she confirmed with a glance out through the uncurtained window at a night sky clearly already lightening with the approach of sunrise.

Cadle... resting at Cadle... resting, resting, resting...

The whispered thought slipped almost unnoticed through her mind. Had it not been for the momentary flicker of the crystal at her throat, she might've thought nothing of it at all, but that single flash of bright blue was enough to put her mind instantly on alert.

"Who are you...?" She hissed softly, keeping her voice as low as possible so as not to disturb Godfrey. Reaching out with her mind even as her fingers rested unconsciously on the pendant itself, Nev allowed herself the weakest of connections with the Shard, holding everything back for fear of losing herself as she had at the Battle of Stewpot Road. "*What* are you...?"

Not even a 'thank you'...? After all, I did save your life... There was more substance to the voice now – enough this time to recognise it – and with a soft groan of disgust, Nev rolled over to face the window on the near wall.

"Oh, *you*... who *else* would it be...?"

There was a faint glow from the corner of the room as a blue haze appeared, shimmering and translucent like the CGI holograms Nev had seen in so many science fiction movies. This time however, it was clearly Percy standing before her with her arms expectantly crossed.

You were expecting Luke Skywalker, perhaps? She asked with a wry half-smile, extending her arms with palms open. *Loki...? James Tiberius Kirk...?*

"Leave me alone, you *bitch...*" she shot back, not even bothering to look at Percy as the apparition swayed and faded in and out. "This is *all* your fault! And what do you *mean*: you 'saved my life' anyway?" She added quickly, anger growing as what Percy had said just sunk in. "You've been trying to do the exact *opposite* since the moment I got here!"

LOL...! You think you managed to take out those big, beefy Blackwatcher boys all by yourself, do you? Percy asked drily, not bothering to hide the derision in her tone. *Hack your way through a couple of dozen well-trained swordsmen, then focus enough Shard power to blow up a warship a couple of kilometres away...? Oh yes, that was* all *you... all you, who's never seen* or *used a crystal before that night on the* Rapier!

"Liar...!" Nev snapped, trying to ignore the logic in her words. "Why would you keep helping *me* when you've already said yourself how much you 'hate me', and how you want to get your 'revenge'...?"

Well, you need to 'level up', of course... Where's the fun in revenge if I'm up against some sooky little 'noob' with no skills and whose only ability is to wander around the countryside moaning 'poor me' to every hunky, young Ryan Gosling lookalike that wanders past...?

"Piss off...!"

That boost of energy you felt out on the Stewpot Road, the moment you opened yourself up to the crystal's full power...? That was *me, you understand? The whole time those old farts were pooling their energy just trying to* block *you from healing the king, I'd 'hacked' in through one of their crystals and 'piggybacked' it right through to the source. They have* no idea *how much power that thing* really *has... although I think that with my help,* you *got a glimpse of a part of it.*

"You still haven't answered my question..." Nev growled petulantly, interested now in spite of herself and propped up in bed by her elbows as Percy affected to sit upon an invisible chair and casually cross her legs beneath a long, flowing skirt.

What... about why I'm helping you? I want a decent enemy... I told *you. These* men *are such fools...* she added, spitting out the word 'men' as if it were a vile profanity. *Here* or *in our world, they're* all *pigs... petty and small-minded and thinking they're* so much better *than all of us. A woman... a* clever *woman with enough power of her own... could control* all *of these idiots.*

"And this Shard God or whatever it is will just let this all happen, will it?" Nev asked dubiously, shuddering as she recalled her last encounter with that booming voice as she fought vainly to save Phaesus' life.

Oh, they know about it all right: they want *me to destroy these fools. The Shard Gods can see it... see it all so clearly. They're sick to death of these morons and their misogynist ways, and they've chosen me to burn all of them. You and this silly 'queen-child' of yours are the* perfect *distraction, and while they're scampering about all over Huon trying to find the pair of you, fighting for every mile and bleeding themselves white, I'll be waiting in the background, building my power and waiting for my chance to strike...*

"Why would you tell *me* this, of all people?" Nev pointed out, almost smiling. "What's stopping me from telling *them* everything you've just said...?"

Oh no! Help... help... you got me monologuing...! Percy actually giggled then. *Sweetie, please* do, *by all means: tell 'em anything you like. It'd be almost worth it to see the look on your face afterward. Have you learned* nothing *about this world yet? Like me, you're just a* girl *to them – not even a woman – and* surely *you've seen already how* little *respect they have for women here? You could go full Chicken Little, running around screaming 'the sky is falling' 'til you were blue in the face, and they'd not even bat an eyelid as a comet came howling right down on top of them. They'd torture you...* rape *you too, no doubt... hurt you in so* many *ways just for fun... but they'd never believe that: that a mere* girl *like you or I could* ever *be a threat.*

"Are you even really here?" Nev asked sourly, pulling a face as she glanced down at the crystal about her neck, still flashing faintly in time with every word Percy spoke. "Can *anyone* see this, or are you just in my mind...?"

Oh, who cares? No one else's business anyway... I just thought I'd drop in to check on an 'old friend'... make sure you're safe and sound...

"What, and find out *where I am* into the bargain, so they can send the Blackwatch after me?" She snarled softly, remembering those first words in her head. "That was what you were talking about to begin with: where I was – what I was doing. Checking up on me for your filthy *new* friends are you?"

That *lot couldn't find their own arses with both hands and a GPS...* Percy sniffed with disdain *...and they're coming to Cadle soon enough* regardless *of whether* you're *there or not. Just found myself at a loss for something to do at five in the morning and thought I'd check* *in with my best friend. We used to text each other* all the time *when we were bored.*

"*That* was before you *betrayed* me by dragging me to this godforsaken little world and nearly getting me killed… *several times…*!"

Oh, tell someone who cares…! Like the old world was so wonderful… like Wonthaggi *wasn't the arse-end of existence anyway! Train, school, study, work… train, school, study, work… that's all you ever* did! *You complain about your life now; what life did you have* back there? *Seventeen years old and you've never even* kissed *a boy yet!* She sneered, throwing a nod in Godfrey's direction. *One week* here *and you've* already *got 'Will Scarlett' there following you around like a love-struck puppy!*

"Shut up!" Nev hissed, too angry to hide the fact that Percy had struck a *very* raw nerve.

Have you kissed him *yet? Bet you haven't…!*

"Shut up, you *bitch…*!" She screamed out loud, the crystal flaring brightly for just a fraction of a second as a wave of energy burst from Nev's mind and dissolved the image of Percy into oblivion.

Woken abruptly by her shout, the apparition had disappeared completely by the time Godfrey was fully alert and fumbling for the sword he'd laid on the floor by the bed.

"What? What is it…?" He barked, brandishing the blade wildly as he turned this way and that, shaking his head to clear his thoughts as he searched for some unseen enemy.

"It – it's okay…" Nev stammered, crying now that the situation was over and she was able to release all the tension she'd been secretly holding inside the entire time. "A bad dream… just a bad dream…"

"By The Crystal, you gave me a start there…!" Godfrey breathed, chest heaving from unexpected adrenalin as he lowered the blade and dropped it onto the mattress in relief. Walking around to sit beside her on the edge of her own bed, he reached out and carefully pulled the covers up around her neck and shoulders against the cold. "Are you all right…?" He asked gently, deeply concerned by her tears and the obvious sheen of light perspiration on her forehead. "Do you want to talk about it?"

"Just a stupid nightmare…" She grumbled softly, fearful of meeting his gaze in case she might somehow give herself away. "Nothing important…"

"You should try to get some more sleep," he ventured, rubbing his eyes and stifling a yaw.

"No point..." she shrugged, throwing a nod toward the brightening sky beyond the open window. "Going to be dawn soon and we need to start getting ready.

"Well, *that* hardly seems fair!" He declared with a grin. "A whole night gone and it barely feels like I've slept a *wink*! Nothing a good, hot bath and a solid breakfast won't fix though, eh? I should go get the rest of my gear and freshen up."

"Can you stay a while...?" She blurted far too quickly as he made a move to get up, cursing her embarrassment even as her hand reached out to rest on his. "Just a bit longer...? I..."

She was scared... scared to be alone for fear that awful apparition might show itself again... but she found she couldn't find the words to explain that she couldn't bear the thought of him leaving the room at that moment – that right there and then, his company was all she needed.

"'Course I can..." he answered with a smile, matching her gaze with one that seemed to reach right into her soul as he took her hand in his, fingers entwined. "...as long as you want..."

"She's at Cadle..." Percy wheezed, almost bend double as she fought to recover her breath. The force of Nev's mental blast had well and truly knocked the wind out her sails. "*Whoo*, she's a feisty little minx! If that girl ever realises how much power she actually has, you lot are in *real* trouble!"

"Yes, yes... *terrible danger*, I'm sure..." De Lisle snapped curtly, clutching at a warm mug of tea as if it were some magical talisman against the chilly morning. "You were 'gone' for some time: is there anything *else* you might want to share? What their plans are, for example? Are they *staying* at Cadle?"

Percy's tent was one of a dozen large and very generic, eight-man canvas models erected not far from the beach as part of Harald's Burnii command centre. She'd been given one to herself in deference to her need for modesty, although placing its only entrance directly opposite the cardinal's had seriously restricted any feeling of actual freedom to at least come and go as she pleased. The tent itself was serviceable enough with a cot, blankets and a few pieces of fold-up furniture along with a small, cast-iron stove at the centre, its flue exhausting straight out through a reinforced opening in the roof.

"Of *course* they're not staying," she replied with a grimace, thinking the answer an obvious one. "Harald's *bound* to head for the fortress eventually, and a single battery of cannon will reduce those walls to rubble in *minutes*. They're not stupid enough to think they can keep the queen safe *there*."

"The army marches on the hour," De Lisle grunted thoughtfully, not telling her anything she didn't already know. "But it's a solid two day's march at best... *plenty* of time for them to make an escape. The Blackwatch has been trying to lock down all the major crossroads heading south but there terrain's too rough and too thick with trees to monitor effectively, and there are too many places where small groups could sneak past undetected."

"Then they're going to slip through... simple as that," she shrugged, not caring in the slightest. "I got the sense they were *definitely* preparing to move out, but *nothing* as to where or in what direction. I doubt they'd tell *her* that anyway, and she probably wouldn't recognise any of the place names if they did."

"And that's *all* you got out of it... after *all* that time...?" The cardinal growled suspiciously, eyes narrowing as if daring her to lie to his face.

"*Yes*, that's all I got..." she replied, doing exactly that. "She wasn't exactly in the mood for chit-chat... although I can't imagine *why*: there's nothing quite like being visited by a blue 'ghost' in your quarters at five in the morning to inspire great conversation..."

"It is *said* that *sarcasm* is the lowest form of wit..." De Lisle pointed out, scowling darkly.

"Really...?" Percy countered, making no effort to moderate her sarcasm whatsoever. "I'd have thought *not being funny* was the *lowest* but then, what do *I* know...?"

"Just keep track of her," he replied tartly, turning to leave and throwing one last instruction over his shoulder. "I'll expect you with me at the head of the column in an hour's time..."

"Looking forward to it..." she called back, but he was already gone.

The rest of the group were already ready and waiting as Nev and Godfrey finally stepped out through the main doors of the palace itself into the bright light of a crisp, cold morning with bags over their shoulders. Randwick sat astride a large stallion at the head of the column, dressed in a fresh set of chain-mail and boiled leather armour, a sword at his belt and his beloved staff slung diagonally across his back, held snugly in place by a leather thong. He wore no hat or helmet, his long grey hair tied loosely at the back of his neck.

William's horse stood next in line, the younger man resplendent in a pristine new set of armour and the same style of white uniform and blue piping he'd worn the first day they'd met, lance once again at his side, standing upright and mounted in a specially-fitted socket fixed to the right side of his saddle. Tied to the lance's shaft just below its pointed steel tip, a large, triangular pennant of bright blue fluttered lightly in the breeze, displaying the falcon's head of the Huon family crest. Both horse and man seemed nervous and eager to be off, his mount snuffling and tramping its feet as it swayed this way and that as if ready to break into a gallop at any moment.

Queen Charleroi waited third in the group, her appearance a marked change from anything Nev had seen in the last few days. Dressed plainly in khaki breeches and a loose-fitting cotton blouse of dark green, her only bodily protection of any kind appeared to be a light vest of fine, silvered mail worn over the top, the whole ensemble covered by a long woollen coat of dull brown for use against the morning chill. A khaki riding cap that was at least a size too large had been snugged tightly over her ears, beneath which her long, dark hair hung heavy behind her in a single 'fishtail' of intricate plaits. A short, jewel-encrusted rapier hung at her belt beneath the long coat while across her back hung a large recurve bow and a quiver full of arrows.

Behind those three, a troop of four guardsmen in uniforms identical to William's waited patiently, their own lances also displaying the same bright blue royal pennant. Four more horses without riders also stood idly by, two clearly intended as pack animals, their backs and multiple saddlebags loaded with a variety of supplies, while the other two wore saddles like the rest.

"No guesses as to who they're waiting for..." Godfrey grinned, resting a comforting hand gently on Nev's back as they stood for a moment on the entrance steps and took in the scene.

"Just give me a moment..." she breathed softly, suddenly captivated by the impressive majesty of the sight and already fumbling inside her jacket pocket for her phone. "I *so* need to get a photo of this!"

"I'll get the horses..." he suggested with a nod, accustomed enough to her eccentricities by now to accept the statement in his stride. "Let's not keep the queen waiting *too* long, yes?"

As he jogged across the cobblestones to the pair of riderless horses and took the reins, she turned the *iPhone* sideways and filmed a long, panoramic shot of the entire courtyard, taking in not only the mounted party but also the crowd gathering to see them off, one that must've numbered at least two dozen and growing (not counting guards watching from the ramparts themselves).

"Mistress Nevaeh, I assume what you hold is this 'phone' device Randwick has told me so much about?" Charleroi called brightly from the saddle, dragging on her reins ever-so-slightly to bring her mount around toward Nev's direction. "I should *very* much like to *see* this fantastical machine in greater detail..."

"It would be my pleasure, Your Majesty," Nev replied quickly, recognising a royal command well enough when she heard one and lowering the phone once more as Godfrey approached with her horse.

"Perhaps at a more opportune time, Ma'am..." Randwick suggested as Nev proceeded to lift herself into the saddle, Godfrey holding the beast steady for her then slinging her sports bag across behind her and tying it down with the saddle strings on either side. "We've had reports of Blackwatch scouts on the Burnii Road south of Bolivar and it's only a matter of time before they march on Cadle."

"Of course, of course..." She conceded with a nod, acceding to his advice. "I'd have you ride with *me* this morning, mistress, if Master Godfrey has no objections...?"

"N – no, Your Majesty... none at all... of course..." He blustered awkwardly, both of them reddening slightly as he quickly mounted his own horse.

"Excellent... it's settled then! Sir William: if you'd do the honours...?"

"Ma'am..." he replied instantly, bowing his head and raising a hand to his hat brim in salute before trotting his horse past Randwick's to take the head of the line. "*Company...*!" He bellowed, lifting himself off the saddle and standing in the stirrups as he turned to call the rest of his men. "Move out... scouting formation! Duclos to point! *For Huon...*!"

"*For Huon...*!" The entire troop of guardsmen echoed loudly in chorus, one of them – presumably Duclos –urging his mount forward and galloping ahead, out through the open main gates with lance lowered and ready. Another trooper fell in beside William, the pair leading the rest of the group out in twos with the remaining two guardsmen bringing up the rear, leading the pack horses.

"*For Huon...! For Huon...!*" Trumpets blared from somewhere up on the battlements, giving fanfare to their departure, and all around the crowd chanted that call, echoing the guardsmen and adding their cheers as the royal party rode out.

"Far to go, Master Randwick...?" Godfrey asked as the troop wound its way northward along the main trail leading away from the fortress at Peaceful Lake.

"Eight miles to the Bolivar Road, give or take," the old man answered after a moment's thought, "and you saw on the way in how it winds through those mountains. Better part of two hours' ride, but it's *after* we reach Bolivar that I'm worried about…"

"Blackwatch…"

"Aye, lad… Blackwatch, right enough… Sixteen miles more of up hill and down dale before we reach the Burnii Crossroads to the west – another four hours during which time we're heading *into* danger rather than away. No reports of those black-shirted bastards that far south *yet*, but their scouts have been spotted as far down as Parra and Hampshire and that's already too close for my liking. They're sure to be marching on Cadle by now and it'll be hard luck for us if they make the crossroads in force before we can pass through."

"Can we go around – push through the scrub instead, maybe…?"

"Aye, we can…" he conceded with a nod, eyes never leaving the road ahead, "but the forests there are as thick as anything you'll come across, and taking *that* route would cost us hours we don't have. I know its springtime now across The Osterlands, but you'd know as well as any how cold it gets down even then, and it's been a *very* cold winter this year. We get caught in the bush overnight and it'll be light a fire or die sure enough, and the light and the smoke from *that* would be seen for *miles* on a clear night…"

"And then south from the crossroads…?"

"Aye, south indeed: I'd *hope* to make Zeehn by nightfall – William has family there and we'll be well be looked after well – but Renison would do at a pinch… don't really care so long as we've somewhere safe and warm for the night. On to Strahn again at first light: I'm *hoping* we'll have a ship waiting when we arrive…"

"'*Hoping*…?'" Godfrey queried, not sure the old man sounded all that confident.

"*More* than a hope…" Randwick grunted, almost allowing himself a grin. "I've a *friend* who's been waiting for us the better part of a week now. S'posed to meet him at Sternley three nights ago but Harald and his cursed lot ruined all that. Instructions were, if we didn't show he was to make for Strahn and wait for my signal. Can't expect him to wait *forever*, but we've a few more days before we need to worry, I think."

"And assuming all goes to plan, where *then*…?"

"Workin' on it…." He replied cryptically, not ready to give too much away just yet despite sensing instinctively the boy could be trusted. "Safest direction right now is west, but only if y' can slip past the Blackships that'll be *guaranteed* to be swarming all over the Deepwater right now. Hard to tell what the reception'll be at the other end either: Croweda might not be particularly *fond* of Harald but they'll not be stupid enough to cross him by helping *us* – *particularly* now he's got these damned cannon as leverage."

"A lot of unknowns, master..." Godfrey observed, trying to sound optimistic but not really managing.

"Aye, lad... more than I'd like and that's the honest truth, but it's all we've got right now and I need to make sure the queen's safe before we even *begin* to think about anything else. *Another* thing..." he added, turning his head at locking eyes with Godfrey for the first time. "Y' can lose that 'Master Randwick' business now. No one's called me by 'Foucault' since I were in junior school, but y' can just use 'Randwick' or *kinsman* if you're at a loss for anything better: you fought hard beside me at Stewpot and you've earned that right, sure enough. Kinsman...?" He added, bringing his mount close in and extending his arm with a nod of encouragement.

"Kinsman...!" Godfrey acknowledged eventually, initially reluctant but urged on by the older man's sincerity as he turned and leaned over in the saddle to accept the offered hand in offered friendship. "Well met..."

"Well met indeed...!"

It's a fine blade you carry, Mistress Nevaeh..." Charleroi observed as the pair of them rode together, a few metres behind the other two. "Master Randwick tells me it's of a design similar to those used by the Sun Empire in the north, but of a quality he's never before seen."

"It's definitely a special one, Your Majesty..." Nev agreed with a nod, trying not to cringe too much over the queen's use of her full name. "It was given to me as a gift from my *sensei* – the man who taught me how to use it. The blade's almost seven hundred years old."

"A fine blade *indeed* then... and you use it well: I saw *that* clearly enough at Stewpot Road. Randwick hasn't told me *much* about who you are – I suspect he doesn't know all that much himself – but what little he *has* said suggests you're not *from* here... not from *anywhere* around here..."

"Not even close, Your Highness..." she answered with a wry smile, not bothering to explain how much of an understatement that was.

"Please... I know it's not 'proper' in public to call me by name, but at *least* use 'ma'am' or 'milady' instead... it seems *ridiculous* for you to have to keep saying 'Your Majesty' of 'Your Highness' every second sentence, *especially* considering what we've already been through together..."

"I – of course... *Ma'am*..." Nev stammered, not *about* to think about how ridiculous it sounded to use that term to address a girl almost a year her junior. "*You* saved *me* once or twice during the battle too..." she added, recalling the image of Charleroi standing atop the log barricade, firing a succession of deadly-accurate arrows into the Blackwatch clustered about Nev as she'd slashed this way and that with her katana. "You *really* know how to shoot!"

"I've Randwick to thank for that..." Charleroi replied with a smile, both forced to raise their voices over the clatter of hooves and the clank and jangle of armoured troopers riding. "I spent *sixteen years* locked up in that castle, and it was either learn things like archery with *him* or *needlepoint* and crochet with one of my handmaidens... not a difficult choice to make, all things considered..."

"*Wow*..." Nev chuckled to herself, finding vague amusement in a joke no one else was likely to understand. "Nerds must've been *scary* before computers!"

XX

KINDRED SPIRITS

Strahn... a remote hamlet of a few hundred people on the wild, west coast of Huon where rather than the great fishing fleets of the north, it was logging ships usually at anchor in her sheltered port; the great forest pines and hardwoods growing there being greatly prized for construction and shipbuilding alike. The town lay at the northern end of Mockery Inlet, a long, shallow body of water that opened out onto the Southern Sea through a treacherously narrow mouth known locally as the Devil's Doorway, ten kilometres south-west of Strahn. Navigating that entrance during rough seas or weather was tantamount to suicide, yet such was the attraction of a hold filled with fine hardwood logs that dozens of vessels made that very voyage every year, sailing in from right across The Osterlands.

Some would never return, but there were riches to be made for those who did and there was always a surplus of cocky captains and plucky crews ready to try. It was for that reason in particular that Randwick and the rest had struck out south-west from Cadle as Harald had continued to solidify his beachhead at Burnii and amassed his forces in preparation for the long march that would precede any assault upon that great mountain fortress.

Ocean Breeze had been the main reason Randwick had decided to head for the wilderness of Huon's west coast in the first place. Ismail Farouk had waited another two days at Sternley before finally deciding to cut and run for safer harbours further south as news of the invasion began to spread. A Blackwater gunboat had sailed into the bay without warning on the evening of that second day and proceeded to shell the docks for a solid half-hour, destroying most of the structures there and leaving that part of town burning furiously.

The ship had escaped damage but the writing was surely on the wall so far as Farouk was concerned and they'd put out to sea by first light, sailing hard for The Takers, an archipelago of rocky islands that lay off the north-western tip of Huon, before turning southward once more for the relative safety of colder climes. The '*Breeze* had finally rowed its way through the Devil's Doorway two days later, taking advantage of a few hours' dead calm to sneak through that narrow causeway into Mockery Inlet.

By contrast, the journey south by land had been remarkably uneventful. The royal escort had ridden hard from the fortress that first day, pushing westward along the Belvoir Road past streams of refugees from all walks of life, most of them also from Cadle and the surrounding countryside. By noon they'd reached the Burnii Crossroads; an unremarkable enough intersection surrounded by thick, forested woodland that to everyone's surprise and relief still remained free of enemy forces.

After a short break at a nearby reservoir to water the horses, the troupe was back on the road again, this time turning south along the Merchant's Town High Road, a narrow carriageway of hard-packed earth and broken patches of tarred surface that wound its way between mountain ranges even more arduous than those they'd left behind. The stream of displaced refugees continued to grow, bolstered by hundreds more coming south from Burnii itself. News had already spread of the king's death and the slow-moving crowds were abuzz with excitement as the queen and her entourage passed by, although it would've been fair to say there were also many shocked by the fact that Charleroi and another unidentified young woman were clearly travelling without visards as protection against the danger of Keepsakes.

Well aware of the reaction that situation was likely to stir up, Randwick remained alert and watchful as a hawk as they'd rode on, and he found himself repeatedly casting a careful eye on William whenever the young officer wasn't likely to notice. The boy had been quite vocal in his opposition when the queen had first declared she'd most definitely *not* be wearing any kind of mask during the journey, and although he'd since kept his mouth shut throughout the ride, the old man nevertheless had a growing suspicion that it was weighing heavily on the guard-captain's mind. Randwick also suspected that hadn't been helped as a number of women of common and noble birth, having noted the queen's lack of visard and the alleged involvement of The Brotherhood in Harald's invasion, had also decided to toss aside their own blindfolds.

Randwick been happy to lose most of the evacuees near the Roseberry Crossing, another otherwise nondescript crossroads where their journey once more turned west toward Zeehn while most of the refugees continued on southward along the high road, making for the safer communities of Glen Anarchy or Arthur's Port on the far south coast: the lesser the crowds, the lesser the danger of awkward questions or of running across some Blackwatch assassin hidden amongst them.

It was mid-afternoon by then and although civilian traffic had thinned out, the escort's ranks had swelled with an influx of additional troops, both mounted and on foot. The shattered remnants of a number of Huon military units had withdrawn from Burnii among the fleeing crowds and many of these had gravitated toward William and the guardsmen as they came through. By the time they reached Zeehn at dusk on that first day, their modest troupe of nine had grown to a small company of foot soldiers and mounted cavalry from at least half-a-dozen different units, all tired and hungry but nevertheless somewhat invigorated by the presence of their new queen and incensed by the news of Baal's betrayal and Phaesus' assassination.

William's family were dairy farmers, and he'd been welcomed with open arms and much emotion from his parents as he'd led the troupe up the rutted dirt track leading past the main farmhouse. Nev and Charleroi had been taken into their home (the fuss made over their son's arrival had quickly paled into insignificance as the queen had made her presence known), and the rest of the company had been provided with food and drink aplenty as a makeshift camp had been set up in the large field out front of the residence.

The bivouac that night was loud and raucous and filled with alcohol and song as the men of Huon – just as soldiers elsewhere were doing in that universe or any other – gathered together to rekindle old friendships and forge new ones, all the while making the most of one precious moment of peace and quiet to celebrate the fact that whatever the new day might bring, right at *that* moment they were very much alive and *very* prepared to make the most of it. The royal party heard little of the celebrations however, all of them exhausted from a hard day's ride and in any case still recovering from the dramatic events of the preceding few days.

They were ready to move out again by first light, many nursing hangovers and wincing at the blinding brilliance of the morning sun as sergeants-at-arms moved this way and that, screaming orders at all and sundry with an intensity that bordered on mania. Two dozen cavalrymen waited patiently in paired columns to one side as close to eighty more foot-soldiers hastily formed themselves into ranks of ten, sounding off in preparation for morning inspection.

It as mid-morning as the long lines of marching soldiers finally tromped down the last hill into Strahn, the entire town lining the main street to welcome them with Queen Charleroi at their head. There was some scattered cheering and the occasional waving of royal pennants, but for the most part the mood was one of subdued apprehension. News of the invasion had already reached the town with the first of the refugees that had begun to appear over the last few days, and the arrival of the new queen heading *away* from the enemy with a rag-tag collection of dirty and bedraggled troops didn't instil a great deal of confidence.

A small fort stood at the water's edge on the other side of town, positioned on a small, rocky peninsula at the centre of the 'Y-shaped' section at the northern end of the inlet where it split off into two separate, far smaller bodies of water. With a three-storey 'tower' barely tall enough for a platoon of coast-watchers to look out across the water over its two-metre stone walls, the barracks buildings within were far too small to accommodate over a hundred men, although some rooms were naturally cleared for the queen and her personal entourage. The rest of the company pitched camp that afternoon in the middle of a large, open expanse of foreshore outside the fort's main gates, their tents for the most part within a short walk of a narrow, sandy beach that opened out onto the cold, dark waters of Mockery Inlet.

The bay itself, although narrow-sided to the east and west, stretched away for many kilometres to the south, the distant shorelines little more than a vague, black-green line beyond the morning haze hanging over the water. The town itself had seemed relatively plain and as 'normal' as any such village might presumably be in a world she'd only arrived in a week ago. There were the same rudimentary stone and mud brick houses that were found everywhere else on the island, although the hard-packed earthen streets seemed substantially cleaner than she'd seen in Burnii or on the mainland.

Villagers made their way back and forth, going about their business in side streets and back alleys beyond the small crowd that had gathered to watch the procession roll in. Carts and hand-trolleys carrying wares and supplies squeaked and rattled up and down between the buildings, and near the centre of town was the ubiquitous temple of The Brotherhood, looking as church-like in general design as anything she'd seen back home. The only difference in this particular case however was that the insignia of the brotherhood – an unmistakable blue diamond obviously intended to represent the image of a Shard Crystal – had been torn down from above the front entrance and now lay smashed and abandoned on the street outside. It seemed that news of De Lisle's betrayal had preceded them and had been received with as much outrage and condemnation there as it had at Cadle.

The only other thing of note as they rode on to the fort was a large and rather inexplicable object left abandoned on the foreshore itself, perhaps two hundred metres east of the barracks walls. Little more than a rusted, skeletal frame, it had presumably once been some kind of vessel run aground – at least, Nev assumed that must've been the case based on its appearance, position and approximate size.

It must've been many decades old judging by the level of degradation, yet was clear enough that *someone* still considered it to be dangerous as the entire site had been cordoned off by white rope suspended by stakes driven into the ground at regular intervals at a safe distance around its circumference. Making a single mental not that the ropes and stakes appeared to be identical to the one's she'd come across surrounding an overgrown mound in the middle of the field on that first morning after she'd arrived, Nev otherwise gave it no further thought as the troop continued on toward the fort and a good chance of more rest.

She was led into a small bunkroom fifteen minutes later. Situated inside the main building behind the watchtower, the interior comprised little more than a pair of bunk beds on either side with a plain wooden chair and a small writing desk in the centre of the far wall. High up in the stone wall above the desk, a narrow window allowed a bare minimum of sunlight to filter through to illuminate an otherwise dreary environment. Nev suspected it had perhaps been used by junior officers, that deduction mainly stemming from the fact that it was directly adjacent to the far more spacious quarters of the commanding officer, which had of course been made available to the queen.

There was no one in the short hallway outside as she poked her head out and took a quick look around, feeling distinctly abandoned and a little on edge over being left alone in a strange place. Godfrey was outside somewhere, helping to organise the troops at William's request, while the queen had retired to her newly-acquired room opposite. Of Randwick there was no sign at all: he'd ridden off to the north within minutes of their arrival, having taken just enough time to make certain the queen was looked after and well-protected before his departure. She knew there'd be guards outside the door at the end of the hall leading out into the courtyard, but that section of the barracks otherwise seemed to be completely deserted.

Nev almost fell backward into her room with fright as the door opposite was suddenly flung open and the queen also poked her head out into the hallway with a broad and distinctly mischievous smile on her face.

"Not doing anything, are you?" Charleroi asked eagerly, casting her eyes up and down the hall to confirm her initial assessment that they were indeed alone.

"Um... *no*...?" Nev ventured cautiously, not at all sure she should be talking to a queen without others present... particularly one who seemed to be acting very strangely in comparison to the poise and demeanour she'd displayed every other time they'd been together.

"Excellent...!" Charleroi stated emphatically, immediately disappearing back inside her quarters as the door swung slowly closed once more, leaving Nev standing in her own doorway with a decidedly bewildered expression on her face.

"Um..." she mumbled again, not at all sure what to do next.

"Well *come on then*...!" Charleroi exclaimed, appearing just as unexpectedly for a second time and pushing Nev even closer to a nervous coronary. "Do I *have* to make it an order? *That's* no way to become friends!"

"Um... *okay*...?" She managed eventually, drawing on every ounce of her public-speaking skills as the queen drew the door back even wider to allow her entry.

The room beyond that door was definitely fitted out for a commanding officer. A huge, leather-topped desk formed the centrepiece surrounded by a trio of large, upholstered armchairs, while a huge set of bay windows behind were bordered by long drapes in Huon blue. A large rack of swords, crossbows and other weapons stood against one wall – all of them dusty enough to clearly be for ceremonial use only – while against the other stood a rather ostentatious four-poster bed that by Nev's reckoning was at least a king-single in size. Several large logs crackled merrily away in a large stone fireplace next to the weapon display and above the mantle, a large oil painting depicted some battle scene that was so generic it could've hung in the officer's mess of any half-decent army *anywhere* back home. Several more works of similar design had been hung about the other walls with what appeared to be an equal level of disinterest.

"Boring, isn't it..." Charleroi observed melodramatically, plonking herself down on the edge of the bed with her chin in her hands. "Stuck in here with *nothing* to do, surrounded by dull old men's toys and even *duller* old paintings."

"Any idea where Randwick's gone... *Ma'am*...?" Nev asked cautiously, taking care to add a title to the end of the sentence just in case.

"Oh, somewhere up north around the bay, I think..." she replied with a casual wave of one hand in that general direction. "I *do* hope he won't be too long... and for *Crystal's* sake, no need to call me 'ma'am' or anything silly like that when we're *alone*: *that's* all just for appearances! My name is Charleroi... *Charli*..." She added, correcting herself, then losing her outward good humour for a moment as the memory of her father came rushing back at the mention of his preferred pet name for her. "Just... Charli..." she managed eventually, mood noticeably dulled but nevertheless still determined not to let any sadness spoil things.

The change in temperament was marked, and Nev figured it didn't take a genius to recognise that having lost her father just days before and *at the same time* be forced to take over the reins of an entire kingdom in the middle of an enemy invasion would be an unimaginable amount of stress even for an *adult*, let alone a teenager who – although clearly pretty sharp and well-educated – had probably grown up in a pretty isolated and sterile environment.

"You don't *mind* if I call you Charli...?" She ventured, feeling as if she were negotiating an emotional minefield while blindfolded (in a completely dark room).

"It... um... my *father* calls – *used* to call me that..." Charli admitted finally, looking like she was about to burst into tears as emotions welled up from within. "I – I don't *have* many friends... not *real* ones, anyway. I wasn't *ever* allowed out of Cadle, and it wasn't protocol to mingle with the children of the palace staff, so there was only really a handful of *noblemen's* sons ever around to talk to..."

"Are teenage boys as *dumb* in this world as they are in mine?" Nev asked with a conspiratorial grimace, thinking she saw a way to break some of the emotional ice.

"What's a 'teenage'...?'

"Oh – uh – it means someone who's between thirteen and nineteen years old – thirteen to nineteen *summers*, I think Godfrey would probably say..."

"Oh... *oh*...!" Charli frowned, the brightened again, grasping the concept quickly. "...*'Teen-age*... that makes sense...! *Oh*...!" She exclaimed, now thinking about what Nev had actually asked. "And you don't mean '*dumb*' as in '*can't speak*' either, do you?" She added, extrapolating. "Oh, *yes*... so, *so* dumb...! All they ever want to talk about is how good they are at riding... or swordsmanship... or *archery* (like I couldn't best most of them at that *anyway*)... or how much *land* their fathers own. It was all I could do sometimes to stay *awake*..." She added with a giggle, her whole face brightening with the smile that followed.

"Yeah... sounds like boys are pretty much the same all over..." Nev grinned in return, pulling around one of the armchairs on that side of the desk and sliding down into its cushiony comfort. "Always going on about football, or what *cars* they like... bragging about how many girls they've... uh..." she paused then, realising that the rest of that sentence might not be appropriate for the teenage queen of a medieval alternate universe. "Well, they *talk too much*, basically..."

"Oh, they brag about that *here* too..." Charli admitted, knowing *exactly* what Nev was talking about and rolling her eyes. "They *think* I don't hear them, but I do... it's *disgusting,* trust me! Randwick always says that chivalry is dead: when I hear the way some of those supposed future lords and nobles talk about women, I'm inclined to believe him..."

"My *friends* call *me* Nev... *everyone* does, really..." she added with another grimace. "I don't have that many friends either... where I come from, I mean. I *had* a friend... or, at least I *thought* I did... but she ended up *betraying* me, tricked me into coming *here* and *nearly* got me killed into the bargain."

"Not *much* of a friend then..." Charli agreed with a serious nod.

"You're not wrong." Nev nodded, giving a wry smile. "You said you were never *allowed* out of Cadle...?"

"Never... at least, not as far back as I can *remember*..."

"But... but, you're – what? – *sixteen*...? *That's* not even unfair... it's *insane*...! Why would... *they* do that...?" Nev asked in bewilderment, managing to divert away from the word 'father' at the last moment.

"Surely you know about the Keepsakes...?" Charli asked sourly, frowning.

"Oh... *that* sexist b- uh – *rubbish*..." she replied, again catching herself at the last moment and thinking it best not to swear in front of a queen regardless of their growing familiarity. "Yes, Godfrey and Lester told me *all* about that when I first arrived. Had to hide in the back of wagons right across half of the Blacklands before we got on the boat that brought us here... well, *most* of the way here, anyway. What *is* it with this place? Is everyone *really* so scared of 'witches' that they make up this kind of crap, or is it just this 'Brotherhood' mob giving the rest of the *men* here an excuse to treat women like second-class citizens?" *Oh God, I'm starting to sound like Perce!* She added silently, not at all happy about the idea.

"They... um..." Charli faltered, not exactly sure how to answer that question, particularly considering her own vested interest. "I... ah... *used* to think it was all just made up. That is..." she continued hesitantly, desperate to share the burden she'd been carrying for so long but also agonising over whether to share her one, huge secret with an almost complete stranger, "...until I *saw* one earlier this week..."

"Wait, you saw... you *saw a Keepsake*...?" Nev hissed excitedly, managing to keep her voice down enough to not make things awkward as Charli glanced self-consciously around the otherwise empty room as if they might be overheard. "You *really* saw one of these stupid things?" She almost giggled in the moment before the seriousness of the situation actually struck home. "So what: you're a 'witch' now...? *You're actually a witch...?*"

"*I'm* not *a witch*...!" Charli snapped instantly in return, forced to moderate her own volume midway through the statement. "I'm *not*...!"

"No...*no*...! Or course you're not – that's not what I meant *at all*!" Nev backpedalled desperately, shaking her head furiously in apologetic denial. "I don't believe there *is* such a thing as witches – I just meant that *they* – this stupid Brotherhood or whatever it is – would *think* you're one because you can supposedly see these 'Keepsake' things..."

"With *Randwick's* help, Father managed to keep that quiet, thank The Shard..." Charli sighed, staring crestfallen at the wooden floorboards below her feet.

"Is it *really* true that only *women* can see them?"

"As far as I know..." she answered with a shrug. "That's what everyone believes: what we've always been *told*, anyway... *No* man can see them, and neither can *most* women... but those who *can* are witches; evil through-and-through and an offence to the Shard Gods. That's why they have that *awful* rule about women not being allowed to travel outside their own safe areas without covering their eyes – they can't risk the chance of someone *seeing* something they shouldn't."

"And they *really* burn women – these 'witches' – at the stake if they catch them?"

"Those that *make* it that far..." she nodded sadly "...the ones that don't kill themselves first, or die while 'resisting arrest'... I've seen it happen, right there in the middle of Cadle courtyard where we waited for you yesterday morning. It doesn't happen often, but it's still *far too many times* to see such a thing! Father *hated* it, but he couldn't say anything against it – even as king, he didn't dare – and I *know* he didn't *believe* any of it deep down."

"That's horrible..." Nev whispered in horror, almost numb with the thought of innocent women and girls being dragged to so terrible a fate that some would rather suicide than go through with it. "Just *horrible*...!"

"They'd have done it to *me* too..." Charli stated with a hollow tone, still staring at the floor. "Wouldn't matter for a *moment* that I was a princess, and there wasn't a *thing* father could've done to stop them:

all because I could see some stupid old *boat* down on the Burnii beach…"

"…Like that old wreck on the beach…?" Nev asked almost absent-mindedly, so enthralled by what the queen was saying that she wasn't thinking anywhere near deeply enough.

"What… the one *right outside*…?" Charli asked in return, a chill rippling through her as she locked eyes with Nev for the first time in a while and the hairs rose unbidden at the back of her neck. "The old wreck up on the foreshore there, about two hundred yards beyond the walls…?"

"Uhh… yeah, I guess…" Nev shrugged, apprehension setting in late as she began to realise too late that she'd said something significant. "Saw it as we were riding in: had those white-topped stakes around it and the rope…"

"Save us from Nethug, that's *one of them*!" Charli exclaimed, leaping to her feet in a mixture of fear and excitement, reaching out to grasp Nev's hands and hold them tight. "That's a Keepsake! You can see them! *You can see them too*…!"

"See *what* too…?" A different, deeper voice asked with mild interest, and both of them jumped and turned in fright as Randwick stood expectant in the now-open doorway, hands on hips and giving a deeply suspicious glare as he took in the scene of two unlikely new friends who'd just discovered they had something *very* special in common.

De Lisle had never seen Cadle in such a state. He'd visited that huge fortress, that spiritual centre of Huon innumerable times over the years, and now it seemed barely a gutted shell of its former self. Corpses lay strewn about the main courtyard and hanging from its shattered ramparts, little more than food for hungry crows now as small bands of Blackwatch troopers moved this way and that on cleaning detail, dragging the limp and shattered bodies of Cadle's former defenders across to the middle of the courtyard where a huge and rancid bonfire burned furiously.

Standing atop a relatively untouched section of rampart near the ruined main gates, De Lisle could stare out over the entire main courtyard and the brutal devastation it contained. The stench of death hung everywhere, mingling with the foetid odours of filth and rotting garbage that were the other obvious remaining after-effects of a battle that'd finally come to an end just hours before. The defenders had stood fast and fought as hard as they were able, but there'd been no way they could've held out against the 5,000-strong army Harald had brought south from Burnii.

It'd been the cannon that had really been the difference of course. De Lisle knew well-enough how strong the Cadle defences were, backed up by months of supplies and a plentiful supply of fresh water pumped from fast-running underground rivers that cut through the basalt, far below the fortress foundations. Cadle could've held against a force ten times that of Harald's army and not even blinked had there not been solid shot and explosive shells to shatter the ramparts and blow apart its thick iron gates.

"That's an *interesting* fragrance they've discovered there..." Percy observed sourly beside him, her voice muffled by the thick, cloth wrap she'd tied across her mouth and nose in a vain attempt to deaden the stench. "*Really* makes me homesick for that *refreshing* country air..."

"There was no *need* for such a waste of life..." The cardinal growled testily, angering over the situation rather than anything she'd said. "I *pleaded* with them for *hours* in the hope of some *amicable* solution..."

"Mmmh..." Percy observed dubiously. "I'm *sure* Harald would've been *very* lenient, had they all just up and surrendered right from the start."

She'd seen enough of the Blackwatch's atrocities, both before and after the invasion, to be fairly certain none of Harald's officers or men were likely to make the shortlist for the Nobel Peace Prize any time soon. She'd become accustomed enough to the violence to no longer be shocked by what she saw, but it nevertheless left her under no illusions regarding the brutality of the regime, nor any regarding how carefully she needed to tread for the time being.

"There *would* have been casualties, yes..." De Lisle conceded with mild annoyance "...but far *fewer* that the wholesale slaughter that's occurred *here* today. A small mercy they were at least able to evacuate most of the women and children..."

"Oh, I'm sure freezing to death in the mountains from hypothermia will be *far* better than finding yourself at the wrong end of a Blackwatch *sword*..." Percy pointed out darkly, pulling a face.

Blackwatch scouts had reached Burnii Crossroads just after noon the previous day, and access to the Merchant's High Road heading south had been cut soon after, leaving hundreds (if not thousands) of refugees trapped north of Huon's forbidding central ranges. It'd been a particularly cold spring so far that year and many peaks were still capped with thick layers of snow. Nevertheless, many had chosen to test their fortune against the unforgiving environment of southbound mountain trails rather than risk being captured by Harald's inexorable advance.

"...Maybe not as *rapey*, at least..." she added with dark sarcasm as a pair of particularly backward-looking individuals tromped past, their armour rattling in time with the march of their feet. She'd momentarily caught the rather unpleasant stare each man gave her and had returned a defiant, side-eyed glare of her own that covered up the shudder she felt ripple through her entire body, making her skin crawl.

"Do you not have *anywhere else* you might be tonight?" De Lisle blurted in exasperation, eyes rolling skyward.

What, and miss out on all the fun...? I wouldn't *dream* of being anywhere else..."

The Shard Gods had decided the girl was important for the time being and had made it clear she should be kept close as a result. A decree of that nature was something even a *cardinal* couldn't ignore or question, yet de Lisle was conflicted by her presence all the same.

She was the strangest and most *irritating* creature he'd ever encountered; someone *completely* unlike any woman native to his world. To a man of such power as himself, whose commands were otherwise obeyed without question, her levels of irreverence and lack of respect for authority were such that he'd already come close to ordering her execution *at least* half a dozen times. Yet for all that, her unconventional cunning and an ability to 'think outside the box' (as she put it), had also undeniably been useful in spite of one or two glaring errors of judgement.

"Besides..." she added brightly, almost sounding sincere "...This is all *your* fault, letting me stand in for that old *filth-monger*..."

"You think that because I allowed you to burn Silas, you hold some claim to his position... his *status*...?" The cardinal snapped curtly, raising an eyebrow. "I think *you* overstep your mark... in fact, I'm *sure* of it! The warning I gave you aboard *Rapier* still stands, and I should urge you not to forget that: you *already* know how quickly fortunes can turn..." he added, and Percy didn't miss the implication that it was the Shard Gods he was referring to.

Percy stared out toward the south, silent for a moment as she contemplated the dark majesty of the nearby mountains beneath the fading light of sunset. She'd been given a long sheepskin cloak to throw over her current attire – a thick, woollen dress of jet black – but it barely kept out the chill in the air. The reports they'd seen so far suggested at least five hundred civilians – *mostly* women and children – had made their way southward in the last hours of Harald's approach, seeking the elusive promise of safety beyond those forbidding peaks. She gave a faint grimace: it didn't pay to think about how long *anyone* might last in such conditions

Instead, Percy concentrated her thoughts on Nev, homing in on her as the pendant at her throat glowed bright for a few seconds. It was impossible to make out exactly where she was – perhaps she'd figured out how to put up some basic blocks against her surveillance – but she could nevertheless sense her presence: distant, but detectable all the same.

A long, thin-bladed dagger lay atop the battlement walls nearby, one of a number of discarded weapons and pieces of armour displaying the crest of Huon inlaid in gold against the broken steel. She reached out and gathered it up, turning it over in both hands and admiring the intricate details engraved into its hilt and guard. The great seal of Huon had been moulded into its pommel, and Percy could only assume it'd been dropped or otherwise cast aside by one of the fortress' defenders in the last moments of the battle. Heavy but well-balanced, the oversized grip felt good in her hand as she held it out in front of her and made a few half-heated, experimental thrusts at the empty air.

"You can sense her... the *other* one...?" De Lisle murmured, instinct and her body language telling him everything he needed to know.

"Not well enough to get a location, although she's further away: *that* much I know... I *think* she might be blocking me now..." she replied sourly, "...but yes, I can sense her; and where *she* goes, the princess will go too..."

"Of *that* I've no doubt," he replied, trying to sound more confident than he felt. "We'll continue our search: so long as the *queen* lives, a risk remains..." he added, unconsciously feeling the need to correct her use of Charleroi's outdated title.

"Where to from here...?" She asked suddenly, changing tack. "...For *you*, I mean...?"

"I go where Harald's army takes me... for now," he shrugged. "The king would claim he needs no counsel in the prosecution of this campaign, yet I would advise him where I can all the same: for the sake of the innocent peasantry, if for no other reason..."

"A cardinal's work is never done..." Percy observed, nodding sagely and with enough sincerity that De Lisle at least wasn't *certain* she was being sarcastic.

"Indeed it isn't, girl..." he agreed with a thin smile. "I'll keep you with us also for the time being..." he continued, correctly deducing the real thrust of her question. "I've a feeling you'll be of use to me yet and I'd rather have you close at hand if we *do* manage to locate this Anderson girl…"

"Just so long as everyone remembers she's *mine*…" Percy growled softly, the coldness of steel in her voice now as she dug the point of the dagger deep into the stonework at her elbow.

"Maintain *your* end of our bargain, and I will make every effort to keep *mine*…" he replied with a nod. "Gods willing, of course…"

You shall have your vengeance soon enough… the voice trickled down into her mind, far softer than usual in its intensity. Following so close after De Lisle's words, it almost caused Percy to flinch in surprise. *Days… months… years: it matters not. Serve me well, and her life will be yours for the taking when the time comes.*

You know I'd make a far *better ruler than* that *ignorant brute…* She replied silently, not bothering to her disdain for Harald the Black.

Do you think so? It asked in return, sounding almost amused. *Perhaps… but it is too early to decide such things: we see* many *possible outcomes and* none *are guaranteed. Serve us well, as we have said…* it repeated with darker intensity *…and there* will *be rewards…*

Her thoughts a thousand miles from the here and now, Persephone Koutroulis stared blankly out into space for a few moments as her free hand reached up and snapped the Shard pendant away from the chain at her neck, allowing several tiny, broken links to fall to the stone beneath their feet with a soft tinkling sound. The flash of Dragonfire enveloped her hands as she clasped the dagger between them, pressing the Shard crystal against the leather-bound hilt, and De Lisle's eyes flew wide as the very metal of Percy's blade began to shimmer and flow, morphing into something completely different. The blue-white glow grew to painful intensity, forcing him to avert his eyes and cover them with one hand as the nearer pieces of shield and broken swords lying on the stones around them began to dissolve into the blinding glare. A gasp forced itself from his lips as he took several steps backward, keeping clear of several large droplets of molten steel as they fell from her hands and sizzled at their feet.

Cooling metal sent faint wisps of smoke into the chilly air and instead of the dagger, Percy now held over a metre of sword in her hands, three-quarters of which was a tapered blade of polished steel. In contrast, the hilt, pommel and cross-guard were plated in gleaming gold, drawn from the inlaid insignia of Cadle's now-dead Huon defenders, and embedded at the very centre of the guard, the Shard Crystal from Silas' pendant glowed dully in the aftereffects of her handiwork.

"There... *that's* better..." Percy declared loudly, still sounding only partially-conscious and a little out of breath as the glow finally began to subside and De Lisle was able to uncover his eyes once more. "Little Miss 'Heaven-Backwards' gets to have a cool, butt-kicking sword... why shouldn't *I*...?"

"It's... it's *beautiful*..." De Lisle breathed, staring wide-eyed at Percy and for the first time unabashedly in awe of the power she's just put on display.

"Of course it is..." she answered glibly, lifting the blade until it caught the reflection of torches burning nearby. "Did a history assignment on Charlemagne once... not that *you'd* know who that was, of course..." she continued absentmindedly. "French king... always thought his sword was *really* pretty: *Joyeuse*, it was called."

"And *this* sword is made in its image...?" De Lisle ventured, making the appropriate leap of logic.

"More or less..." She shrugged. "It's not *identical* – my memory's not *that* good – but it's close enough to do the job. *Better*, really... 'Charlie' didn't have a *Shard Crystal* stuck in the hilt of *his*, for a start..."

"'*Joyeuse*'..." The cardinal repeated, only mildly mangling the pronunciation.

"Means 'joyous'... *obviously*..." she explained, not really paying attention. "*All* special swords need to have a name, didn't you know? *Joyeuse*... Excalibur... *Sting*..." She added with a shrug, swinging the sword back and forth with a few experimental slashes that were close enough to force De Lisle to take another wary step backward. "What shall we call *you*...? I'd a thought perhaps to go one-up on 'Joyous' and call you 'Ecstasy'..." she declared with a grimace "...but then, everyone might start calling you 'Eccy' instead and I never *could* stand the rave scene: *no one* would take me seriously! *Damocles:* now *there's* a good name for a sword... *particularly* considering the danger that's shortly going to be hanging over *someone's* head..."

"I doubt I'll *ever* know what these witches are talking about..." De Lisle muttered softly under his breath, shaking his head in exasperation as Percy continued muttering to herself regardless.

Ocean Breeze lay tied up at a small wooden pier on the eastern edge of Morsel Bay, a short, narrow body of water leading off the very northern tip of Mockery Inlet. A few of Strahn's outer lying homes stood nearby but the area was mostly taken up by ramshackle boat sheds and similar wharfs, where small fishing cogs were moored. A heavy mist lay across the dark water, eerie in the pre-dawn glow spreading across the eastern horizon, and there was a bitter chill in the air as the queen rode out from the fort that morning with a small escort, Nev and Godfrey among them.

Most of those camped outside the walls still slept, just a few shivering sentries on duty vainly trying to warm their bones as they stood at a number of cast iron braziers dotted about the site, the flicker of orange flame licking up here and there amid the general darkness. Those few who were awake watched the small procession with the mild disinterest of those too tired to care, with only the closest making an attempt at coming to attention as they passed.

Farouk was standing ready at the near end of the wharf as the troop rode up, several of William's guardsmen taking the reins of the other horses as the official party dismounted and approached, Randwick in the lead.

"Well met, Ismail..." he acknowledged, hand extended in greeting and readily accepted as they closed.

"Well met indeed, kinsman..." the captain acknowledged with a toothy grin. "And not before time either: there's been reports of Blackships this side of The Takers overnight, and it's only a matter of hours before they make it this far south. If they come with another one of those 'cannon boats', it'll be all over for *all* of us..."

"I've *seen* what they can do first hand," the old man conceded with a single nod and a wry smile, "although I'll warrant *they've* not see what *you're* capable of in a tight spot. All the same, much as it pains me to say so, it's better the queen was away from here without further delay. You're ready to weigh anchor?"

"Ready as we'll ever be."

"Well and good then. A moment if you will, and I'll see to our 'cargo'..." He turned and made his way back to where Nev, Charleroi and the others stood as a small, shivering group, the remaining mounted guardsmen bringing their horses close in to form a protective screen to the landward side.

"This is our ship to safety?" The queen asked dubiously, more concerned about her first sea voyage in general than any comment about the condition or seaworthiness of the vessel itself.

"Aye, lass..." Randwick nodded with a wan smile, not sounding at all pleased about the situation. "Farouk here's as good a ship's captain as any I've seen: he'll see you to safety well enough..."

"See '*me*' to safety...?" She blurted in reply, instantly picking up on his exact wording. "Surely you mean '*us*'...?"

"No, lass..." he replied with a distinct sadness in his tone now, and Charleroi's heart sank with fear as she realised he couldn't meet her gaze in that moment. "...This is as far as we go together for now..."

"No... *no*...!" She barked with a stamp of her feet, finding power in her tone as she attempted to assert her royal authority. "I shan't allow it...!"

"Aye, you will lass... you will..." he countered, shaking his head. "*Someone* needs to stay behind and organise a resistance, but we *must* see you safe away from here until we know we can stop Harald and *hold* his advance. They need me *here* right now – they need all the help they can get – but Huon also needs *you* clear of all this until the invasion is stopped and Baal's either captured or dead. It's best for the kingdom..."

"But... *but*..." she stammered, desperate to find some reason or excuse to not accept his argument and fighting back tears the entire time "...if you stay here... who'll... *who'll*..."

"I'd not see you left alone, my girl... not for all the gold in the Sun Empire and beyond..." Randwick said kindly, managing a smile now as he finally realised the true fear behind her protestations "...but I know you won't *be* alone: not with these two to take care of y' for me..." he added, casting a quick glance at Nev and Godfrey "...ain't that right, mistress?"

"What...? Oh... *oh*... of course... *yes*...!" Nev blustered, caught completely unawares by the old man's question without notice.

"The kingdom needs you safe..." Randwick continued, moving back to solid ground with his argument. "It can't afford to lose you... not when we've lost *so much* already. If you *order* me to come, My Queen, then I'll of course obey, but I think you *know* this is for the best..."

"I'll *miss* you..." She whispered softly, too filled with emotion to meet his gaze and instead electing to stare at the ground between them.

"I've watched you grow up before my very eyes, and I'll miss you more than you could *ever* know, lassie..." he replied with equal feeling, reaching out and gently lifting her chin with one finger until they were again looking into one another's eyes. "But we'll see each other again soon enough, I promise you..."

"Master Randwick, the tide..." came a hesitant warning from Farouk, still standing at the pier with one eye warily on the falling water level.

"Aye, captain, I know you're on a schedule: we'll be done here by and by..." the old man vowed in response before turning quickly back to Charleroi and the rest. "You need to go now, Your Majesty..." he continued, all business now and with greater urgency in his tone. "There's clothes and belongings enough stowed aboard already – I'd prepared for this even *before* Harald sprung his trap at Burnii – and there's no need for you to delay any longer: if they miss the morning tide, we'll *all* be done for!"

Charleroi hugged him then, throwing her arms sightly about his waist and squeezing for all she was worth before he could even react. He returned the embrace after a moment's pause, and it was clear to everyone standing by that Randwick too was struggling to hide his emotions.

"Come on, Your Highness..." Nev suggested gently, realising someone else needed to make a move as she caught Randwick's fleeting, pleading glance. "This'll be your first *ever* ride on a ship... there *has* to heaps of exciting stuff to see: I saw dolphins on the way over from the mainland!"

"Dolphins...*really*...?" Charleroi asked weakly as she separated from Randwick once more, well aware of what Nev was trying to do but too fragile to do anything but go along with it. "Do you think we'll see any on *this* trip?"

"Hope so..." She answered quickly, trying to keep her tone upbeat as she extended an arm as if to guide the young queen toward the pier. "That time was *my* first ride on a ship too... a *sailing ship*, anyway... but I didn't really get a chance to enjoy it..." she went on, Charleroi turning to walk slowly with past Farouk and onto the wooden planks as Nev shouldered her sports bag behind her, the hilt of her katana poking out of the top. "I'm sure *this one* will be *much* more fun!"

"You'll need everyone you can get, I'll warrant..." Godfrey ventured awkwardly, *very* conflicted as his eyes flicked back and for the between the old man and the two young women making their way along the jetty. "Every... uh... able-bodied man who can hold a sword..."

"Lad, I don't know who'll end up protecting *who*..." Randwick observed with a faint, knowing smile, "...but I know well enough where *your* place is, and it's *not* here! I've William here to keep an eye on *me*," he added, clapping a reassuring hand on Godfrey's shoulder. "Keep an eye on *both of 'em* for me, kinsman...?"

"Oh – *really*...?" He faltered in reply, the intent of the old man's words not fully sinking in for a moment or two. "Yes... yes, *of course, kinsman*..." he continued excitedly, reaching out and shaking Randwick's hand firmly as it was offered. "You have my word!"

"Look after her, boy…" he added softly, his tone making it very clear to Godfrey that he wasn't referring to the queen. "She's both stronger *and* more fragile than she knows, and she'll need both your strength *and* yer wisdom before all this is done…"

"I – uh…"

"*Go*, lad…" Randwick urged, more insistent this time. "*Go*…!"

With his own rucksack over one shoulder and sword at his belt, Godfrey Westacre gave one last nod of thanks and acknowledgement before turning to jog after Nev and the queen, catching them up while they were still several metres short of the steep gangway.

Randwick stared and watched as all three made their way up the walkway and onto the deck a moment later, his heart filled with far more fear and apprehension than he dared show. With a single, silent nod of his own, Farouk also bade him farewell and made his own way back to the ship, bellowing orders to his suddenly *very*-active crew the whole time.

"Come on, young fella…" Randwick called out to William eventually, rousing himself from his own melancholy and heading back over to his horse. "There's nowt more we can do here this morning, and plenty still undone *elsewhere* that needs our attention."

"They'll be all right…?" The younger man asked worriedly as their mounts drew near and Randwick pulled momentarily back on his reins. "The *queen* will be all right?"

"Safer where they're going that anywhere *we* could take 'em," he answered confidently.

"And where *are* they going, sir…?"

"Now *that*, young William, even *I* don't know…" the old man replied with a sly grin, lying outright. "Perhaps in time we'll find out…" he added, not wanting to give any great offence "…but for now, the fewer who know *that* information, the better…"

For his part, William accepted that answer without question and headed off to collect his horse, Randwick watching him carefully with suspicion in his eyes.

XXI

Hidden Agendas

Zeehn was already cast in the shadow of twilight as William rode up to his family's farmhouse for the second time in as many days, this time alone. Tying his horse up at a water-filled trough by the front door, he took great pains to shake the dirt from his boots on the mat before entering with a single knock. His mother was *generally* an easy-going soul but she was house-proud to a fault and *no one* in the family was stupid enough to risk her wrath by making the floors dirty.

With her head barely reaching William's chest, she wrapped her arms about him as he stepped through the door and held him tight as his father stepped forward and shook the boy's hand from a distance.

"I can't stay long, mother..." he warned apologetically as they separated. "General Randwick's taking the army south below the ranges to regroup: we're moving out tomorrow."

"So he's a *general* now, is he...?" His father growled darkly, not sounding at all impressed. "Never saw him closer than a *mile* from the front lines the whole time *I* marched me colours, back in the day... *That* was a quick promotion sure enough, with the king dead and the *princess* gone into hiding and all...!"

Taller than his son by several centimetres, Alexander of Zeehn was a tall, solidly-built man with body well-tuned by decades of hard work on the farm and a razor-sharp intellect to match.

"She'd *queen* now, father," William corrected almost automatically, then frowned. "And how do you *know* she's gone, *anyway*? That's *supposed* to be secret!"

"Not much misses our doorstep, son – you should know that by now. I've me own little 'connections' hereabouts who tell me things from time to time, and I hear tell that a ship weighed anchor at dawn this morning with Her Majesty on board, bound for 'parts unknown'. She *ain't* no queen neither – not *yet*, at least: ain't been no coronation to make it official and there's *some* sayin' that may never happen; not if the viceroy gets his way..."

"Amun Baal is a bloody *traitor* and no friend of Huon," William spat angrily in return, having seen some of the man's dastardly handiwork in person. "He *murdered* King Phaesus and betrayed Huon to the Blackwatch!"

"Aye, I been hearin' that too," the old man conceded as William's mother, already bored by political talk, made her way over to the crackling wood stove in the corner where several pots were bubbling for dinner. "And he may well pay for his crimes before this is all done, but mark my words... there's some *strange* tales been getting about these last few days about the '*queen*' too – tales that don't bear thinkin' about *or* repeatin' right now... I'll tell y' this straight: there's like to be a reckoning for quite a few of them royal hobnobs on *both* sides before this thing's good and done. Never mind any 'o that now, anyway," he continued, waving a dismissive hand as William began to respond. "We've little enough time to spend with y' as it is, and I *know* we never agree on politics anymore. I just thank the Shard you're still well and in one piece. You've time to take dinner with us before y' head back...?" He added, clapping a fatherly hand on the boy's shoulder.

"The gen – uh – Master Randwick gave me the rest of the evening at least, and some of Ma's best would be a fine way to say goodbye before I head off."

"You always *could* smell my stew cookin' from a mile away, son," his mother chimed in, beaming with pride as she stirred the largest pot on the stove. "There's a good fifteen minutes or so before its done: go and see your brother and spend some time with him before we eat."

"Rolly...? Rolly's *here*...?" William exclaimed, suddenly excited and not daring to hope for such unexpected good news. "I feared the worst after what happened at Cadle: they've been burning priests as traitors all over the countryside since the news broke that the Brotherhood was in league with Harald."

"He's in the storm cellar," Alexander advised, barely managing a smile. "We thought it best he stay out of sight with what's been goin' on, like you said, and thanks be to The Shard, the Gods have kept him safe so far. Sorry we couldn't tell you last night, with them soldiers about an' all. Head on out and say hello: you know where it is."

"Tell 'im we'll bring some stew out by and by," his mother called out as he strode across the kitchen and threw open the back door.

The main farm buildings comprised the farmhouse and two separate barns behind, one large and the other smaller. William headed out through the rear with an excited spring in his step, making straight for the smaller of the two barns and slipping sideways through the narrow gap between its already-open main doors. The inside was dark and musty, but his father was too careful to ever leave tools lying about or stand for anything being out of place and William had spent enough time playing in there as a child to know his way around blindfolded.

This time however he did find several loose hay bales stacked somewhere they definitely shouldn't be and almost fell over them before he'd worked out what they actually were. With a few soft grunts of exertion, he pushed them aside and reached for the handle of the trapdoor he knew had been hidden beneath. Lifting it high, he was immediately presented with the sight of a large and relatively spacious cellar below, dimly lit by the flickering light of a lantern placed somewhere beyond his line of sight. Without a moment's hesitation, he turned, placed his foot on the top rung of the ladder leading down, and lowered himself inside, pulling the trapdoor back over his head as he entered.

"It's good to see you, brother..." a familiar voice declared from behind as his feet reached the cellar's hard, earthen floor, and as he turned toward the sound, William of Zeehn found himself face to face with Prelate Roland of Cadle.

Ocean Breeze had rounded the heads of Mockery Inlet and turned west, the captain taking her away from the coast and heading for deeper water. A storm had blown in from the south-west by mid-morning, the blustery winds bringing with it a vicious chill and biting rain that kept everyone below decks save for the unfortunate crew on duty. The seas had roughened substantially with the storm's arrival, forcing the vessel to tack heavily through crashing waves as they fought to make headway against the oncoming wind. There'd been not a single thought of dolphin sightings during those first few hours as the cog lurched savagely up and over each huge wave, only to come crashing down again on the other side as any number of stomachs both above and below decks also did more than their fair share of heaving. It was mid-afternoon before the storm had finally passed, blowing away to the east and leaving the skies cloudless from one horizon to the other.

The captain's quarters had been set aside for the queen's use, the spacious cabin placed in roughly the same position at the stern of the ship as Baal's had been aboard *Rapier* (as was the case on basically every other vessel of similar design). A large feather bed the size of a standard double lay in the centre of the space, the headboard backed up beneath windows that covered the entire width of the ship's stern from port to starboard. A low set of drawers stood on either side of the bed, while at least three burning kerosene lanterns hung from the ceiling on short chains, swinging lazily from side to side in time with the rise and fall of the ship cutting through the calming waves.

The bulkheads to port and starboard were lined with further windows, some blocked by several large book cases fixed to the walls with long, narrow slats fitted to the front of each shelf to prevent anything falling out during rough weather. Near the centre of the room, roughly half way between the doorway and the bed, a large, ovoid table stood bolted to the deck surrounded by a number of high-backed wooden chairs with heavy weights attached to their feet for added stability.

Several large steamer trunks filled with a variety of clothes had been brought up to the room, and with seas *and* stomachs now calmer, Charleroi was finally able to break some of them open to cast an eye over the choices Randwick had made without her knowledge.

"Well, at least *half* of these are too *old...*" she grumped softly, her heart not really in it as she and Nev sat at the foot of Farouk's large feather bed "...and some of the *others* are just too *short* now! *Never* let a *man* make wardrobe decisions...!"

"The lace work on these is amazing!" Nev declared, not feeling particularly judgemental but nevertheless silently filing the queen's remarks under 'first-world problems' as she ran her hands over the ornate bodice of a bright blue gown that looked almost Elizabethan. "It must've taken *hours* to make...!"

"Probably *weeks*, I suspect..." Charleroi mused vaguely, not really certain herself but able to make a more educated guess at least. "I think there's only one or two seamstresses in the whole of Huon can even *do* anything this fiddly."

"Uh...yeah... it is *really* pretty..." Nev replied awkwardly, feeling silly now as she realised that – *of course* – the work must've painstakingly been done by hand rather than on some kind of intricate machine.

"I shouldn't complain... without Randwick, I'd not even *be* here to complain about my dresses..." Charli conceded grudgingly, rising from the bed and walking slowly over to the multi-paned windows that ran right across the entire width of the stern, affording a fine view of the darkening ocean and the ship's wake spreading behind them. "I wish he'd at least told *me* where we're going..."

"I'm sure it'll be somewhere safe," Nev assured as Charleroi pushed open one of the windows on its hinges and breathed deeply as cool, fresh air wafted in with the breeze from outside. "I don't know him very well, but he *seems* to be a pretty decent guy... and pretty *sharp* too..."

"'Sharp'..." Charli repeated, glancing back at Nev as she turned the word over a few times in her mind. "You...mean... *smart*, yes...?

Yes, he *is* very smart," she continued, not waiting for a reply as she turned back toward the open window. "*And* a *very* decent man ... finest I've ever known, save for..." Her voice tightened and faded then as she fought against her own grief, knuckles white as her fingers – already resting on the sill of the open window – tightened almost into claws with sudden tension.

"It's okay to miss him..." Nev ventured carefully, eyes moistening with her own surging emotions as she watched a single tear trickle its way down Charli's cheek in the fading light.

"I'm *queen* now..." she whispered softly, bitter defiance in the words as she struggled to retain control. "I have *responsibilities*... a *kingdom* to think of: I'm not *allowed* the luxury of grief...!"

"*Everyone* has a right to grieve..." Nev replied, her tone still gentle but sounding more confident now as the subject moved onto firmer ground. "*Sure*, you're a queen... but that doesn't mean you have to walk around not showing any emotion twenty-four/seven... uh... *every hour* of the day, I mean..."

"History hasn't been kind to the Namur..." Charli observed sadly, turning back from the window and taking a seat on the bed once more. "My father lost his older brother, father *and* his grandfather to war or assassination: we've learned the *hard* way to ignore our sorrow and just move on. It's almost a family pastime. What about *your* family...?" She asked suddenly, trying to brighten a little as she decided it was time for a change of subject. "What are they like? I bet they miss *you*, wherever you come from..."

"I – *um* – I miss my dad... miss him *a lot*..." Nev admitted after pausing for a moment to compose her thoughts. Lost my mum when I was a lot younger; we grew pretty close after that..."

"I'm so sorry..."

"It's okay – I came to terms with that a long time ago... still miss her of course, but it doesn't hurt as much now... not like it did back *then*..." she paused, taking a deep breath as Charli waited patiently, knowing when to stay quiet and just listen. "Where I come from... well, it's *really* different from here. We have machines that can do just about *anything* for us: machines to cook our food... to fly around in... machines we use to speak to someone on the other side of the entire *world*. My dad worked at a mine – they have those here? A *huge* hole in the ground where they dig for coal...? He works lots of hours to pay the bills..." She continued sheepishly as Charli nodded quickly and the question suddenly seemed a little silly. "Sometimes he jokes that it's *me* who looks after *him*, but I'm still just a kid really. I go to school there... *high school*, we call it..."

"I had *personal* tutors, being a princess…" Charli shrugged. "*Most* people in the kingdom don't have that luxury, of course. Used to be that one had to be the child of a lord or nobleman to be given *any* education, but father was *trying* to change that. Even back when he was just a prince, he'd started opening free schools for the commonfolk in the bigger cities and towns. "Father… was *not* popular with everyone…" Charleroi admitted after a long, difficult pause. "He'd *always* been seen as a friend of the *people*, even *before* Uncle Rizal was assassinated, but that was little more than an annoyance as a *prince*, whereas once he became *king*…" She took another moment to compose herself, before adding: "Being loved by the commonfolk often creates enemies *elsewhere* who are far more dangerous… even among your own *relatives* sometimes, it seems…"

"*My* world's history is *full* of stuff like that," Nev admitted with a shrug of her own. "People in charge trying to kill or imprison anyone who tries to give power back to the people… not so usual to see that in a *king* though…"

"My father never *wanted* to be king; never *expected* to be…" Charli explained. "He was a gentle, *decent* man. The only 'crime' he was ever guilty of was that he *cared*…" There was a long silence then as both were momentarily lost within their own thoughts, the only sounds being the faint sounds of the waves outside the windows and the creaking of the ship as it cut through them.

"And now *you're* queen…" Nev pointed out carefully, not sure whether the observation was good news or bad.

"Perhaps not for long as things stand," Charli replied with a thin, rueful smile, "although there's still hope… I'm not ready to surrender *just* yet…"

"How difficult is it to *be* a queen in this world?" Nev asked thoughtfully, considering the other girl's situation in greater depth. "This stupid 'Keepsake-blindfold' thing obviously applies to monarchs as well as commoners: how are you supposed to *rule* a kingdom you're not even allowed to *see* most of?"

"My father and I spoke on exactly that subject just a few days ago…" Charli admitted, her expression darkening "…and we didn't come up with a solution *then* either." She gave an exaggerated '*humph!*' of displeasure and scowled as she picked daintily at her fingernails. "I was pressing my luck daring to travel from Cadle without a visard… not sure even as queen I'd get away with *that* too often. Come to think of it, I *might* even be the first queen ever… I don't know anyone who can remember a time in the Osterlands when there was a queen ruling on her own before. Most of the time, royal families with only girls just keep having babies until they get a boy – which takes care of *that* 'problem' – and those few that are left usually have their daughters *married off* before they have a chance to ascend the throne in their own right..."

"...And I assume the *husband* then takes over everything anyway...?" Nev responded, giving a scowl of her own.

"Not... *officially*..." Charli shrugged, not bothering to hide her own annoyance '...but *everyone* knows what's *really* going on. A royal baby factory: that's all anyone expects a *queen* to be around here..."

"But not you...?"

"Not *likely*...!" Charli spat venomously, eyes narrowed. "Make *me* wear a blindfold, will they? Shard willing, if I see it through this current disaster I'm going to rule my kingdom *my* way, husband or none, and I'll be *damned* if I care what the Kings' Council thinks of that! When have *they* ever done anything for The Osterlands other than maintain the *status quo*? They'd *never* accept a *queen* ruling in her own right. Don't know why I'm surprised; they have *king* in the title after all..."

"Men are such *bastards*..." Nev muttered vaguely, shaking her head.

"Well... not *all* men..." the queen suggested, almost managing a smile then. "There's Randwick, of course... and that Guard Captain, *William* seemed honourable... *and* handsome...!" Her expression turned almost sly in that moment as she turned her head and sent a glance in Nev's direction. "Your friend, *Godfrey* seems quite nice..."

"Oh, for goodness sake: not *you too*!" Nev moaned plaintively, instantly recalling memories of the uncomfortable conversation with Randwick a few days earlier and torn between whether to feel annoyed or embarrassed (or settle for both). "Is there *anyone* who doesn't know about this...?"

"Well... probably *Godfrey*, knowing how slow boys tend to be with this sort of thing..." Charli replied with a conspiratorial wink, taking the tone of a teenager *completely* confident in their comprehensive knowledge of all things. "Maybe he needs more of a hint...?"

"Oh, my God, don't *even*...!" Nev almost choked as the queen giggled, happy her intentional tease had hit home. "I'd be *mortified... seriously*...!"

"So, you *don't* like him, then...?" That next, very intent question was delivered with a seriously-raised eyebrow.

"I – I didn't say *that*..." she squirmed, not quite ready to open up her innermost feelings to someone she'd barely known more than a few days, regardless of their growing bond. "I just… just… I *don't know*…" She ended up blurting, not so much upset or annoyed as she was confused. "He's… nice… *very nice*… and he's kind, and he's about as gorgeous as any boy has a right to be… but…"

"*But*…?"

"*But*… I've been in this world all of a *week*!" Nev replied after a pause, eventually finding her confidence once more along with a stream of logic. "I've been here a week and *already* gotten involved in medieval war, political assassination, some bloody crystal that's magical to the point of being a *cliché*, and a bunch of cultist *lunatics* running about trying to overthrow entire *kingdoms* when they're not spending the rest of their time oppressing women. There's too much going on at the moment to even *think* about anything like that…" she added, working herself around to her *real* fears in a rather roundabout fashion "…and besides… what if he doesn't like *me*…?"

"Dragonfall take me, Nevaeh…" the queen exclaimed with a soft laugh, completely ignoring anything Nev had said about hating that name "…how could he *possibly* not like you…? You're smart, strong, *lethal* with a blade… and stunningly *beautiful* as well! Far too pretty for *any* of them really, and there's no denying it!" She added, *really* making Nev blush now.

"Don't feel very pretty in *this*…" she replied awkwardly, unable to meed Charli's gaze and staring at the floor instead. "I know they *tried* washing my clothes while we were at Cadle, but everything still *feels* dirty somehow and I've been rotating between the same two outfits for a *week* now without a decent change. These greens and browns are *perfect* for sneaking about in the bushes: I'm surprised anyone can see me *at all*!"

"Well then, there's only one thing for it!" The queen declared suddenly, rising to her feet with obvious purpose. "Stand up!"

"What… *why*…?"

"Don't be a spoilsport… *stand up*…!" Charli demanded, hands on hips and a cheeky glint in her eye.

"Oh, *fine*…!" Nev grumped, wary of being made fun of somehow but complying anyway under sufferance. "Whatever…"

"Now, you're a *little* shorter than me…" the queen muttered to herself, eyeing her up and down "…but we're pretty much the same *shape*… *more or less*… soooo…."

She turned and headed straight for the nearest of her steamer trunks, flung the lid open and began rummaging around inside.

"No… no… no… Oh, *Dragonfall*, no: *definitely* not that colour… *aha*…!" She declared finally, hauling something free from the tangled mess she'd created. "*Just* the thing for your hair and complexion, and it's been a few years since I wore it so it *should* be about the right length..." Turning, she held up a folded pile of emerald green silk that she then carefully 'unfurled' into a long and clearly *very* expensive jacket and trousers, looking for all the world like a stylised version of a modern pantsuit. "I have the blouse and some stays for it too... *somewhere...*" Charli continued, half muttering to herself as she continued to rummage about inside the same trunk. "*Ah-hah:* here they are!"

"Oh, I am *so* not wearing *that...*" Nev blurted, almost recoiling physically at the sight of something so alien to anything she would even *consider* appropriate as Charli held up a *very* brief halter top in white that appeared to have a *very* plunging neckline.

"Well, why ever not?" The queen asked with honest surprise as she laid the outfit flat on the bed and wandered off in search of suitable undergarments. "That style is still *very* much in fashion and the only reason *I'm* not wearing it any more is that I grew out of it... well..." she relented, feeling an admission was in order as she carried on with her search "...*and* because it doesn't really suit my hair *or* my eyes, but Matron *did* like it so..."

"I've never worn anything like that in my *entire life...*" Nev declared obstinately, hands on hips now and determined to make a stand, queen or no queen.

"Well, if you ask *me...*" Charli replied brightly, appearing from between two large trunks with a bundle of silk undergarments in hand "...it's high time *you did...*! It *may* still be green – *technically* – but you'll *definitely* stand out in a crowd. Nevaeh, my dear..." she continued, using that despised full name again but somehow managing it in a manner that didn't sound quite as offensive "...although *most* of my so-called 'womanly education' at Cadle was an absolute *chore*, one thing it definitely *did* teach me was how to dress *properly* in royal circles, and *trust me* when I say that *you* will look *incredible* in this...! That young man won't be able to *resist* you!"

"I... don't even know what that means..." Nev admitted bleakly, pausing a moment mid-sentence to think about Charli's last statement. Concern flashed across her face then as another thought suddenly occurred to her. "Oh, my God... what if he's gay? I mean... I don't think... I just *assumed...* But then, I guess if he *was*, then he'd *have* to hide it... for fear of being executed or *tortured* or something horrible like that..."

"'Gay'...?" The queen repeated, frowning. "Why *wouldn't* he be happy about it?"

"Oh... *oops*..." Nev muttered with a sheepish grin. "Never occurred to me that word might not mean the same thing here... *awkward*...! Actually, in *my* world, the word 'gay' doesn't always just mean 'happy'... it *also* means... ahh... *something else*..."

"Which is...?" Charli asked blankly, making her work for it.

"Ahh... well, I'm *assuming* that it happens *here* too..." Nev tried to explain, not sure why she was suddenly feeling so embarrassed about explaining something she she'd always been so vocal in support of back home. "See... 'gay' is one of the terms we use in my world to describe when two people of the *same* gender like... err... *love* each other..."

"*Oh*, you mean '*chasing the rainbow*'...?" Charleroi replied without hesitation, not even batting an eyelid. "Look, one can never tell... and it's *completely* no one else's business if he *is*, *of course*, but I *doubt* it..." She frowned as she considered something else Nev had just said and fixing her with a quizzical stare. "Why would he be *tortured* for *that*, for Crystal's sake? What kind of backward world do you come from...?"

"I..." Nev began, then halted, lost for words again and ultimately able to only give an embarrassed shrug as she raised her hands in surrender, inwardly feeling even more confused than ever. "You know what...? Forget I even said anything..."

"I'm leaving at dawn, brother..." William sighed sadly some time later, seating himself on one of several large crates positioned about a small brazier he'd brought down from the barn for warmth. It filled the cellar with smoke and made it difficult to breathe without discomfort, but it was nevertheless far better than allowing his brother to freeze to death underground during the middle of the night.

"I understand, brother; we must follow where duty leads..." Roland replied with a vague smile, seated on another crate on the opposite side of the fire.

"And what of *you*, Rolly...? Where does duty take *you* with everything that's happened?" The words were framed as a question rather than accusation, yet Roland understood all the same that there was a great deal resting on his answer for a number of reasons.

"This will be a *difficult* time for The Brotherhood, it's true..." he conceded, fingers reaching up almost in reflex to touch the talisman that was the Shard crystal hanging about his neck and giving a faint flicker of blue beneath his fleeting touch. "We shall endure, of course... that cannot be in doubt..."

"Shard Gods willing, I pray so," William responded honestly, touching his own hand to his forehead in the usual manner of respect at their mention. "But this is not like *anything* we've seen before. *Never* has The Brotherhood openly allied itself with one nation to topple a rightful ruler of another from his throne... there's no telling *how* the Kings' Council will react."

"They will understand, by-and-by," Roland assured, almost sounding smug now to his brother's surprise. "The Cardinal has evidence to present to them that will prove Phaesus a traitor and a heretic, and they will *see* why we needed to act: why this demonic folly of giving science and *education* to the masses must be ended once and for all."

"Roland, you're my blood and kin, but what you say is *madness...*" he replied, feeling slightly heated over such a slight to a king he'd held in such high regard; one he'd watched die as he stood by, helpless. "Phaesus was *loved* by his people... he wanted only the *best* for them..."

"Do you think so, brother?" Roland spat, also angering now. "And what would you say if I told you that he *knowingly* discovered a *witch* within the walls of Cadle itself? That instead of denouncing this harpy for what she was, he instead *conspired* with the advisor, Randwick, to have this hell-spawn escape the judgement of The Shard and taken to some unknown place of safety, *far away* from Huon and righteous justice?"

There was a moment – a short, tense moment as both siblings stared defiantly at each other across a crackling fire – before pieces began falling into place regarding what had happened at Strahn the last few days and the reality of it all struck William like a sledgehammer.

"No... *no...!*" He exclaimed in horror, almost unable to even comprehend what the man was trying to say. "She was taken away for her *safety...* because of the *invasion...*" He was almost pleading now, desperate to see *some* hint of weakness or uncertainty in Roland's face and receiving nothing in return.

"And this ship just *happened* to have docked at Strahn by mere *coincidence...?*" Roland asked pointedly, raising an eyebrow as a sneer flickered across his face. "It just *happened* to have several trunks full of the princess' clothing packed aboard through *chance* alone?"

He... *Randwick...* the *general* said..." William stammered, trying to find justification in what he already knew but the more he thought about it, the more everything just didn't add up... the more it seemed that *Ocean Breeze* had *already* been waiting for the queen to board even *before* the invasion… and if that *were* the case, the question definitely needed to be asked as to *why*…

"T'was Garrick who brought it to our attention," Roland explained, softening his tone now he saw that his brother was hooked. "Obtained the *real* reason from one of the chambermaids… and before you ask, *yes*… she *was* tortured, but we're convinced of the truth of it all the same. After the initial report was made, an experienced brother was sent to give a second 'interview', using a Crystal this time, and there's no doubting *those* results. The facts are that soon after their arrival at the Burnii Longhouse, Princess Charleroi was witnessed declaring that she could *see* a keepsake that had washed up on the beach there during the night… 'sea monsters', I think they're called. This was immediately reported to the king and, not surprisingly, *he* immediately gave orders for the princess to be spirited out of harm's way before she might face discovery at the next Endweek ceremony…"

"I… I can't believe this…"

"Then why send her away? Why send her away without visard or proper protection, as the Book prescribes? We're *already* receiving reports that the queen, in company with *another* proven witch, knowingly and openly wore *no visard at all* during their flight from Cadle to Strahn in direct contravention of the Keepsake Law. *You* travelled with them, brother… tell me to my *face* that this was not so… that this did not happen…!"

"Then tell me this instead…" he continued, having paused long enough to be certain William could give no answer, nor look him in the eye in that moment. "What did the princess do when this *other* witch used the power of a *stolen* Crystal to decimate the Blackwatch and destroy one of Harald's warships? Did she object? Did she forbid this *heresy*…? Don't try to deny it, brother: I *know* you were there!"

"She…" William stumbled, recalling the desperate reality of that moment at the barricades and finding himself unable to reconcile it with his beliefs as a Gods-fearing follower of The Shard. "…Nothing…" he answered eventually, sounding almost defeated. "She did nothing…"

"And what did *you* do…?" His older brother insisted then, instantly turning the tables and putting the younger man on the back foot. "Was it *nothing* also? As a *believer* – as one of the righteous – what did *you* do in that moment as *blasphemy* was committed before your very eyes?"

"I protested it! I spoke out against it!" William shot back defensively, knowing he sounded far guiltier than he had any reason to be. "I was ignored! *Randwick* bade me be silent! I'm a guardsman – a low-born soldier with no title or standing: what *else* could I have done…?" In his own mind, he wasn't even lying: under the stress and guilt of accusation, his subconscious had *very* conveniently forgotten all about how quickly his opposition had folded in the face of Randwick's ire, and that Charleroi's had also initially protested Nev's use of the crystal.

"And there you have it…!" Roland declared triumphantly, rising from his seat and pointing an accusing finger across the crackling fire. "Condemned by their *own* actions, they *denied* you when you tried to speak the truth! When you tried to show them *The Way*! They are in *league*, these two harpies – do you not *see* that now? Baal is no traitor to Huon… he is its *saviour*, and with Harald's help, he and The Brotherhood will *purge* this land of the *evil* that lies at its very core – that *sits on its throne*! Let Randwick and the other heretics plead their case to the Council as they will: when the rest of the Oster kings see the *truth* of what's happened here, they'll stand *united* in *cursing* the Namur name and *scouring* it from the pages of history itself!"

"We have him…" De Lisle nodded sagely, pleased with what the vision had shown as Percy had severed her shared link with Roland's crystal and collapsed onto the huge bed behind her, casting aside her newly-made sword and the shard buried within its hilt. Upon arrival at Cadle, she'd claimed Charleroi's old bedroom, seeing it as only fitting after all that she should be treated as she deserved: like a princess.

"We'd better have…" she growled softly, rising to a sitting position once more and straightening her dress, her chest still heaving with exertion. "Connecting multiple targets at long distances like that is *exhausting*… I'd prefer *not* to have to do *that* again for a while…"

"Trust me on this, girl," he declared with confidence, standing by the nearby fireplace as the burning logs within popped and crackled softly. "I know how minds work, and we will *own* that one in time. Brother Roland has sown the seed well; we need only bide our time as it grows."

"He's a clever one, that Roland," Percy conceded, not sounding impressed. "I sensed a *lot* of ambition there: you might want to watch out for him."

"I've faced challenges from stronger minds than his and prevailed," the cardinal replied without concern. "Better I keep *you* under my eye than some zealous novitiate from the western shires."

"You think *I'm* more dangerous?" She asked with a smile, trying to sound innocent and not managing it in the slightest.

"I *know* you are…" De Lisle countered with honesty, intending to give a compliment.

"I'll try not to disappoint then," Percy grinned back, receiving the praise in the spirit it was given.

"Just so long as you're *useful*…" he smiled thinly in return "…and *that* I cannot deny. Whether through practice or by Their design, your powers are growing, girl: what we just did would've required the presence of at least *two* experienced brothers, yet you used the Crystal with *exceptional* subtlety and control."

"Cardinal, my *name* is Persephone Koutroulis… *Percy* to my friends…" she began slowly, tone firm but level as she stared directly at him, her gaze smouldering with its intensity. "It's true that I'm still young – *clearly* much younger than you – but I think the *one* thing we can *all* agree on is that I am *not* a 'girl'. I don't expect us to be *friends* but I think you'll *also* agree I've made a *big* effort to show *you* a great deal of respect these last few days. I would *ask* you *at least* show me the same in return, and a good *start* would be to call be something less *demeaning* than simply 'girl'…"

Standing by that fire with arms crossed, Cardinal De Lisle stared at Percy for a long time, his face an impassive mask as he gave what she'd just said a good deal of serious thought.

"It's *rare* to see such courage in the face of danger…" he observed eventually, a thin smile quirking at one corner of his lips. "There are *few* who'd show such bravery that it bordered on *foolishness*. Even *Silas* in his most 'adventurous' moods rarely made *demands* of me…" he added quickly, almost as an afterthought "…and a *demand* is exactly what that was, regardless of how *pleasantly* it was worded.

"*Yet*, it's true that you *have* made significant effort to *restrain* your usual levels of sarcasm and general impudence, and it's *also* true that you *have* been of great use to me – of great *help* – since we left *Rapier* at Bridgeport. I know that assistance is only provided for reasons of self-interest, but that's of no matter: you *are* helping The Brotherhood nevertheless, and I will acknowledge it. We shall never be 'friends', as you put it – the word '*inappropriate*' would not even *begin* to describe that idea – but you've proven that we can at least work together in a *civil* manner." He raised an eyebrow, barely giving her a wry smile. "Would you not agree, *sister*…?"

"I…" Percy began, then halted as she actually thought about what the cardinal had just said, and about the great concession he'd clearly just made in his own mind to accord her a title at least the equal of any Brotherhood member. "…I'm going to *accept* that…" she decided eventually, the pair of them – with those words – reaching an accord on far more than a simple name. "Have you considered my *other* request?"

"For a larger Shard...?" He asked quickly, his features impassive. "What makes you think such a thing exists?"

"I *know* they exist..."

"Indeed?" He countered with a raised eyebrow. "And if this *were* true, what possible use could you put it to...?"

"You know *exactly* what I'd do with it," Percy shot back with a frown, a little exasperated that De Lisle was being so ridiculously coy. "*More power*! You saw what I did making *this*, yeah?" She continued, lifting her sword from where it had fallen beside her. "*That* took every ounce of energy I could draw from *my* crystal, and even *then* it was only possible because I've *already* had so much practice. *She* has had one of these damned things for only a *week* and she was *already* powerful enough to destroy a warship from a range of a couple of miles... and *that* was without any practice or training! I'm working on experience alone... *she* has something else entirely: something *way* out of my league! When I first brought Nevaeh through, Moloch called her a 'prescient': it said she couldn't be controlled, and I gather from what happened on *Rapier* with that idiot, Silas, that the *last* thing Moloch wanted was for Nev to get her hands on a Shard Crystal. Trust me on this: she doesn't have a *clue* how powerful she is yet, but she *will* soon enough... and when she *does*, *this* pathetic trinket..." she spat darkly, turning the blade to reveal the faintly-glowing crystal embedded in its hilt, "...will not even come *close* to being enough to stop her. This thing is giving me everything it's got but it's just not enough... I need a better connection... more *bandwidth*...!" She declared finally, not even considering the possibility the cardinal might have no concept whatsoever of internet download speeds. "She's got better software..." Percy continued, ignoring the fact that she was crafting a flawed analogy at best, "and the only way for me to beat *that* is to overwhelm it with raw, unadulterated *processing power*!"

"I suspect I'll never understand *half* of what you just said," De Lisle admitted with a thin, wry smile, "but I understand *enough* to grasp the point of your argument. I'll need to discuss this with the Gods and see what can be arranged. We *do* have items such as this pass into our possession at times but they are *extremely* rare and *extremely* dangerous. I'll not allow you control of one unsupervised, and certainly not without clear permission from the Shard God itself."

"It'll say yes..." She shrugged, not concerned in the slightest there would be any other outcome.

"We shall see..." he replied dubiously, a shudder rippling through him as the cardinal thought back over what had just been said. "There was a name you just used... a *name* for the Gods...?"

"What... 'Moloch'...?"

"Yes... yes, that was it..." De Lisle nodded, taking an almost involuntary step away from the fire as morbid curiosity overcame his reservations. "Where did you come by it? In all these years, I've never heard such a name used – I'd always assumed the Shard Gods *had* no name."

"Oh, I picked that one myself," she admitted with another shrug. "Seemed silly to *not* have at least *some* kind of name for it, and it doesn't seem to mind that I use it."

"*Moloch*..." the cardinal ventured, trying the word out for himself and slightly ill-at-ease for some reason over the idea that the Shard God would so readily accept a randomly-chosen title given by an insolent heretic witch. "What does it mean?"

"In *my* world was the name of a mythological god of some ancient civilisation: Canaanite, *I think*. Not sure if he was powerful or not, but he – it *must've* been a 'he', obviously: the *nasty* ones usually are – demanded a high sacrifice in exchange for whatever it was he gave in return."

"And... and what *was this* sacrifice?" De Lisle asked reluctantly, feeling another inexplicable shiver wash through him.

"Hmmm... been a while since I took any ancient history..." she wondered aloud, making an effort to recall "...but I think... if I remember correctly... they used to sacrifice children. Yes, *children*: that was it!"

"I see..." the cardinal replied carefully, not sure if he were more unsettled by the idea of child sacrifice or by the utterly flippant and uncaring manner in which the girl had described the whole thing, as if discussing a walk to the market to purchase bread. *Moloch*... even the name itself sounded dark and forbidding, and as he thought more on it, perhaps it was Percy's throwaway remark about the Shard God not *minding* her giving it that title that disturbed him the most.

"I –I'll *see* what I can do to get you that crystal..." he murmured eventually, finding it difficult to meet her blank, expectant gaze in that moment.

"That'd be *lovely*," Percy chirped brightly, trying to be nice. "It's the *only* solution... I promise you..."

There was a large mirror affixed to the inside of the lid of one of the queen's steamer trunks and as Nev stared into it roughly twenty minutes later, wearing just the pants and blouse, she wasn't entirely sure who she was looking at. Although she still felt like she could've showered for a whole day straight had one been available, she *was* at least wearing something other than the two outfits she'd been forced to alternate through for the entirety of the last week, of which one had been ill-fitting at best.

"These 'stays' – or whatever it was you call them – are a *bit* tough to breathe in…" she observed, wincing a little as she pulled at the bottom of the fully-boned, lace bodice beneath her blouse. Narrowing above the hips, it had the rather strange effect of lifting her bust line and drawing in at her waist while providing a surprising amount of firmness and back support at the same time. Both the bodice and the halter top worn over it were form-fitting and – amazingly – also combined perfectly to *not* show any unwanted details of the body beneath.

"Trust me… the style they make these things in, it's a wonder *anyone* can breathe with them on…" Charli replied with a dry smile, not having the heart to tell her new-found friend that she'd actually gone 'easy' on her when tightening the stays at her back; that women at court were usually expected to wear their bodices far more tightly laced. "It looks *amazing* though: I *told* you it would…"

"I guess it *does* look pretty nice…" she conceded, turning slightly to either side and still feeling a little disconcerted over how much more prominent her bust seemed than she'd ever have allowed back home, particularly considering how low the neckline also seemed to plunge.

The outfit itself was of the finest silk with matching, incredibly detailed collars and cuffs of white, inlaid with a multitude of tiny pearls. Nev had to admit that Charli had been right about the colour too: the emerald green really seemed to accentuate her hair colour, making it seem far redder than her usual auburn tone. She was also surprised by the excellent cut of the design; one which seemed to make her waist seem narrower than was actually the case, although she suspected that effect had more to do with the stays underneath.

The deep neckline was definitely showed a great deal more of her upper body than she'd normally feel comfortable with, although Nev found it wasn't quite so bad once she'd slipped on the suit jacket. The Shard pendant and her drekar necklace, which had been remained well-hidden beneath her previous multiple layers of clothing, were both now clearly on display, resting at the centre of her exposed upper chest for all the world to see.

"That necklace… they're dragons…" Charli noted almost in a whisper, sounding surprised.

"Oh, *this*…?" Nev asked innocently, reaching up and lifting it in one hand as the queen drew closer for a better look. "My grandfather gave me this when I was little. The two dragons represent the figureheads of Viking longships..." she explained, turning it over in her fingers. "He wanted me to always have something close that reminded me of our ancestors..."

"It's beautiful..." Charli breathed, almost unable to take her eyes off it. "Dragons have a *very* special place in our history, as you may have already discovered... *particularly* two-headed ones..."

"You mean 'Nethug'...?" Nev asked immediately, raising a sceptical eyebrow. "Corpse-Eeater... Soul Destroyer...? Yes... Godfrey already told me about *him*."

"Lately, there have been rumours suggest the *real* spirit of Nethug may be one of change – of *revolution* – rather than of outright evil..." Charleroi ventured thoughtfully, recalling what her father had said out on the balcony at Cadle the night before they'd left for Burnii. "Quite a coincidence..."

"It *is*... but I can't see how it could be anything *else*," Nev replied evenly, not ready to consider the likelihood that it was anything other than bad luck and the betrayal of a close friend that had brought her to that moment in a different world.

"And there's the Shard crystal too..." the queen observed softly, still sounding vaguely in awe, if for very different reasons now. "I *saw* what you did with it... what you were *almost* able to do for Father, had they not prevented you..."

"I..." Nev began, halting momentarily with absolutely no idea what to say to that. "I... *still* don't know what this thing actually is *or* why I was able to use it the way I did. I know Percy can use one of them too: she's the 'friend' that stabbed me in the back... *betrayed me*...!" She corrected quickly as Charli's eyes widened in shock. "The *first* time I touched it, some filthy old priest – *Silas*, I think his name was – tried to hurt me with it... I think he called it 'burning' or something like that. I'm pretty sure *he* was surprised when I took it from him and used it against him," she added, almost smiling faintly then as she remembered the terror on his face as she'd taken control of it. "Godfrey had been hit by a crossbow, and Percy showed me how to use it to heal him."

"She *helped* you...? Even after her betrayal...?" Charli asked with a frown, enthralled now as she moved back to the bed and took a seat.

"I know, right? *So* weird! She was going on about 'revenge' and how *she* wanted to be the one to get 'even' with me, *not them*..." Nev shook her head slowly, saddened by both the unpleasantness of it all and the reality behind it. "She's crazy, obviously. Maybe not *all* her fault – I think they might've tortured her after she let me get away – but *nuts* all the same…" Her voice trailed off and she was lost for a moment in her own dark thoughts, fighting off a sudden and unexpected wave of misery as memories of home, her father *and* her mother rose to the forefront of her thoughts. "*Anyway*… I just don't know *what* this thing is…" she continued eventually with a growl, pushing through her self-pity and shaking herself loose. "I sure as hell don't *trust* it, but all the same it feels *important* that I keep it with me for the moment… that I'm going to *need* it in the future – well, more than I have *already*."

"What…" The queen began, almost too scared to ask, "what's it *feel* like… *what happens*…?"

"Heh… I'm not even sure of *that*, to be honest," Nev shrugged, taking a seat next to her and smoothing down the material of her trousers at the same time. "At first, there was only darkness… *nothingness*… and a voice… a voice speaking directly into my head. It's hard to explain: if I reach out for it with my mind, I can *feel* the connection there, always waiting. It does what I ask but it also *shows* me how, like when I was healing Godfrey and your father. It scares me – *more* than a little: Percy warned me not to let it take control of me… that it could destroy my mind… you *saw* what happened when I *did* let it take over… when the Blackwatch attacked us on that hill."

"You said it *talked* to you?"

"Oh yeah – it *definitely* did that. It tried to goad me during the battle – trying to *frighten* me, maybe… just before everything started exploding and I destroyed the gunboat out in the harbour."

"A *Shard God* spoke to you…?" Charli hissed, apprehensive now in spite of her own scepticism. "Father didn't believe in them – he never *said* so, but I could tell all the same… *especially* after he told me about finding the Night Dragon. *I* didn't believe either but to hear you now, saying you've *talked* to one…"

"Whoa, whoa, *whoa*…!" Nev interrupted immediately, raising a hand as a stop sign. "I talked to *something*, yes, but whether it's some kind of *god* is another thing *entirely*! You said your father found a 'night dragon'. I've heard someone talk about Night Dragons and this 'Cleansing' business once before, and I've seen the *wall hangings* in the chapels back at Cadle, but this is the first time anyone's mentioned *finding one*…"

"Father told me a story not long ago of a time when he was very young – younger than I. He'd been looking out through the palace windows at Cadle and had seen a Night Dragon fall behind the nearby mountains, close enough see a flash of light and hear the roar of its landing. He and Randwick rode out to look for it…"

"…And they *found it*, didn't they…" Nev finished the sentence as a statement rather than a question.

"They *did*…!" Charli exclaimed, becoming more excited now. "And you'll *never* believe what it actually *was*…!"

"Let me guess… a *huge* rock in the middle of a big crater?" There was a long silence as a suddenly speechless Charleroi could do little other than stare in surprise.

"How could you *ever* know that?"

"Charli; they're called meteorites and we have them in *my* world too: nothing more than random chunks of rock – big *and* small – that speed through space, mostly minding their own business until they get caught by a planet's gravity and either burn up in the atmosphere or come screaming down out of the sky, and either way leaving a trail of fire behind them."

"Your world *knows* all this?" Charli asked as New simply nodded in reply. "But you already know about The Cleansing, and how the Night Dragons are an integral part…" she continued, alluding to Nev's earlier comment. "You see how it looks then, if what The Brotherhood tells us are fire-breathing demons that fell out of the sky to destroy us are nothing more than lifeless pieces of *stone*? If *that part* isn't true, *what else* isn't? How much of *any* of it can we believe? I *already* doubted, and when father told me that story I was *certain* that none of it was true – that it was all lies…"

"Well, I reckon *most* of it is," Nev agreed, never having had much time for the idea of organised religion herself. "Although there's definitely *something* going on with these crystals and the whole 'voices in my head thing': I'd *really* like to think it's more than just me going *crazy*!"

"But that's the thing isn't it, Nevaeh? If it *is* all lies, then why can only a *few* women see the Keepsakes? Where does the power of these crystals *come from*, and how are the Brotherhood able to use it? How did *you* do everything you've done with it? And if there *are* no gods, what are the voices you're hearing? They never *really* talk about it, but De Lisle and some of the others higher up *must* hear things too… it *can't* just be people imagining things!"

"Well, whatever it *is*," Nev began, thinking seriously on the matter. "I'm willing to put money on it *not* being some 'supreme being' controlling every aspect of people's lives. In *my* world we have a principle called 'Occam's Razor' which contends that in *most* cases, the *simplest* explanation is the most likely to be true. . Maybe we can't explain how these crystals work *right now,* or what those voices are, but that doesn't mean there *isn't* an explanation... it just means we don't know what it is yet.

"My grandpa used to say there wasn't really any such thing as ghosts or magic: there were just things that we can't explain yet. I think the same thing here – I really do. Maybe I can't explain what the voice in my head is *yet*, or how I can do what I do with the crystal just using my thoughts..." Nev continued, stopping momentarily, mid-sentence to take a quick breath "...but the one thing I'm *sure* of is that it *isn't* magic, and that whatever it is behind all this – the thing you all call a 'Shard God' – is anything *but*! After the battle with the Blackwatch, it told me it was 'ageless'... a 'devourer of worlds', so maybe it's some *other* kind of life form – something from *another* planet, maybe..." she added, catching the frown of confusion regarding her last comment. "Either way; if it lives it can be *killed*, and behind all the gloating and the boasting the last time it spoke to me, I got the distinct feeling it was somehow *scared* of me... scared of *us*: *humans*. I know that doesn't make sense, but I felt it all the same. All I need to do now is work out how to use what I know against this thing and *destroy it*!"

"We have no right to ask more of you," the queen began slowly after taking a moment to think on what Nev had just said. "...*I* have no right to ask any more of you..." she corrected quickly, taking responsibility as she knew any good monarch should. "Yet I think Huon will need much *more* of your help before this is done..."

"The morning after I first landed here," Nev began, having taken a good moment or two to think about her answer, "I snuck away from Godfrey and Lester, trying to find the 'portal' or whatever it was that I came through." She paused again, taking a breath and fighting off another wave of emotion threatening to take over. "It was gone – *obviously* – but I *did* run into a bunch of Blackwatch lowlifes who'd have raped and murdered me on the spot if the boys hadn't come to my rescue. I couldn't think of *anything* other than getting back home as *fast* as I could and I *nearly* died because of that. Later that day, Godfrey said he thought that if I *was* ever to get home again, *maybe* there were things I needed to do *here* first. I didn't understand what he meant then, but I think I'm starting to *now*. Maybe it's not things *I* need to do so much as it's things that need to be *done*... by someone who knows how to use a blade *and* a crystal...

"This thing that I hear in my head might not be a *god*, but it's very *very* powerful," she forged on, thinking hard about what she recalled of her first moments in that world, so many days before now, "and I'm *certain* it's behind all of this: The Brotherhood, the

Keepsakes… *all of it*…! It called me something on that first day – a *'prescient'* – and said I couldn't be controlled."

"Perhaps that's *why* it's scared of you…" Charli observed with a cheeky grin.

"It *should* be…" Nev growled, meeting her lighter gaze with a stare that was deadly serious. "I don't know what that word, 'prescient' means, but *it* was scared of me being one… and *now* I have access to the power of one of these crystals too. I *swore* to this thing that I was going to kill it, and that's a promise I intend to keep…!"

We sense… doubt… The words reverberated through De Lisle's psyche, causing him to tremble visibly, eyes screwed tightly shut and fingers clawing desperately at the arms of his communion chair. *There have been times in the past when you have questioned… felt uncertain… but never* doubt. *Have we failed you in some way, cardinal, that you should lose faith in our power?*

"No – *never*…!" He gasped, almost fighting for breath as their power washed over him, coursed through him, and he felt his chest constricting in dull discomfort. "It is *not* doubt I feel… merely *concern* that I cannot see the whole of the problem that lays before us… that there are too many factors in play over which I have no direct control…"

But we *have control…we see* everything. *We see the dangers… your* fears… *We see every outcome and the probability of each becoming* reality *in its turn… You have always trusted us before…*

"This… *girl*…" He continued, struggling to overcome his own fear as be finally broached the subject most at the forefront of his consciousness. "You've had me release her and give her access to another crystal, which I've done… *now*, she requests – *demands* – something larger… something *more powerful*…"

And this *concerns you…?*

"Greatly," De Lisle confided immediately, almost sounding relieved over the even tone of the reply. "She's young and *extremely* unpredictable… *impulsive*… and you *know* that she's failed us in the past…"

…yet her connection with the prescient will be of great use to us. We foresee her as being vital *in tracking down and eradicating this Dragonchild.*

"'*Dragonchild*'…?" The cardinal croaked, not at all happy with *that* piece of news.

"*It is a name she has been given… a name of her ancestors. We foresee the* possibility *that she will invoke it in the name of Nethug… that she will draw upon the power of The Bicephalus itself to guide*

470

her… to make her stronger. The Koutroulis-child can help us in a way no other can.

"You – you think she *should* be given access to a *larger* Shard?" De Lisle asked, almost aghast at the thought.

She should be given anything *she requires…* it answered without hesitation, the force of the reply sending him reeling once more. *Every day the Dragonchild remains free, the greater the danger to us grows.*

"I will of course limit the spread of this as much as I am able, but the rest of the Brotherhood is *bound* to find out…" De Lisle observed darkly. "The brothers *will not* be happy to hear of this."

That is of no consequence to us. We care only *for results.*

"I have *seen* some of what lies within her soul…" he persisted, not ready to accept the decision without at least stating his case. "She *thinks* herself he equal of men – of The *Brotherhood*… she craves power and desires to overthrow all men… *all men*…" he added, leaving unspoken the clear implication that he too was included in that statement.

And again *you speak of matters that have no bearing on what must be. The future is still unclear – we have told you this – and we will make* any *sacrifice to secure our future.*

"You would choose this *girl* over us… *over me*…?" De Lisle demanded, anger in his voice now for the first time. "When I have served you faithfully for an entire *lifetime*…?"

Quisitor Silas asked you the same thing on the day you cast him to Nethug, and what did you say to him then? It asked bluntly, the words so powerful now he feared me might pass out with the pain of it. *…That a millennia of service would not be enough to excuse heresy. Powerful words, Cardinal, but worthless if unsupported by* conviction. *To use* another *phrase you employed in that same discussion, what part of this is* our *problem? Only* our *survival is paramount…* anything else *may be sacrificed to that end and you'd do well to keep that in mind. That you* fear *the Koutroulis-child – fear what she may become – is of no consequence to us. You will give her what she asks…* whatever *she asks… is that clear…?*

"I – I…"

Is that clear…? The voice boomed thunderously in his mind, sending him rigid with agony.

"I understand… *I understand*…!" The cardinal moaned weakly, barely maintaining consciousness under that onslaught.

What you have – everything *you have – is within your grasp* only *because* we *allow it… and it can be* taken *from you just as easily. Do not forget that, cardinal.* Never *forget that.*

He felt the connection break like a crippling weight being lifted from his shoulders and chest and with that, De Lisle collapsed into the chair and blacked out, allowing himself the luxury of oblivion. He awoke some time later, groggy and unsure as to whether minutes or hours had passed. It took a while longer before he was able to gather the strength to lift himself to his feet, finally pushing out of his seat and shuffling around to the rear of the chair.

Near the top of its high back, a large panel was fixed in place with four flat-faced screws, their featureless heads making them impossible to remove with a normal screwdriver. Lifting his Holy Pendant in shaking hands, he took a steadying breath and closed his eyes as the crystal glowed faintly and – each in its turn – the four screws silently rotated themselves out of their holes to a distance of a centimetre or so. Another deep breath, and De Lisle was able to reach out and lightly tap the panel they'd held secure, causing it to fall away from the chair back and drop into his hands.

The Shard crystal held within was huge – at least ten times larger than any found in a Holy Pendant – and it glowed and rippled with a myriad of blue-green hues as he reached in and lifted from its padded socket. The chill of its power washed over and through him, setting his teeth on edge and causing every single exposed hair on his body to stand on end. Still weak and shaking heavily now, he awkwardly slipped the object into one of the large hip pockets sewn into the sides of his ceremonial robes.

"You've got my crystal!" Percy chirped brightly as De Lisle entered through the open doorway of the old princess' quarters, almost leaping from the bed in excitement. "I *knew* you'd be able to manage it!"

"This is the *largest* I have access to..." De Lisle snapped, fixing her with a fiery glare "...and I'll remind you that these things are one with the Shard Gods themselves. It is *not... your* crystal!" He added testily, feeling that fine but important point needed to be made, regardless of how completely it appeared he'd been cut out of the whole process.

"Yes, yes, yes..." She muttered dismissively, barely hearing him at all as she took her sword from where it had lay on the bed beside her and giving it a few experimental swishes as she closed on him. "I *know* Moloch told you to hand it over... so *hand it over...!*"

"You may have the Gods' attention right now," he hissed darkly in return, "but I could *still* make things *very* difficult for you, and I'd caution you to remember that!"

"Your Grace, believe it or not, I'm actually quite *grateful* for what you've done to help me out this last week..." Percy admitted, making an exceptional effort to sound as sincere as she actually felt. "Although you didn't actually do anything to *stop* Silas hurting me..." she continued, fingers straying absent-mindedly to the scars on her cheek for a moment "...you weren't giving the *orders* on that either, so I can't really blame you for it. You know what I want out of this, and that pretty much matches up with what *you* want. Regardless of how the *Shard Gods* treat you, *I* appreciate the effort you're putting in and we *both* want the same thing. Let me work with you *and* for you to help... yeah...?"

His steely gaze washed over her in that moment, every ounce of his pent-up indignation and humiliation daring the girl to make *one* false move or give *one* misspoken word that might justify him unleashing his wrath. Instead – possibly for the first time since they'd met, so long ago now – he found only honest sincerity in her eyes and her tone, and the background chatter he was filtering through his own Holy Pendant suggested it unlikely she was hiding anything or holding back.

"I..." he began haltingly, extremely reluctant to allow his own anger to recede "...I can only warn you that this thing carries *immense* power. You may *think* you know how to handle it..." he went on, shaking again now slightly in fearful anticipation as he slipped his hand into his robe pocket to retrieve the thing "...but you *cannot* imagine the reality of it. Allow it access to your mind only sparingly and in small doses or it will *surely* destroy you."

"I understand..." she acknowledged diplomatically, bowing her head slightly and trying to hide her own excitement. "Perhaps we could access it *together*...?"

"I thank you, but no..." De Lisle replied immediately, shuddering at the thought. "I wish you no harm, however nor do I wish *myself* any either. I've experienced its power before – once, in my relative youth – and I'd not go through that again for *any* price. I wish you luck but I'll not follow you into oblivion, should anything go wrong..."

"Fair enough," Percy conceded with a shrug, unable to fault his forthright honesty. "Righto then..." she added, extending her empty hand with palm open and ready "...let's find that witch for you..."

As quickly and carefully as he was able without dropping the thing, the cardinal hoisted it out of his robe pocket and dumped it into her waiting fingers, snatching his own away again as quickly as he was able. He instinctively backed away a metre or two as Percy's body suddenly turned rigid, sword held pointing straight down at the floor in one hand as the other remained clamped about the huge Shard crystal.

It was already glowing again, rainbow colours coursing through and around it, sending tiny crackles of multi-coloured lightning rippling up her arm where it lay bare at the elbow. Her back arched, and although it was difficult to tell through the growing brilliance of the crystal she held, De Lisle almost imagined he could see her float a centimetre or two above the stone floor. At the same time, De Lisle heard the soft sound of a faint '*thud*' at the back of his mind as if some huge weight had fallen to the ground at a great distance. From experience however, he knew that whatever he was 'hearing' would be *deafening* for Percy and he remembered the almost crippling chill he'd also suffered through many years before as she gasped in shock and pain and a cloud of exhaled breath burst from her lips within that otherwise warm room.

" *Dén to pistévo…*!" she breathed softly in Greek, unconsciously uttering an exclamation her father was fond of as she struggled to cope with the sudden, brutal drop in her core body temperature. "*That* was a *rush…*!"

Percy's eyes fluttered for another moment or two, almost rolling upward inside her head before the tension throughout her body finally subsided and she was finally able to sag forward, taking a few steadying steps and releasing a long sigh of relief. She stood silent for a moment, turning away from the cardinal with shoulders heaving in time with her laboured breathing. Multi-coloured crackles of lightning still rippled faintly up her arm, occasionally arcing across to the smaller crystal embedded in the hilt of the sword in her other hand, causing it to glow brightly also.

"You're all right, sister…?" De Lisle ventured cautiously, not sure what to expect and taking care to remain at a distance.

She turned to face him then, and the only thing more unsettling than the faint sparkle of blue flickering within her normally-dark eyes was the fact that the scars on her cheek were literally healing as she spoke, folding in upon themselves and disappearing into nothingness as a similarly-coloured glow momentarily spread across that entire side of her face, so bright it was possible to see the criss-crossed patterns of veins beneath her skin. The glow faded again within a few seconds, leaving her face as clear and unblemished as the day she'd been born.

"Oh, I'm *way* more than just all right…" Percy wheezed hoarsely, sounding excited and out of breath. "I've never felt anything *like* it…! You want to know where she's going…? Let me take care of that for you!"

Closing her eyes again, she lifted the sword and brought it close into her body, the blade pointing directly upward with the flat of it almost touching her nose. Percy's other hand brought the large crystal in beneath the hilt until she was able to rest the sword upon it, creating a flash and flicker of activity within the object itself. Closing her eyes, she began to concentrate deeply as the brightness of both crystals began to grow in intensity, tiny bolts of static electricity arcing out into the room and crackling their way across the floor and up along the edges of nearby furnishings. With all the good sense and wisdom that came with his years of experience, De Lisle took several more steps backward until he was within easy reach of the open doorway, should he have need of a quick escape.

"Far away now and going *further*..." Percy murmured softly, eyes still tightly shut as wayward strands of her long, dark hair began to lift and float away from her body under the assault of that massive static discharge. "*Hundreds* of miles... *island* somewhere... *west*...!" She opened her eyes then and fixed De Lisle with an intense gaze. "Map...! Get me a map and I can *show* you where it is exactly. We have ships near... *warships*... I could *see* them..."

"*Guards*...!" The cardinal roared, not hesitating for a moment as he called loudly into the hallway beyond that open door. "Guards here to me... *now*...!"

XXII

Moving Forward

Godfrey Westacre was feeling particularly ill at ease, and he was willing to bet that not all of it was as a result of the terrible weather the ship had just sailed through during the bulk of that afternoon. An attempt at sleep following the storm's departure had resulted in several hours of restless tossing and turning interspersed with short periods of fitful sleep, most of which were peppered with dark and unsettling dreams, most of them revolving around Lester's death. As sunset approached, he'd abandoned any hope of rest and instead had wandered out onto the main deck in an exceptionally poor mood, hoping to alleviate his foul humour with some good, honest hard work to occupy his mind.

He quickly discovered that there was little to do however. Most of the crew seemed to have everything in hand already, and the few times he'd attempted to help out had only resulted in him being more of a hindrance than of any real use to anyone. He'd been left at a loose end as a result and eventually found himself mooching around aft, below the quarterdeck, all the while filled with a deep and quite uncharacteristic sense of restlessness as he prowled about near the door to the captain's cabin. He felt vaguely angry and unsettled, and with his dark dreams having long-since faded away into the depths of his sub-conscious, the fact that he now couldn't pin down a specific reason for his ill mood only seemed to make him even more annoyed.

Had he thought about it, Godfrey would likely have considered himself to be a reasonably perceptive person. He was also self-aware enough to know that the confusion and discord currently flowing through him was not at all representative of his usually upbeat and easy-going demeanour, although it was also true that the possibility of having been deeply affected by Lester's death unfortunately never formed in his conscious mind. That he couldn't figure out why was becoming a real source of frustration and all the while, as he paced that deck, his eyes would come to rest on the closed door to the captain's quarters and his anxiety levels would spike again, making him even more irritable.

The pair of armed guards standing on either side of the door frame eyed him with a disinterested mixture of suspicion and disdain.

"Orders of Master Randwick are that *no one* be allowed to see the queen other than at her *specific* request, but if you're concerned for the queen's safety, you needn't be..." Farouk suggested, hanging over the quarterdeck railing directly above. He'd noted the young man's aimless loitering and had rather astutely deduced that Godfrey's interest in the entrance to his quarters to be for one of two likely reasons. "Bronson and Hark are the best fighters I have and they'd not let *anyone* past those doors uninvited..."

"Sorry, captain... the thought never crossed me mind..." Godfrey replied hurriedly, almost flinching in surprise at a voice that had come from an unexpected direction.

"Of course... if it is not the *queen* whose welfare concerns you, then I can assure you that Mistress Anderson is *equally* well protected..." He gave a toothy grin as the younger man turned his face away momentarily, hiding an expression that was equal-parts wry smile and mildly-embarrassed grimace. "From what Master *Randwick* tells me, perhaps I should have Miss Anderson protecting my *guards* instead: I'm told she's a fine swordsman – better than most *men,* if Randwick speaks truthfully."

"He does, and she is..." Godfrey nodded in agreement, deciding his time might be better spent in conversation than brooding alone. Turning to his left, he mounted the wooden later fixed there that led up to Farouk's level. "She charged an enemy cavalry unit at Stewpot Road on the day of the invasion and *singlehandedly* took down a dozen or more of those black-shirted bastards... *and* she was skilled enough to defeat *Garrick* one-on-one. Had I not been there, I'd not have believed it myself."

"Edward Garrick's skill with a blade was well known," Farouk conceded, impressed. "Randwick *also* tells me the two of you have fought together for some time now... and that you escaped the Blacklands together in the days before Harald attacked..."

"Only known each other a week..." the young man admitted, breathing heavier after the climb "...but it sure *feels* like a lifetime."

"You and I *both* know how quickly battle changes things, Master Westacre, *and* how quickly the bonds of friendship can be formed in the thick of it..."

"It sounds like the old man had a *lot* to say..." Godfrey asked, eyes narrowing slightly with mild suspicion. "What *else* did the old man tell you...?"

"Nothing but *praise*, both for you *and* Mistress Anderson," Farouk replied without hesitation, giving a toothy smile. "He passed no secrets that weren't his to tell, if that's what concerns you," he continued, assurance in his tone now, "but us 'old men' have seen enough of life to make the occasional 'observation'. *Sometimes*, we can see things that *young* men cannot in spite of our infirmities and our failing senses…"

"And what 'observations' did he impart, pray tell…?" Godfrey asked with a thin smile, folding his arms expectantly as he leaned casually back against the quarterdeck rail… and ruined the moment for himself by leaning too far, almost overbalancing, and finding himself flailing momentarily to prevent himself from pitching backward over the rail.

"…That youth is *wasted* on the young, Master Westacre…" Farouk declared enthusiastically, laughing out loud and from deep within his frame as Godfrey completely failed to regain his composure or credibility with regard to being serious "…youth *and* love, I promise you that…"

"I… dunno much about that…" Godfrey admitted, staring awkwardly at the deck and suddenly unable to meet the older man's gaze. "Joined The Oster when I was no more than thirteen and I been fightin' ever since – first as a squire and then as a ranger in me own right. Not big on 'community', the rangers… at least, not any community outside our *own*…" he shrugged, the whole thing seeming very simple in his own mind. "My family's never been much: dirt-poor farmin' folk lucky to have two copper to rub together. That's the way it's always been, and I can't see as how things are likely to change…" There was a faint bitterness in his tone now as he recalled the emptiness of the life he'd left behind so many years before, running away to find 'adventure and fortune' with a group of tough-but-fair mercenaries who became much more of a family than his real parents had ever been.

"But you've come a *long* way from such humble beginnings…" Farouk pointed out, surprised at the depth of feeling he'd just witnessed "…*especially* for someone so young. The *queen* knows you… *trusted* you with her *life*: how many *noblemen* could boast such a thing?"

"Lester gave *his* life for the crown, and who's gonna remember *him* in another year save for me and his ma…? They'll praise a *dog* for barkin' whenever a stranger comes by, but that don't mean he'll get to sit at their table or eat outta their *bowl*…" Godfrey muttered, still unable to meet the other man's gaze as his fists clenched in unexpected frustration, Farouk's remarks having clearly touched a sensitive nerve.

"Just a quick scratch behind the ear, then '*away w' ye*' and back outside into the cold night again as soon as the danger's passed."

"If you believe that, sir, you do yourself *and* your queen a great disservice…" the captain countered evenly "…*although*… I do *wonder* if it's the *queen* we're actually talking about?"

"There's high-born and low-born and each keep to their own," Godfrey growled softly, desperate to avoid any glimmer of hope now as the reality of what he was feeling finally began to crystallise in his mind.

"You truly believe that?" Farouk asked, sceptical.

"That's the way it's always been: who am *I* to think I deserve any better?"

"Then let me ask you *this*, Master Westacre…" the captain began, still friendly but taking a more serious stance with feet apart and hands on hips. "What would you say if I tell you the one-pound bars of iron I'm carrying in my hold would sell for around *five* silvers apiece at a Crowedan market?"

"I – uh – I'm no blacksmith, but I reckon that'd be a fair price…" Godfrey replied with hesitation, not sure where the man was going…

"Fair price indeed," Farouk agreed with a grin. "I'm no forge-master either, but I can tell you that if you make those bars into horseshoes, they'll sell for *three times* that much without fail."

"And…?"

"*And*… that same pound of iron made into *sewing needles* would bring a return five *hundredfold* the original purchase price! The point I'm trying to convey, young sir, is that the sum of your life's worth in this world is determined only by what *you* make of *yourself*: the only difference between that five-coin bar and twenty-five hundred silver worth of sewing needles is the amount of *work* put in to make them. The *work* is the difference, and *that* is up to you and you alone. If you're so *certain* that you've nothing to offer this person, then what is there to be lost in asking? If you're correct, your lot is no worse than it was the moment before and you'll *at least* be able to look back on your moment without the regret that comes of never knowing the truth. Better *that* than to be *wrong* and never know at all…"

"Easy to say…"

"And *much* harder to do, *yes*…" the older man admitted with a nod and a wry smile, "but Randwick never mentioned you to be lacking in courage and I see no reason to doubt your valour *now, or* your purity of heart. *You* get to choose the road your life takes on its journey: be brave enough to make the right choices… *and* to make the occasional mistake. I've known many women in my life, Master Westacre, and I've *loved* a few along the way. One or two of *them* even loved *me* in return..." he added, managing to draw a thin smile from Godfrey in spite of himself "...and if the others turned out *not* to be who I thought, then that's *my* poor judgement at fault and nothing more. Give *her* the chance to be the person you *believe* her to be!

"A week's precious little time to get to know someone, true enough," he continued, taking a breath, "but there's *nowhere* like the heat of battle to show a man's true colours... *or* a woman's, for that matter. Would you *die* for her?" The captain asked suddenly, almost catching Godfrey off guard.

"I... aye, I would... in a heartbeat..." he answered after a moment's serious thought, meeting Farouk's gaze now with certainty and fire in his eyes.

"And would *she* do the same for *you*...?" Came the follow-up question with eyebrow sharply raised.

"I – *uh* – I think... yes... *yes*, she would..."

"Then what else is there to know?" The captain asked kindly, tone softening now as he took a few steps forward and leaned over the rail beside him. "There's plenty who've made much out of far less..."

"And if you're wrong...?" the boy asked then, opening up in that moment out of pure desperation, heart well and truly pinned to his sleeve. "If *I'm* wrong...?"

"Then you're wrong," Farouk shrugged simply, "and a friendship forged in battle *still* stands, either one ready to lay down their life for the other. Would that *really* be so bad...?"

Godfrey Westacre turned at that moment and also leaned across the railing, both men staring silently out across the deck at the glowing light of sunset beyond as he thought long and hard about what had just been said.

"No..." he murmured eventually, releasing a long sigh of acceptance as the sensations of anxiety and frustration finally began to drain away. "No, cap'n... I don't s'pose it is..."

Nev and Charleroi come up on deck some time later, arriving in time to catch the spectacular view as the last rays of the sun disappeared on the empty western horizon beneath scattered clouds ablaze with hues of red, orange and pink. Nev still wore the emerald outfit the queen had picked out for her, although in deference to her modesty (particularly when surrounded by a large number of crewmen she didn't know), she'd made sure the jacket was buttoned as high as it would go to cover most of her cleavage. The jacket also served to cover both the crystal and her dragon pendant, Nev thinking it perhaps *not* a good idea that strangers be allowed to see her wearing either.

Both she and Charleroi had been captivated by that stunning sunset, and there was much clapping and exclamations of joy from the queen within moments of their arrival near the bow as a pod of dolphins began leaping in and out of the water ahead, keeping pace with *Ocean Breeze* as the ship cut through the calm sea at a cracking eight knots with a good wind at her stern.

Nev herself was so taken by the sight that she'd even brought out her phone, trying to hide as much of it as she was able while still filming the creatures as they played and leaped about below. It was for that reason Godfrey's approach went completely unnoticed until he was standing right beside her at the railing. Even then, her realisation came a moment or two after anyone else nearby, the queen included, and it'd been duly noted by all that the young man had spent those moments clearly *not* watching dolphins playing.

Godfrey... close! Holding your hand! Leaning in to...!

"You look *beautiful*..." he ventured softly, already close enough to give her such a start as Nev began to turn in reaction to the vision that she fumbled and almost dropped her phone over the side in a yelp of fright.

"Oh... *oh*...!" She stammered, also fumbling for words and not at all happy that particular vision had been cut short as the queen gave a simple smile in response to Godfrey's hasty bow and backed carefully away, allowing the pair a little privacy. "I – uh – *you*...! You're *here*...!"

"Always picked you for being a smart one..." he grinned wryly, inwardly feeling more than a little relief that it seemed he'd gotten his initial compliment past her without any negative reaction. "Been wonderin' when you'd surface... guess it was a bit *dryer* below decks, though I don't figure that storm was much more fun down there than it was up here."

"Oh, we were both sick as *dogs*..." she exclaimed, also relieved to be given a neutral subject to deal with. "I thought I was going to heave my guts up at any moment, and that's *not* a fun feeling to have for a couple of hours straight."

"Don't look like you came through it any worse for wear," he pointed out, making another, more subtle attempt at gallantry.

"What... *this* thing...?" She blustered, *very* happy it was getting too dark to see the colour red at that moment. "I – *um* – the *Queen* found this for me... I – *ah* – I think it's rather nice, actually... once you get used to it..."

"Makes a change from being stuck in a ranger's clothes for days on end, I reckon," he smiled again, turning to stare out across the passing ocean toward the glowing aftermath of sunset, the movement bringing them closer almost without either of them thinking about it. "Captain wouldn't let anyone down below 'cept for a couple of guards on the queen's door..." he explained, sounding less confident now and more than a little vulnerable. "I – I'm glad you came up on deck... I... was worried about you..."

"Worried...?" She repeated, glancing at him for a moment before also turning her gaze back to the ocean. "What was there to be *worried* about? It's not like I could *go* anywhere, and you *know* I know how to look after myself..."

"Aye, I know *that*," he conceded, grinning sheepishly as he lowered his head in mock defeat. "It's just... well... save for you sleeping in the fort last night, we've barely been out of sight of each other for more than a few minutes at a time for a week now and I just... I guess I've gotten used to you bein' around..." He finally admitted, trying hard not to be too obvious as he released a soft sigh of relief over finally getting those words out.

"Well... I will... take that as a compliment..." she decided eventually, smiling faintly as she added: "...I *think*..."

"I missed you..." he said then, finally putting it out there as simply and directly as he was able. "That's... pretty much what I wanted to say..." he went on, feeling even more nervous. "I *missed* you... that's all..."

"I *will* take *that* as a compliment," Nev decided, as reluctant in that moment to show her own relief at hearing those words as he'd earlier been in saying them.

"Standing here on the deck some old cog, surrounded by a ship's crew and with a *queen* looking on wasn't *exactly* the setting I imagined," he grinned again, more of his usual humour creeping back now as their initial awkwardness began to fade, "but I wanted you to know that: none of us know what to expect when we reach where we're going and I didn't want to make the mistake of not saying it 'til it was too late..."

"I'm not going *anywhere* without you – you know that, right?"

"It's not always that simple..." Godfrey replied with a faint shake of his head, good humour fading slightly. "I've seen enough *bad* in this world to know we don't always get what we want..."

"You've saved my life more than once already. I could *never* have made it this far without you..." She stated firmly, finding enough courage somewhere to reach out and rest her hand gently on his on the railing "…and that's not gonna change no matter *what* happens."

"At Cadle, after the battle, you slept so long and so deep that I started to think maybe you weren't going to wake up." His body was wracked by a visible shudder as he recalled the memory. "I… didn't like that… *at all*. I just… *By the Crystal*, it's hard to find the words…!" He blurted eventually, frustration showing through over his own conflicted emotions.

"Whatever it is… just – just *say* it…" she suggested haltingly, her own nerves stretched to breaking point as her heart leaped into her mouth.

"I've never met *anyone* like you… I don't think there *is* anyone else like you … "he said simply, slowly stepping away from the railing slightly and rising to his full height, almost as if coming to attention. "I've been a fighter – a *mercenary* – as long as I can remember… since I was old enough to know what that even was. All there's ever been is The Oster; the only *family* I've ever known – ever thought I *needed* – was The Oster. This is all new to me: I'm no scribe or poet, and I don't *know* the proper words for what I want to say… or describe how I *feel*…" he continued, taking her hand and placing it, palm open, at the centre of his chest, "…but for as long as I still have strength enough to lift a blade… for as long as I still draw breath and my heart still beats… where you go, I follow…"

As Godfrey stood there before her, honest vulnerability on display for all to see, the tense silence that followed that statement was palpable to say the least. A thousand thoughts whirled through Nev's mind in that moment, racing through an entire range of emotions from wildest elation to that darkest speed of doubt, and the only thing she knew for certain was that the intensity of the feelings she was experiencing was greater than *anything* she'd ever known.

"I…" She began, then halted again as her thought processes caught up with her words and she gave *serious* consideration to what she might say next. The queen's words of earlier that evening had very quickly come to mind, giving her courage enough to consider being as open about her feelings as he'd just been, but then Randwick's advice in the chapel had returned, echoing softly at the back of her mind in counterpoint.

Nev knew what she wanted – or, at least, she *thought* she knew – but she *also* recognised that to all intents and purposes she was still a *kid* with almost no experience whatsoever with regard to men *or* relationships. The possibility that her judgement might also be clouded by the fact that Godfrey had been her 'saviour' once or twice and her only constant source of companionship and support during the insanity of the last week was not lost on her either.

"I… don't *know* what I want…" she started over, choosing her words slowly but also with confidence as she turned her hand and closed her fingers firmly about his, still resting against his chest. "I'm still so *young* and inexperienced and, to be honest, I was a bit messed up even *before* I arrived in this world… I don't think I could even *give* a sensible answer about how *I* feel, or what kind of future I see for next *week* let alone the rest of my life…"

There was a momentary pause as she took a short breath and gathered her thoughts before going on, and in those first few seconds of silence it was clear Godfrey had assumed what she'd just said was a negative response. Yet just as quickly as he started to lower his hand and release his grip, she tightened hers and gently but firmly held his hand in place.

"…I don't know what's going to happen, or where *either* of us will end up…" she continued quickly, holding his gaze intently the entire time. "The only thing I know *right now*… is that *wherever* I am… in a week, a month or in ten *years*… I can't imagine *any* of it without *you* being there…" and with the engine fuelling her speed of doubt redlining for all it was worth, added: "…if… if that's what *you* want…"

There was another rather loaded pause of a second or two that seemed to last for years as they continued to meet each other's' gaze and he thought hard about what she'd just said, but Nev had also learned well enough by now to recognise that glint in his eye as he was preparing to be cheeky.

"I – *ah* – all those things I just said *were* out loud, yes…?" He asked as innocently as he could manage, drawing a soft snort of laughter from Nev as she realised how silly her last question must've sounded in light of his earlier statement.

"This is all new to *me too*, y' know!" She chuckled, initially unable to think of a better way to break the tension of the moment and then suddenly reddening slightly as she remembered where the image that had flashed into her mind had ended. "We're *both* going to have to figure this stuff out, I guess…"

"Aye…" he nodded, stepping forward just enough to dramatically increase the intimacy of the situation and send Nev's general temperature settings skyrocketing. "But *at least* we'll be figuring it out *together*…" He began to lower his face even further now, coming in closer to hers in perfect sync with the vision that had flashed into her mind moments earlier.

This is it...! Her *clearly* overwrought emotions exclaimed excitedly as she tilted her head slightly and closed her eyes in preparation, their faces so close now she could actually *feel* the proximity. *He's going to kiss you! This'll be so romantic! Something to - !*

"*Whale*...! Whale off the port bow...!"

"Wait... *wait, what*...?" She blurted, inwardly devastated as she opened her eyes again just in time to watch Godfrey's head pull away and turn in the same direction as everyone else's in that moment.

The bellowed alert came from one of the crew standing watch on the beakhead, a small, tapering platform extending forward below the bowsprit at the very front of the ship, used to provide working space for both the forward rigging and – Nev had discovered earlier with some disgust – the ship's toilets. The cry had drawn everyone's attention on board and as they all craned their necks around in that direction, all aboard *Ocean Breeze* were afforded an incredible view of a large humpback whale leaping half out of the water in the glow of the fading sunlight, no more than a kilometre or so ahead off the port bow.

Well... that *would just about sum up my week*... she grumped silently, also turning toward the call and immediately feeling impressed in spite of herself. ...*My entire* life...!

"By the Crystal, it's *amazing*...!" The queen gushed, overwhelmed with her own excitement as she joined them at the railing and watched in awe as the beast came crashing back into the water with a huge spray. "I've never seen *anything* like it!"

"Why don't you take one of those pictures of yours...?" Godfrey suggested, completely oblivious to her inner frustration, and instantly making it all better in any case by slipping his arm about her waist and drawing her in close against him, side-by-side. "What did you call them: 'selfies'...?"

"Okay..." she laughed out loud as she followed suit by sliding her own arm about his waist in return, finding the experience new and *very* pleasant. "I *think* you're missing the point of it being called a '*selfie*', but that's *actually* still a *really* good idea! Your Majesty...!" She added, turning to the queen as her hand withdrew her phone so quickly from inside her tightly-laced bodice that Godfrey was left none the wiser as to where it'd actually been hidden. "Come and take a picture with us... take a picture with the whale!"

"A 'picture'...?" Charleroi asked quizzically as she moved across from her position at the rail a few metres away, the two guards hovering imposingly in the background. "Are you going to draw something?"

"Don't worry, Your Majesty: it's that phone of hers... she *swears* it's not majik – just a *machine* where she comes from..." Godfrey assured with a wry smile as they separated once more to allow Nev the use of both hands to ready a phone that she'd almost forgotten over the last few days: something that would've been completely unheard of back in her world.

"I *see*..." Charleroi frowned dubiously, the guards taking a precautionary step or two closer before Farouk, watching like a hawk from the quarterdeck still, barked a single order directing them to stand down.

"Okay..." Nev began, extending one arm as a signal for the queen to come on in beside them (as if embracing a monarch was a *completely* normal thing to do) and holding her other hand high with the phone turned to landscape mode and the screen switched to front camera. "Get in here nice and close and we can *hopefully* catch the show in the background..."

"That... that's *me*...! And *you*...!" Charli exclaimed, stunned completely by the spectacle as she realised the tiny screen, assisted by its own backlight, showed all three of them staring back.

"Right... you need to stay very still and smile for a moment, Your Highness..." Nev explained through a tight-lipped grin of her own, concentrating on taking the shot as her free hand now hovered over the shoot button. "That's it: nice and bright...!"

The humpback broke the surface again a moment later, tiny in the background at such a distance but visible nevertheless, and Nev was quick enough to catch it almost at the apex of its leap with three would-be whale watchers grinning like fools in the foreground.

"There we go!" She declared proudly, bring the phone back down and opening up the gallery to inspect the good work. A *bit* dark now... and the *sun's* too close to the horizon on this side..." Nev muttered critically as she offered the phone over for the queen to get a closer look "...but still *pretty good* if I *do* say so myself...!"

"This is me...!" Charli repeated, completely unable to get her head around the whole process and at the same time – rather inexplicably – finding something about it *very* familiar that she couldn't lay a finger on. "*This is me*...!"

"I think its brilliant... just like the person who took it ..." Godfrey grinned, slipping his arm about Nev's waist once more and giving a surreptitious hug that she returned without hesitation.

"Always *knew* you'd be a smooth one..." Nev shot back with a genuine smile, then faltered for a moment as something else occurred to her. "Oh... oh...! After all we just said, I went and asked *someone else* to be in our first photo together... *oh...!*" She exclaimed again, suddenly, foolishly embarrassed that the thought hadn't occurred to her earlier and not hiding her disappointment at all.

"Plenty of time for that..." he smiled back, not in the slightest concerned as he hugged her even tighter. "*All the time in the world...!*"

"I think I like the sound of that," Nev decided, and as they turned back to the railing as one and she hugged him tightly in return.

The docks at Arthur's Port were filled with frenetic activity two days later as Randwick and William stood at the gangway leading up to the deck of a two-masted caravel, a far larger and faster vessel than the average cog that was well-suited to both long-distance trade and exploration. The pair were surrounded by a small cohort of military and civilian personnel, dressed respectively in either their smartest dress uniforms or finest ceremonial robes. Every one of the soldiers present stood waiting and ready with a small but well-packed rucksack at their feet as they all awaited orders to board.

"I wish you luck, *colonel...*" Randwick offered with a grim smile, using the younger man's newly-promoted rank as he extended his hand in farewell.

"Thank you, general," William nodded in return, accepting the hand firmly before offering a more formal salute. "I'll do my best..."

"The fate of Huon itself may rest on your shoulders now and I've no doubt you'll see us proud, boy," Randwick smiled, matching the salute with one of his own. "Bevan and the rest of the diplomatic team will have their work cut out for them, but you know the truth of what's happening here as well as any and we need the Kings' Council to know it also. Barnabas was a soldier, and he was a friend of mine also, once... put your case to him and the rest of the council, fair and square, and you'll see us right, laddie."

"I wish *you* were coming with us."

"Aye, so do *I*, lad, but there's naught for it but to stay here and lead the troops, takin' the fight to the Blackwatch as best we can. The more territory we lose, the easier it'll be for Baal to stake his claim for the throne. Any *other* time, I'd say 'Shard go with you' in parting..." he added ruefully "but perhaps that ain't as appropriate now, with all that's happened. May *good fortune* smile on y', lad... do your duty, and you won't go wrong..."

There was another short round of salutes before William and the rest of the officers and men with him all shouldered their packs, the entire delegation then turning and making their way up the gangway, single file.

"Delegate Norris…" Randwick called softly, addressing the last of the civilians in line as he was about to take his turn heading up to the main deck.

"General…" Norris nodded evenly, making no show of emotion whatsoever. Small of frame and looking to be in his early thirties, he was a man of hawkish, almost pinched features with a pair of tiny spectacles perched precariously across the bridge of his long, narrow nose.

"Young William…" The old man murmured softly, drawing in quite close to ensure his words weren't overheard. "Keep an eye on him for me, would you…?"

"You have concerns, general…?" Came a single question with arched eyebrow.

"Not… *concerns*…" Randwick replied evasively, unwilling to be more specific. "Only the recognition that colonel is a very dutiful and a very *pious* man, if you get my meaning…?" He added, receiving a knowing nod in return. "*Just*… let me know if you see or hear anything out of the ordinary… understood…?"

"*Completely*, general…"

All sign of land had disappeared from the horizon by dawn of the next morning, and *Ocean Breeze* had continued on its north-westerly heading, blessed by a steady tail wind that kept both captain and crew happy as the cog sailed on at a steady six or eight knots for another three days. Farouk would regularly take readings from a large and well-polished brass sextant and although Nev never saw or felt the ship change course, it was nevertheless clear by the third evening that they were now on a more northerly course, the sunset now much further back off their port side than had previously been the case. By the fourth morning, the faint but unmistakeable shimmer of land could once more be seen stretching right across the northern horizon.

In Nev's opinion, one thing that hadn't progressed anywhere near as much as their journey was the new and rather perplexing concept of being (in *theory*, at least) in a relationship. It wasn't that there was no free time to be found; there was actually plenty of that, with neither of them able to help much with the day-to-day duties of sailing a ship. They actually spent pretty much every *moment* of their spare time together… the main problem was that on a so small a ship with just one private cabin (currently occupied by the queen, with Nev sharing), there was absolutely no place they could go that was actually private.

In the days since that first abortive, whale-interrupted 'almost-kiss' moment at the outset, there'd not been a single moment that followed in which either of them, surrounded as they were by dozens of crew, had felt comfortable enough to show any greater display of affection than hand-holding and the occasional embrace. Nev, who'd have been the first to admit her experience of relationships and the opposite sex in general was limited to the point of non-existence, didn't *entirely* see it a bad thing that she was being provided a little breathing space to 'ease' her mind into the concept.

As wonderful as Godfrey was, and as deeply as she cared for him, the thought of 'things' going much further at that moment than they already had was something that Nev found *very* frightening... and her instincts, inexperienced as they were, were nevertheless telling her loud and clear that if that was how she was feeling, rushing things would definitely *not* be the right thing to do. Still, that left her not knowing how *Godfrey* felt about the whole thing... he'd made no indication of how he was feeling about it – *or* whether he was even at all bothered – and as a result, her ever-prepared speed of doubt was racing at full throttle by the time they'd sighted land on that fourth morning.

The pair of them stood up on the foredeck, Nev making sure they stayed just far enough away from the beakhead and the toilets that waited there to ensure nothing untoward came their way with regard to smell *or* sound. Most of that morning and a substantial part of the afternoon was spent making difficult headway against a blustery north-easterly wind that slowed progress to barely three or four knots during that part of the journey. The whole time, the dark shadow of land on the horizon continued to grow until the ship was finally close enough to pick out the detail of scattered trees and waves breaking against distant cliffs.

A faint drizzle had arrived with the wind change: it was light enough that the cloak was sufficient to keep any moisture from soaking through the rest of her clothing (now her usual brown skirt, jacket, leggings and boots) but it nevertheless left Nev feeling chilled and decidedly ill at ease.

"You're all right?" Godfrey asked immediately, drawing her in a little closer with the arm about her waist as he felt a faint shudder ripple through her body. "Cold...? ...Or is something bothering you...?"

"Oh... a bit of *both*, I guess," she admitted, snuggling her body in tight against his and laying her head against his shoulder. "Now we're so close to wherever it is we've been heading, I'm starting to feel more anxious about it all." She signed softly, lifting her head once more and turning to stare up into his eyes. "I don't know... maybe after a week of action with almost no let up, the last four days of doing *nothing* have made me feel a bit paranoid that something *bad's* about to happen..."

"That happens a lot with our veterans," Godfrey acknowledged with a rueful smile. "Seen it a few times with some o' the older Ostermen: they're so used to fightin' and watchin' theirs and their mates' backs every waking moment that they get a bit... *edgy*... when things are quiet. Hard for 'em – the old blokes... lot of 'em don't have family to fall back on if they're crippled or just too past it to fight any more. The Oster does what it can to keep 'em around, though: there's always odd jobs that need doing; sword sharpening, carrying messages... the odd bit of surveillance work here or there when its mostly just sittin' around, keepin' an eye out..."

"You are just *full* of surprises, aren't you...!" Nev exclaimed softly, unable to keep what she suspected was an almost idiotic smile off her face.

"What makes you say that?"

"That was *such* a clever, intelligent thing to say..."

"And that's a *surprise*, is it?" He shot back, trying to sound offended, but Nev was learning how to pick the inflection in his voice when he was joking around and wasn't buying it.

"You *know* what I mean!" She replied as he grinned broadly and gave an 'it-was-worth-a-try' shrug. "How many people in this world even *know* a word like 'surveillance'? You put on this air of being a simple soldier, but underneath that *incredibly* gorgeous exterior lies a lot of smarts... *a lot*..."

"No gold *or* spare time for schoolin' in The Oster, but we make do well enough. There's plenty of those old veterans about to mentor and to lecture, and it pays a young fella to know his letters and how to write 'em down well enough to send a message or decode some orders." He shrugged again. "Guess learnin' just came easy to me... I was always lucky that way..." There was silence for a moment as he considered his next line, actually gave himself a faint nod of approval as he squeezed Nev in another hug, then added: "*Still* pretty lucky, I reckon..."

"You, sir, are a *very* smooth character..." She replied, feigning mild suspicion as they both stared out over the railing at the land drawing ever-nearer in the distance. "But you also have *exceptional* taste: that's *probably* one of the reasons I lo– *like* you so much..."

"*You* were going to say something *else*…!" Godfrey pointed out, imagining a memory of having said those words before and trying to sound scandalised.

"I'm sure I don't know *what* you're talking about," Nev replied airily, knowing she sounded ridiculous and desperately trying to stop herself from bursting into laughter as she discovered that for once, she didn't care in the slightest.

"Is that so…?" He shot back with a dry grin, moving until he was standing behind her and able to wrap both arms around her waist. Hugging her tight, he then leaned down to place a momentary kiss on the top of her head that only sent her into a *mild* swoon. "Well… I hereby declare it to the world that I *like* Nevaeh Anderson…" he continued, the grin widening. "I *like* her with all my heart and soul!"

"*Hey*…!" She protested, struggling to keep the laughter out of her own voice as she gave the hand attached to one of those arms a playful smack.

"Well… I'm sure *you* know what I mean…" Godfrey ventured, resting his chin lightly where he'd just delivered the kiss.

"I can *see* this is going to take some getting used to…" Nev muttered, not at all ready to show she was enjoying every moment but well aware that he knew anyway.

"*Like, like, like*…"

As *Ocean Breeze* continued its northward journey amid a huge expanse of ocean filled with a billion specks of life, two of those specks hugged each other tight and allowed themselves to become lost in the enjoyment of the moment itself. For the first time in over a week and in her entire life, Nevaeh Anderson had begun to hope that maybe – *just maybe* – things might actually work out for the best, moving forward.

www.ingramcontent.com/pod-product-compliance
Lightning Source LLC
Chambersburg PA
CBHW071216250626
47163CB00001B/5